BANKING ON MURDER

Banking on Murder
Three by Emma Lathen

DEATH SHALL OVERCOME

MURDER AGAINST THE GRAIN

A STITCH IN TIME

Macmillan Publishing Company

NEW YORK

Macmillan Publishing Company
866 Third Avenue, New York, N.Y. 10022
Collier Macmillan Canada, Inc.

ISBN 0-02-568870-7

Printed in the United States of America

CONTENTS

Death Shall Overcome

CONTENTS

1 · Fling Out the Banner!

ABOVE ALL, Wall Street is power. The talk is of stocks and bonds, of contracts and bills of lading, of gold certificates and wheat futures, but it is talk that sends fleets steaming to distant oceans, that determines the fate of new African governments, that closes mining camps in the Chibougamou. In the world's great money market, power has forged massive canyons through which thousands of men and women daily hurry to work, hurry to lunch, hurry, hurry, hurry in the shadow of towers tall enough to defy the heavens. Depending upon your point of view, Wall Street is either awesomely impressive or appalling.

No one has ever called it beautiful.

John Putnam Thatcher, Senior Vice-President of the Sloan Guaranty Trust (and, incidentally, a man who had sent plenty of tankers to the Sulu Sea in his day), paid the taxi driver and inspected his portion of Wall Street, which happened to be Exchange Place, with profound satisfaction. It had been turned an exceptionally dirty gray by low-lying November clouds. The chilled hordes streaming past the entrance to the Sloan were an unaesthetic spectacle. Nevertheless, Thatcher felt the real contentment that comes, so we are told, from the sight of an authentic work of art.

"Which proves," he told himself as he struggled into the Sloan's lobby, "that it is all in the eye of the beholder. Morning, Billings."

"Good to have you back, Mr. Thatcher," said Billings with as much dignity as if he were still presiding over the magnificently begrilled oak elevator that had served executives in the old Sloan instead of a pneumatic pillbox.

"Did you have a good trip? It was India, wasn't it?"

"Poona," said Thatcher. "Yes, it was a good trip, but I'm glad to be back."

"I'm sure you are. Here we are, sir."

As he rode up to the sixth floor and the Trust Department, Thatcher considered the warmth in Billings' voice. Was it possible that Billings too had been in Poona?

Miss Corsa, as busy in his outer office as if Thatcher had never been away, had not visited Poona. She welcomed her employer back from foreign parts with her usual calm, then interestedly inspected the length of sheer golden silk he produced from his briefcase.

"It's a beautiful scarf, Mr. Thatcher. Thank you very much."

"Scarf?" Thatcher replied. "It's a sari, Miss Corsa. I noticed that it enlivens an office considerably when the secretary wears something like that. I anticipate coming in one morning to find you looking like a bird of paradise."

Involuntarily Miss Corsa glanced again at the transparent shimmer of the silk. Then she carefully refolded it, stowed it in a drawer, and got down to business.

"And I've clipped the articles in the *Times*, Mr. Thatcher. And the pictures . . ."

"Miss Corsa, it is my intention to forget these past two weeks as rapidly as possible."

Miss Corsa ignored the interruption and made a mental note that foreign travel reinforced her employer's regrettable tendency to levity.

"*Newsweek* had a very good photograph of you in that furry hat. When you were up in the mountains."

"Furry hat!" he repeated irascibly, proceeding into his own office. Banking careers have drawbacks as well as compensations, but not until last week had John Putnam Thatcher added exotic headgear to the list.

"Remind me to send a memo to the chairman this afternoon, will you, Miss Corsa?"

It was the Chairman of the Board, George C. Lancer, who had put Thatcher into that furry hat. He prided himself on a statesmanlike view of the Sloan's far-flung financial commitments, which currently included modest participation in a vast hydroelectric project some two hundred miles northeast of Poona. It was, Lancer had pointed out, only fit and proper that the Sloan Guaranty Trust and the United States of America be represented at the opening ceremonies.

"Certainly," Thatcher had replied. "When do you . . . ?"

"Unfortunately, I'll be representing the bank at the launching of a trawler fleet in Ghana," Lancer had said with a straight face.

Since Bradford Withers, the president of the Sloan, had accepted a luncheon invitation to the White House during the relevant period and the head of International Division was en route to a trade conference in Dubrovnik, it was John Putnam Thatcher who went to Poona, and to an endless round of functions centering on the importance of waterpower—including several religious observances—that culminated in an exceedingly uncomfortable trip to what should rightly have been inaccessible mountain fastnesses. The motley crew of dignitaries accompanying him did not improve the situation.

"Yes. I want to be sure to tell Lancer that the United States was represented by the ambassador, poor fish. And don't let me forget to mention that the Russian technicians outnumbered the Indian officials. *That* will give International something to think about!"

Miss Corsa shook her head disapprovingly, indicated the business at hand, tempered her welcome by pointing out that she had not expected him until the next day, which accounted for the disorder he found (Thatcher's desk was a model of mathematical precision), then withdrew.

With a sigh of relief, Thatcher sank into his own chair, at his own desk. At long last, he had regained the peace and order of the Sloan that had sustained him through the worst moments in India—among which he was inclined to number his own ribbon-cutting remarks.

Almost immediately, reality intruded. Whether from Billings or those members of the staff he had encountered in the hallway—but certainly not from Miss Corsa—news of Thatcher's return roared through the sixth floor like a forest fire. Most of the sixth floor, it soon developed, had urgent need to consult him.

Fittingly enough, Walter Bowman, Chief of the Research Section, was the first to receive tidings of his return, and lumbered in, ostensibly to welcome Thatcher back, actually to argue the merits of Northern Kansas Utilities which he hoped to present to next week's Investment Committee. After this matter had been thrashed out, Bowman solicited Thatcher's impression of the Sloan's Paris branch, visited in passing.

It was not high.

"Just as I thought," Bowman said. "Tell you what, John. I'll send them a list of our reports, and ask for one of theirs. That way, we'll find out what they're doing—if they know."

"Clear it with International, Walter," Thatcher replied. "And remember that Withers' nephew is over there."

Bowman looked innocent as he heaved his great bulk out of the easy chair.

"I'll be tact itself, John. You know that. Well, you'll want to get caught up so I'll go. By the way, I thought India was hot. Why were you wearing that fur hat in all the pictures?"

"Oh, take your tactful self out of here."

This set the pattern. One by one, Thatcher's subordinates cajoled their way past Miss Corsa to lay their problems on the desk of their returned chief.

"I thought Charlie Trinkam was supposed to be keeping the Trust Department running," said Thatcher aloud as he sped Kenneth Nicolls on his way. "And why is young Nicolls looking so tired?"

"I understand that he's been working nights," Miss Corsa replied, depositing a mountain of correspondence on his desk.

"Splendid," said Thatcher brutally.

"He's helping to build a cooperative nursery school in Brooklyn Heights," she continued. "Mr. Nicolls is doing the cabinetwork."

"Another illusion shattered," Thatcher commented. "Miss Corsa, do you think you could manage to keep the rest of the staff out of here. . . ?"

"John! Talk about timing!"

Radiating enthusiasm, Charlie Trinkam stood in the doorway. A man devoted to milking life of the enjoyment it held, he was also a fine trust officer, if unorthodox in method. The unalloyed pleasure in his voice made both Thatcher and Miss Corsa look up with surprise, but Trinkam advanced into the room like a cat stalking a canary. Just beyond him was Everett Gabler, the oldest and primmest of Thatcher's trust officers.

Thatcher narrowed his eyes. Not only was Everett Gabler a born fusser, he was also section chief of Rails and Industrials. This meant that, professionally as well as temperamentally, he was invariably at sword's points with Trinkam (Utilities).

Yet here he was, happily polishing his glasses.

"Well, well, well! It is good to see you back, John." He glanced at Trinkam. "You know, Charlie, I think this solves all our problems nicely. Very, very nicely."

The normal crises that arose when Trinkam assumed nominal authority during Thatcher's absences could never have effected this rapprochement. For a moment Thatcher studied Trinkam and Gabler, both beaming at him with uncharacteristic heartiness, then decided to tread very warily.

"That will do, Miss Corsa. Yes, I got back a day early."

"Great!" said Trinkam.

Thatcher said nothing.

"Have a good trip?" Everett Gabler inquired after a pause.

"Excellent," said Thatcher.

It was noteworthy that Charlie Trinkam did not inquire about Paris.

Thatcher let his eyes stray to his heaped in-box and saw Trinkam and Gabler exchange conspiratorial glances. Charlie cleared his throat.

"Ah . . . John, the reason we're glad that you got back a little early is that we've got a problem on our hands."

"Nothing serious. Things have been going very smoothly," Gabler interpolated.

He was a man in whose jaundiced view things never went smoothly.

"Yes?" Thatcher said courteously.

"You know Schuyler & Schuyler?" Trinkam continued.

Unlimited patience was not John Putnam Thatcher's forte. His voice grew testy.

"Of course I know Schuyler & Schuyler, Charlie. Will you two get to the point, or get out and let me do some work?"

Neither Trinkam nor Gabler budged.

"Had the rumors about Schuyler & Schuyler started before you left?" Gabler asked.

"Rumors? No, I haven't heard a thing. But they can't be in trouble," Thatcher replied, interested despite himself.

Schuyler & Schuyler was a small, well-regarded brokerage firm. Old Nat Schuyler, one of the founders, still ran it with an autocratic hand that guaranteed Schuyler & Schuyler's capital reserves were always well above the required minimum.

"Not the kind of trouble you're thinking about," Trinkam assured him soberly. "No, for the last week or so there's been a lot of talk. Schuyler & Schuyler want to take in a new partner and get him a seat on the Exchange."

"So?"

"He's a Negro," said Everett Gabler quietly.

Thatcher raised his eyebrows. Only someone who had spent almost forty years on Wall Street, someone who knew the Stock Exchange, the investment banks, the great law firms and the brokerage houses could immediately appreciate how much talk there must have been.

He smiled wryly.

"It's Nat Schuyler all over," Charlie said admiringly. "A real damn-your-eyes aristo, isn't he?"

"With a green thumb for money," Thatcher added. "If he can pull it off, it will mean a lot of business."

"He's a smart old cooky," Trinkam said. "But that's a mighty big 'if.' "

John Thatcher sat lost in thought for a moment. Then he asked, "Who's the man?"

Gabler pursed his lips. "That's it. For a while there were a lot of wild rumors . . ."

"I'm sure there were," Thatcher replied, amused.

"He turns out to be somebody named Edward Parry. Walter tells me that his family set up Savings and Loan Associations in Atlanta and Richmond. Worth millions . . ."

Thatcher tilted his chair appreciatively. Not only could he see the furor this must have caused on the Street, he could see the furor growing and growing. He could make a fairly good guess at Nathaniel Schuyler's frame of mind—the man had always played the *enfant terrible* and he obviously proposed to continue doing so even though he must be near eighty. And with some clarity, John Putnam Thatcher could see the shoals looming up before the Board of Governors of the New York Stock Exchange.

"But for the life of me," he said aloud, settling his chair, "I cannot see why this should create problems for the Sloan Guaranty Trust."

Again Everett Gabler exchanged a look with Charlie Trinkam.

"Schuyler & Schuyler sent invitations to most of the big firms on the Street—'To Meet Edward Parry,' " he said. "There's a reception this afternoon."

"The old devil," said Thatcher, after he had considered this. "I wonder if he can pull it off. Well, if anybody can, it's Nat Schuyler. I take it that he's sent an invitation to the Sloan, and you two think you're going to saddle me with it."

"Not quite," said Gabler gently.

Simultaneously Trinkam said, "Hell, no, it's worse than that!"

Gabler proceeded:

"Bradford Withers has accepted the invitation. The chairman has . . . er . . . urgently requested that Charlie or I . . . er . . . accompany Withers . . . to be sure that there won't be any statements . . . uh . . . from the Sloan that aren't what we would want."

Speechlessly, John Putnam Thatcher stared at him. Bradford Withers' role as president of the Sloan was largely ceremonial and, as such, ideally suited to a man whose outstanding characteristic was that he never saw what the trouble was. This rendered him liable to utter, publicly, comments that were hair-raising in their grand disregard of implications. Understandably, it was house policy at the Sloan to keep a weather eye on Bradford Withers in any situation other than the severely social.

"Ev and I don't want to do it," Charlie pointed out reasonably. "And you know, John, you're the only one who can control Brad." He paused to let this sink in, before adding, "And this could get very tricky."

John Putnam Thatcher bowed his head, acknowledging the truth, however unpalatable. In so doing, he caught sight of his wristwatch.

It had taken precisely two hours and fourteen minutes at his desk to transform Poona into a haven of peace and quiet.

2 · Once to Every Man and Nation

TO THE UNTUTORED EYE, all large Wall Street functions seem to be repeat performances played by the same cast. The familiar faces from the big banks, brokerage houses and law firms are everywhere. But in slight fluctuations of personnel, in minute shifts in representation, the experienced eye can read its own lesson.

If, without a word of warning, some astounding feat of levitation had wafted Thatcher straight from the Jockey Club in Poona to the dark-paneled room overlooking Pine Street where he and Bradford Withers found themselves later that day, he would have taken one look, sniffed suspiciously and immediately realized that he was attending a Very Special Occasion.

The first three people he saw were all Governors of the New York Stock Exchange. Further inspection revealed that the Curb Exchange, the commodity brokers, and the over-the-counter houses had satisfied themselves with nominal attendance, as if to emphasize that this was a family problem in someone else's family. The Big Board had their best wishes, oh certainly, but anything more would smack of intrusiveness. And as for the Big Board—the suspicious density of senior partners suggested that many an executive felt with Thatcher that, if a blunder were to be made, he himself would make it, not some middling-to-junior subordinate.

A small, stocky man in his forties had pushed his way to their side.

"Thatcher! I'm glad to see you got back in time. We didn't expect you."

As Thatcher introduced Withers to Arthur Foote, one of the partners at Schuyler & Schuyler, he reflected that Nathaniel Schuyler had organized this affair carefully enough to document the movements of some three hundred men. The old goat must be enjoying himself thoroughly as he prepared once again to shock the Street with a display of his brilliant strategy.

"Look, why don't you come and meet Ed Parry now?" Foote was continuing. "There'll be a mob around him after our official announcement."

Glad to get this accomplished while Bradford Withers was still mindful of the cautions urged on him, Thatcher plodded along in the wake of the other two men.

Edward Parry stood in an alcove with Nat Schuyler. Like everyone present, he looked simonized for the occasion. The lurking fear of television had triggered a wave of five o'clock shaves and clean shirts. In all other visible aspects, Parry was a credit to Nat Schuyler's acumen—that is, he was a replica of a Wall Street financier with a dark skin. The net result was that his teeth and shirt looked cleaner than anybody else's. His slow, considered speech and steady handclasp as he acknowledged their greeting confirmed the impression of integrity, reliability and conservatism. A man of property at every point. In a happier era he might have been a Republican.

The whole thing went like clockwork. For five minutes they chatted on innocuous subjects, thereby edifying the room with a public demonstration of the Sloan's lack of racial bias. That, after all, was what they were there for. Then Arthur Foote's glance strayed over Thatcher's shoulder to the doorway.

"Excuse me. There's someone who wants to meet Ed."

Thatcher turned to his companion, only to realize that once again he had been caught off base by Withers' vagaries.

"A forty-six-foot hull, you say? That's pretty small." Brad shook his head dubiously.

"Yes," agreed Parry. "But plastic makes all the difference. It's not fiber glass, you know. Something completely different. This boatyard in England . . ."

Withers was moved to animation. "I'd like to see that."

The conversation started to bristle with references to the Americas Cup Races and the Bermuda Races. Thatcher's eyes met those of old Nat Schuyler. Above cadaverous cheeks, a distinct twinkle could be seen. Thatcher sighed. His worst fears were confirmed. Schuyler was having a hell of a good time.

"Come on, Brad," he said. "We can't monopolize this corner. Foote is bringing some people over."

Detaching his reluctant superior, Thatcher fought a path to the bar and supplied himself with a Scotch and water. Withers, never one to change course easily, was describing the forty-six-foot paragon to some crony from the Century Club. Vigilance could be relaxed.

A voice broke in on his meditations.

"What are you doing, Thatcher? Making up a roll call?"

Thatcher turned to find Stanton Carruthers at his elbow. He was the trust and estate man for one of the big law firms.

"Counting," replied Thatcher truthfully. "The first thing I saw was three member Governors. I wondered how many turned up."

"Fourteen." Carruthers' reply was prompt. He too had remarked the overpowering display of institutional solidarity.

"What happened to the fifteenth? Dissenting opinion?"

"Oh no! Slipped disk. Poor Bentley is doubled up like a croquet hoop."

Carruthers wriggled sideways to give someone access to the bar. Snatches of small talk could be heard from all directions. Was a corporate reorganization going through and, if so, what would be its effect on second mortgage bondholders? Was Miller, Pierce and Dwyer moving uptown? Was it true what they were saying about the price of landscaping in Mamaroneck? Nobody was talking about the Stock Exchange, its membership—or Edward Parry.

"This," announced Thatcher, "is a very decorous meeting."

Carruthers looked at him speculatively.

"You've been out of town, haven't you?" Then he ventured further. "There isn't going to be any trouble, here. Owen Abercrombie's still making a last minute effort to get Schuyler to withdraw. The trouble will start after the formal application has been filed."

Thatcher nodded. Owen Abercrombie was Wall Street's most vocal ultraconservative.

"And when will that be?"

"Of course I don't *know* anything," said Carruthers cautiously, "but I understand that Schuyler & Schuyler is going to make a statement about that right here."

Yes, that fitted in. Nat Schuyler would want to throw his glove down before as many people as possible. Preferably when they were all nervously on their best behavior.

Not only the guests were nervous. A barman, no doubt overcome by the oppressive atmosphere, let a bowl of ice cubes crash to the table. The ensuing hush was broken only by the tinkle of breakage and one shrill voice carrying its remarks over into the silence by the impetus of its own defiance:

". . . suddenly acting as if they've got a right to be treated just like us . . ."

The speaker stopped abruptly and then compounded his error by flushing fiery red as he became the cynosure of all eyes. Desperate conversation arose from seventy determined voices.

"Couldn't be more unfortunate," said Carruthers with placid detachment. "Thank God we don't act for them. They must be having their hands full." He shuddered delicately at the thought of clients barreling along out of control.

"Who is he?"

Thatcher looked at the speaker disapprovingly. Only sandy hair and the back of a red neck met his inspection.

"Young Caldwell, from Schuyler & Schuyler."

"You mean he's one of Nat Schuyler's partners?" asked Thatcher incredulously. "I don't remember him."

"Well, he's not a partner," conceded Carruthers, admitting some slight meliorative. "But he's their senior analyst. Been giving them a lot of trouble these past two weeks, talking indiscreetly. He's from Alabama," he concluded darkly.

"What about the partners? Let's see. Besides Nat, there was his cousin Ambrose, of course. That's the vacant seat. And then there are Vin McCullough and Arthur Foote. Is there anybody else?"

"No, you've got them all." Carruthers smiled as if encouraging a promising pupil. "It's a small house, and Nat always dominated it. Foote is backing him on this all the way, they say."

"And McCullough?"

"He's by no means enthusiastic about it. But what chance has he got, once Schuyler's made up his mind. And naturally he wants to be careful not to be associated with Abercrombie's group. Oh, hello, Clark. Hello, Robichaux. Just get here?"

Lee Clark, a broker from one of the largest houses, agreed quickly that they had just arrived and went on to ask a question of his own.

"What was that about Owen Abercrombie? Has he been up to something again?"

"Not to my knowledge."

"Well, he will be," said Clark sourly. "As if things aren't bad enough without the John Birchers wanting to burn crosses or something. It's gotten so that you can't get anybody to understand reasonable objections because they've had to listen to some lunatic outpouring from Abercrombie."

Tom Robichaux, who had been busy at the bar, thrust a glass into Clark's hand.

"No use getting worked up," he said sympathetically. "Here! Drink this and calm down."

Lee Clark shook his head irritably. "It's all very well for you, Tom. You don't have a penny at stake. Robichaux & Devane can just sit back and watch the fun."

"Now, that just shows how wrong you are," said Robichaux, stung by the injustice of life. "Francis is keen on moral conscience. I spent the afternoon unloading twenty thousand shares of Stevenson Can at a loss. So we're neither of us feeling funny about anything."

Clark started to explain that there were different ways of losing money, but Arthur Foote had sighted the latest arrivals and was bearing down on them.

"Hello, Lee. Glad you were able to make it." He shook hands cordially and then, with a fine show of indirection, turned to Carruthers. "Stanton, you haven't had a chance to meet Ed Parry. Why don't we get you a fresh drink and go over? Bourbon, is it? And maybe Lee would like to come, too?"

"Oh, for God's sake, Arthur! You don't have to be so subtle about it," grumbled his target. "You know perfectly well that I don't have anything against Parry himself. But I do say, and I'll say it to anybody, that Nat Schuyler is pulling a damn raw deal. And if he thinks that I'm just going to stand still while he jerks the rug from under me, he's got another think coming . . ."

"Well, that's just fine, Lee," replied his host hastily. "That'll be one bourbon and soda and one tomato juice," he added to the barman.

"Tomato juice?" queried Robichaux sternly as the barman complied with the order.

"Ulcers," Foote explained sadly as he led his charges off without further display of hostility.

"He didn't have ulcers last week."

Thatcher inspected Robichaux, an investment banker and lifelong friend. There was no point, he knew, in trying to introduce a new subject of conversation until Tom had settled to his own satisfaction whatever doubts and suspicions had been raised in his butterfly mind by Foote's order.

Finally the tight look of concentration that had been narrowing Robichaux' eyes relaxed.

"You know what? I'll bet all this fuss about Parry has had him worrying. He probably *has* got ulcers. I mean, there's no reason to suppose that going teetotal has got anything to do with all this."

He waved his arm largely to indicate the gathering they were attending.

"Certainly not." Thatcher's tone was bracing. "Particularly as Parry himself was ordering a refill on his Bloody Mary when I left him. You can drink your Scotch in peace without wondering whether it's a clue to your racial sympathies, if any."

Robichaux looked at his companion suspiciously.

"I don't have to have any feelings about this sort of thing. Francis takes care of all that," he explained simply.

Not for the first time Thatcher found himself wondering how that militant Quaker and humanist, Francis Devane, managed to put up with his partner's determined blindness to all extra-curricular obligations except wine, women and song.

Come to think of it, it was surprising that Devane was not playing a leading role in this drama.

It turned out that he was. Arthur Foote, busy on another errand, bustled up. "Have you seen Devane?"

"He's over by the window," said Robichaux. "Said he was going to stay put, in case you wanted him."

Thanking him, Foote sped off in the direction indicated. Robichaux followed his trail with interest.

"I guess the balloon's going up," he said. "Francis is representing the president of the Stock Exchange today. Ponsonby had to go down to Washington."

"Then Nat Schuyler is going to announce that he's filing an application to transfer his cousin's seat to Parry, I suppose," said Thatcher.

"Yes. There's going to be a public statement, with a potted biography of Parry. The Exchange wanted to keep everything quiet, but Schuyler persuaded them that a prepared statement to the *Journal* was better than a lot of inaccurate publicity."

Thatcher said that there were no flies on old Nat Schuyler.

"A buck's a buck," said Robichaux philosophically. "And Nat's little sprees usually bring him a pretty profit."

As usual, when it was a question of money, Robichaux was dead right.

"There they go," he continued as a parting in the crowd revealed Arthur Foote and Francis Devane standing together by the window. Foote was waving across the room to the alcove where Thatcher had been earlier. In response to his signal Edward Parry and Nat Schuyler were advancing to join him. Parry had taken a sheet of typewritten paper from his breast pocket and was carefully unfolding it. Schuyler, bringing up the rear, looked jaunty and triumphant.

"You have to hand it to old Nat," said Robichaux, echoing Thatcher's unspoken thought. "He does manage to get a kick out of things. Look at him. Everybody else there is handling that release as if it were dynamite, but he's full of vinegar."

"My God, have they gotten to the press release already?" demanded a new voice.

Two men had entered from the foyer while Thatcher and Robichaux had been watching history unfold. Expressionlessly Thatcher greeted Owen Abercrombie and Vincent McCullough. What was a partner of Schuyler & Schuyler doing with Abercrombie, today of all days?

As if answering the question, Vin McCullough hastened to dissociate himself from his companion.

"Owen and I caught the same elevator. I'd better get over there and join the firm. Grab yourself a drink, Owen."

Unconsciously straightening his tie and running a hand over his close-cropped graying hair, McCullough advanced to the support of his partners, present and presumptive. Foote, putting on horn-rimmed glasses to study the release which had been handed to him by Francis Devane, threw a questioning glance at McCullough and then at Abercrombie. Thatcher knew McCullough would be explaining the unfortunate proximity in the elevator even before he came to a halt.

"What do you mean, a press release?" Owen Abercrombie's question was literally hurled at Tom Robichaux.

Robichaux repeated his explanation.

"That's absurd. I went out of my way to make an appointment with Schuyler for tomorrow morning to try and bring the old fool to his senses." Abercrombie's bushy eyebrows lowered into a scowl of astonishing ferocity. "He can't get away with this."

"Well, it's not my party, Owen," replied Robichaux mildly. "If you've got any complaints, make them to the management."

"That's what I intend to do! Schuyler & Schuyler will regret this, you take it from me!"

Without further parley, Abercrombie plunged off to the windows where he could be seen haranguing Nat Schuyler. Within seconds he could be heard also. The phrase, "no sense of decency," came winging its way back.

"Wonderful how above-it-all Francis looks," murmured Robichaux appreciatively.

And indeed, Francis Devane, his handsome white head inclined, had engaged Edward Parry in discussion of some point in the release that they were both holding, thereby contriving to protect Parry from Abercrombie's onslaught and to emphasize his own detachment.

Suddenly it all came to an end. From nowhere, Lee Clark and Dean Caldwell materialized. For a moment there was a swirl of activity; then they emerged leading Owen Abercrombie. The altercation attracted the attention of the entire room although a few hardy souls were still doggedly discussing rising office costs.

Arthur Foote took advantage of the near silence to clear his throat and raise an arm.

"Gentlemen! If I could have your attention, please!"

The babble of voices stilled.

"We at Schuyler & Schuyler have asked you to come here this afternoon in order that the financial community may have the earliest intimation of the action we contemplate. I am happy to announce that, together with representatives of the New York Stock Exchange, we have prepared a statement explaining the proposed disposition of the seat on that Exchange held by the late Ambrose Schuyler. If you will bear with me for a moment, I will first read that statement to you, and then be happy to answer any questions which you may have."

Everybody settled into receptive postures. Nat Schuyler and Francis Devane handed Foote the release with gestures that seemed to indicate some emendations to the original draft. Foote nodded comprehendingly, took a revivifying gulp of his tomato juice, and started to read:

"The brokerage house of Schuyler & Schuyler today departed from a time-honored tradition of Wall Street secre—, of Wall Str—"

The speaker suddenly raised both hands to his throat and swayed forward. Those surrounding him leaped to his assistance. Voices rose in a discord of confusion.

"He's sick. Get a doctor!"

"It must be a heart attack!"

"He's collapsed!"

"Clear that couch!"

But even as the couch was cleared and men crouched to lift Foote from the floor, Nat Schuyler rose to his feet and commanded the room with his voice.

"I'm afraid he's dead."

3 · Fruitful Let Thy Sorrows Be

THESE CHILLING WORDS echoed through the room as Nat Schuyler's pronouncement was repeated, doubted, then accepted. Yet, after the first instinctive shock, Pine Street was gripped not by sorrow, but social perplexity.

It was easy enough for the members of Schuyler & Schuyler, who knew what was expected of them. A grave Nathaniel Schuyler positioned himself correctly, like a chief mourner, as he awaited the arrival of the doctor. A step or two behind him stood Vin McCullough beside Edward Parry. Both men looked appropriately solemn.

Dean Caldwell, deputized to handle details, which included obtaining a tablecloth to shield Arthur Foote's sightless eyes, looked shaken as he returned from the telephone to station himself in the formal array. And this, too, was as it should be.

The rest of the room, however, had milled away from the focus of interest, uncertain about the respectful thing to do. It was difficult to shift into formal funeral manner, although there seemed to be tacit agreement that immediate departure would be in poor taste. Accordingly, small groups of uncomfortable men were left to exchange brief, meaningless remarks in hushed voices. After initial confusion, the bartender nodded to his acolytes, and waiters sped through the room, removing half-empty glasses, overflowing ashtrays and other evidence of conviviality. Within a matter of minutes, the atmosphere was that of an extremely awkward wake.

Schuyler & Schuyler's reception for Edward Parry had not been a comfortable social event. Arthur Foote's untimely collapse, however, had injected a new element of anxiety into the assemblage. For the moment, at least, the problem of racial attitudes was displaced by incipient hypochondria.

"But, my God, how old *was* Art?" Thatcher heard a hoarse voice ask.

Fully twenty per cent of the guests, he was prepared to wager, would present themselves for medical examination within the week. Heart attacks among one's colleagues are always unsettling; among one's younger colleagues, they can be downright apocalyptic.

He inclined his head to Watson Kingsley's solemn banalities, while letting his attention range more widely. Across the room, he saw one member of the Board of Governors of the Stock Exchange deep in earnest converse with another. Sad a commentary as it was, he thought as Watson Kingsley mentioned the word "blessing," the fact was inescapable; those of the late Arthur Foote's friends and acquaintances not brooding about their own cardiac conditions were feeling the inconvenience, rather than the tragedy, of his method of going.

"Well, at least this should hold up Nat's scheme about that Negro!"

The voice was suitably low; the sentiment, given the circumstances, was universally offensive. Involuntarily Thatcher and Watson Kingsley (who had moved on to "inscrutable designs of Providence") turned to identify the author. Not surprisingly, it was Owen Abercrombie, still energetically scowling over his own grievances.

Abercrombie was talking to Lee Clark, who was embarrassed. His normally pallid countenance was slightly flushed as he registered the disapproval emanating from their neighbors. He said something inaudible to Abercrombie, who shook his head vigorously.

"No, Nat won't have time to go on with this crackbrained foolishness, Lee. Our troubles are over."

He sounded quite reasonable, a man stating the facts as he saw them. That his way of looking at the facts was brutal had not occurred to him.

It had occurred to Clark, who again murmured something inaudible and moved away with more haste than courtesy. Abercrombie surveyed the room, then strolled through the crush to inflict his brand of reasonableness on other acquaintances.

Thatcher turned to find that Tom Robichaux had joined him. The *bon vivant* looked apprehensive.

"Francis wants me to stand by," he rumbled gloomily. "You know, there's such a thing as carrying Christianity too far . . ."

Thatcher felt a certain measure of sympathy. The high-minded, who gladly shoulder burdens themselves, have a fatal propensity to do so on behalf of their associates as well. However, this was not the time to criticize anyone willing to support Schuyler & Schuyler through the trying formalities surrounding sudden death, so he turned the subject to something that had been puzzling him mildly.

"What's Lee Clark up to?" he asked.

Cooperatively, Robichaux abandoned his own trials and, in his own way, responded.

"You've been away," he said accusingly.

"So people keep reminding me," Thatcher replied. "You'd think I'd been on a desert island for two years."

Robichaux pursued his train of thought to an interesting conclusion.

"I'd like to get away myself," he said with a glance at the funeral party. "But you can't deny it. If you're away from the Street, you lose touch."

"Lee Clark," Thatcher reminded him.

"Oh, that's simple enough."

As usual, once the question came within his professional orbit, Robichaux rose to heights of coherency bordering on the intelligent. He reminded Thatcher of Clovis Greene Bear & Spencer's major coup of some ten years earlier—an expansion into Harlem with plush offices, massive advertising budgets and colored customer's men. This move, for which Lee Clark had been mainly responsible, paid off. Clovis Greene began to enjoy a virtual monopoly of Negro investment in the stock market and became Clovis Greene Bear Spencer & Clark.

"And nobody else ever moved into Harlem," Robichaux continued. "Wasn't worth it with Clovis Greene so big. But if Schuyler & Schuyler gets a Negro partner, then Clovis Greene has had it. And so has Lee."

Thatcher nodded. Really, there were no heights unworthy of Nat Schuyler. It would be a shame if fate had boobytrapped his enterprise by anything so fortuitous as Arthur Foote's heart attack.

"I remember. That's why Clark is so edgy about Abercrombie, isn't it?"

"Well I ask you," Robichaux replied reasonably. "Would you want the Sloan mixed up with someone who wants to send Negroes back to Africa, abolish Social Security and drop the hydrogen bomb on Cuba?"

Thatcher said that he saw Lee Clark's point.

"And then," Robichaux continued reflectively, "I don't think people liked the sound of that trouble up in Katonah. Of course they tried to hush it up—but the story got around."

"What trouble?"

"Abercrombie and Parry both live way up in Westchester, Katonah. When the Parrys built their place a couple of years ago, Owen tried to stir up trouble. Well, nasty letters to the local papers are one thing—but there was talk about pressuring the contractor, and paying off the building inspector and dumping garbage at night. I tell you, people are beginning to wonder if Abercrombie is respectable."

Thatcher, who had been privileged to hear Abercrombie's views on foreign policy ("Send in the Marines!") and fiscal problems ("Abolish the income tax!") tried to picture him slinking around at night with a truckload of garbage.

It was impossible.

It was not impossible, however, to visualize Abercrombie ordering some handyman to do it.

Owen Abercrombie must be causing saner heads at Dibbel Abercrombie considerable discomfort.

This thought reminded John Putnam Thatcher of his own responsibilities. He took leave of Robichaux and hurriedly began to search the room for Bradford Withers.

When he finally located him in a distant corner, however, he discovered his fears had been misplaced; death, like birth and marriage, found Withers at the top of his form. Impeccably formal, he stood exchanging unexceptionable commonplaces about mortality with old Bartlett Sims.

As Thatcher approached, Withers eyed the Schuyler & Schuyler staff still standing guard over their fallen comrade.

"I want Nat to know he can count on us," he said. "But this isn't the time to disturb him."

Thatcher was happy to be able to report that Francis Devane (and his colleagues) were taking care of that. As he spoke there was a stir in the doorway and a small clutch of men hurried into the room. Either Dean Caldwell had been too agitated to report the situation accurately, or the doctors felt it politic to hurry into so august a gathering of Wall Street dignitaries. In either event, their arrival clearly signaled release.

"Why are doctors always too late?" Withers mused. "Well, it's a sad affair, but you know, I think we could slip away."

In no other area did John Putnam Thatcher accept Bradford Withers as arbiter but, in matters like this, he was peerless. Thatcher followed him as he made his way, without unseemly haste, to the door. As others joined them, a general exodus began. Within minutes, only the Schuyler & Schuyler contingent, Francis Devane and the luckless Tom Robichaux remained near the corpse.

The hallway was a relief.

"Thank God that's over," somebody near him said with feeling.

Wall Street being a conventional community, Bartlett Sims immediately replied, "Terrible thing."

"Terrible," everybody dutifully chorused, gratefully going their way.

Fortunately, it was not until they had reached the privacy of a taxi that Bradford Withers shed his public manner for confidences.

"You know," he said, "I can't help feeling that this is a bad sign."

Bradford Withers would not be alone in attributing symbolic importance to the recent catastrophe. Therefore, when they had adjourned to Luchow's for an early dinner, Thatcher listened to his chief with more than usual interest. But, out of touch or no, he learned very little about Wall Street thinking from Bradford Withers' disjointed remarks. Arthur Foote's death was profoundly significant, Withers felt, but he could not specify, to Thatcher's satisfaction, precisely what it signified.

"Well, it's tragic," he concluded with his Linzer torte. "Of course, Nat Schuyler really needs new blood in the office now. Parry sounded very able to me. Did you hear what he said about those new megachrome hulls. . . ?"

"Owen Abercrombie doesn't seem to think that he'll be an addition to the financial community," Thatcher remarked.

Withers put down his cup indignantly.

"You know, Owen is beginning to get positively eccentric. If he were a woman, I'd say . . ."

"What do you think the Board of Governors will do about Parry?" Thatcher intervened to inquire.

Bradford Withers' chief virtue, as well as his most outstanding defect, was transparent truthfulness.

"I haven't the remotest idea," he said with enough hauteur in his voice to suggest that the Board of Governors of the New York Stock Exchange was not the sort of group that a Withers cared to understand. "You know, John, I'm sorry you didn't have a chance to see Jahoda. The maharajah could have given you some fine shooting . . ."

What Thatcher did want to see, after dinner, was his own office. A few hours spent dictating might bring him abreast of the arrears that the Schuyler & Schuyler reception had further delayed. This decision was received by his dinner companion with incomprehension. Going to the office in the morning was, under certain conditions, perfectly reasonable behavior to the president of the Sloan Guaranty Trust. Going there after dinner smacked of the bizarre.

Nevertheless, John Thatcher parted from Withers with less impatience than usual. The Sloan's president was limited, to put it mildly. But he was not an Owen Abercrombie.

Thatcher rather suspected that in the days to come, this might be enough.

He was midway through a letter to a small Massachusetts electronics firm which had recently changed its name and corporate structure in the apparent belief that its stockholders would simply evaporate, when Walter Bowman, who did not share Withers' views on after-hours work, appeared in the doorway.

"I thought I saw you go past. What's this I hear about Art Foote?"

He listened to Thatcher's account of the happenings at Pine Street without revealing how he had received such prompt news of the tragedy. Lost in thought, he lowered himself into the easy chair.

"This might make a difference," he said thoughtfully. "Foote was cooperating with Nat Schuyler to the hilt, you know. He told me he didn't care if Parry was black, blue or green, he'd be worth a million dollars in commissions from Harlem within six months."

With one of the first twinges of amusement he had felt in some hours, John Thatcher mentally saluted his chief researcher. Come typhoon, the return of the ice age, or an epidemic of cholera, Bowman's interest would remain unfalteringly centered on profits and losses. Clearly, here was the man to fill in the lacunae in his own information.

Without regret, he abandoned the ingenuous electronics specialists on Route 128 and did what he guessed much of Wall Street must be doing: considered Schuyler & Schuyler, and Edward Parry.

"Nat did his picking carefully," he observed. "Edward Parry is quite impressive. Did Gabler tell me he had money?"

Bowman grunted.

"Impressive is right. And money, too. I happen to know that Schuyler has been planning this move for months, but to tell you the truth, he couldn't have done better if he'd been beating the bushes for ten years. Parry is the oldest son of Sylvanus Parry. You know, the Savings and Loan man. But he was a millionaire before that—made a fortune out of Atlanta real estate. The son is everything anybody could ask for; he rowed for Yale, he collected almost every medal the Army gives. Then he got a Rhodes Scholarship and spent two or three years in England. Absolutely brilliant, they tell me. Since then, he's been running the family businesses with one of his brothers. And just about doubling the old man's pile."

Thatcher digested this no-doubt abbreviated, and possibly colloquial, but undoubtedly accurate version of the press release on Edward Parry that had not been distributed.

"Tell me, why hasn't this paragon been in the public eye before?" he asked curiously. "God knows, I feel that I've read the life history of every Negro lawyer on the East Coast in the past few years. And minister, too, of course."

Bowman nodded understandingly.

"That's what I wondered. Gus Townely—he's one of our auditors—comes from Atlanta," he said.

Apparently he could not pass on detailed information about Georgia without citing authority.

"He says that the Parry family is simply old money—no publicity, pretty conservative. They're big in community good works —but no politics."

In fact, Edward Parry, spiritually speaking, was another Bradford Withers—with brains, of course. John Thatcher did not say this aloud. What he did say was:

"Really, I've never given Nat Schuyler his due. The one thing that can be said against Parry is that he's a Negro. Is it going to be enough, Walter?"

Like Withers, Walter Bowman did not know.

Neither did Everett Gabler when he drifted in with regrets for having dispatched Thatcher to what had been, in effect, a deathbed.

"It's very hard to tell," he said when Thatcher asked his opinion. "You see, until today, there have only been rumors. Some of them were unfortunate, I grant you, but everything remained vague. The climate of opinion won't jell until Schuyler & Schuyler makes formal application. . . ."

Authoritatively, Walter Bowman corrected him.

"You're wrong, Ev. This is just between the three of us, but I happen to know that Owen Abercrombie has begun circulating a petition. He's just approaching people he's sure of, but they tell me that he's got some important signatures. Including one from Schuyler & Schuyler."

Everett Gabler looked horrified.

"You don't mean McCullough, do you?" Thatcher said. Who had told him that Vin McCullough opposed Nat Schuyler's plan? He forgot. But surely McCullough was too sound to involve himself with Owen Abercrombie.

Bowman lowered his voice while Gabler looked frankly enthralled.

"No, although I know Vin is burned up. He's got a big Southern clientele. Scared to death that a Negro partner will blow his accounts to hell! But basically Vin is decent. He wouldn't get involved in anything ugly. No, it's that Caldwell kid—I don't know if you met him?"

"Briefly," Thatcher said. "Do you mean to tell me that nonentity has been fool enough to ally himself publicly with Owen Abercrombie—against the head of his own firm?"

Walter Bowman's normally good-natured expression gave way to a singularly disagreeable smile.

"He's the last fading flower of the Confederacy. He's . . ." Bowman continued his definition in emphatic terms, finally ending, "He's the kind who likes to call Parry a 'nigra.' Behind his back, of course. The little rat! They tell me Art Foote gave him hell! But I don't think Nat knows about it—yet!"

"Disgusting," Everett Gabler said. "Absolutely disgusting."

There was a moment of silence, then Walter Bowman said, "And I can't help thinking that Art Foote's death is a bad sign."

Suddenly, John Putnam Thatcher felt a surge of impatience.

"Well, this is one bank that's not going to get drawn into somebody else's Roman Circus!" he declared emphatically. "I can see that we can all spend hours on this—but we're not going to. I think we'll have a review meeting of the trust officers tomorrow. At nine o'clock! That should remind the staff of precisely what our business is!"

4 · There Is a Balm in Gilead

THE NEXT MORNING, while John Putnam Thatcher was bringing the Trust Department to its senses, Edward Parry was explaining to his wife how Arthur Foote's death might affect the immediate plans of the Parry family.

"Do you mean Nathaniel Schuyler may back out now?" asked Gloria Parry.

"Oh no. But I wonder whether he might not want to delay things. That's two partners gone in less than four months. The work load will have more than doubled in the firm. He'd have some justification if he decides that he just can't afford to spend all his time politicking up and down the Street right now."

His wife frowned thoughtfully into her coffee cup.

"And what would a delay mean?"

"It's hard to tell. The whole point of Nat's bulldozer approach was to take everyone by surprise. A delay would give the opposition time to organize. And in the end," he paused a moment, reluctant to continue, "it might mean a face-saving way for Nat to withdraw."

At this ominous conclusion, his wife's frown cleared and she laughed softly.

"You're up to your old games, Ed. Trying to prepare for the worst. But I've met your Mr. Schuyler, and I've seen the two of you together. So it's no use trotting out a lot of rational excuses for him to back out, or for you to back out. The fact is, both of you decided to be thoroughly irrational more than two months ago."

Ed Parry looked up in sudden protest. "Now, Gloria, I know you haven't been very enthusiastic about all this—"

"No, I wasn't," she interrupted. "But now—I wouldn't have you stop for anything. What's more, Nat Schuyler isn't used to losing battles, and, in your own quiet way, honey, neither are you. More coffee?"

With a profound sigh of relief, her husband shook his head. "No. I've got to catch the 9:42. I told them I'd be in to see how we stand. You're right, I've just been trying to anticipate the worst. I wouldn't back out for anything now. And while I'm doing battle with Wall Street, how are you going to pass the time?"

"I promised Mrs. Hickey I'd drop by and sign the petition to the Air Force about all these sonic booms."

Her husband grimaced ruefully. "One way or the other, we seem to be spending all our time protesting."

"Well, Mrs. Hickey has a problem with all those greenhouses, and I suppose it was decent of her to ask us. It's only right to try and help her."

"Does she have any concrete suggestions as to where the Air Force should take its jets?"

"Of course not. She just wants them to go away. It's not only a question of the glass. She says the petunias have never recovered."

Ed Parry was still laughing as he put on his hat and coat and went to the garage. But it was not just the thought of the Air Force's elaborately polite response that lifted his spirits. It was the knowledge that Gloria, at first reluctant to accept the inevitable rupture of their privacy which his association with Schuyler & Schuyler portended, had at last decided that the game was worth the candle. Her slowness to come to this decision did not bother him. Gloria was one of those people who, unwilling to disown burdens, have learned in self-defense not to shoulder them lightly.

He was whistling as he came to a conscientious full stop at the end of his driveway before turning onto the county road. As he started to make this turn, all hell broke loose.

It was the grandfather of all sonic booms. It was as if the heavens, rent by some internal fury, had smashed down on him. He flinched against the seat, the windshield starred, and the car swerved. A triumphant reflex brought his foot heavily down on the brake.

The next thing he knew he was canted across the left lane, his bumper locked into that of a school bus. Hastily he scrambled out of the car. He called to the bus driver, asking shakily if the children were hurt.

"Nobody here but me," was the satisfactory reply. "The kids are all at school. I'm taking the bus back to the depot."

The driver climbed down to view the damage.

Looking at his trembling hand, Ed Parry felt a gust of fellow-feeling for Mrs. Hickey's petunias. He was not at all sure that he would ever recover. He would sign any number of petitions to the Air Force, he decided, as he wanly agreed with the driver that that had been one hell of a boom.

"But we're going to have to file a report, all the same," grumbled the driver. "Your grill is all smashed and mine don't look so hot. Probably thousands of reports. You know insurance companies."

Parry joined him to see if they could manhandle the bumpers apart.

"I don't see how they can say it's anybody's fault," he said, bending over to get some purchase. "If the Air Force is going to go around smashing windshields while people are driving, they have to expect—"

"Smashing windshields?"

"Yes. What do you think sent me into that skid? Not only windshields . . ." He was about to detail the depredations committed upon Mrs. Hickey's greenhouses but he was again interrupted.

"Mister! Have you looked at your windshield?"

Parry looked up. The driver had abandoned the bumpers. He was standing bolt upright pointing an accusing finger. Following his gaze, Parry saw that all the cracks in his windshield radiated out in a circle.

In the exact center was a neat round hole.

For two hours he tried valiantly to fight the evidence of his senses. The state police, summoned to the scene by phone, listened, investigated and quietly demolished his theories one by one.

First, he insisted that the windshield must be some freak breakage caused by the boom. Perhaps there had been a structural fault, some weakness in the glass at that particular point which had reacted to stress in this fashion.

The police dug a rifle bullet out of the upholstery in the passenger seat.

Then he suggested that possibly a passing hunter had made an ill-advised shot and, appalled by its consequences, had fled in panic.

"Look, Mr. Parry," said the police lieutenant heavily, "we've got to be sensible about this. You know as well as I do that there are 'No Hunting' signs posted all over the township. And, anyway, what would a hunter be shooting at? You can't tell me he was chasing a deer around here."

He waved his hand at the surrounding landscape. Carefully manicured lawns and clipped hedges rolled back from the road on both sides, with groupings of shade trees dotted at strategic intervals. On the right, set on the breast of the sloping hillside, was the modern Parry house. On the left the Bollingers' Colonial rambled over its level setting.

Ed Parry looked at the scene with discomfort. It was difficult to believe that a bona fide hunter could have fired a shot across this supremely domestic compound. The formal facade was broken only by the Bollinger swimming pool which, together with its surrounding terraces and Colonial cabanas, dominated the front aspect of their house. Parry's own pool lurked modestly in the rear, out of deference to his neighbors' sensibilities. Its placing had been the occasion of considerable discussion with Gloria. She had maintained that the respective wetness or dryness of their skins was irrelevant; the overwhelming fact was their presence. But he, raised in a Southern community which had been shocked to its back teeth by the first sight of colored legs in madras Bermuda shorts, had been anxious to avoid a possible proliferation of irritants.

Now, two years later, he bowed to Gloria's higher realism. He had been guilty of the single eye, seeing only the problems centering on himself, and thereby had done his fellow townsmen—with the single exception of Owen Abercrombie—a considerable injustice. The looming menace of a housing development (for thirty thousand dollar homes) preoccupied them to the exclusion of all other anxieties. They were perfectly prepared to embrace any one-home builder, provided only that he was a multi-millionaire.

A minute later and he was wondering if the police lieutenant had been thinking along the same lines. It would be a help if the man let any expression appear on his face.

"There was some trouble here when you people were building, wasn't there?" the lieutenant asked in a tone suspiciously free from all inflection.

Parry wondered if he were becoming morbid. The man hadn't used any inflection when he asked about the sonic boom.

"There were some minor incidents," he said carefully.

He did not know it, but his voice was the very twin of the lieutenant's.

"Garbage was thrown," said the officer severely. "Paint drums were overturned."

"Nothing more than you could expect," Parry insisted dully. He wondered if he could make this man understand that no Negro had the right to be indignant about garbage while Sunday schools were being bombed.

The lieutenant gazed unseeingly at the horizon. "We don't tolerate that here."

Useless, he supposed, to explain that the Westchester police were not the Birmingham police.

During the ensuing silence, in which both men canvassed and rejected the possibility of further communication, a trooper came running up and drew his superior over to a lane running up the side of the Bollinger property.

Parry was left to his own reflections. He had asked Gloria to stay inside and, on the principle that activity would keep her from worrying, asked her to call the Oldsmobile people about getting the car fixed and sending an estimate to the insurance company. When she predicted that their quiet life was over, she had been right with a vengeance. Reluctantly his thoughts turned to Owen Abercrombie. The police would be asking about him soon. What a mess! This was not the kind of fight anticipated by old Nat Schuyler. Was it possible? Offhand, Parry would have thought not. Abercrombie was not the type to do his own dirty work. But, Parry gloomily admitted to himself, he did not understand the Owen Abercrombies of the world.

He squared his shoulders. The lieutenant was coming back. He would make one last-ditch attempt to have the whole thing passed off as one of those inexplicable freaks of life that occur in the best-regulated communities.

"Lieutenant!"

"Yes, Mr. Parry?"

"I've been thinking. What about a teen-ager? You never can tell. He might have seen a rabbit or something and taken a potshot just for the hell of it. There are rabbits around now and these kids aren't very responsible, particularly if they've got a new rifle."

The lieutenant shook his head. "It's time we got down out of the clouds. You'd better come and see what we've just found."

Together they walked over to the lane. A clump of trees screened it from the Bollinger lawn, and the unpruned shrubbery straggling along its side completed the cover. The area was larger than it seemed from a distance. When they arrived Parry was surprised to see that the little copse had four or five troopers carefully searching the ground. A patch had been cordoned off, and it was to this spot that he was led.

"See those three holes?" The lieutenant pointed to the clearly marked depressions.

Silently Ed Parry nodded. He knew what the explanation would be.

"Those are the marks of a tripod. And we've found some matches and cigarette ashes, not to mention the cartridge. It's as clear as daylight. This sharpshooter"—and his voice was ironic —"set himself up here, took a bead on the end of your driveway, and settled down to wait. He must have had his car turned around, ready for a getaway up the lane. You say you came to a full stop before turning?"

"Yes. That's right." The words were like the tolling of a bell, evenly spaced, evenly accented.

"Well, that gave him his chance to line you up in his sights."

"I guess so."

"I tell you one thing, Mr. Parry. You owe a vote of thanks to the Air Force. You were a sitting duck. If it hadn't been for that sonic boom, you wouldn't be here now, talking about hunters and teen-agers. That threw him off. But he may get his nerve back and try again. You understand that?"

Parry took a deep breath. In a way it was almost a relief to have it out in the open. This was not careful deliberations by a membership committee, or whispered mutterings in a locker room. This was something that there was a word for.

And the word was murder.

His voice was steady when he replied. "Believe me, I'd like to help, Lieutenant. After all, I'm the intended victim. But what can I do about future attacks?"

"It would be a start to find out if there have been any past attacks. Now, I know all about the garbage and paint and the building inspector. But you've been living here now for a couple of years. Has there been anything you tried to shrug off? Or anything you didn't realize was important? Accidents to the car? Fires starting in the outbuildings? Or even," he paused wryly, "even careless hunters?"

Soberly Ed Parry reviewed his life in Westchester. "No, I really don't think so. For the life of me, I can't remember anything."

"It *is* for the life of you," the lieutenant reminded him grimly.

"Of course, this character may just be working himself up to shooting. What about your wife? Has she had any trouble?"

Parry bit back the automatic reply. Not any more than you would expect. No, that wasn't what this policeman was after.

"I'll ask her. But I don't think so. Nothing that she's mentioned, anyway."

"We'll *both* ask her." He held up a hand at Parry's gesture of dissent. "I know. You don't want to have her worried. Well, that won't answer. If there's some crackpot with a gun around, the more worried you both are, the better. What about your kids, anyway? Are they here?"

The children were away at school, Parry told him. Both men looked happier for the news.

"O.K. We'd better go up to the house. I'm going to want you both to figure out what sort of individual grudges you might have started. Anything that might have happened in the last month or so to trigger this off. There's usually something specific if people have been here for a couple of years already."

The suggestion of previous experience with the problem heartened Parry. They were not alone then. After all, Westchester County was a big place. Here and there, scattered among its suburban amenities, were pinpoints of corruption, discharging venom into the community. The police would know all about them, would have records and files charting the outbreaks and subsidences. They would know what to do.

The first thing to do, apparently, was to ask endless questions. It seemed to Edward Parry that he and Gloria told the lieutenant every action and movement in their lives for the past three months. The restaurants they had eaten at, the parties they had gone to, the golf courses they had played at, the stores they had patronized.

At the end of two hours they were all exhausted, confronting each other with blank, defeated faces.

So intent had the lieutenant been on their experiences in Westchester, that only then did he remember the contents of the morning paper.

"Say, weren't you at some party in the city yesterday? Something to do with Wall Street. And there was an accident of some sort?"

"No, no." Parry hastened to reassure him. "It wasn't anything of that kind. Someone dropped dead, a broker. But it was just a heart attack. That's all."

Ed Parry was trying to tell the truth, but he lied.

The twelve o'clock news was the first broadcast in New York City to carry the item about the Westchester shooting. It received only second billing.

The leading bulletin was the announcement that Arthur Foote's death had been caused by nicotine poisoning.

5 · Were You There . . . ?

WHATEVER SUCCESS John Thatcher's nine o'clock meeting had in turning the minds of his subordinates from the problems of Edward Parry to the affairs of the Sloan Guaranty Trust was of so limited a duration as to rob it of any significance. The contents of the twelve o'clock news broadcast were disseminated the length and breadth of Wall Street by the time the last trust officer returned from lunch, and formed the sole topic of conversation.

Poison, eh? Well, that was a new wrinkle. And shootings in Westchester, too. You couldn't say that Schuyler & Schuyler didn't manage to grab the headlines—one way or the other.

Nor was Thatcher himself setting a very good example of austere devotion to duty. He was idly discussing these latest dramatics with Charlie Trinkam, when Miss Corsa entered to announce that a Detective Sergeant Frazier would appreciate a few moments of Mr. Thatcher's time.

Charlie was the first to react.

"You know what, John?" he demanded, with every evidence of satisfaction. "You're a witness. We may yet have the joy of seeing you testify at a trial."

"You already have seen me testify."

Trinkam waved away Thatcher's appearance as expert witness

on the question of the value a going business in McKeesport, Pennsylvania, would have had, if its contractual commitments had been such as were represented to the purchaser.

"I don't mean that sort of thing," he said loftily. "If this Foote business ends up in a trial, it will be for good, old-fashioned murder."

"Yes, and I won't be the only witness," said Thatcher, carried away in spite of himself. "Every bank and brokerage house down here has someone involved."

Charlie grinned. "And a pretty picture it makes, too. I'm beginning to be sorry I missed the fun. What kind of detective do you think the police department has come up with to grill you and Owen Abercrombie and Nat Schuyler?"

"You can see for yourself as you go out," Thatcher suggested pointedly. "All right, Miss Corsa. You can bring in Sergeant Frazier."

The appearance presented by Sergeant Frazier suggested that someone at Centre Street was thinking. He was a clean-cut, serious-looking young man, probably older than he looked. He wore civilian clothes (and natural-shouldered charcoal gray at that). His mode of address was politely deferential, with a formality that for some reason immediately recalled the FBI in its unending round of security clearances. It developed, as time went on, that he was also a skilled interrogator.

He made no attempt to create a relaxed atmosphere. Instead he opened the proceedings by asking gravely if Thatcher had heard the midday news.

"I didn't hear it myself," Thatcher replied accurately. "But everybody is talking about it. They say Arthur Foote was murdered with nicotine poison."

Sergeant Frazier was even more scrupulously accurate.

"The autopsy makes it clear that Mr. Foote died from the ingestion of nicotine in toxic quantities. We have not yet ruled out the question of accident or suicide. But, as the poison was certainly taken while Mr. Foote was at the reception yesterday afternoon, we are naturally anxious to get as clear a picture as possible of his movements there."

Thatcher appreciated the prudence of the police department in refusing to confirm informal announcements of murder. But still, he felt the sergeant's statements were unduly circumlocutory. Probably there was no proof that the poison had been in Foote's glass. After all, there had been that swift clearing up of the premises to remove the unseemly signs of festivity. On the other hand, there was no point in abandoning common sense out of an exaggerated instinct for caution. Lethal doses of poison do not appear at Wall Street gatherings by accident, and Arthur Foote would not have chosen such a locale for suicide. The police in their own good time would, no doubt, produce proof rising to the precision of mathematical logic that neither of these eventualities had occurred. In the meantime, Thatcher was quite content to take a short cut.

"Yes, I can see how you would be interested in Mr. Foote's movements. But I'm afraid I won't be of much help to you. We arrived rather late, and I had only intermittent contacts with Mr. Foote."

"Of course," agreed Frazier earnestly. "Nobody present will be able to give us a minute-by-minute account of the victim. We'll have to arrive at that by making a composite of all the statements. Perhaps you could start by telling me about your own movements at the party, and then we can go into detail on the critical points."

Accordingly, Thatcher cast his mind back to the fateful moment when he and Withers had entered the room and been accosted by Arthur Foote. It was surprisingly easy to conjure up the events of the previous afternoon. Things which he had not consciously noticed returned with startling clarity. The centerpiece on the bar, Nat Schuyler's jaunty posturing as he followed Ed Parry across the room, a little dribble down the side of a bottle of bitters, the tie that Tom Robichaux had been wearing. He spoke slowly, making a conscientious attempt to include the position of every person whom he had noticed at any time.

The sergeant let him complete his recital without interruption.

"That's very good, sir," he said at its conclusion. "Very helpful and clear. Now, if we could just go back over a few points."

They went back to the moment when Foote had waved Schuyler and Parry over to join Francis Devane and proceeded in exhaustive detail down to the moment of Foote's collapse.

Thatcher found himself wondering what there was in his testimony capable of producing such spellbound attention.

"That's very interesting. Let me see if I have everything clear. You say that Mr. Schuyler toasted someone as he crossed the room?"

"Well, it was more of a salute. A gesture, you know. Mr. Schuyler was being playful, I think."

"Yes, of course. And what was in his glass?"

Thatcher was startled. "I don't know. Whisky, I would imagine. Anyway, it was a highball glass."

"And Mr. Parry was unfolding the press release?"

Thatcher nodded.

"And then the press release was passed around and Mr. Devane and Mr. Foote put down their glasses to read it?"

"Yes. And Mr. Foote put on his horn-rims."

Why all this interest in the press release, Thatcher wondered? Surely there was no elaborate theory of its folds containing a minute dusting of powder or something equally exotic.

The sergeant now produced his blockbuster.

"Then, Mr. Thatcher, if I understand the position correctly, there were four men grouped together around this press release, and there were three glasses standing on the table by their side."

"Three?" Thatcher looked up intently. "I'm afraid I don't follow you, Sergeant."

"But you said that Mr. Parry was unfolding the release as he walked over, carefully unfolding it. I take it that he was using both hands to do that?"

The picture was very clear in Thatcher's mind. "Oh yes, he was using both hands."

The sergeant nodded to himself in approval. "Then he couldn't have been carrying a drink, and we have established that no further drinks were delivered to that corner."

Thatcher eyed the sergeant with respect. The damning facts had been extracted from him very neatly. He had an uneasy conviction as to what the next question would be.

"You say you were next to the bar when Mr. Foote ordered his last tomato juice. Did you happen to notice what kind of glass it was served in?"

Oh yes, Thatcher remembered that all right. "It was a double old-fashioned glass."

"Then," said the sergeant as if he were leading a class to the last remorseless line of a Euclid theorem, "the three glasses standing on that table were two highball glasses, containing some kind of whisky, and one cocktail glass with tomato juice in it."

"That is correct."

Confidently Thatcher waited for a battery of questions about Edward Parry's Bloody Mary, although only one mattered—did it look like tomato juice in a cocktail glass? The answer to that was, yes.

The sergeant cleared his throat, smiled blandly and abandoned the party of the previous afternoon completely. How long had Thatcher known Arthur Foote, when was the last time he had seen him before the party, did he know whether Foote had any enemies, had he heard about the ulcer before Foote mentioned it yesterday, what did he know about Foote's drinking habits?

Thatcher explained concisely that he had known Arthur Foote professionally for at least ten years. He had done some business with him by phone in recent months, but had not seen him in person since the preceding spring. He knew nothing about his enemies or his ulcer, and could recall nothing prominent about his drinking habits, which meant that Foote was an ordinary drinker.

Sergeant Frazier punctiliously thanked Thatcher for his co-operation and took his departure, leaving Thatcher prey to a host of questions.

It was clever of the police to have spotted the business about the glasses. And cleverer still, not to press the obvious. Thatcher reviewed his testimony. The last glass of tomato juice must have been the one that had been poisoned. The police were certainly proceeding along those lines.

What had happened after Foote supplied himself with it? Stanton Carruthers and Lee Clark had gone over to meet Parry. Then there had been the huddle over the press release and the more-or-less wholesale abandonment of their drinks by the principals. Then there had been the late arrival of Vincent McCullough, followed by the eruption of Owen Abercrombie and his removal by Lee Clark and Dean Caldwell. During that swirl of activity, anything could have happened. Everybody was trying to pretend that nothing was going on. Half the room could have slipped over and tipped something into one of those drinks.

And most people had been introduced to Parry earlier, when he was rather obviously drinking Bloody Marys. A poisoner, in the natural agitation of the moment, might easily have looked at those three glasses and assumed that Foote's tomato juice was Parry's drink. Particularly if he were familiar enough with the drinking habits of the three regulars so that he would automatically disassociate them from the contents of the old-fashioned glass. In other words, a habitué of Wall Street.

Well, thought Thatcher, that didn't change the picture. Habitués were the only people present, with the sole exception of the guest of honor, who now seemed to have been cast for the role of victim.

John Thatcher was not the only one whose routine had been disturbed that afternoon. Up Wall Street, down Pine Street, along Broad Street, a whole army of serious, polite young men had been making inquiries. In their wake, they left many disturbed executives who, after a round of fruitless introspection, found themselves reaching for a phone. Not surprisingly, some of these calls were to John Thatcher.

The first caller was Bradford Withers.

"John? Somebody from the police has been in my office," he said, rather as if expecting his senior vice-president to send along the fumigator.

"Oh?"

"He wanted to ask me all sorts of questions about that damned party yesterday," the president of the Sloan went on in accusing accents.

Thatcher was soothing. "That's too bad. But I guess we had to expect it, Brad."

"Naturally, I did my best to help him," said Withers, suddenly reverting to his role of responsible citizen. "Don't know why he wanted to know who I talked with. But he did, so I told him."

"Good," said Thatcher hastily. "I'm sure he appreciated that."

"Oh yes," Withers perked up. "And he was interested in that

forty-six-foot schooner. He agreed that they've really got something there."

"Fine."

Withers was not easily silenced. "But the hell of it is, John, that it turns out that fellow Foote didn't have a heart attack. They seem to think he was poisoned."

Grateful that Withers had been spared any appreciation of the horrors lurking before them, Thatcher made appropriate noises of sympathy.

"We've never had that sort of thing before," Withers continued disapprovingly. "I tell you, John, I don't like it."

Cradling the phone, Thatcher had time to reflect that many people were going to join Withers in those sentiments, before he was again summoned by the bell.

"John?"

It was Tom Robichaux, at his most conspiratorial.

"Yes, we've had the police here, too," said Thatcher, stealing his thunder.

"Oh? Did they ask you all that business about the glasses?"

Continuing his policy of ruthless shortcuts, Thatcher replied, "They seemed to think that Parry might have been the target."

"Did they ask you where you were this morning when somebody tried to shoot Parry?"

"Good God, no!"

"They asked us," said Robichaux with simple pride. "Francis was very upset."

Thatcher was perfectly prepared to concede Tom the sensation he had earned. He tried to picture Sergeant Frazier, or one of his ilk, asking Francis Devane for an alibi. He could just manage it. All done very deferentially, with an old-fashioned respect for age and station.

"I can well believe it," he replied. "But why did they pick on you?"

"Actually it wasn't me, it was Francis. I suppose because he's been seeing so much of the whole Schuyler & Schuyler bunch lately."

"Yes," said Thatcher slowly. "I suppose he has been."

"And besides, Francis recommended a doctor to Art Foote. So he knew all about the ulcer."

"What is all this about an ulcer?"

"I didn't know about it myself, until yesterday," said Robichaux, gratified at this proper interest in the tribulations of Robichaux & Devane. "But Foote had been having all sorts of stomach trouble, and then he went to this doctor of Francis' for the tests. So, once they knew it was an ulcer, he started on that whole regimen they have. You know what it's like. God knows, there are enough of them around down here. He gave up drinking last week. Nat says he stuck to it, too, which is more than a lot of them do. Usually he just didn't have anything. And he didn't yesterday either, until he got that glass of tomato juice just at the end. Shows you what drinking that sort of thing can lead to," he concluded on a sepulchral note.

Undeterred by this tempting side issue, Thatcher wanted to know if they had seen Nat Schuyler that day.

"Oh yes, he was closeted with Francis for two hours this afternoon. Don't know what it was all about, yet. You know Nat. He likes to pretend he's organizing the landing at Leyte."

Thatcher agreed that Schuyler liked to be secretive about his plans and asked to have his sympathies conveyed to the much-put-upon Francis Devane. Before hanging up, he asked one further question.

"Tell me, Tom. What did Foote drink before the ulcer? Do you know?"

"Martinis," was the prompt answer. "And brandy after dinner."

There followed, in rapid succession, calls from Watson Kingsley (who wanted to arrange suitable attendance at Foote's funeral), Stanton Carruthers (who *understood* that the police had not been able to dig up a single motive for anyone wanting to kill Arthur Foote. "Makes you think the man must have been abnormal, doesn't it?") and Bartlett Sims (Monstrous! Monstrous! He didn't know what the Street was coming to.).

At this point, Thatcher firmly replaced the phone, told Miss Corsa he would take no more calls and swept Charlie Trinkam off to have a drink with him.

Charlie, while sympathetic, was not encouraging.

"Things have barely begun to hot up," he said as they walked half a dozen blocks north. "You can look at it one of two ways.

Either somebody has decided to liquidate all of Schuyler & Schuyler—and you wonder why some broker's customer hasn't thought of *that* one before—or else somebody's making a dead set for Ed Parry. Either way it means more fun and games."

"Unless the poisoning here and the shooting in Westchester have nothing to do with each other," Thatcher advanced.

"I don't believe that, and neither do you," said Charlie briskly. "Anyway, it wouldn't make any difference if they were unconnected, so long as people think they are. What people think is what's going to make the stink."

Thatcher paused before the revolving doors to consider this. His raffish subordinate had an unerring finger for the pulse of popular conviction.

"Yes, I see what you mean. And either theory will result in an uproar down here."

"Naturally," said Charlie with unabated cheerfulness. "It means one of our little buddies is wandering around with poison and a gun and some unfinished business. For all we know, he may try knives or strangler's rope next time. Just to introduce a little variety."

Oppressed by this catalog of coming delights, Thatcher marched unseeingly into the gloomy interior. It was not until they were hailed that he realized he had been bearing down on a table occupied by Nat Schuyler and Vin McCullough.

"Join us," urged the octogenarian. "We're celebrating."

Vin McCullough pulled out a chair hospitably and grinned. "*You're* celebrating, Nat," he emphasized. "I've got too much sense."

Thatcher and Charlie Trinkam seated themselves, ordered and asked what the celebration was about.

"And," added Charlie, "why is it so ill-timed?"

If Trinkam was hoping to embarrass Nat Schuyler into the realization of a faux pas, he was reckoning without the armor acquired during eighty years of hard work as the bugbear of his more conservative colleagues.

"Naturally, we are both sincerely shocked by Arthur's death. Nor would I countenance anything in the way of a carnival downtown. That's the reason we came up here. But, still, I think that the moment deserves some recognition."

Thatcher preferred Nat Schuyler in his blunter moments. To encourage a return to simple statements, he asked a simple question.

"What have you done?"

Schuyler smiled demonically. "I have just filed a formal application to transfer Ambrose's seat to Ed Parry."

Charlie whistled appreciatively, and McCullough sighed.

Thatcher, who had not lost sight of Nat's goals for a minute, said smoothly, "I don't know anyone who capitalizes on free publicity the way you do, Nat."

"It is not just a question of publicity," said Schuyler with dignity. "After Owen Abercrombie's action, I do not see that I had any choice. Even Vin here agreed with me."

McCullough looked more discouraged than ever.

"What's the old bastard been up to now?" said Charlie, courageously voicing Thatcher's unspoken thought.

Schuyler drew himself up. Ten generations of established New York family could be heard in his voice.

"Owen had the effrontery to present himself in my office this afternoon, with a so-called petition. This petition, after reciting the known facts of the attacks on Arthur and Ed Parry, went on to blame me for—and I quote—'letting loose violence in the streets.' It then ordered me to cease and desist from further attempts to disrupt our American way of life, or be responsible to my conscience and to my fellow citizens for the consequences of my subversive activities."

There was an impressive pause. Schuyler allowed it to prolong itself for the maximum dramatic effect before continuing mildly:

"I showed this document to Ed Parry when he arrived in the office after the assault on him this morning, and we were in entire agreement that we should press forward immediately."

"One can scarcely blame him," said Thatcher reflectively.

Charlie looked accusingly at McCullough. "And you wanted them to hold back?"

"Look, I can understand how Ed feels," Vin McCullough protested. "First, he's shot at, and then he comes in to town to find Abercrombie and his bunch are accusing him of being responsible for violence. But I've already lost a couple of Southern clients, and I was holding on to a bunch of others by the skin of my teeth. If we did this slowly, I could bring them around. But this way, it will hit them like a bombshell, and they'll be withdrawing their portfolios before the week is out."

His superior shed his magisterial quality.

"I know this isn't doing you any good, my boy. But we'll make it up to you with other accounts. It will take some time to arrange things, but I'll see that you don't lose out in the long run. And you're wrong in your idea of tactics, you know. I've been through a good many battles on Wall Street, and that's always the best way to hit people—like a bombshell."

"Oh, come off it, Nat," urged Charlie with a grin. "It may work out as the best way when you're involved, but mostly it's simply the way you enjoy doing things. And speaking of bombshells, people are going to get a bellyful of them. Have the police been around to you yet?"

"Certainly. They were with us this morning," said Schuyler, clearly thriving on a day that had consisted of police inquiries about the murder of one of his partners, the arrival of a potential partner fresh from another attack, an exchange of broadsides with Owen Abercrombie and an extended session with an outraged Governor of the New York Stock Exchange.

Thatcher found himself hoping for a similar wellspring of vitality when he was eighty. No doubt being a professional gadfly helped. He would have to explore the matter.

"They asked a good many questions about the possibility of confusing Parry's glass with Foote's," he offered.

Schuyler was brisk. "Yes, I know. With us they concentrated on finding out how many people knew Ed drank Bloody Marys, before the reception."

"And did many?"

"Oh, almost everybody," was the unconcerned reply. "We've been having a lot of private dinners and lunches for Ed. I tried to get you for one, but you were out of town. So a good many people saw him drinking them—and he never drank anything else as a cocktail—and even more heard about it. I myself heard Abercrombie, at the Recess Club, complaining about it, as if it were some kind of added offense."

Having neatly conveyed the information that Owen Abercrombie had the requisite knowledge to be the murderer, Schuyler seemed prepared to let the subject of his interrogation by the police lapse. Thatcher wondered if he could be drawn further. Probably not. Schuyler, in spite of his surface unpredictability, always knew what he was saying long before the words left his mouth.

"Charlie and I were just discussing the interpretation that's going to be put on these two attacks. We agreed that it's a toss-up between a vendetta against your house, or a campaign against Ed Parry."

"Well, it's not the first," replied Schuyler. "You see, any program to eliminate Schuyler & Schuyler would start with me." He looked around the table with authority. No one contradicted him.

"But, it might start with the name," challenged Trinkam. "By the way, how did Ambrose die?"

Nat Schuyler's innocent blue eyes widened. Vin McCullough sputtered into his drink.

"Now, hold it . . ."

"Just a minute, Vin." Schuyler raised a monitory hand. "I suppose that was a logical question. To reassure you, Charlie, let me say that Ambrose was eighty-two and died of a heart condition that had been troubling him for fifteen years. He was treated by his own doctor on the occasion of his final attack, as well as three previous ones."

"That seems to settle that," admitted Trinkam unrepentantly.

"I should hope so. And now, I really do mean to celebrate the start of my war with Abercrombie. Why don't you all have dinner with me?"

There was a hasty review of plans for the evening. Thatcher immediately accepted. He would not dream of leaving Nat Schuyler while he was in so informative a mood. Charlie Trinkam decided to call up someone and cancel an engagement. Vin McCullough, who would have been a Banquo's ghost anyway, decided that, after one more drink, he would have to be getting home.

"Promised to help my wife," he explained. "We're moving back into the city, now that the youngest has gotten married."

"That's the trouble with all this moving," said Schuyler after McCullough had left to catch his train. "Makes people edgy. I can't understand why people sell their houses when the children go, anyway. We never did that sort of thing," he said, looking back over half a century with some difficulty. "But you can take it from me, that's why he's so impatient about our arrangements with Ed Parry. Really, he has enough to do at the office without dealing with real estate agents and getting rid of furniture. He couldn't have picked a worse time."

This transparent attempt to conceal the very real difficulties that Schuyler's plans were making for McCullough left both Thatcher and Trinkam unimpressed. Charlie spoke for both of them:

"If he thinks there's been a lot of trouble already, he's in for a shock. He hasn't seen anything yet."

6 · Who Follows in His Train?

WEDNESDAY, which in retrospect John Putnam Thatcher was to date as the beginning of The Troubles, provided convincing demonstration of John Maynard Keynes's celebrated dictum about the power of ideas. It was unfortunate, in the light of subsequent events, that so many of these ideas were wrong.

After twenty-four hours, the New York City press put two and two together, produced four, and promptly exploded.

"WALL STREET RACISTS ON KILLING SPREE," screamed one headline.

"POISON AND BULLETS TO KEEP BIZ WHITE," said another.

"WAVE OF TERROR ON THE STREET."

"It's disgraceful, absolutely disgraceful," muttered Everett Gabler.

So indignant was he that he had purchased the tabloids, which under normal circumstances he would not dream of touching, and was now flourishing them at Thatcher.

"Surely there must be some recourse against this grossly irresponsible journalism! Listen to this! 'Wall Street Racists . . .'—why, it's libelous!"

"A little too colorful, I admit," said Thatcher, examining one of the journals. It had managed to invest the murder of Arthur Foote and the attempt on Edward Parry with sexual overtones. Well, they had a specialty and they stuck to it.

"You have to expect the tabloids . . ."

"Hah!" Gabler crowed, thrusting an organ of unimpeachable conservatism at his chief. "And what about this!"

"BROKERAGE EXECUTIVE MURDERED," the headline said chastely. Even the subheadline was restrained. "*Attempt on Negro Candidate for Partnership*," it read.

The article, unfortunately, did not omit the facts.

Wall Street rumors about proposals that a Negro acquire a seat on the New York Stock Exchange were apparently confirmed in violence Monday with the murder of Arthur Foote, 47, a partner in the brokerage firm of Schuyler & Schuyler.

Police are withholding comment on the case, but informed sources report that an autopsy revealed that the victim succumbed to nicotine poison, probably administered during a reception held by his firm for Edward Parry. Mr. Parry, 42, is a Negro.

Although neither Mr. Parry nor the officers of Schuyler & Schuyler were available for comment, it is understood that the firm was expected to admit Mr. Parry to partnership, and support his bid for a seat on the New York Stock Exchange.

Officials of the New York Stock Exchange were not available for comment.

The collapse of Mr. Foote disrupted the reception, attended by many financial luminaries. Barely twenty-fours later, it was learned that an attempt had been made on Mr. Parry's life, as he was leaving his home in suburban Katonah. (cont. on p. 24)

Thatcher looked up. "I don't know what else you can expect," he remarked. "After all, Foote was murdered, it appears. And somebody did take a potshot at Parry."

"Turn to page twenty-four," Gabler directed him sternly.

It was true. Page twenty-four (and page twenty-five, for that matter) was excessive. In addition to the continuation of the front-page story, whose sedate tone was perhaps attributable to the fact that its author was one of the paper's stable of financial writers, there were: a brief biography of Edward Parry (with photograph); a feature article on the Board of Governors of the New York Stock Exchange; for no apparent reason, a description of the Harlem office of Clovis Greene Bear Spencer & Clark, including an interview with Andrew F. Trimmer, Office Manager. (" 'I have no comment,' said Mr. Trimmer. Mr. Trimmer is a Negro.") There was a summary of Negro employment in the financial district, an excerpt from the Civil Rights Bill, and a glossary of technical terms. ("Seat: Membership in the New York Stock Exchange. Only Members can buy or sell securities on the Floor. Floor: The Floor of the . . .")

Unkindest cut of all, there was a list of firms "rumored" to have dispatched representatives to the ill-fated reception.

" 'Rumored,' " said Gabler indignantly. "I tell you it's disgraceful. Well, I suppose I'd better get back to that Rail Summary. I don't know what Ben thinks he's doing out there in Chicago, but I'll write it up for you. I did want to bring all this to your attention."

"Thank you," said Thatcher courteously, letting his eye roam over the biography which substantiated Walter Bowman's informal information:

> . . . Mr. Parry interrupted his undergraduate career at Yale College to enlist in the Army in 1942. He was on active duty in the European Theater of Operations where he rose to the rank of major . . . awarded the Distinguished Service Cross for valor during the Battle of Anzio . . . later attached to the staff . . . Fifth Army . . . crossing of the Rhine . . . wounded . . . medical discharge. After graduating summa cum laude from Yale, where he rowed in the varsity crew of 1946, Mr. Parry attended Oxford University on a Rhodes Scholarship and achieved first class honors in politics, philosophy and economics. Mr. Parry returned to the United States after two years with the London *Economist*. In 1955 he joined his father and brothers in business in Atlanta. Mr. Parry is married to the former Gloria Cole of Philadelphia and has two children, a son Robert and a daughter Louise.

"Yes," continued Thatcher, "it's all very unfortunate."

But Gabler was not settling for anything so tepid.

"Unfortunate!" He brooded darkly for a moment. "I tell you it's inflammatory."

He disappeared before Thatcher could inquire who was going to be inflamed. He was soon to be enlightened.

Miss Corsa arrived within five minutes, technically on time, but far off her own track record. Before she had doffed her raincoat, she too presented Thatcher with an exceptionally large bundle of newspapers.

"Mr. Thatcher, have you . . . ?"

"Yes, I have seen them," he replied gently. Then, because he was only human, he added:

"A little later than usual today, eh, Miss Corsa?"

"My mother didn't want me to come to work," she replied, withdrawing.

For a moment, Thatcher considered this non sequitur. Miss Corsa's large family rarely figured in her conversation. Presumably, then, her comment had been in the nature of an explanation.

"Why," he asked, going to the door to find her composedly settled at her desk, "why didn't your mother want you to come to work?"

Surprised, she looked up. "Why, because of all this trouble. That's why I'm late. I missed my transfer." She turned to the file, in effect dismissing him. If John Putnam Thatcher had time to waste, Rose Theresa Corsa did not.

He retreated into his own office.

"Inflammatory," Everett Gabler had said. "Trouble," echoed a Mrs. Corsa, somewhere in Queens.

"Hmm," said John Putnam Thatcher.

He was not wrong. Mrs. Corsa and Everett Gabler were but straws in a mighty wind. At one minute after nine, his telephone rang.

"Have you seen . . . ?"

"Yes," said Thatcher.

What unfortunate chance had willed that Bradford Withers should choose today, of all days, for prompt arrival at his desk, and for one of his rare perusals of the morning papers?

Thatcher feared deeply that he and the staff were in for one of Withers' captain-on-the-bridge days.

"Damn the Americas Cup," he said to himself.

"Don't like the way the clouds are gathering," said Withers.

"Do you think we should send our people home early today?"

"Good God, Brad!" Thatcher exclaimed.

"These things," Withers said simply, "can turn ugly. We have to think of the women and children!"

With commendable self-control, Thatcher did not reply directly. Instead he pleaded an urgent meeting.

But no sooner was the phone down, than Miss Corsa buzzed again.

"Mrs. Carlson," she announced.

His daughter sounded breathless. "Daddy, are you all right? Why don't you come out and stay . . . ?"

"Laura, what on earth are you talking about?" her fond parent demanded.

"The race riots, of course. Everybody's talking about them. I'm worried sick. . . ."

In this context, "everybody" referred to the Connecticut community where Laura, her doctor husband, and her three—no, four children—resided.

"As I recall," Thatcher observed mildly, "your immediate circle consists almost exclusively of small children and their attendants."

Like her mother, before her, Laura could utilize the pause to communicate impatience. Then she said, "Margo Hillyer called —her husband's at Clovis Greene, you know—and she said . . ."

In the subsequent three minutes, John Thatcher did not form a high opinion of Mrs. Hillyer. Mr. Hillyer, he was fair-mindedly inclined to dismiss because the evidence was so circumstantial. After hearing Laura out, assuring her that he was in no immediate danger, he rang off, prepared to settle down to a memorandum from the Research Department touting Slotkin Corp., an exceedingly dubious operation that purported to see fortunes to be made in secondary oil recovery despite their almost endearing lack of capital.

He had just penciled a question about Slotkin's suspicious ingenuity in the matter of depreciation allowances when the telephone again interrupted him. This time it was Tom Robichaux.

"If you've called to ask me if I've seen the papers," Thatcher began.

"The papers?" Robichaux asked vaguely. "Why should I . . .

oh, you mean the excitement about Parry. It will all blow over. Always does."

But, since Thatcher had introduced the topic, Robichaux cast about for something to add. "Ran into Glover this morning. He tells me that Owen Abercrombie has gone crazy."

"How could he tell?" asked Thatcher with genuine interest.

"Says he's talking about a Wall Street Defense Council," said Robichaux. "With rifles. You remember they had to take his uncle Basil off the Floor in a straitjacket, in '29?"

"I didn't," said Thatcher, considerably entertained.

"Bad blood," Robichaux said. "Francis says that this whole thing is a tempest in a teapot. No reason to anticipate violence."

Normally, Robichaux conveyed his partner's more elevated pronouncements uncritically. But today, perhaps still smarting from having been dragooned into the mourning party, he added a comment of his own.

"Just between you and me, John, I don't think that's the line to take after one murder and one near-miss. But that's Francis' business."

His erratic interest in the subject exhausted, Robichaux reverted to his reason for calling. He had, it developed, a really interesting situation to describe to Thatcher. If he was free for lunch one day this week . . . ?

"What about today?" Thatcher replied.

"Today?" Robichaux was taken aback, as well he might be, since Thatcher normally resisted such bait. "Well, let's see . . . yes, fine, fine. At the Club?"

Only by lunching with Tom Robichaux, Thatcher was convinced, did he have any chance to escape a luncheon conversation centering on Wall Street's emerging racial problems.

That, instead, he was subjected first to a disquisition on Bravura Chemicals ("Synthetic citric acid, John. Don't ask me why, but it's big."), then to one on the current Mrs. Robichaux ("Celestine is sailing someplace with that Greek. Don't really like it, but there you are!") was a small price to pay, he reflected two hours later. It turned out, in fact, to be too small.

"Have you seen the statement the Board just issued?"

Lee Clark, pausing by their table, at least did not ask if they had read the morning papers.

"No," said Thatcher, while Robichaux leaned back, looking unutterably bored.

"A masterpiece," said Clark with a sour smile. "Be sure to read it." He stepped closer to let two men move past.

"I think you're wrong," one of them said angrily. "We could be another Bedford-Stuyvesant. I say that Nat should be . . ."

"Now hold it, Fred," his companion interjected.

As they passed beyond earshot, Lee Clark prepared to follow,

"I can tell you what I think should be done with Nat Schuyler," he said in an undertone.

They watched him disappear into the lounge.

"Letting things get him down," Robichaux commented without approval. He was a firm believer in never letting anything get him down. "Always a mistake to take your troubles to lunch. Now, about Bravura, John."

"I'm inclined to think that Bravura may be one of your troubles, Tom."

They were still disputing the point when they strolled into the lounge ten minutes later. It was unusually crowded. Instead of lunching, then hurrying on about business, Wall Street was sticking together today.

"Have you heard . . . ?"

"Did you see . . . ?"

"You heard about Owen . . . ?"

Somebody, seeking electronic solace, idly switched on the corner television set. Moodily, he stood watching the news. Suddenly, to nobody in particular, he said, "Look at this!"

Like so many Boy Scouts, they crowded around.

"Terrible reception," said Robichaux.

"Sshh!"

The reception, though terrible, was adequate to reveal a hysterical-looking youth draped in earphones and microphones, interrogating a portly, conservatively attired Negro.

". . . Richard Simpson, the well-known novelist."

Mr. Simpson lowered his eyelids briefly.

"And what is the purpose of cash, Mr. Simpson?"

"Cash, cash? Is this one of those quiz programs my wife is always watching?" asked somebody near Thatcher.

"Sshh!"

Mr. Simpson, noted for his simpleminded and successful novels about an expatriate in Paris and his beautiful relationship with a sylphlike busboy, had the resonant voice of an actor, and a firm grasp on the microphone thrust before him.

"The Colored Association of Share Holders," he said, enunciating distinctly.

"Oh my God!"

It was a cry from somebody's heart.

". . . or CASH," Simpson continued, "has been formed today to investigate and combat the gross inequities confronting the Negro in Wall Street."

From around John Thatcher arose a group keening.

"Tell me, Mr. Simpson, how does CASH propose to buck Wall Street?" the young man asked throbbingly.

"Who is that damned fool?" Fenster O'Dowd asked the world. "I've a good mind to call Bill and tell him . . ."

"Sshh!"

". . . using whatever means," Mr. Simpson declaimed. He paused, noted that the hysterical young man was framing another question, and pushed on. "The evidence that the New York Stock Exchange intends to remain lily white has been a shock to thousands upon thousands of patriotic American stockholders who happen to be colored."

Whatever his reception in the saloons on Third Avenue, Richard Simpson could not have asked for a more attentive audience than that standing with Thatcher and Robichaux.

"What are you going to do?" the reporter asked.

Mr. Simpson gave him a look suggesting that he shared Fenster O'Dowd's opinion, and said:

"We have not yet determined what methods are appropriate to counter the racist forces that are denying Edward Parry a seat on the New York Stock Exchange—solely and exclusively because of his color. We do not have our complete strategy mapped out in the face of the kind of anti-Negro forces that were responsible for the death of Arthur Foote, one of the great white men who was a consistent friend to the Negro stockholder. . . ."

He bowed his head. His rich voice was so moving that Thatcher distinctly heard someone murmur brokenly, "Poor old Art!"

"*But*," Simpson continued martially, "I can promise you that

America's Negro stockholders will present a dramatic and moving protest. Including, among our other weapons"—he broke off, staring piercingly into the camera—"including a March on Wall Street!"

"Thank *you*, Mr. Simpson. Now our High-Sky Patrol . . . crackle, crackle . . . an accident on the Long Island Expressway . . ."

At the Club, to use a technical term, all hell broke loose.

7 · Glorious Things of Thee Are Spoken

As MIGHT have been anticipated, Richard Simpson's ominous words, "A March on Wall Street," swiftly relegated the murder of Arthur Foote and the attack on Edward Parry to the mists of ancient history. A number of prominent financiers forgot their newly formed habit of carefully inspecting all nutriment served south of City Hall; in the same area the sales of the collected works of Richard Simpson quadrupled. The financial community, in an orgy of self-absorption, abandoned itself to emotional reactions, ranging from stark bewilderment through cold fury to mindless frenzy. The mighty institutions of lower Manhattan, galvanized by the tocsins of total war and mindful of extensive casualties yet to come, could no longer respond to the tragedy of individual death.

Or perhaps it was even simpler. The targets of Richard Simpson's crusade were the most powerful stockbrokers, the most influential bankers, the most important lawyers in the world. Daily they made decisions that shaped the destinies of men and nations. Naturally, they disliked feeling helpless in the grip of forces bigger than they were. Wall Street was enraged—and surprised —to discover that there were bigger forces. And so, voices were raised with more heat than had been evoked since the nation went off the Gold Standard, and men in expensive tailoring raged with unwonted vigor.

At the heart of the vortex around which these disturbances eddied, was the New York Stock Exchange. The Exchange is a complex body; its work is performed by eleven hundred employees and its ruling organ, the Board of Governors, consists of thirty-three men, twenty-nine representing the individuals and firms which are members of the Exchange, three functioning as nominal representatives of the public, and the President of the Exchange. The President is the Exchange's executive head; his main function is to steer an uneasy course past the demands of the Staff, periodically erupting with policies of its own development, the members mired in internecine politics and time-hardened customs of the trade, and the Board. The President breaks into print in two ways—in the glossy brochures published by the Exchange that cozily remind everyone that stockholders are just ordinary people, and in the public press during his frequent joustings with the Securities and Exchange Commission. The Governors representing the public emerge only when some more-than-ordinarily selfless statement is required. The remaining Governors try to stay on top of everybody else. It is rare indeed that any unanimity can be achieved among these diverse elements. But the specter of Richard Simpson succeeded in awaking several thousand people to a common need.

They wanted somebody else to hold the baby.

The Exchange was opting for a neutrality so rigid that it would justify ignorance of the passions roiling through the Street. In high places telephones began to ring and rolling phrases echoed through the marble halls of the mighty.

"If the financial community were to form a small, independent committee to . . . er . . . ensure that fairness and scrupulous disinterest will be the order of the day, it would be of inestimable assistance to the Exchange," said one of its spokesmen.

"The Exchange and the rest of the community must not be directly involved," said a kindred spirit. "Now a committee could . . . er . . . focus the attention of these dissident elements and allow the rest of us to continue with our work."

A more outspoken representative eschewed nobility for frank

speaking. "God knows *we* can't talk to these people. And somebody has to. Now, if one of *your* partners were to be on this committee. . . ."

It says much for the insularity of Wall Street that by three o'clock the next day it had convinced itself that a committee composed of an outstanding broker, lawyer and banker, all Wall Street denizens, would commend itself to the rest of the world as fair-minded, independent and impartial. Absolutely impartial.

The Committee of Three had as its members Hugh Waymark, Stanton Carruthers and John Putnam Thatcher.

The three defenders of Wall Street had their first meeting in Stanton Carruthers' office, where they eyed each other resentfully.

Carruthers, who had spent a lifetime explaining to clients that he could scarcely be expected to act in the absence of specific instructions, felt the situation most keenly.

"I'll be damned if I can see what we're supposed to do," he said, in effect repeating the statement he had made to the assembled partners of his firm when he had been presented with their ultimatum.

Hugh Waymark hitched himself forward helpfully. While every bit as annoyed as his colleagues at being singled out by a malign fate, he was the only one to cherish any illusion that decisive action might yet cut away the difficulties and reduce his world to that satisfying condition of unchallenged somnolence from which it had been so rudely awakened.

"The way I see it, Stan, they want us to talk some sense into this Simpson. After all, what good would a March on Wall Street do? Has he asked himself that?"

"Pah!"

Even Thatcher was surprised at the noise forced from his lips by sheer irritation. "The buck has been passed to us, that's what. And how are we supposed to talk sense anyway? Do they expect us to hire billboards and sell the world on the proposition that Arthur Foote died of old age, and nobody has noticed Parry's color?"

Waymark looked hurt, but before he could launch a protest, Carruthers intervened:

"Nobody cares about Arthur Foote anymore," he said, sternly

facing facts. "And, as for the rest of it, John is right. We're not supposed to do anything. We wait for something to happen. Then everybody blames us. That keeps the principals in the clear."

Fact facing never has a wide appeal. Hugh Waymark was still grumbling when the Committee of Three prepared to adjourn *sine die*, filled with high purpose and no program. In many ways a comfortable state of affairs . . . certainly more comfortable than what was coming.

There was a muted buzz from the phone and Stanton Carruthers held up a hand. "Would you mind waiting a moment? I told my girl not to put through anything unless it concerned our meeting."

Obediently Waymark and Thatcher halted their progress to the door. Carruthers swiveled around to reach the receiver. His subsequent comments, consisting almost entirely of a series of alarmed grunts punctuated with exclamations of surprise, brought no enlightenment to his audience, but Hugh Waymark glanced up frowningly at his conclusion.

"All right, all right. We'll come right over. Yes, we'll do what we can, but it sounds too late for talking."

Carruthers swung around and up in one urgent movement. He explained tensely:

"That was Clovis Greene. They say they've got a race riot over there. The trouble's down on the Street, and it started over an hour ago. We'd better hurry."

Such was the power of the vision created by these words, that they were down on the street without further questioning.

Stanton Carruthers' law firm maintained its cramped old-fashioned offices on Rector Street. Clovis Greene stretched in expansive grandeur over four floors at the corner of William Street and Wall Street, ten minutes away. Without a word the three trotted toward Broadway. Passing Trinity Church, its gallant spire dwarfed by surrounding colossi, they peered anxiously ahead toward their destination. As usual the vista was obliterated by a solid wave of humanity.

"I don't see any squad cars," muttered Waymark. "I hope to God the police have got things under control."

"Well, if they haven't, I don't see precisely what we are expected to accomplish," said Thatcher shortly.

For half a block, there was depressed silence. Then:

"The main thing is to keep it from spreading," said Waymark, mindful of his own brokerage house a scant three blocks from the disturbance.

Carruthers was more public spirited. "There will have to be some statements made. That's our job—to strike a calming note."

But Waymark, back in the days of his glory as a staff colonel, was viewing the terrain with a keen military eye.

"Good thing there isn't much glass frontage down here. Street fighting won't do much damage. The Chase will just have to take its chances, of course. And you can always raise barricades with cobblestones," he added breathlessly. The pace set by his two companions was incompatible with his figure, no longer what it had been in 1944.

"Are you suggesting that we dig up the asphalt with our bare fingernails?" Thatcher demanded acidly. He was becoming conscious of the spectacle they presented. Waymark's rotundity was balanced by Carruthers' lean length, now stretched forward in hawklike flight. They sped past the Stock Exchange at a lope. The three musketeers, thought Thatcher dispiritedly. And what wouldn't he give for a D'Artagnan, full of youth and fire, prepared to undertake all sorts of ill-advised actions! Carried away by this conceit, he had no difficulty in casting Waymark as Porthos. Carruthers, he supposed, was Aramis. That left him as Athos. Not, he concluded sourly, a congenial role.

Maybe he needed an assistant on this job . . . say, Ken Nicolls. No, he decided reluctantly. The whole point of the Committee was that it should operate personally, borrowing luster and commanding respect by virtue of its distinguished participants. Another objection lay in visualizing D'Artagnan spending his evenings setting up a cooperative nursery in Brooklyn Heights.

Carruthers, leading by a nose, came to a sudden halt at the Seventh Avenue IRT station with an abruptness that brought his two colleagues cannoning into him.

"Where is it?" he asked blankly.

"We'll have to look for it," said Waymark, nothing daunted.

"I thought race riots proclaimed themselves," Thatcher objected.

At this moment there was a slight gap in the scurrying crowds. Carruthers pointed into it.

"Do you think," he asked dubiously, "that *that* can be what they called about?"

He was pointing to a small band of weedy pickets parading before an entrance on William Street with assorted placards. They were treading their stately measure under the disenchanted gaze of three policemen.

"For God's sake! Do you mean this is all there is?" protested Waymark, making no attempt to disguise his disappointment. It was as if Kitchener had fetched up at Khartoum only to find everybody having a friendly hand of five-card stud.

Thatcher maintained a disapproving silence for so long that his colleagues looked at him. He was staring at the placards.

"Tell me," he said, "does it seem to you that these pickets are a long way from unity."

The passing throng paid no attention either to the pickets or to the gimlet-eyed trio which now advanced to close quarters and soberly read each message as it revolved before them. Some people were rushing down into the bowels of the subway. Others were rushing up. Messenger boys from the printers were everywhere, delivering hot proofs of prospectuses, briefs and bank letters. A steady persistent trickle made its way to the small Roman Catholic chapel on Pine Street which provides support and solace for the faithful in the very shadow of Mammon.

Jostled and buffeted, the three musketeers remained motionless, enthralled by their reading. The first sign said that Clovis Greene was racially biased, while the second said that Schuyler & Schuyler were troublemakers. A third, rather confusingly, maintained that "Colored operated is not colored owned," while a fourth demanded simply: "Down with the Stock Exchange." An even more alien note was introduced by a lone theological student carrying a banner proclaiming: "White Turret Restaurant is Unfair."

Thatcher, rousing himself from bemusement, voiced a problem: "Why are they picketing Schuyler & Schuyler here?"

"Didn't you know? They're in this building, too."

"Fine. That's all we need. It makes one thing certain. If there's going to be any fighting, it is likely to be internal warfare among the pickets."

Waymark was eyeing a youth in a turtleneck sweater and

beard. "They look like pacifists to me. Well, I suppose we ought to go up and see Clovis Greene."

"I'd like to see them," said Carruthers grimly. "There's work waiting for me on my desk. What do they think they're doing, pushing the panic button like this?"

"We may have to do more than give Clovis Greene a piece of our mind," remarked Thatcher, nodding at a car that was inching along the street amidst the pedestrian traffic. In the windshield appeared the grim legend: Press.

"Oh, for God's sake!"

"With luck, we have two or three minutes clear," said Thatcher, manfully overcoming the temptation to dive down into the IRT, shoot up to Grand Central and entrain for distant places.

Carruthers was brisk. "You're right. We'd better tell these pickets to address their complaints to us. I'll promise to interview the interested parties and bring them an answer."

Waymark, one eye on the car which now hovered by a truck engineering withdrawal from the curb, threw himself into the fray. "We've got to work fast."

Achieving something of their former urgency, the three marched over and assumed a commanding position. Carruthers raised a courtroom voice to gain attention and introduced the Committee, primarily for the benefit of the suddenly alert police. With an easy stream of professional fluency, he said that they understood the pickets were protesting certain actions on the part of Schuyler & Schuyler and of Clovis Greene, that the Committee would interview these firms and be back shortly with statements as to their contemplated actions. Masterfully silencing all attempts to break into speech and usurp any portion of his precious time, he urged the pickets to continue the responsible citizenship already demonstrated by their courageous, forthright and nonviolent conduct.

A speech embracing a diversity of activities and desires is necessarily generalized, but Thatcher gave Carruthers full marks for conveying the impression that the pickets were regarded seriously and that action was being taken.

The Committee then plunged into the building, timing their entrance so nicely that the closing of the glass door coincided with the descent of a horde of journalists onto the scene.

At the elevator, Carruthers paused in indecision. "Which first?"

"Schuyler & Schuyler, I think," Thatcher replied. "Most of those pickets could be quieted by a statement from Parry. We might be able to get one."

"But what about the Abercrombie boys down there?"

"Nothing will quiet them. They're looking for trouble."

On the twenty-sixth floor, Schuyler & Schuyler was going about its business with a commendable absence of hysteria. Indeed, when they were ushered into Nat Schuyler's office, it was to disrupt a business conference between him and Vin McCullough.

"Come in, come in. Don't mind Vin. I'm snowed under at the moment, and I'm pushing all of poor Arthur's accounts onto him. Between Ambrose's accounts and Parry's application, I don't have a minute to spare."

He smiled up at them genially without mentioning the very substantial accounts in his own name. It was these accounts which had always supported Nat Schuyler's unwavering domination of his firm.

"I heard you three had been formed into some sort of committee. Don't understand what it's all about exactly, but we'll be glad to do anything we can for you."

Thatcher was in no mood to encourage witticisms on the subject of the Committee's mission.

"Tell me, Nat," he said, "do you realize that there are about twenty pickets parading up and down in front of this building?"

Guileless blue eyes turned to him. "Why, yes," said Schuyler thoughtfully, "yes, I believe someone did say something about it."

"And that Clovis Greene has whipped itself into a frenzy on the subject?" Thatcher pressed.

"Now that was what they were saying. That Clovis Greene was calling in the police." Schuyler beamed blandly at the room. "Very imprudent of them, I feel."

Carruthers brought his jaws together with an audible click, while Thatcher stared frostily at the man behind the desk. It was all too clear what was happening. Clovis Greene was being tempted to all sorts of rash, hasty reactions to their present dilemma—and, alas, succumbing to that temptation. Once they had been given ample opportunity to put themselves hopelessly in the wrong, Nat Schuyler would waft himself downstairs and appear on the scene as a white-haired harbinger of peace and moderation.

Nor was any of this playacting aimed at those youthful pickets. Old Schuyler hadn't lost sight of the ball for one single second. It was the pulse of the financial community that he was following with his stethoscopic shrewdness. Given enough publicity, by tomorrow morning a large number of people on the Street would be feeling that Nat Schuyler was the voice of sweet reason. Because the people on the Street, like the residents of Katonah, were basically not interested in Ed Parry's problems; they were interested in their own. And how could you get on with business, if crackpots like Owen Abercrombie wanted you to shoulder a rifle, or oddballs like Clovis Greene tried to call out the National Guard because a couple of students were walking up and down the sidewalk?

At this point in Thatcher's meditations, the door opened and a familiar figure entered. It was young Dean Caldwell.

"Sorry, Nat. I didn't realize that you had people here."

But he was too consumed with the importance of his own activities to make more than a token apology. He continued without pause:

"Do you realize that the police have refused to do anything about what's going on outside? They say as long as the situation is orderly, they won't interfere. Christ! Why don't they admit they don't have the guts to do anything!"

"I wasn't aware that we'd asked them to do anything."

An ugly red tide suffused Caldwell's face. "Clovis Greene has!" he snapped. "Lee Clark says he's going to take it right up to the Commissioner."

"Oh?"

Caldwell took several angry, stamping steps. "That's not the way to handle this sort of thing!" Suddenly he raised his eyes and looked directly at Schuyler. "You may as well know. I called Abercrombie, so he could send a couple of his own pickets over. That trash downstairs won't make any trouble, if they know there's someone willing to take them on."

Did Caldwell realize that he was playing Schuyler's game?

Thatcher thought not. But a healthy instinct of self-preservation would have rung an alarm at Schuyler's next words.

"Did you, now? That was very thoughtful of you, my boy," he said, his voice silkier by the second. "Now that you've assured our personal safety, was there anything else?"

Caldwell stood his ground, but it was at Vin McCullough that he looked. "I've got those reports on the holdings in Art's accounts that you wanted. You can look at them now."

"I don't have time now. You'd better send them along to my office," replied McCullough, pointedly disassociating himself from the departing chief analyst.

Schuyler was amused by the exchange. "You'll have to look at those reports some time, Vin. And he'll make you go to him. So he can sound out your loyalties."

"He makes me sick," said McCullough suddenly.

"Yes. An object lesson to us all. But a very good analyst. The reports will make nice reading."

McCullough relaxed. "They'd better. I got three more cancellations from clients in Biloxi this morning."

"Don't worry," said Thatcher dryly. "I can scarcely believe that there isn't a lot of business heading toward Schuyler & Schuyler. I can almost hear it pattering down from Clovis Greene."

Vin McCullough grinned. He was hardened to Nat Schuyler's tactics but he enjoyed watching their effect on outsiders.

"But those will be Parry's accounts," he said.

"And it is about Ed Parry that we wanted to speak to you. Is he here by the way?"

"No." Nat Schuyler shook his head. "Do you want to see him?"

"Yes. We"—and Thatcher included the rest of the committee in a sweep of his hand—"would like to get a statement from him, urging calm and forbearance on the public scene."

"I think we can do better than that," replied Schuyler, who obviously had the whole statement already planned. "Mind you, I don't know whether Ed will agree to this. But you could suggest that he say he has every confidence in the integrity and fairness of the Stock Exchange. We filed our application yesterday. In the normal course of events, it will be reviewed by the Department of Membership Firms and then by the Board of

Governors. Fortunately, Ed more than meets the personal and financial qualifications involved. That should make approval of the application a certainty, unless he has misjudged the spirit guiding the Exchange. I think he would be willing to say publicly that an imputation of such gross bias and inequality should not be made until the Exchange has had an opportunity to conduct its normal clearance activities."

Thatcher drew a breath.

"That will do nicely," he said firmly. "What you're saying is that all hell will break loose if they don't give him his seat. Our mission seems to be to keep things calm until the Exchange makes its decision. I am not prepared to cross any additional bridges. Right?"

Carruthers and Waymark indicated their approval, and an appointment was finally made for a meeting with Parry on Monday morning. On their way out Schuyler smiled diabolically and asked them to convey his regards to Lee Clark if they were stopping by at Clovis Greene.

"How did he know we were going upstairs?" asked Waymark resentfully.

"Because he's an old devil," said Carruthers, punching the button for the thirty-second floor. "And I am very glad I'm in the law business. We steal our clients from each other much more quietly."

Clovis Greene had the grace to be slightly abashed when its sins were firmly pointed out.

"I'm sorry if they made it sound like a riot, Stanton," said Lee Clark. "We're all on edge. The fact is, we really do have a near riot in our Harlem office. And when the pickets started to show up here we thought it was going to be the same thing all over."

Carruthers had not spent years cross-examining hostile witnesses on disputed wills for nothing.

"Exactly what is going on at the Harlem office?" he demanded.

"The police have got fifteen men there, and I can tell you that they're not putting out that kind of man power lightly. There's a mob in the street that's forced them to reroute traffic, the pickets are inside the office and there's been trouble with the help. And if that isn't enough, there's a line around the block of customers waiting to close their accounts." He ran a hand through his hair and suddenly looked very tired. "I don't know how they expect us to close all their accounts if they frighten the help away."

Thatcher found himself silently thanking heaven that the Committee's geographical jurisdiction might reasonably be held to end at Park Row.

"That is very unfortunate," he said as sympathetically as he could. He knew perfectly well that Lee Clark was looking old and tired because he saw his position at Clovis Greene going down the drain. "We all want to prevent an outbreak of that sort here. Particularly the line of customers withdrawing. Now, are you prepared to join Schuyler & Schuyler in a plea for peace in the streets?"

"Sure, sure." Clark waved his hand vaguely. "You might also say that we have no racial bias. We just don't happen to know any Negro millionaires we can pull out of our pocket."

Thatcher firmly reminded himself that he had already decided not being Owen Abercrombie was enough. Nevertheless the Committee would be wise to expect nothing better than self-pity from Lee Clark in the trying days ahead. He said as much as they drafted hasty bromides on the downward plunge.

"That's that," said Carruthers with satisfaction. "Now, all we have to do is read this to those pickets outside. Then I can get back to work."

But outside was no longer what it had been. From nowhere had come a fleet of trucks outrigged with booms at the end of which perched large cameras and small men. Yards and yards of cable festooned the street, while young men with deep, unctuous voices roamed up and down, microphone in hand.

"And this," said one of them in an oily voice of friendly doom, "is Miss Shirley Glauber from Brooklyn College. Tell our viewers, Shirley, why you have come here to picket Clovis Greene."

Miss Glauber tossed her pony tail and proceeded to harangue the network's listeners in tones destined to carry her far in the League of Women Voters.

Out of the corner of his eye, Thatcher saw two microphones heading for his nose. Well, he thought bitterly, at least he was not wearing furry headgear for his debut on nationwide television.

8 · Tidings from Afar

WHILE *Sturm und Drang* raged on Wall Street, peace and serenity reigned in Katonah, Westchester. That, of course, is why people live there. But Ed Parry, after an hour with the newspapers and mail, looked on his sun-lit lawns with patent dissatisfaction. He had just come in from the hall phone.

"That was the office calling," he explained to his wife. "Nat's bringing Thatcher up here. They're on the way."

"We could ask them to stay to lunch."

"Yes." Parry shifted restlessly. Then he burst out: "It doesn't seem right. Maybe I should have insisted on going in to meet them."

"Oh, Ed!"

Then suddenly Gloria Parry started to laugh.

Her husband looked up in hurt bewilderment.

"What have I said that's so funny?"

She shook her head. "It's not what you're saying, it's what you're feeling. For forty-two years you've been feeling guilty because you haven't suffered with the problems of most Negroes. You've felt like a draft-dodger because money has protected you from most of the nastiness . . . finding a job, or moving into a garden apartment, or getting a decent education for your children. Now somebody's tried to poison you, you've been shot at, and eggs have been thrown at you. And what do you do? Do you stop feeling guilty?" She answered her own question by another gurgle of mirth. "Not a bit of it. You just shift your ground and start feeling guilty because you aren't suffering the tribulations of all the other brokers down on Wall Street. You are! Admit it!"

"It's not exactly that," he hedged. "It's just that I can't help realizing what I've stirred up. After all, I've been in the banking business all my life. I know what's going on at places like Clovis Greene. And all this doesn't help." He flicked a derisive finger at the front page featuring beatnik pickets and Richard Simpson outlining plans for his great March. "And then . . ." he halted uncertainly.

"And then?" challenged Gloria.

"And then I wonder what good it's doing. After all, there aren't thousands of Negroes waiting to buy seats on the Exchange."

"There you go again. Of course there aren't. But you know as well as I do that you can crack an institution much faster from the top than the bottom. It will make a big difference downtown if there's a prominent Negro at the top—a difference in hiring secretaries and customer's men and research analysts. And, Ed, even you can't deny that this has dramatized the question of potential Negro investment."

"I suppose so," he said gloomily. "But at the price of bringing discomfort to a lot of people."

Gloria's tone grew brisker. "There's always discomfort when you change things. Particularly to the people who don't want a change. And even to innocent bystanders. But so long as it's nothing worse than discomfort, the job you're doing is worth it. And, I hope you aren't wasting any of this sympathy on Nat Schuyler."

Suddenly her husband grinned. "No, I haven't lost my mind completely. He's having a grand time, and he knew exactly what he was taking on. The whole thing was his idea, and he's going to make a lot of money out of it." The momentary gaiety faded from his voice. "That seems like a hell of a motive for something like this."

"It's the motive for most financial moves," said Gloria dryly.

"You don't like Nat, do you?"

"It's not a question of liking him. I feel profoundly grateful to him."

"How's that?"

"He's the only thing that makes it all possible. You couldn't stand this if you had to deal with a burning zealot. You'd have to worry about him all the time. But with Nat, you're completely safe. If they dynamite Schuyler & Schuyler tomorrow, Nat will be dug out of the shambles chortling over how he can use the bombing in his next maneuver."

"I don't have to worry about anybody at Schuyler & Schuyler. Even Vin McCullough is going to make a pretty penny out of this, too, in the long run."

"And Dean Caldwell?" asked Gloria slyly.

Her husband frowned. "I may be soft," he replied, "but I'm not crazy. Dean Caldwell can take care of himself!"

"Good! Believe it or not, so can the Governors of the New York Stock Exchange. If you could only realize that they can live through the experience of having to make a lot of statements, and even walk through a picket line, you'd be much more comfortable about the whole thing."

Not for the first time, Ed Parry realized that his wife's armor was thicker than his. Gloria's father had been one of the first Negroes to be elevated to the federal bench—but she had grown up the daughter of a struggling colored lawyer without the protection of a healthy bank balance. The rewards that had come into the Cole family's life had come late enough to be the rewards of endeavor. Gloria Cole Parry bore no burden of guilt, and she had considerable experience with racial problems which her husband had been spared.

"I don't know that I have any right to be comfortable," he concluded glumly. "And I suppose I'm not being truthful with myself, or I'd admit that one of the things that bothers me is the loss of our privacy. I hate the idea of being a professional Negro man of distinction. For years I've gone out of my way not to have articles in the magazines or let myself be exploited by the State Department—and now, this!"

Gloria grinned. "Yes, there's been no nonsense about sticking your toe in to get the feel of the water. You dived in all the way."

She smiled at him with great affection.

Almost grudgingly, he started to return her smile.

"Yes. And I know what you're thinking—even if you don't say it. If I don't have the right to be comfortable, what makes me think I've got the right to be private? And if I get that seat, I will be doing some good."

"When," corrected Gloria firmly.

The smile broadened. "*When* I get that seat," he agreed. "And for somebody who was lukewarm about this whole affair, you certainly are turning into an activist."

"Oh, you'll see me marching with a banner yet."

She did not bother to explain that her motive for activism was the support and comfort of Ed Parry. That would probably make him feel guilty, too. Instead she nodded toward the window overlooking the drive. "That must be your visitors."

Two minutes later and Thatcher was being introduced to his hostess. Ed Parry started off by apologizing for making them drive to Katonah.

"It's the Police Commissioner," he explained. "There was a little trouble Friday night. He wants to give me an escort when I go into the city."

Everybody contemplated the spectacle of a potential member of the Exchange moving through New York under heavy police guard.

"You didn't go into any details about the trouble, Ed, when you called," said Nat Schuyler bluntly. "Was it another shooting?"

No, it hadn't been anything like that. There had been a crowd of hecklers waiting for his taxi when he got to Grand Central. There had been shoving and a few rotten eggs thrown. The police had broken it up.

"Under the circumstances," concluded Parry mildly, "it seemed best to minimize the number of my visits to the city. For everybody's sake."

Thatcher was heartened by this display of self-control. He realized that the Committee, Wall Street and New York could congratulate themselves that they were dealing with sober, responsible adults, not fire-eating young lunatics. Like Gloria Parry, he was beginning to be profoundly thankful that Nat Schuyler, as prime mover of this drama, was so *dégagé* in his motives. Giving partial expression to these thoughts, he said:

"That encourages me to feel that you'll agree to a suggestion made by Mr. Schuyler. It would involve asking the Negro community to suspend judgment until the Exchange has had an opportunity to complete its normal review of your application for membership."

Now that the participants of the meeting were getting down to business, Gloria Parry made an excuse and started to rise.

"No, Gloria, don't go." Her husband waved her back and turned to the others. "This concerns my wife as much as it concerns me. I'd like to have her consider this, too."

The consideration turned out to be protracted, no doubt due to the alarming range of connotations that can be quickened into life by any single sentence in the English language. Happily the group was as one in deploring violence, but . . .

He was the last man in the world to condone mob rule, said Nat Schuyler blandly, but it was every American's God-given right to change stockbrokers. Transferring an account from Clovis Greene to Schuyler & Schuyler did not constitute a threat to the community. Particularly if the customer were moved by certain aspects of the whole man. . . .

It must be clearly understood that the Exchange is as far above a bribe as a threat, John Putnam Thatcher found himself saying. Its rarefied deliberations would pursue their stately course unswayed by both abstention from violence and the hideous specter of mobs chanting at the window. There could be no suggestion of a bargain with the Negro community.

The Parrys, not to be outdone, also had difficulties. They would willingly withhold judgment on the Exchange until presented with irrefutable proof of racial bias. In return, the Parry application must be treated as the normal exercise of a millionaire prerogative. Ed Parry was not approaching the New York Stock Exchange by the back door, hat in hand, humbly asking for a favor. And while he was prepared to plead for peace, he would countenance no suggestion that there had been any Negro violence.

"Because there hasn't been any," he said firmly. "Look at what has actually happened. Aside from a few pickets and a few speeches, there has been only one kind of violence."

"Exactly," chimed in Nat Schuyler. "A series of murderous attacks on Art Foote and on Ed. Not to mention a little egg-throwing."

Parry intervened. "The egg-throwing is a natural result of the situation, Nat. You can't hitch it up with the other two."

"All the same, it must have stemmed from Wall Street."

"Oh?" asked Thatcher.

"Certainly. Ed, here, isn't a household face, and his daily agenda isn't published in the newspapers. That gang must have had some grounds for believing he would be at Grand Central on Friday. Isn't that right, Ed?"

But Parry, who had seen where Schuyler's argument was leading, merely looked acutely uncomfortable.

"I still don't see how that ties in with Wall Street."

Schuyler leaned back expansively.

"Because Ed was going to a dinner with some bond dealers that was common gossip in the luncheon clubs. And there aren't many trains to Katonah after the rush hour. Anybody could figure out when Ed would be showing up at Grand Central. And, of course, a resident of Katonah would know—without even having to think about it."

"Why don't you say it, Nat?" Parry shook his head angrily. "You think Owen Abercrombie arranged that little reception for me at the station. For that matter, I wouldn't put it past him. But that doesn't have anything to do with slipping nicotine into Art Foote's tomato juice."

"You know perfectly well that the police think your Bloody Mary was the target for that nicotine. But I too find it difficult to see Owen fooling around with any sleight of hand with poison packets. He'd be much more likely to spray the room with a machine gun. I do wonder if somebody didn't tip him off about your movements last Friday. Maybe put him up to creating a disturbance. Because what you have to face is that we *do* have a murderer around here. And Owen Abercrombie would make a perfect stalking horse for him."

Unwillingly Thatcher was reminded that the house of Schuyler & Schuyler harbored at least one tipster for Owen Abercrombie. Was that what Nat Schuyler wanted him to think about? Dean Caldwell's name had been carefully kept out of the conversation—but not his image.

Ed Parry was not prepared to let the discussion center around personalities. In fact, thought Thatcher with growing amusement, he was much more the Exchange's *beau ideal* of a member than Nat Schuyler.

"In any event, I think we've made my point to Mr. Thatcher," he said. "What violence there has been has stemmed from the opponents of my application. And it has been directed against our brokerage firm, and not the Exchange, or Clovis Greene. Now, you say that the Exchange is concerned about stabilizing the market in the face of these wild rumors. I am concerned about that, too. After all, I have substantial investments myself. Anything that can be done by calming statements, I'm prepared to do. But I am not prepared to agree that the way to stop these slides is to wrap a curtain of silence over the question of Negro investments. The sooner people start to think about that, the better. Remember, the big slides have been started by attacks on us. If the market is going to dip every time somebody takes a bead on me, then the thing to do is stop this potshotting. There's nothing I can do about it."

Thatcher sighed. Everything that Parry said made sense. One more attempt on his life and the market would have to stop trading.

Gloria Parry came to the support of her husband's intransigence.

"Nor are we prepared to retreat to a cave for the duration. Ed is trying to cooperate with the Police Commissioner, but certain things we have pledged to do and those we'll go through with. You may as well know that we're patrons of the NAACP benefit night at Lincoln Center this weekend. And we're going to it, no matter how anybody feels. It won't be our people who start a riot there."

She looked around the room defiantly.

Curiously, it was Nat Schuyler who was moved to protest. He even started to ask a question, no doubt to emphasize the desirability of keeping the issue simple. Further examination of his hostess's resolute countenance persuaded him to remain silent. This silence was broken by the telephone.

It was for John Thatcher, from Hugh Waymark.

"You've got to get back here right away," said Waymark tersely. Thatcher hoped that his hoarseness was A.T.&T.'s fault. "All hell is breaking loose. The Exchange wants to talk to all three of us."

"I'm perfectly willing to talk to them this afternoon. But I can't leave now. We haven't even worked out a final draft—"

"The draft doesn't matter. This can't wait!"

"What can't?" demanded Thatcher, irritation yielding to curiosity.

Waymark laughed dementedly. "I can't explain. Just turn on your television set."

After hanging up, Thatcher turned to the others. This was no time to break the news that the Committee of Three was already beginning to crack at the seams.

"It seems," he said cautiously, "that something is going on. Could we turn on your television set?"

Gloria Parry obligingly walked over to a sleek walnut hi-fi arrangement and slid back a panel revealing the screen. "What station do you want?" she asked as she started to twist knobs.

But no further information was required. Even before the sound came on, it became apparent that all the networks were carrying the distorted, flickering image of Richard Simpson.

In the ghostly silence that persisted for several seconds, Simpson threw his arms out and opened his mouth in what must have been a bull-like roar. Clearly he was urging some form of Homeric action. In that brief interval of speculation, Thatcher rejected several possibilities as unduly dramatic. Reality for once surpassed his expectations.

". . . Star Chamber proceedings. We demand a fair and open hearing for Edward J. Parry. Let every man stand and be counted! Let there be an open ballot, so that we may know our enemies . . . those consumed by jealousy of the black man must be identified! I call upon you to join CASH in its first show of strength . . . not for us, the sit-in or the wade-in! We are shareholders! Ours is economic power! Use that power! Now is the time for our trade-in . . . each and everyone of you must trade-in Vita Cola! Drive that price down! Bear your losses! These are money changers in the Temple!"

"My God!" said Nat Schuyler, awed by a capacity for freakishness outstripping his own.

"Why?" asked Parry, bewildered.

"I think," said Thatcher gently, "I think I'd better be getting back to town."

9 · They Call Us to Deliver

THE TRIP from Katonah to the Wheatmen's Mutual Building, where Waymark & Sims had their offices, took Thatcher exactly one hour and thirty-seven minutes to accomplish. It says much for the penetrative qualities of modern communications media that, by the time he arrived, Vita Cola had fallen four points.

"The boys over at the Exchange are going ape," announced Waymark, whose conversation these days was heavily salted with service jargon. "They keep saying there must be a law against this sort of thing."

Carruthers shook his head. "You mean they think there *should* be a law against it. What do they want the SEC to do? Prohibit the sale of stock?"

"No, no!" rejoined Waymark, his instincts as a broker coming to the fore. "How the hell could we make any commissions? But isn't this some sort of stock manipulation?"

"Not unless someone is making money out of it. It would be different if these people had sold short. But if they just want to sell their stock at a loss, no one can stop them. I suppose they look on it as a kind of donation to the NAACP."

"Well, that's a hell of a way to treat a portfolio!"

But the protest was a mere formality. Hugh Waymark regarded himself as a man on the firing line. To do him justice this had invigorated, rather than oppressed, him. The large modern office, with its paneled elegance hinting at a bar, sun lamp, vibrating chair and all the other amenities necessary to the demanding business of underwriting, seemed to harbor the whiff of grapeshot.

". . . what we've got to do is map out our strategy," he continued.

Before he could start unrolling maps, Thatcher thought it was time to bring some sanity to the issue before them.

"I admit this Vita Cola move is unnerving," he remarked, "but surely it's a little early for Simpson's supporters to have gotten their sell orders in and effected."

"That's just it," said Carruthers. "It can't possibly be them. They'll hit later today and tomorrow. The brokers and institutions must have started unloading."

Both men turned to look reproachfully at Waymark. "Well, naturally, no one on the Street wants to be hit by an avalanche," he explained glibly.

Under the circumstances, it was scarcely tactful to query the movements of Waymark & Sims in Vita Cola. Carruthers chose a roundabout approach instead.

"But that's just playing Simpson's game. Has it occurred to you what he'll do after he's forced Vita Cola into a real nose dive?"

Waymark stirred uneasily. "The Exchange was mumbling something about his going on to another stock."

His two colleagues nodded soberly.

"Of course, the whole thing may blow over before that problem arises," said Waymark halfheartedly.

"Blow over!" Carruthers sounded harassed. "You'll think twice about that once the word leaks out that we met here today."

Thatcher was curious.

"Are you having trouble at your place?" he asked.

"Pickets!" said Carruthers in tones of loathing. "We have forty of them carrying placards in and out of the reception room, choking up the elevator, parading through the lobby. It's a madhouse."

Idly Thatcher inquired about the message of the placards which had descended on Carruthers, Broadside & Pettigrew.

"That's just it!" said Carruthers with unusual heat. "Most of them simply said 'Justice.' And that's a fine thing to be parading around a law office!"

Gravely Thatcher concurred.

". . . naturally we didn't want to call the police," Carruthers explained. "But how can anybody work, when there are twenty people singing in the reception room?"

"I suppose . . ."

Carruthers shook his head. "No, John, it was not 'We Shall Overcome.' It was some new song."

Both Hugh Waymark and John Putnam Thatcher were conspicuously not interested in new songs. It was, then, with some surprise that they heard the normally polished Stanton Carruthers pursue the subject.

". . . a good strong tune, and some rousing lyrics, too."

"Fine," said Hugh Waymark. "Now, John . . ."

"I expect it may catch on," said Carruthers, speaking with his usual meticulous reflectiveness. "Not that I know much about these things, you understand, but my girl Fernanda seems to buy these records in carload lots."

Thatcher sympathized with the fleeting look of bewilderment that he saw on Hugh Waymark's face. It was gone in a minute; in that minute, Thatcher realized, Hugh Waymark had decided, for reasons known only to himself, that he had let his deep concern over *l'affaire Parry* (or was it *l'affaire* CASH? Or, *l'affaire Vita Cola,* for that matter?) cause him to commit a social solecism.

"Ah yes, Fernanda. She's coming out next spring, isn't she?" he said chattily.

It was Stanton Carruthers' turn to look bewildered. But legal training gave him the edge when it came to seizing conversational gambits and bending them to his will.

"Yes, at my mother's place at Southampton. Now, the reason I mentioned the song is that I want both of you to be prepared."

He waited, satisfied himself that he had their complete attention, and continued:

"It's called 'The Three Wise Men.' "

There was a moment of silence.

Then, with real interest, John Putnam Thatcher said: "Catchy, eh? Tell me, what was the sense of the lyrics?"

"Confused," said Stanton Carruthers, repressively.

Hugh Waymark was manful in the face of adversity. Dismissing folk songs as the least of their current problems, he turned to Thatcher and asked if he had uncovered anything helpful in Katonah.

Thatcher considered the question, and replied truthfully.

"No."

He then relented and provided his colleagues with an abbreviated version of his interview with Edward Parry, together with a description of the statement that Parry had promised to issue.

They listened gloomily. Then, Waymark rose to a height of intelligence that Thatcher had previously felt beyond his reach.

"The real trouble isn't Parry. He's a good man, and he'll do what he can for us, but . . ."

With a short emphatic gesture he indicated the forces now rendering Wall Street hideous. They were indeed bigger than one man, even a man so impressive as Edward Parry.

". . . with open elections," Waymark continued, launching into a résumé of Richard Simpson's latest catalog of demands.

"That man has got the Board of Governors worried."

Possibly because of the folk singers, Stanton Carruthers was less imperturbable than usual.

"Well, I for one am delighted! The three of us are worried. The whole Street is worried. Why the Board should think that it can pretend to be above the struggle has always eluded me."

"You've made one mistake," Thatcher pointed out, recalling Katonah. "Nat Schuyler isn't worried."

"Nat Schuyler!" said Carruthers exasperatedly.

"I don't blame you," Thatcher said with a grin.

Hugh Waymark leaned forward: "Look, Stan, we all agree with you, but we've got to try to do something. I can tell you that the Board is very, very worried. Simpson is stirring up trouble right where they live. They've got their hands full with this new SEC study."

Recalling some of the salvos traded by the SEC and the President of the Exchange recently, Thatcher could well understand their alarm. Both in Congress and in the Commission itself, proponents of increased regulation always become more vociferous when internal policing measures of the Exchange prove inadequate to a crisis.

And if ever a crisis were running away from the optimists in Exchange Place, this was it.

Carruthers was thinking along the same lines. He frowned in thought.

"The Exchange is right to be worried," he agreed. "You know perfectly well that the SEC doesn't care what Simpson is doing.

But it does care about the reaction downtown. If every member firm panics and dumps whatever stock Simpson mentions, then there's going to be a lot of talk about the need for government-imposed discipline. I hope to God they can count on the specialists."

All three men had professional reasons to remember the SEC investigation sparked by the behavior of one or two floor specialists on the day of the Presidential assassination. The job of the floor specialist is to promote orderly dealing in the stock for which he is responsible. In time of panic, he is expected to firm the market. Most of them do. But it takes only one exception to draw nationwide attention.

"And the Parry business won't help," Thatcher mused aloud. "It hadn't occurred to me before, but requiring that no seat can be transferred without the approval of the Board does make the Exchange look like a private club, doesn't it?"

Carruthers nodded. "Not just the seat. They have to approve any new partner in a member firm."

"And why not?" demanded Waymark. "You sound like this Simpson fellow. He's talking about public accommodations and demanding a right of appeal to the courts." A delicate shudder passed over his frame. "By God, you can see where that sort of thing might lead!"

Neither Thatcher nor Carruthers was prepared to stray down this tempting bypath. Instead they wanted to know what Hugh Waymark proposed.

"I've already put an idea of mine to the Board," he admitted. "If they're willing to go along, we could get cracking right away."

In the face of a noticeable lack of enthusiasm, he felt the need to quote precedent. "Remember! Surprise is the essence of attack!"

This stirring battle cry evoked a profound silence which remained unbroken until Waymark's secretary opened the door to announce the arrival of the Exchange's emissary.

His jauntiness unimpaired, in walked Tom Robichaux.

"Don't know why it is," he rumbled in greeting, "but all I do these days is run errands for Francis."

Waymark brushed the complaint aside. "What did the Board say?"

"They say you're to open negotiations with Simpson immediately," said Robichaux, carefully repeating his message. "Francis has every confidence that you will soon have the situation under control."

He looked around the room, examining its occupants, and relaxed his official manner. "Don't know where he gets that idea, but there it is. This fellow Simpson is nothing but a damned troublemaker."

With a start of alarm, Stanton Carruthers said, "I certainly hope you're not making public statements to that effect."

"For God's sake!" said Robichaux indignantly. "That's fine thanks for the running around I'm doing. You don't think I enjoy it, do you? Why I could be—"

Before Robichaux could get well launched on an enumeration of the alternate activities available and preferable to him, Thatcher intervened with a soothing flow of palliatives. At a moment like this, handling Tom required the infinite patience of a tugboat captain piloting the "Queen Mary," which in many ways he resembled.

". . . very inconvenient, I'm sure. But what I don't understand is what we're supposed to negotiate about. It is customary to have something to give, in order to get something."

Before his eyes, Hugh Waymark ceased to be a Leader of Men and became a cunning guerilla chieftain.

"It depends how you work it," he said, rubbing his chin craftily.

Stanton Carruthers drew a deep breath, preparatory, Thatcher guessed, to an explanation that a man who had seized on the Parry crisis with the avidity of a Richard Simpson could not lightly be detached from television cameras, public protest meetings and the leadership of parades. He was forestalled.

"We're not going alone," said Waymark triumphantly. "We're going to have Nat Schuyler at the meeting."

Thatcher closed his eyes briefly.

But it was too late for the voice of sanity to make itself heard. By going to the Board first, Waymark had made a neat end play. Nothing remained but to view the debacle.

The debacle started inauspiciously. By five o'clock the next day, Vita Cola was down eighteen points, and people were play-

ing guitars in the halls of Waymark & Sims. Nat Schuyler, be-
nevolently satanic, received the news calmly as he ushered the
Committee of Three into a suite at the St. Regis.

"Yes, bourbon and branch," said Waymark, rubbing his hands
together. "Been quite a day, quite a day. All hell is breaking
loose over at our place." He chortled in high good humor.

Really, the man was wasted in underwriting when catastrophe
so clearly brought out the best in him.

". . . Berman's making a statement for the TV boys. I thought
that was a smart public relations move. Now, before the others
get here, we ought to clear up a few points. Just the five of us."
He waved to include Vin McCullough by the bar.

"By others, you mean CASH?" Schuyler demanded with a cackle.

"Naturally."

Just then, the chimes sounded.

"And here they are," said Schuyler with gusto.

Waymark looked confused. Under cover of the opening door,
he hissed at Thatcher, "I thought they weren't supposed to get
here until five-thirty."

Thatcher sighed impatiently as they stood up.

The well-known novelist Richard Simpson and aides accompanied their host into the room. Simpson performed introductions.
There was Dr. Matthew Ford, "the well-known sociologist," and
Mrs. Mary Crane. Mrs. Crane, it developed, was well known
in connection with hostilities recently directed against the Board
of Education.

"Oh, I'm really just a wife and mother," said Mrs. Crane, with
a steely smile.

A corporate shudder gripped the room.

Carruthers took one look at Hugh Waymark, who was unnerved by the appearance of female auxiliaries, and twitched the
reins of control from his hands. He introduced his colleagues,
offered CASH Nat Schuyler's liquor and suggested that everybody
settle down to the business at hand.

"Good," said Simpson, accepting a Scotch and simultaneously
flicking the conversation from Carruthers. "We have to get to the
dinner meeting of our executive board."

"Yes," said Carruthers.

Nat Schuyler, carefully crossing spindly legs, looked amused. Before Carruthers could continue, Simpson said:

"You want us to abandon our legitimate protest against the segregationist policies of Wall Street."

He spoke more in sorrow than in anger.

Surprisingly, it was Vin McCullough who protested.

"We won't make any progress that way," he said baldly. "Let's get some facts straight. Mr. Schuyler and I are supporting Ed Parry's nomination. We'll do all we can do to push it. So it doesn't help to call all of Wall Street segregationist."

His emphatic voice brought an impolitic look of surprise to Hugh Waymark, and another smile to Nat Schuyler.

Dr. Ford, the sociologist, nodded. "Yes, we want to be scrupulous about that, Dick." Mrs. Crane simply pursed her lips.

Unrepentantly, Simpson replied, "I stand corrected. We admit that Schuyler & Schuyler is an honorable exception. But you cannot deny that there are racist forces . . ."

He had underestimated Stanton Carruthers. While not precisely denying the existence of racist forces, Carruthers managed to point out that the Stock Exchange was exhausting itself in efforts to be fair.

"Ha!" said Mrs. Crane, causing Hugh Waymark to bridle slightly.

"Owen Abercrombie," added Dr. Ford more specifically.

Hugh Waymark blustered into speech; Stanton Carruthers continued his stately and measured comments on the New York Stock Exchange. Dr. Ford contented himself with sardonic little interjections and Richard Simpson, nettled by Stanton Carruthers' practiced fluency, commenced a moving word picture of the plight of the Negro stockholder in America. Helping herself to another drink, Mrs. Crane joined Nat Schuyler, who was looking on with vast satisfaction.

Under the cover of three, if not four, conversations, Thatcher spoke to Vin McCullough.

"I'm glad you said what you did, but I expected it from Nat, not you."

McCullough smiled wryly. "Because I wasn't crazy about losing money if we took Parry in? Hell, it's too late for that. I'll be damned if I'm willing to dance to the tune of that wild jackass Abercrombie. Do you know, he called me up and tried to threaten Schuyler & Schuyler? Well, nobody pushes Schuyler & Schuyler around—at least not while I'm there. We're going to get Parry a seat on the Exchange if we have to use a cannon to do it."

"That's the spirit!" cried Mrs. Crane, who overheard his remarks. "Fight force with force."

"You're right," said Vin McCullough somewhat grimly.

"Good boy," Nat Schuyler called, sending a knowing glance at Stanton Carruthers.

Who was the idiot who had suggested that Nat Schuyler might be prevailed upon to cooperate? Or Richard Simpson, for that matter?

Simpson, chin up toward nonexistent television cameras, had risen.

"That must be CASH's position. No, gentlemen, peaceful demonstrations and the legitimate use of economic might to further the human betterment of the American Negro cannot be stopped simply because we may embarrass some elements of the community who prefer to ignore one of the crying shames of this city, and of the whole United States."

His breath control, Thatcher conceded, was remarkable.

"No," said Simpson, although no one had spoken. "We shall persist until the glaring inequities which exist upon Wall Street are eradicated forever. We hope and pray that they soon will be."

Mrs. Crane rose to join him. Filling an alarming bosom with a preliminary breath, she spoke vibratingly.

"In this, his hour of peril, we shall stand by Edward Parry."

Dr. Ford also rose. He issued no clarion calls, but contrived nonetheless to loose a blockbuster.

"Coming, Mr. Schuyler? We're going to have to hurry."

"Eh? Oh yes, yes," said Schuyler, busy playing the aged totterton as he got spryly to his feet.

"Just sitting in on this CASH dinner tonight," he explained airily. "Help yourself to the drinks."

With something remarkably close to a strut, he accompanied CASH to the door, paused for the parting civilities, then left.

The door closed on a stunned and indignant silence.

"Well, I must say!" Stanton Carruthers began. "And what's funny?"

For John Putnam Thatcher and, after a moment, Vin McCullough were laughing heartily.

"The old so-and-so," said Thatcher with approval. "Did you know about this, Vin?"

Still chuckling, McCullough shook his head.

"Nat is one surprise after another."

For a moment he leaned back in an attitude of complete relaxation, then determinedly gathered his forces.

"I'd better get along. I'm carrying Art Foote's work at the office until we can get Parry in. And moving house on top of it. So, if you don't need me . . ."

Within five minutes, the Committee of Three was again in executive session.

"So much for that idea," said Thatcher. "Let me make a suggestion. Our one function appears to be that of wasting the time of many people—including ourselves. We can't do much to protect the McCulloughs of the world, but we can save our own necks. Instead of acting as a body, why don't we split up?"

While it was too much to say that the profound good sense of this suggestion cheered his companions, it did appear to be persuasive.

"Mmm," said Waymark. "But we'll meet for progress reports from time to time."

"If you think they're necessary," said Thatcher ambiguously. "But not at the Sloan."

"Or Carruthers, Broadside & Pettigrew," said Stanton Carruthers hastily.

"Or Waymark & Sims." Waymark was mildly regretful. "We sent out forty thousand empty envelopes, by mistake, this afternoon."

Silence descended.

"I suppose you've heard about Lee Clark," Waymark remarked idly. "He's preparing a complaint to the SEC accusing Schuyler & Schuyler of simply using Parry to harm Clovis Greene's Harlem business. Says that Nat doesn't have any real intention of getting Parry a seat."

Stanton Carruthers considered this. "A possibility, I suppose. Clark is pretty bitter, I understand. He's joining forces with Abercrombie, as well."

Again silence, then Hugh Waymark produced a small notebook. "Here are some of the public events the Board would like us to attend . . ."

"We'll toss for it," said Thatcher, seeing the light of endless discussion in his eye.

Three minutes later, Hugh Waymark said, "You've won the ADA tomorrow night."

"What do you mean, won? I've lost."

"Stan gets the John Birch Society, and I get the Committee to Clean Up Wall Street."

"Like Richard Simpson," said Thatcher. "I stand corrected. We've all lost."

10 · No Duty Is Too Lowly

BY THE NEXT DAY the press had surpassed itself in idiocy.

Statements from prelates, the Civil Liberties Union, senators and Black Muslims abounded. Everybody disapproved of the present situation, for one reason or another: it was too violent, it wasn't violent enough, the target was too specialized, nothing could be accomplished without open war between the races. A wealthy church in the downtown area had proposed a solution to the problem which involved dividing Wall Street in much the same manner as Berlin, complete with the introduction of checkpoints and the disarmament of bankers. The Police Commissioner's comment on this plan was a model of fiercely controlled emotion.

In the Bronx, an elementary school which preened itself on its model racial mix (thirty percent colored, thirty percent Puerto Rican and forty percent white) burst into print with a smug analysis of its own virtues. It sent a high proportion of its unending stream of graduates to the Bronx High School of Science, the

High School of Music and Art, the High School of Performing Arts and Hunter High School and took this occasion to congratulate itself on its unfailing wisdom in confronting racial problems that made weaker men blanch. There followed interviews with three selected students: Julia, aged thirteen and Puerto Rican, intended to go to Music and Art for further study of the oboe before ultimate attendance at Juilliard. Snatching a moment from her arpeggios, she said that anybody who worked hard enough didn't have time for all this nonsense. Howard, aged fourteen and Negro, was going to Bronx Science to be a physicist. He felt that science offered opportunities for those facing discrimination in other fields. Sammy, a master chess player at the Manhattan Club, thought it was a mistake to let human passions intrude into any problem.

Thatcher did not approve of encouraging self-satisfied teenagers, but he was forced to admit that their statements compared favorably with those of their elders. Including, he thought bitterly, his own daughter, who was militantly reacting to Edward Parry's problems in a manner that would have won approval from Elijah Muhammad.

A member of the Board of Education tried to refute accusations that racial minorities were deprived of educational opportunity with statistics showing that ninety-eight percent of the graduates of all elementary schools in Chinatown went on to take doctorates. This discouraging vision of horn-rimmed young Orientals standing in serried ranks before something called Whirlwind xxv left Thatcher unreceptive to the counsels of the Chinese Merchants Association serenely prescribing absolute calm for members of the black and white races. In the face of this detachment, he found their references to "our Fair City" unduly proprietary.

The article concluded its massive survey of turbulence and disorder with the announcement that attempts to gather the views of high city officials had been abortive; they were all vacationing out of the country.

No day with such reading matter is a dead loss. Considerably invigorated, Thatcher slapped aside the last page of this comic relief and briskly proceeded to the task of leveling the gigantic pile of arrears accumulated on his desk.

By five o'clock Herculean inroads had been made, Miss Corsa was mollified by a day's work which would have caused many a woman to hand in her notice on the spot and Thatcher, supported by a sense of accomplishment, could anticipate the evening's approaching agenda with unimpaired cheer.

"Where is this ADA banquet I have to attend?" he asked the departing Miss Corsa.

"At the Grand Ballroom of the Waldorf. Six forty-five," she reported.

"Good heavens, how very substantial."

When Thatcher arrived at the Waldorf to join the Americans for Democratic Action milling around outside the ballroom, he realized that his vision of political progressives was outmoded. This smartly dressed, gaily chattering crowd was indistinguishable from any similar gathering of prosperous reactionaries. On both the right and the left, Thatcher noted as he accepted the drink procured for him by a harassed chairman of the program committee, it was the ladies who sounded the most aggressive. He gazed around him with interest. On second glance, he could discern some differences. The ADA ladies were perhaps a shade more intense than the female conservatives of his acquaintance. And, unless he was mistaken, they tended to be a trifle thinner as well. They sported horn-rimmed glasses, not jeweled frames.

He discovered that the chairman's disjointed remarks had been addressed to him.

"I was woolgathering," he apologized, to be rewarded with the news that he had much to be thankful for. Unlike his confreres on the Committee of Three, he was not addressing a specially convened meeting. The ADA banquet had been scheduled many months earlier. A speaker from Washington was on hand.

"And," said the chairman with myopic earnestness, "time will be limited."

"Excellent," said Thatcher.

"So," the chairman continued, "we've had to squeeze you in with the appetizer. I hope you understand."

Thatcher was sincerely delighted. When the assemblage finally trooped into the ballroom and settled down at the banquet tables set up there, his remarks on the Stock Exchange's determination to maintain scrupulous impartiality in the case of Edward Parry's application for a seat constituted an introduction to the shrimp cocktail.

For this Thatcher was doubly grateful. In the first place, he was not intoxicated by the sound of his own voice. Any excuse to keep his statement brief was a source of pleasure. But in the second place, during cocktails he began to fear that the ADA—moneyed, academic and legal—was likely to know a good deal too much about the Securities and Exchange Act as well as the bylaws of the National Association of Security Dealers.

This apprehension was confirmed during the question period following his short statement. References to section numbers and joint committee reports flowed from his hosts in abundance. Thatcher took due notice. When dealing with a pressure group, it is a wise precaution to learn precisely where the pressure is going to be applied. He could now report to the Exchange that the ADA would be camping on Washington doorsteps to demand more extensive federal regulation of the Stock Exchange if Edward Parry were denied his seat. That was not too bad, and, fortunately, hunger kept his audience from laboring the point.

As he left the rostrum, the chairman agitatedly thanked him and said that he was being placed at one of the smaller tables where, the chairman understood, he had acquaintances.

To his surprise, Thatcher found himself joining Charlie Trinkam.

"I didn't know you were a member of ADA," he remarked. If there was one thing noteworthy about Trinkam, it was not the prominence of his commitment to politics of the liberal variety.

"I'm not," Trinkam replied. "Barbara, here, arranged for us to come. Barbara, this is John Thatcher. John, this is Miss Feathers—and Paul and Irene Jackson."

John Thatcher sat down and took stock of his surroundings, brightening as he did so. Any social occasion, however outré, which came about through Trinkam's efforts promised some interest. And the trio with which he and Trinkam were joined was indeed strangely assorted. The Jacksons radiated money, gaiety and knowledgeability. Paul Jackson, smooth-haired and stocky, was, it developed, a thriving criminal lawyer with an extensive and lucrative practice among the city's less desirable citizens. His very attractive wife was a woman obviously deriving considerable enjoyment from life.

Miss Feathers was an economist.

Not for the first time, Thatcher was roused to admiration by the speed with which Charlie Trinkam, given any conceivable public or private problem, could attach himself to a woman with some claim to inside information. Nor were there any limits to his catholicity. Lovely women, social women, intellectual women, dedicated women, family women—all were a source of real interest to him.

At the moment, it was an economist. They were discussing the main speaker of the evening.

"He should have stayed at Harvard," she said, stubbing out one of the cigarettes she was smoking in rapid succession. "But that's the trouble with some of these intellectuals. Stanley is simply power mad."

Thatcher glanced at the head table. Stanley was small, partly bald and possessed of an irritatingly confident smile.

Paul Jackson looked up from his cooling roast beef to remark in jovial accents that he had rarely enjoyed anything so much as Stanley's address to the ADA on the eve of his departure for the White House.

"It was called," he chortled happily, " 'The Challenge to Intellectuals.' "

Miss Feathers' lips tightened as if she reserved to herself the right to criticize Stanley—and all other intellectuals. With his usual soothing instincts, Charlie Trinkam inquired after the subject of tonight's address.

" 'Limitations Imposed on the Intellectual in Washington,' " Miss Feathers replied repressively.

This unhappy, if natural, progression effectively dampened the conversation. The talk, therefore, became desultory, with Trinkam and Jackson exchanging mildly scandalous comments about several friends they had in common and Irene Jackson displaying lamentable frivolity in the face of a lengthy disquisition from Miss Feathers on the subject of the need for More Women in Politics.

"Barbara," said Mrs. Jackson finally, turning to Thatcher,

"Barbara is on the ADA action committee to study the Parry situation."

"Oh yes?" said Thatcher. "What . . . er . . . action do you envisage? Apart from urging increased SEC legislation, that is?"

"SEC legislation!" she said with contempt. "That's all right when it's a question of protecting investors. But this whole Ed Parry affair has triggered violence. It's brought out the lowest hoodlum element. The riffraff of the city." She turned to her left and peremptorily broke in on Jackson's exchange with Charlie Trinkam.

"That's right, isn't it, Paul? You're the one who knows all about criminals and violence after all."

Jackson, amused, denied her charge. "Now wait a minute, Barbara. My clients may go in for violence. I don't get called until it's all over."

Barbara Feathers dismissed this hairsplitting.

"That's not what I mean. But you know that we're not dealing with speculators or defrauders—" she broke off and directed a look at Thatcher that made him wonder if she were including him in this select group "—we're dealing with murderers!"

Jackson was not shaken by her earnestness. "You mean those nut boys of Abercrombie's? They're not professionals, if you know what I mean. They talk big, but I don't think they're ready for anything more dangerous than egg-throwing."

With a quick look at Thatcher, Charlie Trinkam gave the ball a push to keep it rolling. "But somebody has already tried to murder Ed Parry—twice. That's dangerous enough, Paul."

Jackson chose his words with care. "I don't think Abercrombie's crowd is ready for mob violence. As a group, they're not prepared to pay the penalty for it. But, on the other hand, a single individual, resorting to concealed murder—well, that's something else again. As you say, we've got double proof that somebody is willing to try that."

Miss Feathers looked at him with disapproval.

"I don't agree with you about mob hysteria," she said didactically. "Even if these people wouldn't start much by themselves, let them sit around inciting each other for a week—and you don't know what will happen. You have to meet the threat of mass action with a display of mass solidarity. That's why I feel that a big turnout at Lincoln Center is so important. And the committee has finally agreed with me."

Beating down a flicker of sympathy for the action committee, Thatcher asked Miss Feathers if she and the ADA supported Richard Simpson.

"In spirit, we do," said Miss Feathers loftily. "Dick Simpson has a very powerful mind. I don't know if you saw him on the "Today" show, but I personally have never heard a more penetrating analysis of the basically sexual basis of racial bigotry . . ."

"Good God!" said Charlie Trinkam as Mrs. Jackson directed a minatory look at her husband, who obediently broke into speech.

"I think," he said, "the ADA position is that the best way to attack racial discrimination by the Stock Exchange is through pressure on the SEC . . ."

Miss Feathers interrupted him:

"Yes, that's true—as a long-term approach. But when there's violence, we plan to counter it with a massive display of individual support for Ed Parry. We're going to send a thousand members to Lincoln Center Saturday night."

Perhaps sensing John Thatcher's apprehension that the conversation might revert to the sexual basis of racial bigotry, Irene Jackson said brightly, "We wouldn't miss it for anything. It's not every night you can wear your best clothes to a potential riot."

Miss Feathers said, "Charlie is coming with me, Mr. Thatcher. I hope you're planning to attend."

Thatcher framed an evasive reply, inwardly marveling at the sympathetic working of social antennae. Elements as variegated as Gloria Parry, Nat Schuyler, Miss Feathers and the Jacksons all realized that the NAACP benefit was assuming a symbolic significance. Surely it was too much to hope that Owen Abercrombie and his cohorts had not come to the same conclusion.

And what about Owen Abercrombie? Thatcher had noticed that the careful Paul Jackson's statement absolved Abercrombie's followers, while leaving plenty of scope for homicidal action on his part.

And if Owen Abercrombie were capable of dangerous violence, what more appropriate place for it than an NAACP benefit at Lincoln Center?

At this moment, Thatcher's thoughts were interrupted by sounds from the head table that ultimately resolved themselves into a lengthy introduction of the speaker of the evening.

John Putnam Thatcher gave the intellectual precisely three minutes. Then he chose the course of prudence and suspended all thought entirely.

At that very moment, intellectuals were the least of Stanton Carruthers' problems. He hadn't seen anything approaching one for the last two hours. In fact, as he looked at Owen Abercrombie's ponderous, underslung jaw and glittering feral eyes, he was tempted to think that he had receded through several major geological eras and was surrounded by Neanderthals.

The White Association for Civic Intervention (known as "Whacky" the length and breadth of Wall Street) was an offshoot of the John Birch Society, organized by Owen Abercrombie and composed of members disaffected with the moderate views of the parent organization. Its program called for action, and the nature of that action was becoming ominously clear as Carruthers, standing on the flag-draped rostrum before an enormous photomural of the founder, braced himself for questions from the floor.

Or they were supposed to be from the floor. Most of them were coming from Abercrombie himself and started with the phrase: "Do you mean to stand up there and say . . . ?"

". . . I am afraid you may have misunderstood the nature of our committee," Carruthers was saying as he thanked God for a lifetime of self-control under adversarial fire. Only now was he beginning to appreciate the high standards of *politesse* which govern the legal arena. "We want to help promote order during the period necessary for the Stock Exchange to come to a decision with respect to Mr. Parry's application."

Abercrombie, who was also standing, hunched his shoulders forward and let his short arms dangle loosely, thereby emphasizing the simian resemblance.

"You mean to say you people are going to stand back and let them take over?" he demanded.

"The question before the Exchange involves one seat out of over a thousand. That can scarcely qualify as taking over."

"You're opening the door. They'll come pouring in."

Carruthers repressed the desire to ask Abercrombie where "they" were going to get the necessary hundred thousand dollars. Instead he opted for a dispassionate review of the statistics about available seats. It is rare, he pointed out, for more than two seats to fall vacant in any one year.

"Don't try and whitewash this thing with phony numbers!" shouted Abercrombie. "You're trying to cover up the fact that you're scared to stand up for your rights!"

Carruthers permitted himself a tempered coldness. There was, he pointed out, a genuine difference of opinion about exactly what those rights were.

"There's no difference of opinion between honest, God-fearing Americans! We all know there's a Commie line designed to infiltrate our way of life. Are you going to stand up there and feed us Moscow propaganda?"

"I'm afraid I have to contradict you on that, Mr. Abercrombie. The difference of opinion extends to the majority of Congress which passed a Civil Rights Act."

These words were a red flag. A new contestant now entered the fray.

"Civil rights!" shouted Dean Caldwell from the floor. "That's one name for it. I'd like to get this talk down out of the clouds and ask the speaker what he'd do if his daughter wanted to marry one of them. Because that's what it all boils down to! Whether or not we're going to protect the purity of our race and our women!"

In the thunderous ovation which greeted this remarkably offensive question, Stanton Carruthers unexpectedly found himself relaxing, sustained no doubt by the vision of his daughter Fernanda.

With deliberate provocation, he smiled benignly down at the militant young Southerner and told him that, when he was old enough to have a daughter of marriageable age, he would realize that he had precious little to say about anything she did and probably would be damned grateful to anyone who took her off his hands.

Abercrombie, older in the ways of the world than Dean Caldwell, returned to the attack.

"It may be a laughing matter to you," he said, lowering his

voice to a dramatic hiss, "but the defense of our homes and our businesses and our families is something we're prepared to take seriously with every drop of our blood. We are ready for action."

Ovation.

"You come here and tell us you stand for order. You tell us *that* when the Vita Cola specialist collapses and has to be hospitalized—the first casualty on the field of battle. But not the last, let me tell you!"

Ovation.

"Well, we've got something to tell you and your committee. We're the ones who stand for order!"

Here Abercrombie started pounding on the table in a manner irresistibly reminiscent of the United Nations.

"And we're going to protect it and we're going to protect you —in spite of the fact that you're too yellow to stand up and be counted yourselves. We're not afraid to use force against force, are we?"

Arms angled into a stubby vee, Abercrombie received the cheering assent of his supporters. The ugly red tide that had suffused his face when he was exchanging remarks with Carruthers disappeared, replaced by a pale exultant gleam. With his head thrust back he rocked to and fro in a hypnotic interplay of emotion with his audience. He swung forward with each question he asked, and then swayed back under the blast of their maniacal approval.

"Are we going to lie down and take this without lifting a finger?"

"NO!"

"They're all against us. They'll try to muzzle us, try to smear us. Are they going to get away with it?"

"NO!"

"You're the only ones left to defend America. Are you going to let the pinkos take over?"

"NO!"

And then, like a mechanical toy that had been wound tight, he abandoned his dialogue with the auditorium and launched into a wild, disordered peroration, filled with incoherencies and strange quotations:

". . . for the love of God and country . . . no time or place for weaklings, for questioners, for those who would undermine us . . . a solemn duty to which we here pledge ourselves . . . fight force with force . . . let not this cup pass from us . . ."

The evening ended for Carruthers with the frenzied howls of a thousand voices ringing in his ears.

11 · Keep Silence, All Created Things!

AT FIRST BLUSH it would have seemed impossible that the next day should fail to be an improvement over its predecessor.

Not that Thatcher was deluding himself. No one acquainted with Wall Street's passionate attachment to peaceful, if powerful, anonymity—as well as profits—could reasonably expect that listening to intellectuals detail atrocities suffered in Washington would be the only cross to be borne during the Parry Crisis. With Vita Cola still collapsing—in faithful emulation of its floor specialist—Thatcher knew that the demands on him, however incoherent, would be many and urgent.

Nevertheless, when he arrived at the Sloan the next morning, he was unfavorably surprised to find that Miss Corsa had already received four top priority calls.

"First Mr. Carruthers," she reported, consulting a note. "Then Mr. Withers. Then Mr. Devane, and finally Mr. Lancer. They all want you to call back as soon as possible."

"Something must be up," Thatcher mused aloud. "Well, it will have to wait. I'm going to check the papers."

Miss Corsa looked censorious.

"After all, Miss Corsa, possibly the press can explain this new emergency—whatever it is."

"Yes, Mr. Thatcher," said Miss Corsa, ostentatiously buckling down to work.

Thatcher withdrew into his own office and scanned the headlines rapidly. He found nothing to explain why the president of the Sloan Guaranty Trust, its Board Chairman, one of the governors of the Stock Exchange and Stanton Carruthers should be hounding him before nine-thirty. This is not to say that he failed to find anything of interest. There was a front page interview with the Deputy Mayor ("We want to assure out-of-towners planning to visit New York that we have not had one single instance of a tourist molested in the financial district."); a plaintive account of the corporate confusion reigning in Vita Cola's executive offices ("But our profits are thirteen per cent above last quarter!"); and a somber announcement that the New York City Police Department had granted CASH a permit for "peaceable demonstration" ("The right to peaceable demonstration is constitutionally guaranteed to all U.S. citizens," police officials grudgingly declared.).

Nor did the police, if the press was covering the situation (and to find mention of the Soviet Union, southeast Asia or Washington, D.C., for that matter, one had to penetrate to page fourteen of the *New York Times*), have anything to say about the murder of Arthur Foote—or the murderous attack on Edward Parry.

With the newspapers uninformative, Thatcher resorted to the telephone. Within minutes he learned of yet another chore. Edward Parry was finally leaving the amenities of Katonah to come to Wall Street and deliver his long-awaited statement. The Board of Governors of the New York Stock Exchange felt that the presence of the Committee of Three at his press conference would be most advisable.

"Yes indeed," said Thatcher to Stanton Carruthers, who conveyed this information. "It will be a good opening for a few words about the Exchange's scrupulous fairness."

"Yes," said Carruthers, already in the throes of composition.

After learning the particulars—the conference had been scheduled at one o'clock at Schuyler & Schuyler—Thatcher courteously asked about Carruthers' evening with the White Association for Civic Intervention.

There was a long silence. Finally Carruthers cleared his throat.

"Endless and ugly," he said. He debated adding further comment and decided against it. "That sums it up, I think. Well, John, I'll be seeing you this afternoon. And I'll prepare just a few words."

Rather satisfied with his Machiavellian tactics, Thatcher returned his attention to the matters which brought him his substantial salary and gave Miss Corsa and the whole sixth floor of the Sloan Guaranty Trust one of his well-known workouts.

"Well, that should keep you busy," he announced bracingly at twelve-thirty, "I have to be getting along."

Kenneth Nicolls, stunned by the bulk of his impossible assignments, smiled weakly, struggled to his feet and fled. Miss Corsa was made of sterner stuff.

"Where can I reach you, Mr. Thatcher?" she asked.

"Just a press conference over at Schuyler & Schuyler," he replied cheerfully. "I should be back in an hour."

His carefree frame of mind lasted precisely eight minutes—the eight minutes it took him to fight his way through the lunchtime crowds to Schuyler & Schuyler.

There, at the William Street curb, creating pedestrian and vehicular congestion, stood two gaudy trucks. The usual big-city crowd had gathered, well-dressed and to all appearances gainfully employed, rooted to the spot and theorizing freely to account for the appearance of television crews. Fortunately, Thatcher was unable to identify any Sloan employees amidst what he unfairly apostrophized as "brainless time wasters." He pushed his way forward. Around him hypothesis flowed. There had been a bank robbery. There was a new salad oil scandal. Somebody had misplaced securities.

"Probably," said a sleek young woman, "probably some file clerk is threatening to jump from the fortieth floor."

No one, Thatcher noted, looked up.

Well, one thing you could say for Wall Street. If no one was looking up, no one was shouting, "Jump!"

By the time he had worked his way into the lobby a heavy sense of premonition was ripening. By the time he reached the twenty-sixth floor, he found it was all too justified. The Edward Parry conference was being televised.

Schuyler & Schuyler was a madhouse.

"No, no, no," crescendoed a bearded youth with a notebook. "The three camera. I told you, George. If I told you once, I told you . . ."

Thatcher stepped aside for two men manhandling what looked like an irrigation pipe.

"And we'll need more light here . . ."

". . . what about the boom . . ."

"WATCH THAT CABLE!"

"Who are you?"

The last question was directed at Thatcher. It emanated from a large woman with red hair. She did not wait for his reply, but consulted a clipboard and said: "You're Hugh Waymark."

Her conviction made Thatcher regret the necessity for denial.

"Hmm," she said skeptically. "Well, Mr. Waymark—sorry, Mr. Thatcher—you'll have to go to makeup. Willy! Oh, Wil-ly!"

"Now, just a minute . . ."

Thatcher's horrified protests availed him nothing. A harried youth appeared and firmly led him past a gaggle of wide-eyed secretaries, worshipfully watching the invaders.

"In here," said Willy, ushering Thatcher into what in happier days served Schuyler & Schuyler as a conference room. Just emerging was Edward Parry, accompanied by a bitter-looking man who barely reached his shoulder.

Sighting Thatcher, Parry paused.

"Please, Mr. Parry!" cried the bitter-looking man, tearing a cigarette from his lips and grinding it underfoot. "We don't have much time. I'll ask you to read your statement—that's one minute four. Then, when you finish . . ."

Still talking, he led Parry away.

"Here you are, Mr. Waymark," said Willy, indicating a chair for Thatcher.

"I do not propose to let myself be daubed," Thatcher began firmly, just as the large woman reappeared.

"We're running late," she said tersely. Willy burst into agitated burblings and, before he knew what was happening, Thatcher found himself in a chair as a technician advanced upon him with a small tray of cosmetics.

"Oh God!"

For Thatcher was not to be the only victim. Willy was leading Dean Caldwell and Vin McCullough into the conference room. They inspected Thatcher carefully.

"Carruthers," he said with dignity, "neglected to tell me that we were going to be involved in this sort of thing."

Vin McCullough laughed aloud, but Dean Caldwell saw nothing amusing in the situation.

"He's outside," he said sullenly. "God damned circus, that's what it is. What the hell is the matter with Nat?"

Caldwell was still young enough to be submerged by his resentments, Thatcher noted, as he manfully detached his attention from a studious evaluation of his hairline. And, being angry, Caldwell was incapable of hiding it. Despite the technicians moving around, despite the arrival of a sheepish Stanton Carruthers, he continued to voice his discomfort.

"How're we going to get any work done?" he demanded pettishly. "It's bad enough that Nat is steamrollering all of us, but now we have to put on shows for . . ."

"Dean," said McCullough wearily. "Just keep it to yourself, won't you?"

He turned to exchange a mildly ironic comment with Stanton Carruthers.

Caldwell dropped into a chair near Thatcher and hostilely watched the makeup man.

"The whole place is a monkey house," he said in a lowered voice. "And we all know it's Parry's fault that Art Foote got killed!"

Thatcher reflected that the problem of disciplining junior staff members was handled better at the Sloan. He did not, however, propose to concern himself with this petulant young man. Moreover, his bedizenment achieved, he was free to go.

He rose.

"Doesn't know his place," Caldwell was continuing. "And you know what?"

Irritably McCullough moved past Thatcher to take the seat indicated for him.

"What?" he repeated.

Stanton Carruthers was silently radiating disapproval.

"Some people are going to do something about it. And I'm going to be with them."

"Can't someone shut him up?" Carruthers whispered to Thatcher.

"Apparently not," he replied. "Let's get out of here."

But before they could escape, they were privileged to hear McCullough evenly pointing out the advantages of self-control to Caldwell. The technician woodenly continued beautifying both of them.

"No, I'm not getting into trouble, Vin. You'll see."

His slyness would have roused suspicion in a man far more obtuse than Vin McCullough.

"Look, Dean, I'm just trying to give you some good advice. At a time like this, the prudent thing to do is to keep your mouth shut and watch your step."

"That's the trouble with everybody," said the younger man sullenly. "They're so busy being prudent, they forget they're men."

McCullough interrupted impatiently.

"I know you don't want to be slow and cautious. You've got some crazy idea about strutting down to Lincoln Center Saturday night with your friend Abercrombie and making trouble for Ed Parry."

"So you think you know all the ideas in my head, do you?" smiled Caldwell unpleasantly. "Say what you want, Owen Abercrombie is more of a man than anybody else down here. He doesn't run around licking people's boots."

"He doesn't have to," said McCullough dryly. "He's head of his firm. You're not."

"You're a fool if you think Owen wouldn't be man enough to do what he knows is right, whether or not he was a partner."

McCullough retreated from his attack on Caldwell's mentor. "Maybe so, maybe so. God knows he's crazy enough! But, Dean, let me tell you, starting riots at Lincoln Center is no business for an employee of Schuyler & Schuyler, even if he is the best research man we've ever had."

Caldwell preened himself in the mirror as the makeup man finished his ministrations. "It may turn out that Schuyler & Schuyler needs me more than I need them. And, anyway, what's so important about Lincoln Center?"

"It's the NAACP benefit. Half the bigwigs in the city will be there. If you start anything there, the networks will play it up all over the country."

"It's time they did," said Caldwell defiantly. "They've been hiding things from people long enough."

Vin McCullough brought his fist down on the counter. "For God's sake, will you listen to sense! And try to talk some into your friend Abercrombie."

"Pu-leese!" said the beautician haughtily.

Caldwell's reply was lost to Thatcher and Carruthers.

"Well, McCullough tried to talk turkey to that boy. But if you ask me, not a word got through," said Carruthers.

Thatcher grunted disapprovingly. "I don't think any word could get through."

"You're right," said McCullough, catching up with them in the corridor and overhearing. "I suppose it isn't worth the trouble."

"Well, the effort does you credit," said Thatcher, not mincing matters, "but frankly I didn't like the way he seized on Lincoln Center."

McCullough groaned. "I know, I know. But we can't tiptoe around watching every word we say, for fear that boy will get himself into trouble. He's got to get used to the idea we're going to have a Negro partner."

"Don't we look fine!" trebled Willy, darting up to them. "This way . . ."

Within minutes all chaos was resolved. Thatcher, Carruthers and the late-arriving Hugh Waymark sat at one side of the long table, facing the staff of Schuyler & Schuyler, including a glowering Dean Caldwell. Nat Schuyler, together with Edward Parry and the interlocutor, who was the forceful and bitter man, sat at the head of the table.

Upon a signal that transfixed everybody, Edward Parry cleared his throat. Then, in his pleasant resonant baritone, he carefully read his statement. It was, Thatcher decided, about as much as they could have hoped for. Parry first expressed formal confidence in the New York Stock Exchange's fairness. He was, he continued, opposed to violence and extremism.

Parry spoke calmly and without embarrassment. Thatcher mentally applauded him. He knew enough of the man to know he must detest this whole performance—almost as much as Dean

Caldwell, if for different reasons. But Edward Parry had learned self-discipline.

When he finished his remarks, the interlocutor asked Nathaniel Schuyler a question. Schuyler was at his best, exuding venerability, wisdom and saintly tolerance.

". . . and I would be most interested," he said with a straight face, "in hearing the opinion of our distinguished representatives from the Stock Exchange."

When Stanton Carruthers responded without hesitation, Thatcher thought he discerned a fleeting look of disappointment in Schuyler's benevolent eye.

"o.k.!" shouted somebody.

Everybody relaxed.

"Very, very good," said Nat Schuyler, rising stiffly. "I think that was excellent, Ed."

Turning, John Thatcher happened to catch sight of Dean Caldwell watching the head of his firm congratulate Ed Parry.

It provided him considerable food for thought.

12 · I Was a Wandering Sheep

TWENTY MINUTES LATER, Thatcher was returning to the Sloan, a prey to new and unwelcome sensations. Ordinarily devoid of self-consciousness, he now sensed every eye upon him. His ears turned scarlet as a muted giggle broke from two stenographers behind him. Common sense told him they were deep in discussion of their own affairs. But what price common sense, when a man has been subjected to ordeal by television?

Rising to haunt him were the numbers proudly flaunted by networks in pursuit of sponsors. Our daily news program is watched by ten million viewers . . . by twenty million . . . by fifty million. In fact, by everyone between the ages of ten and eighty.

"Good God!" And he almost said it aloud.

For weeks to come he would be dogged by reminders of the

horror so recently undergone. Mrs. Corsa, out in Queens, would have something to say. Charlie Trinkam would be more outspoken. There would be the housekeeper of the Devonshire, the elevator operator, taxicab drivers . . . The list was endless.

It almost seemed worthwhile to discover important business in Poona.

Then he remembered the furry hats.

This is the tragedy of our time, Thatcher thought as he strode along. The illusion of refuge is gone. No comfortable sensations of security rise at the thought of Tahiti, the Himalayas, or Arabia Deserta.

Things have changed. Nowadays, Gauguin's family in Paris could enliven dull evenings by following the adventures of their levanting husband and papa among dusky island beauties. The Grand Lama of Shangri-La would conduct a Sunday morning program of spiritual uplift, and Lawrence of Arabia would be interviewed on camelback about the Cyprus question.

"Tell me, Monsieur Gauguin, what exactly made you decide to give up banking for painting? And perhaps we could introduce this young lady to our viewers?"

"Now, the Reverend Grand Lama—do I have that right, sir? —will give us his views on attaining personal serenity."

"If you could just hold that dynamite a little higher, Colonel Lawrence, our listeners could see exactly how you go about blowing up a train."

There is no sanctuary. A man might as well face it out on Wall Street.

Thatcher's spirits began to rise. If there was nothing to be gained by exile to polar snow drifts or glaring deserts, then he might as well enjoy his notoriety in the comfort of New York, where, in addition to central heating and indirect lighting, he had the advantages of rank and position. Millions of people might be dying to tell him what they thought of his television performance, but the combined efforts of Miss Corsa at the Sloan and the entire staff at the Devonshire should insulate him from the more immediate manifestations of this peril.

Unfortunately, one of the people from whom not even the redoubtable Miss Corsa could protect him was the Sloan's Chairman of the Board. The message to call George Lancer was marked urgent.

"What's this all about, Miss Corsa?" Thatcher asked, frowning down at the memo slip.

With a monumental lack of interest, Miss Corsa professed ignorance.

"But Mr. Lancer's secretary did say it was very important, and would you please call back as soon as you got in."

Thatcher sighed.

For Lancer to be in a flap about something which had escaped Miss Corsa was ominous.

There was only one way to find out. Grimly he nodded to his handmaiden and within seconds was greeting the Chairman of the Board.

"John? Thank God!"

This was scarcely reassuring.

"What seems to be the matter, George?" asked Thatcher, already displaying that tendency to belittle trouble that comes to the best of us, when faced with strong displays of anxiety.

"It's that damned lunatic, Withers. We ought to keep him locked up."

There was a moment of appalled silence. Thatcher knew perfectly well that only extreme provocation could have sparked this trenchant candor.

"What's he done this time?" he asked, treading warily.

"You know about the tour for UN junior staff?"

Thatcher did. An annual event arranged for the benefit of UN financial types new to New York, the tour included important and historic spots in the Wall Street district. Among them, naturally, was the Sloan, where Bradford Withers was in the habit of making a short ceremonial speech of welcome. It was the kind of thing he enjoyed doing, and did well.

"But what can have gone wrong?" demanded Thatcher. "He does it every year."

"Well, this year he had some extra time on his hands, and he insisted on escorting them up to see the new employees' dining room. You know," Lancer added in bitter parenthesis, "how loony Brad is about that dining room. We never should have let him pick out the murals himself. Anyway, as soon as they got there, somebody from Tanzania asked him about segregated eating facilities."

"Oh, God! What did he say?"

"I gather that part wasn't so bad," Lancer admitted grudgingly. "He made some stately remark about the Sloan not tolerating that sort of thing and this wasn't Mississippi. In fact, the whole thing would have blown over except that some little twerp from the Congo insisted that the colored dining room was being hidden from the tour, and finally it dawned on Brad that the guy was calling him a liar."

"And then?" asked Thatcher with sinking heart.

"Then he blew up and said Wall Street didn't want outsiders telling it how to run things, particularly outsiders with plenty of riots themselves. That got picked up by every wire service in the country. Wait a minute . . . I've got the damned thing here some-where . . . I'll read it to you."

There was a pause while George Lancer could be heard shuffling the papers on his desk and adjusting his glasses. His voice had a savage bite as he continued:

" 'Wall Street wants no outsiders,' declared the President of the Sloan Guaranty Trust today in discussing racial tensions in the financial community with a delegation from the United Na-tions. Bradford Withers went on to deplore violence among groups seeking admission to the select downtown community' . . . and so on . . . and so on. Got the picture?"

So much for distracting attention from the Sloan by not hold-ing meetings of the Committee of Three on its premises. Thatcher could already hear the guitar-strummers beating at the front door.

"Yes," he said wearily, "I've got the picture."

"So naturally we've got a press conference scheduled. To try to correct the impression that's gone out—"

"You're not going to let Brad talk to them?" Thatcher made no attempt to conceal his alarm.

"Of course not. You and I are taking them on. It won't do any good," said Lancer with defeatist realism, "but it's the least we can do."

Three hours later, with Bradford Withers safely packed off to start a long weekend on his estate in Connecticut, Thatcher found himself giving guarded answers to a young man from Tass. No doubt the interview would enliven the front page of tomorrow's edition of *Pravda*. The young man asked long, involved questions to which there was no innocent answer. Thatcher delivered elaborate statements which were totally unresponsive to any question in the world. Lancer had already performed yeoman service in a more acrimonious exchange with a representative from the official organ of the Rhodesian Association for National Union.

Under Thatcher's right hand rested a hastily compiled file setting forth statistics about the original hiring, subsequent promotion, present salary and future prospects of every Negro employee of the Sloan, as well as past public statements, union clauses and internal memoranda on the subject. Curiously enough the chief emotion exercising Thatcher at the moment was pure, undiluted chivalry. He was prepared to go down fighting in defense of the privacy of a woman he had never met. Her name was Mrs. Joyce Morse, and she was the only Negro teller employed in the main office of the Sloan. Should her existence ever be revealed, she would spend the rest of her life being hauled in front of television cameras, while unctuous young men asked offensive questions about what it was really like in the ladies' room.

"No," he said, sadly shaking his head at the man from Tass as if the necessity for denial were a personal grief. "I am afraid it is against our policy to release a branch-by-branch breakdown of our figures. I can tell you that one hundred and thirty-two Negroes are employed in the capacities you have mentioned. That is for the bank as a whole, of course."

The man from Tass then asked a long question designed to show that, even though the Sloan's dining facilities were not segregated, things were as bad as though they were.

Thatcher countered with an equally lengthy reply challenging the Soviet Union to produce one black bank president, and implying that, if the Sloan knew of a qualified candidate, they would rush out and hire him at once. As he mouthed this inanity, he reflected that they could scarcely do worse than with the president they already had.

With the honors about even, Lancer rose to take on Reuters. In many ways these innings with the foreigners were a warm-up, centering as they did on facts and situations. The domestic press, Thatcher feared, would be much more interested in personalities.

He was right. After the London *Economist, Le Matin* and *Der Spiegel* had had their sessions—and after the man from a Bombay daily had made it clear that, in India, John Putnam Thatcher was a household name—there was a muted hush of expectancy. Then the dam burst.

Where was Withers? Was he hiding? Had the NAACP communicated with the Sloan? Had Thatcher heard what Richard Simpson said about Withers' statement, and did he care to comment? Was it true that Lancer was making a personal apology to Edward Parry? Was the Sloan supporting Owen Abercrombie's attempt to blackball Nathaniel Schuyler from two luncheon clubs? Was City Hall declaring the Sloan off-limits to the UN? Had all the Negro employees of the Sloan been given two weeks' vacation, a bonus and orders to go to Las Vegas? Had the Stock Exchange demanded Thatcher's resignation from the Committee of Three? Did Edward Parry and Bradford Withers belong to the same yacht club? Was the Secretary of State closeted with the Sloan's Board of Directors?

And on, and on, and on. When the last journalist had been ushered out by the still feebly smiling representatives of the Sloan, a great silence seemed to fall on the room.

Lancer's first action was to summon brandy. Then he looked at his associate.

"Well, what do you think?"

"I am past thought," said Thatcher acidly. "All I can rely on now is my will to survive."

Lancer poured two healthy snifters before mopping his brow. "We're going to have to produce Withers," he said unhappily.

"Yes. But in our own time, and in our own way. That's all we could hope to gain."

"I suppose so. If we could just prevent questions . . ."

Thatcher pondered. He was reminded of Nat Schuyler's trafficking with CASH. A little of the same kind of duplicity seemed indicated.

Meanwhile, the Chairman of the Board was dispiritedly reviewing the possibilities within the Sloan's staff.

"It's useless to think we'll get any help from the public relations people. They're the ones who organized this massacre." He stared around the recently vacated room balefully.

"I don't think that's the right line to pursue," said Thatcher slowly.

Lancer looked at him hopefully. "You've thought of something."

"Yes," admitted Thatcher. "You may think this is crazy. But the man who could help us is Edward Parry."

Soundlessly the chairman whistled. "Well, it's a different approach all right. What exactly were you thinking of?"

"We could get Parry and Withers together on a platform somewhere, with Brad more or less appearing under Parry's egis. Ed Parry would understand the kind of occasion we want—something where Brad can do a public *mea culpa* in sympathetic surroundings. God knows Parry must have occasions by the handful right now."

"Would he do it?" asked Lancer doubtfully.

"I don't know. He might. This isn't the kind of publicity he wants, any more than we do. And," concluded Thatcher in the tones of one summarizing the thirty-nine Articles of Faith, "he is a banker."

The chairman brightened. "Then I'll leave it to you. If you can find the right way to approach him—it will have to be done delicately, you know—then go ahead. But, if it's going to do us any good, it'll have to be done pretty fast."

One thing Thatcher was learning from this whole mess: every horror can be outstripped by some subsequent outrage. For the past week his life had consisted of events, any one of which should have been a climax of discomfort to be recovered from at leisure, lingering in the memory as an eminence towering above its surroundings. But at the pace he was now living, recollection could barely stretch back for two hours.

Thus when his daughter's call came through, interrupting his appraisal of possible approaches to Edward Parry, he was momentarily bewildered by her opening remarks.

"Daddy? We watched your show. It was grand."

What in the world was she talking about?

"What's that? What was grand?"

"Your television show, Daddy. At lunch today," she added impatiently. "Timmy wanted to know why you looked so stern."

In the host of diabolic viewers he had envisioned, he had never imagined his ten-year-old grandson. No wonder family authority was breaking down everywhere. Briskly he counterattacked by demanding to know why Timmy was watching television instead of attending the fifth grade.

"Oh, he saw the rerun at four o'clock. I saw it live. Mr. Schuyler must be a fascinating man."

Thatcher agreed that he was. He could think of other descriptions, unsuitable for his daughter's ears.

"I'm *so* looking forward to meeting him," trilled Laura in the tone Thatcher recognized as preliminary to an unwelcome request. Even so, he could not resist following up this statement.

"When are you going to meet him?"

"At the benefit at Lincoln Center. That's what I wanted to talk to you about."

In some ways Laura and the young man from Tass had a great deal in common. She too phrased her questions so that there was only one possible answer. After much beating around the bush, it developed that Dr. Benjamin Carlson was going to be busy the day after tomorrow and Laura would thereby be deprived of her husband's escort that evening. She wanted her father to step into the breach.

"That's what you get for marrying a surgeon," said her father brutally. "If you want to go to this Donnybrook, it's your business and your problem. I have enough of my own."

"Oh, Daddy!" Laura was used to sweeping over *pro forma* displays of opposition. "It isn't just that I want to go. I have to go!"

"What do you mean, you have to go?" he demanded suspiciously.

"I'm a patroness. Together with Mrs. Parry. I must have forgotten to tell you. And everybody knows I'm your daughter. Can't you see what people would say if your daughter backed out of supporting Mrs. Parry at a time like this?"

Thatcher could see all too vividly. Nor did he credit Laura's forgetfulness for one minute. She had him in a cleft stick, and they both knew it.

"Can't you get anybody else?" he asked, fighting to the last ditch.

"But it can't be just anybody else. Not on a night like this. And Gloria Parry likes you. She told me so."

Dimly a plan took shape in Thatcher's mind. Much as he disliked the whole idea of benefit concerts at Lincoln Center, he began to see that it might be his duty to attend. In fact, Laura had given him the answer to his problem. And he had never deceived himself with the hope that the solution was going to be attractive.

But he had his paternal position to maintain. It was with a great show of reluctance that he let Laura force him down the path of compliance, inch by inch.

It was not until ten minutes later that she was saying: "Oh, thank you, Daddy. I knew I could count on you."

13 · Or Roll of Stirring Drum

IN TRUTH, John Putnam Thatcher was happy that his children still counted him among the strong buttresses of life. He did, however, regret that rendering support to his daughter, Laura, so often required formal attire. The check he had mailed that morning to one of his sons was, in many ways, a smaller price to pay.

"A very, very successful evening."

The speaker, a portly middle-aged Negro, was decked out, like Thatcher, in white tie and tails. He was surveying the great lobby of Lincoln Center, tonight aglitter with the hard brilliance of crystal, the honey gleam of marble, the shimmer of fluid satin and the sparkle of diamonds. His gaze encompassed elegantly gowned women, floating like butterflies through the iridescent beauty of the setting; even among their escorts there was an occasional peacock. Tonight, Thatcher saw, ribbons were being worn; silhouetted against a column was the magnificence of a rich purple turban; just sweeping in through the great glass doors was the crimson splendor of ceremonial African robes. And, to light and sound, there was added the special, unforgettable scent of powder on bared shoulders, the attar of a hundred perfumes, the rich leaf of tobacco, and the smoky pungency of furs touched by the fog's damp fingers.

"It is indeed a successful evening," said John Putnam Thatcher. He had fallen into this stilted conversational exchange after Laura, resplendent in a black taffeta gown that may have explained why her husband was finding it necessary to work hard these days, spied an acquaintance and swept away for a moment. Thatcher's chance companion, while projecting substance and a certain proprietary satisfaction, had the look of a man similarly cast adrift by a woman. Before he could continue their exchange, he was reclaimed.

"There you are, Fred! Where have you been?" a pearled matron emerged from the crowd, collected Fred in a practiced fashion and bore him away. As he passed, his eyes met Thatcher's with an expression age-old to man, regardless of race, creed or color.

"Women," it said.

"There you are, Daddy," said Laura. "I've been wondering where you were."

"I haven't moved an inch," Thatcher replied mildly.

Strong-mindedly, Laura ignored this.

"Isn't it wonderful that the evening's so successful," she said, nodding regally to a passing couple. This moment of graciousness was immortalized by a photographer who exploded a blinding flashbulb at them. Thatcher only wished he could believe that he would appear on the Society Page. But, since Bradford Withers' gaffe, he very much feared that a vice-president of the Sloan Guaranty Trust was frcnt page fodder.

"I've been saying the same thing as a matter of courtesy," he said irascibly, "but, with my own offspring, I feel constrained to point out that it's a little early to decide this is a successful evening, in view of the fact that it has barely begun. And why, may I ask, is it necessary for us to promenade about?"

Like her mother before her, Laura had a splendid way of dealing with this kind of fractiousness. She smiled brilliantly.

"Oh, Daddy," she said in perfunctory protest. "Good evening, Mrs. Bertolling . . ."

As Thatcher escorted his daughter through the crush, exchanged civilities with acquaintances, then fell back to let the ladies discuss civil rights (or, occasionally, culture), he had plenty of time to think.

Without a doubt, if volume were the criterion, the NAACP gala was a success. Over intervening heads, Thatcher could see that the endless string of limousines was still debouching magnificently attired concert parties at the door. Unfortunately, he also saw four raincoated policemen, guarding the barricades that kept the corridor under the canopy free of idle sightseers—or worse. Out of sight, but not out of mind, beyond further barricades, were the inevitable pickets, undeterred by foggy drizzle or by the police caution which was keeping them far distant from the festivities. Glum and depressing, they stood in the rain, beneath placards which were also depressing:

CIVIL RIGHTS FOR WHITES

NO MINORITY RULE

And, inevitably:

IMPEACH EARL WARREN

Of course, these poor wretches posed no threat to the assemblage of wealth, prestige and power (black and white) gathering in the stylish premises of Lincoln Center, to attend a concert, then a late supper, to swell the coffers of NAACP, and to support civil rights in general, and Edward Parry's rights in particular.

But were there any other threats? Thatcher looked around. It was hard to believe that anybody in this animated gathering—and he saw a U.S. senator laughing in a hearty professional way—felt any threat imminent. Negro or white, the dignitaries were smiling unconcernedly, conversing happily, exuding fellowship, optimism and goodwill.

But, Thatcher knew, many things are hard to believe. Some of the men and women floating grandly up the stairway to the balcony had had firsthand experience with the dark forces of hatred and bigotry—and recently. Could anyone—say, Owen Abercrombie—be planning further damage? Something more meaningful than ugly words on placards, carried by life's rejects?

John Putnam Thatcher profoundly hoped not. The ladies were excited enough already. Add an "incident" perpetrated before their eyes, and the ailments afflicting Wall Street would include enraged Carry Nations, marching in and out of brokerage houses, axing ticker machines.

"Mrs. Parry," said Laura. "Hello, Gloria."

Thatcher roused himself. The first thing to meet his eyes was a vision of calculated and artful magnificence. He spoke the words that came into his mind.

"You are in great beauty tonight, Mrs. Parry."

This old-fashioned formulation delighted Gloria Parry, who briefly gleamed the smile of a warm, vital woman instead of a poised and disciplined public personage. Laura dimpled her approval, rather as if her father were young Timothy, doing something precocious and, for a change, socially acceptable. Yet Thatcher spoke no more than the truth. Mrs. Parry wore a gown of amber lace with emeralds. The effect was impressive.

Thatcher glanced around to see if Edward Parry's composure were equal to the trying task of escorting a really dazzling woman. A word with Parry, he reminded himself, could go far toward relieving the Sloan Guaranty Trust of its current embarrassments —and so render tonight's discomforts a simple extension of his professional obligations.

"Ed's talking to Mr. Kingsley over there," said Mrs. Parry, reading his thoughts. What she really meant, Thatcher knew, was that she had dispatched her luckless husband to take care of her furs, then blithely sailed away into the crowd, leaving him to search for her.

"Have you met Mrs. McCullough?" Gloria Parry continued.

"I wonder where Vin is?" Mrs. McCullough replied after greetings had been exchanged. She looked around, vaguely expectant.

This was the only way in which Mrs. McCullough resembled her companions. A tall, slim woman, she wore her hair in the long blond sweep that had, no doubt, made her an exceptionally attractive college girl some twenty-five years earlier. She was not evincing pleasure in the gaiety of the occasion, like Laura who was becoming more organization-minded with every child. Nor did Mrs. McCullough have the aura of enormous physical attraction coupled with superb (and expensive) plumage that marked Gloria Parry. She was, it soon developed, another, not uncommon, type of American woman.

". . . just about dead on my feet," she said in a firm voice.

"Oh really?" Laura began. But despite her four children, she was too young to have perfected social armament against the Julia McCulloughs of this world.

"We went to Arthur Foote's funeral today," Mrs. McCullough continued commandingly. "So depressing. Of course, Virginia is prostrate, poor dear. But I understand that Art had very good insurance, which is something. . . ."

Gloria Parry was old enough to be able to deal with this phenomenon. Moreover, her upbringing had brought her to a finer cutting edge (socially speaking) than would ever be necessary for a Laura Thatcher Carlson. But she, too, was effectively immobilized. Anything concerning a Schuyler & Schuyler partner— even a murdered partner—was necessarily interesting to Edward Parry's wife. Gloria Parry was not a politician's daughter for nothing.

Nevertheless, she indulged herself with an alarmingly intelligent look at Thatcher, before murmuring:

"What a tragedy . . ."

"Just awful . . ." Laura echoed dutifully.

". . . but of course, there are the children, which makes it hard," Mrs. McCullough forged on, her voice quarantining her unwilling audience from the general surge of bright social chatter, the graceful semiwaltz movements of the fluid festive crowd and, Thatcher saw with sudden indignation, from the champagne cocktails being made available (rather than served) at a table beneath an extraordinary ton of metal which was, it was to be presumed, a piece of statuary.

"I know how it is. My sister's husband died just last month, and Vin and I had to support Carolyn through the whole thing. And it wasn't the money . . ."

"No, indeed," Gloria Parry said through a glaze of boredom.

Laura, Thatcher regretted to see, was incapable of even this.

". . . because he was a doctor and left Carolyn quite comfortable, thank God! But Vin was executor, and there was all the trouble of settling his effects, and closing up his office—and so suddenly. Then, telling the boys was simply terrible. I said . . ."

Without compunction, Thatcher withdrew his attention. At a distance he sighted Nat Schuyler. Nat was looking subdued. Was he worried, Thatcher wondered. Or, was it simply the small round woman at his side (black velvet and lace, a plethora of chains and other hangings, and completely improbable black hair)?

Idly, Thatcher's gaze wandered on. There was Tom Robichaux, with an extremely decorative blond young woman. Was that Celestine, returned from the sinister Greek yacht?

As Thatcher recalled—and he was the first to admit that he might be in error—the current Mrs. Robichaux was a striking redhead.

"John! Good to see you!"

Clearly Charlie Trinkam had not let social niceties keep him from the champagne cocktails. He was enjoying himself thoroughly. In his way, the man was a marvel. Beside him, looking handsome, if severe, in black brocade was Miss Feathers.

"I'm glad to see that the Sloan Guaranty Trust is out in full force tonight," she observed after a round of introductions.

With a raised eyebrow, Charlie inspected the crowd. "Brad here? I haven't seen him, have you?"

"God forbid!" said Thatcher under his breath.

Fortunately, his words were lost in a lecture from Miss Feathers:

"In view of the really appalling situation developing on Wall Street, I can only say that if the large institutions . . ."

Her earnest tactlessness—and the real terror of what she might feel impelled to say—galvanized Gloria Parry and Laura into protective measures. As of one accord, they turned to Mrs. McCullough, and cooingly said:

"And you're moving too, aren't you?"

"Oh, moving is such a chore!"

Mrs. McCullough, who had looked Miss Feathers up and down and decided that she did not like what she saw, sighed dramatically. The enlargement of her audience did not, however, materially alter her peculiarly confiding tone.

"I am just about frantic. We're selling the house, now that the children are grown up . . ."

Miss Feathers, as befits a lady intellectual, interjected a comment designed to inflate Mrs. McCullough's troubles into a sociological generalization.

"Have you noticed how housing starts are shifting heavily into multiple dwelling units . . . ?"

Even the normally imperturbable Charlie Trinkam was moderately taken aback; Mrs. McCullough simply raised her voice slightly.

". . . a terrible wrench, leaving Stamford. Not to speak of how terribly rents have risen. You wouldn't believe what we're paying for a simple six-room terrace apartment on the East Side. I told Vin he'd have to take care of selling the beach cottage himself. Really, what with talking to real estate people, and trying to get everything into storage and getting rid of the second car— and then having to go to funerals, I am thoroughly exhausted. Not that Carolyn . . ."

Her detailed recital continued. Mrs. Parry merely endured. Laura allowed herself the luxury of nodding to fortunate passing friends, and Miss Feathers listened as if Mrs. McCullough were an aborigine encountered on a particularly arduous field trip.

"By God!" said Charlie Trinkam in a low voice. "Look over there, John."

Thatcher glanced toward the entrance.

Just strolling in was a small party of men, all decorously attired in evening clothes. In their midst, enormously pleased with himself, was Owen Abercrombie.

"Do you think that means trouble?" Charlie asked in an undertone. "Lee Clark is here, too."

"Lee Clark is no threat," Thatcher said, keeping his voice down. "He's just trying to protect his Negro business. But I don't like this. . . ."

He broke off when he noticed that Gloria Parry was following this exchange, quiet as it was. She too had seen Owen Abercrombie enter. She raised her chin fractionally.

Good girl, Thatcher applauded mentally.

She was smiling her beautiful smile as Ed Parry made his way through the crowd to her side.

"There you are," his wife said calmly. "I was wondering where you were."

"Yes," said Ed Parry. "Well, I think we should be getting inside. . . ."

In the ensuing stir, John Thatcher managed to have a few quiet words with Parry concerning a brief talk between the two of them at some point during the evening.

"I'll bet it's about Withers," said Parry with an appreciative grin.

"It is," said Thatcher.

"We'd better talk about it. We can have coffee together after dinner," Parry said, still smiling.

He was as impressive as his wife, Thatcher decided.

Because Edward Parry, too, had seen Owen Abercrombie, and he knew what that meant. He was remaining not only calm, but cooperative.

"That'll be a help," said Charlie Trinkam, as a discreet stirring showed that the assembly was being shepherded into the concert hall.

"Where on earth is Vin?" Mrs. McCullough asked the world. "Oh, there he is . . . Vin! Vin!" Smiling kindly, she bade them a general farewell and plunged off toward her husband.

"You've got the tickets, Daddy?" Laura asked anxiously, after making punctilious *au revoirs* to the Parrys, who were moving toward the farther entrance.

He did.

Using them, however, took time. Progress down the aisle was slow, interrupted by greetings, brief conversations and general confusion. Only when they had finally located their seats (next to the head of the State Liquor Authority) did Laura whisper a confidence.

"Wasn't she a perfectly dreadful woman?"

"Mm," said Thatcher, noncommittally, idly flicking through the fat program. He had met worse but he did not say so, knowing this would only elicit a lecture from Laura. She turned to reply to friends yoohooing across two rows and her father, to ensure himself against meeting any eyes, continued leafing through a compendium of advertising and good wishes from every major commercial institution in New York City.

He smiled wryly. Clovis Greene Bear Spencer & Clark sent best wishes to the NAACP. CASH did not. Possibly they had been formed too late to make the publication deadline. Robichaux & Devane also sent good wishes. The Sloan Guaranty Trust,

Thatcher discovered with approval, sent nothing; it had merely taken two full pages.

On the whole, he was inclined to think that the NAACP was the group to value this above quarter-page "good wishes." Particularly when, as he found riffling on, good wishes were also emanating from Dibbel Abercrombie.

Well, fund raisers, like public relations people, couldn't be deflected by little things like reality.

"Oh my God!" It was an involuntary exclamation, made as the last of the violins finished his cacophonous wailing and joined the rest of the orchestra in staring at the audience, willing it to still the magpie chatter that was keeping the maestro in the wings.

"What's the matter?" Laura asked as the lights began to fade.

He had stumbled on the evening's program, sandwiched between eloquent statements of faith from Chock Full O' Nuts and Macy's. Pre-intermission he was safe: Bach, Brahms and Schumann. But post-intermission? He read it again.

INTERMISSION

ROOTS   AARON BOATMAN
to a text by Richard Simpson

Soprano: Lucine Asmara
Tenor: Jan Arrow
Bass: William Barlick
Narrator: Alicia Pontandante

PREMIERE

"*Roots,*" fluted Program Notes, "is an orchestral 'happening' by Aaron Boatman, the musical rendering of the mellifluous verse by Richard Simpson. It is scored for twelve violins, fourteen trumpets, a marimba and the full percussion section of the orchestra with arias by the soprano, tenor and bass, contrapuntally painting the pastel musical nuances of the long anguish of suffering humanity evoked by Simpson's agonizingly immediate word images. First, the Narrator reads Simpson's powerful and moving "Where Are My Roots?" against the background lament of the richly conceived atonal choral . . ."

"Do you mean . . . ?" he began with deep indignation.

"Sh!" said Laura. She determinedly stared ahead, applauding the arrival of the conductor. Her father eyed her. Without turning, she laid down the law:

"And Daddy, we are staying after the intermission!"

Thatcher fell back, strangely relieved. Obviously Fate could have nothing worse than *Roots* in store—at least this evening.

14 · And Only Man Is Vile

TWO HOURS and thirty-four minutes later, the music crashed into its penultimate bar. The only thing sustaining Thatcher was the dim air of *finale* that had crept into the otherwise unidentifiable melodic workings of the evening's last selection. There was a shattering dissonant chord for three beats, a quarter rest, another chord, a half rest and finally a vast tumult that defied definition as a chord, suggestive as that word is of some relationship between individual notes.

Then a horizontal flick of the conductor's baton brought silence, blessed silence. But not for more than ten seconds. Too long had human beings been coerced by mere instrumental chaos. A mighty clamor arose from thousands of human voices, hands, feet. From the balcony, a demented claque from Juilliard howled for the composer. The conductor bowed alone, then graciously lofted the orchestra to its feet with one sweeping gesture.

Wild applause continued. Thatcher himself was still clapping, he realized. It was understandable. No matter what the critics might say, this was enthusiasm for release, or, more simply, the human propensity to raise cain in any socially acceptable manner. Functionally speaking, *Roots* was not music but an outlet that left everyone happy without constituting a threat to life or property. Presumably, at a performance by a teen-age idol, Thatcher reflected as the ovation continued, it was at this point that high-strung adolescents proceeded to wreck the premises. Although he wondered why the young were always described as supercharged dynamos perilously close to eruption. The ones he knew personally, those employed by the Sloan as file clerks or messenger boys, displayed a languor profound enough to approach the pathological.

Twenty minutes later, Thatcher was still lapped by the tide of well-being, but the tide was ebbing fast. The audience had been marshaled back into the great lobby for supper. Now, against the dramatic backdrop of glass planes and other geometric complexities, there twinkled a myriad of tables resplendent with crystal and silver damask. As the guests seated themselves, each table assumed a distinct personality. Thatcher saw Charlie Trinkam and Miss Feathers join the Jacksons to fill out a circle of NAACP notables. The Schuylers and Parrys were throwing the mantle of Wall Street over their own little enclave. Unfortunately, Thatcher could not join them or have his discussion with Edward Parry during supper. His own table, alas, was heavily musical, housing, as it did, the composer of the evening, Aaron Boatman.

But the food was excellent and the wines even better. Much could be forgiven. While the woman on his right insisted on discussing the technical merits of a tone poem that he intended to forget as soon as possible, on his left, Mrs. Boatman was interested in nothing more alarming than finding an apartment in Manhattan suitable for small children.

Diligently working his way through a crumbling paté, a memorable lobster bisque and veal as it is too seldom encountered, Thatcher contented himself with small nods of comprehension to the right and rather more helpful comments on real estate to the left. The wine waiter was assiduous in attendance, and the end was in sight.

It was with the appearance of artichokes in *sauce vinaigrette* that Thatcher's attention was wrenched back to the menace at hand. Mrs. Boatman's comments had turned his private thoughts to banker's calculations. Once their children were grown, many people, like the McCulloughs, were moving from the suburbs back to the city and cooperative apartments without lawns. Construction was meeting this demand. But what about the Boatmans, with their small children? Were they an isolated instance, or the newest of *nouvelles vagues*? Perhaps new building was required. Deep in real estate syndicates, construction bonds and first mortgage holders, Thatcher was only distantly aware of his right-hand neighbor swaying to one side to allow a change of plates.

"Oh, dear, there he is!" she cried.

Thatcher murmured something politely interrogative.

"Henry will be furious if there's trouble. He didn't want to come, but I said that he was always looking for an excuse to get out of concerts. And I said, 'Henry, this is Aaron Boatman's latest!' "

Without understanding her, Thatcher experienced a marked fellow feeling for the unknown Henry.

"That did it, I suppose?" he suggested helpfully.

"Well, no," she admitted. "He still said it was dangerous. So we made a bargain. We decided to come as far as the door, and see. Henry said that if there was a mob we'd go straight home. But there wasn't, was there?"

She appealed to him with large, watery blue eyes.

He composed his face into an expression of manly reassurance, but Mrs. Boatman took the bull by the horns.

"Do you mean Owen Abercrombie?" she demanded. "That *awful* man. Aaron was so worried that he might try to ruin *Roots!*"

To avoid a comment, Thatcher turned. Owen Abercrombie and his party were dining at an inconspicuous table near the far wall. Thatcher inspected them. He wished to be fair-minded but they did not look like music lovers. There was an air of rented livery about six of the evening attires.

"A friend of yours?" he asked his neighbor to the right, wondering if these were now fighting words.

"Certainly not," she said coldly. "But I did see him on television yesterday."

Hastily, Thatcher turned the subject. He did not succeed in turning it from Abercrombie.

Mrs. Boatman was glaring at Abercrombie's group. "Philistines!" she said. "And those men with him look more like a bodyguard than anything else!"

Clearly, any threat to *Roots* brought out the beast in Mrs. Boatman. Since Thatcher could think of nothing pleasant to say about the composition, he was at a loss.

Fortunately, Mrs. Davis again contributed her mite. "Oh dear! You don't suppose that it's true what *everybody's* been saying? That he'll try to kill that *dear* Mr. Parry again?"

Thatcher waggled his eyebrows furiously at his daughter. The ladies had drawn the attention of the whole table, and worse still, the attention of Owen Abercrombie himself. Noticing their unwavering interest, he was now staring back with imperial arrogance. Across half the width of the room, Thatcher could feel the lordly self-satisfaction.

The man was aching for a scene. For the first time, Thatcher wondered if Abercrombie were certifiably insane.

In the meantime Laura Carlson was proving herself worthy of her descent. As titular hostess she raised her voice into a sweet clarion, addressed a question to Aaron Boatman and then remorselessly involved the entire table in a discussion of the inspiration for *Roots*.

"Only now are we beginning to understand the mainsprings of the baroque . . ."

". . . suitably modified by the demands of a mechanistic age . . ."

". . . but, Mr. Boatman, isn't automation the most important facet . . ."

"Too long have we allowed a slavish adoration of the romantic . . ."

"The time has come to recognize we are in the midst of a new Renaissance. The twentieth century *is* the sixteenth century. What the *cinquecento* was to art . . ."

Thatcher watched it all with relief and some amusement. His daughter, as nearly as he could tell, was going to skip being a young woman entirely. Incredibly, she had managed to remain a girl, albeit an attractive and considerate one, until the birth of her fourth child. Then, without pausing for breath or putting on an ounce of weight, she had started to unfold matriarchal petals. He was not sure that he approved. He remembered the thirty-five-year-old women of his youth nostalgically. It had been an interesting time of life.

And what of his own role in all this? Matriarchs, he felt, should have managed to shed at least their ancestors, and better still, their husbands. What future was there in being the father of a dowager? With extended life expectancy, one generation after another would soon be impinging on each oher's jurisdiction. Modern society would have to create new forms to absorb the ever-extending period between extreme youth and extreme age.

Entrancing as these speculations were, he did not forget his duty. He agreed seriously with Mrs. Davis that we have much to learn from the East. The West had been too absorbed with the diatonic scale. Counterpoint had preoccupied some of our ablest men to a grievous extent. There was the simple charm of single notes to be rediscovered. Mrs. Davis, it developed, had been to Tokyo. Even worse, she knew from *Time* that Thatcher had been to India. While he would not, offhand, have assumed that a short trip to help open a dam made him an authority on yoga and Shinto, it was enough to convince Mrs. Davis of certain sympathies. Inevitably the conversation broadened.

"Nowadays everyone realizes that theirs is a much more gracious way of life. Don't you agree?"

"Oh, absolutely."

"All those rock gardens and almost no furniture. It gives the mind so much more room."

"Just so."

"Then one can concentrate on the really important things. It's not surprising that they're so far ahead of us in things of the spirit, is it? Why, I do believe that it's time for coffee. The time has just flown talking with you, Mr. Thatcher. It's so rare to meet someone who understands. Of course, I say it's impossible unless you experience it yourself. And you have to be receptive. There's no point unless you can open yourself to new impressions. Henry, I'm afraid, isn't . . . Oh, he's waving at me. You'll have to excuse me. We're taking coffee with Mr. Hornstein, the concertmaster, you know."

Thatcher assisted her to rise and watched her sweep off on the arm of the unfortunate Henry. That, of course, was one way of passing the middle years. He went to the head of the table to claim his own.

"Ready, Laura?"

"Yes. And there comes Mr. Schuyler." She waved at the Schuylers and Parrys, who were threading their way forward as Thatcher pulled out her chair. Her eyes laughed at him. "Now you can be comfortable. And, remember, I took care of Aaron Boatman."

Nat Schuyler overheard her last remark. "Did you get stuck with the composer, Thatcher? We got the chairman of the NAACP finance committee. Tonight was a great success from his point of view."

Thatcher was too relieved at his deliverance from Mrs. Davis to comment on Schuyler's ability to land on his feet. He congratulated him on his luck and Mrs. Parry on the financial prospering of the evening. He did not get far before he was interrupted by alarmed cries.

Turning, he saw Owen Abercrombie and his followers bearing down on them. Abercrombie was in the lead, shouldering his way forward with a reckless disregard for the comfort or safety of his victims which augured ill for his intentions. Several women were already clutching the arms of their escorts in the wide wake that the group was leaving. Abercrombie's dark eyes glittered under the busy eyebrows, and a vein in his neck twitched visibly over the starched white collar. Out of the corner of his eye Thatcher saw two stolid men close up on Edward Parry.

Abercrombie stepped forward and grasped Nat Schuyler's sleeve.

"Just a minute, Schuyler! We've got some business with you and your playmates," he growled.

Schuyler was superb. He stood still, unalarmed and quietly disdainful. His face expressed only inquiry at this rupture of the evening's decorum.

"I'm sure you have a great deal to say, Owen. But I have no intention of helping you create a brawl. You can come to my office Monday morning and say anything you want."

"You can't get away with that! You and your protégé have to take what's coming to you. We've had just about enough of your troublemaking. The time has come to settle things."

Abercrombie was so engrossed by this exchange that he could not check on his subordinates. They were in some disorder. Two of them, eyeing the approach of several uniformed policemen from the corridor, were uneasily trying to slip away.

"You're making a fool of yourself, Owen. Now we're leaving."

As he spoke, Schuyler broke his arm abruptly free from Abercrombie's clasp and stepped forward. Unfortunately this left Abercrombie face to face with Edward Parry. Without pause, he closed the gap, grabbed Parry's shoulder and gave a bull-like roar that sent spittle streaming down his jaw:

"Well, *you're* not getting away, my fine colored friend. Think you're somebody, don't you? I'll show you just what you are . . ."

Parry did not try to emulate Nat Schuyler's contemptuous hauteur. Instead he doubled a workmanlike fist. But, at that moment, the two stolid men behind him oozed forward. One of them firmly removed Abercrombie's hand from Parry's shoulder.

"Now, we don't want any trouble here tonight, Mr. Abercrombie . . ."

"HOW DARE YOU TOUCH ME?"

The strong hand on his wrist seemed to rupture Owen Abercrombie's tenuous hold on sanity. The twitch spread from his neck to his face, working convulsively from jaw to brow. With an inarticulate shriek of encouragement at his followers, he shook loose from the detective and began to flail against him. The second detective instantly grasped his left arm, uttering professional injunctions to take it easy and come along quietly.

These were lost. With his right arm thrashing wildly, Owen Abercrombie suddenly fumbled in a pocket, then brandished a small black revolver.

"Hey!" shouted the detective, pushing forward.

There was one deafening shot.

Knocked off balance, Abercrombie had fired while he was still struggling. The bullet hit one of the chandeliers. There was a cascade of tinkling glass. And from somewhere came a frightened wail.

"Let me alone . . ."

"Watch it, there . . ."

"Get back, get back . . ."

With a madman's strength, Owen Abercrombie, still clutching the revolver, struggled against the two burly detectives, struggled to level his gun on his enemy.

Then Edward Parry shook off restraining hands and stepped

forward. With a clublike fist, he smashed a blow down on the gun so savage that Abercrombie's high, thin scream of pain almost blanketed the thud of heavy metal striking the marble floor.

15 · Tell Me the Old, Old Story

FOR A MOMENT that seemed to extend itself into an eerie vacuum of sound and movement, everybody was immobile, staring dully as the revolver bounced along the tiles and shards of falling crystal rang a series of notes that spaced themselves further and further apart. It was almost as if they were waiting for a second finale.

Then, abruptly, there was a convulsive milling as the uniformed police pushed their way forward, hurrying to the scene. By the time they arrived, Owen Abercrombie, restrained by Edward Parry and one of the detectives, was shrieking and raving, twitching and sobbing, mouthing inarticulate exhortations and obscenities. The police shouldered Parry aside and grasped Abercrombie competently, before turning their attention to his companions. These, they lined up and searched on the spot.

"Two more guns!" was the final tally.

"Aiiihheee . . . !" Abercrombie's unearthly screech made Thatcher's skin crawl.

"Leave him alone!"

The shout, urgent and angry, rose above the growing buzz of conversation.

"I said, leave him alone!"

Dean Caldwell paused in his struggles against constraining arms to watch disbelievingly as a gibbering Abercrombie was moved swiftly toward the exit. Then he resumed his defiance.

"Who do you think you are? You can't do this to him, you filthy . . ."

The officer in charge broke in. "Oh yes, we can. And you're next, buddy."

He nodded a command, and two of his men efficiently frog-marched Caldwell away to the waiting riot car.

They passed in front of Thatcher so that he saw the blank stupefaction descending on the angrily twisting face of the Southerner.

It was all over in minutes.

"My God!" somebody said. "Abercrombie tried to murder him in front of a thousand people . . ."

"I tell you he's crazy . . ."

"Oh, Henry . . ."

"Daddy!"

Laura, white-faced and suddenly defenseless, had moved close to him.

"It's all right, baby," said Thatcher, tucking her hand reassuringly in his arm. "Just a passing ugliness."

But it was more than a passing ugliness. Gloria Parry, breathing hard, was stroking the sleeve of her husband's coat to reassure herself that he was still there. Parry himself was still clenching and unclenching his fists. Mr. and Mrs. McCullough, who had hurried over, stared blankly at the door through which the police and their prisoners had gone.

Thatcher looked down at his daughter. "No, don't talk about it. Let's have some of that coffee we were aiming at."

Mrs. Parry seconded him. "Yes," she said, and her voice shook only slightly. "Yes, I think I'd like some coffee, too."

But once the initial shock was over, Owen Abercrombie's arrest cried aloud for comment. The NAACP banquet, once recovered, discussed it in a brittle near-hysterical way until late into the night.

As Wall Street did, on Monday morning.

According to the Sloan's Chief of Research, no arrest unconnected with storage tanks had aroused so much talk for decades. Walter Bowman was having the time of his life, trumpeting into the telephone, sounding old contacts, opening new pipelines of information. His subordinates were lashed into a frenzy of activity.

"The New York City Police Department employs over forty

thousand people," he thundered. "One of you must have a contact. Think!"

He refused to admit that very few budding young bankers do know a cop. Neophytes in the Research Department, accustomed to appraising their circle of acquaintance in terms of potential tipsters to mergers and acquisitions, suddenly found themselves remembering that dim daughter of their mother's Cousin Susan who was rumored to have married somebody in the police public relations office. Irately they reviewed their relatives, their classmates, their neighbors. Wait a minute! Didn't their roommate at the Business School have a brother who was a pathologist, somebody who did autopsies? Spiritually, the Research Department rang with cries of "Mush!"

In spite of this self-flagellation, very little meat was added to the bare bones of the official press releases. These were massively uninformative. Owen Abercrombie had been formally charged with violating the Sullivan Act by carrying concealed weapons, with breach of peace, malicious mischief and a host of misdemeanors and minor felonies. Bail, however, had been denied, indicating that a more serious charge was in the offing. His cohorts had also been the subject of miscellaneous holding charges. Indeed, two of the thugs were wanted in Rhode Island for armed assault. Dean Caldwell was out on bail.

"And that's about it," Bowman summed up for Thatcher. "Not much so far. But we'll keep working at it. By tomorrow—"

He was interrupted by the entrance of Charlie Trinkam, who beamed at them in high good spirits while draping himself on the windowsill.

"Hashing over this Abercrombie business?" he asked. "I just got all the dirt from Paul Jackson."

Thatcher nodded approvingly. A criminal lawyer had the contacts they needed. He would know everything there was to know. But perhaps it was more than a question of knowing the right people. So far there had been no announcement of an attorney for the defense. This delay had inspired the White Association for Civic Intervention to an angry denunciation of incommunicado tactics by city officials and confused mumblings about *habeas corpus*, which had hitherto been incapable of provoking

"Whacky's" recognition, let alone its approval. The Police Commissioner had wearily countered by disclosing that the defendant had already seen his wife, his son, his doctor, his partner and three lawyers whom he had refused to retain.

"Is Jackson going to undertake the defense?" asked Thatcher.

"They asked him to, but he said no."

"Good man," murmured Bowman.

"Oh, it isn't that." Charlie shook his head. "He'll act for anybody. But he says that it's a million to one against this coming to trial, so it's not his cup of tea."

Bowman began to protest this view of the situation, but Trinkam held up a restraining hand.

"It's all very interesting," he said. "You know Abercrombie is a rich man. Well, he threw out his son a couple of years ago when the boy decided to go and be a poet in a beach shack out in California. They'd been having trouble anyway, since Owen's second marriage."

Rapidly Walter Bowman scanned his mental files on the personages of the financial community. "That's right. He got married about five years ago. To that model."

"Exactly. And the honeymoon's been over for some time. Personally, I think Owen lost interest in sex when he discovered segregation. So, guess what happened as soon as the news hit the radio. The boy flew into town in the middle of the night, and he and the wife put their heads together. Their theory is for Owen to beat the rap by being pronounced insane."

"Ah-h-h," Thatcher was appreciative. "Then he'd be legally incompetent to handle his estate."

"Sure. They get themselves appointed guardians, then they hold the purse strings, and the beauty of it is that Abercrombie doesn't have any financial liabilities. He's piled up a mess of criminal charges but there aren't any civil damages, no big tax bills, nothing. It's just a question of putting him quietly away in a private sanitarium for a couple of years. Hell, he's going to have to spend more than that in jail anyway if he doesn't agree. Public opinion won't go along with a suspended sentence, particularly when it comes out that those two thugs from Providence got their guns from him. And that's even if they don't get him for the two earlier attempts on Parry."

"Yes, it doesn't seem as if Abercrombie has any choice. But you say he's resisting the idea?"

"The way I hear it, he's barely able to get out a coherent sentence. When his own lawyer advised an insanity plea, Abercrombie threw him out. Sure, he'll fight it at the start. But then he really hasn't taken in the fact that he's a criminal. The wife and the son have got the old man in a squeeze. He doesn't have any choice. And even if he does contest it all the way, the family isn't going to have any trouble producing a string of witnesses. Quite apart from his performance last night, a lot of people think he's loony."

"Then that takes care of Abercrombie for the duration," said Walter Bowman out of the depths of his experience. "The courts can settle a lot of things fast when they want to, but the one thing that takes months, if not years, is a family quarrel about control of an estate. And part of that estate is his partnership interest in Dibbel Abercrombie. Had you thought about the mess this is going to make over there?"

Everyone present agreed that even customers with a strong enough stomach to deal with Abercrombie *qua* broker during the past few weeks were going to fight shy of a house that managed to foul itself up into a situation worthy of *Jarndyce v. Jarndyce.*

Thatcher's interest, however parochial, was not confined to this aspect of Owen Abercrombie's arrest.

"Are they going to charge him with the other attempts on Parry?"

"Not if he sets up a successful insanity plea."

Thatcher waved away this technicality. "Of course not. But do the police think he did it?"

Charlie shrugged. "They don't know, according to the poop from Jackson. They tried to check his alibi for the shooting, but you can guess what they came up with. The wife doesn't get up till noon, and Owen drives to the station himself. He lives in the same town as Parry, after all, and the whole thing took place during commuting hours. He could easily have slipped over for half an hour and then gone on his way to New York. But that holds true for everybody in that neck of the woods. All of Westchester and the Connecticut shore."

"Connecticut? How does that come in?"

"While the police had their hands on Dean Caldwell, they decided to run a check on him too. He lives in Greenwich, and he has the same itinerary as Abercrombie. Solitary drive to the station and time of arrival in New York unprovable within an hour or two. I think what the police are really pinning their hopes to is finding the rifle. They've got both the bullet and the cartridge case. And the way Caldwell has been talking makes him a good second-string suspect. Personally, I think it's a lot of hot air. At least he wasn't carrying a gun last night."

"That doesn't mean anything," Bowman objected. "He had a good motive, and the attempt in Katonah was pretty safe. He'd be smart to let Abercrombie take the spotlight at Lincoln Center where no one but a nut would try anything."

"Maybe so." Charlie was still unconvinced. "But look, John. If you really want the latest, why don't you have lunch with Jackson and me. I fixed it up with him for one-thirty."

"I'd like to," said Thatcher, "but right now I'm interested in what you said about a motive, Walter. I thought young Caldwell was simply giving vent to his spectacularly unpleasant racist feelings."

"Don't you believe it," said Bowman wryly. "Sure, he's from the South and he thinks exactly the way he talks. But what really put the bite into his venom was the situation at Schuyler & Schuyler."

Both men turned to him respectfully and Bowman visibly expanded under their attention. Trinkam might know criminal lawyers, but when it came to what was going on behind the scene at any brokerage house in the world . . .

"You've got to go back to the time when Ambrose Schuyler died. That's a small house they have over there, but even so it was obvious that they were going to need a new partner. Even before Art Foote died they were understaffed. Now, that kid Caldwell's got a swollen idea of his own competence. He decided that he was going to be the new partner. Normally that idea would have been squelched damned quick when it became obvious that Nat Schuyler was talking to all sorts of prospective partners. But Nat played the whole Parry scheme close to his chest, and the negotiations dragged on for a couple of months, even after Nat located his man. In the meantime Caldwell convinced himself he was as good as in. I saw him around that time and tried to get him to backpedal a little, but it was useless. Then, when he finally found out what was going on, he exploded. As far as Caldwell is concerned, Ed Parry stole something that was his. And he doesn't have a doubt in the world that, with Parry out of the way, he could have it back."

Thatcher frowned. "You say you tried to discourage him even before you knew about Parry? But how did you know he was wrong, Walter?"

"Because nobody in the world would have offered him a partnership. He was never even in the running. Dean Caldwell is a good enough research man," replied Bowman with all the serenity of a man who knows that he is the best of all possible Chiefs of Research and has no further ambition, "but there are others. And he's lacking on almost every other score. He has no pull, he's not a salesman, he doesn't get on with people and he doesn't have the judgment to be a particularly good trader."

Trinkam whistled at this comprehensive indictment.

"I wonder if the police know about this," mused Thatcher.

"Jackson will be able to tell you," said Bowman handsomely.

"Sure, they've dug up all that business about Caldwell's bid for a partnership," said Paul Jackson, spearing his butter with a breadstick. "All these people seem to be complete blabbermouths. Caldwell must have spent his entire working day complaining to people about how Parry did him dirt."

Jackson did not approve. His own clients were noted for taciturnity.

"Amateurs," Trinkam murmured indulgently.

"You said it," agreed Jackson heartily. "They're having a hell of a time finding out whether there's a gun missing from Abercrombie's collection. It seems they found an arsenal at his place in Katonah—rifles, shotguns, machetes. The only thing he was short on was pocket weapons. I guess that's why he only outfitted two of his boys."

"I'm surprised the others didn't march into Lincoln Center shouldering shotguns," Thatcher observed.

"The boys wouldn't go for that." Jackson was perfectly serious. "But the fact remains that the bullet and cartridge don't match anything in the Abercrombie house now. I understand they're sifting through the Katonah dump. It would be just like that lunatic to toss his rifle there."

Trinkam was sympathetic. "Hell of a job."

"Oh, I don't know. It's a model dump. Won a prize or something," Jackson said, displaying yet another piece of esoteric information. "Just the sort of thing Katonah would have."

"Then it's the kind of dump that will probably have vaporized this rifle within twenty-four hours."

"No," said Thatcher and Jackson simultaneously. Charlie Trinkam every now and then displayed a powerful ignorance of life as it is lived outside the confines of a metropolitan district. He would have been far more at home in the center of Peking than in South Orange, New Jersey.

"Scavengers," explained Thatcher clearly. "In fact, in Katonah, it's probably antique dealers who inspect the throwaways."

"That's right. A good rifle would be picked up right away. One of the dealers got a fine Oriental off the trash heap up in Westchester."

Charlie moodily pecked at his salad, unprepared to contemplate this strange and exotic way of life. Jackson tactfully turned the conversation.

"The police are pretty hot on the idea of Caldwell as their boy. They figure it this way. Practically everyone at the poison party lives within striking distance of Katonah. In fact, Nat Schuyler is about the only one they care to cross out. He lives in Princeton, and hasn't driven his own car in years. Even so, he could probably still have done it if anybody can think of a reason why he would want to. So, unless they can find the gun, they've pretty well had it on the shooting. But then, there's the poisoning. And that's where you come to an interesting point."

"But everyone at the party could have done that too," Thatcher protested. "It still leaves you with the same group of people."

"Not exactly. First of all, they've compiled a monster timetable of movements at the party. They were lucky there. They got to people right away, the next morning in fact, while the details were still fresh in everybody's minds. And they figure they got as much as they ever will by that route. So they haven't been around again. But they've been working on it."

Thatcher realized with a start that he had almost forgotten that gravely deferential young man who had interviewed him so efficiently. But Centre Street had not forgotten. All through these past days people had been sitting in offices piecing his statement together with seventy others and amassing a very accurate picture of that ill-fated party.

"And poison isn't like a gun," Paul Jackson was continuing. "This won't be a case of someone having nicotine around the house for years. If they ever pin this one on anybody, access to the poison will be a big part of the case. Anybody can have a rifle innocently. It's a lot harder to pull that as a defense with nicotine."

"People in cities don't have rifles," said Trinkam, still obsessed with his unfortunate glimpse of exurbia. "And, anyway, I thought people in these estate areas had weed killers and insecticides by the ton. That's what the pharmaceutical firms are always saying."

"Foote wasn't killed with any weed killer," Paul Jackson replied. "It was the pure alkaloid. You don't come across that often, and it's damn hard to explain away."

It was apparent that Jackson was already readying himself for the arduous task of defending the poisoner, if and when brought to trial. His dark eyes glinted with interest and he elaborated further.

"The police will really have something to sink their teeth into if they can find a solid motive—and I don't mean one of these 'Let's Keep Wall Street White' things—and access to poison. I assume they can prove opportunity with their charts."

"That still doesn't narrow things down at all."

"Ah, but if you think of it as a rational crime, then you get to the point about the confusion of the glasses. That's what I meant about the police being onto something interesting. They're concentrating on the people who had reason to know that Foote was on the wagon. Someone who wouldn't have been put off by finding four men with three glasses."

"Does that narrow it down much?" asked Thatcher dubiously.

"Does it ever!" replied the lawyer exuberantly. "What with old Nat Schuyler spending all his time squiring Parry around, and someone having to take up the slack in the office, poor Art Foote was pretty well chained to his desk, except when he was helping on the Parry bit. His contacts were much more restricted during his last week than normally. And practically everyone he saw was at the reception. Of course there was one group that heard about his ulcer morning, noon and night, and that was the people at Schuyler & Schuyler." He ended on a triumphant note.

Thatcher was forcibly reminded of canny old Nat Schuyler's comments on the use of Owen Abercrombie as a stalking horse. He said as much.

"Of course it makes sense. Anybody could play these racists like a piano. And there's not much doubt that somebody's been doing it from Schuyler & Schuyler. Abercrombie was a gift from heaven to the murderer." Jackson grinned brilliantly around the table. "And he's going to be even more of a gift to the guy's lawyer."

16 · Day of Wrath! O Day of Mourning!

JOHN PUTNAM THATCHER set off for his office Tuedsay morning in high spirits. Since no sane observer could derive satisfaction from the current state of affairs, this left him to conclude that he was an unregenerate earthling, as opposed to the rare Eastern spirit Mrs. Davis had apparently discerned. An excellent breakfast, including first-rate eggs, bacon and hashed brown potatoes, real coffee and the other necessities, was followed by the discovery that the sun had finally reappeared, bathing the world outside the Devonshire with a vitality which endless days cf gray drizzle and fog had drained from it. After this, Thatcher found it impossible to let the existence of Owen Abercrombie affect him.

Except favorably. Was it possible, he asked himself as Brewster summoned a taxi, that the Abercrombie arrest had eclipsed Bradford Withers' *bêtise*? Was it too much to hope that gunfire at Lincoln Center had diverted CASH's attention from the Sloan Guaranty Trust?

After all, Owen Abercrombie's maniacal outburst did tend to monopolize attention. How long had it been since anybody thought of that quite likable man, Arthur Foote? Of course the police were still pursuing his murderer, but there was no doubt that Wall Street was much more interested in the attack on Edward Parry.

To the extent of assuming that Arthur Foote's poisoner and Edward Parry's assailant were one and the same man.

But were they?

And if so, why?

No good answer suggested itself, so Thatcher leaned back and watched the sun brighten the colors worn by the clerks and secretaries streaming up from the IRT. Indefatigably nature touched the aridity of even this man-made desert, nourishing the human spirit as surely as it fed flowers and bushes.

It rapidly developed, however, that nature had an uphill fight. Thatcher got his first intimation of this when the taxi turned off Broadway, only to be waved to a halt by a uniformed policeman.

"What the——?" demanded the driver, who gave no evidence of having breakfasted well.

Usually Thatcher let these little exchanges complete themselves without his participation. Today, however, a general predisposition toward peace and harmony caused him to hitch himself forward. But before he could contribute to the conversation, a squad car screamed to a halt beside them. As they turned to watch, three blue-coated policemen flung open the doors and pelted down to Exchange Place, nightsticks in hand.

"——do you want me to do?" the cabby snarled.

The policeman was willing to tell him in some detail. After completing a picturesque recitative, he withdrew.

"Officer," Thatcher called out, handing his driver a bill and hurrying to alight. "What's going on?"

The policeman, busy fending off other taxis who were now creating a tangle that would last for some hours, had time for only four words.

"Trouble at the Sloan!"

"Good God!" said Thatcher.

He started to struggle through the huge crush, at the same time mulling the possibilities. Embezzlement? Then, why the police horses, dancing dangerously down Exchange Place, with grim-faced riders, wielding sticks, shouting commands that the surging mob get back?

Fire? Then where were the fire engines, the alarm bells? Only the whine of police sirens rent the air. Thatcher was jostled slightly as another team of uniformed men, breathing hard, charged past him. Above the din of thousands of people trying to see, trying to get to work, trying to move, there were shouts and confused noises from ahead. From, John Putnam Thatcher realized, the Sloan Guaranty Trust.

"Here, there, you can't . . ."

A human chain of policemen behind a barricade of wooden horses barred the approach to the Sloan lobby.

"What's going on?" Thatcher demanded.

"Just move on."

With a spurt of rage, Thatcher elbowed his way to the red-faced policeman who was shouting directives.

"Now listen here. I'm a vice-president of the Sloan," he began in icy tones. "And if . . ."

The harassed policeman capitulated immediately. "O.K., O.K. Let him through. Get in there, and see what you can do!"

Thatcher barely had time to digest these ambiguous words as he slid past the policemen and hurried the twenty-five steps to the great glass doors (intact) of the Sloan Guaranty Trust.

Without pause, he pulled them open—then stopped dead in his tracks. The nature of the problem was instantly and painfully clear.

The lobby of the Sloan Guaranty Trust (terrazzo with mosaic inlay) was totally obscured. Kneeling on every available surface were, perhaps, five hundred Negroes (with a sprinkling of white faces among them). They were singing, very beautifully and very softly. Instead of the muted clacking and cheerful clicking of a busy bank, the great glass lobby with its tortured friezes and ele-phantiasis-ridden foliage was—except for the muted hum from outside which became a punctuating burst whenever the doors were opened—echoing with the solemn harmonies of devotional anthems.

Well, there was one question answered. CASH had not forgotten.

The staff, naturally, was confused. But respectful, thought Thatcher, edging inside. He noticed Henley, the office manager, back to the wall, fix horrified eyes on four young girls at his feet as they clapped their hands softly and reverently.

"Well, here you are, John!"

Even Everett Gabler was whispering. He came sidling along the wall to Thatcher. As he did, he inadvertently trod on a brown hand.

"Oh, I'm so sorry," he said anguishedly.

"That's quite all right. Didn't hurt a bit," replied a pleasant-faced matron. She resumed her singing.

Gabler whipped out a handkerchief and mopped his brow.

"What is all this?" Thatcher inquired.

"A kneel-in," said Gabler.

"A *what?*"

"A kneel-in," Gabler replied. "The minute the doors opened this morning at eight o'clock, these people marched in and started all of this—praying and singing! Shocking thing to do in a bank, but it is imposing in its way, don't you think?"

Thatcher agreed that it was and suggested retreat to the Sixth Floor and the Trust Department, leaving Commercial Deposits to handle its own problems. As he spoke, Henley, the manager, finally reached their side. Behind him, looking baffled, was a policeman, resplendent in gold braid.

"Thank heavens you're here, Mr. Thatcher. Mr. O'Hara is in Washington, and I don't know what to do!"

"We can clear 'em out," said the policeman in a low growl. Then, conjuring up violence and bloodshed, he gloomily added, "That is, if that's what you want!"

Thatcher sighed inwardly. It was not, technically speaking, his responsibility to deal with this. But Henley was clearly out of his depth (and O'Hara, fortunately in Washington, would also have been out of his depth, he thought uncharitably). It was obviously unthinkable to let Bradford Withers handle this. Henley, wringing his hands, broke in:

"I understand they're protesting Mr. Withers' remarks," he said, looking anxiously over his shoulder at the congregation. He was not mistaken; the tempo of the singing was picking up.

"Perhaps we should try to get to your office to talk," Thatcher suggested. At this, Henley registered enormous relief; well might he. He had just shifted his burden to other, stronger shoulders.

Reaching the office was not easy. All available floor space was packed. Standing behind the counters, looking beleaguered, and rather bemused, was the depleted staff.

"A lot of people can't get in," said Henley apologetically over his shoulder as he led the way. "Oops! Oh, sorry, sir!"

"Quite all right," caroled back an elderly black gentleman, without breaking the beat. "Rock, chariot, I told you to rock!"

"Oh dear," moaned Henley, picking his way forward.

They followed him, Indian file, until they had reached the comparative comfort of the tellers' area. There, Thatcher noted with a gleam of amusement, one of the young women had momentarily forgotten that her first allegiance was to the Sloan Guaranty Trust. Caught up by the rhythm, she was tapping her foot, and softly joining in:

"Rock, chariot, I told you to rock!
Judgment goin' to find me!"

As the dignitaries passed, she put hand to mouth in an endearing gesture of guilt. Neither Henley nor Everett Gabler noticed her. John Putnam Thatcher did.

With a sudden grin, he winked at her.

He was, however, grave and sober as he marched into Henley's office and listened to his plaints, and to the ominous, though less voluble, prognostications from Captain Bielski.

"Well, it seems clear enough," he said decisively. "If these people are determined to stay, we certainly are not going to throw them out."

Bielski looked relieved. So did Henley, until he thought about the day's business.

Thatcher cut his lament short.

"The major problem seems to be order outside," he said.

"Don't worry," Bielski reassured him. "The riot squad is on its way."

They looked at him in silence for a moment.

"Ah . . . yes," said Thatcher. "Well, that should convince the staff of the value of physical fitness, if nothing else does. Now, Henley, all you have to do is hold the fort down here. We'll try to work something out."

At some stage, Thatcher knew, the singing would end and Richard Simpson would emerge.

"Yes, yes," said Henley, perceptibly reviving. "What about the employees who are late today?"

With an effort, Thatcher reminded himself that Henley, in the last analysis, was a clerk, not a banker.

"I'd just forget about them," he said gently.

Henley was disappointed.

"Low level tyrant," Thatcher said to himself, pondering this unattractive type as he and Gabler escaped to the executive elevator bound for the sixth floor.

He missed Everett Gabler's critical remarks on Walter Bowman's latest research report.

"Sorry, I didn't hear you," he murmured as they stepped out of the elevator. Here, too, there were gaps in the familiar ranks normally stationed behind files, calculating machines and typewriters. But since the trust officers to a man preferred using the executive entrance, they were all present. Thatcher entertained no illusion that they were working. Predictably, only Everett Gabler could rise above five hundred Negroes singing spirituals in the lobby.

"Pharmaceuticals," he was saying with spinsterish disapproval. "Now, John, you know as well as I do that the drug houses are already overpriced. I see no reason . . ."

"Do I detect a moral disapproval of oral contraceptives?" asked Thatcher, leading the way to his own office in time to shock Miss Corsa yet again. "No, Everett, I don't have time for that right now. We've got a lot of things to do. . . ."

Just then Charlie Trinkam arrived, reporting cheerfully that the throngs on Exchange Place were growing. And the television crews had arrived.

"That's another thing," Gabler began disapprovingly as Miss Corsa rang through. Bradford Withers was on the line.

"John!" The voice was vague and faintly aggrieved. "John, what is all this? I don't know if you've noticed, but there's some sort of fracas going on downstairs. Somebody should do something about it."

Thatcher counted to ten. Then:

"The police are doing what they can," he said carefully, ignoring Trinkam's broad grin.

"The police? What is all this . . .?"

"Brad, we're having a kneel-in. Yes, K-N-E-E-L- . . . yes, protesting your remarks . . ."

The telephone erupted into turkey gobblings.

Rather sharply, Thatcher retorted, "No, I don't think it would be a good idea for you to go down. Yes, we're keeping an eye on the situation. Yes . . . yes . . ."

He hung up and sighed. With considerable tact, his subordinates did not comment.

Instead, they started a brief consideration of Bowman's critique of the pharmaceutical industry. This, unfortunately, caused Thatcher's attention to revert to one of the day's earlier musings —the poisoning of Arthur Foote. It was not so odd that it had slipped from the center of attention—not when Wall Street was being reminded of the attacks on Edward Parry by kneel-ins, trade-ins, by television interviews—and by the dread specter of the coming March on Wall Street.

"Good God!" he said aloud. "If a kneel-in can disrupt one of the Sloan's divisions, can you imagine what a full scale March on Wall Street will do?"

Trinkam raised his eyebrows. "To be honest, I haven't been able to think of anything else."

Determinedly, Thatcher brought a fist down on his desk.

"We've got to strike back!"

"But how?"

For a moment Thatcher pondered.

"They're singing the 'Battle Hymn of the Republic'!" said a new voice.

Ken Nicolls stood in the doorway. It was evident that the junior trust officers, delighted to have their routine interrupted, were making periodic reconaissances of the lobby situation.

Suddenly Thatcher snapped his fingers and smiled broadly.

"That's it!" he announced.

Trinkam, Gabler and Nicolls stared at him.

"That's it," he repeated. "Now, Charlie, I want you to get

over to Philborn and tell him to get the glee club ready. Nicolls, call the custodian . . ."

With a martial air that Hugh Waymark would have envied, John Thatcher dispatched his junior officers to a number of urgent tasks.

"And hurry!" he said in parting. "Now, Miss Corsa, I want you to get Ed Parry for me. No, I don't know where he is but . . . what's that?"

"Mr. Robichaux," she countered briskly.

"No, I don't want Robichaux," said Thatcher authoritatively.

"He's on the line," she reported.

There was no escape.

"Tom, I'm in a hurry . . ."

"Understand you've got trouble over there," Tom shouted.

"To be precise," Thatcher replied, "a kneel-in."

There was a long pause.

"Well, good for them," said Tom Robichaux astonishingly.

Thatcher removed the receiver from his ear and inspected it. What was Robichaux saying?

"You know," the hedonist continued, "I had a little talk with Francis last night, and by God! It hit me."

"What hit you?" Thatcher inquired with genuine interest.

"Why, this civil rights business," said Robichaux. "Never really saw it before. But, dammit, I'd be kneeling-in myself . . . No, I'd be breaking your glass windows, that's what I'd be doing. . . ."

In a world gone mad, it was not particularly strange that Tom Robichaux was going mad with it. The picture of him heaving rocks through the Sloan's great windows was, in fact, irresistible. But Thatcher was still curious to discover how the wily Francis Devane had managed to engage his partner's support for the civil rights movement. Robichaux was happy to explain.

"Well, Francis put it to me. 'How would you like it,' he said, 'if you had fourteen million dollars, and they wouldn't let you buy a seat on the Exchange, simply because you're a Negro?' Well, that hit me, John, I don't mind admitting it. Never thought of it in that light before. But for God's sake, what does color matter when a man has fourteen million dollars—that's the way I see it."

"I'm sure you do," said Thatcher. There was much to be said for an uncomplicated outlook.

Robichaux' voice dropped into a confidential range. "Of course, this may cause me trouble. But I'm a man of principle . . ."

"Trouble?"

"Celestine. She's big in the UDC—United Daughters of the Confederacy, you know. She comes from Macon. But on a thing like this . . ."

"Who was that lady I saw you with last night?" Thatcher could not resist asking. Robichaux did not recognize the quotation.

"You mean Saturday night? A very interesting woman, Zelda. She's a social worker, would you believe it?"

Thatcher, who would not, indicated again that he was in a hurry.

"Yes, well the reason I called you was that I wanted you to hear the latest. They've just told Francis. The SEC is going to come out with a statement later today, something about investigating racial bias in the New York Stock Exchange, with a view to legislation. The Governors want to beat the timing."

Nicolls stuck his head in the door, nodding.

With an uplifted hand Thatcher held him motionless as he continued to listen to Robichaux.

"That's fine, Tom. It works in with something I have in mind. You'll have to clear it with Francis. Now, listen, this is what I want you to do . . ."

A moment later he was turning to Nicolls and listening to his report.

"Fine," he said, consulting his wristwatch. "We don't have much time. Now, you'd better root out the electrician and be sure we have the microphones ready."

Nicolls nodded and listened to further instructions. Over his shoulder, Thatcher saw Trinkam dispatching clerical help on errands.

"We'll have to hurry," Thatcher said.

"Yes, sir!" said Nicolls, suppressing a salute in the nick of time.

"And, Nicolls," said Thatcher, "I need scarcely tell you that if that kindergarten of yours in Brooklyn Heights does not turn out to be fully integrated, your employment at the Sloan is hereby terminated."

With a brisk wave, he strode down the hall toward Walter Bowman's office.

Nicolls stared after him blankly.

Miss Corsa, handling three telephone calls simultaneously, took pity on him.

"Don't worry. That was one of Mr. Thatcher's little jokes."

17 · Sing Ye Heavens and Earth Reply: Al—le—lu—ia!

AT THAT VERY MOMENT, Richard Simpson was cleaving his way enthusiastically toward the Sloan.

He had a very clear idea of how the next two hours would shape themselves. The early morning kneel-in, coupled with a careful leak from his own staff about an important announcement, had ensured the presence of all the major networks. Cameras would abound, while young men with microphones hung deferentially on his every word. Against a solemn background of choral spirituals he would deliver an eloquent statement about the rights of man and the sanctity of selling off Vita Cola. Then there would be a few stern questions, cast in a rhetorical frame, addressed to the iniquities of Bradford Withers.

Perhaps at this point the Sloan might produce some mindless helot to stammer out a few transparent evasions. It didn't matter. At this peak of dramatic crescendo, possibly with a single basso intoning "Deep River," he would signal the timing of the March on Wall Street for the day after tomorrow. Then there would be a powerful fade-out of his right profile looking firm and exalted. In fact, a good deal of Richard Simpson and precious little of anything else.

It was not to be. Simpson, happily riding the crest of a situation created by others, failed to realize that the opposition had not yet begun to fight. Like many an agitator before him, he was about to learn that it can be difficult to control the powers one has unleashed and virtually impossible to upstage them.

John Putnam Thatcher's blood was up. The invasion of the Sloan had touched off emotions normally associated with the desecration of the home. Like a good general, he first planned his strategy. Then he alerted his intelligence, deployed his troops and summoned reinforcements. The nature of his tactics might have come as a surprise to an orthodox military mind—say, that of Hugh Waymark, last heard from in the clutches of the Committee to Clean Up Wall Street.

Thatcher's conference with Walter Bowman apprised him of the exact nature of Simpson's forthcoming announcement. The trouble with contrived leaks is that anybody can get hold of them. Bowman's information merely confirmed Thatcher's intuitions.

"And I think," he declared, "I think we're taking the right steps."

These steps were many. Workmen moved to the front lobby the giant television set in the Directors' room used for closed-circuit communication with the Sloan's scattered operations. It boasted a thirty-six inch screen. Meanwhile, the members of the Sloan Glee Club, together with their musical director, were hastily summoned from their desks and assembled on the balcony overlooking the lobby, where they were in the habit of serenading holiday crowds with Christmas carols during the yuletide season. They were not a group to be despised, as even the critic of the *New York Times* had admitted after their ambitious rendition of Handel's *Messiah*. Messenger boys were returning from all the local bookstores with every available collection of Civil War songs. All employees had been given permission to join the festivities. And best of all, Tom Robichaux, the light of conversion beaming from his vagrant eye, was hurrying to the scene of battle.

Thatcher's aim was quite simple. The Sloan Guaranty Trust was going to steal Simpson's thunder. The spirit of Mahatma Gandhi was going to be displaced by that of John Brown. People who got up at dawn to take the A train the length of Manhattan to Broadway and Nassau had feelings to rouse. What Julia Ward

Howe had done for the Union, she could do again for the Sloan.

A scant two minutes before Simpson's arrival, Thatcher stepped into the lobby, flanked by his ADC's. Summoning the press to him, he declared in stentorian tones that he was in momentary expectation of an important message from the Stock Exchange. A representative would be with them immediately. Then, dead on time, he wheeled to the doors and welcomed Richard Simpson with a ringing speech which placed the Sloan so far in the vanguard of the civil rights movement that it left Simpson looking like a Ku Klux Klansman. There was a tumultuous ovation from the lobby and then, as the CASH leader collected his scattered wits to reply, seven hundred voices thundered forth, "The Battle Hymn of the Republic."

In the face of this welter of noise the television cameras, understandably enough, abandoned the principals and panned over the singers. There was much to reward any cameraman. The kneelers were singing with passion, their eyes lifted upward. And as the lens followed their gaze into the architectural heights of the lobby, it came to the glee club, equally exuberant, and being conducted with demonic energy. Pages fluttered as chorus after chorus unfolded. Then down came the camera to another enthralling scene. Tom Robichaux had come through the doors and, after taking in the picture before him, reverently removed his homburg to lay it across his breast while he stood at attention.

> Glory! Glory! Hall-e-lu-jah!
> Glory! Glory! Hall-e-lu-jah!
> His Truth goes marching on!

With the last chorus echoing through the marble halls, Thatcher and Robichaux relentlessly advanced on the microphones, where Robichaux announced that the Board of Governors of the New York Stock Exchange would meet on Thursday morning to deliver its decision on the transfer of a seat to Edward J. Parry.

This news had two happy results. It sent the entire financial press scampering from the scene to attack the President of the Exchange in his lair, and it cut the ground from under Simpson. By the time he could get to the microphones to paralyze his listeners with a call to the great March on Thursday, he sounded like a man determined to have his March whether or not there was any reason for it. As he incoherently accused the Exchange of deliberately undermining his schedule, he sounded neither firm nor exalted. He sounded petulant.

Thatcher let him maunder on until the conductor reclaimed the attention of his chorus. Then, to a telling accompaniment of "We Are Coming, Father Abraham," Thatcher really let himself go. In rip-roaring accents he reminded the kneelers, the television audience and most of Exchange Place of the gigantic rally at Madison Square Garden the next evening for all March sympathizers.

"And we of the Sloan Guaranty Trust, including our president Bradford Withers, will join with you—and Edward Parry—for this occasion!"

Ovation!

The proceedings were then brought to a climax by a final anthem. Emotions had reached new heights. The elevators, the halls, the stairways were crowded with employees joining in. If that fire-proof, water-proof, earthquake-proof building had any rafters, they rang as never before. Not until he saw the young woman teller from Commercial Deposits openly laughing at him did Thatcher realize he himself was singing. Like many a farm-boy from New Hampshire in 1862, he could not resist the "Battle Cry."

> We will rally from the hillside,
> We will rally from the plains,
> Shouting the battle cry of freedom!
>
> We will fill the vacant ranks
> With a million free men more,
> SHOUTING THE BAT-TLE CRY OF FREE-DOM!

With the Sloan achieving the spiritual renaissance that figured so largely in the supper conversation at Lincoln Center, with sandwich boards demanding "Justice!" in the corridors of Stanton Carruthers' law firm, and a hootenany in progress at Waymark & Sims, the Committee of Three found it difficult to select an unobtrusive site for the deliberations which would produce the press release being promised to the *Wall Street Journal* at this very moment by Francis Devane. They had long since become resigned to their hoodoo impact on their surroundings. No normal commercial establishment could be expected to welcome them with open arms.

These considerations, plus the prevailing atmosphere of insanity which was beginning to topple strong minds, explained why, although the blustering November afternoon had ominous gray skies overhead and a brisk breeze whipping in from the northeast, Thatcher and his colleagues were assembled on the pitching deck of the Staten Island ferry plowing their way endlessly back and forth across New York Harbor. Nor were they united by any common reaction to their plight.

Thatcher himself was so uplifted by the success of his give-'em-hell tactics that morning that he could have taken an entire armada in his stride. Repressing a tendency to burst into "Anchors Aweigh," he buoyantly reminded his companions that he had a great deal to do. He still had to see Edward Parry, check Bradford Withers' speech so that it was foolproof, absolutely foolproof, and—as a concession to Francis Devane—invite Lee Clark to join the Sloan and Schuyler & Schuyler in appearing at the March on Wall Street Rally.

"Let's get down to business," he urged.

But Hugh Waymark wasn't going to do anything until he had relieved himself of his accumulated grievances.

"That Committee to Clean Up Wall Street," he sputtered angrily, "it was all a fraud."

Thatcher pointed out that it didn't matter what they were. The only reason for speaking to them was to prevent uncontrolled action.

"You don't understand. They didn't care about Parry. They were nothing but . . ." He cast around wildly for the *mot juste*. "Nothing but nonbelligerents. In fact, civilians," he concluded, much as Rommel or Montgomery might have described a stray Bedouin wandering over the fields of Alamein to a water hole.

"But I thought they wanted to clean up Wall Street," objected Carruthers, emerging briefly from his reverie.

"They mean it. Literally. They want trees on the sidewalks and a flower box in every window." Waymark's voice rose in scornful mimicry. "A sapling now will provide shade and spiritual comfort to future generations." He resumed his normal tones.

"It seems there's some sort of a deal you can set up with the Department of Sanitation. They provide the tree and care for it during the first year. Then it's yours. Not a bad idea, really. I wouldn't mind having one in front of my place uptown. But is now the time for that sort of thing?"

No one could say that the Committee of Three wasn't learning about life, thought Thatcher. He had found out all about the prizes won by the Katonah dump, and Waymark would soon be tending an infant oak in Sutton Place. But perhaps the strangest result of their flight to the sea was to be found in Stanton Carruthers. He was standing by the rail, inhaling deeply.

"Haven't been on this ferry in years," he said expansively. "Really it's a great place to get away." He gazed yearningly at the Statue of Liberty in a posture suggestive of the newly arrived immigrant, one leap ahead of the Gestapo.

"Yes, yes," said Thatcher impatiently.

But Carruthers also had things to get off his chest. He told them in loving detail about his little ketch at the Greenwich Yacht Club, lamented Vin McCullough's sale of a fine schooner consequent upon his removal to the city, and said that young men today were faddists. Always taking things up, and then dropping them. One year it's sailing, and the next year it's birdwatching. Sad, sad. No stamina, no fixity of purpose. For those with the sea in their veins . . .

In the end Thatcher wrote the release himself.

Francis Devane no doubt meant well when he suggested that inviting Lee Clark to join the Sloan Guaranty Trust and Edward Parry on the rally dais would be both courteous and politic. Clark didn't see things that way at all.

"It's an insult, that's what it is," he growled at Thatcher.

"Oh, come now. The Board of Governors knows that this has been a hardship on Clovis Greene. This would give your firm an opportunity to publicize your connection with the Negro community."

"Connection!" Clark twisted his knuckles until they cracked. "We're just another victim. Schuyler & Schuyler is responsible for this whole mess—and they're reaping a damn big profit!"

Thatcher was not going to indulge in meaningless platitudes.

"They certainly hope to do so. But Devane thought you might be able to stem the wave of withdrawals with a personal appearance. We all know that you can't recoup your losses completely."

"You can say that again. But you don't understand what the damage has been so far. Look, we've picked up a couple of clients from Schuyler & Schuyler. Some of their Southern customers who dropped McCullough when they heard the news. Well, they've had to wait two weeks for their portfolios. And you know why? Because they're so busy over there handling the new business. We've lost over five hundred accounts. So what do you think a little speech from me is going to accomplish?"

Possibly losing another five hundred, Thatcher yearned to say. Instead he repeated the invitation.

Clark showed his teeth in an unpleasant smile.

"Oh no. Nat Schuyler and I are going to have a reckoning. And that reckoning doesn't include smoking any peace pipes in front of all of Harlem."

Thatcher had saved his conference with Edward Parry for last, because he expected it to be the least taxing of his many duties that day. But there he neglected to reckon with the eddies of passion swirling through the corridors of Schuyler & Schuyler. The first thing he heard as he stationed himself before the receptionist was the voice of Dean Caldwell, raised somewhere in the nether regions to a shrill yell of defiance.

"So you think you can throw me out and wash your hands of me! Well, you've got another think coming!"

Dim, inaudible rumblings intervened. They did not sound particularly placatory. The receptionist, Thatcher noted disapprovingly, did not measure up to Miss Corsa's high standards of indifference. Visibly nervous, she asked Thatcher to take a seat.

"I don't know whether Mr. Schuyler and Mr. Parry are free right now," she babbled distractedly, giving Thatcher a good idea of the identity of the disputants.

"I haven't gone through all this to be given the boot for some nigger! You can't get away with this!"

The voices were coming nearer. Evidently the disturbance was roiling its way to the exit. A good thing in many ways, but

Thatcher could find it in his heart to wish that his own movements had detained him from the house of Schuyler for another fifteen minutes.

Caldwell burst through a door into the reception room. He came backward, whether because he was turning to yell at his companions or because he was being hustled along, Thatcher could not tell. Ed Parry and Nat Schuyler were right behind.

"You planned it, the three of you!" shrieked Caldwell. "You and Art Foote and this colored boy. You ganged up on me. That's what you were after all along, to get rid of me!"

"That's enough, Caldwell," said Nat Schuyler sharply. "You're hysterical and you're upset. I have some sympathy with you. But if you're not out of this door in two minutes, I'm going to call the police."

Schuyler paid no attention to the other occupants of the room. Nor was he making any attempt to hide the fact that his lapels and shirt collar were rucked up, as if violent hands had been laid on them.

For a moment Caldwell glowered silently at him but, as Parry stepped forward and Schuyler turned to the girl at the switchboard, the Southerner suddenly let out his breath and his shoulders sagged.

"All right, all right," he muttered, stumbling toward the door.

But with his hand on the doorknob he seemed to recover some of his defiance. He turned for one parting shot.

"But you haven't heard the last of this. I've got plenty of friends, and I'm not taking this lying down!"

The door banged behind him.

The girl at the switchboard kept her hand on the dial, unwilling to recognize that the crisis was over. Parry and Schuyler looked at each other helplessly. Then Nat became aware of Thatcher's presence.

"I'm sorry," he said sheepishly, as if embarrassed at a display of emotion unseemly for a brokerage house. "I have to get cleaned up. You can probably figure out what happened, Thatcher. Anyway, Ed'll tell you all about it. You'll have to excuse me. In spite of everything, I can't help feeling sorry for that boy."

Then, moving very slowly, but still erectly, he left the room. There was a moment of silence.

"Whew!" breathed Parry at length. He took out a gleaming white handkerchief and mopped his brow. "Sally, we'll be in my office. Send us some coffee, will you? And find out if there's anything Mr. Schuyler wants."

He ushered Thatcher back into what had once been Ambrose Schuyler's office. There were lines of worry around his eyes. "I hope all of this isn't doing Nat any harm. He's not a youngster, you know."

"Did Caldwell attack him?" asked Thatcher bluntly.

Parry shied at the word. "Well, the boy jumped him," he admitted unhappily. "I pulled him off. Nat fired him."

"Under the circumstances, that can scarcely have come as a surprise to Caldwell."

"You'd think so. But then you weren't here. I could swear that he was completely taken aback. It sounds impossible, but I don't think he expected Nat would. I guess he thought he was indispensable." Parry shook his head. "He went berserk. As if the whole world had suddenly turned upside down."

Thatcher tut-tutted sympathetically, recalling Walter Bowman's opinions of Caldwell's self-esteem.

"Maybe he'll calm down once the shock has worn off," he suggested.

Parry looked dubious. "I've been hearing a lot about him lately. You know, when I first agreed to join the firm, the people I saw were Nat and Art Foote. I worked out the deal with Nat and did a lot of office work with Art Foote. He spent most of his time here filling me in on the house's business. It's only recently I've gotten to know Vin McCullough and this Caldwell kid. Vin and lots of others have let me in on how Caldwell feels. I don't think it's going to die down. In fact, it seems to be growing stronger and stronger."

Here was more confirmation of the police view as expounded by Paul Jackson. Look at Schuyler & Schuyler, they said. These were the people who knew about Art Foote's drinking habits. These were the people who had something really riding on Edward Parry's admission to the firm.

And, it developed, these were the people who thought in terms of assault and inciting others to assault.

It was an effort to return to business.

"Now, about the rally," he began.

"Oh my God!" said Edward Parry from the heart.

18 · Hasten the Time Appointed

TWENTY-FOUR HOURS later, John Thatcher recalled this comment.

"Where to?" asked the cabby.

"Madison Square Garden," said Thatcher. One thing, and one thing alone, could be said for his current peripatetic rounds; he was revisting many New York City landmarks. After all, how many years was it since he had last taken the Staten Island ferry? Or been to Madison Square Garden? He remembered the long count, but nothing since. Probably it was time that he revisited Madison Square Garden.

At this point reality broke in. Were there any solid reason for a return trip to Madison Square Garden, a hockey game would be infinitely preferable to a CASH March on Wall Street Eve Rally.

Featuring, as his baser self cravenly pointed out, placatory remarks by Bradford Withers, designed to dissipate the Simon Legree attitude he had foisted on the Sloan.

"Geeze, I hope there ain't no trouble," the cabby remarked turning right on 50th Street behind a bus emblazoned: PASSAIC CASH JOINS MARCH ON WALL STREET. It was the last of a long string of buses. "I mean, just look!"

Handing him a bill, Thatcher looked. The sidewalk, as far as he could see through the tangle of buses, cars and trucks, was thick with Negroes, well-dressed but determined-looking. Their placards also were determined:

FREEDOM AND EQUALITY

NO SECOND CLASS CITIZENS

THE TIME HAS COME

With difficulty, he began to struggle indoors. The lobby, too, was thronged. From the auditorium there thundered great organ crashes, with ringing voices uplifted in accompaniment:

> "There's a little black train a-comin',
> Get all your business right;
> There's a little black train a-comin',
> And it may be here tonight!"

Thatcher stood aside to let a large family party pass him hurriedly. The father, anxiously surveying his brood, had a mischievous little girl perched on his shoulder. The mother, lips compressed with silent but firm control, was supervising two frankly rambunctious boys, perhaps ten and twelve. And, also in Sunday best, the grandparents forged ahead.

It was not Richard Simpson's labored exhortations that were propelling thousands upon thousands of Negroes into Madison Square Garden tonight, to listen to speeches and songs. (The music within had moved on:

> "Joshua fit the battle of Jericho,
> Jericho, Jericho!
> Joshua fit the battle of Jericho,
> And the walls came tumblin' down!")

Thatcher was, accordingly, deep in unrewarding thought, when he heard his name called.

"John! There you are!"

He looked up. A frowning Vin McCullough waved vigorously, then plunged cross-stream against the inflowing tide to join him.

"Brad's here," he reported, suggesting that he, at least, had had some doubts about Withers' appearance on the scene. "He's down in one of the offices with some of the officials. We might as well get on down. . . ."

If there was one thing Thatcher could have done without, at the moment, it was officials. Nevertheless he followed McCullough along battered, utilitarian halls, where hawkers were selling huge buttons: CASH MEANS RIGHTS, into a small bare room where he first saw Nat Schuyler, deep in converse with Dr. Matthew Ford, the noted sociologist. Well, he was getting plenty of grist for his mill. Nearby stood Bradford Withers.

To do him justice, he did not look intimidated by the muted distant roar, transformed by some acoustical oddity from simple musical enthusiasm to the screams of Romans eager for Christians.

"No," he was saying, "I still don't like it. . . ."

"Please, Mr. Withers!" His vis-à-vis, a thin, balding young man, was a member of the Sloan's legal staff, Thatcher recalled. For some reason, he seemed to be on the brink of tears.

"Still think . . . oh, hello there, John."

Bradford Withers was sounding very like himself, Thatcher saw. That, of course, was both good and bad.

". . . I still think that I should just get up and explain, informally, don't you know?"

"Please," the lawyer pleaded emotionally. "Please, Mr. Withers, just read the statement. I'm sure . . ."

"Well, dammit, it isn't fair . . . oh, hello there, Stan . . ."

Hard on John Thatcher's heels, the rest of the Committee of Three appeared. Stanton Carruthers, he was glad to see, though sorely tried, still felt that he must rally to the aid of a junior (and outmanned) member of his profession.

"Hello, John. Now, Brad, what isn't fair?" he asked in the heavily soothing voice common to lawyers and dentists. Outside, somebody was performing a stirring march with trumpet flourishes and great responsive shouts. Both Nat Schuyler and Dr. Ford were looking smug.

"Dammit, nobody can claim that I'm anti-Negro," said Bradford Withers heatedly. "Oh, hello there, Parry. Listen, when this is over tonight, I'd like a word with you about that shipyard. . . ."

Parry's look of strain momentarily gave way to the flicker of incredulous amusement that Bradford Withers so often evoked. A tremendous thundering from the auditorium quickly erased the amusement. He looked troubled as he nodded his greetings and moved over to join Schuyler and Ford.

"Nobody claims that you are anti-Negro," said Stanton Carruthers with care and no accuracy. "It is merely that your remarks lent themselves to misinterpretation. . . ."

"Well, then, if I just explained . . ."

"Which is precisely what the statement does," said Carruthers, plucking it from the young lawyer's nerveless fingers and quickly scanning it. "Yes, perfectly clear . . ."

It was true, John Thatcher knew—and suspected that Edward Parry knew, if nobody else in the room did. Bradford Withers simply divided the world into two groups: Witherses and non-Witherses. The appalling misfortune of being born a non-Withers overshadowed such minor disabilities as race, creed or color.

Thatcher settled back to let Stanton Carruthers continue his good work. He discovered that he was sharing a battered desk with Napoleon after Waterloo.

Or possibly Robert E. Lee, bidding farewell to the Army of Northern Virginia.

"After our long efforts," said Hugh Waymark, gazing bleakly into the jaws of defeat. "And, God knows, we strained every sinew. Yet we haven't been able to save the day."

Ford and Schuyler were deep in a conversation that Thatcher had no desire to join. Vin McCullough and Edward Parry stood exchanging desultory remarks, both of them flinching at each full-throated roar that reached their ears.

"It sounds like another one of those damned sonic booms," Thatcher heard McCullough say in a strained voice.

Parry nodded absently.

"Just a few friendly words," Bradford Withers was saying earnestly. Stanton Carruthers allowed himself a slight frown.

"Perhaps the statement might be more prudent . . ."

"How," Thatcher asked Waymark, "how have we strained our sinews in vain, Hugh?"

Waymark shook his head sadly.

"We've played our last card. I don't think that there's any doubt about it. Tomorrow . . . tomorrow there's going to be a March on Wall Street!"

In view of the fact that nineteen thousand people had assembled to listen to speeches, songs and organizational details concerning tomorrow's March on Wall Street, Thatcher was tempted to make an acid retort. Then, casting his mind forward to the horrors yet to come, he decided to hold his fire.

". . . sad for our comrades-in-arms," said Waymark. Clearly he was ready to organize a Veterans of the March chapter.

"Oh, John!" called Stanton Carruthers, as Thatcher had known that he would. "Perhaps we could have your opinion . . ."

In the end, it took the united efforts of Thatcher, Stanton Carruthers, Hugh Waymark, Vin McCullough and Nat Schuyler to convince Bradford Withers that he should not depart from the script prepared by the Sloan Guaranty Trust's legal and public relations departments. (And there, thought Thatcher, was a collaboration that made the blood run cold.) They were just in time.

"I think," said Dr. Ford, consulting his watch with a deprecating smile, "I think we should be getting up to the platform."

One thing can be said for the financial world. It teaches discipline. To a man, they rose.

"Can we trust that damned fool?" Nat Schuyler did not bother to lower his voice as he joined Thatcher.

"You don't really care, do you, Nat?" Thatcher replied with acerbity.

Schuyler took this as a high compliment. He was still wheezingly chuckling as they filed out of the office and began the long walk down the aisle to the bunting-draped platform in the center of the Garden floor.

"Oh my God!" Thatcher heard Edward Parry say again. He could well understand it.

Noise, like a hammer blow, smote their ears: the blare of horns, the explosion of flashbulbs, the monotonous incitement of drums and the abandon of thousands of human beings, roaring in defiance, in enthusiasm or in sheer exultation. Completing the grotesque distortions were the wild careening of spotlights, stabbing the darkness with blinding gleams of light. As they moved into the auditorium, the world narrowed to a tangle of arms and hands, waving or pointing at them, in one instance grasping at Parry's jacket. The party proceeded into the pandemonium through a weird human arch.

Bradford Withers, who was leading the way with Dr. Ford and Nat Schuyler, simply sailed on, superbly untouched by this tumult, as by the rest of life. Both Vin McCullough and Edward Parry, however, lacked his natural insulation. Both of them were visibly shaken.

Bringing up the rear was the Committee of Three. Stanton Carruthers, mindful of the Chief Justice of the Supreme Court, was weighty and dignified. Hugh Waymark, that gallant officer-gentleman, smiled bravely in defeat.

Thatcher was last to clamber up the wooden steps to the platform. It was already crowded with Richard Simpson, Mrs. Mary Crane, two ministers, two rabbis, a quartet of spiritual singers, the deputy mayor, three technicians and Miss Feathers.

In subsequent days, Thatcher was to maintain that this exceeded all of the nightmares to which he had been party. As they took their seats—rickety folding chairs—the noise did not abate. Nor did it abate thereafter. Thatcher looked out on an endless sea of faces, shuddered inwardly, and tried to withdraw into his own thoughts. The kaleidoscope of sound and light made this easier than might have been expected: the official program, to those seated on the platform, was nothing more than unintelligible electronic booms, followed by frenetic responses.

". . . March on Wall Street!" shouted Richard Simpson into the microphones, flapping a telegram in the air.

A tidal wave of noise broke over their heads.

Thatcher felt Vin McCullough stir beside him.

"Impressive, isn't it?" said Thatcher.

"Terrifying."

But it was Edward Parry, on his other side, who had replied.

". . . and education!" screamed Mrs. Mary Crane, who had succeeded Simpson. From nowhere, four drum majorettes appeared bearing a huge banner:

READING, 'RITING—AND RIGHTS!!!

In the upper level there was an explosion.

"Just a balloon," Hugh Waymark said, in effect dismissing anything less than a howitzer.

With some apprehension, Thatcher glanced toward Bradford Withers, sitting near the lectern. Once again he was pleasurably surprised; Withers had managed to reduce this holocaust to a social occasion. He was deep in conversation with a bishop of the African Methodist Church. Unless the cleric was a sailor, it was hard to conceive what they might be discussing, but they seemed to be getting on famously.

". . . housing!" bellowed the latest speaker.

The roar that greeted this made McCullough stir again.

"Well, I've done my bit," he said. "Sold the house today, to a Negro doctor."

Thatcher was not sure that he approved of small talk under the circumstances. On the other hand, sitting there and being yelled at was very difficult.

"Did Nat approve?" he asked.

"Happened too fast," McCullough said as somebody in the balcony hurled tons of confetti into the air, further confusing the whole scene. "I haven't had a chance to mention it to him yet."

Edward Parry, forcing himself to speak lightly, leaned forward. "You can give the doctor my name as a reference," he said. "I may have some tips for him."

But McCullough and Edward Parry could not sustain casual conversation. The spectacle of the emotion-packed auditorium, veritably pulsing with life, and hope, was palpably daunting.

". . . Sloan Guaranty Trust!" shouted somebody.

Thatcher refused to betray tension. He knew that, while the audience was raptly watching Bradford Withers, who was ponderously taking his adieu from the bishop and moving with statement in hand to the improvised lectern, eyes on the platform, particularly those of Richard Simpson and Mrs. Crane, were fixed on him.

He had no trouble masking his reaction to Withers' speech. This was because he had none. The words were totally inaudible. Despite his heavy responsibilities to the Sloan Guaranty Trust, Thatcher was profoundly grateful.

Withers spoke at length. Whatever he said provoked an outburst. For one terrible moment, Thatcher feared that the president had cast prudence to the winds and had indeed just spoken a few words from his heart; in which case he was to have the rare opportunity of seeing a president of the Sloan Guaranty Trust torn to pieces by a howling mob.

But, watching Withers punctiliously shake hands with Simpson and Dr. Ford, he concluded that the *mea culpa* had been, if not effective, at least inoffensive. Stanton Carruthers, he noted, while not moving a muscle, managed to exude vast relief.

". . . Caldwell," said Edward Parry.

"What was that?" Thatcher was forced to ask over the combined voices of two hundred choristers from Howard University.

"He came into the office today to clean out his desk," said Parry. "I'm a little worried about what he's likely to do tomorrow, during the March."

"And now, ladies and gentlemen," said Richard Simpson. "About the March!"

Despite Hugh Waymark, Thatcher regarded the worst as over. It was not humanly possible to follow the rest of the proceedings, although they consumed another hour.

So, in the midst of emotional whirlwinds, benumbed by the eloquence of speaker after speaker, Thatcher did, at last, withdraw into private communings.

About Arthur Foote.

About Edward Parry.

About Dean Caldwell.

And murder.

"Of course," he murmured softly to himself, waking to virtual silence.

The bishop, an immense figure, had his arms outstretched. In a deep beautiful voice, he was praying.

With sadness, Thatcher listened to him.

". . . and forgive our enemies. Let us seek peace and understanding. And let our needs and hopes teach us to understand the needs and hopes of others. Thy will be done. Amen."

"Amen," said thousands of voices.

"Amen," said John Putnam Thatcher.

Then, as the platform came to life, he moved swiftly to intercept the man he needed—Nathaniel Schuyler.

"Great evening."

Thatcher looked at him.

"No clowning, Nat. Listen . . ."

As he spoke in a low urgent voice amidst the satisfied hubbub surrounding them, he saw the color drain from Schuyler's face.

"No!" Schuyler protested when Thatcher had finished.

Thatcher said nothing.

Schuyler bowed his head for a moment. Then, straightening with an effort, he said:

"Do you want to go now?"

"I do," said Thatcher grimly.

They were going to the offices of Schuyler & Schuyler.

19 · The Day of March Has Come

IT WAS VERY LATE. The usually bustling office lay in shadowed silence. Nat Schuyler closed the last folder.

"Another one," he said harshly, handing it to Thatcher.

Thatcher took it and ran his eye over the neatly typed contents memo, then tossed it onto the large pile of similar folders on the desk.

"You were right. No escaping it," Schuyler said. There was no remnant of his original shock at Thatcher's revelations; hour after hour of proof had forced him into bitter acceptance of the identity of the murderer.

"Question is, what do we do now?"

Thatcher, himself a little tired, raised an eyebrow. Nat Schuyler was old enough to take a philosophical view of life and death, having seen too much of both to respond emotionally to any single incidence of man's inevitable end. Was he extending this same tolerance to murder—and to a murderer?

Schuyler answered the question for him.

"Too late to call the police now," he muttered, rising stiffly. He gathered the pile of documents on his desk. "I'm going to put these in the safe. He'll know—but by that time he'll know anyway."

Thatcher watched him suit action to word, then turn to add:

"I propose to meet you first thing tomorrow morning. Eight-thirty will do. Might as well get this cleaned up before business tomorrow."

"I suppose you're right," said Thatcher doubtfully, also rising. Delay did not seem desirable but it was already past three o'clock. Alerting the police now would serve only to take horror into an innocent home. Better let the arrest take place in the impersonality of Wall Street.

It was, after all, a peculiarly Wall Street murder.

"All right, eight-thirty," he said, stifling a yawn. "Shall I meet you here?"

Nat Schuyler drew his spare frame upright. "No," he declared. "Not here. At the Centre Street police headquarters!"

This was not precisely how John Thatcher would have chosen to proceed, but he did not protest. In a manner of speaking, this was Nathaniel Schuyler's show. It was only courteous to let him, temporarily, retain the illusion that he was still calling the shots.

Unfortunately, it had slipped his mind that eight-thirty tomorrow morning was going to be a very busy hour.

Indeed, by seven o'clock, the quiet suburbs and the somnolent exurbs were already humming with preparations for the day.

"I wish you didn't have to go in today," said Gloria Parry.

Edward Parry looked at her, but she did not give him a chance to reply.

"I know," she said. "You think it's your duty! You think this whole noble March is because of you, so you're going to go in. But, Ed . . ."

Gloria Parry rarely let herself get upset, and never let herself sound upset. Parry reached across the breakfast table to grasp her hand reassuringly.

"Now, Gloria," he said, "I promise to be very careful. I promise not to take any risks. And I'm sure the police will be watching me like a hawk!"

"That doesn't comfort me!" she flashed back.

"Me neither," he said with a half smile. "But I do have to go in today. No, it isn't just heroics. There's something important I've got to do at the office."

Twenty miles away from the luxurious environs of Katonah, a variant of this scene was being enacted in Greenwich.

"I wish you didn't have to go in today," said Mrs. Dean Caldwell, automatically fluttering her eyelashes while at the same time efficiently shoveling oatmeal into her younger son's mouth.

"Now, Varena," Caldwell replied. Hysterical youth though he might be in the office, in his own home he was very much the *paterfamilias* (if not the Old Massa). In fact, a good deal of trouble would have been avoided had the rest of the world accorded him the respect and admiration that Varena did. There were drawbacks to this role: Dean Caldwell was still wondering how to tell Varena that he was now a member of the Great Army of the Unemployed.

"I just get so worried, Dean honey," she continued, carefully wiping her son's chin. "And, young Dean, you finish your toast!"

Old Dean looked around his kingdom, recalled Robert E. Lee's moving observation about his footsteps guiding the young and, persistent in error, attempted something equally memorable.

"A lot of colored rabble can't make trouble for a Caldwell," he declared with quiet dignity. He remained pleased with the apothegm until young Dean spoke up.

"Then what can, Dad?"

The accent (Greenwich, Connecticut) and the spirit (dispassionate inquiry) were alike offensive to Caldwell.

Quickly, his wife said, "Now that's enough from you, young man!"

"Gee, what'd I say?"

Only after an ungenteel wrangle could Dean Caldwell resume the subject.

". . . and besides, Varena. I have to go in today. I've . . . got something important to do."

Four miles away, Mrs. McCullough called to her husband, who was rummaging through the closet for his coat.

"I wish you didn't have to go in today."

"Oh, the March will be orderly," he murmured.

Julia did not hear him. Nor, it developed, was she concerned about his well-being. She rarely was.

"The storage people are coming for the crates. Then I promised the real estate people that I'd get an estimate on that garage door, and if that isn't enough, I've got to have lunch with Dot Pervin, and you know what that means! She'll be furious about our selling the house . . ."

"I've got something important to do at the office," McCullough said.

Julia was still talking when he left.

And as the clock crawled on, the access routes to Manhattan began to swell, to choke and to jam with the millions of toilers in that vineyard. They came by the IRT and the BMT, by the Independent and the Hudson & Manhattan tubes, by the Long Island Railroad and the New York, New Haven & Hartford. They came on roads, through tunnels and over bridges, and in their midst they floated thousands, coming for another reason.

At Union Square, one of the preliminary rallying points, the last of the Connecticut buses had arrived by eight o'clock.

"You're in the group over there," shouted a young Negro, hurrying up and consulting a master plan on his clipboard. "They've already got your banners."

Three hundred people started moving toward the standard:

CONNECTICUT CASH WANTS CONFIDENCE IN WALL STREET

They passed the Washington, D.C., representatives, already milling around in place.

CAPITOL CASH FOR CAPITAL WITHOUT COLOR

Having arrived on the five-thirty Pennsy, Washington, D.C., was raring to go, and scornful of late-arriving Connecticut.

"C'mon, let's get this show moving!" shouted one of its members (owner of a substantial amount of IBM).

His exhortation was drowned out by the roar of three large open trucks that came lumbering in and ground to a noisy halt. Approximately seventy-five Negroes began clambering down.

"Is that the best that Delaware could do? I mean, trucks?" asked the assistant director for New Haven; he was still smarting from D.C.'s scorn.

"Delaware!" the young man with the clipboard shouted. "Oh, good! We were afraid that breakdown with your bus might have held you up. You're over there . . ."

He gestured to a distant placard:

DELAWARE WANTS COLOR-BLIND DIVIDENDS

"Oh, I don't like that . . ."

"Now's no time . . ."

"ATTENTION!" boomed an authoritative voice through a megaphone. "We're about ready to get started!"

A chorus of cheers rose from the ranks.

". . . we're picking up the New York representatives at our rendezvous point on our way downtown . . ."

Cheers, laughter, cries of "Hurray for New York!"

"Now, before we get started . . ."

"C'mon let's go, go, go!" This was a shout from Delaware. The delegation, though small, was spirited.

"ATTENTION! Now, I just want to review some last minute reminders . . ."

"We know, we know . . ."

"First, keep together while we're at Washington Square. There'll be a lot of students, and we don't want to be separated. That's our official starting point, and each state will be notified of its position in the lineup. Second, remember the route. Down Broadway, over to Foley Square, through City Hall Park and then right on down to Wall Street. And last, keep in ranks until we get down to the Exchange itself. Orderly ranks. The police will be lining the route so there probably won't be any trouble, but if anybody starts anything, it's up to you to stop it as fast as possible."

The assorted stock and bondholders listening to him nodded vigorous agreement, but there were faint catcalls from a small clutch of white folk singers who, though totally devoid of any investment in American business, were bringing up the rear. They, frankly, were itching to encounter the American Nazi Party; they were folk singers second, the University of New Hampshire football team (second squad) first.

"Fine. Now, if anybody feels faint, or gets overcome by the heat . . ."

Since it was a clear, bitterly cold morning that promised to become a clear, sunny and cold November day, this caused a Cleveland, Ohio, dentist to turn to his neighbor, a teacher from Philadelphia.

"What's he talking about?"

"He learned the ropes at the March on Washington," the teacher explained knowledgeably. "I'll bet he doesn't realize that this is a roast beef crowd. That's the trouble with these specialists."

He was right.

"Red Cross stations are at Washington Square, City Hall and Trinity Church," said the speaker. "Now what else? . . . oh yes!

Lunch at Battery Park after the March. No chicken, egg or tuna sandwiches . . ."

The assemblage had already been instructed to the point of exhaustion. Moreover, it possessed mimeographed sheets presenting essentials both more clearly and in greater detail than the speaker. It stirred restively.

Even though he was not particularly sensitive (and a man who makes a career directing demonstrations cannot afford to be too sensitive), the speaker registered this reaction.

"O.K. That's all. I just want to tell you that there will be over ten thousand of us marching . . ."

Deafening cheers!

"And I've just received news that we're not alone. Our friends in Paris are staging a sympathy sit-in at the Bourse. The eyes of the world are on us!"

On signal, the band struck up "Marching through Georgia." Eagerly the ranks surged forward.

At eight-thirty on the dot, John Putnam Thatcher was struggling into Centre Street Police Headquarters against a similar eager surge—this time, blue-coated, determined policemen charged with the onerous task of keeping order on Wall Street.

"Without anything which could, under any circumstances, be construed as brutality—by anybody!" the commissioner had said emotionally, thus contributing to the general thanklessness of police chores.

The powerful wave of blue had wedged Thatcher into a corner when suddenly a flashbulb exploded at him.

"New York Times!" shouted a voice above the others. "What are you doing here, Mr. Thatcher?"

"I have nothing to say," he barked, jamming himself forward as a circle of newsmen turned their attention from the police to him.

"Is the Sloan expecting trouble?"

"Why are you here today?"

"Nothing to say!" Thatcher shouted.

"Can we quote you?"

Thatcher turned to snarl, and in so doing caught sight of a disheveled Stanton Carruthers.

"John!"

"Not a word here," said Thatcher, indicating the *New York Times*, busy demonstrating its superiority by abandoning the police and sticking with a vice-president from the Sloan Guaranty Trust.

"Certainly not!" said Carruthers, offended.

A few low words with the desk sergeant told them what they wanted to know.

Not until they had driven off the *Times* and were alone in the dusty second-floor corridor, did Thatcher discover why Nathaniel Schuyler had abdicated in favor of Stanton Carruthers.

"It was Min Schuyler. She got the whole story out of Nat when he got home and decided that it wouldn't do to have him come down here. She said," Carruthers quoted carefully, "that the excitement might harm his health."

Thatcher snorted.

A full-scale riot wouldn't disagree with leathery old Schuyler. What Min really meant was obvious; she didn't want a Schuyler mixed up with the whole distasteful affair. He personally wished that a Thatcher weren't mixed up with it. And a fat lot of good that was doing him.

". . . so I came along to help," said Carruthers. "Once we lay this information before them, we can let the police . . . er . . . do their disagreeable duty, and . . ."

"Get back to our own business," Thatcher finished for him.

"Certainly not. We'll join Hugh Waymark at the Exchange."

At first this program moved smoothly. It took but ten minutes to lay certain financial facts before the poker-faced individual behind the desk. Scrupulously, Thatcher simply outlined technical information, without once mentioning murder—or Arthur Foote.

"We wondered about him. Everything was clear—except the motive," the policeman said, after giving him a long hard look. He spoke slowly, but he was pressing buttons in his intercom. He snapped orders into it. "And now you've given us the motive. We'll pick him up before he gets into the building," he said.

And that, it appeared, was that. After the officer hurried out, both Thatcher and Carruthers delayed leaving; it is no little thing to deliver up a murderer.

"Well, we'd better get over to the Exchange," said Thatcher, recovering.

It was precisely thirty minutes later that he first began to wonder if he had indeed delivered up a murderer.

He and Carruthers were still on the fringes of City Hall Park, trying to battle their way down Park Row. The sidewalks were solid with humanity, not the inadvertent solidity of men and women hurrying from different directions to a standstill, but the contented motionless solidity of viewers and spectators. The narrow streets were given over to official vehicles; there were squad cars, ambulances, motorcycles, two Red Cross mobile units, three television trailers, several radio transmitter cars, a Civil Defense truck and—for no reason that John Thatcher could dredge up—a Brinks armored car.

Over the talk, the occasional mysterious noise of officials communicating with each other, and the roar of the motorcycles, the beat of a band was distantly audible. A brass band. A marching band.

By strenuous exertions, Thatcher advanced about six paces.

"We made a mistake," he said to Carruthers.

"What was that . . . oh, sorry. Yes, Madam, I am truly sorry that I trod on your foot . . . good heavens! What did you say, Thatcher?"

"We made a mistake," Thatcher declared. "The police won't be able to get to Schuyler & Schuyler in time. When he sees that those files are gone, well, he'll know . . ."

His hat knocked rakishly over one eye, Carruthers pointed out that giving the police certain financial information (which, incidentally, enabled them to identify a murderer) was really the extent of their duties. Apprehension of the miscreant today, or in the near future, was a police problem.

". . . and it doesn't concern us, at all, thank God . . . ouch!" In a savage undertone he continued, "I wish you would tell me why that woman needs an umbrella on the finest day in weeks."

His grumbling was submerged by a clash of cymbals as the CASH band strutted by, on the move again, followed by the stern leaders of the movement—including Richard Simpson and Mrs. Crane, Thatcher saw over intervening heads. Mrs. Crane was in precise step with the music. Simpson, all too predictably, was not.

Next came a uniformed group representing veterans (who were presumably also stockholders); then a contingent of school-children; then, as far as the eye could see, row upon row of other marchers.

"We've got to get to the Exchange before they do."

With judicious use of the elbow and aided by a general seepage southward, they managed to inch themselves through the crush while CASH members from fifty states, so it seemed, strode by in stately array on Lower Broadway, which was being kept clear for this purpose by at least four hundred policemen. Across the street, far behind the police lines, Thatcher could see a small group of pickets. They had no more chance of disturbing the parade than did the distant (but also hostile) governor of Mis-sissippi. Vin McCullough had assured his wife that the March would be orderly, and it was.

The trouble period, however, was still ahead, at the technical terminus of the March where ten thousand marchers would be assembled, however peaceably, before the New York Stock Ex-change, an area definitely not designed to accommodate such gatherings.

Would Richard Simpson be able to resist the temptation to say a few words?

Thatcher very much doubted it, although the police had ex-pressly forbidden any speeches before Battery Park.

Yet, under the circumstances, what would the police be able to do?

And, more germane to John Thatcher's responsibilities, what would the Stock Exchange do?

"Sorry, I have to get through," he said frigidly to a stenog-rapher who was audibly wondering who he thought he was, shoving that way.

Their painful voyage to the Stock Exchange was accompanied by other freely voiced criticisms. Accordingly, neither Thatcher nor Carruthers was feeling particularly peaceable (or even orderly) when they reached the first of twenty concentric semi-circles of security forces well ahead of the March.

"My God, they're not planning a siege!" Thatcher shouted in exasperation to an obtuse and unyielding member of the Ex-change's own guards. Fortunately, at this moment, Hugh Way-mark emerged.

"Let 'em through, Powers," he ordered. "Good man, Powers," he continued, dropping his voice. "I've deployed only veterans out there. Come on in . . ."

With the density outside approaching disaster proportions, Thatcher was happy to do so.

Hugh Waymark had been assigned or had assumed the military precautions at the Stock Exchange. Within the building, Thatcher discovered, somebody else had decreed that it was to be business as usual.

Somebody, Thatcher decided, following Waymark upstairs, without much horse sense.

"Volume's way down," Waymark remarked over his shoulder.

Thatcher glanced into the pit; there were traders and specialists as usual, if perceptibly fewer; there were the familiar druggists' jackets. But business? No. This site of so many frenzied scenes, normally abuzz with men rushing in and out, with buy or sell orders falling like snow onto the Floor, was a study in lethargy.

"How's Vita Cola?" he asked.

"They haven't opened yet . . . what is it?"

For Stanton Carruthers had suddenly stepped forward to grip Waymark's arm, halting him.

"Look!"

Following his pointed finger, they saw a member of the New York Stock Exchange stroll onto the Floor.

"Why not?" Waymark asked curiously.

"Because he's a murderer, that's why!" Thatcher said grimly. He had been right. One look at the looted office had been enough to sound the murderer's alarm. He had fled—into a street swarming with police. And now—here.

Hugh Waymark instantly became the leader of a posse. "We'll just go down . . ."

Stanton Carruthers kept his eyes fixed on the trim figure. "He's behaving quite normally," he said. "Possibly he doesn't know the police are after him."

"I doubt that, Stan," said Thatcher.

"I do too," said Carruthers. "And, Hugh, this man is a murderer. This is police business."

Waymark, looking mulish, launched into protest but Thatcher was thinking rapidly.

"There's no use calling the police," he said, turning to return to the stairway. "If their lines aren't jammed, ours certainly will be. The thing to do is to get some of those men outside."

"I'll do it!" Hugh Waymark cried, bounding athletically ahead, briefly so transfigured that he forgot one of his favorite possessions, his tricky heart.

With resignation, Thatcher watched him sprint ahead. This, as he was subsequently quite ready to concede, was one of the most serious errors he had ever committed.

Waymark reached the heavily guarded entrance just as the last of the March on Wall Street had snaked ten thousand members of CASH (actually 8,495) onto New Street. Richard Simpson had assumed a commanding position in the shadow of the Stock Exchange's angled brass doorway, and was now turning to face his followers.

Police, on the one hand unwilling to let him flout the law, and on the other hand extremely sensitive to the delicacy of the whole situation, were trying to close in on Simpson, and move him off, without actually touching him. Just as they began their deliberate stalk, Simpson seized his advantage: flinging his arms wide, he bellowed:

"We demand to be heard! We must talk to the Board of Governors! About rights—for Edward Parry!"

A huge roar went up from the multitude, including those on the steps of the Treasury Building, those around the corner on Broad Street and those hanging out of every window in the district.

At this moment, the forbidding doors swung open. Instantly, all noise ceased. In the almost painful silence, Richard Simpson turned.

Hugh Waymark strode outdoors. Masterfully ignoring Simpson (and his 8,495 followers), he sought the nearest high-ranking police official. His eye fell on a harassed captain, not ten feet away.

"We need you in here," he said in clear carrying tones. "We've got your killer!"

There was a moment—a brief one—during which Hugh Waymark's second heart attack could have been averted. Then, he simply disappeared beneath the tidal wave.

A subsequent SEC investigation revealed the following facts:

a) 1,847 unauthorized personnel rushed into the sacred precincts of the New York Stock Exchange. 138 of them managed somehow to get onto the Floor.

(The uniformed forces caught up in the onslaught caused less distress than others.

"But, Madam!" shouted old Bartlett Sims shortly before she shoved him to his knees, "WOMEN ARE NOT ALLOWED ON THE FLOOR OF THE EXCHANGE!")

b) For three hours and twenty-eight minutes, no business—at all—was transacted.

(In Iron Mountain, Michigan, Mr. Fred Lundeen called his broker.

"What's the latest on Bessy?" he asked, prepared [he thought] for the worst.

The broker sounded drunk. "We haven't had a single quote for the last fifty-eight minutes."

"Oh, I see," said Mr. Lundeen, hanging up. He reflected deeply, then sadly spoke to his son, who was in business with him:

"Duane, those bastards have dropped the Bomb!")

c) Approximately $28,405 damage was done to the N.Y. Stock Exchange's physical plant.

("There he is!" shouted a policeman, carelessly propelling a tally clerk through a plate glass window. The murderer, after one comprehensive inspection, had ripped off his jacket and was moving toward the stairs leading to the balcony.

"What do we do now?" an enthralled Stanton Carruthers inquired.

"Remove ourselves," Thatcher replied. This was only prudent; hard on the murderer's heels was a motley crew, some bearing placards, some swinging nightsticks, all of them pounding along like stampeded buffaloes.)

d) Almost one million dollars in commissions was lost during the period of the disturbance, see prorated transactions schedule, Appendix A.

(The murderer, realizing that he had inadvertently started a wild race that was only drawing attention to his own flight, ducked into a convenient cubicle [a statue was being replaced] and let the mob surge past. Then, with a quick look for watchful eyes, he slowly began to sidle downstairs again. The Floor was a cauldron, but in its disrupted pandemonium he could be momentarily safe. He quickened his steps, past two policemen intent upon a short pugnacious order clerk. In so doing he cannoned into the U.S. Steel specialist who had, somehow, lost his tie and a portion of his shirt. He was also bleeding slightly from a small cut over his left eye.

"What the hell is going on?" he demanded, breathing hard.

"God knows!" said the murderer. He sounded frightened and panicky, but so did the steel specialist.

"There he is!"

Incredibly, a policeman had sighted him again, a policeman who recognized him.

The steel specialist at that moment sustained a painful swipe in the neck from a fiercely brandished placard [CASH WANTS PEACE AND JUSTICE]. He turned angrily and saw a new covey of police who were ignoring offenses in their immediate vicinity to struggle toward him.

"My boy," he said softly, "I don't know why they want you, but . . ."

With that, he pivoted and landed a competent rabbit punch. He followed this up with a short, powerful jab. The murderer folded. [He did not slump to the ground since he was held erect by the crushed tangle surrounding him.] The U.S. Steel specialist might be sixtyish and overweight, but he had not boxed at Dartmouth for nothing.

Moreover—he looked around, shuddered and moved aside to give a nearby fistfight decent room—this sort of thing was Letting the Exchange Down.)

The SEC report, combining schoolteacher disapproval with maternal anguish, continued its list of outrages connected with the March on Wall Street for many pages. It did not, however, contain two interesting items:

1) At 10:32 (approximately eighteen minutes before Hugh

Waymark disappeared, and some four minutes before the March reached the Exchange), the Board of Governors completed its formalities and approved the application of Schuyler & Schuyler to admit its newest partner to the Exchange with all the rights and duties of a full member.

2) At 11:16 (approximately nine minutes after Hugh Waymark regained consciousness, but long before order was restored), another Schuyler & Schuyler partner was removed from the Floor by four burly policemen.

His name was Vincent McCullough.

20 · There Is a Line, By Us Unseen

"SO IT WAS Vin McCullough all along." Edward Parry shook his head. "From the way Nat talked, I was almost sure it was Dean Caldwell. Seems incredible. But then everything has, this past week."

He was not the only one finding it difficult to reemerge into a workaday world. The financial community, which had survived the threat of race riot and the reality of murder, suffered its greatest casualties in the termination of the great March on Wall Street. As the news had spread into every side street and alleyway that Edward Parry was now a member of the Stock Exchange and his would-be murderer under arrest, the March had mushroomed into a celebration. Wall Street, whose meanest resident was something of a connoisseur of ticker tape parades and welcomes for the returning hero, had never seen anything like it.

A mad, impromptu fiesta sprang up with dancing in the streets, confetti and, of course, music. Everywhere there were stirring marches, moving spirituals and ribald folk songs. As catchy marimba bands on Broadway vied with devotional gatherings in Bowling Green, the scene resembled some enormous cross-breeding between a Latin American gala and a Salvation Army crusade. The infectious enthusiasm of clapping, laughing, stamping, sobbing proved too much for the denizens of the concrete barracks towering overhead. They poured forth into the streets, leaving behind companions to fling out the refuse of thousands of punch card machines, tickers and typewriters, until a blizzard in rainbow-colored hues floated down from the heavens.

Thatcher was to retain many hectic memories of that day, not the least of them being Miss Corsa and Everett Gabler, driven into temporary alliance, looking on in outrage as Kenneth Nicolls swung his secretary in a lusty square dance. Perverse thoughts inevitably germinated in this fertile soil. What would happen if he asked Miss Corsa to rhumba?

Unthinkable. After all, he had obligations to the unknown Mrs. Corsa in Queens.

With such a carnival of merrymaking and revelry on Thursday, Friday reeled under the monumental aftereffects. Thatcher took in stride the Sloan's massive list of absentees, and even his own brief notoriety as a leader in the civil rights movement. His composure was undiminished as he declined an invitation to address an investment club of Negro women in New Rochelle, arranging for Nicolls to appear in his stead. What was really wanted, he reflected, was a special Lenten season for Wall Street. Forty days of fasting and shriving would set everybody to rights and had the further merit of historical tradition. Instead, he began to receive calls from Washington. It was these that brought him to the luncheon table looking like a veteran of street warfare.

"There is not the slightest justification for it. I have been willing to take a good deal, but this," he announced incisively, "this is outrageous."

The lunch was also a celebration. The three men were eating at the Stock Exchange Club, and Thatcher was present as the guest of its newest member, Edward Parry. The occasion was a gesture and, for the sake of the gesture, they were all prepared to put up with the food.

"What's so outrageous?"

Thatcher explained that Washington wanted to appoint him ambassador to a small, new African country.

"There'll be a lot of that sort of thing coming your way," said Ed Parry wisely. "With me, they always tried to push the UN."

Nat Schuyler waved away these irrelevancies. He was displaying the resilience that had brought successive generations of Schuylers unscathed through every major American crisis. Five short months ago he had had three partners—his cousin Ambrose, Arthur Foote and Vincent McCullough. All three were gone, and now he had one—the man across the table. But business was coming in as never before.

"Have you heard anything more about McCullough?"

Thatcher reported that Paul Jackson had undertaken the defense, but it seemed a hopeless task.

"The trouble is that once McCullough was suspected, the evidence was lying around, waiting to be picked up."

"I never did understand why you and Nat raced away from Madison Square Garden that way," interjected their host.

"It was McCullough telling me he sold his house to a Negro doctor."

Parry grinned.

"So?" he challenged softly. "What's so incriminating about that?"

"It certainly wouldn't have alerted me," Nat admitted. "I might have been furious, but I would have assumed he had gone crazy. Almost everybody else did, in one way or another."

"But that's the point. McCullough's posture was that of a man who resisted Ed's admission into the firm on perfectly business-like grounds. Then, when the whole issue became fraught with racist ramifications, he began to cooperate with you, Nat. That was credible. He certainly wouldn't do anything to hurt the firm. But selling his house to a Negro could have been disastrous, simply by distracting attention from the central issue. Anybody could have predicted you would be furious. You had all you could do the other day to keep quiet—when Mrs. Parry said she was going to Lincoln Center. Every single person responsible for this Exchange seat transfer has been anxious to keep it simple, to keep it undistracted. The reason we objected to Richard Simpson was that he insisted on clouding the issue. And, in a different way, so did Owen Abercrombie. Now, Gloria Parry had a good reason to insist on Lincoln Center. But Vin McCullough didn't have any apparent motive for introducing an additional complexity. Particularly at a time when he depended on you to make up for his lost clients. In anybody else, you would say that he sold that way because it was an easy, fast, profitable sale. Right?"

They both nodded.

"And then, when you started thinking in those terms, we had been hearing a lot about McCullough selling things. A house, a boat, a summer place, a car. What did it all add up to? Vin McCullough needed money desperately and quickly. His wife said that the rent they were going to pay was high. That meant he wasn't making an investment in a cooperative. Nothing was being replaced, and a great many things were being converted into hard cash, under cover of a move into the city. It was clever of him to realize that so many sales could be made to appear normal that way. You expect a change in life when people move into an apartment. And what Carruthers said about faddists was true, also. If a man is moving downtown, you're not surprised to have him change from an outdoor type to a city type. The theater and nightclubs quite naturally replace country clubs and yachts. But once you started to think of McCullough as a man in urgent need of money, a lot of things came floating to the surface. Most suspiciously, the slowness with which he was returning portfolios to his customers."

"Now that I hadn't heard about," Schuyler broke in to say. "My ears would have pricked up if I had."

"Exactly. Lee Clark got it from some of the customers themselves. He thought it was a departure from normalcy because of your newly acquired business."

"Nonsense! The last thing in the world a brokerage house wants is a reputation for not delivering on request. It's as if a bank couldn't come up with funds to meet a legitimate withdrawal. The next thing would be a run on the bank. The same thing would happen to us. Let people once get edgy about whether they can withdraw, and they will."

Even now, with all danger past, Nat Schuyler waxed indignant at the possibility of such a rumor spreading forth and undermining the house of Schuyler & Schuyler. It would take him several moments to recover his equanimity.

"And then there was something else." Thatcher turned to Ed Parry. "Everybody accepted the fact that two tries had been made to murder you, as indeed they had. Well, why did they stop?"

"I was just grateful that they did," Parry admitted. "I suppose, if I thought at all, I thought it was police protection, my isolation in Katonah, that sort of thing."

"Yes, and there was a good deal of merit in that position. If you had come into the city within the next few days, something would have been tried. All right, so far as it goes. But after Lincoln Center, you did start coming in again. You were here when Nat threw out Caldwell, you came in before the Madison Square Garden rally. But nothing happened. It looked as if somebody had lost interest. Why?"

Parry frowned in thought. "You're right. Not only did I come in, but all the most obvious suspects knew about it."

"And that takes us back to the original motive. McCullough didn't want you in the firm for the very same reason he gave you. Because it would spark many of his customers into withdrawing. What he didn't add, was that he was in no position to return their portfolios, because he had stolen them. And it didn't make any difference to him whether the Stock Exchange ultimately denied you a seat, or deliberated about it for two years. Just let there be enough publicity about Schuyler & Schuyler wanting you, and the damage was done. His fraud would be revealed, and he would be discredited. And that would be the end for him—discovery, prison, no future. The thing that infuriated him the most was that it was all a question of timing. He had stolen to get the cash for a really big plunge. He had what he thought was a sure thing. Two months more and he would be in the clear. That's why he started off by urging Nat to go slow, advising caution, trying to delay things. When that didn't work, he took steps to end the threat to himself. He went to the reception with nicotine in his pocket and tried to poison you."

"And instead got poor Art Foote," said Schuyler with sad solemnity.

"And was just as badly off as ever," added Parry. "Or even worse. Now he had to worry about exposure for murder as well as fraud."

But Thatcher shook his head. "Things weren't that simple. Although he thought so at first. That's why he tried to shoot you first thing the next morning. He was in a desperate hurry. Already customers were backing out. Thanks to that sonic boom, he missed. You remember that the police were satisfied Caldwell could have been responsible for that attempt. But McCullough lived in Stamford—which hasn't been troubled with sonic booms, by the way—next door to Caldwell in Connecticut. The geography was as easy for him. But that failure sent you into isolation up in Katonah, and McCullough had time to look around. Then he discovered a very odd fact."

"What? I presume that's what made him stop trying to kill me. Or was it that, by the time he had another chance, the damage had been done?"

"There was that of course," agreed Thatcher. "But the real thing was that Nat, here, gave him Art Foote's portfolios. After all, while he couldn't easily get at you in person in the city, there was nothing to prevent his sending you poison packages or blowing up your house. He had already shown he was unscrupulous in his methods. No, the thing that did it was the discovery that Art Foote's death was almost as good for his purposes as yours would have been. True, his customers withdrew, but he used Foote's portfolios to make up the difference. Supplied the actual shares when they were the same, or sold off and converted when they weren't. And in so doing left a damning record behind him. Because all of these transactions were recorded on the books, if you knew what to look for—name of share, amount, date of purchase. Take Continental Can, for instance. One of his customers held two hundred shares which he had stolen. There were some in one of Foote's accounts. So he supplied those. But the records show that he supplied shares purchased two years after those bought on his account. And it's even easier where he wasn't able to make a replacement from Foote's inventory."

Parry nodded his comprehension. "So that's why you and Nat rushed off to the office after the rally."

"Yes. We spent most of the night going over the records, and we matched over forty-seven transactions."

"He could never have kept it up," said Schuyler. "We would have had the usual audit after a partner's death."

"That explains the need for cash, and that's why I said the timing was so important. It's one thing to have people howling for something you can't deliver. It's another to go out and raise money before a routine audit. He managed to accumulate well over a hundred thousand dollars in cash from his sales. With his credit standing and position, he probably could have borrowed another hundred thousand. That would have seen him through, even if he didn't make his pile before the audit."

"It's a good solid motive, all right."

"Oh yes. But the police have a good deal more than motive, you know. First, they found the rifle. His treatment of that was simple enough. Instead of making any attempt to destroy it, he let his wife send it into storage along with all their excess belongings—furniture that wouldn't fit into the apartment, boating gear, country clothes. He thought, and quite rightly, that as long as he wasn't suspected, all he had to do was get it out of sight. If he was suspected, there was so much other evidence against him it wouldn't matter much. I wouldn't be surprised if he didn't plan suicide in the unlikely event of the police probing into his accounts. Of course everything happened too quickly in the end, and he just panicked."

Schuyler looked worried. "Suicide? Do you really think so?"

"I don't know. Not any longer, I expect. Paul Jackson has a way of heartening his clients. But I suspect that he's just heartening this one into a good frame of mind for his prison sentence. He can never explain away the poison."

"That was something to do with his brother-in-law, wasn't it?"

"Yes, McCullough was executor for his brother-in-law's estate. And his brother-in-law was a doctor. There were all the poisons any murderer could want, right at hand. And the police have gotten hold of the office nurse and the poison log. They're in a position to show that there's nicotine missing. The pure alkaloid, too, whatever that is."

Damning, agreed Parry. "But the thing that's so hard to believe is that he could do all that, then settle down to being a hard-working broker again."

"Oh, he didn't just settle down. That's when he began his career as an *agent provocateur*. It wasn't comfortable for him to have a full-scale investigation into the murder going on. He felt reasonably safe about the shooting. But the poisoning was a different matter. If the police continued their painstaking inquiries, their suspicions would be roused, then they would be onto the question of access to nicotine."

"I don't see how," grumbled Parry. "I probably did as much thinking about it as anybody, and it never occurred to me to suspect Vin McCullough."

"You did a lot of thinking in the absence of facts," Thatcher corrected him. "Inevitably, that means you were thinking about who would want to kill you. And that led you into the whole morass of the race question. But the police, very sensibly, thought in terms of opportunity. Probably going on the assumption that almost anybody there might want to kill you. And that worried McCullough. Everybody knew the police were working on a timetable, and the possibility of confusion about Foote's drink. Well, the one thing that emerged was that the people at Schuyler & Schuyler had the best chance to know about Foote's regimen."

Ed Parry raised his eyebrows. "I hadn't thought of that one."

"Once the police had gotten that far, what else would they discover? That Vin McCullough had arrived late. Everybody else from your brokerage house was present long before Foote took that glass of tomato juice. And Foote was with your group most of the time. Assuming the murderer had kept an eye on his potential victim, if only to be able to locate him, he could scarcely miss the fact that Ed walked over without a drink to join Foote, who did have a glass. The tomato juice was actually ordered in front of Lee Clark and carried back to both of you. Caldwell was in the room. It's barely conceivable that he might have missed this activity, but one thing was sure. McCullough was certain to have missed it, because he hadn't yet arrived. You recall, he didn't come in until you were all huddled together over the press release. Then there was the business of Owen Abercrombie charging over and being pulled off by Caldwell and Lee Clark. Clark was virtually cleared, unless it was Foote he was aiming for all the time. The other two might have done it. But the one with the best opportunity was McCullough, and that's the kind of situation that makes the police think. McCullough wanted to short circuit that line of reasoning. And that's where the whole race question became a godsend to him, just as it had promised disaster earlier."

"You mean because it was so easy to divert attention?" probed Schuyler. "Yes, I can see that. But he was still extraordinarily lucky that Abercrombie and Caldwell made such fools of themselves."

"Luck, I think, had very little to do with it," replied Thatcher dryly. "McCullough was not the man to sit back and wait for fortune to bestow its favors. You were on the right track when you first suggested Caldwell might be using Abercrombie, but you had the casting wrong. Caldwell, in his own perverted way, was sincere. It was McCullough who was the mainspring, and he was much more subtle than young Caldwell could ever have been. He played the role of trying to save Caldwell from himself. I caught him at it during the television broadcast. He was warning the boy not to be fool enough to try anything at Lincoln Center. It was obvious that, up to that moment, Caldwell hadn't even thought about the concert. I remember asking McCullough if it was wise to let Caldwell know. He looked a little self-conscious, but said that he wanted to give the boy some good advice. At the time I accepted the explanation in good faith. The world is filled with people doing the wrong thing from the best motives. But McCullough had accomplished just what he intended. First, he had conveyed information. Then he also made sure that Caldwell and Abercrombie would do something surpassingly silly by waving a red flag at Caldwell. By the time he was done with his propaganda effort, he was virtually certain that they would draw attention to themselves in some way."

"But he couldn't know that Abercrombie was going to pull a gun," protested Parry. "Even Caldwell didn't know that he was carrying one, and I doubt if he intended to use it. It's hard to explain, but I think he was carrying it simply to show . . ."

"To show how warlike he was," supplied Schuyler, who was not going to shilly-shally around for terms defining Owen Abercrombie's eccentricity. "Undoubtedly that incredible lunatic had talked himself into a frame of mind where it seemed the manly thing to do."

"And never dreamed of using it until that detective injured his sense of *amour propre* by touching him."

"Exactly. Except for that intervention, Abercrombie would probably have harangued you in abusive terms and made a number of vague and disagreeable threats. Which would have suited McCullough very well. You have to realize that he had no thoughts of anybody being convicted for his actions. No one knew better than he the unlikelihood of proving access to poison for Abercrombie or Caldwell. But if the two of them persisted in adopting a consistently homicidal attitude, he had every reason to hope that the police and the public would ultimately assume one of them was the murderer. It would be another case closed for lack of hard evidence. There would be grumblings from civil rights workers until the next big headline came along, and that would be that. McCullough was in a paradoxical position vis-à-vis the race question. On the one hand, he saw himself forced into murder because of his clients' reaction to the problem; but on the other hand, he had a very strong protection against anyone spotting his motive, for just the same reason."

"That may be the way Vin sees it," said Schuyler loftily. "I prefer to say that he was forced to murder because he chose to rob clients of our brokerage house."

The other two men bowed their assent. The head of Schuyler & Schuyler was understandably unsympathetic to such activities.

Parry, after a moment's silent propitiation of these sentiments, returned to the original question. "But still he had luck. He must have been hard put not to stand up and cheer when Abercrombie went mad at Lincoln Center."

"Oh, he had luck," Thatcher agreed. "More than he expected and more, even, than he realized. Jackson tells me that, when the police started to investigate Abercrombie with a view to poisoning, they didn't find anything. But when they tried the same thing with Caldwell, the first thing they hit was a visit of his to some pharmaceutical firm two weeks ago. They were bending every effort to find out if he could have picked up some pure nicotine while he was there."

"Good heavens! I'd forgotten about that," exclaimed Schuyler. "I sent him to Downbill's myself. They're going public, you know."

"Well, Downbill's maintained he hadn't been anywhere near their stock of nicotine, but it was enough to keep the police interested. And, of course, nobody could have expected Abercrombie to be mad enough to lose his instinct for self-preservation."

"Is he really mad?"

"That's his story. He's entered a plea of insanity on all those charges, you know. His son, I understand, is giving up California. Now it's a villa in Majorca."

"It would be. Next thing we know, he'll be publishing his poems in little lavender volumes."

Schuyler nodded knowingly. "You remember Owen's Uncle Basil?" He shook his head sadly. "And now Owen. Terrible, the way these old families go to seed. The boy will probably end up the same way. Blood tells, you know."

Parry grinned cheerfully. "It may be that the air of Wall Street goes to their heads. Anyway, the beatnik strain has something to recommend it. I hear that the boy has sent a check for five thousand to the NAACP."

"Wait until he hits Majorca," advised Schuyler darkly.

"And what about Caldwell, Any sign of atonement there?" asked Thatcher, genuinely curious.

"I wouldn't know," said Schuyler distantly.

Parry brayed his laughter. "Not on your life! He's got a job with a broker in Atlanta. I think he may intend to tangle with my father." A deep chuckle rumbled. "He doesn't know what he's taking on. Well, live and learn."

Sight unseen, Thatcher was prepared to credit the prowess and acumen of any Negro who had marched into Atlanta in the 'thirties and emerged a multimillionaire.

"It may be the making of the boy," he agreed gravely. "By the way, do you hear something odd going on out there?"

Out there was the vestibule. And, indeed, there seemed to be some sort of low-keyed disturbance in progress. There were cries of: "But it's all over!" "Hey! You can't go in there!" "Not with the guitar, sonny!"

And then they streamed in. The Troubles had left in their wake a small and determined band that had found a new way of life. When the sun rose each morning, like cocks crowing, like magnets turning to the north, like lemmings entering the sea, they took to the IRT and headed for Wall Street. So finally, Thatcher was able to gratify his ambition. The tune was the "Battle Hymn of the Republic"; the lyrics came through loud and clear as the little group followed its bearded, strutting leader: and "The Three Wise Men" resounded once again:

There's a mighty storm that's blowing on the Street
    that's known as Wall,
Where the fat cats with their bowls of cream
    are heading for a fall,
With a broom that's new, we're going to brush
    the rascals one and all,
Helped by Three Wise Men!

Waymark, Thatcher and Car-ru-thers!
Waymark, Thatcher and Car-ru-thers!
Waymark, Thatcher and Car-ru-thers!
Wall Street's Three Wise Men!

We are marching for Ed Parry, we are Marching
    for the Seat,
We are tearing triumph from the bankers' howls
    of defeat,
Tempered by the flames of justice, we are
    turning on the heat,
Helped by Three Wise men!

Waymark, Thatcher and Car-ru-thers!
Waymark, Thatcher and Car-ru-thers!
Waymark, Thatcher and Car-ru-thers!
Wall Street's Three Wise Men!

Let the brokers count their money, let them
    count it day and night,
Let the lawyers and their lawbooks try to keep them
    lily white,
There are thousands of us ready who are girding
    for the fight,
Helped by Three Wise Men!

Waymark, Thatcher and Car-ru-thers!
Waymark, Thatcher and Car-ru-thers!
Waymark, Thatcher and Car-ru-thers!
Wall Street's Three Wise Men!

Murder Against the Grain

CONTENTS

Prologue

From New York, New York:

RUSSIAN-AMERICAN TRADE TREATY SIGNED
COLD WAR THAWS OUT
100 Million Tons Grain for USSR
Consulates Opening New York and Frisco

American foreign policy scored a major success today when the Soviet Union accepted the proposals of American negotiators in Geneva and signed the Russian-American Trade Treaty. The Treaty is the first phase of a step-by-step program designed to dissipate US-Soviet tensions. Prominent features call for major purchases of US grain by the Soviet Union and opening of Soviet consulates in New York and San Francisco later this month.

"The first step was bound to be the most difficult," said the Secretary of State in his press conference immediately after the accord was reached. "The peaceful goals of the American people had to be communicated to the Soviet Union so that they would be willing to lay aside their distrust and suspicion. . . ."

From Moscow, USSR:

US-SOVIET TREATY SIGNED
Grain shipments this winter

Representatives of the United States today accepted Soviet proposals in Geneva and signed the US-Soviet Trade Treaty. Thus the first step has been achieved in the program of the Central Committee to reduce areas of conflict between the capitalist and communist worlds. The treaty calls for major sales of US grain to the Soviet Union and the establishment of American consulates in Leningrad and Odessa.

The Foreign Minister said here that it was a source of great personal satisfaction to him to have succeeded in bringing home to the American people the peace-loving aspirations of the Soviet peoples. He is confident that American belligerence and aggression will melt before the . . .

From Paris, France:

The French Government of course applauds any diminution of world tensions caused by the mutual distrust and ignorance of the non-European great powers. It would, however, warn that any attempt to bypass the European community in the settlement of world problems cannot be acceptable . . .

From Bonn, Federal Republic of Germany:

Germany has the most to gain by the lessening of prospects for a third world war which would necessarily be fought on German soil and with German blood. However, agreement with the Soviet Union on collateral problems, without first reaching accord on the question of German reunification, is a direct violation of the commitments to the Federal Republic of Germany made by the United States.

From East Berlin, German Democratic Republic:

. . . and with German blood. However, agreement with the United States on subsidiary problems, without first reaching accord on either German reunification or the Oder-Neisse territorial demarcation, is a direct violation of the commitments to the Democratic Republic of Germany made by the Soviet Union.

From Peking, China:

And thus the hostile forces encircling the Peoples Republic of China have joined hands to further the course of imperialism in Asia. The Soviet Union, once again abandoning the principles of Marxism-Leninism, has embraced the bastion of capitalism in a transparent maneuver aimed at the enhancement of right-wing deviationism. . . .

From Manchester, England:

A LONG COOL LOOK AT THE TRADE TREATY

But existing undertakings do not spell out how the rapprochement is to be effected. Both powers are acutely conscious of their commitments to their allies and some of those commitments are disturbingly at variance with the immediate goals of the pact. Close agreement between the United States and the Soviet Union on policy in Central Europe will therefore be the yardstick by which any major realignment will have to be assessed by future British governments. . . .

1

Sing a Song of Sixpence, A Pocket Full of Rye

"MISS CORSA DID SAY IT WAS AN EMERGENCY, Mr. Thatcher!"

Miss Turvin delivered this message, cast a frightened but defiant look at the startled conference table, then fled. She had interrupted an Investment Committee meeting and even the newest employee of the Sloan Guaranty Trust knew that never, under any circumstances, should this occur. No messages, no calls, no announcement of visitors waiting in twenty-five important offices. The Investment Committee's solemn deliberations were sacrosanct.

Yet Miss Turvin, a veteran of twenty years' service, had not only shattered tradition, she had compounded the offense by transmitting his secretary's message to John Putnam Thatcher, who was senior vice-president of the Sloan, presiding officer of the Investment Committee, and currently acting executive officer of the bank. It took Miss Turvin several days before she could think of the whole thing without shuddering.

"Hmm," said John Putnam Thatcher thoughtfully, while a muted buzz sped around the vast conference table. Leaving the Investment Committee at this particular juncture would constitute a departure from protocol. In addition, there were certain perils: Walter Bowman, the perennially exuberant chief of research, was waxing dangerously eloquent about a dubious investment in liquid sandpaper.

On the other hand, if Miss Turvin could be believed, the imperturbable Miss Corsa was running up storm signals.

"Charlie, do you want to take over?" Thatcher decided finally, pushing back his chair. "I'd better look into this."

"Sure," said Charlie Trinkam with his usual cheeriness. "But if we're on fire, be sure to tell the firemen that we're up here, won't you, John?"

The Investment Committee's proceedings resumed before Thatcher had left the tower conference room, but as he strode vigorously toward the waiting elevator, he knew that twenty-five bankers' brains were running over the list of mishaps that could befall a bank. The list was varied and, unfortunately, virtually endless.

When Billings, the elevator operator, debouched him at the sixth floor, a rapid glance told Thatcher that at least no one had run amuck in the Trust Department. (It had happened once, in 1934.) Typewriters were clacking, file drawers were rolling, and trust officers were telephoning with their usual hushed efficiency. Thatcher strode down the corridor to his corner suite with the athletic vigor that belied his years, catching fleeting glimpses of offices as he passed; nothing looked out of order.

In his outer office Miss Corsa sat at her desk, calmly checking the monthly portfolio summary reports. She looked up as Thatcher entered and announced:

"It's Mr. Quentin, Mr. Thatcher. He's waiting."

Without wasting time, Thatcher continued into his office. There, the acid angularity of modern architecture and décor was moderated by the old-fashioned and comfortable furniture that Thatcher had wrested from the original Sloan by brute force. In a big, red leather chair sat Victor Quentin, chief of the Commercial Deposits Division of the Sloan Guaranty Trust. One look told Thatcher that, as usual, Miss Corsa had spoken only the literal truth: this was an emergency. Victor Quentin was flushed and shaking with suppressed emotion.

"John! Thank God! I told Miss Corsa that I had to talk to you . . ."

Deliberately slowing his pace, Thatcher circled his desk and settled himself, maintaining an imposing air of calm. One question was answered: whatever it was, it was big. Victor Quentin was normally quiet-spoken, competent, and—if the truth were told—something of a cold fish. As Thatcher watched, he ran a shaking hand through hair that was carefully brushed to lie flat and smooth.

". . . God knows I didn't want to call you out of the Investment Committee, but I couldn't sit on this any longer . . ."

Thatcher interrupted. "No, that's fine, Victor. It was a pretty dull meeting. What's the trouble?"

". . . you know this new Russian-American Trade Treaty? Well, of course, we've arranged to handle some of the commercial paper from the wheat sales . . ."

Quentin seemed to find it difficult to stop talking. Thatcher raised a hand to silence him. Then, without a hint of impatience, he said:

"Forget the background, Victor. Why don't you just tell me the bad news in a sentence? We'll get to the details later."

Momentarily Victor Quentin looked panicky. Then, after a deep breath, he said:

"Four days ago we were robbed of $985,000."

There was a moment of silence. In the distance Miss Corsa was typing.

"Yes," said Thatcher with measured appraisal that was perfectly genuine. "Yes, that is quite a sentence."

Quentin, to do him credit, tried to smile. He did not succeed. "When this came over me today," he said with a catch in his voice, "I thought I must be going crazy."

Thatcher nodded. The Sloan Guaranty Trust is a big bank, but $985,000 is a lot of money. And four days is a long time. For that matter, the Russian-American Trade Treaty was a very important document. Question after question leaped to his mind. He did not ask any of them. Instead, studiously neutral, he said:

"Well, Victor, you'd better fill me in on some of those details. What happened?"

"God knows!" Quentin replied, sagging back in his chair. But with Thatcher implacably waiting, he made an effort to marshall his resources and explain; the familiar workday terms served to revive him slightly. Thatcher watched the shock recede. Victor Quentin was once again the quiet-spoken, eminently competent head of the Sloan's Commercial Deposits Division.

"It all began with the Russian trade treaty," he said.

"I'm sure it did," said Thatcher tartly, and to himself. The opening of wider channels of trade between the U.S.S.R. and the United States had already involved him in ceremonial festivities including gala performances by the Bolshoi Ballet, dinners addressed by Soviet and American dignitaries, and more bad luncheons than he cared to remember. Still, it seemed excessive that it should also involve a theft of $985,000 from the Sloan.

With growing self-assurance, Victor Quentin continued his recital. One of the first actual transactions to be consummated under the newly liberalized trade agreements was the sale of forty million bushels of U.S. wheat to Russia. This colossal undertaking required the efforts of hundreds of grain brokerage firms, flotillas of ships—and many banks, including the Sloan.

". . . and Russian ships," said Quentin, sounding bitter. "That's why it was possible, John! My God, nobody could pass off forged bills of lading from an American ship on me. But this was the first time I had seen these damned Russian bills . . ."

What had happened was this: a week earlier, the grain brokerage firm of Stringfellow & Son had called the Commercial Deposits Division of the Sloan to report that the first Russian vessel had begun loading. The news had been confirmed by the Port Authority. Three days had passed, culminating in a second call from Stringfellow's office—his secretary reported that Stringfellow expected the final papers any minute. These documents would be speeded to the Sloan, where financing to the tune of $985,000 had already been arranged in a long, tedious series of conferences.

"So I made out the check," Victor Quentin went on, goaded by the recollection. "After all, it was perfectly standard procedure . . ."

"Yes," said John Putnam Thatcher, walking the narrow line between sympathy and authority.

"Well, in about two hours a messenger brought in the package from Stringfellow. Of course, I examined it carefully—checked to see that the bill of lading was okay, and the invoices, and the consul's certificate. Hell, they looked fine!"

He shook his head.

"So, I assumed they were all right. I signed the check. And since Stringfellow had asked me to send it to him at the Registry of Deeds—he's buying some land out in Jersey—I sent it right out since the messenger was going there anyway. And that was that . . . just a simple little $985,000 . . ."

Before he could relapse, Thatcher prompted him. "That was that until . . . ?"

Quentin shuddered. "Until two hours ago—when Stringfellow called me. He said he was sending down the *Odessa Queen* papers, and would I ship that check to him as fast as I could! My God, John, I don't know how I finished that call! The minute Stringfellow was off the line, I rushed out to look at the papers I had accepted—and Goddammit, they still look good! But an hour ago, the messenger brought these—and hell, you can see!"

He almost flung the envelope onto Thatcher's desk as he went on savagely, "Oh, it's a beautiful job, all right. They got the letterheads—from Stringfellow and from the Russian Consulate! That's what made it look so good—but the rest is a forgery! A smooth, high-class forgery!"

Thatcher picked up the envelope and opened it. Inside were two bulky sheafs comprising the familiar, elongated receipts given by the ship's officers on loading of goods, the promises to pay on delivery, and all the documents that constitute the commercial paper of trade which—in some circles, including the Sloan Guaranty Trust—is virtually indistinguishable from cold cash.

"The check has been cashed, I suppose," he said finally.

Quentin nodded somberly. "I've started an investigation, but I think we can take that for granted."

Thatcher agreed. That was the point of the theft, after all. "That means, presumably, that the messenger did deliver the check, it was picked up—what's the matter?"

Quentin slumped forward again. "I didn't use a bank messenger. Baranoff's chauffeur brought in the Stringfellow package. Since I knew he was going up to the Registry of Deeds—well, I made him wait and take up the Stringfellow check . . ."

Thatcher repressed a sigh. Quentin was clearly bent on self-flagellation. It made no difference at all who had carried the check; the point in question was who had cashed it. Abe Baranoff was an important Sloan customer. His many employees were all used, at one time or another, as couriers for checks, contracts, securities, and other financial instruments of their master's far-flung empire of theaters, movies, concert tours, and real estate deals.

"Unless Baranoff's chauffeur has taken to crime," he said somewhat pointedly, "it doesn't make much difference whether he carried the check or the U.S. mails did. The question is, who cashed it? I wonder . . ."

Hopelessly, Victor Quentin watched Thatcher frown in thought.

"I don't suppose that there's any possibility of a mix-up at Stringfellow," Thatcher mused aloud.

Quentin hitched himself forward. "That's why I wanted to talk to you, John. I don't know whether it would be wise to call Stringfellow. It would certainly cause a lot of talk if . . . if . . ."

If, in fact, word leaked out that the Sloan Guaranty Trust had been fleeced of $985,000.

Thatcher closed his eyes. Unbidden came mental pictures of Russian ambassadors shaking presidential hands, of U.S. trade missions talking to Russian trade missions, of speakers dwelling lovingly on the rich potential for peace inherent in growing trade between the great Union of Soviet Socialist Republics and the United States of America. Let Russian vessels steam into American ports to load agricultural bounty for the long trip across the seas to Russia. Let American fleets anchor in Baltic waters, for vodka, gold, and furs to be brought to the Western Hemisphere. Transform the armadas of war into harbingers of peace. Let peaceful trade herald the promise of a new dawn. . . .

"No," said Thatcher wearily. "We certainly don't want to rouse any talk if we can avoid it. But we have to check with Stringfellow." He drummed his fingers for a moment, then came to a decision. "I've got it!"

Without waiting to consult Quentin, who had obviously passed beyond constructive thought, he stabbed the buzzer on his desk.

In a moment, it produced Miss Corsa.

"Miss Corsa," said Thatcher. "We need your help with a little problem."

Composedly Miss Corsa waited, untouched by the tension in the room.

"We want you to call Stringfellow & Son. Get hold of Stringfellow's secretary—do you knew her name, Victor?"

Quentin started. "What? Oh, no, no I'm afraid not."

"Well, say that you're closing out a report—or something of that sort. The point is that we want to know if Stringfellow has got our check—yet. And we want to make it seem like a simple, routine question—nothing to get excited about. Do you think you can?"

"Certainly, Mr. Thatcher," said Miss Corsa, in effect reminding him that she was never excited about anything.

She moved to the extension phone and Thatcher marveled, not for the first time, at the psychological power of that instrument. Miss Corsa had been raised by loving but strict parents and carefully trained by the good sisters of Our Lady of Lourdes School for Girls. In consequence, she had a painfully high regard for veracity, as Thatcher knew to his cost. Yet put a telephone in her hand, and she could lie like a trooper—without the slightest sense of guilt. Nothing transmitted by AT&T was a sin in Miss Corsa's catechism.

Silently, he and Quentin watched her find a telephone number. Then, with the artificial courtesy of telephonic discourse, Miss Corsa located Mr. Stringfellow's secretary—a Miss Marcus—and launched into an elaboration of Thatcher's sketchy instructions. Her side of the conversation bristled with references to "closing out the check count" and "drawing up account records." There was a silence; Miss Corsa added something about "a new girl here in the office." Then:

"Yes . . . yes . . . well thank you, Miss Marcus."

She hung up.

"Well?" cried Victor Quentin.

"Miss Marcus says that they just sent the *Odessa Queen* papers over this afternoon. They're expecting our check later today—or the first thing tomorrow."

Again there was a pause as Miss Corsa waited for further instructions.

"That's all, Miss Corsa," said Thatcher. "And thank you."

"Certainly, Mr. Thatcher."

She had barely closed the door behind her when Victor Quentin burst out:

"That means that we've been swindled out of $985,000! By forged paper! Now what do we do?"

For the first time in their interview John Putnam Thatcher let steel show.

"What do we do? We call the police!"

He knew where his duty lay: Washington and Moscow could look to their own interests. Now was the time for him to concentrate on the Sloan Guaranty Trust.

2

Separating the Chaff

"BASICALLY THE SITUATION IS QUITE SIMPLE, Inspector," Thatcher was saying an hour later to the large, smooth-faced man from police headquarters. "It's as if someone had passed a forged check. Unfortunately the details are a little more complicated."

"I knew it," said Inspector Lyons, congratulating himself and sounding rueful at once. "Can you give me the bare outlines?"

Reducing the intricacies of foreign trade to bare outlines is not a task for everyone, but Thatcher was willing to try. "You know, foreign sales are usually made by what we call a letter of credit. Let's say that we're selling something abroad—wheat to Russia, for example. Now the Russians will pay for that wheat only when they get control of it. The seller of the wheat—that's Stringfellow & Son in this instance—wants to get paid as soon as it hands over the wheat."

Quentin nodded encouragingly, but Lyons merely looked wary. "Okay," he said.

Thatcher hoped so.

"That's where the banks come in," he said. "The Russians have a bank account in London. And the London bank has an account here at the Sloan. When the wheat seller—Stringfellow & Son—presents us with the loading documents that prove he has handed over the wheat, we pay him. Then London pays us later. That's the whole transaction in a nutshell."

Lyons was game. "And those loading documents were your forged check?"

Thatcher nodded. "That's exactly it. When you're shipping wheat, the steamship company gives you a bill of lading after the wheat is safely aboard—and that bill of lading is what Stringfellow brings to the Sloan. We pay, and in the normal course of events, we send the bill of lading to London and they pay. Unfortunately . . ."

He let the sentence trail off and kept from looking at Victor Quentin. Unfortunately this bill of lading was a high-class forgery; the Sloan should not have handed over $985,000 for it—and the London bank certainly would not.

Lyons thought for a moment, then spoke with resignation. "I suppose it's more complicated than that in actual practice?"

Technical questions had a beneficial effect on Victor Quentin, Thatcher was happy to observe. Quentin sat up. "Yes indeed," he told Lyons. "For instance, there are insurance certificates and export licenses and tax exemption forms. What Stringfellow & Son ships to us is really a packet of official documents—but the bill of lading is basic. That's what says the wheat is aboard ship."

"And that was forged," said Lyons.

He deflated Quentin.

"It was. And the invoice too," Quentin said.

Lyons groaned. "What's the invoice?"

"The invoice is the paper that Stringfellow & Son prepared—specifying how many bushels of wheat were sold."

Lyons was trying to sort this out in his own mind. "Let's see if I've got this straight. The Sloan is responsible for this wheat really being on board the ship . . ."

Thatcher and Quentin were both horrified.

"Certainly not," said Quentin. "Banks don't get involved in responsibility for the quality or even the existence of goods."

Thatcher saw the bafflement on Lyon's face. "Look, Inspector," he said, "it really is like a check. If you give a check to a car salesman, your bank isn't responsible if the car turns out to be a

lemon. You can even write a check to buy the Brooklyn Bridge—
and the bank doesn't care."

Lyons smiled. As it happened, his last car had been a lemon.
"So, on this letter of credit—all the bank really cares about is
whether or not those bills of lading—yeah, and the invoice—were
forged or not."

There was a silence during which Thatcher and Quentin looked
at each other.

"On letters of credit," said Thatcher with real regret, "things are
more complicated."

"Somehow I thought they would be," said Lyons.

"Normally the Sloan would only be responsible for determining
that these documents were in order. We're not expected to spot
forged signatures or anything like that. We are responsible for
noticing that the paper we accept comes from the correct ship. Do
you see?"

Lyons thought that he did. He also thought he had spotted
something new. "But since these forgeries are all in order—from
the right ship and everything—doesn't that mean that the Sloan
isn't going to be responsible? You said that Mr. Quentin here isn't
expected to be able to verify signatures."

Thatcher sighed. "The key word is 'normally.' You see, this
wheat shipment isn't at all normal. Half the wheat is being shipped
in American bottoms, half in Russian. And the Soviet government
wants the wheat as quickly as possible, so they're sending over
every boat they can lay their hands on."

"Boats from the Black Sea," said Quentin gloomily. "From the
White Sea. Even naval vessels. The *Odessa Queen* is a converted
troop transport. She's never issued a bill of lading in her life. And
there aren't any steamship offices in New York—to check."

Lyons was not unduly impressed by this catalog of woes. "But
couldn't you see the foul-up coming? Couldn't you prepare for
it?"

Quentin simply shook his head, but Thatcher spoke for him.
"We did," he said. "We prepared, and the Russians did too. So the
arrangement requires that every bill of lading has to be authenti-
cated by an official certificate from the Russian Consulate here—
with signature and seal—"

"And that . . . ?"

"Yes, that was forged too."

Lyons was developing some sense of identity with the Sloan. "That's what's going to sting you, eh?"

"Who knows?" said Thatcher philosophically. "It certainly raises a tricky legal problem for our lawyers. They'll probably be working on it for years. I just want you to see how abnormal this whole transaction has been. And the forger seems to have known every detail of it. Just look—he forged a bill of lading from the *Odessa Queen*, he forged Stringfellow's invoices, in triplicate, he forged consular certificates with Russian seals and signatures, and this draft . . ."

As he went down this melancholy list, he tossed photostats of these documents across the desk to Lyons. The originals had already been dispatched to laboratories and specialists. Lyons looked at them without enthusiasm.

"There's just one more point, Inspector," Thatcher said.

"Yes?"

"You do realize that when Washington hears about this all hell will break loose? This Russian-American Trade Treaty is important—and the whole wheat sale is, too. I'm afraid we've got to be ready for tremendous repercussions if we don't handle this right."

Lyons, a man who knew you can't fight city hall, expelled an exasperated breath. "Senators!" he muttered. "The FBI! The CIA! All of them underfoot, all of them hamstringing us . . ."

Thatcher was pleased with this realistic and ready acceptance of the inevitable. "I've already spoken to Lancer—he's our board chairman—and he's breaking the bad news to Washington. I think we've got to keep quiet about it until the Russians have been officially informed . . ."

"Fine," said Lyons irritably. "And how do we talk to Stringfellow, without letting him know what's happened?"

"We don't," said Thatcher incisively. "It's out of the question. And believe me, you cannot regret it as much as the Sloan does."

Lyons acknowledged this with a smile. "Still, the trail is already four days old," he said. "If anybody knows anything, he's rapidly forgetting it." He thought for a moment. "I'll tell you what. We can still talk to the chauffeur. We won't have to explain anything to him. And if Mr. Quentin here is right about just shoving the check into his hands—well, that leaves him clean!"

These musings were simply the tools of Inspector Lyons' trade, and his brutality was quite unconscious; it sufficed, however, to turn Quentin ashen again.

Thatcher considered this. "That's all right," he decided cautiously. "But all things considered, I think the Sloan should be represented at the interview."

Lyons nodded. "You said the man's name was Denger? I'll give the office a ring. They'll be able to track him down."

The sign above the double overhead doors read "Halloran's Garage." The doors were up, leaving both driveways clear and forming the only entrance. Inside, fluorescent lighting cast a bright, metallic glow over the fleet of glistening, black cars. One car was being raised on a hydraulic lift, while others were being washed and greased. A mechanic extracted himself from underneath a hood and strolled over to them, swinging a greasy rag.

"Do something for you?" he asked in a genial shout over the prevailing din.

"August Denger around?" asked Inspector Lyons.

The mechanic shook his head. "He's out on a job.": He looked at them doubtfully, suspicions dawning. "You want a car? You'd better see the office."

Lyons didn't move. "No, we want Denger. When will he be back?"

"No idea."

Lyons reached for his wallet. Flipping it open, he displayed his identity card. "All right. Fun's over. The police."

The mechanic's eyes widened slightly. "I don't know what the trouble is, mister, but now I'm sure you'd better see the office." He lifted his voice over the stillness that had spread like magic at the sound of the word *police*. "Hey, Ed! Get Rita! It's the cops!"

A man at the far end of the cavern was busy talking through a glass window in a stud partition. "Rita says to come into the office," he relayed, turning back to the garage. "Through that door."

As they filed across the littered floor to the whitewashed door labeled simply "Accounts," Thatcher leaned toward Lyons. "Where are we? I thought Denger was Abe Baranoff's chauffeur."

Because Lyons, after a brief discussion over the phone, had bustled them all into a taxicab, and they had rolled up First Avenue to Halloran's Garage in the upper eighties.

"It's more complicated that that. The Hack Bureau says this is where Denger works."

Victor Quentin was distressed. "But I know he works for Baranoff. He's been running Baranoff's errands for years."

Lyons pushed open the door. "We'll know in a minute."

The woman sitting behind the desk was white-haired and vigorous, probably near sixty. She waved them into the hard wooden chairs and then kept her hand stretched out suggestively. "Eddy said you are police."

Lyons handed his wallet over and she whistled soundlessly. *"Inspector* Lyons, eh? I guess we're not talking about a traffic accident. I'm Rita Halloran, by the way."

"No, it's a lot bigger than a traffic accident. And it may not have anything to do with your operation, except incidentally. We'll know more after we've talked to this August Denger."

Mrs. Halloran made a long arm for a clipboard hanging on a nail in the wall. "Gus is out right now," she announced, "but he should be back any minute. I'll tell Eddy to get him the minute he checks in." She pushed at the sliding panel and spoke crisply to Eddy. When she turned back to them her forehead was creased in a frown. "You can't tell me anything more about this?"

"Not yet."

Mrs. Halloran did not push the point. The garage business seemed to encourage acceptance of the unknown. Inspector Lyons settled himself more comfortably before pursuing the conversation.

"By the way, we were a little surprised to end up here. The way I heard it, this Denger was Abe Baranoff's chauffeur."

"Well, that's simple enough," she said. "This isn't just a car-hire business. I do some hiring for an evening or a weekend, naturally, but mostly it's contract work."

"Come again?"

"Most of our customers don't run their own cars. While they're in town they rent a car and driver from me. And the ones who've been on the books a long time always have the same man. That means the driver gets to know their habits and their ports of call, so they have most of the benefits of a private chauffeur. This Baranoff, for instance. You know about him?"

"Just the usual. Brings a lot of foreign companies over. He's produced some movies, and now he's big in real estate."

"That's right. He spends about six months of every year in New York. When he's in town, he has the exclusive use of a Caddie and of Gus Denger. This has been going on now for about six years. I can look up the exact time if you want."

"There's no hurry," said Lyons easily. "I just want to get the picture. So the fact is, Denger really is Baranoff's private chauffeur for about half the year. The rest of the time he's on call for other jobs."

Rita Halloran nodded. "That's right. He doesn't have any other regular customers because Baranoff's schedule is so irregular."

"Most of your business like that?"

"A lot of it is."

"You use just Caddies?"

"No, I use everything they want. Caddies, Continentals, Rolls Royces. Most of them like the idea of a limousine for New York."

Thatcher had taken no part in the conversation, content to listen to the Inspector and Mrs. Halloran. He was always willing to learn about the ways in which money is made and business is serviced. But now he had a question of his own.

"Did you start out this way or did you work up to it?"

"Hell, this isn't the way we started." Mrs. Halloran took a cigarette from a package on the battered desk and seemed surprised to find Quentin presenting her with a light. "Frank began with one car he drove himself. Frank was my husband," she explained. Her tone became reminiscent. "And what a rat race that was! Calls at all hours. Then he got a bank loan after the war and began expanding. Still mostly the hire-car business, but he had four or five cars and a bunch of drivers. I came down to take over the office end, and when Frank died, I simply kept going. I went into the contract business to simplify things, but it's paid off. Getting bigger and bigger by the year."

Thatcher's unspoken question had been answered. He now knew why Halloran's Garage was run by a woman.

The woman meantime was answering a tapping on the sliding panel. Eddy was again at work.

"Gus is back," she told them. "Here he is. Gus, this is Inspector Lyons from police headquarters. Help him out, will you?"

Without further parley, she left the office and the floor to the Inspector.

Denger stood in the doorway through which she had passed and surveyed the assembly truculently. He was a short, squat man with the beginnings of a beer belly. His feet planted well apart, he rocked back on his heels slightly so that he was peering upward. The requirements of Halloran's Garage saw to it that he was clean-shaven, with a fresh haircut.

"I don't know what you think you've got. But I'm clean. My ticket is as good as the day I took it out in 1949."

"I'm not from the Hack Bureau, Denger. I want to ask you about some errands you ran for Abe Baranoff."

A slow and rather unpleasant smile crossed Denger's face. "So the King's got his feet wet, huh? That'll be a change from sitting on his ass in a Caddie."

"Well, come in and we'll find out," urged Lyons heartily with a brief glance at Thatcher. Denger was not wedded to the Baranoff interests. And that might make things easier.

"What makes you think Baranoff is in trouble with the law?" Lyons asked when they had finally become settled.

"It stands to reason, doesn't it? Everybody knows he started without a cent. Now he's rolling in dough. Nothing's too good for him. It's caviar and champagne and Sardi's. You should see the parties he throws!" Watery gray eyes searched for approval. "Now, nobody makes a pile like that who's legit. Naturally he's been pulling some fancy stuff. And it must be something big."

"Oh?" Lyons encouraged.

Denger expanded with seedy authority.

"Sure. First off, everything about Baranoff is big. And then it's got three of you tracking him down. Two of you big shots from Centre Street." He paused to look at his interrogators knowingly. Apparently John Putnam Thatcher conformed to his idea of the kind of policeman necessary for somebody as tricky as Abe Baranoff. "And then, to put the lid on, the third one is from the Sloan. That means there's a helluva big stink—about something."

He had recognized Victor Quentin. Thatcher felt a small knot of anxiety dissolve. He was not unmindful of the ambivalence of Quentin's position. Denger's recognition of Quentin was confirmation of Quentin's supposed recognition of Denger.

"Now what can I do for you gentlemen?" asked Denger condescendingly.

"I want you to think back to last Thursday," said Lyons. "Give us a blow-by-blow account of your day."

Denger pushed his visor cap to the back of his head and scowled. "Thursday? Let's see. Oh, sure. I got you. That was pretty confused. Bound to be with His Majesty sailing. That's always hell."

"Sailing?" Lyons broke in sharply. "You mean Baranoff?"

"That's right. Mr. Big himself. I took him and that nance secretary and the whole crew down to the pier at ten o'clock in the morning. And it was no joke, let me tell you. That pier was hell on wheels. You wouldn't believe there were so many bums ready to sit in the sun for a week and relax from the heavy partying they do."

Lyons waved aside Denger's notion of travel on the North Atlantic in early March. "Now let me get this straight. At ten o'clock in the morning you went to the pier. Do you know what time the ship sailed? And also what ship?"

"The *Queen Mary*. Nothing but the best for us. We always go an hour before sailing time. I didn't hang around though. Don't know what time they got away. I had plenty of jobs to do for His Nibs."

"How long did that take?"

"Christ, he left enough for the whole day! He always does. You'd think I'd get a couple of hours for myself after trailing him around for six months. I don't go on to other work until the day after. But not once. . . . Okay, okay," he said as Lyons made a gesture of impatience. "Let's see. I ran around uptown and midtown on my way back from the pier. Then I brought the car in here to be gassed up while I went to lunch. Naturally by the time I got back that bastard had thought up something else for me to do. Luckily it fitted in with the downtown jobs I was holding for the afternoon."

Thatcher wondered if Denger managed to moderate his sullenness when he was driving Baranoff. Lyons, however, was concentrating on the narrative.

"Now wait a minute. I thought you said he'd sailed."

"Yeah, sure. You don't think somebody like Baranoff calls a chauffeur direct?" Denger replied sarcastically. "He'd gotten hold of his office. Some girl there told me he left some stuff at the pier for me to deliver right away."

Tense stillness settled on the little room. Even Denger had abandoned his self-satisfaction. With clumsy curiosity, he said:

"I suppose that's what this is all about, huh? That's the package I took to Mr. Quentin here."

"Let's take it in more detail," said Lyons slowly, carefully. "The girl told you Baranoff had left something for you at the pier. Did she tell you what it was?"

Was Denger alarmed by this question? Thatcher thought he sounded apprehensive as he answered:

"Are you crazy, mister? I'm just the errand boy in that outfit."

"And what exactly happened at the pier? I mean where did you go?"

"Where I always go. You know that kind of booth they have, where you can leave fruit and flowers and telegrams for the jokers who're sailing?"

Lyons nodded.

"Well, it works the other way too. The jokers can leave stuff for messengers. I asked for the package for Baranoff's chauffeur, and the guy there looked at the mess of stuff in the back and gave me an envelope addressed to the Sloan. I had to fight to get it too. There was a real mob of deliveries."

"I see." Lyons was getting grimmer and grimmer. "Now tell me what happened at the Sloan."

"I don't know why you pick on me." Denger was certainly uneasy now. "Mr. Quentin here can tell you as well as I can. I gave him the envelope. He said to wait while he checked it. So I waited, didn't I?"

Lyons gave Quentin no opportunity to reply.

"You gave it personally to Mr. Quentin?" he snapped.

Denger was openly puzzled.

"Sure. It was marked 'Personal Delivery.' A lot of Baranoff's stuff is that way. It means I don't settle for secretaries or assistants. I hand it to the big cheese himself. Say, what is this?"

"And then?" Lyons pushed.

"Like I said, he checked the stuff. Then he was just telling me everything was okay and I could go, when he saw this other envelope I was carrying addressed to the Registry of Deeds. So I let him smooth-talk me into doing the Sloan's errands. He went away for a couple of minutes and brought back an envelope addressed to somebody called Luke Stringfellow at the Registry. I took it to the Registry." Denger nervously ran a meaty hand over his chin, then hurried on, "When I got through the doorway there, a guy came up to me. Asked if I had the envelope for Luke Stringfellow. I said sure and handed it to him. And that was that. I left the rest of Baranoff's stuff with the clerk and beat it."

Quentin was white as this recital came to an end. His mouth opened, but the look from Thatcher forced him back into silence.

Thatcher knew exactly what he wanted to say. It is not every day that someone walks up to a messenger and gets $985,000 without even showing identification. Not that it would have made any difference. The man undoubtedly had ample identification—all forged.

The Inspector was the first to recover.

"Describe the man."

Again Denger ran a finger along his jaw. "God, I didn't really look at him much. It was in that dark entrance way. He had on a topcoat and a dark hat and a scarf of some sort."

"You must have noticed something about him," Lyons pressed.

In his surly fashion, Denger was trying to be responsive.

"Well, there was nothing strange about him, if that's what you mean. Nothing out of the ordinary. He was about medium build I guess. Maybe a little taller than me. He was wearing some kind of glasses—horn rims—and yes, yes, he had dark hair showing around the hat. And that's about it."

His listeners sat silent and disappointed. Denger was relaxing when Inspector Lyons took a new tack.

"All right. Now this girl who called you. What about her? Did you recognize her voice?"

"Nope. I didn't take the call. The message was just waiting when I got back."

"Dear God, couldn't you have told me that before?" Lyons ground his teeth in exasperation.

"You didn't ask me." Denger grinned again in good humor. He enjoyed scoring off mankind in general. But Lyons had abandoned him and was at the door.

"Mrs. Halloran!"

"Yes?" Rita Halloran raised her eyebrows as she appeared from around the corner. She cast a sharp glance at Denger, Thatcher noted.

"Is there any way we can find out who took a call from Baranoff's office during Denger's lunch hour on Thursday?"

"I don't—oh, wait. Was that the call telling him to go down to the pier? If so, I took it myself. I was eating a sandwich at the desk when it came through."

"And could you recognize the voice?"

Mrs. Halloran stared at the Inspector as if he had suddenly gone mad. "Not a chance in a million. You don't know how many calls like that we get from girls in offices."

"Game, set, and match," said Thatcher when they were out in the street again. "An unknown voice on the phone for the pick-up. An ordinary man with no distinguishing characteristics for the drop-off. A complete dead end."

"We'll see about that," Inspector Lyons promised grimly.

But three hours later, Thatcher was doing some grim promising himself.

He had just emerged from an extended session with George Lancer in which he had been privileged to learn the views of the State Department and the United States government in the matter of honoring Luke Stringfellow's second draft.

"And it will interest you to know, Miss Corsa," he said savagely on returning to his own office, "that any delay on the part of the Sloan will be viewed as tantamount to declaring a third world war."

Miss Corsa was far too experienced to be flushed into discussion by this ruse.

"Mr. Quentin has phoned five times. He says it's urgent," she said.

"All right. You can put him through. Not that I have any doubts about what he wants."

Victor Quentin wanted to report that Luke Stringfellow had called repeatedly for his check. Obedient to instructions, Quentin had merely replied that he was still checking the documentation. "But I can't go on saying that forever."

"You don't have to," Thatcher replied shortly. "Lancer has made his decision. Do you have the check there? He can have it tomorrow."

The day, for John Thatcher, reached its climax of unsatisfactoriness when he sat foursquare at his desk and appended his signature to the buff slip just below the words "Nine Hundred Eighty-Five Thousand Dollars and No Cents."

3

A Jug of Wine,
A Loaf of Bread . . .

THE SLOAN GUARANTY TRUST was as mindful of its public responsibility as the next great bank, but there is a limit to high-mindedness, and $985,000, it turned out, defined it pretty neatly. From the directors' room and other important offices came a strong feeling that somebody should do something. Thatcher mildly pointed out that any such action would have to be circumscribed in view of the Sloan's agreement to observe momumental discretion and tact.

"We have complete faith in you, John," said George Lancer, departing.

For a moment, Thatcher considered alternatives. Then, because he was opposed to aimless forays on principle, he decided to make the best of a bad situation.

"Miss Corsa," he told the intercom. "I want you to make some calls. First, Inspector Lyons. Then I suppose that State Department man. Then . . ."

Miss Corsa remained serene.

The next morning, Thatcher stopped at the Sloan only long enough to collect Victor Quentin, who seemed to have lost ten pounds overnight. Thatcher thought briefly of reminding him that it was not Sloan policy to start heads rolling at every setback, then decided against it. It was all too probable that Victor Quentin would have to go; it would be a false kindness to pretend otherwise.

"We're going to see if we can find out how those *Odessa Queen* papers were faked," he explained briskly. Then, to the waiting taxi driver, he added, "Pier Twenty-two."

Apathetically, Quentin clambered into the taxi and asked: "Do you think we can learn anything at the *Odessa Queen?*"

"Not really," said Thatcher truthfully. "But we can see how the bills of lading should have moved. That might suggest something about how our thieves were able to operate."

Quentin looked skeptical, and the driver, who turned right in front of a Broadway bus, splashed dirty rain water from the gutter onto pedestrians waiting for the light.

Thatcher maintained a bracing tone. "Inspector Lyons has gone down to the Cunard Office to see what he can find out about the package that was left for Denger. He suggested we might tackle the *Odessa Queen* at the same time. He'll join us if he gets through early enough."

"I don't see what he thinks he'll uncover at the Cunard pier," said Quentin, rousing himself. "You know what they're like on a sailing day."

"He's just checking anything he can check. God knows there isn't much. And Denger is worth a second look."

Quentin was surprised. "Denger? But I told you, I almost forced the check on him. And he told a perfectly straightforward story."

"The story was straightforward enough." Thatcher was silent for a moment. Then he continued: "Maybe it's just his manner that put me off. You've seen him under different circumstances. Tell me, is he always that pleased with himself?"

"Well, I've only seen him when he was running errands for Baranoff. But, yes, I suppose you could say he's pretty cocky."

Thatcher shook his head dubiously.

"It wasn't just cockiness," he said, almost to himself. "It was as if he were enjoying a secret joke."

The taxi driver, running a red light at Chambers Street, narrowly missed a delivery truck illegally backing out of an alley.

"Jerk!" he summarized over his shoulder to his passengers.

As a rule, Thatcher did not encourage taxi drivers, having long since discovered that what passed for philosophy among simpler minds palled rapidly. But Quentin was sunk in a dejection profound enough to be contagious; moreover, now that he came to think of it, he had a technical question, and here was an expert of sorts.

"Wouldn't it be easier work if you were with one of the private chauffeuring outfits, instead of driving a cab?" he asked.

The lecture lasted until Franklin Street. Private garages, Thatcher and Quentin learned, were slave drivers, exploiting their hapless employees with impossible schedules and endless nagging about standards of service.

". . . and you get a minute, for Crissake! You gotta polish the goddamn car! Who wants to polish a car? You get a bash on the fender, and they dock your pay. . . ."

The biggest liveries in Manhattan were Waley Car Hire, Custom Chauffeurs, and Halloran's Garage.

"About Halloran's Garage," Thatcher began delicately.

"Boy, there's one tough dame!" said the cabby with unstinted admiration. "Got a tongue that would blister paint. And around that garage, does she know what she's doing!"

Thatcher agreed. Running a garage at an enormous profit was not as simple as Rita Halloran had tried to make it sound.

"A lot of garages handpick the chauffeurs," continued the cabby. "But Halloran's is the only one I know that handpicks the customers too. Well, with her money she can afford to."

He braked to an abrupt halt in a truck-throttled street. "Can't get no closer!"

Thatcher would be willing to bet that Mrs. Halloran's drivers could. He did not say as much, but paid the driver and slipped out into the middle of the street after Quentin. The docks were gray and dirty under a leaden sky. There was the usual din of machinery and wares being manhandled along rough bricks, of shouts and cries, of engines churning. Beyond the echoing warehouses, out of sight, tugs shrieked impatiently above the rumble of the traffic.

"Yes, here we are," said Thatcher, threading his way to the curb.

The smell of the port assailed them like a blow: salt water, rotting garbage, damp and decaying wood, bilge. Overhead, gulls wheeled and screamed insults at one another.

At Pier Twenty-two, a small contingent of police stood about, curiously immobile in the midst of moving men and freight. Thatcher presented credentials and asked if this were routine.

"Nope," said the guard, checking a list. "You're okay. No, we got the boys out at all the Russki ships. You can't ever tell what some nuts will do. Just yesterday, we had twenty-five Hungarians down here. You go right on up."

"You know, I never thought of that," Quentin said as they trudged upstairs. "The theft could be political, couldn't it, John? Some White Russians, or something like that?"

"From what I've seen of White Russians," Thatcher remarked, "they'd find it difficult to break into a piggy bank, let alone forge papers well enough to take you for $985,000, Victor."

"Or some Albanians," Quentin continued.

Who was Thatcher to dash hopes? He did not reply.

In the great echoing cavern, there were longshoremen, customs officers, and other officials, but no sign of Lyons. At the berth, they could see the *Odessa Queen*. Thatcher was no seaman, but the *Odessa Queen,* sitting low in the scummy water, looked both squat and utilitarian to him. At the foot of her gangplank was a representative, not of the New York City Police Department, but of the United States Navy.

"Now what?" Thatcher murmured in exasperation as they moved forward.

The man, with the keen innocent face of the military and the usual dazzling show of ribbons, stepped forth, ascertained their identity, then introduced himself: "Commander Richardson." A pause, then: "United States Navy." This last, Thatcher inferred, was in case they should confuse him with a member of the Coast Guard.

Quentin and Thatcher let their hands get shaken strongly and projected cautious curiosity. Commander Richardson cleared his throat, stepped aside as a burly stevedore rolled toward them with an enormous, canvas-covered load.

"Bureau of Naval Intelligence," he explained cryptically. "New York Branch."

"Move it, mister!" shouted somebody behind him.

This revolted the leader of men in Richardson, but wisely deciding that he would cut no ice with a member of the longshoremen's union, he stepped aside. "A little naval discipline would do them a lot of good," he said tightly. "Well, I'm here because we heard, from unimpeachable sources, that you're boarding the *Odessa Queen.*"

It sounded as if they were going to do it with daggers between their teeth.

Thatcher was beginning to feel the dank chill. "You mean the police informed you?"

Commander Richardson again took a quick look around. Thatcher expected a reply concerning enemy ears; instead the Commander hissed, "Washington wants a representative of the U.S. Navy present."

Thatcher repressed a sigh. In view of his other troubles, he did not feel inclined to take on the U.S. Navy. Accordingly, he indicated that Commander Richardson was most welcome to join them, looked around in vain for Inspector Lyons, then decided, as they had agreed, to carry on without him.

"Let's go aboard," he said in smart tones of command.

"Yes sir!" said Richardson, going over the top.

They were welcomed aboard the *Odessa Queen* with a tremendous flurry of salutes. Then the Russian officer said, "If you will please come . . . ?"

He led the way; Quentin, Thatcher, and Commander Richardson—who was looking keen—followed. Six sailors fell in behind.

After walking the length of a short deck, they turned and proceeded down narrow stairs. The *Odessa Queen* had an odd musty smell; somewhere distant machinery was producing vibrations. The officer turned a corner and finally went down a long passageway to the single cabin door.

"Captain's quarters," Richardson explained in an aside.

The door opened; they were ushered into an unexpectedly cozy cabin, dark with heavy oak furniture and betasseled red velvet draperies. There was a large table supporting decanters and glasses; a gallery of family portraits covered a shelf beneath an oval mirror.

A huge, red-faced man in a rumpled uniform rose as they entered.

"Captain Kurnatovsky!" he bellowed, seizing Thatcher's hand, pumping it and powerfully drawing him in before passing on to Quentin. "Captain Kurnatovsky!" he repeated, reaching Commander Richardson. With a happy shout, he pounded him soundly on the back. The door closed behind them and Russian sailors, Thatcher had no doubt, took up stations outside.

The Captain's quarters on the *Odessa Queen* were not large, yet as Commander Richardson pulled himself together and attempted introductions, Captain Kurnatovsky grinned broadly and stepped aside to reveal three companions. Two of them advanced to cover his flanks and joined in the bedlam of greetings. One was a harassed man, very correct, bearing a briefcase; the second was a dark, vivacious young woman. To the rear hovered a slightly younger man, his broad shoulders stooped and his face paled by anxiety, with "assistant" written all over his deferential posture. The young woman, anything but pallid, was built along lines that made Thatcher regret Charlie Trinkam's absence. Charlie was the Sloan's most serious student of Woman; here was a notable example.

It was she who started the ball rolling.

"Unfortunately Captain Kurnatovsky does not speak English,

and I will have to interpret. I will do my best to be helpful." A quickly suppressed twinkle suggested that her best, in all arenas, was very helpful indeed. Sternly she returned to business and indicated the briefcase bearer. "And Mr. Liputin is from the Embassy in Washington."

Liputin gave a formal bow.

"I speak English," he announced. "Not too fast, please."

This augured ill for a fruitful exchange of information, but Thatcher merely nodded and waited for the final introduction.

"Mr. Voronin is an assistant commercial officer with our consulate in New York."

"How do you do," murmured Voronin tonelessly.

"Excellent," Thatcher said. "Tell me, Richardson, do you speak Russian?"

"Certainly," the Commander answered, implying this was standard equipment at the Bureau of Naval Intelligence.

Thatcher's worst fears were realized. All the seconds could communicate freely. Only the principals were to be prevented from doing business.

But business, it developed, was not to be the first order of the day. There was an explosion from Kurnatovsky, who waved his huge arms and thrashed his way to the bottles.

"The Captain says we begin with a toast," said the interpreter approvingly.

Ominous glasses of colorless liquid appeared, thrust into their hands by the Captain, who was bellowing something high-spirited.

"To full peace and understanding between our countries," said the interpreter.

Manfully, Thatcher quaffed; the interpreter might be young and attractive but he suspected her accuracy. From what he could see, Captain Kurnatovsky was likely to use less lofty formulations as a prelude to a drink. And the Captain was tossing off vodka with a down-to-earth competence that was in sharp contrast to Commander Richardson's prudent sipping. Under the circumstances, Thatcher felt a patriotic pang; if the United States Navy insisted on meddling in the Sloan's affairs, they could have had the decency to produce a real sea dog, someone to yo-ho-ho for a bottle of rum with the best of them.

Liputin, who also managed his vodka with praiseworthy dispatch, opened the subject.

"From Washington I have come upon learning of this crime. The *Odessa Queen* has nothing to do with it. Captain Kurnatovsky knows nothing of it."

"Oh, certainly," said Thatcher.

Captain Kurnatovsky again bellowed something, produced a bottle and replenished Richardson's drink. Victor Quentin, staring at him with awe, nervelessly held out his glass.

"You comprehend," said Liputin earnestly, "that Captain Kurnatovsky is a simple sailor. He knows not of details. He loads the *Odessa Queen* with wheat, and that is all. . . ."

The interpreter, translating for the Captain's benefit, had reached this point when the simple sailor burst into a torrent of impassioned speech that brought tears to his own eyes and apprehension to those of Commander Richardson.

"The Soviet people are friends of the American people," ran the suspiciously concise translation.

"Hear, hear!" said Victor Quentin (who afterward explained that somebody had to say something, and what could you say?).

"More vodka!"

Much clinking.

Thatcher had no particular desire to break up a promising party, but the Sloan Guaranty Trust had lost $985,000.

"We appreciate that Captain Kurnatovsky and the *Odessa Queen* have nothing to do with this theft. . . ."

This produced relief from Liputin.

"That is what the Ambassador told me," he said.

The Captain, when the gist of Thatcher's truncated remarks was relayed, shouted vast approval. There was a thin line of perspiration on Victor Quentin's forehead. Determinedly Thatcher avoided more vodka.

". . . but we are simply trying to trace details about the bill of lading."

There was a pause for translation. The Captain looked at Liputin, produced a pipe, busied himself lighting it. Then, through a haze of foul black fumes, he spoke.

"He asks," the interpreter said gravely, "what is a bill of lading?"

The Captain rumbled further. Compressing her lips, the young woman turned large, dark eyes on Richardson. "He asks if you, a fellow naval officer, know what is this bill of lading?"

"Bill of lading?" Richardson repeated blankly. He fulfilled at least one sea dog qualification. His eyes, now firmly locked onto the interpreter, had abandoned the rest of the gathering.

"Mr. Liputin, I merely wish to find out a little more about how the *Odessa Queen* issues its bills of lading—since a forged bill was used to rob us."

Liputin nodded intelligently.

"Perhaps you can tell me how . . ."

Liputin drew a deep breath. "The Ambassador tells me that we regret this crime but we have no knowledge of the criminals. Perhaps fascists who wish to destroy Soviet-American trade have done this. We will make no public statements, and we are very much approving that there is no publicity maligning the Soviet people or the *Odessa Queen*."

In desperation, Thatcher turned to the third member of the triumvirate. Voronin was slightly withdrawn from the group, sitting well back and missing approximately two out of three rounds of vodka. Thatcher's simple question, repeated for the third time, produced a reaction beyond his wildest anticipation. Voronin, who had shown himself completely at home in the English language during the introductions (with traces of a BBC accent, in fact), now retreated hastily behind the language barrier. He addressed himself exclusively to the interpreter in Russian.

"Mr. Voronin," she intoned, "is present only as an observer. He has no authority to discuss these matters."

Liputin seemed to take savage exception to this remark. He rounded hotly on Voronin. Within seconds the interpreter had been sucked into the dissension, and all three were tossing around Slavic polysyllables with frantic abandon. Thatcher resisted the temptation to think that he had thrown the Soviet representatives into a panic. A lifetime of international negotiations had taught him that almost any exchange in a foreign language can sound alarmingly dramatic to the uninitiated.

At length the disagreement resolved itself, and the interpreter again turned to him:

"The details that you desire are obtainable at the offices of the consulate. Mr. Voronin suggests that you make an appointment to speak with Sergei Pavlich Durnovo there. He regrets that he himself must leave us now. He extends to you his best wishes in your inquiry."

Voronin's hasty departure, whether on his own initiative or at Liputin's behest, made it clear that he was not laying himself open to further questions. Thatcher watched him go with a sigh. There went the only man likely to provide them with any information. Accepting the inevitable, he turned to his remaining hosts and said:

"Perhaps I should have expected this. I think the best thing we can do is follow Mr. Voronin's advice. Quentin . . . Quentin!"

Withdrawal from the *Odessa Queen* proved a lengthy process. When Captain Kurnatovsky learned their intention he launched into a lament punctuated by several rounds of vodka and urgent invitations for Thatcher, Quentin, and Commander Richardson to come again, to consider the *Odessa Queen* as their own, to visit Kurnatovsky in Kiev any time. Liputin looked impassive. Surprisingly it was Victor Quentin who replied in kind with warm offers of hospitality at the Sloan.

As he left them at the gangplank an hour later, Mr. Liputin repeated the Ambassador's strongest representations that dastardly as this crime was, it had nothing to do with the Russians.

Unless it was an anti-Russian plot.

"Whew!" said Victor Quentin, wobbling slightly as they left the ship. "I'm not used to drinking so early in the morning."

Neither was Commander Richardson. But, queried as to the recent Russian bickering, he waxed informative.

"That was just one of their bureaucratic squabbles. Liputin wanted Voronin to get permission to answer questions, but Voronin insisted on bringing Durnovo into the picture. Said Durnovo was his boss, and those were Durnovo's specific instructions. Anything else I can do for you?"

Receiving a negative reply, the Commander accompanied them to the street with dignity, then smartly saluted and went his way.

"What good he did, I don't know," Thatcher said sourly, though in fairness he would have had to admit that Richardson had been no more obstructive than any other of the agencies present. He succeeded in flagging a taxi and extracting Amtorg's address from Quentin.

"Well, that's two hours wasted," Thatcher summed up.

Quentin leaned his forehead against a cool metal crossbar and surreptitiously lowered his window. But even with the world spinning around him, he was still functioning.

"Why are we going to Amtorg?" he asked.

"To see this Durnovo," said Thatcher patiently. "The man who can answer a few questions, and won't let anyone else."

"You're not going to make an appointment?"

"Not unless I have to. After all, Voronin left an hour before us. That's given him plenty of time to brief Durnovo, which is certainly what he's been doing."

Quentin started to shake his head, but thought better of it. "Anyway, the consulate isn't with Amtorg anymore."

"I thought they were sharing offices."

"They got too big. They've taken a brownstone of their own on Seventy-third Street."

Thatcher relayed the new instructions.

This driver was melancholy rather than choleric.

"Why not?" he asked sadly as he sped uptown. "Why not sell wheat to them Russians? They're human, aren't they? That's what I say. Anyway, it can't do no harm to anybody."

He was wrong.

How wrong they were soon to learn. As they swung east on Park Avenue, they encountered a crowd that was excessive even for New York lunchtime standards. A group of pickets waving placards was being herded across the street by mounted police, cars were screaming up to the curb to join the cluster of patrol cars and motorcycles.

"Can't get nearer," the cabby announced with gloomy pride as people nearby began to break into a run.

Thatcher paid him, roused the somnolent Quentin and began to struggle through the press. Even so, it took several minutes before he could make any headway and confirm a growing suspicion. The center of the disturbance was the anonymous brownstone which was his goal. But the density of the crowd made any further observation impossible. He paused for thought.

"I suppose it's not worth it," he grumbled, reluctant to give up at this point. "Whatever they have on their hands up there isn't going to leave them any time for our fishing expeditions. The only thing to do—"

His meditations were brought to a halt by a new arrival.

"Thatcher! Quentin!"

Detective Inspector Lyons was alighting from a squad car that had forced its way to the curb.

As Thatcher turned, he caught the word "murder" being passed around the crowd.

Lyons hurried to his side. "I'm glad you're here. You'd better come and take a look."

"We were just leaving," protested Thatcher, naturally recoiling from the detective's suggestion. "This isn't any of our business."

"It is, if the radio in that squad car was right," Lyons rejoined grimly.

Without further discussion they prepared to follow him. Quentin was moving like an automaton. Lyons' ID card brought them to the foot of the steps.

The door remained closed. But several men stood looking down at a body spread-eagled, face down, in a pool of blood.

"Shot," said somebody nearby. "Dead before he hit the ground."

Uniformed attendants with stretchers were moving through the crowd. Lyons knelt down with one of them and helped turn the body over, grimacing with distaste as his hand touched the sodden jacket.

The visored cap fell clear as the face came into view.

"Oh, my God!" said Victor Quentin in a sick voice.

Lyons nodded in macabre satisfaction.

"The radio wasn't wrong," he said harshly. "It's Gus Denger all right!"

4

. . . with a Grain of Salt

IT WAS TOO MUCH to hope that a violent murder on the steps of the Russian Consulate in the midst of New York City's lunch hour should not start political hares in the minds of television announcers reviewing the event. Particularly as the police release confined itself to identifying the victim and specifying the locale. The pundits of radio and television, with these bare bones, were swift to spy sinister political significance. The presence of New York City police outside the consulate at the time of the shooting was underlined, the small band of Ukrainian Nationalist pickets became a fiery uncontrollable mob bent on assault, and the name August Denger by some miracle of pronunciation was invested with heavy Slavic overtones.

After several early afternoon broadcasts in this tenor, the powerful minds at the State Department and in the Russian Embassy concluded that disclosure of the million-dollar theft would be, on the whole, less prejudicial to the Big Thaw than the continued excitement of Ukrainian passions.

"Because you can't tell how this thing will go," said Wright Dixon. "We have a lot of Ukrainians in this country."

Piotr Rostov lifted weary eyes. "There are quite a few in my country too," he pointed out. This was not irony but simply the transmission of information.

Dixon considered one of those complicated statements maintaining that New York has more Irish than Dublin, more Italians than Milan, more Jews than Tel Aviv, and more Ukrainians than whereever it was, but rejected the idea. There were more urgent problems at hand.

"Let's check this press release once more."

Accordingly the evening newspapers carried the entire story of the Sloan robbery, with full details on August Denger's role as pick-up and drop-off man. The murder was firmly attributed to Denger's criminal accomplices. Without actually misstating any of the few known facts, the release finally issued from Washington laid the whole affair at the door of gangland rivalry.

And what Washington doesn't know about stretching facts is scarcely worth knowing. So ingenious were the drafters of this document that it provoked a whistle of admiration from Charlie Trinkam.

"You have to hand it to them. Those boys haven't missed a trick, John."

"And not a single outright falsification," commented Thatcher.

Everett Gabler, the Sloan's oldest and most conservative trust officer, was rigid with indignation at this coupling of the Sloan to the Cosa Nostra. "It's outrageous. Surely we have some recourse."

"You can't let your feelings run away with you, Everett," Trinkam replied. "Look at the job they've done. They've even managed to bury the fact that he was shot twice with a pistol. It's somewhere in the middle of the biographical statistics. The general idea is that he was given the once-over with a tommy gun from a speeding car."

Thatcher leaned forward, his interest roused. "Biographical details? Where are they?"

"I've clipped them for you, Mr. Thatcher." Miss Corsa, not one to be diverted easily, was still trying to return to the dictation interrupted by the descent of Trinkam and Gabler.

But Gabler also had a one-track mind. "It may well be defamatory. We should consult our attorneys. Or release a statement ourselves. After all, this was a respectable theft."

Thatcher had long ago stopped trying to live up to Everett Gabler's high, if idiosyncratic, notions of propriety.

"There was nothing crude about it, I agree. And highly efficient. The most money for the least effort," he concurred.

"At least a word to the *Times*," said Gabler militantly.

"I'm afraid it would have to be a word to the State Department."

Charlie Trinkam grinned. "Well, you're going to have a chance. They're due here at four-thirty."

"That's all we need," Thatcher muttered absently as he perused the brief biography. "Denger seems to have led the life you'd expect. High school, Korea, milkman, United Parcel truck, then Halloran's Garage. Nothing there to tell anybody anything."

"Wait until tomorrow. They'll have him the righthand man to Capone."

Certainly by that evening, television had neatly reversed its position. The entire criminal sequence of theft and homicide was now admittedly home-brewed.

The general insistence on a "Made in USA" tag for the crimes was reflected on a more elevated plane by *Pravda*, which wanted to have its cake and eat it too. The crime was undoubtedly the result of America's well-known and flourishing criminal element—oh, undoubtedly—but its purpose was to embarrass the Soviet government. Displaying the egocentricity to which that venerable organ occasionally falls prey, the editorial firmly refused to believe that a million dollars could be sufficient motivation for the crimes.

> We are not deceived, nor are our readers. War-mongering elements in the United States, alarmed at the successful overtures of the peace-loving Soviet peoples, have turned to their natural allies, thugs and hooligans, to introduce division and

factionalism in the implementation of the great Soviet-American Trade Treaty. As a new dawn for a great concord of amity between these nations sheds its first golden light, militarist and materialist have joined hands to prolong the black night of dissension. They shall not prevail. The American people will not be confused by this transparent attempt to attribute an exclusively economic motive to these outrages. They will demand the identification of those social groups and class enemies . . .

"They don't know much about Americans," Thatcher muttered to himself over his breakfast coffee.

The article then went on to castigate the Ukrainian mobsters in front of the consulate and, perhaps fortunately, strayed into the quagmire of the Russian national problem.

The New York papers, however they may have bent to the wishes of the State Department in their own treatment of the story, had stuck to their guns and republished the *Pravda* article on their front pages—where it made very strange reading in the midst of articles bristling with references to the Brink's robbery and a gangland slaying in a hotel barber shop.

It was a copy of the *Times* which was spread out on Luke Stringfellow's desk when John Thatcher and Everett Gabler descended on the offices of Stringfellow & Son shortly after the opening of business.

Everett Gabler's protests at personal involvement had been overborne by Thatcher.

"If it's good enough for the Sloan, it's good enough for us."

Calls to Gabler's sense of service rarely failed. He had yielded, but he was still inclined to find fault and he was now inspecting Luke Stringfellow's milieu with a critical eye. The receptionist had passed them on to the inner office with a minimum of formality. Stringfellow himself was in shirt-sleeves, reading pertinent snatches of the paper to his secretary. She was sitting on the corner of the desk immersed in a tabloid. Both held cartons of vending machine coffee.

It was not the way Gabler liked clients of the Sloan to face the world.

Stringfellow hoisted his burly weight from his chair, looking doubtful. "You're Thatcher from the Sloan? Your office called and said you were on the way over. Of course, I expected someone as soon as I saw the paper. I can see you've got your problems, but so have I. What about my check? You can't blame us if . . ."

His voice trailed off as Thatcher, without attempting to stem the garrulous flow, simply reached into his pocket and produced the familiar buff slip. Laying it on the desk, he said:

"There. I think you'll find everything in order."

Stringfellow picked up the check and examined it admiringly. "Now how about that? I thought you were going to give me a hard time. But this is all right. I'll say one thing for the Sloan. They don't try and stick anyone else for their mistakes. I appreciate this, Thatcher, I really do. There's a big deal hanging fire, waiting for this. And I know a lot of banks would have had me running around in circles before they finally came through."

At his driest, Thatcher said: "You'll appreciate, Mr. Stringfellow, that it would be best if you paid this into your account or dealt with it personally at the bank. It will be a long time before anybody at the Sloan is casual about anything connected with these wheat shipments."

"Once burned, twice shy, eh!" Stringfellow exploded into laughter and turned to his secretary. "Say, Tessie, give Kay a call and ask her to bring in more coffee."

By the time the coffee arrived, their host's elation had subsided enough for Thatcher to return to business. "You understand that, while we have honored the letter of credit a second time, we are extremely anxious to get to the bottom of this affair."

"My God, I believe it! Almost a million dollars! It'd be a cold day in hell before I forgot anything like that."

"Exactly so."

"But say, why isn't Vic Quentin in on this? He was the one I really expected to see."

"Quentin is busy with the police. It seems safe to say that he'll stay that way for some time," Thatcher replied.

In spite of his physical bulk—he was a big man, in both height and weight—and in spite of the crew cut rigidly disciplining his coarse red hair, Stringfellow seemed very youthful as he alternated spontaneous outbursts of fleeting emotion with carefully conventional expressions of sympathy.

"Poor Vic! It's a damn shame! About the robbery of course. But t's even worse that it happened to Vic. Why, Tessie and I were just saying that he must know more about shipping documents than anyone else in the business."

"Yes, he's upset about it all," Thatcher said tersely.

Stringfellow detected no constraint in Thatcher's voice. He

shook his head in commiseration. "I remember when I took over this business from my dad about fifteen years ago. Every week practically, Vic would have me on the phone to straighten me out on some angle I'd overlooked."

Everett Gabler put down untasted coffee and introduced rigor to the exchange:

"You see, our immediate problem, Mr. Stringfellow, is to determine how much inside information was required to forge the documents," he said precisely.

"Yes, you'd have to have some, I can see that." Stringfellow paused to absorb the implications. "I guess this murder made me forget that. The papers are talking about a bunch of hoods. I suppose Denger was just a messenger, and he had to be shut up."

"Nobody seems to know. You've never heard of him before?" Thatcher asked.

"No. Who was he? Just some guy who worked for a garage, wasn't he?"

Thatcher decided the time had come for a calculated indiscretion. To a man the papers had been silent on the connection between August Denger and Abe Baranoff. It was impossible to say whether this was due to lack of knowledge, to soft-pedaling of the Russian connection, or to fancy footwork on the part of Baranoff's public relations men. But the more Stringfellow knew, the more likely he was to be of assistance.

"The garage was his formal employer. Actually he worked as private chauffeur to Abe Baranoff."

Stringfellow pursed his lips. "So that's the way the wind blows. Baranoff is the one who's always bringing over those Russian troupes, isn't he?"

"That's right."

"So he must have a lot of official Russian connections? Boy, this thing gets bigger and bigger."

"And murkier and murkier," agreed Thatcher. "But what we are particularly interested in is the Stringfellow invoice that accompanied the forged bill of lading. Perhaps you'd like to look at a photostat."

He produced it. Tessie was the first to comment.

"It's one of ours, all right, Luke. It's even a good imitation of your signature. I think it would fool me."

"The police experts say that it was traced. I suppose it wouldn't be difficult to get access to one of your signatures?" Thatcher asked.

"Don't see why. Aside from all the commercial paper I sign, almost anyone could write me a letter asking for some sort of a quote and get an answer with a signature. Say, the invoice is supposed to be in triplicate, isn't it?"

Thatcher nodded. "Yes, there were three copies all right. The others were just carbon copies. I didn't bother to bring them. But it suggests that someone had no difficulty laying hands on a supply of blank invoices from your firm."

Luke Stringfellow was quick to resent the suggestion of office laxity. "Now, wait a minute. We run a pretty tight shop here. I'm not saying a mastermind couldn't figure out a way to pinch some forms. But I don't see how he did it, off the top of my head."

"May I make a suggestion?" It was Everett Gabler's second contribution to the conversation.

"Yeah?"

"I noticed as we passed through your reception room that the young lady at the desk was typing something. She had a box of forms by her side. If she does typing for the office, I presume that she occasionally does invoice work."

Stringfellow shuffled uneasily. "Hell, I never thought about that. We don't have enough reception work to keep Kay busy. So she pitches in and helps out with odd jobs of typing."

"Including invoices?" Gabler was at his severest.

Stringfellow looked helplessly at his secretary. "Tessie assigns the office work."

"There's no sense in dodging it. Sure, she does invoices. Almost every day." Tessie was not apologizing for anything in her office management.

Before Gabler could comment, Thatcher intervened. It would be just as well if Everett were prevented from developing his impersonation of an MKVD interrogator. There was no point in putting Stringfellow's back up, particularly as Gabler's rigidity sprang not from suspicion but from personal affront at the entire situation.

"Then I think we can regard that as settled. The young lady would naturally be absent from her desk occasionally. Any steady visitor to your office could abstract some empty forms—if he were willing to wait a few weeks. But more than access to forms was required. You realize that the documents presented to the bank conformed exactly to the requirements of the letter of credit. And those requirements were rather unusual."

"I'll say they were." Stringfellow's hearty bonhomie had been replaced by a tough, workmanlike attention to detail. "Those consular certificates were a real joker. It took us almost a whole day to get one out of the commercial attaché. What was his name, Tessie?—Oh yes, Durnovo. The one with that suit—well, he didn't look like a communist to me. He insisted on going down to the docks too. Still, I see what you mean. Somebody had to know all about the deal."

"That was what I had in mind."

"It's not going to help you much, you know. This wheat deal was a big thing. Even after we got rid of the boys from Washington, the place was a madhouse. We had a whole bunch of giant conferences. Hell, we couldn't even use an office. We had to go to the Statler."

Thatcher had expected something like this. But it still could be helpful in narrowing things down. "And who attended these conferences?"

"Every wheat broker in the city, for a start," said Stringfellow firmly. "Then we had the big freight forwarders, the banks—Vic Quentin was there, by the way—the Atlantic steamship lines. And that's not mentioning a few odd men, like the grain elevators in Jersey, the elevators in Chicago, the railroad people."

"And all these people were in on all parts of the conference? I mean, were people concerned only with transshipment from Chicago to New York present at sessions concerning payment by the Russians and ocean shipment?"

A frown of concentration was accompanying Stringfellow's attempts to recollect the meetings. "Now there you've got me. Some Chicago people dropped out early, I remember. And—yeah, now wait a minute—some of this is coming back. That's right. We had to have a Russian interpreter when we hammered out this business about consular certificates. Vic Quentin will remember. The banks were there, and somebody from the consulate and a whole pack of Russian ships' officers. The man from the *Odessa Queen* was one of them. Not that it did much good when he doesn't speak English. Their interpreter is damn good, but it does slow things down."

The frown had been transferred to Thatcher. "I hadn't realized that the ships' captains were actually in on the conferences. I thought all that was being handled by the consulate."

"No, captains, too. Understand, only some of them were there. The ones who got over here early."

Thatcher's gloom was deepening. "We'll have to talk with the Captain of the *Odessa Queen* again. That will mean another round with the State Department, the Russian Navy, the Russian Embassy, and probably a conference in Geneva."

"No, it won't. I thought you realized. It's been forty-eight hours since I sent you the bill of lading."

"Realized what?"

Stringfellow spread his hands. "The *Odessa Queen* sailed yesterday."

5

Flailing About

THERE WAS A MOMENT of silence before Everett Gabler announced the obvious conclusion.

"Then, we have established one fact. The personnel of the *Odessa Queen* was informed about the details of the letter of credit. Now they are beyond the reach of questioning." He eyed the gathering sternly. "It seems incredible that they should have been allowed to decamp in this fashion."

Gabler's intractable sobriety sparked a demon of perversity in Thatcher.

"Not so incredible, when we recall that the entire purpose of the trade treaty was to have this wheat shipped as soon as possible, Everett. And remember, the State Department has made it perfectly clear they do not intend to let our troubles stand in their way."

"Now wait a minute," protested Stringfellow. "I don't want you two to get me wrong. The Captain was at some of our meetings. But how much he found out, I couldn't swear to. There's one thing we didn't discuss, I know for a fact, and that's the business of triple invoices. That's so commonplace no one would raise the point."

"Because everybody already knows it," Gabler argued.

"I don't want to disillusion you, Everett, but it will be a long time before I credit the slightest commercial knowledge to anyone in a naval uniform," Thatcher objected, mindful of his experience at the docks.

Stringfellow was undeflected by this exchange. "And there's another thing. No Russian has been hanging around my office with his hands free to snitch things from the reception room."

"Maybe we should reverse our tactics," suggested Thatcher. "I've been trying to find out the widest circle of people who might have known the details of your arrangements. What about the narrowest circle? Those who absolutely had to know? Besides the brokers and the banks, of course."

"Let's see." Stringfellow passed a hand over his stubble of red hair. "The big freight forwarders. You know, one of our problems was trying to synchronize the deliveries to Russian ships and American ships. The forwarders broke us down into subgroups based on our elevator holdings. One elevator, one subgroup. That's how they decided to handle it, and it's worked pretty well so far."

"And your subgroup?"

"Just Willard & Climpson and Stringfellow & Son. We two are the biggest single purchasers in the whole wheat deal."

"And I suppose each subgroup met for discussions?"

"With our bankers. Sure."

Thatcher's meditations on this point were interrupted by the buzz of the telephone. Stringfellow's face sharpened into joviality as he identified his caller.

"Hello . . . That you, Len? . . . How's the boy? . . . Yes, I was just going to call you. The check's come through. We can go ahead with the deal. . . . No, I'm expecting Yates. What about this afternoon? . . . What ? . . . Just a second."

He laid the receiver on the desk while he turned to consult his secretary. "You know that surveyor's report, Tessie? Len wants to know if the right of way is blocked in. What the hell is he talking about?"

"It's the Farquarson right of way. I went over it with him."

Stringfellow turned back to the phone. "Len . . . say, I've got some people here. Tessie's coming on. She knows all about it. Okay? . . . Yeah, that's right. See you this afternoon."

Thatcher was pleased to see the conversation cut short. Time was running out. But he was also interested to have received corroboration of the Stringfellow real estate purchase. He watched Tessie root out a folder from the filing cabinet before moving the phone to a side table and starting to speak about the surveyor's report with brusque competence. She was the kind of secretary he had come to associate with the Stringfellows of this world. Men who were specialist traders, buying and selling in large sums out of small, untidy offices; simple men who did one thing and did it quite well but needed a steady no-nonsense woman to run the office, manage the paper work, and listen to their domestic troubles.

Tessie must have been in her late thirties, Stringfellow about forty-five. Thatcher was willing to wager that Tessie had worked for him fifteen years, had called his wife by her first name for the past ten years, and would be as willing to arrange a Nevada divorce as a gala party to celebrate his twentieth wedding anniversary. With Luke Stringfellow she was friends, but it was to Stringfellow & Son that she was committed.

During this lull Stringfellow had gone to have a word with his receptionist. He now returned with a visitor, a dark-haired young man busy unbuttoning his topcoat.

"This is Dave Yates. John Thatcher, Everett Gabler from the Sloan. It's a good thing you dropped by, Dave. We're just trying to figure out who might have had the savvy to pull this forgery. You've read about it, haven't you?"

"First thing this morning," Yates nodded. "That's why I called in. Wanted to know if it was going to make any difference in how we handle things."

Stringfellow turned to the bankers. "Dave is a partner at Willard & Climpson. The brokers in our subgroup, you remember. He may be able to dredge up something I've forgotten."

Thatcher acknowledged the introduction and said:

"Before we go into that, let me answer Mr. Yates's question. There won't be any basic changes. But there will be a meeting of all the banks and brokers to tighten up procedures somewhat."

"I guess nobody can complain about that." Yates smiled diffidently. "This is my first big deal as a partner and I thought procedures were already complicated enough. But apparently not."

Stringfellow grinned at the younger man. "Don't let it throw you, Dave. You can spend your life in the grain business and not have this sort of thing happen again."

"You seem pretty chipper, Luke. I suppose this means that the bank hasn't made any . . . er . . . difficulties?"

Stringfellow's grin broadened. As Tessie took issue with the phone in the background, he produced the check and waved it aloft. "Right on the button."

"That's a relief," his colleague exhaled.

"Believe me, Dave, it isn't always this easy," said Stringfellow with a return to grimness. "But what the Sloan particularly wants to know is who knew all the shipping details besides the obvious people at the meetings."

Yates pulled at his lower lip reflectively. "That's hard to say. I'll tell you one thing, though. By the end of last week the chief longshoreman did. You remember, Luke, that day I came in to tell you that the *Odessa Queen* was loading and you called Quentin on it? Well, by that time Riccardi knew all the details. In fact," said the young man with a burst of frankness, "Riccardi was the only person at all helpful I could find on the docks."

On the basis of his limited experience, Thatcher could well believe the statement. But all he said was:

"You sound dubious, Mr. Yates. Don't you think this Riccardi is up to something as complex as these forgeries?"

"Oh, I expect he could manage it. No, it's the time I was thinking of. Most of the details sort of percolated down to him, bit by bit. I doubt if he had much information before last week. And these forgeries took a lot of time, didn't they?"

Everybody agreed they did. What's more, Luke Stringfellow was prepared to swear that the chief longshoreman had never been to the offices of Stringfellow & Son.

And that seemed to be that. Neither of the brokers had any further suggestions.

"After all," said Stringfellow, "you don't pass the time of day at the clubhouse bar describing letters of credit down to the last dotted 'i.' "

"That certainly wasn't much help," Gabler complained as he and Thatcher reviewed their findings in the taxicab. They were on their way uptown from Hanover Square to their next call—the Soviet Consulate.

Thatcher shook himself free of the reverie into which he had fallen. "No, it wasn't much help. It all comes down to the same thing. You can, by a vivid stretch of the imagination, picture freight forwarders and Russian naval captains and longshoremen pulling this fraud. But the natural suspects are the wheat brokers themselves and the banks with which they dealt—nothing alters that."

"If anything can be regarded as natural in a business conducted with such astonishing carelessness."

"Oh, come now. I daresay it might be possible to abstract a few blank letterheads from the Sloan."

Gabler's disapproving silence made it clear that it might be possible from John Thatcher's office, but certainly not from Everett Gabler's. In this, he did Miss Corsa an injustice.

Thatcher allowed a few moments for his companion's irritation to dissipate before returning to his chief concern.

"I hope you realize the reason I'm belaboring this point, Everett. It is because the New York City Police have two people in mind. Victor Quentin and Luke Stringfellow."

Gabler was in the habit of finding fault with everything. His colleagues were accustomed to his criticisms; very few of them had ever heard a word of commendation. But like most conservatives, once his back was to the wall, he was prepared to concede that his associates of long standing were, on the whole, not quite so unsatisfactory as the rest of the world. Now, he lost no time in making his position clear.

"Victor Quentin? That's out of the question! I've worked with him for twenty years. He may have been negligent. But dishonest? Never!"

"Then turn your mind to how we can persuade the police of that. And, as a starter, you might consider this point." Thatcher knew that he now had Gabler well and truly hooked. "We are agreed that the banks and brokers are suspect. But if a man were planning such a crime, wouldn't he avoid involving his own firm? Just so that he wouldn't immediately appear on Inspector Lyons' short list?"

"He would if he could. But the reason these men are suspect is because they have detailed inside information."

"That's why I was interested in this curious subgroup feature. As nearly as I can tell, Yates knows as much about Stringfellow's cargo as Stringfellow does. We're going to have to go into this in more detail with Quentin."

Gabler was eager to expand the list of suspects, but it was beyond his power not to raise objections.

"What about that call from Stringfellow to Quentin, the morning before that chauffeur turned up? That can't have been an accident. If it hadn't been made, Quentin probably would have checked back with Stringfellow."

"Didn't you hear what Yates said? He was with Stringfellow during the call. Or at least, one of them. And they seem to live in each other's offices. You heard Stringfellow say just now he was going over to Willard & Climpson."

"There may be something we don't know," Gabler said cautiously. "For instance, whether they had equal access to Russian forms."

"We can ask this attaché we're going to see," replied Thatcher as the cab drew up at their destination.

Aside from two policemen the sidewalk was bare. No demonstrators had put in an appearance this morning. Either they were afraid of being involved in a murder investigation, or they were put off by the possibility of another round of gunfire. Somebody might be taking potshots at anyone in front of the consulate. After all, this was New York. You couldn't tell what some people would do for kicks.

The receptionist was expecting them. Within moments they were being ushered into an office.

"Good morning, gentlemen. I am Sergei Pavlich Durnovo, commercial attaché seconded to the consulate. I believe you have already met my assistant, Feodor Voronin."

Durnovo was a tall, slim man with a suavity of manner that suggested the experienced and successful diplomat. He did not affect the rumpled, homespun look of lower-echelon Soviet officials. Sleek silver-gray hair was set off to advantage by the charcoal of his suit and the carefully matched greens of tie and handkerchief. Italian silk tailoring flowed smoothly as he punctiliously seated his guests.

After the introductions were completed, he began solemnly to convey a message from the consul. The rolling sentences unfolded into a statement which met even Gabler's high standards of formality. There were no shirt-sleeves or cardboard cups here.

Thatcher, armed with his morning's reading of the newspapers, was not surprised to find Durnovo passing from sorrow at the robbery (and shock at the murder) to a review of the Ukrainian problem.

"They are misguided. Yes. They are foolish. Yes," he said in slow march time. "But they are not murderers."

Apparently the Ukrainians, however apostate, were assured of a true loving socialist welcome if they would return to the fold.

"It is the passion of conviction with them. You must not judge them harshly. We understand them."

Thatcher yielded the point. Gravely he assured the company that he would not judge the Ukrainian Nationalists prematurely. He had come because he knew he could rely on the cooperative spirit of the consulate. He had no wish to involve the Soviet government in his travail; only a matter of detail required clarification.

"I am sure that you have heard the general outline of the forgery. We have already established that a blank letterhead was stolen from the wheat broker involved. I wonder if we could do the same for the consular certificate used."

He produced the certificate for inspection. Durnovo examined it slowly while Voronin bent over his shoulder.

"There is no question that the Consul's signature is a forgery. I have here a genuine specimen."

Thatcher had realized that they would insist on an acknowledgment of this point, whether or not he had already conceded it.

"Yes," he agreed politely. "The signature is a forgery. The seal too."

"As you say, the seal also."

"But the letterhead?"

Minutes passed. Everyone knew that the letterhead was genuine. The attaché had surely received very precise instructions on this point. But damaging admissions are not lightly made by great powers.

Slowly Durnovo rested elbows on the desk and steepled his long tapering fingers into a graceful arch. Light was reflected from the beautifully polished and shaped nails.

"On the basis of my inspection, the letterhead would appear to be genuine." He glanced down at the paper in his hands and frowned.

Everett Gabler was nodding approvingly. Suggestion and agreement were proceeding with the slow solemnity he relished. It occurred to Thatcher that Everett would make a fine Soviet foreign affairs officer.

"We understand that a number of the people taking part in these wheat sales have conferred with you here at the consulate. In your opinion, would it have been possible for them to abstract one or two of these letterheads?"

Another pause. Like Luke Stringfellow, Durnovo did not appreciate reflections on his office management. Suddenly Voronin whispered several sentences in Russian to his superior, whose face brightened.

"My assistant has reminded me of something I had forgotten. A Soviet delegation, including several of our captains and both of us, attended a conference at one of your hotels. The purpose of that meeting was to review Soviet requirements for documentation. As an illustration, we took a box of letterheads to the meeting. That would have been sometime last month, would it not, Feodor Ilyich?"

"Yes. I can give you the precise date." A pocket diary was flourished, and Feodor Voronin announced that the date had been February 2. Almost six weeks ago.

"And the letterheads could have been taken at that time?"

At a sign of assent from the attaché, Voronin expanded. "Very easily, I am afraid. Several copies were handed round—oh, five or six, I would say. But that is not all. It was a large meeting and during one of our pauses, the papers were left spread out on the table so that those in the back could examine them. At the end of the meeting, I collected the papers on the table. I think it would be impossible at this date to be more specific about who returned which paper."

Thatcher nodded. "Then it seems probable that the letterheads were taken there, rather than here."

"Yes," agreed Voronin. "Most of the brokers who have come here to the consulate have conferred with me in my office, and I assure you that they have not been left unattended at any time."

Thatcher accepted the statement without reservation. In fact, it was almost a pleasure to have one avenue closed. This seemed to be the only office connected with the entire far-flung transaction which had made any attempt to restrict the freedom of its visitors.

He turned away from the serious assistant, repressing the thought that civil servants look the same all over the world. Voronin could have been any forty-year-old employee of the Bureau of Weights and Measures.

"There is one further point. I don't suppose it will help us much, but there are a few lines of Russian typed at the top." Thatcher tapped the heading. "Are there any blunders in the language? Does it suggest that someone who knew no Russian used a dictionary carelessly?"

Durnovo was interested. He leaned forward almost eagerly. But in a moment he was shaking his head. "There is no room for pitfall here. You understand, these are not sentences. Only unconnected phrases. The name of the ship. The number of tons of wheat. The classification of the wheat. For what it is worth, the itemizations are all correct."

"Then I am afraid there is nothing further for us to do than thank you for your courtesy and for your time."

But Durnovo had fallen prey to abstraction. He roused himself and replied that the Soviet Consulate was willing to do everything in its power to identify and punish the miscreants. They were not unmindful of the loss suffered by the Sloan, or the signal contribution to world understanding inherent in the Sloan's immediate decision to honor its commitments.

"Indeed it is a lesson to men of good will everywhere."

And a damned expensive lesson, thought Thatcher, as Durnovo unwound toward his conclusion. For a diplomat, the fellow had seemed reasonably short-winded until now. Leave-takings probably brought out the lurking ambassador in all foreign service officers. Or was he talking for time? If so, nothing seemed to happen to make it worthwhile.

At the conclusion of the amenities, Thatcher reached for the forged consular certificate. Durnovo abruptly abandoned his public platform manner.

"I wonder if you would permit us, Mr. Thatcher, to photostat that document? Although I am afraid we have not been of much assistance this morning, it is possible that further examination might reveal something I have overlooked. Indeed, I am asking Feodor Ilyich to make further inquiries among our staff. And such a photostat would be helpful to him."

This seemed to be Voronin's first intimation of his new assignment, but he pulled himself together and looked decorously eager. Thatcher raised no objection. The photostating was accomplished in record time, and the Sloan party was bowing itself out when Durnovo's secretary delivered a message.

Inspector Lyons had called and suggested that Mr. Thatcher might wish to join him at Halloran's Garage when he completed his business at the consulate. There were new developments.

6

Keep Off the Grass!

INSPECTOR LYONS was waiting for them in Rita Halloran's office. He was looking pleased, in marked contrast to Thatcher's companion. Their trek northward had been enlivened by a return of Everett Gabler's fractiousness.

"I don't see what we can expect to accomplish by dashing around to garages, John. And to be honest with you, I hate to think of what Charlie may be up to—while you and I are out of touch."

One of the many burdens of Everett Gabler's life was the nominal superiority in rank enjoyed by Charlie Trinkam at the Sloan. During Thatcher's absences, Trinkam was acting head of the department and, according to Gabler, in strong need of a restraining influence.

The no-frills exterior of Halloran's Garage and its utilitarian premises did not allay Gabler's alarms. Thatcher had not expected them to; the blast of a hydraulic jack, the echoing clatter of tools, the begrimed mechanics staring incuriously were calculated neither to exorcise the specter of raffish Charlie Trinkam plunging the Trust Department—if not the entire bank—into chaos, nor to encourage the conviction that they were on a foray worthy of the Sloan. Field work would never be Everett's cup of tea.

"This is one of the largest car rental agencies in Manhattan, Everett," Thatcher offered in propitiation, as he forged his way to the rear of the building.

Gabler continued to register fastidious disapproval. Big money without the proper accessories left him untouched. The only two institutions ever known to have elicited his wholehearted approbation were the old Union Pacific (back in the days when a railroad was a railroad, by God!) and Du Pont. It was not to be expected that Halloran's Garage could compete in this company.

The introductions caused a further compression of his lips. Inspectors of the New York City Police Department rang no bells for Everett. In a better world, the Sloan would simply have been granted full police powers.

"We're waiting for Eddy," explained Inspector Lyons. "It seems that he's got something to tell us. Although he may be getting cold feet about it."

"Eddy is a fool," Rita Halloran said in a perfectly level voice.

Whether this remark pertained to Eddy's story or to his cold feet was not clear. Nor did the lady's tone encourage a search for clarification. Thatcher certainly felt no temptation to pursue the subject, and Gabler looked as if he had just sighted his first native in Basutoland and didn't like it.

But Lyons was made of sterner stuff.

"Not enough of a fool to skip, I hope," he said easily. "That could make trouble for everyone."

Rita Halloran looked at him unenthusiastically. "Don't worry, Inspector. He's just sneaked out for a pick-me-up. The boys will find him."

"Good! We all know how much this means to Halloran's Garage."

Mrs. Halloran's lips tightened.

"Don't waste your time painting me a picture, Lyons. I'm willing to play ball with you. Hell, I've got to! You can ruin me, and we both know it. But don't push it!"

"Nobody's done any pushing"—there was an artful pause—"yet."

"You don't have to. I've gotten enough bad publicity from Denger's murder and the Sloan robbery. Any more, and I can kiss good-bye to the good will of Halloran's Garage."

Lyons settled back more comfortably. "That would be a shame," he said.

Mrs. Halloran's eyes narrowed.

"It's not going to happen," she announced flatly. "I've spent too many years building this up to watch it go down the drain."

The Inspector was prevented from supplying further provocation by a head suddenly appearing in the hatchway.

"Eddy's here. He's right outside."

"Well, come on," called Mrs. Halloran peremptorily. "Come in, and let's get this over. I've got to get seven Caddies out for the Home Show crowd this afternoon."

Thatcher's recollection of Eddy was immediately refreshed. Small, ferret-faced and grimy, he hesitated in the doorway, avoiding Rita Halloran's eye. He ducked a shoulder in greeting to the rest of the assemblage before taking up his position, leaning against a battered filing cabinet.

Lyons nodded quietly. "Oh, I know you're busy. But then, we're all busy, what with the murder of one of your drivers and the big robbery he helped pull."

"That's a lot of—"

Realizing abruptly that she was playing the detective's game, Rita Halloran stopped in midstream and drew a deep breath. Her voice steadied and fell back into its normal register. "Now, just tell your story, Eddy."

Eddy, once again the focus of attention, ran a dirty hand down his shirt.

"I just thought it might mean something. After I read about that big haul and after they got Gus. Hell, I don't want to make trouble for the garage, or anything like that. I just thought . . ."

Without turning to look at him, Mrs. Halloran interrupted: "The garage is clean, and you know it. We all know it."

"Sure," Lyons agreed amiably.

For the first time Eddy and Rita looked directly at each other. It was an exchange of two troubled glances. They were both unnerved by the Inspector's reassurance. Eddy, in fact, started to edge backward.

"The story, Eddy," she reminded him remorselessly.

"Like I said, I thought it might mean something. So I told Rita and—"

"And I said we better call you, Lyons," Mrs. Halloran finished smoothly.

This simple statement deprived Eddy of what wits he had. He goggled speechlessly at his employer.

"That's fine. Now suppose we hear this story."

Eddy produced a crumpled pack of cigarettes from a shirt

pocket and struck a match. He drew a deep lungful of smoke before speaking.

Stripped of false starts, of broken sentences, of panicked silences, Eddy's story was short and simple. The day that Gus Denger was shot on the steps of the Russian Consulate, he and Eddy had slipped off for a mid-morning beer. (Here Eddy cast a frightened look at the sphinx-like Mrs. Halloran. If, as Thatcher suspected, beer during working hours was forbidden, there was more to Eddy than met the eye. Flouting one of Mrs. Halloran's rules was not something to be undertaken lightly.)

". . . and Gus, he says to me, he's got a good thing going. No . . . hell, no! He didn't have anything to do with the robbery—God, I'd swear to that on my last dollar. No, he's got something else—a little easy money coming his way. So I ask him if it's the horses, and he says no, it's a lot surer than that. So he makes this phone call, see?"

They all saw.

"Well, I been thinking about it, and I see the name in the papers . . . and we don't do no work for them, so why is Gus calling him? Hell, Rita, I thought it was the right thing to do . . ."

Thatcher had had a trying day, and he had no intention of straying again into the tangled relationship that seemed to obsess Eddy and Mrs. Halloran.

"Well, get on with it! Who did he call?"

Almost sullenly, Eddy ground out the cigarette under his heel.

"Stringfellow. This guy, Luke Stringfellow."

Thatcher saw Mrs. Halloran's lips move soundlessly. He wished he knew what she was saying.

Inspector Lyons had listened, without interruption or comment, to the broken narrative. Now he proceeded to take it apart, straighten it out, examine it from all angles and put it back together. He took Eddy backward and forward through his story, again and again, until the mechanic's eyes glazed, and he lost all awareness of his surroundings, even of Rita Halloran's measured appraisal. But though the words varied (Denger was first too "honest" to be in on the Sloan robbery, then too "chicken," and finally too "small-time"), and the details changed (the one beer had become two by the end of fifteen minutes), though Eddy produced some surprisingly ingenious speculations of his own, though he hemmed and hawed about what "a little easy money" might be in round numbers, the two basic facts remained un-altered. Denger had said that he was onto a good thing, and this had prompted him to place a call to Luke Stringfellow.

The question raised by these facts also remained constant. Was it this call to Stringfellow which had caused the shooting of Gus Denger some three hours later?

Finally Lyons was satisfied. "Okay. I guess that's all."

But Eddy, wound up like a top, couldn't leave it alone. "I just thought . . ."

"You thought!" remarked Rita Halloran with good-natured contempt. "From now on, you leave the thinking to me."

Somehow, peace had been tacitly established in the midst of that labored recital. Perhaps Rita had feared some disclosure which had not come. Certainly Eddy no longer feared mysterious reprisals. He sighed with immense relief.

"Sure, sure thing, Rita," he agreed eagerly.

Lyons, while missing nothing of the byplay, was not to be distracted from the central problem. "It's interesting," he summed up. "Denger knew something. He was keeping it under the rug, thinking he could parlay it into a roll, somehow." He looked mildly at Mrs. Halloran to see how she took the suggestion.

She was not as ready to leap to Denger's defense as Eddy had been. She was too busy defending her own interests. She paused for thought, before pronouncing judgment.

"Denger was no big-time crook. You heard his story yourself. Did it sound as if he thought he had a piece of a million dollars? Besides, my boys are bonded, and they get checked up and down the line. I'm not saying they don't like pickings. That's only natural. They see a lot of loose expense-account money floating around this business. The smart ones settle for tips on the market. With the rest, it's five bucks, maybe ten bucks, for keeping their mouths shut about something. Hell, what do you expect? You don't get plaster saints lining up for a job pushing hacks."

Shortly thereafter, Lyons, Thatcher, and Everett Gabler were adjourned in a small nearby cafeteria.

"What was going on back there?" asked Thatcher. "Between Eddy and Mrs. Halloran, I mean."

Lyons was amused.

"The old lady was sore because Eddy blabbed. The less she has to do with the papers or the police, the better, as far as she's concerned. But Eddy was big with his story and told someone. My bet is that he told his beer klatsch about it this morning. Anyway we got an anonymous call at Centre Street advising us to ask Eddy what Gus Denger told him the day he was shot. Then about an hour later, Rita Halloran called me."

"Hmm," Thatcher mused. "You might almost think she had something to hide."

"You might," Lyons agreed carefully. "A surprising number of people do. And if so, Eddy's in it with her. Eddy is her nephew, by the way. Or her husband's. He's got a stake in the garage, too."

"Of course, Eddy could be lying," Thatcher observed. "He's clearly not one of the world's truth tellers."

Lyons nodded. "Yes, but we've got confirmation of his story. The telephone at Tumulty's is at the bar, and old man Tumulty thinks he heard Gus making this call . . ."

Waspishly Gabler said, "Luke Stringfellow was most emphatic about not knowing this man Denger." He lofted a dripping tea bag and glared at it. "I suppose we are sure that it wasn't Luke Stringfellow himself who picked up that check."

"We aren't sure of anything, Everett," Thatcher said, exchanging a glance with Inspector Lyons. "But I certainly got the impression that Denger was telling us the truth about that when we talked to him. He said that he handed over that check to an essentially anonymous man—middle color, middle height, middle weight." He recalled Stringfellow's burly build, shock of red hair, and weather-beaten face. "And whatever else you can say about him, Luke Stringfellow is not anonymous looking."

"No, he certainly is not," said Gabler, making it sound like an accusation.

Lyons thoughtfully stirred his coffee and thoughtfully rose to Thatcher's bait. "You can bet that we'll be double checking on Luke Stringfellow. But I agree with you, Mr. Thatcher. I thought Denger was telling us the truth . . ."

"Then why was he calling Luke Stringfellow just before he was killed?" Gabler asked unanswerably.

They thought in silence while a busboy collected crockery and managed to remove Gabler's teacup before he was quite finished.

"There is something going on at that garage I don't understand," Thatcher said suddenly. "I didn't like Denger's smugness when we questioned him. And now we know he was hiding something. I don't understand what Mrs. Halloran is up to or what she's so furious about. And why is Eddy acting as guilty as if he had just murdered five people in a row? Somehow it all seems to center right there."

But even as he spoke Thatcher wondered if he was being fair. Halloran's Garage was, after all, in serious peril; the carriage trade does not hire limousines associated with robbery, with murder, or with the police. Fast deals do not flourish under official scrutiny.

On the other hand, a blue-ribbon livery would certainly provide an excellent opportunity for extralegal activities ranging from the transport of call girls to the dispatching of checks, Sloan checks, out of the country—fast.

No doubt Inspector Lyons would be investigating this as well.

"A very competent woman," said Thatcher as they prepared to leave.

"But not a lady," said Everett Gabler. "John, I do think it's high time that we got back down to the Sloan."

7

Not by Bread Alone

THE SLOAN to which they returned was scarcely the Sloan of Everett Gabler's fond recollections.

While they had been pettily preoccupied with the recovery of their money, more powerful intelligences were grappling with the international implications of the sordid tangle in which the Sloan had become enmeshed. The governments and agencies pursuing these investigations had varying goals; but they were united on one issue. The Sloan was not, by a puerile insistence on its commercial rights, to imperil the unexpected accord which had suddenly emerged between East and West.

George Lancer, after extended consultation with his own legal department and with almost every law firm on Wall Street, could see one small ray of hope. The Sloan might be able to pass off some of its loss onto the foreign bank representing the Soviet

Union. If so, the foreign bank might insist on penalizing its client.

"My God!" remonstrated the long distance line from Washington. "Do you want to play into the hands of the Chinese?"

Lancer, who occasionally wrote articles on international events for *Foreign Affairs,* hastily denied the charge. Hadn't he been one of the first to recommend exploitation of the Sino-Soviet rift? He was advised darkly to stay in the realm of theory and leave the implementation to the professionals.

Victor Quentin, finally managing to devote a few hours to his professional duties, succeeded in tracing the first check for $985,-000 when it came in for payment. Three telephone calls gave him further information. The check, he reported, had been paid into a Puerto Rican bank account and the funds immediately withdrawn to buy Mexican bearer bonds. Should he go further?

"No, no!" shrieked a voice from Washington. Any attempt to interfere with the liquidity or anonymity of Mexican bearer bonds would be regarded as provocation by the Organization of American States, and could constitute a death blow to the Alliance for Progress. Tactful inquiries on a government-to-government basis would naturally be made, but private intervention would only endanger the already delicate balance of interests in the Western Hemisphere. "Do you want to play right into the hands of Castro?"

Victor Quentin, as befitted his lower station, did not have George Lancer's pretensions to a statesmanlike view of the Sloan's international operations. He didn't care whose hands he played into if he got his money back and the police off his neck. But long and lively experience with Mexican bearer bonds led him to acquiesce in the Washington policy. For all practical purposes, the thieves and murderers now had $985,000—in cash.

At this point, an even humbler employee made an interesting discovery. The Sloan did not have the massive insurance portfolio affected by most industries. Banks do not expect to bear risks; they expect to fob them off onto their unfortunate customers. The only area in which they protect themselves heavily is that of the peculant employee. But young MacDonald thought it worthwhile to take a look. And amidst the lavish piles of certificates from bonding companies, richly crackling with their 100 per cent rag content, there reposed a rather unusual policy with Lloyd's of London—a testimonial to that firm's readiness to insure against bizarre risks. Hours passed as heavy legal case books were consulted. Yes, MacDonald thought, he rather thought, that just possibly there might be a chance. Inflamed at the prospect of solving a problem which had baffled mightier minds, he wrote a memo. Within hours his phone was jangling.

"Do you know what you're doing?" a voice sternly inquired. "Do you know that there's a by-election coming up in England?" The election, it developed, was going to turn largely on the question of the future of NATO, thereby giving the electorate of Little Puddingford a respite from the cares of Rhodesia. And NATO meant only one thing to Washington. "Do you want to play right into the hands of DeGaulle?"

Well no, now that the subject had been raised, young MacDonald did not want to play into the hands of DeGaulle. It had never occurred to him that they were on playing terms.

It has been given to few American institutions to become the involuntary ally of China, Cuba, and France within the space of a few days. The Sloan, ever willing to break new ground, might have sustained the role with fortitude. But Washington was not content to stymie all the bank's moves toward recovery; it insisted on reporting to the Sloan the results of its own efforts. Accordingly, almost every major officer of the Sloan was closeted with an emissary from some government agency.

And bank business ground to a halt as effectively as if Exchange Place had suffered a direct hit.

"Yes," said the man from the CIA to the directors' meeting especially invoked for his benefit, "I think we can assure you that this was not a plot on behalf of the Soviet government."

"But—" said someone at the table.

The CIA man raised a calming hand to quell the riotous relief evidenced by old Bridewell's polishing his glasses. "Of course, it's not final yet. We still have to receive verification from some of our sources. I don't want you to think we're being precipitate. But so far, we haven't raised a flicker of suspicion."

"These sources?" asked a doubting Thomas. "Do they know anything?"

"Some of them are assessed as being alpha reliable," was the dignified reproof. "I can't go further than that. It would not be in the national interest."

"That's all right with me," said the first director. "The whole point of this trade treaty was that the Soviet Union had lots of gold and no wheat. Doesn't make sense for them to endanger the delivery of wheat, in order to steal some money. Right?"

"You're trying to look at this as a simple commercial transaction."

"Well, it is a commercial transaction."

The CIA man smiled bitterly.

The FBI man didn't get the full board. He got Charlie Trinkam.

"Communism," he explained kindly, "isn't the simple thing a lot of Americans think it is. It's a worldwide conspiracy, and there are dissensions and failures of discipline there, just like every place else. We never thought your robbery was Russian inspired. We've had our eyes elsewhere."

Charlie Trinkam tried, without conspicuous success, to summon an appearance of decent interest. "Oh, where's that?"

"The New Left! You're surprised, huh? Sure, a lot of their money comes from the C.P., but to them Russia is just another great power. And they're against all great powers. They'd welcome the chance to throw a monkey wrench into the works."

"So that's what you've been doing, is it?"

The FBI man looked around cautiously before admitting: "Some of our best men have been at work in Berkeley for a long time now."

"And what do they say?"

"Not a peep about robbing the Sloan." He sighed heavily, then tightened his jaw. "There it is. You can't blink at facts."

The Internal Revenue was pleased to report that their investigation had failed to reveal any link between the Syndicate and the bank's loss.

Everett Gabler was sufficiently startled at the source of this information to break his seething silence.

"And would *you* know?"

The thin man across the desk permitted himself a restrained chuckle.

"We know more about their income than they do."

The Office of Foreign Commerce announced this was not a plot by other wheat-exporting nations, the Bank Examiners asked the Sloan to set an early date for a conference, the United States Navy offered to post guards at the Sloan for the duration of the wheat shipments, and every bank in New York wanted a careful run-down on exactly how the swindle had been worked.

And last but not least, Capitol Hill in the form of an old friend of Lancer's called to pass a veiled warning. The report on the theft now circulating in Washington had roused congressional interest. Lancer would be well-advised to leave a week free in his schedule to testify before the inevitable House investigation.

"What report?" Lancer growled resentfully. "For God's sake, how could anybody write a report at this stage? What did they do? List the conspiracies that aren't involved?"

"Well, there wasn't an awful lot of material," said his friend, "but they managed to spread it over thirty pages."

George Lancer went out for a drink.

John Putnam Thatcher had avoided the tidal wave by abandoning the premises. He was keeping his feet dry by fraternizing with yet another of the Sloan's dubious allies. Only Miss Corsa knew that he could be reached at Centre Street, in the office of Detective Inspector Philip Lyons.

Lyons had naturally lost no time in confronting Luke Stringfellow with the information extracted from Eddy at Halloran's Garage.

"Not that it got me anywhere," Lyons grumbled. "Stringfellow sticks to his story that he never heard of August Denger."

"You mean he denies the call was made?"

"No. That, at least, would tell us Stringfellow was lying. We've got definite confirmation of the call from Tumulty's Bar. It's less helpful than that. Stringfellow was out of the office, and says he never heard of Denger. The call was taken by that girl of his, Tessie Marcus. She told Denger that Stringfellow wasn't in and went through the usual routine about leaving a message. Then, as nearly as she can remember, he just told her to say that Gus Denger called."

Thatcher looked at the Inspector appraisingly.

"And do you think she's telling the truth?"

Lyons nodded. "Yes, I do. She's loyal to Stringfellow, but she's no fanatic on the subject. I doubt if she'd try to cover for him."

"Yet she didn't volunteer the information."

"She says she wanted to talk to Stringfellow first, which is reasonable enough under the circumstances. And she didn't get a chance, until after the murder was announced. Stringfellow didn't come back to the office until late in the day. Their story is that they were coming around to see me if I didn't get to them in the next day or two. Myself, I think they were a little more elastic than that. She decided she'd answer any questions, but she wouldn't take the initiative."

The Inspector's easy, measured judgments underlined the fact that he had spent a lifetime with cases of fraud and embezzlement, and knew a great deal about how innocent bystanders reacted when their testimony about friends and associates became critical.

But to Thatcher's alert ear, the judgments were a little too easy. By rights, the detective should now have been baying at full throat after Luke Stringfellow.

"There's something else, isn't there?" he asked. "Something that points away from Stringfellow?"

Lyons smiled his acknowledgment. "Yes, there is. I wanted to see how it sounded to you. Denger's last hours that morning seem pretty important. We've been over and over this with everybody at that garage. Calling Stringfellow wasn't Denger's only activity. He also called Baranoff's office and asked when Baranoff was due back in the States. Then he asked one of his shopmates if he knew what a certain brownstone on Seventy-third Street was. The guy can't remember the number now, but it was in the same block as the Russian Consulate. And they don't have any kind of sign outside. Then, if it means anything at all, Denger received a couple of calls at the garage. No one seems to know from whom. Does all this begin to add up to you? One point sticks out."

Thatcher frowned as he considered the information. Stringfellow . . . Baranoff . . . the Russian Consulate . . . of course! He leaned forward.

"But all this happened before there was any news release on the Sloan robbery! And we didn't tell him anything, when we questioned him. So he must have found out someplace else that the consulate was mixed up in this. And he was calling everybody involved. And Eddy said Denger was onto a good thing, didn't he?"

"We're thinking along the same lines." The Inspector was pleased. "He was trying to sell something. Our visit probably tipped him off to the value of his information. He may not have known how big a swindle it was, but once the Sloan and the police were on the scene, he knew it was big enough to be worth some money to him. Or, more money than he'd already gotten. So he started to call everybody in the picture."

Thatcher interrupted firmly. "Not everybody," he corrected. "He didn't call Victor Quentin."

"No, he didn't call Quentin." Lyons paused as if reaching a decision. "Look, Thatcher, there's no point beating around the bush. We both know that the two men in the driver's seat on this deal were Stringfellow and Quentin. It's only right that those are the two I'm looking at first."

"Of course it is," Thatcher agreed quickly. "The Sloan has every reason to be grateful for the thoroughness of your investigation. I suppose you've already gone into the question of alibis for Denger's murder. Quentin was with me, you recall, on the *Odessa Queen*."

"Oh, he's clear on the murder," Lyons conceded promptly. "So if the robbery was a one-man job, he should be okay on that too. Only thing is, there's no reason to say it was a one-man job."

Nor was there any reason to say it was not, Thatcher reflected. He decided to abandon the question of Victor Quentin's guilt and move a little farther from home.

"And Stringfellow?" he asked.

"Stringfellow of course was out of his office. That's why he didn't get Denger's call. All day, he was hopping from place to place. He ate lunch alone in a cafeteria uptown. There's at least an hour when he isn't covered. And I can tell you one thing. It's going to be the same for everybody we question. You know what lunch hour is like in New York. Unless there's a business meeting set up, people wander around."

Yes, Thatcher thought, that was probably why the murder took place then. Quite apart from the fact that Denger was unlikely to be able to go to the consulate except during his lunch hour.

Or did that assume the murder had to take place at the consulate?

He shook his head irritatedly at this circular reasoning and returned his attention to Lyons.

"I did get one piece of interesting information when I was checking into Stringfellow's movements," Lyons continued. "On the day the letter of credit was cashed, Stringfellow left his office for the day after telling his girl to call Quentin. He went over to Jersey to look at some property. So Quentin couldn't have checked back with him when Denger showed up, even if he'd wanted to."

Thatcher absorbed this item in silence.

"It works both ways," he finally pointed out. "If Stringfellow was guilty, he wouldn't want to be available. If he was innocent, then it was a great benefit to the guilty party to have him out of the way. Unless you can narrow down the number of people who knew he was going to New Jersey, it doesn't seem to be much help."

On this discouraging note, both men lapsed into their own thoughts. As he stared out the grimy window, Thatcher was reminded of David Yates's perpetual presence in the Stringfellow office. He had been there during the Quentin call. He probably knew about the trip to New Jersey. But it was idle to speculate with so little data. There might have been other people in the office. Anybody could have called and ascertained Stringfellow's absence. Someone could even have instigated the trip. The trouble was that there weren't enough facts.

"Do you know anything about Stringfellow?" he asked, pursuing this train. "His general background, I mean."

"Quite a bit." Lyons reached for a folder. "We've checked into Stringfellow and Quentin and Denger, so far. That is, we've checked their current position. We're not getting an awful lot of attention from Washington—as far as national records go." The Inspector's voice shaded into irony. "Not that it makes much difference with the first two. They've been doing the same thing for a long time. Quentin's been at the Sloan for over twenty years. He's lived in Scarsdale for over thirty years. Got a big house with the mortgage all paid up. He keeps talking about getting a smaller place now that his kids have grown up and married, but doesn't do anything about it. Let's see, they belong to the club and go there occasionally on Saturday night. Quentin golfs and has picked up quite a bit of business at the club. By and large, they live quietly and don't seem to have any trouble, either between themselves or with the kids. The only known debt is on one of the two cars they run. They seem to live well within their income."

Thatcher contented himself with a silent nod. He did not point out that, with a man in Quentin's position, the Sloan had its own system for being alerted to blatant overspending.

"Stringfellow's a little flashier. He inherited the business from his father and has been running it for fifteen years. He and his wife left the city twelve years ago. They've traded up on houses three times. Now, he's got a big place in Huntington and keeps a boat at the yacht club. They like to step out some. Two kids in high school, one in grade school. They've got mortgages on the house and boat, and are still financing two of their three cars. What's this?" Lyons peered in perplexity at the paper. "Oh, it must be one of those little foreign sports jobs. Probably the kid's car. Anyway he's getting a lot of mileage out of his income, but nothing beyond reason. My information about his income is from Quentin."

"Who knows what he's talking about, I'm sure. Well, all that sounds predictable enough. What about Denger?"

"Also predictable. Lived in a rooming house, passed his evenings in a tavern mostly. I managed to get hold of his brother. Seems he had a marriage that went sour a long time ago, no kids. According to the brother, most things did go sour for Denger, he was that kind. Liked to play the horses, liked the idea of easy money in general. But he had no big criminal ideas. Brother thinks he wouldn't have burned his fingers on this deal if he'd known how big it was. Just an ordinary small-time bum, maybe a little more surly than most."

Thatcher decided to enter an objection. "I realize that you have to look into people's financial position, but it isn't really relevant, is it?"

"How so?"

"Because this was a theft of almost a million dollars." Thatcher paused to emphasize his reasoning. "And nobody really *needs* a million dollars. You might discover some irregularity in the Stringfellow or Quentin background. They might have betting losses, they might be blackmailed, Stringfellow's business might be in trouble. But not to the tune of a million dollars. Neither of them could have gotten unsecured credit for that amount, in the first place."

Lyons nodded encouragingly, as if Thatcher were following some path he had already explored. "Blackmail?" he suggested. "A bank officer would be very vulnerable to that pressure."

"What kind?" Thatcher insisted. "If someone were blackmailing

Quentin on personal grounds—someone who didn't know anything at all about the wheat deal—he'd ask for forty or fifty thousand dollars. Quentin could raise that on his property. No blackmailer could expect him to raise a million dollars. If you're talking about a blackmailer who didn't want money from Quentin but wanted to use him as an accomplice in this theft, then you're talking about somebody who knew all about the wheat deal. That takes us right back to where we started—to another insider."

Lyons followed Thatcher's reasoning, step by step. Then, almost sheepishly, he said:

"There's another angle. It's what I always call the new life approach, people who want to get away from everything and start all over again. Sometimes that's set off by financial trouble. That's why I'm trying to get an idea about domestic backgrounds. If Stringfellow, for instance, was fed up with his wife and kids already, then his business was suddenly in the hole for fifty thousand —*that* might be enough to trigger him into trying for a new life in Brazil."

Thatcher was intrigued. "I hadn't thought about that," he confessed. "But it makes some sense. Now that I come to think of it, almost all the major coups that have been outright thefts—I don't mean the financial juggler spinning to keep himself alive—have been on your new life principle. Very few people, after all, are in a position to have a million dollars flow into an old life without raising a good many questions."

"I'm glad you agree." Lyons grinned broadly. "When it comes down to money, there's nobody I'd rather listen to than a banker."

8

Sowing the Wind

WITH THE SLOAN still smarting from a $985,000 theft, and with unknown sharpshooters littering bodies over the steps of the Russian Consulate, the entire situation could fairly be described, in Everett Gabler's terms, as a revolting muddle. It was only to be expected that the passing days should produce fresh convulsions.

What surprised John Putnam Thatcher was their nature; the last thing he expected to see introduced into an already roiling scene was a troupe of one hundred and twenty-two highly trained otters.

These otters were no ordinary otters, if various respectful but guarded press reports could be believed. Not for them the mere balancing of rubber balls on shapely noses, the disjointed tooting of childlike tunes.

No, these were Russian otters, fresh from a triumphal tour of Europe, quivering with eagerness to show American audiences that the genus *lutra* had nothing to learn from the Lippizaners. These otters could sing *The Volga Boatman,* dance a rousing mazurka, and assemble a three-stage rocket. Their leader, a strange otherworldly zealot named Plomsky, had devoted thirty years of his life to creating Plomsky's Otter Ensemble and was known in some circles as the Stanislavsky of aquatic mammals. He was also a Hero (Second Class) of the Soviet Union.

"Such otters," Abe Baranoff told the press on the chilly deck of the newly docked *Cristoforo Colombo,* "such otters America has been waiting for. They are artistry in motion, beauty of form, a not-to-be-believed grace . . ."

"For fish?" suggested somebody from the *Times* (who had already learned that Plomsky's Otter Ensemble had boarded the *Cristoforo Colombo* only after the Cunard Line had politely, but firmly, declined to place a first-class cabin at the company's disposal).

"Fish?" replied Baranoff, drawing a silk scarf against the icy wind whistling up the Hudson. "Fish for artists like this? Would we give fish to Callas? To Rubinstein? To Horowitz?" He brandished a malacca walking stick. "Tell them, maestro."

He inclined his majestic head as Plomsky commenced a detailed description of the sugar pellets used to coax prodigies of effort from his protégés.

"Soaked in champagne," added Baranoff grandly. He cared more for the spirit than the technique of the performing arts.

Pained, Plomsky protested.

"But no! Not champagne. Sometimes, when they are tired, a little vodka, yes! But champagne . . . no!" He resumed his lecture. "You understand, of course, that not every otter has it in him to become a Plomsky virtuoso. First, we must find unusually intelligent otters . . ."

With a lordly gesture that, in effect, dismissed Plomsky and the gifted otter, Baranoff gathered the journalists around him like a cape and began a proconsular stroll through the departing crush of passengers and porters, toward his cabin.

"In America, Plomsky's otters will swim in champagne!" he declared.

In a word, Abe Baranoff was back, and already busily working to insure full houses in Boston, Rochester, Dallas, and anywhere else Plomsky's Otter Ensemble was booked. A practiced impresario, he brought to bear the tools that had worked so successfully with the Anatolian Puppet Theater, Grimya Pelaguin, the noted Peruvian counter-bass, the Upsala Boys Choir, and the many other cultural and artistic events introduced to an eager American public for well over forty years under the banner: "Abe Baranoff Presents . . ."

Besides being time-tested, his method was simple. First, he provided a tantalizing glimpse of his stars (to a photographer from *Life,* if possible). Then he gave vivid, and sometimes accurate, descriptions of mad opening nights in Madrid, Rome, and London. Then last, but by no means least, he would lead the whole group to his cabin, where today he seriously incommoded secretaries, assistants, and the functionaries of the *Cristoforo Colombo* by insisting that champagne and brandy be produced for his good friends, the ladies and gentlemen of the press. Since Abe Baranoff tipped, as one steward put it, like a Grand Duke at Monaco in 1908, he got what he wanted.

"Ah, little did I think when I was a small boy in Omsk that one day I—Abe Baranoff—would have the privilege of introducing this great ensemble of Russian artists to America," he confided, settling himself next to the *Daily News.* Baranoff was a great believer in the personal touch and did not intend to let Plomsky and the otters upstage him. "A childhood dream come true."

The *Daily News* was sipping Piper-Heidsieck with other goals in mind.

"Abe, did you cut your European trip short because this chauffeur of yours was involved in the Sloan robbery?"

Abe Baranoff was wounded. Magnificent eyes under overhanging brows became infinitely sad.

"What does Baranoff have to do with bankers?" he said. "Bankers, always bankers. Ah, if my mother—who starved to buy me a violin—if she should know. But, at least God has let me play my small part, although I could never be a great artist. I have helped bring the finest talents of our times to America. And today, I am bringing Plomsky's Otter Ensemble—that is why I am back! I know nothing of robberies . . . yes, what is it?"

This last was directed to the slim, pallid aide-de-camp hovering nearby with a sheaf of cables. Silently the underling handed Baranoff the papers. The impresario sighed deeply, then produced glasses from a pocket, affixed them, and with lightning rapidity riffled through the sheaf, meanwhile dictating replies.

". . . no answer to this . . . send this to Weinstein and tell him to get an estimate . . . tell Myra to make me an appointment. . . . My God! Who does this swine think he's dealing with? I said ten per cent, and I'm not going one penny higher . . ."

After making a few notes, the young man retrieved the papers and disappeared.

"Business, always business. It pursues me," said Baranoff, removing his glasses and holding out his hand for more champagne. "Ah, if Mother could see this, her heart would break. Now, what was I saying?"

"You were saying," said the *Daily News* with a straight face, "that your interest is centered on otters—not on the chauffeur of yours who got shot."

"Ah!" Was this a tribute to the champagne, or to something else? "Ah, such otters! My friend, when you see them your heart will quiver . . ."

He rose and moved off, to give *Time* a revealing glimpse into the heart of a great artist *manqué*.

After he had completed his circuit and his confidences, Abe Baranoff donned a billowing coat, lofted his walking stick, and prepared to debark from the *Cristoforo Colombo,* still touting the brio of Plomsky's otters.

(His entourage managed the usual leave-taking amenities: "Always nice to have Mr. Baranoff with us," the cabin steward said obsequiously.

The pale young man, who was charged with distributing largesse, smiled humorlessly. "Isn't it?")

But ashore, things proved to be different. The press swooping down on the Baranoff party here had not been hand-picked by Baranoff's very wily press agent. And of course, they had not spent the preceding twenty minutes drinking champagne.

"Hey, Abe, what about this driver . . . ?"

"Baranoff, got anything to say about the robbery?"

"Pete, get a picture of them here . . ."

The press agent, alerted by a minatory look from Baranoff, forged his way to the head of the group.

"Gentlemen please, we're here to introduce a great company of performers . . ."

The gentlemen merely continued to howl.

"The world is too much with us," murmured Baranoff tragically in *The New Yorker*'s ear.

Little did he know. More important forces were conspiring to distress Abe Baranoff. They were lying in ambush at the Customs Office. Within twenty minutes his accent had deepened, and shifted from vaguely French to wildly Mittel-Europa. In thirty minutes, Abe Baranoff was, to put it baldly, screaming:

"Quarantine! What nonsense is this! I have a letter of clearance from the American Ambassador! I have certificates of vaccination . . ."

A meaty-faced official gazed at Baranoff's long hair with mild dislike and repeated something about regulations.

"Regulations! What regulations? I'll call my Senator! I'll call the White House! George, you dummy! Why are you standing there! Get me Weinstein! Get Mulloy! What do I pay these lawyers for when they're not here when I need them? Regulations! We'll see . . ."

The ensuing uproar did not alarm Baranoff's retinue, all too accustomed to angry cries for lawyers. The customs officials, who had dealt with the furor when Baranoff brought seventy-two Lapland reindeer to America (for a Christmas spectacular), stared into space.

"They can't do this to me!" Baranoff howled, speeding George to a telephone for legal reinforcements. The press, except for those who knew Baranoff well enough to review his performance without seeing it, scribbled furiously.

"Assassins! Cossacks! Bureaucrats! The curse of my life! All I want to do is bring beauty and art into our country . . . and this!" With a gesture worthy of a nineteenth-century Hamlet, he placed a manicured hand on his heart. "And for this, I am persecuted."

The customs officials not only had the imperturbability of civil servants; they had coped earlier with a middle-aged Idaho lady trying to smuggle four Florentine leather purses in her corset. They watched Baranoff impassively.

"These otters," he told them vibrantly, "have performed before all the crowned heads of Europe."

Grigori Plomsky gave an anguished yelp.

"Now what?" Baranoff demanded, goaded beyond endurance by human folly.

"Crowned heads?" Plomsky said. "Baranoff, are you trying to kill me?"

Baranoff was nettled. "Kill you? Listen Plomsky, leave these details to me. Let Abe Baranoff take care of you as he has taken care of the Astrakhan Folk Ballet . . ."

But the dread specter of royalism had touched Plomsky on the raw. Moreover he was not a mindless ballet master. To some, otters might be non-ideological, but not to Grigori Plomsky, artist and intellectual. He stood up.

"I want to see my consul," he announced. "This confusion . . ."

"Viper!" shouted Baranoff.

"Viper, perhaps," said Plomsky with dignity. "Revisionist, no. I want my consul!"

Baranoff hurled himself into a torrent of invective. Remaining aloof, Plomsky folded his arms, stared over Baranoff's head, and maintained a cold silence.

"Stabbed in the back," said Baranoff brokenly. "Always stabbed in the back!"

But despite being stabbed in the back, Baranoff was constitutionally incapable of emulating the silence of Plomsky and the customs officials; he must talk. Accordingly the press finally managed to divert the Niagara of his eloquence from otters to matters of greater interest to the newspaper reading public of New York, including John Putnam Thatcher.

"Denger? What should I know of Denger? No, I gave him no orders to pick up papers . . ."

"What was he like, Abe?" somebody yelled.

"What was he like?" Baranoff repeated, his imagination fired. At his elbow, the press agent spoke urgently. "Be careful? Why should I be careful? No, I, Abe Baranoff knew this man. I understand such men as he. . . ."

He lowered his head in ponderous thought.

"Denger was . . . not ordinary."

A groan went up from the assembly, and the customs men began inspecting their watches.

"Ah, you do not understand," Baranoff declaimed. "One had to look beneath the surface. He was not an artist, no. There was no music in his soul. And that an artist is born with or he is . . . he is nothing."

The press stirred restively. They had all been exposed to the Baranoff theory of soul music. Ever sensitive, the showman realized he was losing his audience. Hastily he shifted gears.

"But still, he had something. He had the thoughts, but he could not put them into practice. It is the tragedy of so many." Here the great figure drooped in a pantomime of suffering. "And so he was frustrated. By the knowledge that he was a failure. By the sight of others who were not."

It was clear to everybody who was the biggest success in Denger's immediate circle.

"Could he plot a big crime?" somebody shouted.

"He could plot; he could not plot well. I understand them, the failures." The arms swept out in a dangerous gesture designed to embrace the failures of the world.

"Listen, Abe, lay off this!" his press agent pleaded, anticipating Weinstein. But Abe Baranoff was caught up by his own performance. When someone asked what he and Denger had talked about, he had his lines ready.

"What do they all talk to me about? Their hopes, their fears, their hidden dreams. Ah, the pathos of it! The dreams of little men!"

"Why was he shot?"

"Who knows? Something in his own miserable life. But nothing to do with me . . ."—and here an idea visibly came to Baranoff—"and nothing to do with the great Russian nation. A people with a profound and reverent esteem for the arts . . ."

In the corner, Plomsky's head went up slightly.

"Abe, did you know Luke Stringfellow?"

Cut off in midstream in his observations about the culture-loving nature of the Slav, Baranoff was momentarily off balance. With a quick look at his press agent, he said:

"Luke Stringfellow? Who is Luke Stringfellow? I have never heard of him . . . Ah, Weinstein, at last! About this quarantine! You must do something!"

Weinstein, who looked depressed, managed to do one thing at least; he put a speedy end to Abe Baranoff's public utterances.

"Hmm," said John Putnam Thatcher, finishing a rather tidied-up version of the scene in that evening's paper. "Of course, the question is whether or not Baranoff knows the difference between fact and fiction."

Everett Gabler, who was in Thatcher's office on quite another matter, was torn between personal dislike for anybody photographed in a fur-trimmed coat and a certain decent respect for substance.

"He does have that string of theaters," he said unwillingly. "And God knows how much real estate, in one holding company or another."

"True," said Thatcher idly, letting his ever active imagination play with the possibility of dispatching Everett to Plomsky's Otter Ensemble. "Still, it's hard to believe that anybody who waxes lyrical about otters is a good judge of men. Think of those unbelievable books. But Baranoff probably was right about Denger . . ."

To his surprise he had touched a chord.

"These otters are quite remarkable from what I hear," said Gabler, gathering up papers preparatory to departure. "I understand that it takes years to train them. Fascinating."

Thatcher watched him leave in some mystification. He had forgotten Everett Gabler's enthusiasm for animals, if not for human beings. He buzzed Miss Corsa.

"Miss Corsa, I think I'd better talk with Abe Baranoff. Will you try to make an appointment for me? I don't know exactly where you can get in touch with him . . ."

Miss Corsa received these instructions with calm.

"They are having a terrible time about those otters," she informed him. "Temporarily they have to keep them on Ellis Island. I'll try there first."

Since Miss Corsa was conspicuously not interested in animals, this could only mean that, not for the first time, she had anticipated him.

"In the meantime . . ." he began slyly.

"I've got the forged documents here for you to look at again," she replied.

He recognized defeat when he saw it.

"Thank you, Miss Corsa."

9

Cover Crop

TRACKING DOWN ABE BARANOFF was not easy, but it was naturally well within Miss Corsa's powers. Her step-by-step campaign promised to last most of the day, however, with some of the minor engagements fought under Thatcher's eye after she started taking dictation during the lulls. Fascinated, he overheard her converse with informants backstage at the Metropolitan Opera (even across the desk he was exposed to the vibrations of a *Heldentenor* limbering up), and the administrative offices of the Bronx Zoo (strange grunts and yips suggesting that their offices were livelier than most), and at the Fulton Fish Market (still stranger grunts and yips).

When the phone next rang, Thatcher expected another report from Miss Corsa's intelligence network, but she turned to him and murmured:

"Mr. Voronin of the Russian Consulate would like to speak with you."

Foreign names did not provoke in Miss Corsa the half-hesitations and false starts of the self-doubter. She simply decided how she was going to pronounce them, then did so firmly and swiftly. She might be wrong, but she was never embarrassed.

Voronin, while wrapping the matter in courtesies, wanted Thatcher to come up to the consulate and was unwilling to say why. Thatcher did his bit for world peace by agreeing to go immediately.

In the taxi, he surrendered himself to speculation. Voronin was the subordinate assigned to further investigation of the forged consular certificate. Obviously he had come up with something. Thatcher was not such an innocent as to think that Voronin had promptly reached for the phone to tell the Sloan all about it. There must have been a session among the reigning powers at the consulate; they had decided on this action.

In other words, what Voronin had discovered was hot enough to require transmission to the Americans. On the other hand, the consulate did not wish to attach to it the importance that would surround participation by either the Consul himself or Durnovo, the commercial attaché. So the scene had been laid for a casual, underplayed approach.

Just how casual, he had not bargained for.

When Thatcher presented himself at the receptionist's desk, there stood the commercial attaché, Sergei Durnovo. He was staring at an envelope he had picked up from the desk. His surprised recognition of Thatcher was masterful.

"Mr. Thatcher! What an unexpected pleasure! I did not know you were to visit us today."

Thatcher had too often pulled the same trick himself—who has not?—to be taken in. But he was perfectly prepared to play the game.

"Yes, I received a call from Mr. Voronin. I'm on my way to see him now."

An elegant frown flitted over the high, domed brow. The smooth silver hair added the suggestion of statesmanlike concern.

"Ah, yes, he was looking into the question of those forged certificates, wasn't he?"

Without a quiver, Thatcher agreed.

"Allow me to show you the way to his office. It is just down the corridor from mine."

Durnovo indicated the way to the stairwell and fell into step beside Thatcher. The abandoned envelope fluttered back to the desk.

"I believe that Feodor Ilyich did say he had uncovered something that might interest you. We are naturally anxious to inform you promptly of any little fact we unearth, no matter how insignificant. We are so unversed in your tortuous ways of finance that you must excuse us if we trouble you with trifles."

Thatcher confessed he was without sufficient words to express his unbounded sense of obligation. Then he waited to see if there was more to come.

There was.

"Naturally," murmured Durnovo gently, "had we dreamed of these official seals being put to improper use, we would never have exposed them to any casual passerby walking in from the streets. Now, of course, we will take more rigorous precautions. It is, I am afraid, another case of locking the stable after the horse has been stolen."

Durnovo had oiled his way silkily to Thatcher's destination and now, with one last beautiful smile, delivered him into the hands of Voronin's secretary.

While the intercom was being brought to life, Thatcher reviewed the points made by the commercial attaché so casually.

First, whatever Voronin had learned was insignificant to the point of triviality. Second, the seal, which had obviously been found in some Soviet purlieu, had been used for the forgery by someone who wandered in off the street. (And who wanders in off an American street? An American!) Three, the Soviet personnel stationed in New York were such lambs in the jungles of American finance that they could barely understand its complexity, let alone bring off brilliant strokes of fraud. (And what an admission *that* was from a commercial attaché who had probably cut his eye teeth on letters of credit!)

That was a lot of information to pack into a charming two-minute chat. Thatcher decided that Sergei Durnovo's professional eminence was indeed well earned.

Meanwhile the intercom had produced not only Voronin, but a visitor he was ushering out.

"You made excellent time in the traffic, Mr. Thatcher," he commented. "I don't know whether you know Miss Marcus."

Thatcher recognized Luke Stringfellow's Tessie, as she greeted him staidly.

"Luke is getting ready to load a second boat," she announced. "Mr. Voronin and I have been going over the papers."

"You can understand our concern, Mr. Thatcher," said the Russian. "There will be no mistakes in the papers this time."

"Well, there weren't any last time. Not in the real papers. God knows we spent enough time working out the details. And much good it did us," Tessie ended grimly.

Thatcher examined Stringfellow's secretary with interest. Her manner might be as brusque as ever, she might be cooperating with Inspector Lyons, but she could not hide the fact that nobody at Stringfellow & Son was relaxing until official suspicion ceased to center on Luke Stringfellow.

"I don't think you'll have any trouble with your second ship," he promised her. "The Sloan's only interest is in seeing that the remaining deliveries go through as normally as possible."

"That's what we're all hoping," said Tessie as she picked up her plastic portfolio and departed.

Voronin came straight to the point.

"I've discovered an interesting fact, Mr. Thatcher. Perhaps it isn't important enough to justify disturbing you, but we would like you to have all the information that is available to us."

Thatcher expressed appreciation and concluded that Voronin was ignorant of Durnovo's end play.

"It's about the seal. You recall we agreed that it wasn't the consulate seal."

Suddenly Thatcher recalled more than that. He remembered how Durnovo, after examining the seal, had become absent-minded and then suddenly wanted a photostat.

"Yes?"

"Although the seal was not from this consulate, it did have characteristics which were familiar. So I have been checking the seals and stamps in use by Soviet agencies in this city—the Intourist Agency, Amtorg, our office at the U.N."

"What an excellent idea," said Thatcher.

"Of course if the seal had been in use any length of time, we would have recognized it. But it turned out to be comparatively new."

"Then you succeeded in locating it?"

Voronin nodded. "Oh, yes. Some months ago we opened a permanent trade show in New York, primarily to display Soviet-produced articles. A small section, however, operates as a store. Purchases can be made only for delivery to individuals in the U.S.S.R."

"I remember. It's somewhere on Fifth Avenue, isn't it?"

"Yes, near Fifty-third Street. I have already spoken with the manager by telephone, and he cannot explain the use of their stamp," Voronin continued. "However, as it is only used to indicate that the processing of an order is completed, there is no elaborate security procedure. I am about to go to the store and inquire further. Perhaps you would care to accompany me?"

When Thatcher said he would be delighted as well as interested, it was no mere civility. If his days and nights were going to revolve around Russian-American trade treaties (and the attitude of both governments to the Sloan's little embarrassment suggested that the wheat deal was the first of many), then he might as well familiarize himself with the Soviet agencies in New York.

On Fifth Avenue they were greeted by a delegation of two—the manager and the vivacious young brunette who had been the one bright spot in Thatcher's visit to the *Odessa Queen.*

"We shall do everything we can to help," the manager assured them. "Everyone on our staff speaks some English, but only those on the floor of the store are fluent. Katerina Ivanovna will be available as an interpreter when you speak with the office staff."

Voronin interrupted. "But will it be necessary to speak with the office? I thought the stamp was used by the clerk taking the order?"

"It is not quite that simple. You understand our operations have become rather more complex than we had anticipated. Let me show you."

The manager led them down an aisle flanked by large pieces of machinery, bristling with cogwheels, levers, and oversized tires. Labels identified these industrial items as: "grinders," "lathes," "drop presses," and other objects rarely seen on Fifth Avenue. As they progressed to the back of the store, however, the atmosphere became more familiar and the goods smaller. Here, under a sign that said "For Sale" were clerks, instead of engineering consultants, and display cases of watches, sewing machines, radios, toys, and bicycles.

The manager halted at a case filled with cameras. Picking up a small 35-millimeter model, he continued:

"Suppose a customer wishes to buy one of these cameras. The order, of course, will be filled from stock in Moscow and delivered in the Soviet Union."

"Very rapidly," interjected the smiling clerk, obviously a born salesman. "On this model, which is extremely popular, we have been making delivery in under a month."

The manager waved away this ill-timed enthusiasm. "Yes, yes. In the procedure we originally set up with the consulate, the customer would have made payment and the clerk would have stamped the order. But two problems have arisen. On our more popular items, the Moscow inventory may be temporarily exhausted. This was particularly troublesome last fall when everyone wanted delivery for Christmas. Then another problem arose." He turned apologetically to Thatcher. "Most of our customers have relatives in the Soviet Union and are sending presents. But occasionally we wonder how much they know about their relatives! We have had addresses that turn out to be in Turkish Armenia, or in

Finland. And, as for Poland! Of course, we realize that the last fifty years have been eventful for Poland, but you would think they would know what country their sister is living in. Then, we have Americans who wander in, who seem to think that all of Eastern Europe is part of the Soviet Union. It makes things very difficult."

Thatcher and Voronin nodded their sympathy to these geographic woes.

The manager continued:

"It has, therefore, become necessary to verify the addresses our customers give us. The sales clerk takes care of the obvious ones, like Prague, but all others go to the office. Under our new system, therefore, the order goes back to the office, where it is cleared by the inventory clerk and by the address clerk, before it is stamped with the seal. Only then can the salesman accept the order and take the money."

Voronin's face had been falling steadily during this recital. It was apparent to Thatcher what had happened. Durnovo and Voronin had seen the original procedures calling for stamps in the front of the store. The consulate, when it made its discovery about the provenance of the stamp, had assumed that a stamp could be stolen, or at least used, by any customer who wandered in. But the change in procedure since adopted made this impossible. Access to the stamps now rested with the office staff—all Russians.

So much for Durnovo's tactics!

"I hope I have made it clear," the manager asked anxiously.

"Extremely." Voronin paused, trying to make the best of a bad bargain. "I think the next thing for us to do is locate these stamps in the offices."

The manager led the way. Thatcher was not surprised to find Voronin pulling ahead for a quick Russian conversation with the manager, leaving Thatcher to bring up the rear with Katerina Ivanovna.

"I am afraid our robbery is adding considerably to your duties," Thatcher said to her.

She smiled at him with a shade of mischief. "I know the robbery is a great misfortune and, of course, I am sincerely sorry. But it has made my work much more interesting. I am seeing so many places that I would otherwise not have seen."

"That is true for me too," he said appreciatively. "I would not have come to this display without the robbery."

"And I would not have visited the docks."

"And I would not have met Captain Kurnatovsky."

Katerina laughed as she recalled the festivities aboard the *Odessa Queen.*

The next hour was spent in following the route of order slips and stamps. Voronin was more morose than ever when they finally reemerged to the display room and came to rest by a pile of paid orders waiting to be pouched and shipped.

"And this is the end," announced the manager. "At this point, our duties are completed."

Voronin sighed. "It has all been most instructive," he said heavily as he picked up an order form and looked at it with distaste.

Thatcher knew that the man from the consulate did not wish to discuss their obvious findings here. Tactfully he disassociated himself from the final exchange and idly leafed through the orders, looking at the addresses. Ekaterinburg, Kazan, Vladivostok, Irkutsk, Smolensk. . . . It all sounded very romantic. Orenburg . . . shades of the Trans-Siberian Railroad.

Suddenly alerted, he looked at the order more closely. No, it wasn't Orenburg that had caught his attention. It was the customer's name.

David Yates.

Could it be? It must be. It would be too big a coincidence to have another David Yates on the scene.

There might, of course, be some perfectly innocent reason for Yates to be sending a record player to K. I. Ogareva in Orenburg. For all Thatcher knew, Yates was married to a Russian and sending presents to his in-laws. Or even simpler, he was making a gesture of appreciation to a business colleague. After all, Yates must have met a good many Russians in the course of negotiating his share of the wheat deal. He might merely be doing errands for Willard & Climpson. But, still, it was interesting, very interesting, to have found a wheat broker in the vicinity of the misused Russian seal.

Thatcher roused himself to thank the store manager for his courtesy. A round of farewells, during which Katerina dimpled roguishly at the visitors, released Thatcher and Voronin to the sidewalk where they eyed each other cautiously.

"I think we should discuss what we have learned," said Voronin.

Thatcher looked at his watch.

"Then let's do it over lunch," he suggested. To his surprise, Voronin agreed. Thatcher had expected a return to the consulate and a briefing session with superiors to precede any discussion. But he had underrated his man. Feodor Ilyich recognized that briefing sessions were fine, when they could serve to regulate the flow of information. But once the cat was out of the bag, facts had to be faced.

"I know what you are thinking," he said over his salmon after they had been served. "Naturally, you suspect an employee of the trade display. But for my part, I am thoroughly bewildered. I do not see how anyone connected with that store could have obtained detailed information about the wheat sales."

"Yes," Thatcher agreed. "I reached that stumbling block too. The one thing we know is that the forgeries were too accurate to be the work of an outsider."

Voronin showed his relief. He had thought he would have to fight for this point. "Did you hear me ask the manager when they changed their system? He said it was during the beginning of their rush, last October."

It was Thatcher's turn to frown. "About six months ago. Hmm? That's a long time, but it's not impossible. It was before the meetings during which your consulate letterheads were probably taken."

"Exactly. Months before."

"So if it was done then," Thatcher mused aloud, "the store's seal must have been stolen outright. It wasn't a simple question of using it for a moment, because the thief didn't have the letterheads yet. Did you ask the manager if they were missing a stamp?"

"No, I did not." Voronin shook his head. "You understand, I would prefer to have the Consul decide how rigorous an investigation he wants. You saw for yourself that there seemed to be many stamps lying around."

"If it's like most offices, it will turn out that three or four stamps have simply evaporated," said Thatcher, who had a difficult time with his own ballpoint pens.

"I am afraid so. But we shall let you know what we discover. We only wish to protect our personnel against premature judgments." Voronin hesitated a moment, then proceeded: "It is all most awkward. That this should have happened here, of all places."

"A major loss of this kind would be awkward wherever it occurred," said Thatcher, defending New York.

Voronin remained serious. "That is not what I meant. I was thinking of it from the viewpoint of a commercial attaché. In other countries, where the Soviet Union has more normal trade activities, everything is not a crisis. But here, everything is sensitive, every single little transaction."

"Yes, I can see how that would make New York a more difficult appointment than most. Have you been here long?"

"I came here from London two years ago. Several of us under Mr. Durnovo worked on the wheat sales. We started at Amtorg—and moved to the consulate when it opened."

Thatcher was relieved to learn that Voronin had had some experience with the city besides gigantic thefts and homicides in broad daylight. "And you liked London better?" he inquired curiously.

"The work was certainly subject to much less pressure. But it is difficult for me to judge the two cities. My daughter was living with me in London. She is now married, in Moscow. It is better so. It is no life for a young woman, living with a widowed father."

Thatcher agreed wholeheartedly. His own wife had, thank God, lived to see their children's marriages. He would not have liked to be left with Laura on his hands. He said as much.

Voronin laughed. "Daughters, they need mothers first, and then husbands. There is not much place for fathers. Sons, I do not know about."

Thatcher could have contributed a few pithy comments on the requirements of sons, but he abstained. Instead, he expressed the hope that Voronin would remain in New York long enough to see the consulate return to normalcy.

"It is a kind hope, and I thank you for it. But I will be content if we can merely live through these wheat shipments without any further explosions."

It was a modest ambition, but not destined to be realized. As they paused at the desk for Voronin to buy cigarettes, they could see the television set over the bar.

"And now for further developments in the ill-omened wheat shipments to Russia," the newscaster intoned expressionlessly.

"Longshoremen servicing New York's docks, after an emergency meeting this morning, have set a midnight strike deadline. Officials of the Port Authority expressed confusion as to the nature of the strikers' demands. The Mayor, after a personal visit to the scene, has announced that he sees no hope of an early settlement. All loading is expected to come to a halt late this evening, even as a new flotilla is steaming toward New York waters. This promises to be the worst tie-up since . . ."

"No!" said Voronin in agonized disbelief. "Oh, no!"

It was, of course, not the kind of normalcy that John Putnam Thatcher had envisaged.

10

International Harvester

THATCHER MADE HIS WAY back to the Sloan at a more leisurely pace than was usual with him. He was not lost in thought, since this would be tantamount to self-immolation on Exchange Place during business hours, but he was reviewing the morning's work.

The trouble, he thought, was that he was spending too much time with, among others, Russians. Thatcher was not exceptionally xenophobic (although he had had his fill of Swiss bankers). It was simply a matter of efficiency; as yet, despite the interesting revelations at the Trade Display on Fifth Avenue, the correlation between Russians encountered and time lost was too high.

As Miss Corsa informed him when he reached her desk, he was about to change all that within the hour. He was going to waste time with a real red-blooded American.

"Mr. Lancer asked if you could fit a Mr. Hosmer Chuddley in," she reported.

"I suppose I could," said Thatcher without enthusiasm. "Who is Mr. Hosmer Chuddley?"

With uncharacteristic doubt, Miss Corsa double-checked her impeccable notes. "Miss Spence"—Lancer's secretary—"Miss Spence *says* that he's a farmer."

Manufacturers, wholesalers, retailers, engineers, consultants, factors, speculators—a whole spectrum of economic specialists regularly passed before Miss Corsa's uninterested gaze. But rarely, if ever, a farmer.

Thatcher was able to reassure her.

Hosmer Chuddley, he now remembered all too well, was the celebrated Iowa farmer who had entertained a former Premier of the Soviet Union, who had visited the U.S.S.R. as the highly honored guest of the Ministry of Agriculture. He could afford such activities since he was several times a millionaire—but what did he want with the Sloan Guaranty Trust? Or, more to the point, with John Thatcher?

As Thatcher learned five minutes later when Miss Corsa ushered Chuddley in, he wanted accomplices.

"Chernozem!" said Chuddley, after greeting Thatcher in a hearty manner consonant with his calling and his healthy corn-fed frame. "I say, chernozem!"

Thatcher circled his desk and remained silent, a technique he found invaluable at moments like this.

Hosmer Chuddley, red in the face with earnestness, elaborated.

"Chernozem! Finest wheat-producing soil on earth! Just like our own prairies. I've seen them, and I know what I'm talking about."

"I'm sure you do," said Thatcher. He only wished that he did.

Chuddley shifted a considerable, if muscular, bulk. "And I'm all for Russian-American friendship, I guess I've showed that . . ."

"I guess so," Thatcher murmured.

He was beginning to feel for all those Russian delegations of agronomists and technicians who were inevitably doomed to a weekend of real American hospitality ("with all the fixin's") at the Chuddley farm near Parched Stream, Iowa.

". . . but I said, and I'll say again, this wheat deal is a lot of political hogwash! Oh, it's going to give a lot of people jobs, but it's not the way to do things. It's a lot of . . ." Chuddley broke off, searching for a word that was not too rural and finally settled on repetition, ". . . a lot of hogwash."

Thatcher, whose own exposure to the hoopla connected with the wheat deal had not impressed him favorably, pricked up his ears as this noted friend of Soviet-American friendship flayed the cookie pushers and bureaucrats—on both sides of the Atlantic—who were bungling the whole thing, because none of them had ever seen a farm. (Most of them had never seen a window box.) What would cement Soviet-American relations was a solution to the pressing food problems. That solution was not going to be reached with grandstand plays and trade deals.

"Mmm," said Thatcher.

Real farmers were needed—not chairbound politicians. "Draft the Aggie students, if we have to," Chuddley argued. Then organize an Agriculture Corps to be dispatched to instruct Russia on up-to-date agricultural methods. That was the only answer to recurrent crop shortages. Why those people were still plowing under fallow cropland. . . .

Resolutely, Thatcher kept his head in a flood of nitrogenous fertilizers, hot feeds, and corn-hog ratios.

Finally he said:

"This is all most interesting, Mr. Chuddley, but I'm not altogether sure where the Sloan enters into it."

Chuddley enlightened him. He was about to organize a Stop the Wheat Deal Program.

". . . not destructive, but progressive! I've already lined up a lot of support."

Thatcher remained expressionless.

". . . and since you people already got stung, I thought you'd be interested. You mark my words, this whole wheat deal is going to be rotten with robbery and graft."

Chuddley continued in this vein, and Thatcher did not dispute him, largely because he could see that it would be a waste of time.

"You won't forget your appointment at the aquarium, will you, Mr. Thatcher?" said Miss Corsa, interrupting Thatcher's thoughts and Chuddley's speech.

"No," he said, grateful that his guest hailed from Parched Stream, Iowa, not nearer home. It is one thing to propel visitors out of one's office by imaginary appointments; it is another thing to become fanciful.

Thatcher sped Hosmer Chuddley on his way to the New York offices of the American Farm Bureau Federation with assurances that the Sloan would give an Agriculture Corps serious and immediate consideration.

"Oh, by the way, Miss Corsa," he said, pausing to phrase his reprimand as tactfully as possible. "About the aquarium . . ."

Miss Corsa looked up. "Mr. Baranoff said, would you mind

meeting him there? Then you could go on. He doesn't seem to know exactly what his schedule will be this afternoon. His secretary said something about fish."

Her message, however bizarre, conveyed, Miss Corsa returned to her chores.

For a moment, Thatcher stared. Then, thanking his lucky stars that he had not put himself irremediably in the wrong by groundless protest, he said:

"Fine! And if any important calls come for me—say, concerned with the running of this bank—you might try catching me at the Brooklyn Botanical Gardens."

Miss Corsa made a note of it.

Once before, many years earlier, Thatcher had dealt with Abe Baranoff. He forgot the details, although he dimly recalled that it involved financing a sea-borne shopping center, but he remembered the atmosphere. Therefore, before setting forth for the aquarium, he armed himself with a witness.

Unfortunately Charlie Trinkam, possibly the best fitted of the Trust Department's personnel to deal with flamboyancy, was deep in negotiations with the Teamsters. (And Thatcher made a mental note to review *that*.) This left him no choice.

"I am not sure I understand why we have to meet him at the aquarium," said Everett Gabler, shrugging himself into his overcoat.

"Neither am I," said Thatcher. "Hurry up, Everett. We're late."

They did not have to plunge into the shadowy deeps of the aquarium. Abe Baranoff and entourage were just emerging as the taxi pulled up. When both parties joined, Baranoff shook hands heartily.

"Those otters," he said. "You would not believe the troubles. Now it is fish. Special fish, they must eat. Max, you take this cab and go down to Fulton Street. But . . ." Fatalistically Baranoff shrugged. "I am glad to see you again, Mr. Thatcher. Ah, yes, Mr. Gabler. Here's my car . . ."

Whatever he might confide to the press about the sordidness of money, Abe Baranoff evinced no acute discomfort at the arrival of two distinguished representatives of the Sloan Guaranty Trust. Exuding graciousness, he led them to a waiting limousine, pausing only for instructions to various minions before joining them in the cavernous back seat. The pallid young man climbed in front next to the chauffeur.

"Is this a Halloran's Garage car, Mr. Baranoff?" Thatcher inquired innocently.

"Ah hah!" said Baranoff with a shrewd and amused look. "Mr. Thatcher, could I afford anything but a Halloran car and driver—now?"

It was an answer worthy of a worthy antagonist. Everett Gabler brightened and looked more on his mettle.

Baranoff settled back. "I am sorry to hurry you off this way. Something has just come up. There are so many things to do . . ."

He continued a fervent description of the various difficulties raised by Plomsky's Otter Ensemble.

"They are, thank God, off Ellis Island. With the governor, the mayor, I got them off Ellis Island. But now, they are in isolation in an armory in South Orange, New Jersey. You wonder why South Orange, New Jersey? Well, so do I."

This at least explained the George Washington Bridge over which they were speeding as the car skilfully maneuvered out of the city.

"Now, about this Denger," said Baranoff, producing a gold-tooled case and offering them cigars. "No? They are from Havana. Well, as I told the police, I know nothing about what he did. For me, he ran errands, he picked things up. The police are checking with my lawyer, with my secretaries—but that is what they will find. Denger ran errands for me—but so do many others. It is true, he sometimes took things even to the Sloan Guaranty Trust, but as you know, I am doing business with the Sloan. Apart from that, I know nothing. . . ."

Thatcher took advantage of Baranoff's dramatic pause to disabuse him of the notion that the Sloan was subjecting a valued customer to anything so mundane as police grilling (although at this very moment, three Sloan secretaries were searching the files for anything on which the name Baranoff appeared).

"Whatever you want to ask," Baranoff invited him. "I have nothing to hide."

"I wanted to ask you about the Russians," said Thatcher. "You have been dealing with the Russian government recently, and I know you've had dealings with them in the past. Can you think of any reason why the Russians might be party to this kind of thing?"

It was Thatcher's recent experience that inviting people to comment on the Russians was more revealing than the Rorschach test.

"No," said Baranoff promptly. "No, this would not be the Russian way of doing things. First, what advantage would they get? They need the wheat we are selling—that you can see in the markets in Moscow."

"It was the sailing of the *Odessa Queen* that raised suspicion in some quarters," said Everett Gabler, quite probably in all sincerity. Almost everything raised deep suspicions in him.

Baranoff smiled a melancholy smile.

"Ah, that is easier to understand. The *Queen* was loaded, orders were to sail. Why not? Why stay to become involved with questions, with delays . . . ?"

After deliberating a moment, Thatcher briefly told Baranoff about the day's discoveries concerning the forgery of the Russian consulate seal. Baranoff, he saw with interest, grasped the significance of this immediately.

"Ah," he said, "now that—that will make a difference. My Russian friends, you understand, are suspicious, and awkward. Underneath all the noise, they fear to be thought uncultured. So when crimes happen, even when bodies are found on their steps, why, they say: 'No! It is nothing to do with us!' I have known tenors like this. But . . ."

"But?" Thatcher prompted.

"But they are not simple fools," Baranoff said reflectively. "They have scientific minds. When they see that they really have something to do with the crime, and perhaps with the murder—well, then, they will act!"

"How?" Everett Gabler demanded, sounding breathless. Abe Baranoff, Thatcher saw, was a master showman.

"What the Russians will do, only the devil can tell. An old proverb—I just made it up. Here we are? Good, good. Come, let us go in."

They had pulled up before an abandoned National Guard Armory in a derelict corner of South Orange, New Jersey—a community that Thatcher had previously thought lacked derelict corners. Baranoff descended, took one haughty look at his surroundings, said "Pfa!" and strode in. Amused, Thatcher followed.

Within the ancient edifice, distant barking sounds brought a rabbity look of expectation to Everett Gabler. But as they proceeded into the hall, Thatcher was noting, for future reference, that Abe Baranoff was not only a subtle and devious personality—he had the mechanics of the wheat deal at his fingertips. Of course, he might have been born with such details at his fingertips.

"My God! I am surrounded by imbeciles!" Baranoff shouted into the echoing amphitheater.

From crates piled along the wall, from seven occupants of an improvised rink just before them, from Plomsky, secretaries, aides, workmen, discontent echoed back.

"Smelt! Give me smelt!" Plomsky said passionately. "Here, Mitya, we are still practicing. Bad otter!"

Four young men, bearing sheafs of paper, immediately cut Baranoff off from his companions, while an incredibly constructed blonde in incredibly high heels stood nearby, balancing boxes of sugar cubes. At the far end of the hall, beyond the rinks, a small orchestra added to the din by taking advantage of the interruption to reprise a tricky portion of "Lady of Spain."

"The music must be Russian!" Plomsky howled. "And smelt! We were promised smelt . . ."

Up came Baranoff's great head. "Call Weinstein! Get me Weinstein . . ."

"Please, Abe, will you look at this?"

"Smelt . . ."

"Abe . . ."

For thirty minutes, Thatcher and Gabler indulged themselves by watching the whole fearsome spectacle. Plomsky, placated upon learning that Max was bringing smelt, turned to attack the orchestra.

"The time, it is important! Mitya enters on the down-beat!"

"Abe, will you tell this clown . . ."

"Pig!"

"Mitya! Bad otter!"

"Get me Weinstein!"

Punctuating the strains of "Meadowlands," to which the otters marched in serried ranks, were hurried arrivals, each clamoring for Abe Baranoff's undivided attention.

After allowing Everett Gabler the privilege of five minutes with Plomsky, made possible by the performing otters' need for a sugar break at regular intervals, Thatcher decided to take advantage of Baranoff's offer of a limousine.

He made his way through the crowd to take his leave. Baranoff shouted at his aides, shook a fist at somebody across the hall, and accompanied Thatcher a few steps.

"A pleasure, Mr. Thatcher. A real pleasure. And," he lowered his voice, "if there is anything else . . . well, remember I have many contacts."

"Now what did he mean by that?" Everett Gabler demanded once they were speeding into Manhattan.

Conscious that ears from Halloran's Garage might be listening, Thatcher said only, "I wonder?"

And the Jersey flats sped by to Everett Gabler's measured approval of Mitya's solo.

The limousine deposited them at Exchange Place long after the Sloan's customers, clerical help, and middle-rank executives had departed.

But Walter Bowman, the large, jovial chief of research, predictably was still at his post. Moreover he had the look of a man with a blockbuster as he followed Thatcher into his office.

"It came over the tape," he said. "You mean you haven't heard?"

"You don't keep up with the ticker when you're driving to and from New Jersey," said Thatcher, idly inspecting the notes Miss Corsa had left for him. "What is it, Walter?"

Bowman drew a happy breath; for him, life had few pleasures greater than the breaking of news.

"The Cuban Navy is blockading the port of New York! The Russians have threatened to send gunboats . . ."

Startled, Thatcher let the papers fall. Had Bowman's mind finally given way to the strain of overwork?

Everett Gabler retained his waspish calm. "For heaven's sake, Walter! Cuba doesn't have a navy."

Bowman smiled broadly.

"You ain't heard nothing, yet . . ." he said, as he began a complex tale of small mosquito boats flying the Cuban flag and disrupting harbor traffic with their zigzag maneuvers.

When the lurid catalog was complete, Everett Gabler had the appropriate comment ready:

"That's one in the eye for the longshoremen!"

11

Cereal Story

HOSTILE NAVIES ENCIRCLING New York might be an embarrassment to the United States government, but other people had other problems. In a small frame house in Astoria, the brother and sister-in-law of Gus Denger wrestled with the vexations of interment.

"All I want," said the brother for the twentieth time, "is to do the decent thing."

"Sure you do, Al," replied his wife, "and, believe me, I'd be the last to grudge the expense, if anybody was going to come to see it. But who is there?"

Gloomily Al shook his head. "It doesn't seem possible that Gus lived over forty years without leaving someone who wants to come to his funeral."

Elsie, being no fool, did not remind him what Gus had been like. Instead she discussed tactics.

"How about his rooming house? Did you tell them when it will be?"

"I called yesterday. What could you expect from guys in a place like that? They've all got something else on . . . they say. That means sitting around having a beer and picking their horses."

His wife had gone on to further problems. "What are we going to do about the mass? After Father Fitzsimmons has gone out of his way to help. And you know what he must be thinking."

Al was stirred to pugnacity. "Look, I'm not the only one in this parish with a bum in the family, and Father Fitzsimmons knows it!"

Elsie refused to be drawn into a discussion of Father Fitzsimmons, a subject on which the couple did not agree. "It's going to look awfully funny if no one but us shows up."

"Now, honey, don't worry about it. That Mrs. Halloran at the garage said she wanted to come. I'll just give her a ring and let her know the time."

As he headed for the phone, his wife slumped back in her chair. "Will I ever be glad when this is over," she muttered. "Gus has never been anything but trouble, trouble, trouble. First it was that tramp he picked up, then it was liquor and the bookies. Now he can't even have a respectable funeral."

"Yes," said Rita Halloran. "I've got that. Ten o'clock at Saint James. And I'll bring a few of the boys along. Anyone who isn't out on a job."

She checked the thanks evoked by this offer and cradled the phone. Mrs. Halloran had years of experience with her drivers. Half of them were much-married men living in the midst of rampant fecundity. But the other half were rootless drifters, like Gus Denger. She knew all about the problems associated with their funerals. She had managed one or two herself.

"Denger's funeral," she said in brief explanation to the client across her desk.

"You are going to it?"

"Yes. There won't be many people there, and it'll be a help to the relatives. Particularly if the press shows up."

"The press?"

Abe Baranoff straightened. If he had been the kind of man who waited for opportunity to knock at his door, he'd still be waiting behind that door in Omsk. For a moment he nursed the malacca stick planted between his knees, then reached a decision.

"Reassure these relatives! There is no need for concern. I shall attend!"

The audience for Gus Denger's funeral obsequies had just trebled. For where Baranoff went, so did his entourage. Even now a platoon of them lurked uncomfortably just outside the office, in the midst of hydraulic lifts and air hoses.

Rita Halloran stared at her visitor in open amazement. What was he up to now? Did he know something? Could he possibly have found out anything after only two days back in the country? And what was he doing in her office? The Baranoffs of this world do not come to garages (unless, of course, they have just unearthed the world's finest troupe of Armenian mechanic-acrobats).

He said he wanted to discuss his contract. Baloney! He would call, or send a flunky. But here he sat, shrewd eyes taking in everything, in no hurry to move on. A man with a hundred irons in the fire! Acting as if he had nothing to do but drop in for a casual chat. Rita Halloran's nerves were not as strong as they had been a week ago. She thought to herself, if this fat slob goes on like this, I'll throw back my head and scream!

But Abe Baranoff had exhausted his pleasantries and was now getting down to brass tacks. He sighed heavily.

"This Denger business," he brooded, "it could mean trouble, real trouble."

The press *did* cover the funeral. What's more, the murder, which had almost been lost in the shuffle of Soviet-American relations, reemerged as front page news. Official records had yielded additional details about Gus Denger's early life—an obscure high school in Queens accepted the responsibility for his education, the army admitted that he had advanced to the rank of technical sergeant during his Korean duty. There was a picture of Albert and Elsie Denger looking shellshocked. Their determined bid for respectability had been blasted sky-high. Predictably, the funeral had turned into a Baranoff spectacular.

Luke Stringfellow shoved the paper aside and stared blankly at the wall. He was sick with apprehension. Everything was coming to a head at once. Some invisible net was closing, shrinking around him with each passing day. My God, there must be something he had overlooked, something he had never considered important! How had he ever gotten involved in this? If he could only think, if he could only think, there must be some way out.

Tessie had to speak to him twice. She was slitting open the afternoon mail.

"It's the grain elevator," she persisted. "They want to know what's going to happen with this strike. Jim says—"

"Tell him to drop dead!' snapped Stringfellow.

Tessie examined him in silence. She hadn't expected Luke to go to pieces this way. God knows, trying to run the office as if nothing had happened was hard enough anyway. It was going to be damn near impossible if he started having hysterics.

"All right," she said at length. "I'll tell Jim he knows as much as we do. We'll all have to wait and see."

Stringfellow did not bother to answer. His thoughts were already a mile away. Imperturbably she continued to read the mail, scribbling a note here and there. It would be a waste of time to consult him now. When she finally rose, the movement made Stringfellow give a sudden start. Almost accidentally, their eyes met. He shifted under her level gaze.

"Look, Tessie, I don't feel so hot," he said, running a finger inside his collar as if suddenly choking. "I think I'll call it a day. I can catch the four-ten if I leave now."

Tessie stared at him, more disturbed than she wanted to admit. "Alice is picking you up in five minutes. You're going up to West-chester with her. Remember?"

"Oh, my God! That's all I need! Today of all . . ."

He was still at it when Alice Stringfellow arrived. A tall, volup-tuous blonde, normally in good temper with herself and with her world, she narrowed her eyes as her husband made his prepara-tions for departure. He barked a few commands at Tessie, jerkily shoved some papers into a briefcase, reached for his hat, then dropped the hat to recheck his papers. With an exclamation of annoyance he plunged out of the office. Tessie called after him:

"You might sign those letters on my desk, Luke."

"All right, all right!" he exploded as if subjected to some in-tolerable nagging.

Alice Stringfellow lost no time after his exit. "What's the matter with him? He's as jumpy as a rabbit."

"He says he's not feeling well. He's been edgy all afternoon."

"All afternoon!" snorted Mrs. Stringfellow. "More like all week! What's gotten into him?"

Tessie suppressed a sigh. Being in the middle was the price you paid for being on good terms with both. "There's been a lot of pressure about this Sloan robbery, Alice. Luke's involved, whether he likes it or not."

"It's more than that," said Alice stubbornly. "He's been like a cat on a hot stove since this whole Jersey business." She looked at Tessie out of the corner of her eye. "He's been spending a lot of time out in Jersey, hasn't he?"

"It's a big deal, Alice," Tessie said pacifically, "and Luke isn't used to real estate."

Alice closed her mouth with an exasperated click. She should have known better than to try to get anything out of Tessie. Tessie had raised to a fine art the science of keeping her eyes open and her mouth shut. Normally that was fine. But if things were going to blow up, Alice Stringfellow wanted to know. She wasn't the lying-down type, and there was something very funny going on. She could smell the difference in the office.

"Okay, let's go." Her husband had reentered and was now in a frenzy to be gone. "Come on, honey, we'll be late. Tess, don't forget to ring Quentin about the strike."

Tess nodded as she watched the two leave. Usually they were a

well-matched couple. The easy-going tolerance which characterized both of them could float their marriage over ordinary little
sore patches. Unfortunately, neither of them had any real sympathy on which to fall back when they hit serious trouble.

Tessie shrugged. That was up to them. They were both adults
and could look after themselves.

"Yes, I understand, Miss Marcus," said Victor Quentin for the
last time before hanging up the phone. Two minutes later the
entire conversation might never have taken place. His thoughts
were again circling frenziedly, like rats in a maze, around the two
papers on his desk. What would happen if he walked upstairs and
thumped them down before John Thatcher? Was it too obvious?
Maybe nothing would happen. Maybe he was losing his mind.
With a shaking hand he started to shift the two documents, first
that on the right, then the other. One thing was certain, he wasn't
cut out for his sort of business.

Victor Quentin had lost all resemblance to a cool, competent
executive. These days he was pallid and indecisive. Desperately he
fought for control. There was a chance, just barely a chance, that
if this was handled right, it would shift suspicion away from himself. This was the only card he still held. Should he play it now—
or later?

Victor Quentin had been in the financial world all his life. He
knew that unless someone else were firmly saddled with the Sloan
theft, his career as a banker was over. And that had not been in his
plans at all.

David Yates was nominally on duty at his office. But he had
swiveled his chair around and rested his feet on the windowsill, so
that he could gaze sightlessly out the window. Willard & Climpson
paid an extravagant rental for that window because it embraced a
wide view of the busy harbor.

Now, of course, the longshoremen's strike had left the harbor
moribund. The only sign of activity was from the sea gulls, swooping and squawking against the brilliant blue sky. Their outraged
complaints rose and fell with melodic monotony. The strike had
interfered with their way of life too, interrupting the steady supply
of refuse that kept them sleek and shining.

David Yates was not thinking about sea gulls, but about David

Yates. He was very pleased at the way things were going. The main thing was to keep it cool. Some people, of course, would say he was playing with fire. Well, there was nothing wrong with fire if you didn't get burned. And the game was worth the candle, there was no doubt about that. In this life you had to decide early if you were going to go around half-dead because you were afraid to do what you wanted to do. Most men after all wanted the same things —Americans, Russians, Laplanders. They hated being tied down by suffocating routine, but most of them were afraid to take chances. Most men—

At this point in his reflections, a spasm of irritation crossed his face. Most men, yes. But women were different. They positively liked being tied down. Remorselessly, his thoughts turned to his fiancée, Dorothy. Dorothy wanted to be tied down, and the sooner the better. What a time for her to turn on the heat for an early wedding! Little did she know! Yates shrugged Dorothy aside and began to dream of distant lands.

Things were better at the Russian Consulate. Nobody was brazenly daydreaming. People were at least pretending to work. Katerina Ivanovna was, in fact, prettily attentive as Feodor Voronin gave her some last-minute instructions before entering the conference room.

Women, as David Yates had just discovered, do think differently from men. Katerina Ivanovna for instance. She had decided that if her activities in New York were not precisely what the Soviet Union had in mind when it assigned her there as an interpreter, then the way to keep everybody off guard was to look as conscientious as possible. This policy had paid handsome dividends. Not only was she establishing an enviable dossier, she was becoming one of the most mobile of consular employees. She went here, there, and everywhere. As a natural consequence of this activity, her location at any given moment was hard to pinpoint. Which was very, very convenient. True, she was walking on eggshells, but that was what gave spice to life. Nothing ventured, nothing gained. It wasn't as if she didn't have her final goal clearly fixed.

Her inner amusement welled up into that expression of dancing high spirits that her colleagues knew so well. But she said gravely:

"Of course I shall remain on duty this evening, Feodor Ilyich, if it will be of assistance to you."

Feodor Voronin could have used some hidden springs of amusement to get him through that conference. The embassy in Washington, alerted to the latest developments, had descended in full force. Unhappily the consulate staff reviewed its findings for the visitors, produced seals, explained the workings of order clearance at the Fifth Avenue Trade Display. The conclusion was inescapable.

Unbelievable as it was, incredible as it must appear to every right-thinking Soviet comrade, there was certain evidence—yes, they agreed weakly, you could call it irrefutable evidence—that some representative of the Soviet Union in New York had, in some undefined way, conspired to steal from the Soviet Union, to attack the sanctity of Soviet credit, to endanger the shipments of wheat, to take bread out of the mouths of babes, and to imperil the relations between East and West.

In a word, something was rotten in Denmark.

As the awe-inspiring itemization of crimes came to an end, the senior representative from Washington summed up the sentiment of the meeting.

"It is the presumption of it that turns my stomach. A junior official—not even an embassy official—to have the impertinence to meddle in these affairs!"

Somebody said cheerfully there was no proof it was a junior official. After all, there was always the U.N. delegation.

This remark received a chilly reception. Piotr Vassilich had never been noted for his tact.

But all this Voronin had expected. What he had not anticipated was that his superior, Durnovo, should so determinedly try to wash his hands of the whole business.

"No, no," said Durnovo over and over again. "You will have to ask Feodor Ilyich. He handled all the details. I had nothing to do with this."

Subordinates all over the world are acquainted with the maneuvers of their superiors to shift the blame, any blame, onto lesser shoulders. But in a long career as a subordinate, Voronin had never seen a comparable performance. Iron control enabled him to maintain an even voice and a dutifully receptive expression as Durnovo made one resolute attempt after another to hand his assistant's head around the table on a platter. Durnovo was making a tactical mistake. Inevitably others besides Voronin were asking themselves the question: What is Durnovo trying to cover? Why is he so nervous? What is he hiding?

But the only tangible expression of these inquiries came from the Consul himself when he finally interrupted his commercial attaché:

"My good Durnovo! In my report I congratulated both you and myself on our negotiation of the shipment details. Little did I realize that all the credit belonged elsewhere. We must rectify whatever false impression has been created."

After this, it was not altogether surprising that the meeting decided a rigorous investigation was required.

"And not, I think," said the Consul, "by anyone from the New York staff. I would prefer that the embassy send someone from Washington."

The representatives from the embassy agreed with an almost sinister enthusiasm. But they went one step further.

"Not Washington. It shall be someone from Moscow!"

12

Alien Corn

As THESE MEN and women of assorted ages, stations, and nationalities grappled with the problems nearest them, their governments —following Machiavelli's great dictum—were left to cope with strains in the fabric of the general well-being.

The Cuban Navy was a case in point.

After an initial hour of complete pandemonium, the New York Office of the Bureau of Naval Intelligence pulled its socks up and came to a conclusion: despite large homemade signs saying "Viva Fidel," the garbage-hurling vandals were not Cubans. Like Everett Gabler before them, BNI seized on the fact that Cuba does not have a navy. Hurried inquiries were initiated. As the hours wore by, the little boats seemed to bear charmed lives—dashing out, megaphoning insults at Russian and American ships—then darting away, to hide as darkness fell. All the relevant authorities were outraged, but the first hard information came from Halifax, Nova

Scotia, not New York. These gadflies were French-Canadian terrorists.

Precisely why French-Canadian terrorists should be intruding themselves at this juncture, nobody, least of all the BNI, knew, but the State Department dispatched a stiff note to Ottawa, then informed the Russian Embassy that there was no need for Soviet gunboats. Should convoys become necessary, the United States Navy would provide them.

Gunboats, said the Russians austerely, existed only in the fevered imagination of the New York press.

The State Department mopped its collective brow and phoned the White House. An irascible voice replied that it didn't want to be bothered with a lot of details when something really important was at hand—the longshoremen's strike.

"Oh, yes," said the State Department weakly.

The White House snarled, hung up, then got in touch with the Department of Labor, a Supreme Court justice, and David Dubinsky. Within three hours, the Mayor of the City of New York, flanked by a glowering union president and a federal mediator, stood on the steps of Gracie Mansion to make an announcement. He didn't get a chance to open his mouth.

"They're twisting our arms," growled Mike Finn. "So we'll take a seven-day cooling off period! But then we're going out, sure as hell!"

The Mayor tried to smile.

While these public and private passions seethed, John Putnam Thatcher sat quietly at his desk, reflecting on the odd figures attracted to his world by recent events.

For example, Hosmer Chuddley. According to the *News,* he was trying from a small headquarters on Ninth Street to rally public opinion by distributing bumper stickers which read: Farmers Not Flunkies for Food.

Thatcher tossed the paper aside and continued to waste time. Chuddley was not the only newcomer on the Wall Street landscape. On his own peregrinations, Thatcher was beginning to recognize the phalanx of anonymous young men who trailed in his wake. They waited for him to emerge from the Sloan; they strolled casually outside the Russian Consulate; they were probably keeping sharp eyes on Plomsky's otters out in Jersey. Thatcher did not think for a moment that he was their only quarry, but just who was maintaining this surveillance remained unclear. The New York City Police Department, the Federal Bureau of Investigation, and the State Department, upon being taxed, denied responsibility.

More newcomers put an end to his dereliction from duty. The Export-Import Bank wanted the Sloan's assistance in setting up a meeting of the financial institutions involved in the wheat exports. The American Banker's Association wanted Sloan advice on their latest position paper; the ABA was going to come out strong against bank robberies. The New York Federal Reserve Bank, charged with supervising the handling of Russian bullion, developed deep fears about potential gold snatchers infiltrating Wall Street and presented an elaborate security scheme. The State Department told Thatcher that everything was very, very serious.

And His Excellency, Muhammed Ali Fervan, ambassador of Buganda, asked the Sloan Guaranty Trust to underwrite a vast reforestation scheme to the tune of $985,000—which Thatcher could not believe to be pure coincidence. Apparently the Bugandans had been much taken with how little $985,000 meant to the Sloan.

When, at the end of the morning, Miss Corsa announced that the Russian Consulate was on the phone, Thatcher was by no means pleased. He had, he felt, already done more than his duty by the Sloan's high obligations to help maintain public order and international amity. Nevertheless, he wearily reached for the phone, mentally reviewing the Russians he had met.

It was the suave commercial attaché, Sergei Durnovo himself. His phrases rolled as smoothly as ever.

"Mr. Thatcher, if you will not think it positively discourteous, I should like to invite you to dine with us this evening . . ."

Surely this was a departure from the Russian Consulate's punctilious standards, thought Thatcher, moderately taken aback. He was casting about for an excuse that would not unduly emphasize the point, when Durnovo came to the end of his elaborate apologies and continued:

". . . but although it is at short notice, I think that you would be interested to meet Mikhail Maseryan . . ."

"Oh?" said Thatcher. There are times when even trying to be helpful is useless.

"He has just arrived. From Moscow," said Durnovo sounding almost human for a moment.

"Oh yes. I see," said Thatcher, who did. He chalked up another unlikely visitor enticed to New York.

Durnovo drew a deep breath and explained what was already quite clear to Thatcher. When Thatcher and Durnovo's assistant, Voronin, had placed the Fifth Avenue seal squarely in Russian hands, Moscow had started putting two and two together. The other suggestive item was the forged documents from the *Odessa Queen.* And two and two had produced a change in official thinking.

"It was decided at the very highest level," said Durnovo impressively, "that every possibility—however remote—must be explored. You understand?"

Thatcher said that he did.

"Yes," said Durnovo. "Comrade Maseryan has been sent to . . . to look into things. He is a most interesting man. And he has said that he would be honored to meet with you. So, if you do not object . . ."

In other words, another policeman.

Thatcher put an end to Durnovo's suspense by replying that he would be delighted to meet with Maseryan that very night.

"Splendid," said Durnovo with relief. No doubt when ordered to get Thatcher for dinner, he was expected to produce. "He has decided to stay with our Soviet Trade Mission tonight so we will dine there. At seven-thirty. I shall send a car . . ."

Accordingly, at six-thirty, John Putnam Thatcher stepped from the Devonshire Hotel into an exotic limousine driven by a silent, frozen-faced chauffeur. It was too dark to see the expressions of the anonymous young men strolling past the Devonshire, but Thatcher was sure that he had triggered a flurry of some sort of activity. He settled back for the long drive to Huntington, Long Island, and the mansion that had once been the home of Chester Hollenmajor, the famous Sugar King, presently the home of the Russian Trade Mission.

Presumably those members of the consular staff joining him at Huntington were using other transport—transport uncontaminated by the presence of an American banker. He knew that the consular staff, latecomers to New York, had to be satisfied with civilian city apartments instead of North Shore estates.

The party assembled in the lordly living room consisted mostly of Russians with whom he had already dealt. Standing in the background, like model civil servants, were Durnovo and Voronin, who nodded formally to him. The young interpreter, Katerina Ivanovna, favored him with a charming greeting, then quickly returned to utmost gravity.

"We are delighted you could join our little party this evening," said the Consul, whom Thatcher had encountered some months earlier at a banquet. He introduced a middle-aged, motherly woman as Mrs. Grabnikov, his wife, then continued, "And permit me to present to you our distinguished colleague from Moscow, Mikhail Maseryan. Mr. Maseryan is in our Ministry of Foreign Affairs."

Maseryan proved to be a small bulky man with a luxuriant black mustache, a hooked nose, and shrewd eyes. He greeted Thatcher in serviceable English and said, by way of idle conversation, that this was his first visit to the United States. Thatcher replied suitably, meanwhile noting that this exchange seemed to have mesmerized the company. Durnovo in particular wore a frozen smile. Fortunately, a manservant circulating with drinks broke the trance; Thatcher was happy to see martinis on the tray as well as those ominous clear beakers.

"I have often wanted to visit your country," Maseryan said, after doing justice to his vodka.

"And I have wanted to visit yours," Thatcher replied. He was beginning to be almost unnerved by the painful intensity of the listening silence. Katerina Ivanovna and Voronin were too taut to do more than clutch their glasses.

There was a pause.

Mr. Grabnikov bestirred himself. "Seeing a country that is not one's own is educational," he finally contributed.

"That is very true," said his wife.

Feodor Voronin and Katerina Ivanovna murmured agreement and took tentative sips.

Emboldened, Sergei Durnovo went even further. "It teaches one to value one's own country," he said after clearing his throat.

"That is true."

"Very true."

Maseryan, Thatcher was pleased to note, looked as disheartened as he felt. A second round of drinks and lavish silver cups of caviar did nothing to lighten the atmosphere. Nor could the dinner, once they removed to the medieval vault that was the dining room, be described as a sparkling social moment.

"Tell me, Katerina Ivanovna, what do you do in New York

when you are not working?" Maseryan spoke playfully, in the avuncular tone that a very pretty girl frequently elicits.

"I go to concerts," said Katerina Ivanovna quickly, apparently not recognizing either playfulness or avuncularity. Indeed, she sounded like a guilty schoolgirl.

Her colleague, Feodor Voronin, gallantly came to the rescue. "The concerts in New York," he said, "are excellent."

"Yes."

"That is true."

Katerina Ivanovna threw Voronin a grateful look, then concentrated on her bread. Maseryan rolled his eyes slightly and returned to his soup.

For a while, it seemed that the excellent fish might be consumed in total silence. Finally Mr. Grabnikov took the bull by the horns and launched into a long, boring recital of the New York colleges he had recently visited.

". . . then the City College. And the University of Columbia. And, later, out to Queens College. And to the ladies in the economics department of Hunter . . ."

Thatcher himself essayed a brief discussion with Feodor Voronin.

"At least we are spared the longshoremen's strike for a week," he remarked.

"Yes," said Voronin in a low voice. "Yes, that is very fortunate."

Thatcher was not by inclination chatty but he felt an obligation to say something at a dinner table. Accordingly he persevered.

"And I understand that two Russian ships cleared port today."

"Yes, yes, they did."

Thatcher gave up.

Under the circumstances, dinner seemed interminable. Mikhail Maseryan, whose knowing eyes and half smile did not seem intimidating, positively paralyzed his colleagues. Of course, Thatcher thought, as he irritably speared an asparagus stalk, who knew what dark forces Maseryan represented? The knout?

Or was he out of date?

At any rate, he could discern no sensible reason why he should have been introduced into this scene of Dostoevskian gloom. Fortunately, Maseryan appeared to agree. As they left the table, he briskly suggested that he and Mr. Thatcher—if Mr. Thatcher would not object—might take their coffee in the library.

Mr. Thatcher would have taken his coffee in the cellar to be spared more of this.

After they settled in Chester Hollenmajor's library (Gothic arches and matched sets), it developed that Mikhail Maseryan had been as oppressed by the atmosphere as Thatcher.

"I must apologize, Mr. Thatcher. I had thought that a congenial evening with people known to you would be a fitting prelude to our talk. But . . ." He shrugged, spread his thick fingers in an eloquent gesture. "But this . . . wake, is not what I anticipated."

"Of course, the staff of the Russian Consulate is anxious, these days," Thatcher began diplomatically.

Out went Maseryan's fingers again. "No, it is me! These block-heads worry that I shall report things. They are all the same. Moscow sends me to find a connection between any Russian and the robbery of your bank, and the murder as well—and do you know what these people are afraid of? Of buying high-fidelity sets on the installment plan! Of romantic attachments! Of listening to jazz music, or studying modern painting! Bah! They read too much of your propaganda, I tell you!"

Maseryan drew black brows into a fierce frown, then energetically grasped the brandy bottle and splashed two healthy drinks. When he put the bottle down, he glared at the label.

"And I can tell you this, my friend. The head of the Russian Trade Delegation is wondering if perhaps he should not have put the French brandy away, and served Crimean brandy, while I am here. You would not believe the places I have had to drink Crimean brandy! Paris, even!"

Thatcher, although entertained, was not inclined to underrate Maseryan's abilities.

"Of course," he suggested, "somebody might have a guilty conscience."

Maseryan looked at him shrewdly from under those beetling brows. "They all have guilty consciences, Mr. Thatcher. All good Russians enjoy New York, Paris, Rome—and they always feel that it is wrong, that it is a betrayal of their Mother Russia. It is a national characteristic. You Americans are the reverse. You go to London, Paris, or Rome and enjoy yourselves, then you think that you are the first persons clever enough to have done so."

Thatcher smiled. "I notice that you do not include Moscow in that list."

"No," said Maseryan gravely. "Not yet. But soon. However, I

am keeping us from business. It is true that my friends from the consulate all show signs of bourgeois error, but I do not think that all of them are involved in a major crime. We can dismiss that. Let me explain our position . . ."

The Russian position was simply that the discovery of the seal, together with the real competence of the forgeries, suggested the possibility of Russian participation. Technically this meant that the staff of the United Nations Delegation, the Trade Mission, the Intourist staff, and even the embassy in Washington were being considered.

"But of course," Maseryan said, refilling his glass and sketching an offer in Thatcher's direction, "first we concentrate on our friends of the Russian Consulate in New York. On Durnovo, on Voronin, on Ogareva . . . Did I say something to interest you?"

"Who is Ogareva?" Thatcher asked.

Maseryan looked at him. "The little Katerina Ivanovna, who goes to concerts when she is not working. Was there something . . . ?"

"No," said Thatcher, not quite truthfully. "I simply had not heard her name before."

"I see," said Maseryan, studying his glass. "At the same time, you understand, my colleagues in Moscow are investigating the crew of the *Odessa Queen* . . ."

"Do you really think that Captain Kurnatovsky is up to high-class forgery?" asked Thatcher, amused.

"Ah, he is more cunning than you think," said Maseryan. "Already, we have uncovered interesting, but strictly forbidden trading in nylon stockings."

"Well I hope that does not mean serious trouble for him," said Thatcher, who recalled Captain Kurnatovsky's uncomplicated approach to life with considerable appreciation.

"Some trouble," said Maseryan, "but not big trouble."

Thatcher was left to ponder this as Maseryan continued to explain that since in this instance the interests of the Sloan Guaranty Trust and the Union of Soviet Socialist Republics marched hand in hand, his government formally requested cooperation. "And," he added, "may I say personally that I would be most grateful . . ."

This eloquence roused the competitor in John Putnam Thatcher. Where Russia led, could the Sloan fail to follow?

"First, I should say that I welcome your presence. Not that I am

convinced that a Soviet national is necessarily implicated in this
. . . er . . . dastardly crime . . ."

"Let us hope not," said Maseryan formally. "But in that case, it
is an American, which is also regrettable."

"Quite so," said Thatcher. "It is too much to hope for somebody from an uncommitted nation. At any rate, I am most happy
on behalf of the Sloan Guaranty Trust to offer you what assistance
I can," he concluded. If he had not topped Maseryan, he decided,
he had at least matched him.

"Thank you," said Mikhail Maseryan, who then dropped the
high manner and outlined a long list of requests ranging from an
interview with Victor Quentin to a tour of the Registry of
Deeds. "And, Mr. Thatcher, we will clear this up, I think. If it is a
capitalistic crime, why, you are the expert. If a communist has
betrayed his cause, then I am the expert. Between us"—the thick
fingers guillotined quickly—"we are more than a match for
him."

"Certainly," said John Putnam Thatcher. "Whoever he is."

13

Snap . . . Crackle . . . Pop!

THE NEXT MORNING found Thatcher on his mettle. Mindful of the
luxury in which he had been rolled out to Huntington, he firmly
directed Miss Corsa to commandeer the Sloan's most impressive
automotive transport. He felt, as he so often did these days, that
the honor of his country was somehow at stake. At ten o'clock he
picked up Maseryan at the Russian Consulate in something long,
low, and streamlined. They did not drive to the Sloan; they crested
the air waves.

After two hours of solid labor, Thatcher was mentally calling
down blessings on Moscow. They had sent him a worker.
Maseryan must have stayed up far into the night absorbing his
notes of the previous evening. And now he was grimly wading
through the material provided by the Sloan's research staff. He was
well on the way to qualifying as an expert on letters of credit and

the geography of New York City with respect to loading docks, the Cunard piers and the Registry of Deeds.

By God, the Soviet Union was going to learn that when the Sloan decided to cooperate, it cooperated to the hilt!

Thatcher's spirits lifted. A realist if ever there were one, he had abandoned all expectation of help from the federal agencies of the United States within twenty-four hours of the theft. But now, for the first time since the crime, Thatcher entertained the possibility that the Sloan might yet recover its missing funds. He had already lined up Inspector Lyons for dinner. Idly he played with the thought of a triumvirate—Lyons, Maseryan, and Thatcher. Each with his own expertise, his own sources of information, his own access to the leading performers in the drama. Yes, there was a fighting chance.

His visitor having thus become precious to him, Thatcher turned to thoughts of his welfare. Soon it would be lunchtime. Where should he take Maseryan? For a moment Thatcher considered the Seamen's Refuge—a fitting chop house for an upholder of the proletariat. But he had a better idea. If he himself were visiting Moscow as a representative of Wall Street and a notorious exploiter of the downtrodden (witness Miss Corsa), he would like to see his enemies face to face. Maseryan probably felt the same way. Without further ado, Thatcher made a reservation at the Bankers Club, regretting only that J. P. Morgan was not still alive and on the scene.

At twelve-thirty he removed with Maseryan to that Valhalla of capitalist hopes. On the way, mindful of his duties to a tourist, he pointed to some pockmarked striations in the granite wall they were passing.

"Those marks date from the anarchist bombing of Wall Street in 1920," he commented. "There are more across the street."

Determinedly Maseryan crossed the street to examine the evidence. He was not impressed.

"Slovenly work," he decided. "These anarchists. No organization."

Thatcher was amused. "Would Marxists have made a better job of it?"

"Marxism-Leninism has always abhorred isolated acts of terrorism. They serve no useful function in preparing for social revolution," his guest reproved him. He gave a final look at the marks, gazed up at the unscathed buildings looming overhead, and added: "But if Marxists had been involved, they would have been more efficient."

"Almost anybody would have," Thatcher agreed. "I could have done better myself. At least I would have found out when the bankers went to lunch."

"Lunch?"

"Yes. The custom here is that the clerical help goes to lunch from twelve to one, and the executives go at one. The anarchists came at the wrong time and got the wrong people—hundreds of the wrong people."

"But we ourselves are lunching between twelve and one."

"Yes, I thought you might be sick of reading those reports we gave you."

"So, we go at the dangerous time. Maybe I will be bombed by an anarchist."

This put Maseryan in high good humor. He was roaring with laughter as they entered the Bankers Club. A fortunate circumstance, in his host's opinion, as the sounds of merriment brought to the occupants' faces that expression which most of the world associates with bloated capitalists. Thatcher was particulary pleased to see old Bartlett Sims in a corner, looking like a petulant whale.

But a born worker cannot be long deflected from his task. Maseryan looked around, approved the vodka, and then turned to the business at hand.

"It is interesting how little the criminal had to do on the day of the theft," he said. "Regardless of when the seal was stolen, there is no doubt that the consular letterheads were taken many weeks ago. And you say the letterheads from Stringfellow could have been obtained at any time?"

Thatcher nodded. He had already described conditions at the office of Stringfellow & Son.

"Then the paper work was all done a long time in advance. After that, the criminal simply waited for the *Odessa Queen* to near completion of loading. Do you not think that the timing was critical?" Maseryan asked.

"Yes. The papers would hardly have passed Quentin's inspection if there had been discrepancies with an earlier set. I think it was essential that they should be the first set of Russian papers to cross his desk."

"So our criminal simply waits for a suitable day with relation to the *Odessa Queen*," Maseryan continued. "On that day, all he does is deliver the papers to the Cunard pier, call this chauffeur—you know which one I mean, the one who was murdered."

"Denger."

"He calls Denger and goes to the Registry of Deeds. It is not an onerous schedule."

"No," Thatcher frowned, "but there are other things involved. I'm willing to assume our criminal had some luck. But still, there are a lot of coincidences or questions of timing that remain. First, there's Baranoff's departure. Now Baranoff is a public figure, and his comings and goings get a good deal of publicity, but still—"

"Ah, I know what you are about to say. Probably no one in New York knows as much about these Russian trips by Baranoff as the consulate. It is undeniable. Consider that point accepted."

There was much to be said for Soviet realism, Thatcher decided. He continued:

"There's another point—those calls by Stringfellow to the Sloan before the arrival of the forged paper and the fact that he then disappeared for the day. One of them might be a coincidence. But I doubt if both were. I think we have to assume our criminal either knew about the calls or about Stringfellow's trip to Jersey."

"Now I see why you are frowning. That information was probably not known at the Soviet Consulate. But it might very well be known in your own circle of wheat brokers."

"Exactly."

These were heretical sentiments for the Bankers Club, but Thatcher had come to the same conclusion some time ago.

For a moment they sat in silence. Thatcher was the first to speak.

"We need more facts. I thought we'd start at the docks," he said. "The one element in his timing that the criminal couldn't control was the loading of the *Odessa Queen*. We may be able to find out who was unusually interested in that."

At about the time that Thatcher and Maseryan were hailing a cab, Rita Halloran put down the phone, stared angrily around her small office and arose.

"I'm going to be out for the rest of the day, Phil," she said to a passing mechanic. "You cover the office."

Phil nodded and asked if she wanted one of the cars.

"I'll grab a cab," she said, briskly heading toward the street.

On the principle that leads dairy farmers to use oleomargarine instead of butter, Mrs. Halloran rarely used one of her limousines for her own travels. This was sound economics; a limousine that could be earning as much as a hundred dollars a day was no car for a businesswoman.

But today Mrs. Halloran had a special reason to prefer public transport. She had no intention of having everybody at Halloran's Garage know that she was consulting her lawyer.

Joe Kiley's offices were in a shabby building on Lexington Avenue. Joe himself was similarly shabby, with a too-red face, spots on his tie, and a wide range of expressions from piety to ferocity that all looked artificial. Many an opponent had been misled into thinking he was an aging second-rater, but nothing was further from the truth. Kiley had a roll of clients that would have been the envy of some downtown firms.

"You're looking fine, Rita," he said when she had settled down opposite him.

He moved a pile of documents to another corner of his desk so they could see each other.

With a gesture that both acknowledged and waved away the compliment, she said, "Joe, I think I've got trouble coming."

Kiley raised his eyebrows. "Well, I know your mother told you to tell the truth to your doctor, your priest, and your lawyer—so let's have it."

She turned to him. "Abe Baranoff came down to see me the other day."

Kiley waited.

Mrs. Halloran fiddled with her purse. "I guess I told you that, didn't I?"

"Yes, you did," he said with elaborate patience. "You said he was worried about Denger. And we both know that Gus was up to something—else he wouldn't be dead and buried. Still, that's the legal end. And apart from that, I don't see that you've been getting too much bad publicity—all things considered. What's troubling you? Is business falling off?"

Some women might have been offended by this uncompromising appraisal of their genuine interests, but Mrs. Halloran was not one of them. "No, business is all right. Most of the regulars don't care one way or the other. It's the slow season, of course—no, this morning I got *this!*"

She fished a letter from her purse and thrust it at him.

Kiley unfolded it and read. Then he read it again. Then he looked up.

"Well now, this seems like a bona fide offer from a bona fide buyer for Halloran's Garage. At a very good price. And that is a good price, Rita. Now this lawyer I don't happen to know—but the New York Bar's full of Weinsteins, so I'll get the scoop on him." He tossed the letter aside and looked at her again. "I don't see trouble."

She shook her head vigorously.

"I don't like the way things are going, Joe. First, the garage isn't up for sale—never has been. Then, out of the blue, here's someone offering to buy it—at, as you say, a good price! I want to know who—and why!"

Kiley regarded her, then said. "Shame the devil and tell me the whole truth, Rita. What's worrying you—exactly?"

"I'm afraid Baranoff's behind this," she said bluntly. "And I don't like it! Why now?"

Kiley tapped the letter with a nicotine-stained finger.

"If that's all, let's put your mind at rest. I can find out by this afternoon if Baranoff's got a finger in this pie. But listen, Rita. Don't you trouble yourself about why anybody should want to buy Halloran's. Remember, it's a good, going business. And people— *any* people—may be asking themselves why Rita Halloran, who's a wealthy woman, should want to go on working all her life. Maybe she's ready to sell out, to travel, to see the world. After all, Rita, you don't have young ones to leave it to—there's just Eddy, and I know how you feel about Eddy—so why not sell out while you can still enjoy life?"

She looked surprised. "Is that what you think, Joe?"

He indicated exaggerated denial. "I'm not telling you what I think—but what other people may be thinking." He dropped into a sober tone. "Now Rita, take it easy and just put this from your mind. I'll find out who's behind it. And in the meantime . . ."

She leaned forward.

"In the meantime, you give a little thought to the idea of selling," said Joe Kiley. "This wouldn't be a bad time—at all."

Mrs. Halloran left Kiley's office both relieved and troubled in mind. With all its problems, with its ever changing cast of different Gus Dengers, Halloran's Garage and its clamorous phones, its echoing caverns, was home to her.

But, as Kiley said, there were other things in the world.

With a sudden spurt of amusement Rita Halloran saw herself down at the docks, ready to board a great liner, to see a new and different world.

"Even Russia!" she told herself. That would be a nice twist.

Currently at the docks were John Thatcher and Maseryan. They had arrived in search of information about the *Odessa Queen,* more particularly anybody who had shown interest in her. From that point of view, the docks were a waste of time.

Otherwise, it was worth the effort of getting there. The seven-day cooling-off period, which represented such a triumph for the city and federal negotiators, had ensured the shipment of substantial quantities of wheat, but it had not quenched the ill-defined fervor which had caused the strike vote in the first place. There were pickets everywhere.

A genuine strike would have created less turmoil. Frenzied efforts were being made to move wheat before the seven days elapsed. As a result, oversize crews labored valiantly while oversize picket lines got in their way. To add to the confusion the United States Navy, alert for the hostile mosquito boats, had posted observers. Between cranes and feed bins and derricks, between sweating stevedores and fiery pickets, moved naval spotters, their work rendered hideously difficult by the armada of pleasure craft afloat in the harbor, hoping to witness a naval incident.

Understandably, the port authorities had no time to waste on Thatcher and Maseryan.

"The *Odessa Queen?* My God, that was back in the good old days! I can't remember that far back. What? . . . Out of my way! . . . That canoe can't land here!"

"Sorry, I'm special dock police drafted in from Philly. Don't know anything about this port."

"Are you the union people? Well, somebody's got to shift those pickets. There just isn't enough room. No! No! No!"

By dint of perseverance and, more effective still, by making it clear they were not leaving without satisfaction, they did get some information.

In the halcyon days before strikes and garbage-throwing French Canadians, the port authorities had had time to give information to busybodies. And had done so freely. The entire world had been interested in the movement of wheat to Russia—the domestic press, the foreign press, the commercial press, the diplomatic world, the grain world, the banks, the railroads, the exchanges.

Not much wiser, Thatcher and Maseryan finally found themselves back at the entrance hall. Thatcher consulted his guest.

"We aren't meeting Inspector Lyons for two hours. We'll be working with him all night, so I think we could take some time off now. What would you like to see?"

Maseryan reflected. When he spoke, it was with some hesitation.

"You understand, we in Russia are very interested in your problems, your agriculture and space programs and defense efforts, but even more in the problems we do not share. We see the headlines, we see the pictures—oh, those pictures! so compelling, so dramatic!—our curiosity is naturally stirred. And so . . ."

"Yes?" encouraged Thatcher, bracing himself for a tour of Harlem and the inevitable comments.

"And so," continued Maseryan, "I would like very much to see your al-i-en-ated youth," he rolled the words out cautiously. "Do I have that correctly?"

"Yes. That's the current phrase." Thatcher's mind shifted gears hastily. The trouble was that American preoccupations came and went so quickly, there was no way to predict what foreigners would want to see. Alienated youth, however, was better than that Yugoslav fifteen years ago with the wife who read American ladies' magazines: he had wanted to inspect togetherness.

Thatcher stalled for time.

"That may be rather difficult," he said.

The great advantage with Harlem, he reflected, was that it stayed put.

As always in time of travail, his thoughts turned to his secretary. Minutes later he was in a phone booth.

"Miss Corsa, do we have anyone young at the Sloan?"

For once Miss Corsa was shaken. She struggled nobly to meet the challenge.

"Well, there's always Mr. Nicolls," she said doubtfully.

"No, no," he said hastily. "I mean *really* young. Someone who would know about beatnik hangouts. I thought maybe one of the secretaries. . . ?"

Miss Corsa's silence reminded him more plainly than words that beatnik propensities in candidates for secretarial employment at the Sloan did not impress the personnel manager. Not favorably, that is.

But now that a decent, limited objective had been defined, she was willing to try. She rather thought that some member of the staff might know somebody who was young. There was always the possibility of a brother or sister. Would Mr. Thatcher wait while she investigated?

So while Thatcher held the line, irritably fumbled for additional change, finally hung up and waited for the return ring, Miss Corsa gallantly assaulted the barrier between the generations—which quite a startling number of sociologists would have been prepared to tell her was impenetrable.

Within a short space of time Miss Corsa was back on the line dictating addresses and pertinent comments:

"May get rough later in the evening . . . a tourist trap . . . favored by beat writers . . . not for mixed couples . . . possibility of drugs . . . strong on folk songs and Vietnam." She did not reveal her sources.

Armed with this information he returned, only to have Maseryan balk at the cab rank.

"I thought we could take the subway. I hope you do not mind," the Russian inquired anxiously. "After all, we are two strong men."

Thatcher stared. "I don't see how that's going to do us much good."

Maseryan's eyes hooded. "They prowl in packs, I know. But how large?"

"Who?"

"Those subway hooligans."

"Ah!" Thatcher understood now. "Yes, we can take the subway. But its not hooligans we have to worry about. It's the rush hour."

The subway ride, uneventful from the point of view of a commuting New Yorker, filled Maseryan with awe. On the platform he was swept off his feet and bodily impelled into the wrong train, from which Thatcher extracted him (with the help of two burly sailors) in the nick of time. Ensconced in the right train, he was separated from Thatcher and crushed like a sardine without any means of support. At one point, as the express swayed and bucketed around a corner and the entire mob keeled over, a sharp cry told Thatcher that Maseryan had just learned about stiletto heels the hard way.

As they climbed the interminable stairs at West Fourth Street, Maseryan sounded exhilarated. Filth, bad manners, lack of air, and shrieking noise left him unmoved. The Moscow press had prepared him for all that. But the hardiness of the travelers!

"It is amazing! It is truly a communal experience. And how can they say you Americans are soft? Why, I saw little old ladies in there. There was one with an umbrella. You should have seen the way she got a seat! Not nice, no! But efficient, without a doubt."

Getting Maseryan three blocks to a coffeehouse was harder than Thatcher had anticipated. The Russian was fascinated by the paperback bookstores. Approvingly he noted the signs that proclaimed twenty-four hour availability, the hordes of returning commuters, students, artists, residents who poured in and out. But the grunts produced by the display racks in front of each store were more equivocal. By one rack, he remained rooted to the spot as he read the titles:

Some Notes on Swamp: In-ness in our Time
Wrecking Balls: Urban Renewal in America
The Camel and the Chickadee: The Poetry of Urgency
Abortion without Tears: A Medical Study
Seminarian: An Intimate Journal

"But where is the Shakespeare?" Maseryan demanded. "Where is the Hemingway? Where is the infinitely necessary input-output theory?"

Eventually they were deposited at a small round table. Smoke filled the room but did not obscure the art gallery which formed its walls. A group of three people, all in beards and sandals and sweat shirts, stood before the pictures, engaged in furiously contested analysis. A young couple discussed their sex life (unsatisfactory, it appeared) in forthright terms. The illusion of free love was shattered by the proximity of a small baby in a carryall. Girls in what seemed to be shiny black oilcloth sat about in a welter of hair and boots. The high-fidelity record player poured forth with crystal clarity the strains of a guitar and a young voice lamenting unrequited love. Everyone was talking, talking, talking.

Thatcher leaned back satisfied. This he felt sure, was the right place. But Maseryan, looking around narrowly, seemed to be disappointed.

"No drugs," the Russian finally protested.

Miss Corsa was nothing if not thorough. Thatcher reached for his list.

"Well, there's a place further down the street that's rumored to be a source of heroin," he said. "Although I'm afraid they just distribute it there."

Maseryan waved aside heroin. "No, no. I do not mean heroin or cocaine. I mean the drugs your universities have been perfecting. You call them hallucinatory, I believe."

"Oh, those."

"Your young people take them gathered together in order to have a group experience. And I have heard of the powerful effects they induce."

"So have I," said Thatcher austerely.

He went on to explain that the home of the hallucinogenic drug was now in Little Forks, Idaho, the authorities of Massachusetts, Mexico, and Texas having proved successively hostile to the march of science.

Philosophically Maseryan accepted the disappointment.

"Ah, yes, I can see that. The work goes on in your provinces because your metropolis is overwhelmed with other problems. New York must build housing and provide social services and deal with its unemployed."

Maseryan's words were unfortunately audible at the next table. A foxy-faced young man took instant exception and interjected himself into their conversation.

"Ranch houses, white-collar jobs!" he sneered. "That's all you and your kind think of. You can't stand the sight of non-conformity. You have to impose your middle-class attitudes on everybody!"

"Middle-class attitudes! Me!" Maseryan was deeply affronted. "You miserable, pampered offspring of privilege! It is the petty bourgeois like you who stand in the path of social progress."

"Petty bourgeois! Me!" A dull red tide suffused the youth's face as his companions snickered. "You don't know what you're talking about. Why, I was a dropout!"

"Until the draft," goaded an habituée.

Long training in Marxian polemic gave Maseryan the edge over his opponent. Fox-face reeled under charges of "parasitism" and "materialism," but came rattling back when the indictment spread to "philistinism."

"Philistine!" he squeaked. "Why you wouldn't recognize a work of art if it was under your nose."

Maseryan's English failed him. "I can recognize a —— when I see one," he announced ferociously, filling the gap with a few well-chosen Slavic expressions.

The lack of a real common language was probably fortunate, thought Thatcher, enjoying himself. There was no need for him to worry about his guest. Several of the familiar clean-cut young men had entered hard on their heels and were closing in on the disturbance.

Separating the combatants was not difficult. Fox-face's experience had led him to believe that all adult men who wore hats were easy game. The brisk counterattack, particularly with its strong socio-economic frame of reference, jolted him. He was persuaded to change tables even as Maseryan recommended a year or two in a factory as a tonic for his underdeveloped sense of social responsibility.

Thatcher ordered more coffee to indicate they were not abandoning the field. Everybody in the room looked more cheerful. These little excitements do brighten life.

"Me, middle-class? How dare he!" rumbled Maseryan.

"He only means that you're over thirty," Thatcher translated.

"You cannot be serious. Who is to lead youth, if not the experienced?" asked the Russian, displaying that feel for discipline which has made the Red Army what it is.

Thatcher unveiled further horrors. "There's a group of students out in Berkeley who have taken a pledge not to speak to anyone over thirty."

"Incredible."

"Or a blessing for all concerned," said Thatcher drily.

Maseryan reviewed the whole problem of youth. "Of course it is different in our country," he said at length. "Our system does not have the organic deficiencies, the economic and class antagonisms, that form the basis of conflict between generations."

"How interesting!"

"I would not deceive you though. We too have young people who are disturbed, who are unwilling to commit themselves whole-heartedly to the mainstream of Soviet life, who cultivate the culture of the West and reject the individual's responsibilities to contribute to the welfare of the community along prescribed lines." His voice grew steadily less confident as he proceeded. "But with us, this must be attributed to inadequacies in education, in the party's ideological indoctrination."

"Curious," said Thatcher blandly, "how such divergent causes result in virtually identical symptoms."

Maseryan brooded darkly for a moment. Then: "But what do they want? It is clear enough what they are against. But what are they for? That is what I ask myself."

"God knows, I'm no authority," Thatcher replied. "But as I understand it, these people are stronger on the attack than on a purposive program."

"Nihilists! That's all they are! Believing in nothing."

"Well, they always say they're for love and communication."

"Bah!" The word was an explosion. "That is childish. Presumably even Nihilists copulated."

"Presumably," Thatcher agreed gravely.

But he was thinking that it would be hard, after this, to return his guest's thoughts to their engagement with Inspector Lyons and all that it portended.

If he had been wiser, he would have pursued the problem of love and communication in a divided world.

14

Kernel of Truth

ALTHOUGH COMRADE MASERYAN, between bouts with contemporary youth and dinner engagements with New York City detectives, was scarcely ever inflicting his presence on his much-tried compatriots, his spirit nonetheless cast a decided pall over the consulate on Seventy-third Street.

"A trying day," admitted Sergei Durnovo, consulting a wrist

watch. He turned to his companion graciously. "Those papers can wait for tomorrow, Feodor Ilyich. There is no need for you to work tonight."

His assistant looked up. "Thank you, Sergei Pavlich, but I might just as well finish them. I have nothing to do this evening."

"Well, in that case . . ." Durnovo shrugged. Then, instead of departing, he produced a cigarette, sat down, and prepared to while away the idle moments in social exchange. He was still at it, twenty minutes later, when Katerina Ivanovna and a young man from the records department looked in.

"You will not be needing us?" she asked.

Voronin shook his head.

"No, no, Katerina Ivanovna," said Sergei Durnovo. "Work is over for today. Enjoy yourself."

But Katerina Ivanovna did not wave farewell and depart with her companion. Instead, after a hesitant glance at Durnovo, the two of them entered Voronin's small office and joined the party.

"Because I am quite free to help you if you need me," she said, shaking out her hair after removing a rakish little beret.

"No, no, I assure you . . ."

In a few minutes the group was augmented by the stout woman in charge of secretarial services and by the single statistician with the mission. After some transparent excuses for the interruption had been offered, the conversation became severely general.

Now, anyone who has ever worked in any office anywhere, will realize that smoking, drinking coffee or tea, and exchanging gossip is a prominent and time-consuming part of the working day; only under the most exceptional circumstances does this activity lap over into off-duty hours. In this case, the exceptional circumstance was Mikhail Maseryan. There was a pervasive feeling that now was not the time to gain a reputation for clock-watching. Should Comrade Maseryan chance to call long after closing time, how satisfactory to be able to answer the phone in firm, workaday accents.

In addition the Russian Consulate, normally as faction-ridden, competitive, and at odds as any office in the world, was united by the descent of the man from Moscow to the point of needing the company of fellow-sufferers.

Every member of the consulate staff was a highly trained specialist of some sort; even stout Tamara Andreeva had been chief secretary at the disarmament talks in Warsaw for a period of time. This accumulation of brains, experience, and knowledgeability could not fail to grasp the obvious. Suspicion might fall on the United Nations delegation, on the embassy in Washington, even on ships' captains, but it fell most naturally on the staff of the New York consulate.

"Not that I am convinced that any Soviet citizen was implicated," said Durnovo when the preliminaries were over and the subject finally broached.

Anton Vassilich (records and regrettably pert) made a sardonic bow. "With all respect, Sergei Pavlich, it is not what you are convinced of but what Maseryan is convinced of . . ."

This speech alone demonstrated the changing climate in the consulate. Sergei Durnovo was usually far too conscious of his superior rank, of his growing reputation as a man making his mark, to tolerate familiarity from an underling. Today, however, he was somewhat awkwardly encouraging a comrade-in-arms atmosphere.

There was a shiver of silence broken by Tamara Andreeva.

"Well, I for one do not believe that Mikhail Mikhailich is convinced that someone here was responsible. No, not at all. He was sent for the sake of appearance—because it was the correct thing to do. It was decided it would look odd not to cooperate. But, you will see, it was some American who did this. Violence, murder— these are American habits, not Russian."

There was a murmur of assent.

"You do not agree, Feodor Ilyich?" Katerina asked anxiously.

Voronin shrugged slightly. "I do not know. I simply do not know. I hope you are right—but those Soviet documents? All that detailed knowledge of our procedures—no, I do not know what to think!"

"That is not the attitude for us to take! We know that we are all innocent!" Durnovo was annoyed. This was no way for a comrade-in-arms to talk! "It is not for us to adopt a pessimistic attiude . . ."

But he could not meet Voronin's eyes.

The situation at the consulate was difficult; it would have been even more constrained if the participants could have overheard the conversation in a little known, but highly esteemed establishment on Mott Street. Tactful inquiry had disclosed that Maseryan was not letting the Sino-Soviet rift interfere with his enjoyment of Chinese cuisine.

Through the abalone soup Maseryan and Lyons had fenced warily, taking each other's measure. Over the Peking duck, Lyons, with the air of a man throwing caution to the winds, had relayed to Maseryan all his hard-earned information about Denger, Quentin, and Stringfellow and followed up with an elaboration of his "new life" theory.

Maseryan had listened carefully, responding to the information with a series of grunts and to the theory with rapt silence.

"It is interesting, what you say," he announced at last. "The new life, I can see that. Not clearly, you understand, but more clearly than I can see a Soviet citizen planning to steal a million dollars and continue his old life."

Inspector Lyons then went up several notches in Thatcher's estimation by abandoning the immediate problem and entertaining them over the steamed bass with a lively description of Baranoff's antics at the Denger funeral. Nothing in his manner suggested that he expected, or even hoped for, a *quid pro quo* from his Russian counterpart.

". . . that clown actually had a flag over the casket that he insisted on presenting to the sister-in-law. The poor woman was so embarrassed she didn't know where to look."

Maseryan was intrigued. "It is not customary to drape flags over your deceased chauffeurs?"

"Only chauffeurs being handled by Abe Baranoff," said Lyons, laughing.

His tactics paid off. By the time they were sitting over their melon, Maseryan had made up his mind.

"I know very well you are frustrated by not having access to the records of Soviet personnel who might be concerned in this crime." He examined Lyons shrewdly. "You are welcome to the background information I have. But, truthfully, I do not see that it will be of much help."

He was as good as his word.

Durnovo, they learned, was a rising man. Younger than he looked (he was only forty-five), he had capped a promising early career with a series of professional successes during the last ten years. Until he came to New York, he seemed to have a knack for being in the right place at the right time. It was no secret that he was destined for early advancement to a distinguished niche in the

Ministry of Foreign Affairs—provided, of course, that he survived the current debacle.

"An enterprising man," Thatcher remarked.

"In more ways than one," said Maseryan sourly. "Ten years ago he married. His father-in-law is very superior in the Ministry. You see, I am frank with you."

Thatcher, mindful of Bradford Withers' nephew wreaking havoc in the Sloan's Paris office, refrained from witticism. Instead he suggested they pass on to Durnovo's assistant.

Feodor Voronin was forty-seven. He had been something of a war hero in his youth and entered the Ministry after a distinguished academic career. He had seconded important missions on every continent except Africa.

"This one married early," Maseryan said with approval. "His wife died three years ago. They had one daughter."

"And Katerina Ivanovna?"

She had graduated from the University of Moscow with the highest grades in English, French, and German ever achieved. Her career at the Interpreter's Institute in Geneva had been equally notable. She had come to New York after short tours of duty in London and Geneva.

Maseryan concluded her biography with one further fact.

"She is, of course, a very attractive young woman."

"I haven't met her," said Lyons with genuine regret. "And you're right. None of this sounds as if it's going to do us any good. But I've got something for you besides background material. We've finally dug up a solid fact, and I think it will interest you, Mr. Thatcher."

"Yes?"

"Baranoff finally gave us a list of the papers Denger was taking to the Registry of Deeds for him. Christ, I thought he was going to plead the Fifth Amendment! That lawyer of his made him cooperate."

"Well?" Thatcher could not keep all impatience from his voice.

"The papers were filed the day of the robbery, all right. But they use a time stamp at the Registry, and the papers are marked 4:30 P.M."

Maseryan leaned forward, his eyes bright with interest.

"But surely that is much too long. The Registry is not far. It—"

"Denger should have been there before two-thirty, if he went directly from Quentin to the Registry," Thatcher cut in.

"Then," continued Maseryan, "he had over two hours in which to dispose of your check. In two hours he could have gone to a great many places."

Thatcher frowned in thought. "Of course, there might be some explanation unconnected with the theft. He could have been drinking, he could have been placing bets, he could have been buying socks for all we know. But it doesn't sound reasonable. He told us himself that he would be free for the day when he finished Baranoff's errands. You'd think that if he wanted time for himself, he'd rush through his work to have the rest of the afternoon off."

"That makes sense," Lyons agreed. "And there's one other point that makes the whole thing screwier than ever. One of the women at the Registry thinks Denger was there twice that afternoon, the first time shortly after lunch. She says she couldn't swear it was him—just caught sight of him in the doorway—but she's pretty sure. That would square with what he told us. That he turned the check over in the entrance shortly after leaving Quentin. We didn't ask him what he did with the rest of his afternoon, so we don't have his testimony on that."

"Denger's testimony," Thatcher observed realistically, "is getting more and more suspect, isn't it?"

Even as he spoke he remembered how Denger had looked, peering up at them, the visored cap pushed back, unable to conceal his spite, his smugness . . . his amusement. Was that the cause of his amusement? That they had failed to probe his activities after handing over the check?

Meanwhile Lyons was still musing: ". . . those two hours could be damned important. That must be when Denger cottoned on to something. Nobody could have known he was going to deliver the check. He found out something, but he didn't know what he had until we showed up at Halloran's. Then, what does he do?" Lyons glared around the table. "He rushes to the phone to call Luke Stringfellow."

"And becomes curious about the Russian Consulate," Maseryan reminded him severely.

"And wonders when Baranoff is coming back," Thatcher added, in duty bound.

"All right." Lyons shook his head as if there were flies buzzing around it. "I've got my boys going through everything we've got on Stringfellow. And I'm tackling him again in the morning. The same thing goes for Baranoff. As far as the consulate goes, I don't see what we can do. Hell, he didn't even know it *was* the consulate. Just asked what that brownstone on Seventy-third Street was. Anyway, that's not my department. But I still think—Yes, what is it?"

A waiter had come to announce that Centre Street was on the phone. Maseryan took advantage of Lyon's absence to pursue his own concern.

"Tell me, what he said just now, is it accurate? That Denger was asking about a brownstone on Seventy-third Street without knowing what it was?"

Thatcher frowned. "Yes, that's right."

"But don't you see? If he did not know what the building was, he could only be interested because it was associated with some person. And if he knew what the building looked like, then it would be because he had seen someone entering or leaving it. As you know, there is no insignia or sign identifying the building."

"That's true. But where does it take us? Every single person involved in this case has a perfectly good reason for visiting your consulate. And they have all been doing so, quite regularly. Except . . . but no, that's ridiculous." Thatcher had suddenly been reminded that there was one person who should not have been entering the consulate on the afternoon of the robbery.

Maseryan had become tense. "What is so ridiculous, my friend?"

"I was thinking that Denger would have been very interested to see Baranoff enter any building in New York that afternoon. But I can't believe that Baranoff wasn't on that boat. It's so easy to check."

"It is certainly easy to check that someone using Baranoff's name was aboard. Baranoff himself could have flown over later in the day."

Thatcher shook his head. "No," he said stubbornly, "I refuse to believe that any man slipping in and out of the country clandestinely would encumber himself with a hundred and twenty-two otters."

Maseryan was prepared to debate the point, but he broke off his argument as he saw Inspector Lyons striding across the room with sudden urgency. Imperiously the detective summoned for the check. He did not sit down when he reached the table.

"Having the boys go through Stringfellow's file again paid off," he announced tightly. "A car is picking me up in a couple of minutes. I'm going out to Huntington right away. If you want to come along, I'll explain as we drive."

Luke Stringfellow was alone in the big house in Huntington. They could hear the mechanical chattering of a television set in the distance as the door swung open. Their host was not pleased to see them.

"Everybody's out. I thought I'd get a little peace . . ."

Red-rimmed eyes finished his accusation for him.

"No use offering you a drink, I suppose," he said defensively, grasping his half-filled highball glass.

Maseryan interrupted an awed inspection of Alice Stringfellow's robust notions of elegance (currently including three oversize geometric paintings and a huge, weathered Buddha ensconced on an ivy-twined pedestal) and replied:

"Excellent! It has been a dry day. And with all this talk . . ."

Luke Stringfellow smiled, a little contemptuously, and moved to open a Venetian-mirror door. Behind it was a small well-stocked bar, with vodka for Maseryan and Scotch for Thatcher. Even Inspector Lyons yielded, if beer can be described as yielding.

"Now, what's this all about?" demanded Stringfellow, sounding less truculent.

Lyons carefully put down his glass and described the latest discoveries about Gus Denger's movements on the day of the robbery. As he spoke, Stringfellow listened without expression. Thatcher, watching him over his glass, knew that he had been tensed for something quite different.

"So, why come to me?" Stringfellow said when Lyons finished.

"I want to go over this call Denger made to you."

Stringfellow slammed a big hand on the table with enough force to move the heavy cigarette lighter. "Look, why don't you try changing the record? I've told you Denger never got through to me. I know he called because you say so—and Tessie says so. *Why* he was calling me, I don't know! I do know that I don't know a damned thing about the robbery! Somebody used Stringfellow paper—but it wasn't me! Hell, for a while it looked as if we were going to get stung for $985,000 instead of . . ."

"Instead of the Sloan," Thatcher supplied when his outburst came to an abrupt end.

Stringfellow grinned at him. "Sorry, Thatcher. But you can afford it better than we can."

"Especially now that you're investing in that industrial park in Trenton," said Thatcher. Whatever his intention was—and in retrospect he was not altogether sure he knew—he had touched a nerve.

"That's right," said Stringfellow almost savagely. "Here, I'll top that up for you."

Maseryan agreed to this suggestion with enthusiasm; his performance as early-vintage MGM Russian was impeccable. Lyons gave him a calculating look as Stringfellow busied himself at the bar. Maseryan rolled his eyes slightly.

From the bar, Stringfellow spoke with a weariness that struck Thatcher as quite genuine. "I don't have any idea—at all—why this Denger should be calling me . . ." Suddenly he broke off and his head went up. "I think I hear my wife. Excuse me a minute . . ."

Without waiting for a reply, he hurried from the room. There certainly had been sounds from the hallway but, to Thatcher, Stringfellow suggested a man suddenly struck by an idea. An unwelcome idea, at that.

The three men sat in silence while Luke Stringfellow alerted Alice to the usurpation of her living room. Her reception of the news was quite audible:

"Luke, you've got to tell me what's going on. You were drinking all afternoon, you wouldn't go to the Shaw's, and . . ."

The voice died away as if Stringfellow were drawing his wife farther from the living room. But the indistinct rumbles went on for some minutes before he returned, more red-faced than ever.

"Alice is upset," he said, trying to play the protective husband. "She's frightened at having police in the house. You might have gotten me in the office in the morning."

Lyons put his empty glass down deliberately. There was nothing easygoing about him when he next spoke.

"If you'd come clean, Stringfellow, we wouldn't be barging into your house."

"Look, Inspector, I don't have to take that kind of talk from you," the wheat broker blustered. "I've been willing to try and help you guys out—"

"If you want to be helpful, Mr. Stringfellow, tell us about your military service," said Lyons with dangerous calm.

Stringfellow went white.

"The service?"

"More particularly, your service in Korea. You could tell us what outfit you were with."

"Now look, I can explain all that."

"Can you?" Lyons let the silence grow for a moment. "You're going to explain to me how you and Gus Denger served together for over eight months without your noticing him?"

"My God, I can't be expected to remember every man out there. I was a captain and he was a sergeant."

"Remembered his rank, have you? And the fact that he was in your artillery unit at Pusan."

Stringfellow mopped his brow.

"I know it looks funny." He looked around the unbelieving circle. "Goddammit! I did forget! That was a long time ago, and there wasn't anything special about Denger."

"And his being in the headlines for a week didn't remind you?" Lyons pressed remorselessly.

"All right, all right! I did remember after it was in the papers about his being murdered. But not before! It wasn't until I saw that he'd been in Korea with my outfit that I remembered. You didn't even tell me he was Gus Denger when you first asked me about him. You called him Augustus or something."

"He remembered you, all right. That's why he was calling you."

"I can't help that. I didn't have anything to do with him for over fifteen years!"

And from this position, Stringfellow could not be moved. Lyons kept at it, alternating accusation with cajolery, threatening a massive investigation into Denger's movements, but Stringfellow's answers were all the same. He had not recalled Denger until he read the accounts of his murder in the newspapers. Then he hoped to keep the connection a secret from the police.

And since Luke Stringfellow, by turn belligerent and self-exculpatory, stood accused of no crime, the three investigators eventually found themselves back in their car.

Lyons was far from displeased.

"We've got him rattled, that's for sure."

"Tell me, I am unfamiliar with your army," said Maseryan. "Is it possible that he did not remember Denger?"

"It's possible," Thatcher was trying to be fair-minded. "Denger was not particularly notable and would have been less so as a young man in the army. His captain would not have seen much of him. And it is a long time ago. What's more, some men forget their military experiences very easily. It's a different life altogether."

"One thing's certain," Lyons announced grimly. "Whatever Stringfellow forgot, Denger didn't forget him. It stands to reason. Stringfellow is a kind you remember, and he's stayed the same. Burly, bull-necked, red-headed. Then there's the name. You don't meet two Luke Stringfellows. We've found out something. When Denger handed over that check, he knew it wasn't to Luke Stringfellow."

"Yes, I think that's obvious." Thatcher pondered a moment. "One point might help. Do we have any idea whether Denger asked for Luke, or for Mr. Stringfellow, when he called Stringfellow's office? That should tell us if there had been any recent intimacy."

"I don't know. But we'll find out right now. We can stop at Tessie Marcus' place in the Village."

Maseryan nodded approvingly. Swooping down unexpectedly on people late in the evening accorded perfectly with his ideas of police investigation.

But not with Thatcher's.

"It's after ten, Inspector," he protested.

"She'll be expecting us. We'll warn her over the phone." Lyons grinned. "But we'll phone from the corner. You can't be fussy in this business, Mr. Thatcher."

In spite of the call, made from a booth on West Eighth Street, Tessie Marcus looked stunned, almost frightened, when she opened her door to them. She also looked unexpectedly human. A turkish towel wrapped around her hair, the ironing board they could see set up in the living room, attested to a domestic evening into which a vice-president of the Sloan Guaranty Trust, an Inspector of the New York City Police Department, and a visiting Russian investigator were now intruding.

"I always wash my hair on Thursday night," she said unguardedly. "What do you . . . I guess you'd better come in . . ."

It was a small room. Awkwardly they watched her unplug the iron and remove it to the kitchenette that led off the living room. The ironing board pointed an accusing finger at them. Tessie Marcus disappeared into the darkness beyond the kitchen for a few minutes, then reappeared in a white blouse and full black skirt instead of the maroon wool robe. Her coarse black hair was combed and wet; she had put on lipstick. Her unstockinged feet were still in flat, shapeless slippers.

His own Miss Corsa went home to Queens to a large, food-loving, multi-generationed family, Thatcher was suddenly happy to remember. But how many of New York's Tessie Marcuses lived their real lives in their Stringfellow & Sons and came home to drab apartments, to washing their hair every Thursday night?

To a solitude so profound that visitors rattled, and finally, cracked the hard protective shell.

"It's crowded," said Miss Marcus after directing them to the sofa and the easy chair and bringing a hard-backed kitchen chair out for herself. "My mother died last year, so when I moved in here I brought some things from the old place . . ." She looked around, seeing the overstuffed furniture, the polished old-fashioned end table, the betasseled lampshade for the first time. "I suppose I should have thrown this junk out and started from scratch . . . but I didn't get around to it . . ."

There are some people who enjoy stripping the pretenses of others away, exposing the naked flesh. John Putnam Thatcher was not of that kidney and neither, he was pleased to see, were Lyons and Maseryan. Lyons' voice sounded surprisingly gentle:

"My mother went four years ago," he said, "and I've still got St. Francis staring down at me every time I have a beer. And I haven't been to confession for forty years . . ."

The Slavic approach was more direct.

"Miss Marcus," said Maseryan with sincerity, "is it discourteous to ask if you would make coffee? I do not know in America but . . ."

Tessie Marcus became Miss Marcus as she busied herself in the tiny kitchen alcove. By the time excellent coffee was steaming in the four flower-decorated cups, she was herself—as much as she could be away from Stringfellow & Son.

"Now, why are you here at this hour?" she asked. In her own home, she sounded almost vulnerable. Maseryan sipped his coffee with appreciative noises and examined a large file of records near the turntable and loudspeaker at his elbow. Lyons looked unhappy.

John Putnam Thatcher made a note to demand more money—much more money—from the Sloan if his official duties were to include much more of this sort of thing. He cleared his throat. "Miss Marcus, we are sorry to burst in on you like this . . ."

"But this is a real home," said Maseryan with the approval Huntington had failed to elicit. "You have Oistrakh, I see . . ."

Tessie Marcus was torn. In a room this size it was hard not to respond to Maseryan's overpowering personality.

"Music always meant a lot to me," she said to Thatcher, making it sound like a shameful confession.

He forced himself to persist, ". . . but it was about that call from Denger."

As far as wet hair and slippers allowed, Miss Marcus became all business. Gus Denger had called the office of Stringfellow & Son. He asked to talk to Luke Stringfellow.

"Luke? Not Mr. Stringfellow?" said Lyons trying not to lead the witness. The Russian was still engrossed in the records.

Tessie Marcus frowned in thought. "I just don't remember. I think he said Luke Stringfellow—but I can't be sure. We all call him Luke . . ." She let the sentence trail off.

"He didn't say anything else?" Lyons asked.

"Not a thing."

"Sure, Tessie?"

Thatcher was appalled by this familiarity, but Inspector Lyons had apparently recognized a kindred native New Yorker and, more important, Tessie had too.

"Oh God," she said with a half smile that transformed her heavy features into a kind of bittersweet beauty. "Sure, Inspector. 'Is Luke Stringfellow there?' 'No, he isn't.' 'Click.' That was it."

Inspector Lyons pressed her on this point several times but to no avail. Then, without warning, he told her about the Korean connection between Stringfellow and Denger.

"Oh, Christ! So that's what it was!" She looked at the three intent faces awaiting her reaction. She took a deep breath that was almost a sigh. "I knew there was something. Luke's been behaving like a maniac the past week. But you don't know him." She threw out a hand that pleaded for understanding. "It probably happened just the way he said. He didn't remember anything until he saw the papers. He loses his head, you know. When things go wrong, he gets scared and then makes them ten times worse."

They dropped the subject. Thatcher, at least, was reminded that Alice Stringfellow had not felt it necessary to enter her living room and explain to them that her husband panicked in times of crisis. In this threesome, that was Tessie Marcus' job.

Inspector Lyons accepted this. Maseryan seemed to as well; he also apparently felt that Miss Marcus could be of use.

"What excellent coffee. Well, yes, another cup. Four lumps of sugar, if you don't mind. Oh, the trouble with those four lumps! When I was a young man, enemies said they showed I had bourgeois tendencies. Now Miss Marcus, you are an intelligent woman. Will you help me?"

Tessie Marcus grew wary, and Thatcher did not blame her.

"You said that you cared for music."

She looked as though she regretted the admission.

"Now, you must tell me. Here in New York. Imagine a woman —a young woman. She works hard, but she does not make much money—not as much as capitalists like my friend Mr. Thatcher, here, or his friend Mr. Victor Quentin . . ."

"You mean she's a secretary," said Tessie Marcus tartly.

"Yes, say, a secretary. Now here, I see that drink costs much money. To go to the theater in New York—that is for the rich . . ."

"You can say that again," said Tessie.

Maseryan was momentarily puzzled, but continued: "Can a secretary afford to go to concerts? Is not this music too expensive, like the theater?"

Tessie Marcus could not resist the opportunity to impart information. "Have another cup . . . and I've got some plum brandy. No? Well, yes, your secretary could afford concerts. You see . . ."

Only after an exhaustive description of Town Hall concerts, of subscription series at City College, of standing room at the Met, did they escape. At least, Miss Marcus seemed more like herself.

"And she could go to the Y," she called down the ill-lit hallway after them.

On the sidewalk, they all relaxed.

"I tell you I'm glad that I haven't got any sisters," said Lyons. "That is, sisters who don't have six kids."

"Ah," said Maseryan, ambiguously. "Ah, you Americans. In Russia, *that* one"—he jerked his head in the direction of the apartment they had just left—"that one, with that intelligence, she would be a doctor. In fact, that is one of the trifling drawbacks of our society. There are too many women doctors. It can be very embarrassing . . ."

"Observe," said Maseryan, as they were dropping him at the consulate, "observe a part of American life that is not generally seen. All this going to concerts! Think of it!"

He disappeared within. Lyons and Thatcher looked at each other.

"I suppose he meant something by that," said Lyons.

"He meant something," Thatcher agreed. "But what?"

15

The Bread of Adversity

THE NEXT DAY STARTED inauspiciously. Thatcher had barely, and tardily, reached his desk when Miss Corsa came in with a message; Mr. Lancer would like to see him.

"And," she added, noting that her employer was beginning a survey of the morning papers, "Mr. Quentin is waiting outside."

As she spoke, Quentin himself materialized at her elbow. He looked anxious.

"Can I have a few minutes, John?"

Much as he would have liked to, Thatcher could not refuse this plea.

"Come in, Vic," he began as Miss Corsa, apparently disgusted, contributed the last word.

"Mr. Lancer," she announced inexorably, "is coming down in fifteen minutes."

She then withdrew, ostentatiously washing her hands of the whole situation, including the menace implicit in Lancer's Coming Down. This left Quentin apologizing and Thatcher wondering what was exacerbating Miss Corsa; true, he had promised her time for correspondence and she was clearly not going to get it. But was this the moment for Miss Corsa to turn on him?

"No, Vic. That's fine. You heard Miss Corsa. Let's see what we can do before George gets here . . ."

Courtesy and kindness alone produced that invitation. Quentin was oblivious to the lack of enthusiasm. He was obsessed by his own difficulties.

"John, I'd like your advice . . ."

Instinctively Thatcher stiffened. The words, ominous at best, here had a doomsday ring. It was too early in the morning for a confession. He was casting about for a noncommittal response when Quentin hurried on:

"I'm sorry to barge in this way—I know you're busy—but, my God! that Russian has been taking up hours . . ."

Thatcher relaxed as the quiet, bloodless voice droned on with nothing more alarming than extraordinary demands on time and staff, interruptions to work schedules; at the same time, it told Thatcher clearly—if without words—that Mikhail Maseryan had shaken Victor Quentin badly.

Without really listening, he heard out Quentin's recital, which still lacked shape and form.

Maseryan, of course, was a man of considerable force of character, and the arm of a powerful agency, whatever its initials were. But why had this disturbed Victor Quentin? Particularly after what Quentin had already survived?

Perhaps there was an innocent explanation; Quentin was simply not up to Maseryan's weight.

Or perhaps the explanation was less innocent.

With what he liked to think was lightning decision (actually, a longshot player's hunch), Thatcher interrupted:

"I know you're being pushed down in Commercial Deposits, Vic. I'll see what I can do about getting you some help. But at least"—he carefully kept from looking at Quentin—"at least you're not in as bad shape as Stringfellow & Son."

Quentin took out a cigarette, although Thatcher seemed to recall that he smoked only after meals. "That's true enough, John. I went over the other day. And I did sense a real change. They used to be—well, almost too easygoing, if you know what I mean. Now, they're pretty tense . . ."

Awkwardly, he relit the cigarette that had gone out.

"Are there . . . has anything new come up? At Stringfellow, I mean?"

Without editorial asides, Thatcher described Luke Stringfellow's military history, and the questions this raised. Quentin sat motionless as Thatcher concluded with the discoveries that Lyons had made about Denger's two trips to the Registry.

"That's interesting," Quentin finally said. Thatcher suddenly realized how often those words are spoken without truth; Quentin was not interested, he was fascinated.

"Yes," Quentin said almost to himself. "That makes it bad for Luke . . . I see that . . . Not that I think he could . . ." He broke off.

Quentin was still plunged in thought when George C. Lancer appeared

"Busy, John? Oh, Vic . . ."

During the highly stylized ritual that got Quentin out of Thatcher's office and Lancer firmly settled, Thatcher let his thoughts wander. First it occurred to him (as Lancer, speaking a shade too loudly, sped Quentin on his way with injunctions not to worry) that Lancer's brushing past Miss Corsa could produce no softening of that redoubtable young woman's current disapproval.

His second thought was less frivolous; he had given Victor Quentin grounds for hope. But what the devil had he given him to cause so much tortuous thinking?

"Poor fish!" said Lancer with his customary ease. "Looks like hell! I don't suppose . . . no!"

"No," said Thatcher firmly. "Now, George, what is it . . .?"

In the interests of variety alone, he hoped that he was not about to learn of another large theft from the Sloan.

George C. Lancer, statesman-banker and utility businessman-intellectual, had the grace to look slightly embarrassed.

"Potato chips."

Thatcher maintained his equanimity. "I know you're going to expand that, George."

George did. Several years earlier, a Soviet premier had toured the United States. Commuter traffic, expressways, even Hollywood left him cold. Disneyland had been closed to him. The only two aspects of American life that had made a hit were Hosmer Chuddley's farm at Parched Stream, Iowa, and potato chips.

"Very interesting," said Thatcher ironically. He was beginning to feel that the inmates were running the asylum.

"Now, John," said Lancer, "just bear with me."

The net effect of the premier's enthusiasm for potato chips was a desire to introduce this comestible to the Russian cuisine. As a result, delegation after delegation of Soviet specialists had been forced to round off tours of U.S. farms, universities or laboratories with pilgrimages to the nearest available potato chip factory.

"Fine," said Thatcher. They had their troubles, and he had his.

"Now, I don't know if you keep up with potato chips," said Lancer with due caution. He knew full well that, while he was composing replies to George Kennan, John Putnam Thatcher was keeping up with American industry—including small local potato chip producers. "You may have noticed that they have just formed an American Institute of Potato Chip Producers . . ."

"I missed that," Thatcher admitted.

Lancer continued. Three important happenings were converging; the trade association was launching itself on the waiting world with the usual hoopla; an enterprising potato chip producer was unveiling a new, automated facility (with significantly increased capacity) in Bridgeport, Connecticut; and a Soviet delegation, sent expressly and solely to study the potato chip, was arriving.

"Today," said Lancer heavily.

Thatcher temporized. He saw, all too well, where this was leading. "Tell me, why this enthusiasm for potato chips? After all, they've had several premiers since . . ."

With his usual expertise in these matters, Lancer could cite findings from Harvard's Russian Research Center, where eminent kremlinologists had analyzed Russian agricultural programs, Politburo personalities, the narrative poems of youthful rebels, and come up with a conclusion: Russia had a lot of potatoes.

"Well, George, this is all fascinating," said Thatcher, letting his eyes stray meaningfully to the thick folder that was currently exercising Miss Corsa. "It will no doubt be a great day for potato chips. I don't quite see . . ."

Lancer hitched himself forward and interrupted. In view of the precarious state of current U.S.-Russian trade relations, it had been decided—"at the very highest level, John"—that potato chips, and visiting Slavs, merited red carpet treatment.

"Fine," said Thatcher.

Furthermore, since the Sloan was so intimately connected with the darker side of U.S.-U.S.S.R. trade, it was felt that the bank should send a high-ranking representative.

"To show the flag, as it were. I'd like to go," Lancer assured him, "but I've got to testify this afternoon . . ."

Three hours later, despite silent but burning reproaches from Miss Corsa, John Putnam Thatcher sat not at his desk but in the stifling luxury of an improbable limousine, part of the cavalcade of sixteen such behemoths being escorted up the Merritt Parkway by snappily uniformed motorcycle police. Brilliant cold sunlight bathed a frozen landscape as they sped through. Inbound traffic, comfortably multihued and winter-grimed, stared curiously at all this black splendor snaking its way north. They were wondering, Thatcher knew, what politician had died.

Thatcher repressed a sigh and inclined his head to the stately enunciations of the chief dietician of the American Institute of Potato Chip Producers. She was a formidable female who was describing the many ways to cook with potato chips. There were two other occupants of this car; the agricultural attaché of the United States Embassy in Moscow (who had been winkled out of home leave in Laconia, New Hampshire) projected bad temper; the senior agronomist of the Murmansk Institute of Horticulture was actively confused.

". . . crumble potato chips, add mushroom soup, then bake in a 300° oven!" Miss Rorely concluded triumphantly.

"Mushroom soup?"

The Russian was probably regretting Joseph Stalin, whose shortcomings, whatever they were, had not included efforts to supersede borscht.

Thatcher himself was regretting—for perhaps the first time in his years at the Sloan—the absence of Bradford Withers. According to postcards, Withers was inspecting Angkor-Wat, but Thatcher doubted it. In any event, his chief's innocent enjoyment of ceremony would have removed potato chips from Thatcher's overcrowded agenda.

Chippsies, Inc., was a photogenic one-story building carefully centered in a genteel grove. Americans in the official party descended from the transport to look around with open pride. Russians nodded approvingly.

"Er . . . these cars," Thatcher overheard the undersecretary confide to the notable he was escorting, "all those cars belong to our workers."

The Russian was stolid.

"Your undersecretary," said a sour voice in Thatcher's ear, "he, too, reads too much propaganda. We know about American workers—and their cars."

Thatcher turned to find Mikhail Maseryan falling into step beside him as they neared Chippsies' neo-colonial entrance.

"You don't know about potato chips, do you?" Thatcher retorted. "Otherwise we wouldn't be here."

"There is truth in that," Maseryan conceded, looking elsewhere.

His game was just alighting from the last limousine, Thatcher saw by glancing over his shoulder. He had overlooked Sergei Durnovo, Katerina Ivanovna, and Feodor Voronin at the assembling ceremonies in New York.

"Yes," Maseryan said placidly following his gaze. "I watch my friends from the consulate go about their daily chores. And you would never guess how much they travel . . ."

Thatcher had no opportunity to reflect on this. Almost immediately he was plunged into the wonders of modern potato chip manufacture. With moderate interest he obeyed the guide and watched a complex piece of machinery scrub, wash, rinse, then slice two tons of Maine's best.

Nodding sagely, the Russians crowded closer to study the apparatus with concentration. They sustained this attention at dipping vats, at ovens, at conveyer belts moving mountains of chips toward a demonic bagging machine.

"Now, here in our Broken Chip Department . . ."

The party moved past a watchtower where white-coated technicians twirled knobs with the eagle-eyed dexterity of test pilots.

After too long, it was over. "Now, to our Chippsies Research Kitchens!"

It was as the technology of potato chips was being unveiled— "Now, at 400 degrees fahrenheit, the chip remains crisp, with absorbative vegetable oil capability"—that Thatcher felt the tap on his elbow.

The sleek young woman looked worried. "They said you were Mr. Thatcher."

Thatcher wrenched his attention from waffle-cutting techniques and admitted it.

"Good. You're wanted on the phone."

If her name card could be believed, the young woman's name was Nona and she was Chippsies' Potato Girl of the Week.

Thatcher sighed and backed out of the kitchen to follow Nona to the phone.

For a reason he was unwilling to explore, Thatcher knew who must be calling.

"It's me, John. Vic Quentin."

"Yes, Vic," he replied with extreme caution.

"I think we've found something important."

There was no excitement in the voice, nor any exultation. With his customary quiet-spoken competence, Victor Quentin outlined a standard operating procedure; the thoroughgoing search of the Sloan files had unearthed an application from Barling Realty Corporation to transfer certain titles and credits in Trenton, New Jersey, to one Luke Stringfellow.

Thatcher had a vivid picture of Quentin's recent reaction to news of a possible Stringfellow-Denger connection.

"We already know that Luke Stringfellow is planning to buy into real estate in New Jersey," he began, matching Quentin's calm.

"But *Barling*," said Quentin with understated professional emphasis. "John, Barling is one of Abe Baranoff's real estate operations!"

He succeeded in startling John Putnam Thatcher. So much so that, not until several days later did Thatcher find himself asking the question that should have leaped to his mind—potato chips or no:

"Vic, just *when* did you discover this?"

While Thatcher was on the phone, the official party had proceeded into the Chippsie Pub, where several pretty girls offered them their choice of remarkable meals consisting of chippsburgers, chippslaw, chipps foo yung, tuna chip salad, and like fare. This kept Katerina Ivanovna fully occupied; moving from table to table she interpreted and tried to explain to her bewildered compatriots precisely what their hosts were saying. The difficulty did not rest in finding Russian equivalents for the English words but in convincing the assorted Russians that she was not making the whole thing up.

"Now that cannot be right. Chipped steak? You must have made a mistake . . ."

"I assure you, Ivan Ivanich, that is precisely correct. Americans take steaks, dip them in crushed potato chips, then broil them!"

The Red Army had given Ivan Ivanich the opportunity to travel abroad some years earlier. Reaching back into memory, he came up with an appropriate comment.

"Wunderbar!"

"Yes, isn't it?" said Miles H. Orville, of the American Institute of Potato Chip Producers. "And, miss, do tell him to try this chocolate-chip cookie!"

At a small table, Sergei Durnovo looked at Feodor Voronin with amusement and resignation. Like all officials stationed abroad, he had learned to conceal his intense boredom (and annoyance) when visiting parties of dignitaries passed through town, demanding aid, comfort, and amusement while disrupting normal operations, then returned home to point out that the Russian Consulate in New York was staffed with wastrels and worse.

"They could not have chosen a more awkward time to come," he remarked to his assistant.

Voronin, watching Katerina Ivanovna with sympathy, was unwilling to join Durnovo, whom he now distrusted, in indiscretions. "These are busy times," he said.

Durnovo recognized the rebuff and did not like it. Voronin was his assistant, but he was far from being a comfort. Still, despite the basic discord between the two men, they shared a common awareness of the awkwardness, even the dangers, of their current position —as well as a suffocating awareness of Mikhail Maseryan's bright eyes watching, always watching.

As they sat in silence, they saw Thatcher return to the room, catch Maseryan's eye, and make a brief summoning gesture. Maseryan rose from a nearby table and went out into the hall.

"What are they doing, do you suppose?" Durnovo asked with unguarded venom.

Voronin absentmindedly ate some virgin potato chips. Like Durnovo, he was so deflected by curiosity that he forgot their profound lack of sympathy.

"I do not know," he replied. "Mikhail Mikhailich spent all morning with me, asking question after question."

"Not all morning," said Durnovo in the tone that Voronin had come to loathe—suggesting as it did Durnovo's sense of official and personal superiority (as well as Moscow contacts). Voronin saw he was being unjust when Durnovo continued, "He spent a goodly portion of the morning with me. With, as you say, question after question."

Voronin, the older if the junior man, was also the more reflective. "Since it is apparent that anyone in our consulate could have doctored the fraudulent invoices, I do not see how these questions contribute anything."

Durnovo made a gesture of distaste. For a moment they sat isolated from the bustle, talk, and laughter around them.

"And the banker," Durnovo added unwillingly. "What he is doing I cannot see."

Voronin took a sip of his beer. "I know that both of them are spending much time with the police. No doubt they are cooperating . . ."

Durnovo's slashing gesture spilled beer over the table. Only after a waitress had rushed over to mop up, smile kindly, and depart, did he reply, "Cooperation! I tell you, Feodor Ilyich, I do not like the way things look. All these questions! All these telephone calls! It is clear to me that they have decided to find a criminal! And who knows who may be cast for the part . . . ?"

Voronin looked at him with real surprise. The agitation in Durnovo's voice was a far cry from his usual armored nonchalance. And naked emotion made it difficult, indeed impolitic, for Voronin to comment. Before the silence could become embarrassing, they were interrupted.

"Whew!" said Katerina Ivanovna, dropping into the chair beside Voronin. "This is exhausting. Never will Yuri Blekhov believe what I am saying . . ."

Despite his anxiety, Voronin smiled at her. The irrepressible smile, the sparkling eyes, always reminded him of his much beloved daughter. His heart warmed to Katerina Ivanovna—and, sometimes lately, ached for her youth and vulnerability. But Voronin was not the man to reveal such feelings.

"You are a very fine interpreter," he said in his precise way.

"But I know nothing about cooking," she replied. "Now, about good restaurants . . ."

She broke off guiltily, shot a look at Sergei Durnovo. He had not been listening.

"Now they are coming back," he muttered, almost to himself.

Katerina Ivanovna followed his gaze. "Who? Oh, them."

She was elaborately indifferent. Voronin suddenly felt very old and afraid.

Thatcher and Maseryan had resumed their places in the Chippsie Pub only because of the difficulties of transport in America; the one efficient way to return from Bridgeport to New York City at this hour of the day was via official cavalcade.

"And besides," said Thatcher as he dialed. "It may be difficult to track Baranoff down. Miss Corsa? Good. Will you see if you can line up Abe Baranoff for me? I'd like to talk to him tonight, if that's possible. Yes, it looks as if we'll be here for quite a while . . ."

(There were to be official ceremonies during which American Potato Chip Producers presented the chip-starved peoples of the U.S.S.R. with two potato slicers of advanced model and design. Thatcher knew this could not be accomplished without considerable oratory.)

He gave Miss Corsa the number and turned to find Maseryan sunk in thought.

"You have told the police?" the Russian asked.

"I told Quentin to call Lyons," said Thatcher.

"I would like to talk to both of them now," said Maseryan with emphasis.

If Maseryan talked to Quentin again, thought Thatcher, the Sloan might as well write off Commercial Deposits.

"Neither Stringfellow nor Baranoff is likely to run away," he said as they strolled into the Chippsie Pub, unconscious of Sergei Durnovo's almost feverish gaze.

"We will see," said Maseryan. "We will see."

By the strange logic governing current events, John Putnam Thatcher should not have been surprised that the discovery of a link between Luke Stringfellow and Abe Baranoff propelled him from the frontiers of modern potato chip manufacture (in Bridgeport) to the basketball courts of City College of New York. Maseryan, he had expected to accompany him. But Dmitri Vlozhnov, analytical chemist from the Smolensk Institute of Food Research, was something else again.

As Thatcher had foreseen, Miss Corsa located Abe Baranoff and called Thatcher back only minutes before the presentation ceremonies ended and a general exodus toward the cars had begun.

It was, therefore, seven o'clock before they returned to the United Nations Plaza. There, Thatcher had already decided, the simplest thing to do was bolt.

Upon prearranged signal, he and Maseryan turned on their heels, marched briskly, and snaffled the first available taxi without looking back.

This was when Dmitri Vlozhnov manifested himself. As the taxi accelerated, they suddenly saw that they were not alone.

"Look here!"

Russian expletives!

The newcomer presented a face last noticed over a chippsburger. Thatcher relaxed. Maseryan thundered imperious questions. The cabby sped toward Twenty-third Street.

Vlozhnov was a small, nut-brown man with thick glasses and a merry manner. He recovered his breath during Maseryan's furious tirade, and replied at length. Maseryan translated. Vlozhnov had been so weighted with instructions to follow his guides that when he saw two members of the party set off to the street, he had fallen into comprehensible error; wrongly assuming that this was the official route, he had hurtled after them. Here he was. With open faith, he surveyed them.

Maseryan's reply did not shake his trust.

"If we take him back to the United Nations," Thatcher said after consulting his watch, "we may miss Baranoff. Miss Corsa said that he had an appointment later this evening."

Rounding on Vlozhnov, Maseryan spoke savagely. Vlozhnov chuckled and replied.

"Bah!" said Maseryan. "I told this idiot they will think he has defected. Do you know what he says? They will know better. He says that after potato chip soup, no one would defect . . ."

Fortunately at this moment, the driver pulled up to the gymnasium of City College. Miss Corsa had reported that Abe Baranoff expected to be here and Thatcher trusted Miss Corsa. He did wish she had more curiosity. It had not occurred to her to find out why Abe Baranoff should be using basketball courts.

The explanation became speedily apparent. Baranoff was not in sight under hanging baskets. What met their eyes was the Leningrad Symphony, members of Baranoff's retinue, fourteen weedy students moving wooden chairs, and several sharp-featured dark-haired women brandishing instrument cases.

"Ah!" It was a cry of pleasure from Vlozhnov as a violin scale wafted toward them. His nose wriggled slightly, he quickened his pace.

"Another music lover! As if I did not have enough!" said Maseryan, putting out a restraining hand. "Where is Baranoff?"

Thatcher had just located the ubiquitous George. He was standing, nay drooping, amid a healthy group of floppy-trousered men.

"Where is Baranoff?" Thatcher yodeled. He was forced to repeat the question at higher volume when Vlozhnov hailed his compatriots in a jovial slavic outburst. George was pained.

Maseryan shook his charge slightly, but this did not abash him. Inconsequentially Thatcher decided that, for an analytic chemist, Vlozhnov was remarkably perky. As such, he compared favorably to George.

George minced forward and in refined accents vouchsafed the information that Mr. Baranoff could be found in the small office off the far end of the courts.

There Baranoff was, hunched over a battered desk, bellowing into the telephone. The plain room was lit with a single naked bulb; the rightful owner of the room—who was an official of the CCNY credit union—as well as his secretary, stood looking on with resentment.

"So, Weinstein, be sure to check with this Kiley . . ."

After more shouting, Baranoff hung up, waved a manicured hand at his visitors, and addressed the secretary.

"Now, be a good girl and remember to call my downtown office. Tell them to send a car for me in about an hour . . . and if you will type the rehearsal schedule . . . well, Baranoff will see to it that you get something nice tomorrow."

He patted her cheek and rose to join Thatcher. The secretary, a thin intelligent young woman who had attended Hunter, glared after him, but Baranoff swept out of the office he had highhandedly preempted, exuding pleasure upon seeing Thatcher again.

"So, you do come to Baranoff again, to talk. Ah, Maseryan, is it? Yes, I have heard that name. Dr. Vlozhnov? Enchanted. Here, we can talk in here . . ."

He led the way into somebody else's office. Soon they were settled at the desk. Baranoff, Thatcher observed, had quite unselfconsciously chosen to seat himself behind it.

"This morning, the Leningrad Symphony arrived," Baranoff

said. "Since Lincoln Center is busy, we telephoned here. They must practice. Ah, such artists . . ."

Dmitri Vlozhnov uttered an ecstatic comment. Baranoff turned to look at him absently. "Better to talk English . . ."

"Have you forgotten your Russian?" Maseryan asked softly.

Baranoff was put out. "No. I have not forgotten my Russian! But with Mr. Thatcher here, it would be discourteous . . . ah, George!"

His call halted the minion who swept into the office, looked around with patent contempt, and presented Baranoff with a paper before leaving.

"George! Close the door!"

The door cut off the distant thunder of drums, the throat clearing of cymbals, shouted commands and pleas. The silence in the bare little office was sudden, complete, and almost ominous.

Dmitri Vlozhnov, unaffected by the atmosphere, began a scientifically thorough study of the portraits lining the walls, although it was hard to see what luminaries of bygone City College basketball greatness could mean to him.

Baranoff thrust a telegram into a pocket and confronted his visitors.

Trying to free himself from an oppressive sense of unreality, Thatcher said, "Mr. Baranoff, are you Barling Realty?"

The flamboyant showman facing him narrowed keen businessman's eyes.

"Do I need Weinstein?" he asked in a low voice.

Thatcher was back in a world he knew very well. "No, you do not need your lawyer when you talk to us. I have no doubt that the police will be speaking to you later—as a matter of form, the Sloan has informed them. I'll leave you to decide if you'll want legal counsel then."

Baranoff raised heavy eyebrows, shot an unfriendly look at Maseryan, who was waiting to pounce, and said:

"All right, Mr. Thatcher. I am Barling Realty—yes . . ."

Before Maseryan could intervene, Thatcher described the problem in bald terms. "Barling Realty just sold five acres in Trenton, New Jersey," he said. "To Luke Stringfellow."

Baranoff's mobile face was a study in conflicting emotions. Did fear or surprise predominate? Thatcher could not be sure, but he soon saw that whatever emotions Baranoff felt, his brain was working at its customary high speed.

"When I talk to the police," he said with a half smile, "I will have Weinstein."

He was as quick as Maseryan and Thatcher to see what this suggested; collusion of some sort, collusion that had first used Gus Denger, then contrived at his murder. Baranoff was, for once, choosing his words with care.

"I have many interests. I buy and sell. Not all these sales do I personally know about. After all, each year I spend many months in Europe, on the coast. And when I am away, my business does not stop . . ."

Maseryan stared at him. "What? Do you claim that you did not know that you sold this land to Stringfellow?"

It did not take a communist to feel suspicious of a man who admitted selling something worth nearly a million dollars, and professed ignorance of the details, including the buyer's name.

Baranoff looked angry. "My friend, I do not claim—I tell you! Of course I knew that land was sold—and I knew the price. I did not know who bought it—because I was in Iran, at the time. That is what my lawyers are for . . ."

"An odd way of doing business," Maseryan reflected aloud. "I come all this way to find a capitalist from Omsk—and what do I find? A very odd way of doing business."

Abe Baranoff swelled with rage. "We are not in Omsk now!"

Maseryan was acid. "And that is lucky for you!"

As their voices rose, Dmitri Vlozhnov turned to stare at the protagonists with disapproval; then he returned to CCNY's notable fives. Thatcher felt obliged to interrupt the exchange, which showed signs of growing even more acrimonious; for some reason, Omsk had sparked ancient enmities.

He said mildly, "I agree that the police are going to be hard to convince."

Baranoff broke off his glaring duel with Maseryan and shrugged. "That, Mr. Thatcher, is what I pay Weinstein and the others for!"

Baranoff leaned back at these words. A glint of cold uncompromising light struck a gold thread in his richly embroidered waistcoat as he did so. These were the wrong surroundings for him, Thatcher thought suddenly. Abe Baranoff was not at his best in shabby functional offices.

He kept his eyes on Thatcher, but there was no doubt that he was addressing Mikhail Maseryan.

"I hire many lawyers, Mr. Thatcher, in order that I do not have to convince the police of anything. Weinstein and the others will do it for me. And no doubt this—did you say the name was Stringfellow?—no doubt he will agree with me. And his lawyers, also."

Maseryan leaned forward with a ferocious smile. "Then tell me this, my friend Baranoff, why do you talk so seriously to this woman who owns the garage? Why are you so interested in this Denger—if he was only a chauffeur. Denger—who knew Stringfellow? Are you sure you did not tell him to do something . . . ?"

"How do you know that I have been to Halloran's Garage?" he demanded.

Maseryan rubbed the side of his nose with a thick forefinger. "Is it then a secret?"

Abe Baranoff fell into stylized outrage. "Then you are following me? Well, do so, Comrade Commissar! We are not in Omsk now!"

His voice again mounted and gathered strength. Thatcher withdrew into his own thoughts. Could the U.S.S.R. have placed an agent in Halloran's Garage? A short week ago he would have snorted at the idea, but now . . . When he returned to earth, Abe Baranoff had moved from fury to awful irony. "And remember, Comrade Commissar, I am a rich man. A very rich man. I buy and sell—and talk to many people, about many things. And I do important business in my car. Sometimes I say things there that not everybody should know." He broke off, directed a knowing look at Thatcher. "As Weinstein reminds me. Naturally, when I learned that this Denger was a crook, I was worried . . ."

Thatcher could believe this too. Not all the details of every business transaction—even those of less swashbuckling businessmen than Abe Baranoff—would benefit from indiscriminate publicity.

"So there is your truth!" This explosive sentiment signaled the return of Abe Baranoff, entrepreneur of the arts. "Wonder if you will—that is all I can tell you!"

It also signaled—unmistakably—Baranoff's intention to terminate this conference. For a brief moment Maseryan looked at him, almost contesting the dismissal. But, at a sign from Thatcher, he shrugged and rose.

Baranoff let a small breath of anxiety escape. Then he rose and magnificently flung open the door to admit the great cascades of Tchaikovsky's *Fifth* that were echoing through the high-roofed auditorium.

"But we cannot sit here—talking about such things! Not when these great artists are bringing magic into our lives! Even you, Comrade Commissar, must be stirred. Ah, listen to the crescendo . . ."

Still declaiming, he led the way to the corridor.

As they followed, it was apparent that only Dmitri Vlozhnov was completely satisfied.

16

Harrowing Details

JOHN PUTNAM THATCHER had been too modest in his appraisal of the forces flushed to the surface by the current difficulties. He had neglected one group that was all but taking over the act—namely, the People.

Long ago the citizenry of a nation minded its own business. It farmed its land, raised its family, fended off the elements, and limited its relations with any governing body to the payment of ridiculously small taxes and occasional participation in some brief martial endeavor. Affairs of state were left to those paid for the job, and bad cess to them.

But, we were told, this was no way for a democratic electorate to act. Democracy depends on you! Know the issues! . . . inform yourself! . . . keep abreast of the personalities! . . . reach your own conclusions!

Any government in its right mind would have thought twice, had it known what was coming. But governments—or the men who compose them—are the same everywhere. Until reality intrudes, they always imagine that participatoin is synonymous with support. They see a keen-eyed, clean-cut, diligent populace reviewing the aspirations of its leaders and shouting enthusiastic approval.

And sure enough, that's the way it began. American voters

started by trooping obediently to the polls. Magazines sprang up to slake the sudden thirst for information about the country, the world, the personalities, the issues. Television came, and it was no longer possible to be totally ignorant. Then support occasionally faded into criticism. Even worse, critics sometimes seized the initiative.

The Soviet Union, undeterred by this appalling precedent, started lecturing its own nationals on social responsibility. Predictably, the same pattern unrolled. First, they cooperated, then demurred, then went on the rampage.

Suddenly every great power found small groups not only giving it advice, but turning ugly if that advice were not immediately followed. Young men burned draft cards in Central Park. The rich declared war on poverty. Poets in Moscow told Russia what was wrong with it.

In this heady atmosphere, no matter how prudent the official actions of the United States and the Soviet Union, it was only to be expected that various individuals and groups would insist—loudly, clearly, and in as inconvenient a manner as possible—on some eerie policy of their own. And all too often they discovered the power to implement that policy without recourse to any higher agency.

An obscure bus driver for Intourist somewhere in outermost Siberia was the first individual to take power firmly by the horns. Abandoning his cargo of thirty-six American tourists and their Intourist guide in the middle of nowhere, he departed with his bus after being inflamed by a tacky, uninformed article about the longshoremen's strike in New York.

"If they don't carry Soviet wheat, I don't carry American tourists," he announced. From this position the tearful pleading of the Intourist guide was unable to budge him. The party was totally isolated for a day before the gallant efforts of the guide ultimately brought them to a town from which news of their dilemma flashed west.

Unfortunately, that evening it reached Kharkov where an American opera company on tour was preparing to give a performance of *Boris Goudonov*. Futile alike were the demands of the company's director, the impassioned reasoning of the local leader in cultural exchanges, and the call for solidarity among artists delivered by the principal of the Kharkov Musical Academy. Instead of performing *Boris,* the company marched on stage en masse and launched into a deafening rendition of "The Star-Spangled Banner." The Kharkov critic assigned to the event, a man who did his duty with the heavens falling, conscientiously reviewed their performance. Never had he heard anything like it. But then, he added, never had he heard it performed by the world's leading basso supported by two hundred trained operatic voices. There had been a subtlety of phrasing, a command of nuance, too often lacking in familiar pieces, that gave the intelligent listener pause for thought.

Among those who paused to think were the members of a Soviet track team in Cleveland, Ohio. Mutinously downing their fibreglass poles and spiked shoes, they first threatened a whole medley of Russian music, starting with the *Internationale.* Cooler heads, however, advised against competition with trained musicians. "Leave that to the Leningrad Symphony," counseled the world's champion broad jumper. He himself was tone deaf. "For us, the two-minute silence!"

So Cleveland track fanciers were subjected to the moving spectacle of the Soviet team, standing grimly at attention, as seconds passed in the lofty stadium. Broadcasters, trying to emulate their brothers in Kharkov (if with less material), did what they could. "Well, sports fans, this really is something! On the left of the Russian line-up is Konnie Levsky, who broke the outdoor record in Tokyo in 1964. And now a message from Gillette . . ."

Each incident inspired some fresh partisan reprisal. The great vortex, spiraling wider and wider, caused wild-eyed government agencies to cast about blindly, seeking the intervention of responsible, sober non-belligerents. Notables in every field were pressed into the service of urging their more inflammable fellow-citizens to maintain absolute calm. But no sooner was one hole plugged than another would start spouting, as patriots, determined to show their bureaucrats what the national will demanded, kept springing into ill-advised action.

"The amazing thing is that so many of them are on the other country's soil," said Mikhail Maseryan, as he called to break an appointment so that he could go soothe, gag—and, if necessary, kidnap—some Russian astronauts pugnaciously on their way to an international space program.

"If this is what happens with restricted travel, it makes you think twice about opening up the borders," Thatcher agreed tartly.

Maseryan had no trouble assigning a cause to his irrascibility. "And you, whom do you have to calm?" he asked.

"Hosmer Chuddley," replied Thatcher. He rejected the thought of further comment. Nothing that came readily to the tip of his tongue was going to bolster the image of the United States or promote international harmony.

When they met for a belated lunch at Luchow's, Maseryan reverted to the topic.

"I do not quite understand. I thought Chuddley had already made his protest."

"Oh, you saw that article in the *Times?*"

"I do not know what makes you think we have to resort to the papers where Chuddley is concerned," Maseryan said wearily. The astronauts had been determined young men. "He keeps descending on our Trade Delegation, telling them what is wrong with our agriculture program."

"I doubt if you'll be seeing much of him now," Thatcher said. "He has other fish to fry."

"Does he ever!" exclaimed Inspector Lyons, who was with them. "He wants the Commissioner to crack down on some meeting in Washington Square."

Maseryan was puzzled. "But there are no Russians meeting in Washington Square."

"He's protesting the other American protesters," said Lyons in a confused attempt to clarify. Almost all attempts to explain Hosmer Chuddley became confused, sooner or later.

"He likes to be in a minority of one," said Thatcher. "He thinks the rest are just claim jumpers."

Actually what had bothered Chuddley was the quality of his unexpected supporters.

"What have they ever done?" he had demanded of Thatcher. "Why should people listen to them?"

Chuddley, like many a millionaire before him, regarded the acquisition of great personal wealth as a prerequisite to the expression of views on public matters. The only prerequisite.

Anxious to get the man out of his office, Thatcher had cunningly argued that the new protesters must have been swayed by the eminent good sense of Chuddley's highly publicized statements.

He had no intention of telling Maseryan any of this. We all occasionally feel the necessity of sweeping something under the rug in the presense of foreigners. But his intention to introduce a change in topic was forestalled by the police inspector. Lyons was not only shifting the conversation, he was doing so to some point.

"I see Dave Yates is eating here too," he said, indicating a table across the room. "That's a good-looking girl with him. His fiancée, I suppose."

Thatcher and Maseryan looked across the room. The dark, vivacious features were familiar. There was a long silence. Finally Maseryan spoke:

"That is not Mr. Yates's fiancée, whoever she may be. That is Katerina Ivanovna Ogareva, an employee of the Soviet Consulate. As Mr. Thatcher knows—and as I suspect you do, too."

Lyons was mildness itself. "I'm not acquainted with either of the young women. But it seems to me that I did hear something about this."

Ever since the discovery that it was the attractive Russian interpreter to whom Yates was sending presents, Thatcher had expected some development. If Yates bought his presents in Russian stores and the two lunched together openly in places like Luchow's, it was inevitable. But he had hoped that the *eclaircissement* would not have to be made by Americans to Russians. Apparently this was not going to be necessary.

"You must think we are idiots," grumbled Maseryan. "I have known of this for some time. After all, I have access to Katerina Ivanovna's dossier. She probably does not realize herself why she was transferred so suddenly from Geneva."

"Happened before, has it?" inquired Lyons, lapsing into his easygoing interrogation methods.

Maseryan's face suddenly saddened, as if with some knowledge old to the human race. "There are girls like that, you know. We have a proverb in Russian about them. About how the wind will blow them a man wherever they are."

"We do too, as a matter of fact," said Lyons, suddenly erudite. "Only with us it's a poem."

"That is very interesting. So you are familiar with the problem."

Thatcher made a gesture of impatience. "I expect the Bantus have found it necessary to have a tribal legend on the subject."

"But this could be important," Lyons persisted. "A combination between Yates and this girl would give us just about everything we need."

"Yes, but what do we know?" objected Maseryan. "These two, they have a romantic attachment. It is not a state of affairs that recommends itself to me, no. But it does not make them murderers and thieves. Oh, it is possible, that I admit. So far, Katerina Ivanovna has been lucky. This time, she may have been unfortunate."

"You mean?"

"I mean that she is an attractive young woman with a taste for adventure in these romances of hers. So far she has attracted men who wanted from her the normal, obvious things. But if she attracted one of the other kind, someone who saw in her a very useful accomplice—and Katerina Ivanovna has a top rating as interpreter-translator—someone who could engage her affections, then I do not know what would happen. I would have thought that basically she was too firm-minded, but who can tell with women?"

"We don't have to tell about women in general," said Lyons bluntly. "But isn't it about time that we found out about Miss Ogareva in particular?"

Maseryan frowned. "This is a matter of some delicacy. Part of my mission is to protect our nationals from suspicion by the American police. We would not consent to an interrogation of Katerina Ivanovna by anyone other than a Soviet official. That duty I intend to undertake myself. However, having taken this position, it becomes awkward for the Soviet to urge the American police onto an American citizen. You see what I am driving at? We are not going to get anywhere unless Katerina Ivanovna and your Mr. Yates are both questioned. But I do not think that I can ask you to undertake the second task if I will not surrender to you the first."

"Look," said Lyons with heavy patience, "this has been the problem all along. You people—both of you—want this mess cleared up. You want our help in doing it. But you want to call all the shots. Okay, I'm not objecting right now. I know we've all got problems. But don't think if this turns out to be a joint deal by Yates and his girl friend, that the New York City Police Department is going to sit back and let everybody else carry the ball. Like I said, for now it's all right. It doesn't have to be me that talks to Yates."

Across the room, David Yates rose and instinctively they all turned their faces downward. Yates drew the lady's chair, tossed a bill on the table and began threading his way out behind Katerina Ivanovna. She laughingly said something over her shoulder; with a grin, he reached forward and put a proprietary hand on her elbow.

Katerina Ivanovna was dressed so simply that it could have—and did—pass for elegance in the company of David Yates. They were both obviously bursting with youth, health, and high spirits.

Thatcher heard somebody—he thought it was Maseryan—sigh.

When normal conversation could be resumed, Thatcher was not surprised to have Maseryan and Lyons look meaningfully at him. He had seen this new aspect of their strange international cooperation coming for some time. But his thoughts were elsewhere.

"Yes, yes," he said briefly, "I'll talk to Yates. Although there's very little I can do, if he refuses to discuss the matter with me. But there's something else you said that interests me. You said that he was engaged. Somehow I assumed he was married. Not that he looked married, I grant you."

"No," replied Lyons, "he never has been. We've got some information on him, if you want it." He flourished a small notebook. "Let's see. He's twenty-nine, came to Willard & Climpson a year after he left Yale. Spent the year traveling abroad. His family owns the firm, or a big chunk of it anyway. Has a nice income, both from the firm and a trust fund. About thirty-five thousand a year. He has an apartment on the East Side—one of those expensive, bachelor-service affairs—and a cottage on Fire Island. Got engaged about six months ago to a girl from an old New York family with money of her own. Debutante, charity balls, a society figure. The wedding certainly hasn't been rushed through. There doesn't seem to be any reason for them to wait around. That could be important." He looked at Thatcher. "You remember we were talking about the New Life theory the other day?"

Thatcher shook his head. "I don't agree. It's not surprising the wedding's been delayed if Yates has started this affair with Miss Ogareva. On the contrary, the engagement has made me think David Yates may be totally unimportant in our concerns."

Even so, with Katerina Ivanovna fresh in his mind's eye, he felt rather sorry for that unknown debutante from an old New York family—money of her own, or not.

17

Comin' Through the Rye

ALTHOUGH THATCHER THOUGHT David Yates unimportant, he was nonetheless anxious that the young man prove this to be the case. But his opening move ran into an obstacle he had not anticipated.

"I would like to speak with you, Mr. Yates, about something that's come up," he said into the phone later that afternoon. "If you have time, I could come over to your office right now."

Yates did not hesitate. "Of course, I'd like to help you out, but I'm all tied up right now. Maybe we could get together some time later in the week."

Thatcher frowned slightly. This was the first actor in their drama unprepared to lay everything aside for the pressures of the investigation. To be fair, however, Yates was also the first person encountered who might legitimately consider himself a bystander. Thatcher decided to be more specific.

"I'm sorry to insist," he replied, "but later in the week would be too late. I understand that Miss Ogareva is being questioned now."

There was a lengthy pause. When he resumed speech, Yates sounded harassed. And, as he was speaking to someone else, this was not surprising. "It's all right, Dottie," he said in an audible aside. "This won't hold us up. I'll be with you in a minute, dear. It's just about the wheat shipments." Then he spoke again to the phone:

"Look, Mr. Thatcher, I am busy right now, and will be for the next couple of hours. Could you drop by my apartment about seven-thirty or eight this evening?"

Thatcher agreed at once. But he was far from satisfied when he hung up. It was unfortunate, of course, that Dottie—presumably Yates's fiancée—should have been in his office at the moment of the call.

But why did the young wheat broker want time? Was it simply to shed his fiancée? Or was he going to prime her to corroborate his denial of serious involvement with Katerina Ogareva. He could always admit to a lunch or two on the grounds of business courtesy.

When, later that evening, Thatcher debarked from his taxi in the upper sixties and gave his name to the doorman, he was still uneasy. A discussion of Yates's Russian romance conducted in the presence of Dorothy would not necessarily embarrass Thatcher. He was old enough to make sure that the embarrassment fell elsewhere. But it would cloud the nature of Yates's reactions. And one thing this case could do without was transparent evasion for no purpose other than the demonstration of fidelity.

But Yates was alone when he arrived on the sixteenth floor. Alone and mildly apologetic.

"Hello, Thatcher. Sorry to cut you off on the phone that way, but my fiancée was with me. And you can understand, I didn't want to discuss Katerina in front of her."

He took his guest's coat and hat and urged Thatcher to a seat near the glass doors overlooking a terrace and the city lights beyond. From the closet, he spoke over his shoulder:

"I had to squire Dottie to a cocktail party at her parents'. But I managed to leave early."

"I hope I haven't upset your evening," said Thatcher with insincere civility.

"No, you haven't. You also haven't explained why the hell I should talk to you about Katerina. What business is it of yours? You're not even my banker."

Yates was perfectly pleasant, even amused, as he seated himself, but there was a challenging tilt to his eyebrows. Just for a moment the suppressed laughter in his voice, the dancing eye, and the rumpled dark hair made him look very much like Katerina Ogareva. Thatcher could easily understand how they came to be attracted to each other.

"You're telling me that your affairs are none of my business, and indeed they are not. But this theft from the Sloan *is* my business."

Yates merely looked puzzled. "Sure it is, but what's that got to do with my love life?"

"It has been suggested that you and Miss Ogareva, together, would have had no trouble in acquiring the expertise needed for these forgeries. The authorities"—and there, he thought to himself, was a nice ambiguous word to cover the strange alliance he represented—"have had trouble figuring out who could have known both the Russian end and the wheat broker end. Then they stumbled across this partnership of yours. Inevitably the question arose—"

Yates broke in impatiently: "Why in the world should Katie and I run around robbing the Sloan?"

The question was reasonable. Inspector Lyons' answer was not. Nevertheless Thatcher dutifully advanced the detective's hypothesis.

"If your attachment became deeper than you originally contemplated, you might have wanted to run away with each other. A million dollars would come in handy for a new life somewhere."

The laughter was no longer suppressed. Yates roared. "But why?" he sputtered between spasms. Calming down, he continued: "I grant you, we might have decided to get married. But where do you get the running away business? I mean, what's wrong with just getting married and living happily ever after in New York?"

"There is this matter of your other engagement," Thatcher remarked.

"Engagements are broken every day," Yates reminded him. "I don't say there wouldn't be a little embarrassment. But what's that in the face of a grand passion? As a matter of fact, Katie and I haven't considered marriage and, speaking personally, I don't intend to."

Thatcher could only nod. It was the first thought that had occurred to him upon hearing Inspector Lyons' encapsulated biography. He could have pictured a married Yates fleeing with his Katerina. A wife entrenched behind the barricade of domesticity and maternity could make divorce so difficult that a man might well cut and run. But no mere fiancée could be such an impediment.

Conscientiously he continued to play the role of prosecuting attorney. After all, he was here as Inspector Lyons' proxy.

"That would be true if Katerina were American, but she is a Russian."

"So?" challenged Yates. "That wouldn't make any difference, and you know it. What would the Soviet government do? Even if they objected, it would be more in sorrow than in anger. And the U.S. government? They wouldn't refuse to let Katerina become a resident. In fact, the way things are going right now, both governments would probably celebrate the thing as a joyous omen. And it wouldn't make any difference to me. I'm not running for election, I'm not a top-security scientist. Nobody would be interested."

Emotions are fine for the young; eminent bankers are interested in something else.

"There's still the question of a million dollars."

"But I don't need money. And, if I did, Dorothy has plenty waiting around the corner. Anyway, what's a million? Say fifty or fifty-five thousand a year. I'm already in that league, and I'll be doing better in another ten years' time."

At this point Thatcher dismissed David Yates from further consideration. The mind that automatically thinks of a million dollars as a capital sum for prudent investment is not the mind that robs banks and streaks for South American beaches.

Yates, satisfied that he had disposed of any suspicions, moved toward his liquor cabinet. "You'll have a drink, won't you?"

Thatcher absently agreed to a Scotch and water. "It's a shame," he murmured, half to himself. "Collusion between a Russian and an American would solve so many problems."

Yates paid no attention. When he did speak, it was to continue his answer to Thatcher's original accusation.

"The thing is, I'm happy. I even like being a wheat broker. I've done a lot of thinking about my life recently, and I realize how lucky I am. Most of my classmates went into management training programs of some kind. Now they're assistant to an assistant to the assistant division manager. Of course, I know I couldn't have stepped into my spot if my family didn't have connections. But now I've got the spot, I sure as hell am not leaving it. There aren't many operations left where you can be involved in million-dollar deals and still have a small outfit. Willard & Climpson is one of them. There isn't so much goddammed red tape and paper work. Most important of all, we're not cogs. Everybody's still a human being."

Thatcher grunted. What Yates said was true insofar as it concerned himself. But remembering Tessie Marcus' life, as opposed to Miss Corsa's, he doubted if the clerical help at Willard & Climpson enjoyed the high degree of rounded individuality permitted to Yates.

Yates was continuing: "No, if somebody's planning to skip to Brazil, you want to look for someone with problems. Me, I don't have any problems."

That final declaration would have roused anyone.

"None?" Thatcher inquired genially.

Yates flushed. "You're thinking about my engagement. Look, I don't want you to get the wrong idea about Dorothy. Six months ago I was closer to her than any other person in the world. And, it may seem a funny thing to say, but I think I still am. She's a girl in a million. But the day the ring went on her finger and that damned notice was sent to the papers, I tell you I felt as if someone had dug a deep, cold grave for me."

"Quite a few men feel that way just before they're married," Thatcher said automatically. Usually he had to produce this sentence on the steps of the church.

"It's not the ones who feel it before getting married who worry me. It's all the ones who seem to feel that way afterward," Yates retorted. He rubbed a hand over his hair. "I don't know. Sometimes I think the guys who get into harness when they're twenty-one have got the right idea. Then they never know what they're missing."

"The realization is merely postponed," said Thatcher dryly. "The thought does finally emerge."

But he could not give full rein to his irritation. Much as he disliked being made party to elaborate analyses of marital—or premarital—discontents, he had brought this on himself.

"I suppose so," Yates said, lapsing into gloom. Then, with a sudden burst of frankness: "You know, you tried to make something about Katie and me wanting to get married and running into trouble because she's Russian. I tell you, half the reason I fell for Katerina is that we can pretend it's the Iron Curtain that's keeping us apart. We don't have to think about marriage. Sure, Katie's a damned attractive girl, but the final attraction for me has probably been that I can list her as unattainable. And I wouldn't be surprised if the same thing holds true for her."

Thatcher smiled in spite of himself. He wondered how many hours of self-analysis had been required for young Yates to realize that Katerina Ivanavna was impelled by the same motives as he was. "You think she's just giving way to her sense of adventure?" he asked, recalling Maseryan's phrase.

Yates nodded. "Sure. I doubt if she's ever given a serious thought to me. She's having a good time and she will, for another year or two. We're a lot alike, you know. But when she does settle down, it will be with a good, solid Russian, believe me. Because she's basically just as contented as I am. And I'll bet it won't be a

Russian in the foreign service. That was all right for sowing her wild oats. But when she puts the toys on the shelf for good, it will be with an engineer or a doctor in some suburb of Moscow. Just the way it will be Dorothy and Westport for me. We both need a sobering influence. And as for your robbery," he concluded with a rueful grin, "if you want to know, it's been a damned nuisance for Katerina and me. Everything was fine before. Nobody paid much attention to what Katerina was doing off hours. Nowadays they're watching everybody at the consulate like a hawk."

"Aren't you worried about Katerina? I gather you're fond of her."

"Certainly I'm fond of her," Yates said hotly, "but there wasn't anything to be worried about. It never occurred to me that anybody would think of us in terms of the robbery. It's only that with all this surveillance, somebody may catch on to us."

"And that isn't anything to worry about?"

"Not according to Katerina. She says that when they find out, they just transfer you instantly. It happened to her before in Geneva." Yates paused. "They never found out in London."

Thatcher was amused. Katerina Ivanovna was more perceptive—and more enterprising—than Maseryan knew. It was as Yates had said. She was contented. She was young, attractive to men, competent at her work and seeing the world. But it was only a youthful deferral of adult responsibilities. When she did settle down, it would be far from the temptations that might concern a prospective husband in Moscow.

"You've convinced me at any rate, and I doubt if Miss Ogareva will have any more difficulty convincing the Russians," he said at last. "The combination, I confess, always seemed unlikely. But it fitted our requirements so neatly."

For the first time Yates became really interested in Thatcher's problem, rather than his own. "Why is this combination such a good thing? I thought everybody and his little brother knew about the wheat deal."

"In general, yes. But specific knowledge was needed to carry through the forgeries. It involved both Russian and American documents, you know."

"I don't know anything," Yates declared. "The press just said forged shipping papers. And Luke—Stringfellow, that is—hasn't seemed to want to talk about it much."

Thatcher was glad to have his host's attention. Here was somebody inside the wheat world. Maybe Yates would have some suggestion. Thatcher had forgotten how few people knew all the details of the forgery.

"Perhaps you'd like to look at some of the documents involved. I'd be glad to have your opinion," he said, pleased that he had brought photostats along.

Yates agreed readily, pulling over a table and producing a pair of horn-rims for the inspection. Thatcher left him to his examination and looked around the room. There was none of the impersonality often found in luxury bachelor housing. The service kept the place clean, the furniture polished, the windows washed, but it had not tidied the apartment into sterility. Probably Yates's habits made that impossible.

There was a long cabinet-and-shelf-unit housing a hi-fi apparatus on which records in gay colored jackets were tumbled. The collection would have won the approval of Tessie Marcus and must have pleased the Russian in Katerina Ivanovna. Here were the concerts Katerina had mentioned. No wonder she had blushed! A lively Mexican rug brightened the wall opposite the terrace, and part of Yates's sports equipment had escaped from its assigned quarters. Ski boots and golf balls jostled together on top of a chest.

In a way, all this comfort was a shame. If Yates had not succeeded in making his bachelor quarters so cozy, he would be looking forward to marriage with more enthusiasm. If this building had found a way of providing home-cooked meals, Dorothy might have a long wait.

Yates had finished his inspection. "I don't see anything that socks you in the eye," he admitted. "Of course, I don't know much about the Russian stuff. But I can see how you might think a Russian was involved. The typewriter alone is enough to make you think so."

"The typewriter?" said Thatcher, suddenly alert. He had been awaiting Yates's judgment on the American documents, not expecting anything from the others. "What do you mean by that?"

"It's not easy to get a typewriter with Russian characters. Several times, when the Russians wanted to make changes in some bilingual agreement, they've had to send all the way uptown for the typing to be done."

It was so obvious. Yet no one had mentioned it. Maybe Lyons had not commented because of its obviousness. Maseryan was probably unaware of the difficulties.

Yates was taking back some of what he had said. "Of course, there are Russian typewriters around. NYU once let us use one. But they're hard to come by."

"Anything else?" asked Thatcher.

"I was wondering about the Stringfellow invoice. It's certainly a beautiful forgery. Even uses their abbreviations."

What a mine of information Yates was proving to be, thought Thatcher. Aloud he said: "I thought abbreviations were standardized."

"Well, they are and they aren't. Some things, there are one or two variants, and firms get into the habit of preferring one usage. Here, I've got some of our invoices. I'll show you."

In a few moments he had produced some Willard & Climpson invoices from the corner desk and was proceeding:

"See, we use f.o.b. in lower case. This invoice uses FOB in upper case, without the periods. That, I know, is the way Stringfellow & Son does it. I've noticed it before. And the same thing for 't.' and 's.t.' We abbreviate the word 'ton' and they abbreviate 'short ton,' but we're both using the 2,000-pound ton. Now about this, I don't know," he said, pointing to the destination. "We use periods in 'U.S.S.R.' Some firms omit the periods and write 'USSR.' I don't know what Luke's people do."

The question in Thatcher's mind was not whether Yates knew, but whether the forger knew. Patiently he kept the young man plodding through the invoice, stopping to question each period, each comma, each abbreviation, each formalized use of numbers. By the time the job was done, they had a list of eight points in which the forged invoice differed from Willard & Climpson's usage, three points being marked departures from trade custom.

Now Thatcher was in a hurry to be gone, to disrupt Victor Quentin's evening, to examine genuine Stringfellow invoices. For if the eight points were all duplicated in the Stringfellow file, then the odds that the forgery had emanated from the Stringfellow office became very, very good.

"I can't tell you how helpful you've been," he said, taking a hurried farewell. Yates seemed surprised at the genuine warmth of his guest's thanks.

"Anything I can do to help, you know—" he started, but Thatcher was already impatiently ringing for the elevator. His mind seethed with speculation. Why hadn't Luke Stringfellow pointed this out? Why hadn't the helpful Tessie Marcus? The woman who, according to Lyons, would answer truthfully but would never volunteer information against her employer.

Or was he being too harsh? Was it simply that all invoices looked that way to the workers at Stringfellow & Son? That no question had ever occurred to them?

Harsh or not, three hours later he was uttering a triumphant shout across the desk to a bedraggled, shirt-sleeved Victor Quentin. Open files were strewn over the office.

"Got them, by God!"

All eight points had checked out. Two of them had been used by Stringfellow & Son only once in the past five years.

18

Thrashing It Out

VICTOR QUENTIN stared at him, and Thatcher beat down a flicker of impatience.

"My God, Victor, don't you see what this must mean? It has to have been a Stringfellow insider . . ."

Quentin shook his head. "No," he said. "The police will still think that anybody who did a lot of business with Stringfellow could have done it . . ."

Thatcher was incisive. "No, Vic," he said, "nobody could have picked up these details from a few invoices. We had to go through five years of files to find them. They just happen to be the way somebody works."

Quentin smiled sourly. "Try convincing Lyons of that," he said.

Thatcher thought for a moment. He had already suggested that Quentin take sick leave, instead of running Commercial Deposits during these trying days—but Quentin, gritting his teeth, had been determined to stick it out. Thatcher understood, and sympathized;

the man's resolve to salvage his old life argued forcibly that he was the last person on earth to steal a million dollars for a new life. Still, the strain was showing.

Well, Commercial Deposit's customers would simply have to like it or lump it. Since Commercial Deposit's customers were borrowing money they would, Thatcher knew, lump it.

Wearily Quentin rose and resumed his jacket.

"By the way, John, did anything come from that Stringfellow-Baranoff connection?"

When Thatcher shook his head, he shrugged. "All these damned coincidences! I give a check to Baranoff's chauffeur to give to Stringfellow! Stringfellow and Baranoff are doing business! And it's all coincidence—coincidence that's drawing a noose around my neck!"

"No," said Thatcher. "Both of them claim that it was a routine commercial transaction. Their lawyers back them up, naturally. And, for all we know, Vic, it could have been. At any rate, the police had to let Stringfellow go."

"Then I can expect the police first thing in the morning," said Victor Quentin as they were emerging into the darkened lobby to be greeted by the guards and let out into a deserted Wall Street.

Gallows humor, but it was better than none.

But morning did not bring the police for Victor Quentin; nor did it shake Thatcher's strong and growing certainty that only somebody at Stringfellow & Son could have duplicated the Stringfellow invoices with such meticulous fidelity.

This virtually narrowed suspicion to a single point—a single point, moreover, already interrogated and released by the police.

Could trickery explain the Stringfellow invoices?

Could somebody have been gulled into preparing the fraudulent *Odessa Queen* papers in all innocence? Could the Stringfellow insider even now be ignorant of having been a murderer's accomplice?

Deep in these tentative explorations, Thatcher strolled into his office. Miss Corsa, no respecter of executive daydreams, greeted him with a full docket of work. Mr. Trinkam, Mr. Gabler, and Mr. Bowman had all expressed urgent need to confer with their superior.

"Fine!" said Thatcher, who wanted time to think. "Send them all in . . ."

Miss Corsa protested. "I believe they wanted to see you separately."

Thatcher was stern. "Miss Corsa, since I am on twenty-four-hour call by the Department of State, the Russian Embassy, the New York Port Authority, and God knows who else, it is apparent that the only way we can get any business done in this bank is to use the efficiencies of mass production. I didn't watch those assembly lines in Detroit for nothing! It's all of 'em—or none."

He stalked into his office, leaving behind a palpable atmosphere of disapproval. This, in turn, injected a note into Miss Corsa's voice that was immediately identified by the secretaries of Messrs. Trinkam, Gabler, and Bowman. Thus, when they converged on Thatcher's office, they were prepared to tread warily. The most explicit channels of communication at such institutions as the Sloan Guaranty Trust do not rely upon mere words. Charlie Trinkam, tuning his ebullience low, reported quickly and succinctly on new and unwelcome developments in some Sloan-held securities.

"What do you know about it, Walter?" Thatcher demanded.

His big, comfortable chief of research was not the man to break under fire.

"Not a damned thing!" he replied forthrightly.

With the cameraderie born of common misfortune, Everett Gabler turned the discussion; he had spotted an accounting irregularity in the annual report of a New England electronics firm. He wanted to summon the lawyers. He, too, could stick to his guns.

"We'll have to think that over," said Thatcher shortly. "At the moment, let's put it on ice."

His subordinates, being no fools, neither pressed their issues nor tried to prolong this session.

". . . so, if you'll just sign that Angleworth estimate, John," said Trinkam, "I'll put Nicolls onto it."

"Send it up," said Thatcher.

His staff was departing, faces carefully composed to conceal relief, when Walter Bowman felt the call of disinterested duty which frequently afflicts the conscientious professional.

"Oh, John . . ."

Thatcher, already deep in a file Gabler had left, looked up.

"I heard a rumor you might be interested in," Bowman said.

"Down at the Travel Analysts Association, they're saying that Halloran's Garage is up for sale . . ."

"What?" Thatcher was jolted out of his bad temper.

Bowman was too experienced to reveal satisfaction.

"Ev here told me that that Halloran woman was involved in the robbery. Just thought you might want to know."

Before Thatcher could demand particulars, Bowman hurried on.

"I picked this up an hour or so ago. I've put Phil Neale onto it. As soon as I get more info, I'll shoot it up to you . . ."

With this, Bowman lumbered off, feeling, quite rightly, that he had handled the Thatcher storm perhaps more adroitly than his colleagues.

They were in the corridor outside Thatcher's office when they saw a new Christian heading for the lion.

Charlie Trinkam summed up. "Poor bastard."

But, as he settled across from Thatcher's desk, Mikhail Maseryan was met with a different kind of impatience. Thatcher was eager to compare notes with him. An internal metronome had started to race; Thatcher knew that solution of the murder was in sight, if not within grasp.

Why the enigmatic Mrs. Halloran was pulling up stakes was not instantly apparent to him, but it added to Thatcher's conviction that things were, in some way, breaking.

Now he studied his visitor. There was, he noted, a certain weariness about Maseryan.

"I came down," said Maseryan. "It seemed easier. At the consulate our friend, Comrade Capitalist, is talking about bringing Russian horses to race at your Aqueduct—is that right?—so there is no peace."

Thatcher interpreted this without difficulty. Abe Baranoff had taken possession of the Russian Consulate, his outriders rushing in and out with important messages, or usurping other people's secretaries. As Maseryan said, no peace.

". . . so, I thought it best to come to you," Maseryan continued. "I have talked to Katerina Ivanovna. I have again looked at that forged seal. I have studied these consular forms again. And I have looked for a Russian typewriter . . ."

The grim cadence in Maseryan's voice puzzled Thatcher. However, he was not letting anybody else claim a monopoly on dogwork.

"I interviewed David Yates last night," he said, frowning slightly.

"Yates?" said Maseryan. His eyes became bleaker than ever. "Ah . . . Yates."

This dredging up of a name from the ocean deeps of memory nettled Thatcher, since it was the real possiblity of criminal, as opposed to amorous, alliance between Katerina Ivanovna Ogareva and David Yates that had sent Thatcher to Yates's apartment and those interesting insights into life and love among the young.

Maseryan, however, was retreating into Russian melancholia and spoke, almost to himself:

"It can be no other way. It was someone at the Soviet Consulate. Who else knows these formulations for certificates? And" —his voice dropped heavily—"who else can find a Russian typewriter?"

These ruminations testified that Russian dramatists were not exaggerating when they put speeches into the mouths of their soul-tormented heroes. Thatcher was interested to note that, despite his abundant misery, Maseryan had not failed to register the point made by David Yates—it is difficult to locate a Russian typewriter in New York City.

Thatcher smiled slightly, which set Maseryan off again.

"Does it please you to learn that the criminal is Russian? Oh, unworthy . . ."

"We bankers," Thatcher retorted, "are scrupulously non-ideological." There was no point in trying to out-Jeremiah Maseryan. "I take it your research has more or less duplicated mine."

With economy, he described his interview with young Yates. The details of the relationship between Yates and Katerina produced a head shaking.

"Precisely what she told me," said Maseryan. "She called it only a passing friendship. I fear little Ogareva is falling into very unfortunate patterns. It must be back to Moscow for her."

Thatcher relayed David Yates's opinion that Katerina Ivanovna was destined to end up in the Soviet equivalent of Westport.

"Ah, he is not such a fool, that young man," said Maseryan. "I myself think that . . . but, no. These young people are incidental. The important part is what you have learned about the Stringfellow invoices."

Thatcher repeated his findings. There could be no doubt that the extreme accuracy of the duplication of the Stringfellow procedures pointed inescapably to a Stringfellow insider.

With an oath, Maseryan slammed a heavy hand on Thatcher's desk.

"How can it be? It was assuredly someone who knows the Soviet consul's forms. Only a Russian . . ."

"And I say it was someone from Stringfellow," Thatcher persisted. "Now look here. It was, after all, the possibility of a Russian-American conspiracy that set us off after Yates and this girl of yours. Although if David Yates had anything to do with it, I'll eat my hat . . ."

Thatcher was just hitting his stride when Miss Corsa cast routine to the wind and buzzed him. Fighting a feeling that he was a whale surrounded by minnows, Thatcher demanded enlightenment.

"It's Mr. Withers on the phone," Miss Corsa reported.

Not even the president of the Sloan Guaranty Trust was enough for Thatcher in his present mood.

"From Katmandu?" he demanded.

"From Rome," said Miss Corsa impassively. "He wants to talk to you about bringing back a new Alfa Romeo to be used as the bank's car . . ."

The frustrations of a frustrating morning came to a boil.

"Tell him I've left for Alaska!" Thatcher snarled. "Tell him he can bring in a dozen matched Rolls-Royces, for all I care! Tell him . . ."

Pointedly, for she too was having a trying day, Miss Corsa left the switch down so that Mr. Thatcher could hear his message relayed:

"Mr. Thatcher suggests that you contact Mr. Brady when you get to Paris about the customs forms . . ."

Abruptly he switched off. Automatically he began to describe Walter Bowman's hint about Rita Halloran, before suddenly snapping his fingers.

"That call!" he said.

Mikhail Maseryan was courtesy itself. "I am impressed. Alfa Romeos, Rolls Royces—like so many potatoes. It is capitalistic exploitation, no doubt—but I do not deny that it is impressive."

Again Thatcher smiled. "It may well be capitalistic exploitation —but it is also the solution to our murder!"

19

Reaping the Whirlwind

"WHAT DO YOU MEAN?" Maseryan demanded.

John Putnam Thatcher was not smiling now; instead he somberly paused to marshal the facts that damned two criminals. This mental review uncovered no loopholes, no further unknowns. His argument, when he began to speak, was as logical and complete as any report he submitted to the Investment Committee.

For a full five minutes Maseryan listened without interrupting, his eyes narrowed as Thatcher moved from link to link along the chain of robbery and murder.

"It was Miss Corsa's call just now that made me see it," said Thatcher in conclusion. The facts he had described were irrefutable, and depressing. "I don't know whether or not I should tell her that she showed me how the whole scheme was arranged."

"No," said Maseryan absently. "Perhaps it would not be conducive to high office morale."

They fell silent. In Thatcher's outer office, Miss Corsa was typing, blissfully unaware that she had just demonstrated exactly how to weave an intricate pattern of crime.

"You are right," said Maseryan with heavy finality. "You explain everything—first the robbery, then the murder. And they are the only ones who could have done it. But"—he made an angry gesture—"but now, our clever murderers will wait for a week, then disappear with a million dollars!"

"A week, or a month," Thatcher amended. "They're very careful and prudent, remember. But even if knowledge is power, I'm not sure where this leads us. There isn't any indictable evidence here—the murder took care of that. And I confess I don't look forward to the prospect of waiting for weeks or months."

Maseryan smiled in an exceptionally ferocious manner.

"Waiting? No, I am not by nature a patient man. As I have said, my friend, we are a good team. You have seen how these crimes were committed—yes, I am convinced that you are right. Now I will play my part. I will make the criminals condemn themselves. That we Russians know how to do."

Thatcher's heart sank as Maseryan spoke. It was true that his own reconstruction of the crime was no more than ingenious hypothesis, without the support of hard evidence. On the other hand, Russian methods concerning self-incrimination, although undeniably effective in their sphere, were inadmissible here. Or, so the Supreme Court kept saying. He was casting around for a way to express this when Maseryan forestalled—and relieved—him.

"We will bait a trap for them!"

Cautiously Thatcher projected skepticism.

Maseryan hitched himself forward. "Let me explain."

After hearing him out, Thatcher made the only comment suitable under the circumstances.

"Oh my God!"

In later days, he was to maintain that, had he been given any choice, he would—at that moment and subsequently—have opted to write off the Sloan's $985,000 to experience and leave the miscreants free to enjoy their ill-gotten gains. Moreover, as he never failed to point out, as things turned out, he would have been saving the Sloan money.

But the choice was not to be his. The prospect of definitive action exhilarated Maseryan. He was bulldozing ahead with zest.

"Theoretically it could work," Thatcher finally conceded.

"It *will* work," Maseryan assured him. "But to make it work, we must bait the trap. There are arrangements to be made . . ."

Unfortunately, these arrangements involved sovereign nations and major financial policies; they further involved four full days. And, indispensably, John Putnam Thatcher's cooperation.

Maseryan had barely left his office before Thatcher set to work. The whole Russian-American Trade Treaty had triggered extravaganza after extravaganza already; what did one more matter?

His first telephone call was to George C. Lancer. Lancer listened to Thatcher's terse recital, squared his already square jaw, and said, "Good work, John. I'll get the Ambassador on the phone . . ."

This in turn was followed by further telephone calls, and inevitably conferences with: the director general of the International Monetary Fund; His Excellency, Manuel Ribiera y Ribiera, Minister of the Treasury of the Republic of Mexico; Otis Hammer (of the Wall Street exchange specialists Hammer & Hammer); three men from the U.S. Treasury; and platoons of underlings.

The result of this activity, and of certain powerful arguments advanced jointly by the governments of the United States of America and the Union of Soviet Socialist Republics, finally budged rigid Hispanic ideas of national dignity.

"But of course," said Señor Ribiera with the feline grace that had not deserted him even when Baker, from the Federal Reserve, broke down and wept. "But of course, if it is within the province of the Ministry of Finance of the Republic of Mexico to cooperate with our great friends, the United States of America and the Soviet Union—we are most happy to do so." But Señor Ribiera y Ribiera had, to put it bluntly, been leaned on. He wanted his pound of flesh. "Permit me to say, furthermore, how happy my country is to witness this eager cooperation between two great nations . . ."

He allowed himself to embroider this theme. Across the table assorted U.S. and Russian officials glared at him. Thatcher pointedly averted his eyes and studied the dour features of a portrait on the wall. He, at least, was willing to pay the price of listening to a lecture; he had got what he wanted.

This was a small notice in the financial press.

Tessie Marcus called it to Luke Stringfellow's attention the next morning. In her flat, matter-of-fact way she had spent a good part of the morning advancing small pieces of information like this toward him, trying to spark some interest, to revive the Luke Stringfellow she had known. The silent, brooding giant slumped in his chair, listlessly watching clouds through the window, disturbed and rather frightened her.

Without interest, Luke Stringfellow took the newspaper she handed him and obediently read, " 'The Ministry of Finance of the Republic of Mexico, having been advised of certain defects in series four of its 1979 50,000 peso bearer bonds (A8273 to TC 9483) hereby recalls such bonds. Holders may present them for redemption or exchange at any Mexican bank within the week. Thereafter such bonds may be redeemed only at the Ministry of Finance.' . . . yeah. So what, Tessie?"

She fought a temptation to shout at him to be a man, to hold up his head, to show some pride.

"Don't you see it's a trap, Luke?" she said harshly, and only an intimate would have realized that she was pleading with him. "Lyons tried to get you this morning. He said they've traced that

Sloan money to Mexican bearer bonds! And now they're calling them in! That means that the thieves are going to have to cash them in Mexico within the week. Otherwise they'll be stuck for years and years."

He looked at her dully, and she broke off. "For Crissake, Luke!" she snarled. "This means that maybe they'll clear everything up! Don't you see what that means?"

Stringfellow swivelled to stare out the window again.

"If they catch them," he said. His voice sounded distant.

Tessie Marcus slammed a desk drawer viciously.

Katerina Ivanovna Ogareva, looking woebegone, listened while Durnovo and Voronin discussed the item.

"It is clear enough," said Durnovo with a revival of his superb condescension. "Mikhail Mikhailich tells me that this will cause the criminals to panic. But I tell you that—had I been asked, which I was not—I would have pointed out that this will not work."

He paused. Voronin exchanged a quick look with Katerina, then dutifully asked:

"Precisely why will it not work?"

Durnovo expanded. "Because the criminals have already cashed these bonds! Already they are far away . . ."

He developed this theme at length, before departing to his own office.

Voronin frowned. Then, although he regretted having to do so, he asked a personal question. "What is the matter, Katerina Ivanovna?" His voice was low, troubled.

For a moment her eyes were bright with unshed tears. "I thought you must know. They have recalled me."

In his heart of hearts Voronin had known that this was inevitable. Nevertheless he looked at her with comprehension and worry. There was little comfort he could offer. Helplessly he said, "It could be worse."

Her voice grew hard as she stood up and prepared to leave. "Yes. It could be much worse."

Joe Kiley's telephone call came just after Rita Halloran finished a long talk with Phil about a dented Rolls Royce fender. It found her in a salty mood.

"No, I don't read the financial pages . . . well, what does that mean?"

Kiley was not put off by her tone.

"It means that they're closing in," he said with the authority of someone with good police contacts. Still choosing his words carefully, he continued, "I think it's a trap, Rita . . ."

Keeping one eye on the work she could inspect through the hatchway, she listened. "Yes, I'm still here . . . well, Joe, that's their problem. When are you going to have those papers done? I'm in a hurry."

Kiley was unhappy. "You're rushing this through awfully fast, Rita. Are you sure you want to sell?"

"It was your idea," she snapped. "Now that I've made up my mind, I don't want to hang around waiting longer than this week."

Kiley forced himself to ask another question.

"What are you going to do?"

"Travel," she said grimly.

There was a long pause.

"Well then," said her old friend and lawyer, "just remember, Rita, the world's a mighty small place these days!"

David Yates read the financial pages because he read the entire paper every morning, not as a prelude to work but as an integral part of it. Secretaries and accountants at Willard & Climpson were not allowed to indulge themselves this way, but read the morning paper at breakfast, on the subway, anywhere—so long as it was on their own time. Young Mr. Yates, however, was a partner, and the morning paper was part of a long-established ritual.

His pleasant features gave no hint that his thoughts were racing furiously even as he read an editorial about Albany, even as he read the obituaries of New Jersey dentists, even as he read about Mexican bearer bonds. But David Yates, who was not given to introspection, was thinking, as indeed he had been thinking since John Thatcher's descent on his apartment. Finally he put down the paper, drummed his fingers on the desk in a final moment of indecisiveness. Then he reached for the phone:

"Dottie? . . . oh, I'm sorry, I thought you'd be up . . . yes. Listen, Dottie, I've been thinking . . . yes . . . we ought to set a date . . . soon. Yes, Dottie, I know that it's eleven o'clock in the morning . . ."

"Weinstein! Did you see the *Journal?*"

Weinstein moved the receiver several inches from his ear and acknowledged that he had.

"I've got to see you right away! Do you understand?"

Weinstein did.

"That's going to flutter a lot of dovecotes," said Walter Bowman when he inspected the notice in the morning papers.

Thatcher, who had put in virtually eighteen unbroken hours of negotiation to achieve that notice, evinced no sympathy for those members of society who require numbered accounts or bearer bonds for their assets.

"Those dovecotes, Walter, can take good care of themselves."

"I agree," said Bowman. "You don't catch me crying for the Mafia. Or for tax evaders either, for that matter. And just how in the hell did you get Mexico to go along?"

This was a question that was going to be asked in many quarters when the full story came out, Thatcher reflected. The answer, however, must not leave the confines of the Sloan. Happily, Señor Ribiera y Ribiera was not likely to make any statements on the subject.

"The United States is helping out with a desalinization project off Yucatan. The U.S.S.R. is building a dam . . ."

"And the Sloan?" asked Bowman, incorrigibly parochial.

Thatcher was resigned. "I expect that we're investing in low-income housing near Acapulco . . ."

Bowman did some mental arithmetic. "Adds up to eighteen or twenty million—to get back $985,000," he commented.

"This proposition," said Thatcher with genuine weariness, "has become strictly noncommercial."

It was easier to say what the proposition was not than what it was. Enormous efforts were being made, but Thatcher was not sure to what end. His own travails, however acute, were comprehensible; unwillingly, he had started out to retrieve the Sloan's money. The low-income housing in Acapulco simply testified that once again he had underestimated high-mindedness, public responsibility, and a number of other attributes of which he had become heartily sick. Why the Russians were building a dam he would never understand.

"So," Bowman summed up, "the criminals can trade the bonds in Mexico for the next couple of days pretty freely. After that, there'll be a lot of questions when they try to get their money. Right?"

"Right," said Thatcher.

"Well, I understand that much," said Bowman. "But how do you think you're going to catch them before they break and run?"

"That," said Thatcher, "is Maseryan's problem. He and Lyons have been thick as thieves this last two days. Presumably they're hatching an elaborate system to trap these poor fools. But exactly what it is I don't know."

At this very moment, Miss Corsa buzzed.

Flags fluttered in a cold wind. A dull gray sky sneered at the efforts of men and nations to make galas in the Northern Hemisphere before summer came. The men and nations persisted and, currently, gleaming limousines bearing high U.S. and Russian officials were proclaiming an event. This time, however, there were no potato chips in the offing. The site was Kennedy International Airport, and photographers were immortalizing yet another historic step in the Russian-American rapprochement by snapping shots of important men and women ducking into the great terminal.

There were even pickets; these hurried-up arrangements had caught Hungarians, Ukrainians, and the American Legion short; not so the enraged citizenry of Jamaica, Long Island, up in arms about jet noise.

"Let the Reds Keep Their Jets Home!" screamed a sign borne by Mrs. Barbara Benbine, present, indignant, and the mother of two cold infants.

For the occasion of this latest gathering of luminaries was the expected arrival, at any minute, of the mighty Ilyushin-62. Aboard would be Vladimir Lusklov, deputy premier of the U.S.S.R., plus thirty-two leaders of high-achievement Stakhanovite stations.

This august party was being welcomed to the new world by the Vice President, the U.S. Secretary of Agriculture, the president of the American Farm Bureau Association, and the president of the Farmers Union.

(Which proved, Thatcher reminded himself as he moved out of the path of a large congressional party from wheat-producing states, that Maseryan had considerable power and authority indeed; what explained the presence of the Vice President, he refused to contemplate.)

On hand with political, commercial, fraternal, and professional greetings was a very large cast. There at the desk, handsome in a mink stole and cream wool liberally bedecked with diamond clips, was Alice Stringfellow. Beside her, Luke Stringfellow smiled at a representative of the Food and Agriculture Organization. Dark shadows under his eyes attested to his recent ordeal. But he was still out of jail, and perhaps that was enough for Luke Stringfellow at the moment.

As Thatcher looked on (and made no move to near this part of the throng), David Yates pushed through a group of Indian economists to join the Stringfellows. He was glancing impatiently at his wrist watch. The Ilyushin was ten minutes late; Maseryan, nowhere in evidence, had probably arranged that as well. Already a certain impatience was stirring the huge crowd that was milling around the airport's angular waiting room; cigarettes were being smoked, then stubbed out too quickly. Small groups were forming and reforming in a minuet of polite restlessness.

For two criminals, the minutes must be dragging.

Yates, however, looked suitably grave and untroubled. The picture, in fact, of the solid young businessman.

Was his mind exclusively on the business of selling wheat to Russia, Thatcher wondered?

Over intervening heads he could see the Russian delegation stationed in ranks near the corridor, ready to greet their distinguished compatriots. They showed the slightly embarrassed, forced geniality that characterizes welcoming parties. Behind the head of the United Nations delegation, Thatcher thought he saw Durnovo. Far behind him, in the midst of a less orderly group of lower officials, he noticed Feodor Voronin stepping aside to allow an airline official to pass.

There was no sign of Katerina Ivanovna Ogareva.

Thatcher sighed. Wherever she was, he hoped she could still smile.

"Flight twenty-six, American Airlines Astrojet to San Francisco, is ready for departure . . ." The disembodied voice intoned, barely audible over the steadily rising din.

Thatcher shifted slightly as the Mayor of New York strode into the terminal accompanied by four uniformed policemen. The other policemen present, Thatcher knew, were decorously disguised as farm economists.

"Great day for the city of New York . . ."

"Great day for Soviet-American friendship . . ."

"United Airlines Flight two oh one, non-stop to St. Paul . . ."

In the mounting uproar, Abe Baranoff had managed to corner a reporter and was busy telling him something. The crush, however, hampered his style; he could brandish neither arms nor cane.

The Ilyushin was now eighteen minutes late, and even the vast confines of Kennedy International Airport began to take on that tattered look that a large mass of impatient people impart—smoke hazing the air, crumpled cigarette packages littering modernistic furniture. Some of the waiting throng even abandoned their postures of spurious eagerness and rested briefly. With increasing desperation, official told official that it was a great day.

Finally the hum of private conversations was stilled, the thousand fidgetings and stirrings were frozen. Triumphantly the loudspeaker spoke:

"The Ilyushin-62, non-stop from Moscow, has just landed on runway six and will be unloading . . ."

Thatcher watched the quick return of party manners as Russians, Americans, wheat dealers, policemen straightened ties, smiled brightly, and began slowly seeping toward action stations. From somewhere, two little girls with baskets of flowers were produced and ruthlessly shoved ahead of the Russian delegation, the Mayor and three directors of the Kansas Cooperative Council.

This was John Putnam Thatcher's signal. If those long hours of debate with Señor Ribiera y Ribiera had any meaning, now was when he would find out. He turned and began to walk down the nearby corridor that snaked away from the main terminal. Each step that bore him away from the subdued roar of the official party rang louder and louder as he hurried on. With only its normal quota of bona fide travelers, the corridor managed to impart an illusion of emptiness.

But unless Mikhail Maseryan and Inspector Lyons had made grievous blunders, Thatcher was but minutes behind another member of the official welcoming party—a member who had slipped away earlier.

He turned a handsomely paneled corner and glanced at his watch. It was all a matter of seconds now. The Ilyushin-62 had set down precisely on schedule; not, to be sure, the schedule of the airline or Kennedy International Airport, but a schedule, all right, that was tight as a drum. Elaborate calculations had produced a kind of certainty, in some minds at least; the Ilyushin-62 was coming in just as a Panagra Turboprop took off for Mexico.

And Thatcher's goal was the ticket counter of Panagra Airlines.

He sidestepped a small group of dark men and women greeting each other with gusto and hurried forward to the Panagra waiting room. It was almost empty. The passengers were already aboard ship, waiting to be lofted skyward and southward.

But at the desk a man was hurriedly stuffing tickets into a pocket, the tension of his stance identifying him as late, hurrying to catch his plane.

As Thatcher stood at the door watching, Mikhail Maseryan appeared on cue from the office near the counter and moved swiftly to block the way to the loading gate. The tardy passenger snatched up his bag and swiveled to take the last steps toward freedom.

He saw Maseryan—and was turned to stone.

Despite the blank, familiar ticketing clerks, the gay travel posters, the sudden eruption of two small children with blue flight bags from a nearby bank of leather sofas, the scene was chillingly stripped of the commonplace.

"Hurry up! They've called . . . Oh God!"

It was a cry Thatcher would never forget. Tessie Marcus was half running as she appeared under the sign pointing to Gate 7. For a moment she stood rooted in horror, until Inspector Lyons appeared behind her. As he put a hand on her elbow, she gave a compulsive shudder and broke into agonized sobbing.

Mikhail Maseryan had not looked up at her cry. Nor did his face have the involuntary pity that Thatcher could see in Lyons'. Maseryan looked darkly implacable as he slowly approached his motionless quarry.

Feodor Voronin's face remained carefully, painfully blank.

20

In Clover

ONCE AGAIN Kennedy Airport was en fête. The Soviet dignitaries who had arrived only the week before were now returning home in a blaze of glory. Their short stay had seen the recovery of the Sloan funds, new hopes for the Big Thaw, and the completion of yet another trade treaty promising further grain shipments in exchange for platinum and bauxite. Sweet harmony was everywhere. American operatic companies, Soviet track teams, Intourist bus drivers, and New York longshoremen had all returned to duty amidst pledges of undying fraternal affection.

The Ilyushin-62 was waiting to fly the distinguished visitors back to the Soviet Union. Its silver flanks glistened in the brilliant sunshine under a clear blue sky. Fountains tossed feathery spume in the breeze, brass bands stood ready to launch triumphal refrains, and throngs of spectators lined the roadways. The whole world seemed to have joined hands in a giant *entente cordiale*. Nothing marred the occasion. True, the Ukrainians were still dissenting but, as their nationalist purism prohibited the expression of their views in any language other than Old Ukrainian, they could not hope to find an appreciable audience.

While joy and amity reigned supreme on the field itself, John Putnam Thatcher was lurking with his companions in the shadows by the Air France loading gates. He had been lurking steadily now for seven days. His successful excision of a malign international growth had produced hysterical gratitude from Washington and Moscow which, to Thatcher's mind, bordered the pathological. The Soviet government wanted to give him the Order of Lenin. The State Department wanted to arrange a solemn presentation ceremony in the Rotunda of the Capitol.

And Abe Baranoff had offered to handle him.

Even worse, George Lancer, apparently brainwashed by his recent experiences into viewing the Sloan Guaranty Trust as an extension of the World Court, had been receptive to this appalling proposal. ("Naturally I don't want to twist your arm, John, but think what it would do for our image!")

Long ago Thatcher had learned that you can't twist the arm of a man who isn't there. Accordingly, he had decided to remain on the move until the departure of the Soviet deputy premier effectively removed all threat of dramatic galas with himself in a leading role.

But deliverance was at hand. Another hour and the peril would be over. He had broken out of his solitary haunts to pay farewell respects to Mikhail Maseryan. It was Maseryan who had arranged this rendezvous. Now four men stood in the shadowy corner. Thatcher was supported by Victor Quentin and Everett Gabler.

It was a new Victor Quentin. The apprehension of the culprits and the return of the missing $985,000 had trimmed twenty years from his face. Relief was already giving way to curiosity.

"Tessie Marcus! Of all people!" he exclaimed. "I've worked with that woman for over ten years, and I could have sworn she didn't have a thought outside her job at Stringfellow's."

"It would have been healthier if she had," Thatcher replied. "That was one of the troubles."

Everett Gabler, whose life was filled very satisfactorily by Rails and Industrials, was unprepared to let the conversation stray into undesirable generalities. "But what made you suspect her?"

"Looking back, I find it incredible that we didn't spot it sooner. But I suppose you could say that light began to break when Maseryan, here, proved conclusively that the criminal had to be a Russian, and I proved it had to be someone at Stringfellow."

Quentin blinked. He was a slow, thoughtful man. Flights of fancy were not up his alley. "I don't see how you could do that."

"The forgeries were too good."

The old bitterness momentarily reappeared on Quentin's face. "They certainly were. They fooled me completely."

"If you will forgive me," Maseryan interrupted, "that should not have been too difficult. You had never seen Russian documents like these. Nobody in New York had. Much less accurate forgeries would have sufficed. Only the absence of the Consul's signature and seal betrayed them. How then was the thief able to produce certificates prepared exactly as the consulate would do them? When there were no previous papers to copy from? The answer was obvious. They were forged by someone familiar with this type of documentation, from his work with a Soviet trade delegation in another country. Hence a member of the Soviet staff."

Quentin nodded slowly. To Everett Gabler the whole thing was clear as day. This was what came of shifting people around the world willy-nilly. You didn't find the Sloan acting that way.

Thatcher took up the story. "But none of the Soviet officials was an old hand in New York. They were all comparative newcomers, brought over within the last year or two. And the criminal had to be someone from the New York wheat world, who knew exactly how you worked, Victor. The critical period in the entire crime was the interval during which you were examining the shipping papers and releasing the check. You had been conditioned for over a week to act exactly the way you did. On top of that, the same observations could be made about the Stringfellow papers that were made about the Russian ones. Where there was nothing to copy from, still the forger went ahead and produced an invoice exactly the way Stringfellow's office would have done it. Inevitably, we were forced to think in terms of collaboration between a Russian and an American."

"But how could you narrow things down any further? Theoretically, any combination of two people would have been possible." Gabler's normal testiness had been mellowed by the Sloan's recovery of the loot. Personal outrage no longer underlined his every reference to the robbery.

Thatcher shook his head.

"Theoretically, perhaps. But actually, no. Try to imagine an American wheat broker and a Soviet official first suggesting a million-dollar theft to each other. Think of Yates and Durnovo, for instance. It simply doesn't stand up. Total strangers don't make that kind of suggestion to each other. There has to be some sort of intimacy first, some grounds for thinking the proposal will be acceptable."

"And life being what it is, the intimacy would be between a man and a woman." Maseryan was nodding like a Mandarin sage. "We have had some experience with the intimacies of Soviet personnel abroad, and that is always how trouble starts. A man and a woman."

Gabler snorted. "Not just with Soviet personnel!"

"We had no trouble getting that far," continued Thatcher. "That's why we were so attracted by the possibilities of the situation between Yates and Miss Ogareva. But when that didn't stand up, we were at a loss. We've all been so indoctrinated with the myth of young love, that we didn't think in terms of a woman of thirty-eight and a man of forty-seven. If I had paid more attention to the realities of life, I would have been thinking along the right track as soon as I talked with Yates."

"But you redeemed yourself nobly, my friend," said Maseryan generously. "Your insight was positively brilliant."

"What insight?" Quentin demanded. "That's what I want to know. What made you zero in?"

Thatcher leaned against the building to collect his thoughts. "All along I was bothered by the luck our criminals had. Stringfellow's calls alerting the Sloan, Stringfellow's absence in Jersey on the critical day, Stringfellow's contemplated land purchase being brought to our attention so that a delivery at the Registry of Deeds was reasonable. That's what I meant about conditioning you, Victor."

Quentin was no longer unnerved by references to his innocent but vital role in the fraud. He was moved to enter an objection.

"But we proved that an outsider could have found out about these things."

"Finding out wasn't enough. This robbery was planned months in advance. The criminal's problem wasn't finding out himself. It was making sure these things happened—and that you, at the Sloan, knew about them. The timing of Stringfellow's movements and the timing of the *Odessa Queen* were interlocked. It looked almost as if the criminals had to be moving Luke Stringfellow around, arranging his calls and his trips. All that was explained if Stringfellow were the guilty man. Indeed, the suspicion was reinforced by the exceptionally tense atmosphere at Stringfellow & Son after the theft, when they hadn't lost a cent. It didn't seem possible that it could be anyone else. And then I asked Miss Corsa to make a call for me."

Gabler's mellowness had its limits.

"Well?" he demanded impatiently. "That's what she's there for. To make your calls."

"Exactly. But I told her to say one thing and she, quite properly, said another. To be honest, I told her to tell Withers that I'd left for Alaska, and she translated that into some acceptable message. If anybody had asked me four days later, I would have immediately agreed that I told her to give *her* message to Withers. And Withers would have said that he got that message from me.

We both think of Miss Corsa as my alter ego. But it started my thoughts along a certain path. Who makes calls for me? Who arranges my appointments? Who can make absolutely sure that at a certain moment I will be at the aquarium meeting Abe Baranoff? Who, in short, can push me around the board like a chess piece?"

He received an unexpected reply.

"It is a great mistake, my friend, to allow yourself to be managed by a woman," said Maseryan broodingly. "You should assert your authority."

Thatcher snorted politely. It was all very well for Maseryan to talk big, here safe in Kennedy Airport. In his only face-to-face encounter with Miss Corsa, the Russian had been mild as milk. Thatcher was ready to swear that somewhere in the Kremlin, or wherever Maseryan maintained his office, there was a soft-voiced, strong-minded young woman named Ludmilla who saw to it that Comrade Maseryan toed the line.

"Never mind that," he said diplomatically. "All this made me think of Tessie Marcus in a new light. We all agreed that it was unfortunate the last call to Quentin before the forgery gave him the impression that the *Odessa Queen* papers would be delivered any minute, instead of any day. Stringfellow adopted the language of the call unhesitatingly. But actually the call had been made by Tessie. She could twist it to leave any impression she wanted. And she could easily arrange her superior's movements to suit herself. Finally, the atmosphere at Stringfellow & Son could result from her tension, rather than Luke Stringfellow's. Anybody who doubts that simply has to visit my office when Miss Corsa is displeased."

Quentin still had difficulty with the outlines of the plot. "I see all that. But how in the world did you move on, to her liaison with Voronin?"

"That was the easiest of all," said Thatcher sadly. "That's why I should have listened to Yates. He told me that happy people do not rob and murder to start a new life. And he was right, of course. But a simple examination of the records eliminated quite a few people. Compare Voronin and Durnovo, for instance. Durnovo is the classic example of a man on his way up. Every year has seen an improvement in his position. Before the robbery, he had clear sailing for a brilliant future. Voronin was exactly the reverse—brilliant beginnings petering out into mediocrity. A war hero, a top student, then downhill. That might have meant nothing by itself, but his personal life had become equally unsatisfactory. First he lost his wife, then his daughter got married and left him alone to move to a strange city. Tessie Marcus' mother had died two years ago, leaving her to solitude. They were both probably very unhappy. They had been working with each other on these wheat shipments for over a year. What more natural than that two lonely people should come together?"

"Have they spoken of this at all?" asked Maseryan. He had lost touch with the criminals after their arrest. Voronin's diplomatic immunity had been waived by the Soviet Union; he was now imprisoned in New York, under a charge of first-degree murder.

Thatcher's information was more recent, and he was able to reply.

"Yes. Tessie Marcus has told Lyons all about it. She's not the least bit remorseful. She says she'd do it again if she had the chance. She and Voronin met quite accidentally at a concert one evening almost a year ago. You were right about all that music being a link. They had coffee together afterward. Within a month, they were living together. Within two months, they had decided they couldn't live without each other. It's a great mistake to think it's the young who take their love affairs seriously. People like Miss Ogareva and Yates still have the illusion of inexhaustible time and opportunity. And it's not such an illusion. Yates can find himself a new attachment any day. Katerina Ivanovna knows very well that she has only to lift a finger to bring a man to her side. It's the middle-aged, the lonely, the failures, who bring the edge of desperation to their relationships. As far as Voronin and Tessie Marcus were concerned, this was their one, their only chance to seize happiness."

Everett Gabler was markedly unsympathetic. "That may explain why they persisted in an improper relationship," he said stiffly. "It does not explain why they found it necessary to rob the Sloan of a million dollars."

"Ah, you are not acquainted with Feodor Voronin's record," Maseryan interjected. "He was what you might call a perpetual assistant, constantly being moved from country to country, whenever there was need of extra personnel."

Thatcher had a vivid recollection of the first time he had seen Voronin on the *Odessa Queen,* sitting modestly withdrawn from

Captain Kurnatovsky's convivial circle; then later at the consulate hovering deferentially at Durnovo's elbow. After twenty years of being the deferential assistant, a man begins to be weary.

He tried to explain this to Everett, although he knew that Everett was beyond understanding.

"Look at the situation they faced. It was very different from the Yates-Ogareva tangle. Voronin would soon be transferred away from New York. And he couldn't even defect successfully. He had spent his entire professional career as a junior Soviet administrator and was virtually unemployable in any other capacity. He didn't know anything that would make him a catch to American intelligence. Quite the contrary. In the present climate of good relations between the two countries, even sanctuary would have been extended reluctantly. And Tessie? Was she willing to go on dedicating her life to the affairs of Stringfellow & Son? No, of course not. They had both reached the point where they were ripe for the attractions of what Inspector Lyons calls the new life in Brazil. And between them, they had an ideal opportunity to achieve it."

Quentin was still preoccupied with the aspects of the robbery which had impinged on him personally. "And Denger? How did he come into it?"

"He wasn't supposed to come in at all. When Voronin was casting about for a way to deliver the forgeries anonymously, he remembered how Baranoff would settle down at the consulate, ordering the nearest secretary to call Halloran's and deliver instructions to Denger. Remember, Voronin never dreamed it would be Denger at the Registry of Deeds. He thought it would be a bank messenger from the Sloan. By a terrible fluke, Denger knew Stringfellow . . . knew him well enough to realize a second after he made delivery that an imposter was concerned. So he followed Voronin back to the consulate without any idea of what was involved. That's how he spent the time between his first call at the Registry and his second. As soon as the police became active, he realized his information must be worth money to somebody. Tessie says it was the biggest shock of her life when she picked up the phone and Denger announced himself as an old Army buddy of Stringfellow's. He told her he'd followed Stringfellow's stand-in back to Seventy-third Street."

"We shouldn't have overlooked that," Gabler said reproachfully. "That call was the only one in which Denger actually spoke with a suspect. It must have been the motivation for the murder, and the person involved was Miss Marcus."

"Yes. She acted very promptly too. Got Denger's number and promised to call back. Then there was a hurried consultation with Voronin, and they set Denger up for the murder. They were in hourly danger that the papers would report the Sloan robbery. After that, they couldn't count on Denger's staying away from the police. There was bound to be a sizable reward from the Sloan."

Maseryan shook his head at violence by a Soviet citizen. "It was Voronin who did the actual shooting, after making an appointment at the consulate with Denger. He was very familiar with the terrain. He was back inside, by a rear door, almost before the alarm had been given."

Thatcher drew Quentin's attention to a point he might have overlooked. "That's why Voronin left us so abruptly at the *Odessa Queen*. He was uptown an hour before we were, waiting to keep his appointment."

"And Mrs. Halloran didn't suspect Denger of being up to something?" Gabler asked dubiously.

"Oh, she suspected all right. She was desperately afraid that the entire robbery had been engineered from her garage. And she thought there might be other things going on that she didn't know about. That's why she was eager to sell. And the closer we seemed to be coming to a solution, the more eager she was to be free and clear before the revelations were made."

Gabler, with his usual concentration on the fine print of commerce, had an inquiry.

"But exactly why did Abe Baranoff buy Halloran's Garage?"

John Putnam Thatcher rarely found it possible to score off Gabler in this context.

"Because, Everett, Baranoff is always ready to buy—in a buyer's market."

To add to Gabler's pique, Mikhail Maseryan chose to illustrate this truth by quoting from Marxist scripture.

"Accumulate, accumulate . . ." he said with disapprobation.

Before Maseryan could continue into a denunciation of Baranoff's habit of buying garages with the right hand and selling real estate with the left, Victor Quentin dragged the conversation back to the straight and narrow.

"I understand Abe Baranoff," he said, incurring a frigid glare from Everett Gabler, "but Luke Stringfellow beats me. Why was he so upset? I know you say it was Tessie who made the difference in that office, but Luke was on edge too."

Thatcher cleared his throat. "Well, Vic, I wasn't going to bring this up right now, but perhaps it's just as well. If I were you, I'd be careful of the business Luke Stringfellow brings to Commercial Deposits these days."

Quentin gaped at him.

"Yes," Thatcher agreed. "It's hard to believe, after all this, but it seems that Luke's up to his ears in trouble, over that Jersey real estate operation. It's a highly dubious deal, I gather. And the rumor is that Luke Stringfellow is acting as strawman. Not exactly illegal, but flirting with it, you might say."

"Tsk, tsk," said Maseryan.

Quentin flushed. "Stringfellow? After all this? John, believe me, I'm going to watch him like . . . like . . ."

Since words failed him, Thatcher came through. "Like a hawk. Yes, I would. At any rate, that's why he's been so worried about bank and police attention. It's reasonable . . ."

Both Victor Quentin and Everett Gabler embodied an outraged Sloan Guaranty Trust, but Quentin still retained enough human frailty to experience personal emotion.

"This whole thing, the robbery and the murder, has been unbelievable," he said.

"*Now* it is unbelievable," Maseryan told him sternly. "But it should have been foreseen. Our friend Sergei Durnovo will have to answer for this. His future may not be as bright as he—and his father-in-law—expected. This went on for months, under his nose. Voronin should never have been exposed to such . . . such temptations. As soon as his daughter left, he should have been transferred back to Moscow. Two years of home duty, and he would have been contentedly remarried!"

"No one could possibly have expected such irregular conduct." Everett Gabler did not anticipate human shortcomings. He demanded the ideal. When he didn't get it, he was incensed.

"To expect is one thing. To defend yourself is another," retorted the Russian.

With some amusement, Thatcher intervened. "As you have, I understand, with Katerina Ivanovna."

"What has he done with Katerina Ivanovna?" demanded Victor

Quentin, who had pleasurable, if hazy, memories of the *Odessa Queen* party they had shared.

Mikhail Maseryan met the question with dignity. "She has been appointed my secretary, in Moscow," he said blandly. "That way I can assure myself—that she does not get into further trouble."

Confronted by undisguised incredulity, he hastened to change the subject. "But you are wondering why I have brought you out here for this meeting. I wanted to introduce you to Voronin's replacement. He has just arrived on the flight from Paris. Ah, there he is."

They turned to watch a baggage-laden group being ushered over by Maseryan's driver.

"And I suppose that this time you have protected yourself against any possibility of unhappiness or loneliness?" Thatcher asked skeptically.

"He may be unhappy," said Maseryan, "but I guarantee that he will not be lonely."

The handsome blond couple in the lead were introduced as Akim and Anna Maltsev.

"And you must introduce us to the others," urged Maseryan.

Proudly Akim Maltsev stepped aside to reveal the tail of the procession and began the enumeration:

"And this is our little Vanya, our little Sasha, little Volodya, little Natasha, little Olya, little Doonya, little Grisha . . ."

A Stitch in Time

CONTENTS

1 Medical History

WALL STREET is the money market of the world and its outward trappings of power are plainly visible. Proud bastions rise from high priced curbs with glass walls, contemporary decor and pampered foliage to bespeak financial might. From Brooklyn to the Bronx, whole armies of men and women are drafted to service Wall Street by carrying papers, typing letters and answering telephones. On occasion, one of the grandees of the street can be sighted, the healthy tan of his countenance marking him out from the pallid herd of the common folk.

In an era which puts a premium on visual communication, the face of Wall Street is entirely satisfying.

John Putnam Thatcher came to this conclusion one damp May afternoon as he strolled back to his own particular outpost, the Sloan Guaranty Trust—third largest bank in the world. Possibly a leisurely lunch explained the idle tenor of his thoughts, more possibly it was the inexplicable lull in his duties as senior vice-president of the Sloan and head of its Trust Department.

On the other hand, it might have been native tenacity. Thatcher was still trying to find something good to be said for the new Sloan Guaranty Trust, an opulent palazzo of glass, marble and brass that had replaced the stately and venerable edifice on Pearl Street where Thatcher's banking had begun many years earlier.

Undeniably, the new Sloan looked impressive.

But, Thatcher thought as he proceeded unhurriedly in the midst of desperate secretaries returning to their desks in frantic hobbled dashes, this cosmetic effect was misleading. Wall Street's power is not embodied in its profligate real estate, in its streams of myrmidons or even in its throbbing pulse of activity.

These, after all, could be duplicated on Seventh Avenue. Or, if modern architecture were the nub of the matter, in Dallas, Texas.

No, the real power on Wall Street lurked unseen behind this façade, in the hands of men who could make one telephone call and raise the price of steel. They did this, as they shook hands on four-million-dollar deals, very calmly indeed.

Tom Robichaux, thought Thatcher, entering the Sloan lobby, was a case in point. Robichaux, an investment banker and lifelong friend, had been his recent companion at lunch.

As this protracted meal had testified, Tom Robichaux was markedly untouched by the tensions of high finance that etched lines in the faces of his subordinates at Robichaux & Devane. He had even found it difficult to summon passing interest in the bond issue of a sports arena outside Boston, the ostensible reason for their meeting.

"I'll send this prospectus over to Bowman," Robichaux had said, critically studying his steak *au poivre*.

"Fine," Thatcher replied. He had sensed a certain abstraction in Robichaux, but ingrained caution kept him from explicit inquiry; all too frequently his friend's preoccupation signified another change in marital status. Over the years John Thatcher had perfected an all-purpose response to tidings of divorce, marriage, alimony, alienation of affection suits and remarriage which conveyed sympathy devoid of any desire for detail.

"Are they thinking of an enclosed arena like the Houston Astro-Dome?" he asked.

Robichaux seemed to have forgotten what they were talking about.

"The Boston bond issue," Thatcher prompted.

Robichaux grounded his coffee cup decisively.

"To tell you the truth, John," he rumbled after close scrutiny of the adjoining tables, "I've got a little problem. . . ."

The rest of the conversation was devoted to a conflict between Robichaux and the current Mrs. Robichaux, a Melinda who had hitherto escaped Thatcher's notice. Melinda, Thatcher concluded, was decidedly original. She did not want diamonds, ermines or Balenciagas. She wanted an island.

". . . so I said that Gardiner has an island because he inherited it, for God's sake!" Robichaux reported indignantly. "He didn't buy it! You don't buy islands around Manhattan!"

Thatcher reflected on this as the Sloan's elevator bore him up to his offices on the sixth floor. Tom was right. A prudent man contented himself with buying stocks and bonds, industrial parks and warehouses of cocoa beans. That was what Wall Street was for.

Within the hour, Thatcher was to learn that money could take even more mysterious forms than he thought. Together with one of his junior trust officers, he was reviewing the affairs of a hydrofoil company hovering on the brink of bankruptcy. Suddenly they were interrupted by sounds of raucous merriment from the outer office. Thatcher's eyebrows rose in mute question; young Kenneth Nicolls showed more open surprise.

Just as Tom Robichaux could carry out chancy deals for a million dollars without evincing strain, so the Sloan Guaranty Trust was in the habit of conducting profitable operations without audible gales of hilarity.

Both Thatcher and Nicolls knew that these sounds were not emanating from clerical minions. The outer office was guarded by Thatcher's secretary, Miss Corsa, a young woman clearly designed by nature for the motto: *We are not amused*. Rose Theresa Corsa believed in decorum and propriety to a degree that sometimes oppressed Thatcher, and she was fully equal to the task of suppressing indecorous yelps from messenger boys.

She could keep Kenneth Nicolls in line, too.

This meant that the rioters were so exalted that Miss Corsa was powerless to impose her own standards. Considering her attitude to her employer, that boiled down to two starters—the Chairman of the Board and the President of the United States. Lesser mortals would need nerves of steel.

"We've got to find out about this," Thatcher said, rising to throw open the door and advance upon the scene.

The disturbers of Miss Corsa's peace were two middle-aged men. One of them, his elegant form topped by a Homburg, was applying a handkerchief to eyes streaming with the force of his glee. He was promptly overcome by another paroxysm.

"Better than a fifty-fifty chance!" he crowed. "It was beautiful! Unbelievably beautiful! And Chisolm . . ."

He became speechless at the memory.

His vis-à-vis seemed to understand him, if Thatcher and Nicolls (and Miss Corsa, for that matter) did not. Sitting in a chair, doubled over in pleasurable agony, three hundred dollars' worth of discreet tailoring hooted triumphantly:

"Chisolm's face! If I die tonight, it will be worthwhile!"

"I think," said Thatcher to Nicolls, "I think that we can abandon hydrofoils for the moment while I deal with this."

This dismissal was unfair and Thatcher knew it. On the other hand, he did not want junior members of the staff present while their elders and betters were losing control.

Obediently, if regretfully, Nicolls departed, leaving Thatcher to survey the intruders. Despite tears, bellows, backslappings and incitement to further delirium, he recognized the two figures.

The Homburg hat, now pushed back to a regrettable angle, crowned his second-in-command, Charlie Trinkam. Trinkam, the most ebullient trust officer of the Sloan, had always been notorious for the gaiety he brought to a vigorous bachelor life, but so far he had not broken down during office hours. The tailoring encased the form of Paul Jackson, one of New York's flourishing trial lawyers.

The strangest feature of the whole business was that both men seemed sober. Perhaps, not so strange. Thatcher had seen them both drunk and exercising more control than at present.

Charlie Trinkam finally acknowledged his superior's presence. Clutching at a desk for support, he gasped:

"Oh God, John, you missed the scene of the century!"

Banishing everything but mild curiosity from his voice, Thatcher said:

"What have I missed? What have you two been up to?"

A diabolical smile crossed Paul Jackson's lips.

"Freebody v. Atlantic Mutual. To both questions."

Then it all came back to Thatcher.

Pemberton Freebody had been a wealthy and childless widower, living out a comfortable old age at the Waldorf Towers until the onset of cancer. Freebody contemplated the lingering pain and indignity in prospect. Then, without undue regret, he put his affairs in order, named the Sloan Guaranty Trust as executor of his estate, got into his Cadillac and drove safely and slowly out the Long Island Expressway to a small wooded area he remembered from his distant youth. There he punctiliously affixed a note to the dashboard, proceeded into the trees and shot himself in the chest.

At this point, Pemberton Freebody's plans went awry. A passing truck driver was alerted by the shot. Braking abruptly, he plunged into the woods to find the old gentleman still alive. Forthwith giving the lie to theories about the alienation of our times, he slung the frail body into a fireman's lift, hurried back to the highway and sped to nearby Southport. At Southport Memorial Hospital, emergency stations were manned, the chief of surgery summoned and every resource of modern medicine brought into play. Despite the intervention of these well-wishers, Pemberton Freebody finally did manage to die—four days later. He had not escaped the indignities, but at least he had never regained consciousness.

So exit Freebody, and enter the Freebody estate. The bulk of it had been left to the newly formed Institute for Cancer Research at Hanover University. Included in the large estate was a hundred-thousand-dollar life insurance policy with the Atlantic Mutual Insurance Company. Atlantic Mutual quickly informed the Sloan that the suicide invalidation clause of the policy was still in force; Hanover would have to do without this particular one hundred thousand dollars.

Almost immediately, Atlantic Mutual came up against three powerful forces. First was Hanover's deep disappointment. It was delighted with the amount it had inherited, but it still regretted that one hundred thousand dollars.

"For cancer research, we need every cent we can get!"

Second, came Charlie Trinkam's native instinct to spread happiness. More as a theoretical exercise than anything else, he had said: "Of course if we hinted that we were willing to go to court, we might get some sort of settlement. . . ." After that, as Trinkam himself was the first to admit, he lost effective control of the situation.

Third, the trial lawyer chosen to lend substance to this hint was Paul Jackson. Trinkam had reported this to Thatcher.

"When Hanover insisted we retain Paul Jackson—well, John, I figured there'd be a laugh or two in it, if nothing else."

Thatcher had asked why Jackson, a noted criminal lawyer, had consented to take the case.

"He likes to get his teeth into insurance companies."

Recalling these words as he ushered the two men into his office past Miss Corsa's frosty disdain, Thatcher could only suppose that Jackson's teeth had found a nice, solid grip.

"You should have seen it," Charlie Trinkam murmured once again.

"Well, I didn't," Thatcher announced tartly. "Suppose you tell me about it."

His professional instincts roused, Paul Jackson leaned forward:

"It's really quite simple. Atlantic Mutual put on its suicide defense. The usual thing, rounded off with the people from Southport Memorial—the hospital where Freebody was taken. A couple of nurses and the surgeon who cut out the bullet."

"Beautiful, just beautiful," Trinkam provided as light accompaniment.

Jackson grinned an acknowledgment.

"Then I got started, cross-examining Dr. Martin, the surgeon. And was heaven watching out for us today! He was perfect, an arrogant cocksure bastard who wanted to tangle with me." He turned for an aside to Trinkam. "I don't know what was bugging that guy but we couldn't have asked for anything better."

"You played him like Paderewski."

"Martin's built to be a keyboard!" snorted Jackson. "All he wanted to do was contradict me. I could have gotten anything from him. But what I got was the jackpot. It all boils down to his saying two things. First, I wanted to know why the hell they operated—if the man was on his deathbed and nothing could save him anyway. Martin snapped right back at me: *The patient had better than a fifty-fifty chance for recovery. The bullet was nowhere near the heart. I operated to improve his chances.* All very lofty and professional. Everybody in the courtroom was hating Martin already."

"Except us," Charlie said irrepressibly. "We were ready to take up a collection for him. Then Paul really twisted it home. Asked why Freebody died if the chances were so good. And he answered—"

"Let me," pleaded Jackson. He held up a hand and seemed to be quoting holy writ. "Martin said: *The operation was perfectly successful. But the patient was seventy-six years old, and dying of cancer. He was an aged and enfeebled man in no condition to withstand any unusual or extended strain.*"

Jackson stopped and looked across at Thatcher with a broad grin.

Thatcher did not hide his restiveness. "I have grasped the fact that Martin said exactly what you wanted him to say. I can even see that something else is coming. But until I know what it is, I'm outside this ring of self-congratulation."

Nothing could ruffle the high spirits of his visitors. Charlie Trinkam took a deep breath and delivered the denouement in one long stream.

"Then Dr. Martin stepped down and Paul called the man who did an autopsy on Freebody for us. The autopsy revealed that seven hemostatic clips had been left in the body!"

Jackson and Trinkam grinned at Thatcher like two imbeciles.

"Now wait . . . let me get this absolutely clear," he said. "You mean we now have a case that Freebody did not die as a result of shooting himself, but as a result of these hemostats?"

"That's it!" Jackson sang out. "And the beauty of it is that De-

Luca, the expert we hired for the autopsy, refused to give an opinion as to the cause of death. He wouldn't swear it was the hemostats—but he wouldn't swear it was the bullet, either. DeLuca, by the way, is a big gun in postmortems."

"The whole thing seems to have gone beautifully," said Thatcher, not stinting his praise.

"We were lucky in our man. If the surgeon had been a remorseful young resident, we might not have had it so easy. But this Martin is pure poison. You should have seen Chisolm's face when he realized what he was stuck with."

"Who's Chisolm?"

"He's the lawyer for Atlantic Mutual. This Dr. Wendell Martin, the surgeon, is his witness. Couldn't be worse." Paul Jackson smiled beatifically. "And the jury is going to see a lot of Dr. Martin, believe you me."

"Where do things stand now?" Thatcher asked.

"Oh, Chisolm got an adjournment. To do research, he said. What else could he say? He was flabbergasted!"

Thatcher said that he could understand and, in fact, sympathize with this.

Paul Jackson, however, was too deep in hilarious speculation to pity his fellow attorney.

"You know what they'll do, don't you? They'll beat the bushes trying to find doctors willing to say they always forget seven hemostats! And is Chisolm going to have a hard time! I can just hear the doctors! Every one of them will swear that he's never known of seven hemostats left in a patient. No experience with it at all. . . ."

Since Jackson showed signs of giving way again, Thatcher intervened.

"What about the hospital—at Southport, was it? Will they support the doctor?"

Jackson pursed his lips thoughtfully and continued his predictions.

"As soon as Southport Memorial Hospital realizes what's hit it, they'll lower an Iron Curtain. Nobody will know anything—or remember anything! Oh, we're still not home clear on this case, John. But we are a lot closer than we were yesterday."

Jackson sighed dreamily.

Charlie Trinkam was ready to pass judgment here and now. "I've got to hand it to you, Paul. You've really set the sparks flying!"

2   *Heartburn*

IF IT WAS sparks at the Sloan Guaranty Trust, it was more like a forest fire in Southport, Long Island. Southport Memorial Hospital was one of the town's proudest possessions, so it was only natural that in Segal's Drugstore, in Muriel's Bake Shop, in the park and the bus stop, nothing else was discussed.

"Isn't it awful!" Southport asked and reasked. "Just awful!"

The medically devout then moved on to a litany featuring illustrations culled from their own operations.

Southport's Christian Scientists shook their heads more in sorrow than in anger.

"Seven hemostats!"

"Hemostats, nothing! Do you remember that rubber glove two years ago?"

Only a few professional optimists in the Chamber of Commerce were able to dredge some satisfaction from the metropolitan press coverage. "Well, this sure puts Southport—and Suffolk County—on the map!"

There was some merit in this observation. In 1925, Suffolk County had been much as it was during the American Revolution. Fifty miles stood between the easternmost portion of Long Island and Manhattan. Behind this buffer, Suffolk County slumbered in agricultural languor, cultivating potatoes, ducks and market produce. Its rural fastness suffered only one annual interruption during the brief hysteria of summer vacations, but otherwise Suffolk County was unaffected by the vast population of New York City. A geographic truism explained its protection: fifty miles is too far to go to work.

World War II changed all this. Work came to Suffolk County. The sandy soil began to produce aircraft, gyroscopes and secondary radar instead of asparagus. With the work came workers, and soon the potato farms were giving way to housing developments. Following hard on the heels of these consumers was free enterprise, in the form of shopping centers, discount houses and used-car lots. The great suburban ball was rolling.

The stage props for *Freebody v. Atlantic Mutual* arrived with another phenomenon. Having been provided with jobs, houses and stores, a multitude of Americans still found time hanging heavy. Despite a forty-hour week earning money (rather restful on the whole), despite a fifty-hour week spending money (totally exhausting), people still managed to divorce each other, abandon their children, commit crimes, read books, play tennis and get sick.

There was an anguished wail for social services. Authority, slower off the mark than entrepreneurs, belatedly recognized the need for more schools, marriage counselors, libraries, courts, jails, parks, social workers and hospitals. New agencies proliferated like fruit flies; old institutions donned new paint and flexed their muscles.

Among the older institutions struggling with the population explosion, none had been more successful than Southport Memorial Hospital. Originally built in 1927, Southport Memorial was remodeled in 1949; a new wing was added in 1959, and by 1966 a full-scale expansion was projected.

It was, Southport learned, one fund drive after another.

Expanding with the hospital was the medical staff. Nurses, orderlies, analysts, X-ray technicians, laboratory specialists and nurses' aides jostled for parking space. The top of the totem pole was, of course, reserved for the doctors—obstetricians, internists, surgeons, neurologists, endocrinologists, gynecologists, dermatologists, pathologists. Many specialties and many men. But, as in any hospital, the doctors who really ran things could be numbered on the fingers of one hand.

Two of them were showing the flag, as it were, at Segal's Drugstore. On the whole, they were giving a fine performance of men oblivious to the vulgar gossip around them.

"That's him, isn't it?" the customer at cosmetics hissed at the salesgirl. "Martin, I mean. Over there, at the tobacco counter."

The clerk emerged from under the counter and looked across the store.

"That's him, all right. The short one. The big man with him is Dr. Wittke, the head of the hospital. Dr. Wittke's a real gentleman."

"Did you read about what Dr. Martin did? I tell you! Imagine leaving all that junk in that guy. Killed him just as if he put the bullet in him, that's what I say!"

The salesgirl lowered her voice confidentially. "Listen, nothing Dr. Martin does would surprise me! He's always rushing around and snapping someone's head off. He probably leaves things in his patients all the time!"

This libel was the result of personnel practices at Segal's Drugstore. At lunchtime, the salesgirl covered the tobacco stand, and Dr. Wendell Martin was particular about his cigars.

At the back of the store, a salesman from one of the big drug houses was deep in knowledgeable talk with Harry Segal, who was Sid's younger boy.

"I see Dr. Martin got himself in hot water," he said.

"He's sure making the headlines," Harry agreed neutrally.

"He'll find some way to duck the whole thing," the salesman said with a knowing smile. "He's a smart cooky when it comes to taking care of old Number One."

Harry looked up from the price list. "I didn't know you knew him."

"Met him a couple of times," said the salesman. "I don't deal with him, thank God! Give me the druggists any time. You can have doctors!"

Harry smiled carefully.

"Still," the salesman continued, "I saw Martin yesterday just after he got back from the trial."

"Oh?" Harry abandoned the price list and leaned forward. This was the closest he had come to an eyewitness report.

"Yeah. I was over there at the hospital pharmacy. Not that I ever sell them much. They're as bad as you. All the doctors want to do is cut, cut, cut. Boy, if they made as much money from prescriptions as they do from operations . . ."

"Martin? What about him? You saw him?"

"Sure. I was just packing things up when he came sailing in. So help me God, he was purple! Looked like he was going to have a stroke. Of course, at the time, I didn't know what was the matter. . . . But boy! When I read the evening papers—well, if he looked like that by the time he got back here, I hate to think of what he looked like in court."

"It would upset anybody," said Harry.

"Upset, hell, he was mad! Slammed the door to his office—like a cannon. But one thing I'll say for him. He sure got busy. Right away, the loudspeaker was blasting away for Dr. Wittke and Dr. Neverson—and you know what that means."

Harry shrugged. "Oh, the big shots will take care of it. Now we're going to need a thousand units—"

"A thousand units! You're crazy! You gotta stock at least five thousand. . . ."

At the soda fountain, three middle-aged women argued over sundaes.

"I don't care what you say," the center woman announced defiantly. "Just because you work in the hospital kitchen you think you know all about the doctors. Well, I work there too!"

"What's the kitchen got to do with it, anyway? It's in the papers, right there in black and white. They wouldn't say that Dr. Martin killed that man if he didn't!"

"Papers will say anything! All I know is, when Burt had the gall bladder, Dr. Martin was marvelous!"

Her companions scoffed.

"It's two years now and you've forgotten all about it. Day after day, you kept saying how Dr. Martin wouldn't tell you anything. Wouldn't talk to you—or to Burt!"

"Who wants a doctor to talk?" she demanded unanswerably. "You want he should do a good job. And in two years, Burt hasn't had a day of trouble—knock on wood!"

Ceremonially she knocked twice on the formica counter.

At the candy counter another viewpoint was being aired.

"Well, as soon as I saw that story, I called our GP," said the man, holding out a five-dollar bill absently. "I put it on the line! Faulkner, I said, I'm holding you responsible. I won't have Dr. Martin within ten feet of Alison!"

"But I thought you said Alison and the baby were coming home day after tomorrow," the other objected. "Why should a surgeon go near her?"

The new father accepted a beribboned two-pound box of Whitman's and swelled protectively. "Let him try!"

At the cigar counter, Dr. Wendell Martin was continuing his thoughtful inspection of the stock, deaf to the conversations around him and untouched by the atmosphere. Sid Segal waited patiently, his shrewd eyes partially hooded by drooping eyelids. The tableau was not wasted on him. Nothing ever was.

Dr. Martin's companion, Dr. Philip Wittke, did not smoke. But Dr.

Wittke had felt it politic to accompany Wendell Martin on this expedition as a public demonstration of professional solidarity.

"Of course, this notoriety is unpleasant for all of us, Sid." He shook his head sadly. "But that's the way things are these days. Journalists have no qualms about exploiting misery to provide sensationalism."

"It's tough, Doc," said Segal.

Wittke drew a deep breath and allowed his volume to expand slightly. Nothing obtrusive, Segal noted appreciatively, but enough so that anyone could overhear him.

"I always tell young men just starting their medical careers that they have to realize every hospital is going to have a certain number of terminal patients. We'd like to save them all, we do our best, but in the end it's in Other Hands. In the first shock of loss, you have to make allowances for the survivors. We have all of us faced hysterical accusations and other unpleasantness, from time to time. But I tell my boys that the thing to do is to be patient, and remember that time is the only healer."

If Sid Segal found it hard to visualize Hanover University rending its face and tearing its clothes in grief for Pemberton Freebody, he kept the thought to himself.

Wendell Martin finally finished preparing a cigar and stuck it jauntily into a corner of his mouth. A moment later, fragrant smoke enveloped the threesome. Dr. Wittke's voice continued from somewhere within the cloud.

"The important thing for a doctor is to know that his colleagues support him," he said, coughing slightly. "They're the ones who've seen his work, who know how he responds to pressure. Only his fellow doctors can value a fine professional. And that"—here he weakened slightly and looked beyond Segal to the larger audience— "that is what we have at Southport Memorial! A fine group of dedicated professionals, proud of each other, standing shoulder to shoulder!"

"Standing shoulder to shoulder," said Sid Segal, "that's always a good idea."

Wittke indicated accord, glanced at the wall clock and gave signs that he and Dr. Martin had to return to their great work of healing. Their departure, dignity itself, did not end discussion of them.

Waiting for the light, Wendell Martin was disposed to grumble.

"I don't know what good that did," he said sourly.

Paul Jackson might wonder what was producing Wendell Martin's sourness, but Philip Wittke did not. Wendell Martin's sourness was nothing new. Unfortunately, Wittke reflected as they crossed the street, it was allied with a positive genius for alienating people—as Martin's lamentable performance on the witness stand demonstrated. He debated suggesting a more cooperative stance in future courtroom appearances, then rejected the notion.

Dr. Wendell Martin did not react favorably to even the sanest suggestions. Short, stocky and abrasive, he was Southport's chief of surgery; in the hospital, his word was law, his opinions valued and his foibles deferentially pandered to. Small wonder that he acted and thought like a dictator.

Dr. Wittke, who liked power as much as the next man, was another one of Southport Memorial's titans, but he eschewed the Napoleonic manner. In part this was temperament: Wendell Martin did not mind having people hate him. Dr. Wittke liked to be liked.

Still, as they strolled up the drive to the entrance, he had to conclude that Wendell Martin's unshakable self-assurance was an advantage at the current juncture of affairs.

Wittke shot a glance at him. Wendell Martin was strutting along, as if he had not left seven hemostats in Pemberton Freebody. It might have shattered a lesser man; it would have shaken Dr. Philip Wittke. Dr. Wendell Martin was simply angry, angry at the demands made on his time, angry at the presumption of the lawyers, angry at Pemberton Freebody for having died.

Well, it takes all kinds, Philip Wittke decided, smiling at Mrs. Stosser, the director of nursing, who was hurrying back from lunch. For himself, power—even unlimited power—at Southport Memorial was not enough. Philip Wittke looked to wider horizons. The profession knew that he ruled Southport Memorial Hospital's Executive Committee and controlled the outside doctors who wanted hospital privileges. More than once unfriendly voices had accused him of using this power to discipline doctors whose views on medical insurance and group medicine did not have the imprimatur of orthodoxy. But footling criticisms did not bother Philip Wittke; his election, some years earlier, as delegate to the national convention of the American Medical Association had heralded his arrival in the bigger world of medical politics. The Wittke Clinic was being run—and very successfully—by his two sons these days; the elder Dr. Wittke had become a familiar figure on the public platform and the television discussion show, either appealing for funds or denouncing Medicare.

He cultivated a confident, genial voice and silver hair, both calculated to contribute to his aura of massive distinction.

Lowering that confident voice slightly, he said, "Well, Wen, I am glad that you've agreed to have a little talk with Roy and me. It should be most helpful."

Martin gave a snort of impatience. He had never been guilty of considering any well-being other than his own, but Wittke had convinced him that his Southport colleagues had a vested interest in the disposition of *Freebody v. Atlantic Mutual.* It was characteristic of the man that he thought of the forthcoming conference in terms of his own needs and desires.

"All right, Phil. But I'm going to want a strong statement of support. And while we're at it, we may forward a protest to the medical association about that postmortem. . . ."

Wittke evaded a reply. This was no time for Dr. Wendell Martin or Southport Memorial to be protesting anything. He wondered if Martin could be brought to see this.

"Another thing!" said Martin imperiously as they strode into the lobby. "When the trial is resumed, they're going to call those nurses! Now I want to make it clear to them what their duty is. . . ."

He had not bothered to lower his voice, despite visitors in the waiting room, two young doctors glancing with masked curiosity in their direction, the girl behind the desk. This sublime indifference to the needs of the moment nettled Philip Wittke, but with an effort he contemplated the harangue that Martin could be expected to inflict upon the nurses who had assisted during the Freebody surgery. Repressing a shudder, he masterfully led the way to the privacy of the office corridor, then said:

"Yes, although on the whole I feel that perhaps your talking to Doyle and Gentilhomme might well be . . . er . . . misrepresented by the lawyers. You know lawyers. Why don't you let me have a word with them?"

Wendell Martin halted outside his office and narrowed his small eyes at Wittke.

"All right, Phil, you talk to them. Just be sure that you get them to understand—completely!"

"I think," said Dr. Philip Wittke authoritatively, "I think I can promise you that they will!"

3   Symptoms

BY THIS TIME a number of lawyers and doctors were mobilizing to fight *Freebody v. Atlantic Mutual* if it took all summer. None of the lawyers, and only a few of the doctors, underestimated the magnitude of the engagement. It was the clear destiny of those seven hemostats to become as hotly argued as if they moved in interstate commerce.

At Jackson & Jackson, Paul Jackson directed a large stable of legal yearlings through grisly precedents, himself lunched steadily with Dr. Edmund Knox and other medical bigwigs from the Institute for Cancer Research and, as he reported to John Putnam Thatcher, unearthed proof that any medical treatment beyond prescription of two aspirin tablets was grossly overpriced and probably potentially lethal.

"What are our chances?" asked Thatcher, upon whom medico-legal anecdotes were beginning to pall.

The phone temporized. "Well, we've still got Wendell Martin going for us," it said. "He'll be a big help. But the hospital is backing him. I'll have to fight to get a word out of anyone. Oh, say, seventy-thirty!"

On the opposing shore, the Atlantic Mutual Insurance Company, in the persons of its Eastern Manager, Dexter Loomis, and its counsel, Andrew Chisolm, was also performing prodigies of research. Telephone calls flowed out to obscure clinics in hunting areas, several recuperative miracles were dusted off and readied for citation, and some extremely plain talk was directed at Dr. Wendell Martin. But, as Andrew Chisolm was the first to admit, with seven hemostats going against you, it would be foolish to offer any odds.

Nor was the cooperation being offered by Southport Memorial Hospital enough to make him alter this assessment.

"No," said Dr. Wittke to the phone, "it's no trouble. I'm having a small conference this afternoon—quite informal. We'll talk things over and reassure Wendell that Southport is supporting him—"

The phone erupted.

"Yes," said Dr. Wittke soothingly. "Wendell can be difficult—a fine doctor, of course—but we'll try to talk sense to him. You will be happy to know that I've had a friendly little chat with Mrs. Doyle and

Miss Gentilhomme—the nurses, you recall. They are fully alive to their professional obligations."

He listened for a moment, then more sharply said, "Yes, we fully realize that it will do Southport Memorial no good . . . yes . . . I think I can say that everything here is well under control."

So began a week of surprises. To lawyers and doctors, *Freebody v. Atlantic Mutual* might appear to be a question of fact and logic. But, in addition, it touched many corners of many lives. This, as John Putnam Thatcher could have foretold, guaranteed the intrusion of antic, authentically human unpredictability. By the time *Freebody v. Atlantic Mutual* resumed, nothing—and no one—was well under control.

Dr. Wittke wished to speak to Dr. Martin and Dr. Neverson—a summit meeting in effect, since this was the triumvirate that dominated the hospital. To allay any such impression, Dr. Wittke suggested meeting in his home, a majestic structure commanding a wide view of Great South Bay from its acre of ocean frontage on Southport's choice Rocky Point.

They sat in the large sunny room overlooking the bay. Roy Neverson, the youngest man present, gazed idly out at the sparkling waters and repressed a sigh. A beautiful day to be out in the boat!

He glanced down at the watch contrasted against his darkly tanned wrist. Thirty minutes already, and they were still where they had been when they started!

Neverson forced himself to sit still. He had made his mark early; it had taken just ten years to fight his way from resident to the best internist at Southport.

He hadn't done it by sitting around trying to reason with Wendell Martin, a waste of time if there ever was one. On the other hand, he had not made it to the top by letting his opinion of the chief of surgery show.

"This court case shouldn't pose a serious threat," he said. "But we have to decide how to handle it."

"What is there to decide?" Martin burst out. "You know you have to back me up. Loomis and Chisolm have explained the whole thing. I don't know why you got us out here, Phil."

A short, brutal gesture transformed the gracious room into a tawdry pool hall.

Wittke retained his equanimity. He felt it proper to shoulder the burden of the conversation, but realized that his platitudes were not piercing Wendell Martin's armor. As he downed his cup of coffee, he shot a quick glance at Roy Neverson.

Neverson hitched himself forward. Trying hard for friendly frankness he said:

"Look, Wendell, Southport *is* backing you! That's already been decided! Nobody is testifying—except the nurses! We haven't answered any questions—and we won't! But Phil and I want to be sure you realize that this isn't simply a malpractice suit with some John Doe trying to make hay out of a little slip. It's the Sloan Guaranty Trust and Hanover University—with the most expensive lawyers on Wall Street! Under the circumstances, you see, this is bigger than a question of professional support. . . ."

He discovered that he was talking slowly and distinctly. Wittke, at any rate, nodded measured approval.

Wendell Martin glared at him.

"For God's sake! You make it sound as if they're the only ones involved. What about Atlantic Mutual? Don't forget them! It's their job to look out for us! And let me tell you, I'm going to give them hell! I'm their witness, after all! And look what they let me in for . . ."

For a moment, Wendell Martin's view of his place in the universe stupefied his companions. Although there was a gap of thirty years between them—and all that implies in style and substance—Neverson and Wittke found their eyes meeting.

Wittke cleared his throat.

"Now, Wen, I don't like to hear you say that about Atlantic Mutual. They're some very fine people over there. And we must remember that they do have some grounds to be . . . er . . . less than happy with you, at the moment. . . ."

Inwardly, Neverson grinned. This was Wittke at the top of his form. Not many people could take so Olympian a view of seven hemostats.

Martin did not see it this way.

"They're not pleased?" he repeated in outrage. "What have *they* got to complain about!"

"One hundred thousand dollars," Neverson could not keep from retorting. "Now look, Wen, you're not the only doctor they'll call—"

"So what!" Martin snarled.

Neverson made another effort to keep his voice steady.

"So that means, the questions haven't started yet!"

Despite himself, the sentence came out like a bullet. He turned to look at the bay again. "That's what we want you to realize. The longer this goes on—the worse it's going to be. There's going to be publicity, and more questions—and it's going to be tough on you, and on us. It could be disastrous." He paused. "The sooner this is over, the better!"

Again Wittke waded in.

"The important thing for us is to maintain a united front."

"Of silence!" Roy Neverson was urgent. "Look, Wen, we realize that you're taking the knocks. But we've all got to keep as quiet as we can. We don't have to say who was in the hospital, what they were doing, or what we were doing. Unfortunately," he added almost unwillingly, "we're stuck with those damned hemostats!"

The last words undid his good work. Martin was affronted.

"Those hemostats could have happened to anybody!" he snapped, pushing cup and saucer away. "Phil's a surgeon. He understands!"

Whatever Phil understood was interrupted as a melodious gong echoed through the house.

For a moment, naked consternation leaped into his eyes.

"Who could that be . . . Virginia is out . . . didn't say anything. . . ."

"It's Dr. Bullivant, Dr. Wittke."

The housekeeper stood on no ceremony. With so many doctors present, what did one more matter?

Edith Bullivant was in the doorway, gazing at her colleagues with her usual placid and maternal good will.

"Coffee? Well, I call that nice!"

"Yes of course. . . ."

Philip Wittke, notorious for his sangfroid, was not equal to Edith Bullivant. She sailed past him. Patients found her reassuring; young nurses were known to refer to her as "Aunt Edie." Without haste, she sank into a comfortable chair and expelled a sigh of relief. Then, with small delicate hands that were surprising in so substantial a woman, she accepted a cup of coffee with unstudied graciousness.

"What a day!" she remarked humorously. "I had a terrible breech delivery this morning. Well, you don't want to hear about my little troubles, do you? Thank you, Phil, just sugar, please. I wanted a

word with you"—she smiled brilliantly at Martin and Neverson—
"and they said that you'd gone home!"

An indistinct noise from Wittke led her to add: "And I remembered how you—and Wen and Roy—like to have your business meetings here!"

"Oh yes," said Dr. Wittke.

"I'm not interrupting you, I hope," said Dr. Bullivant gently.

Wendell Martin could barely restrain a growl, and Dr. Bullivant's
voice grew more emphatic.

"Although, of course, you—we—all have a lot to talk about now,
don't we?"

"Dammit—" Martin began.

Swiftly, Roy Neverson cut in, although he was somewhat amused
by the womanly ruthlessness of Dr. Bullivant. "Yes, Edith. We're just
agreeing that the best thing for us to do—in connection with this case
of Wendell's—is to help it die down, fast. We've agreed that we won't
have anything to say, to lawyers or newspapermen."

There was nothing in this speech to give Dr. Bullivant food for
thought, yet she knit her fine brows. When she did speak, it was in a
heavily practical tone.

"Have any of you thought what will happen if somebody comes
up with Harley Bauer?"

There was an appalled silence.

Both Martin and Wittke stared at her.

"That's one for the old girl," Roy Neverson thought silently.

"I mean it won't look good, will it?" she asked the room at large.
"In fact, it could look quite bad."

Harley Bauer had been, until very recently, Southport Memorial
Hospital's pathologist. He had been dismissed.

Wendell Martin recovered himself. "What does Harley Bauer have
to do with anything! This isn't a case of a questionable operation, let
me remind you, Edith! There was a perfectly simple medical situation, and there's a perfectly simple medical question as to the cause
of a patient's death! There's no need for a pathologist's report. This is
not an investigation into *your* medical practice!"

The naked animosity in his voice left Dr. Bullivant untouched.

"We don't want to get involved in old quarrels now, do we, Wendell?" she asked sweetly. "After all, you have enough to worry about.
. . ."

Wearily, Roy Neverson tried to salvage the discussion.

"That's the point I'm making. On the whole, the best thing is to let other doctors dispute about what killed Freebody. We should keep quiet!"

"And cooperate with the people at Atlantic Mutual," said Dr. Wittke quickly. His immovable hostility to group insurance did not preclude approval of joint action in other areas.

"That's right," said Roy Neverson, still trying to sell the idea to Martin. "Let Atlantic Mutual fight with the Sloan! The two of them can slug it out by themselves. We don't want them nosing around here! Right?"

There was probably no possibility of success for his appeal, but Dr. Bullivant assured its failure.

"Unless, Wendell, you decided to modify your opinion?"

Martin paled in rage.

"You mean, say that I killed Freebody? Would *you?*"

Dr. Bullivant sipped her coffee. Then, quite deliberately, she said: "You practically have said so, you know!"

In a voice that was choked, Martin spoke as he jumped to his feet.

"I've had enough of this! And thanks for the coffee, Phil!"

He had slammed out of the room before anybody could move.

"Isn't it fortunate," said Edith Bullivant quietly, "that he has a devoted wife to go home to."

Roy Neverson's wife and two children were now living in Michigan, not Long Island. But he did not rise to Dr. Bullivant's bait.

"Isn't it?" he agreed. "Well, I'll be pushing on. . . ."

"I hope I'm not driving you out," said Dr. Bullivant cheerfully.

"No, I think we said what had to be said." Neverson paused before the final thrust. "And, Edith, give my regards to Giles."

Wendell Martin's devoted wife heard him before she saw him.

"Lucille! Lucille!" His voice resounded through the sprawling ranch house and reached her as she was bending over her golf bag, putting new balls in the pocket. Without hesitating, she put them aside and hurried into the living room.

Her husband stood before the built-in bar, brandishing a bottle in one hand.

"Lucille, there's no soda water!"

In the hospital this would have been a vicious accusation. Here, in his own home, however, Wendell Martin's disappointments with the world put a faint plaintive edge on his voice.

"Oh, Wen, wait," said Lucille Martin reassuringly. "I've got one in the kitchen."

When she returned, he was sitting on the sofa.

"It won't be cold," he said angrily.

Without comment, she made him his drink. Then, making herself a much weaker one, she reminded herself to call Natalie and beg off golf this afternoon.

"Are you going out?" Martin finally asked.

"No," said Lucille Martin serenely.

He looked at her suspiciously.

"If you are . . ." he began.

Lucille Martin was too experienced to fall into this trap. Instead, she asked what kind of day he had had.

"What kind of day would you expect?" he asked. "First, I've got those damned fools at the insurance company on my back. Then Wittke and Neverson keep talking nonsense. And that damned Bullivant woman . . ."

As he warmed to his narrative, Lucille Martin unobtrusively re-filled his glass, occasionally murmured agreement or, simply, comprehension and continued to look faintly indulgent. A smartly out-fitted blonde with a clear fresh complexion and untroubled eyes, she managed to maintain an atmosphere of healthy calm despite Martin's endless complaints and outbursts.

". . . all that woman does is try to shaft all of us! She's so jealous she's green!" he concluded, sounding almost cheerful.

"I've never liked her. Or that husband of hers!" Lucille Martin lied. She neither liked nor disliked the Bullivants; she simply never thought of them. Her attention had remained centered on the children when they were still at home; now it was focused on running a house smoothly and efficiently.

And coping with Wendell.

"It isn't a question of liking them," he began happily.

Unfortunately, at this juncture the maid entered the room with a vase of flowers.

"Why wasn't the soda water put on ice?" he snapped.

"Wen—"

"No, Lucille, I don't see why you should be worried about these things. What's the girl for? And"—he was growing more excited—"look at the condition of these glasses! My God! Where were you brought up! Haven't you ever heard of infection? You can damn well take this whole tray back to the kitchen and wash them again. I don't know what you do with your time. And see that they get clean this time!"

Lucille watched the girl retreat to the kitchen. Despite desperate sniffing, the sobs started at the door. Well, it was another toss-up. Would the extra five dollars a week—plus choice culls from Lucille's wardrobe—balance Wendell?

On the whole, she thought not. Gladys had been snapped at just once too often.

Well, that would give her an occupation for the next few weeks. Finding a new girl.

Running Wendell Martin's house smoothly and efficiently was no small task.

4   Exploration

JOHN PUTNAM THATCHER knew nothing of Lucille Martin's domestic problems, but within days he was privileged to learn that running a trial smoothly and efficiently with Dr. Wendell Martin on the premises was no picnic, either.

Paul Jackson fixed his eyes on the witness.

"Dr. Martin, I put it to you that on the basis of your own testimony, Pemberton Freebody—quite apart from his gunshot wound—would have been unable to survive the strain imposed by the presence of seven hemostatic clips for over four days."

"Put it any way you want!" Martin snapped. "That man died of his wounds, and my operation had nothing to do with it!"

"Is it not a fact, Doctor, that the patient had begun to recover the morning after the operation? That he suddenly collapsed that afternoon, as if affected by severe strain?"

"You can't tell how a patient will react to major surgery. In nine cases out of ten—"

Jackson was peremptory.

"You must be more responsive, Dr. Martin. I am not asking for a generalization about what *most* patients do. I am asking what the late Pemberton Freebody did."

"In my opinion—"

Again Jackson cut in.

"I am not asking for your opinion, Dr. Martin. I want the facts."

"What kind of facts? You're asking me for an opinion as to the man's condition."

"Isn't it true that the patient's pulse, blood pressure, temperature and breathing were adversely affected the day after the operation? Isn't it true that, before this, there had been marked improvement?"

"If you know so much—"

Paul Jackson appealed for assistance. "I must request the defense to keep its witness in order."

"Perhaps I can perform that duty," the judge intervened. "Dr. Martin, I shall remind you that you have sworn to speak the truth and the whole truth. You must answer these questions!"

Wendell Martin crossed his arms.

"I'll answer reasonable questions," he declared. "These questions are out of order. They're a violation of medical ethics—"

The gavel slammed down.

"In this court," the judge said severely, "I am the arbiter of the propriety of counsel's questions, Doctor."

"I'm not going to let him—"

Gavel, gavel.

"I think," said Thatcher in an undertone to Trinkam, "that this round is ours!"

"Now, Mrs. Doyle, as chief operating room nurse, you were present throughout the operation on Pemberton Freebody, performed by Dr. Martin?"

Mrs. Doyle stared at Jackson coldly. Her navy-blue linen sheath, like her bright blond hair, was beautifully disciplined. But Mrs. Doyle did not suggest hospital austerity; her figure, well-fleshed if mature, was displayed to advantage. Cosmetics and costume jewelry had been applied with a lavish hand.

"Yes, I was," she replied. Her voice, like her person, held the hint of boldness in reserve.

"Then, can you tell us how many hemostatic clips were inserted by Dr. Martin during the operation?" Jackson asked.

"I don't remember."

Jackson raised his eyebrows. "Oh come now, Mrs. Doyle. Do you mean that a nurse of your experience did not note such an important factor?"

"I don't remember."

"Can you tell us how many hemostatic clips were removed from the patient at the conclusion?"

"I don't remember."

Alice Doyle kept her eyes fixed straight ahead of her expressionlessly.

"Can you tell us how long the operation lasted?"

"I don't remember."

"Tell me, Mrs. Doyle," said Paul Jackson, passing from sarcasm to a certain playfulness, "can you remember whether Dr. Martin was present?"

Mrs. Doyle narrowed her eyes in dislike. She was under orders not to abandon the security of mechanical response, Thatcher was willing to bet. But she was clever enough to yield fractionally to pressure. A tremor crossed her carefully schooled features.

"Yes, Dr. Martin was present."

"And, I presume, Pemberton Freebody as well?"

But Alice Doyle had recovered the hard unforthcoming tone.

"That is correct."

Paul Jackson appraised her for a moment, then turned away, speaking almost casually. "Now, on the first day of this trial—before we learned the results of the autopsy performed on Pemberton Free-body—you told us about the condition of the deceased when he was being prepared for surgery. You also described his condition during and after the operation. You agree that you did so?"

Mrs. Doyle could have been miles away. "That is correct."

There was nothing playful about Jackson now.

"But today, Mrs. Doyle, you claim you don't remember who was present or what instruments were used. You don't remember what was done to recover clips and sponges. Even though these things are your responsibility—and the condition of the patient is not?"

The nurse was as emphatic as Jackson.

"That is correct." Her words were evenly spaced.

Jackson moved his shoulders slightly.

"Thank you, Mrs. Doyle, that will be all. Thank you for your cooperation."

"And that round?" Charlie Trinkam asked.

Thatcher thought for a moment. "Let's call it a draw!"

But Paul Jackson professed satisfaction with the morning's work when he joined John Thatcher and Charlie Trinkam for lunch. His enthusiasm was so infectious that he managed to convince them to remain for the afternoon session, promising developments with a high entertainment value.

"And dollars and cents, too, I trust," Thatcher remarked. "Other-wise, I've had enough of well-rehearsed nurses."

"Sometimes," said Jackson with gusto, summoning a second round of drinks, "sometimes the rehearsal is perfect, but the performance is lousy!"

On this enigmatic note, the conversation turned to the unmanning behavior of an outstanding investment analyst who had recently withdrawn to a Trappist monastery.

Andrew Chisolm, Dexter Loomis and the assembled representatives of Atlantic Mutual Insurance Company enjoyed no such surcease. Moreover they had charges to chaperone.

Loomis slid into heartiness as he approached the Southport contingent at the back of the courtroom and suggested one large luncheon table. That table would not have to be overlarge, since the Southport group at the trial was limited to Dr. Martin, the nurses, and a Dr. Kroner, who had been present in the Emergency Room when Pemberton Freebody was carried in.

This was not pure chance; Paul Jackson was lavishly inviting all interested parties—from the Sloan to the Red Cross—to drop in on the trial. Atlantic Mutual was not. Indeed, a very frank exchange with Dr. Wittke had produced consensus: Southport Memorial Hospital should keep its nose to its own grindstone and boycott legal byplays at the New York County Courthouse.

Unfortunately, Loomis's suggestion foundered, as had so much else, on the idiosyncrasies of Dr. Wendell Martin.

"No," said a stripling from the insurance company, still peering around the crush outside the courtroom, "I don't see Dr. Martin, sir."

"Well, we'll just go on to lunch," said Loomis briskly, aware of the perils raised by increasing public interest and journalistic coverage.

Not that he looked forward to lunch. Chisolm had cravenly begged off, pleading the need for further research. This left Loomis with an ill-assorted group of guests. There was Mrs. Doyle. A quick look told him that Mrs. Doyle was still nursing the bruises from Paul Jackson's rough handling. Moreover, to Dexter Loomis, Mrs. Doyle was not— quite—ladylike. Handsome, yes. Well turned out, yes. But not what he would call a lady.

The second nurse, Miss Gentilhomme, was a pale depressed girl in a limp seersucker suit. Her plump shining face was innocent of the rouge and lipstick so luxuriantly evident on Mrs. Doyle. Perversely, this did not hearten Dexter Loomis.

Dr. Kroner (Karl, according to Dexter Loomis's notes) was courteous, gentle and totally nondescript. He was not proficient in English.

"We'll just go off and enjoy ourselves without Dr. Martin," said Dexter Loomis robustly.

If Dexter Loomis enjoyed lunch, he did it alone. Mrs. Doyle, after three martinis, remained edgy. Miss Gentilhomme refused a drink in a frightened voice suggesting either awe of her surroundings or terror of her forthcoming appearance on the witness stand. She remained dumb. Dr. Kroner's desire to please foundered on the language barrier.

"Very nice indeed," said Loomis desperately, signaling for the check. "And, Miss Gentilhomme, there's nothing at all to worry about. . . ."

The worst was yet to come. His aide hurried up, bad news writ large on his face.

"I've located Dr. Martin," he announced breathlessly.

Mrs. Doyle and Miss Gentilhomme stared; Dr. Kroner leaned forward eagerly.

"I hope he's had lunch," said Dexter Loomis, who hoped something else.

"He hasn't," said the aide. "He's been in the corridor, giving every newspaperman in New York an earful."

"He's *what?*"

"Been talking for about an hour," said the aide, relishing the magnitude of the disaster. "I got Chisolm to shut him up finally. But from the way the reporters set off—I think Dr. Martin got a lot off his chest."

"The goddam fool!" But this cry, Loomis kept to himself.

The same thought was expressed aloud by one of his guests.

"Dr. Martin," said Dr. Kroner with great care, "Dr. Martin is not always wise."

Dr. Martin's confidences to the journalists, suitably edited, were rushed into the afternoon papers. A number of people read them with interest.

At the office of the District Director of Internal Revenue, a young man checking a file nodded to his superior.

"You were right. We do have this Dr. Wendell Martin down as due for an audit."

His superior read further. "Holy Christ! He says he does hundreds of operations a year . . . listen, have an examiner call for an appointment. My God, I thought the first thing they taught them in the medical school was to keep their mouths shut. . . ."

"And ask for payment in cash!" his subordinate added.

"Now, Will, you're getting cynical!"

At the office of the American College of Surgeons, telephone calls alerted a gray-haired man. He read, and did not like what he read.

"But why won't he say anything about who refers patients to him?"

"I can guess," said a colleague.

Gloom descended. "The whole world can guess he's milking kickbacks," the gray-haired man mused. "What about a word to the wise?"

"To Wendell Martin? You're kidding."

The local medical association felt the need to act more imperatively.

"I don't like this. Martin is giving the whole profession a black eye. Now, who do we have at Southport? Wittke, isn't it? Can't he give Martin some advice?"

"He'd better try!"

Even as far away as Wilmington, Delaware, the afternoon papers were making themselves felt. Albert Martin, Wendell's brother, listened to the account read over the phone to him, whistled, then rang off.

"No brains. That's Wen's problem! No proportion. He wants to take on the whole world."

He drummed his fingers on the desk for a while, debating a telephone call to Lucille.

In her way, Lucille Martin could manage Wen, he knew. Certainly better than he could. But Lucille had always confined herself to house and home. As a matter of policy, she chose to remain ignorant of Wendell Martin's business.

Al envied her, at the moment. Then he started running down a list of names: Wittke, Neverson, Bullivant . . .

Dr. Harley Bauer was bubbling over about a young Puerto Rican mother who had managed to have twins in a shopping center when his wife called.

"Harley!" she said excitedly. "Your Wendell Martin has got himself into an awful jam!"

Dr. Bauer, still full of little Jesús and Anastácia, had to ask her to repeat her remarks.

"Oh, Harley," his wife wailed in mock despair. "You are absolutely the only man in the world who could forget someone who got you fired!"

"Now, hon," he said. "I didn't forget. What is it?"

"Get a paper!" she directed him. "And what time will you be home tonight?"

Harley sent his nurse out for a paper and snatched a moment (between a tricky thyroid condition and a small staph infection) to read the details, shaking his head as Dr. Wendell Martin's intemperate outburst unrolled before his eyes.

"Boy," he said. Suddenly, something in column two captured his attention. Since he was by nature gregarious, he drifted out of his office across the hall.

"Stan, you read this about Dr. Martin?"

Dr. Stanley Fink's dental offices were almost as spanking new as Dr. Bauer's.

"You mean your esteemed colleague who left the stuff in that patient?" Fink asked, disengaging himself from an open mouth. He moved to the doorway. In his waiting room, Harley Bauer was now reading aloud.

"Yeah . . . say, listen to this! February 17 . . . you know what that means?"

"Just a few minutes, Mrs. Ober," said Dr. Fink, firmly closing the door on his equipment-festooned victim. "No, what?"

"That's the night that I got bounced from Southport!" said Bauer.

Fink plucked the paper from him and read avidly. "You mean this jerk really was your colleague?" he asked. "He must think he's God Almighty! He wants to take on everybody. Listen to this! He's going to sue the AMA and demand a public apology from Hanover! On top of that, nobody's got any right to ask *him* questions about anything!"

"That's Martin, all right. He was chief of surgery out at Southport. He got me fired as pathologist."

Fink remembered the details of this disaster. "February 17? He fired you the day of this operation? So he was upset. That's why he left the kitchen sink in this poor guy."

Bauer was too engrossed to respond to the habitual mockery.

"Wendell Martin upset? Why should he be?" he said, rescuing his paper and turning to an inner page. "I was the guy that got canned. And believe me, Martin was tickled to do it. He was always out to get me . . . him and that Bullivant bitch. I told you . . ."

Stanley Fink's interest in non-dental matters was limited. However, with his customary good sense, he pointed out that this might have been a blessing in disguise. Bauer's new practice was getting off the ground nicely; it would do a young man no good to be associated with any hospital currently rating Southport's headlines.

"I mean," he amplified, reading one aloud, " '*Southport Mem Operation Challenged.*' "

He cocked his head. Muted voices from his office suggested restiveness or worse on Mrs. Ober's part.

Bauer, however, was deep in his own thoughts. His open, normally good-natured face was solemn.

"I can't help wondering if there isn't more than a coincidence here."

Fink asked what that was supposed to mean.

"I told you about . . . the trouble," Harley said.

"Yes," said Fink. "Listen, I've got to get back inside. Why don't you and Joan drop by for a drink tonight?"

"It might be a good idea for me to run out to Southport, just to see what's going on," Bauer continued. "That way I could get the real lowdown on Martin."

Dr. Fink shook his head sadly. "Always afraid you'll miss something, Harley," he said reprovingly. "Remember, curiosity killed the cat."

But Bauer protested that Southport Memorial Hospital held no further dangers for him. This time Wendell Martin couldn't get anybody else to take the rap for him.

Fink shrugged. "You may be right," he said, opening the door to his office. "You still have friends out at Southport, don't you? Here we are, Mrs. Ober. I think we're just about ready now. If you'll just open a little wider. . . ."

Dr. Fink did not hear Harley Bauer's response to his observations.

"I've got friends out at Southport," said Harley Bauer slowly. "But I've got enemies, too."

An apprehensive Marie Gentilhomme finally mounted the witness stand. John Putnam Thatcher, whose partisanship had sharply defined limits, watched with pity. Lambs always had this effect on him.

Paul Jackson, ostensibly mellowed by an excellent lunch, smiled.

"Miss Gentilhomme, were you present at the operation on Pemberton Freebody?"

Trying to emulate the spartan conduct of her elder, she quickly said:

"I don't remember."

The ripple of laughter through the courtroom surprised her into blushing.

Paul Jackson became a comforting father figure.

"I'm confusing you," he reproached himself. "Now, let's start farther back. How long have you been qualified as a registered nurse, Miss Gentilhomme?"

"For nine months, sir. Since last September."

"And how long have you been employed at Southport Memorial Hospital?"

"Since January."

"So, on the night of February 17, when Pemberton Freebody was brought into the hospital, you were on night duty, weren't you?"

Silence.

"Come now," he said gently. "You have already told us that you were."

"Yes," she said, sounding scared.

"And did you see the patient before he was brought into the operating room?"

"Oh, no!" The truth and her relief was transparent.

"But you saw him in the operating room?"

"I don't remember."

"Oh now, Miss Gentilhomme, you must have noticed him."

Miss Gentilhomme was younger and more vulnerable than Mrs. Doyle.

"Well, I did just notice him."

"Where were you throughout the operation?" Jackson asked with flattering interest.

"I was removing instruments from the sterilizer, bringing them to the table and taking them away. Most of the time, I wasn't even at the table."

"But when you were—I suppose you glanced at the patient?"

"I . . . I don't know."

Lunch had not really mellowed Paul Jackson. The questions were coming faster now and the witness, showing confusion, was trying hard to distinguish between innocent questions and questions about the patient. Jackson helped her to her destruction by snapping his queries about Pemberton Freebody, and relaxing the pace on others.

"You were too busy with the instruments?"

"Oh yes! I barely saw the patient or the doctors!"

"You were busy bringing instruments to the table and removing them, too?"

"Yes, sir!"

"And you started to take things away after the bullet had been removed from the patient?"

"That's right," she said, shying again at the word "patient."

"So you did notice when that part of the operation was finished, didn't you, Miss Gentilhomme?"

"Only because I started taking things away. But honestly, I wasn't noticing the patient!"

Jackson seemed to yield to the pleading in her voice.

"All right. But if you weren't noticing the patient, perhaps you were noticing what Dr. Martin and Mrs. Doyle said about him. You did have to listen, didn't you—so that you'd know what instruments were wanted?"

"Yes, but I didn't really pay attention—not unless it was about the instruments." Marie Gentilhomme had her moment of innocent triumph.

"And when you began taking the instruments away, Miss Gentilhomme, when did you first notice that hemostats were missing?"

The lawyer's voice was free from tension as he asked this critical question. He reproduced the slight decrescendo that Marie Gentilhomme had come to associate with safety. Without missing a beat, she fell into the trap.

"I didn't notice until Mrs. Doyle told Dr. Martin."

"And what did Dr. Martin say?" Jackson asked casually. Mentally he, Charlie Trinkam, John Thatcher (and the judge as well) were anathematizing the spectators who let their gasps become audible.

"He said not to bother him because he'd made his own count, and anyway he'd completed the sutures. . . ."

Abruptly, Miss Gentilhomme's hearing caught up with her speech. A hand flew to her mouth as the echoes of her last two replies hung in the now-silent room.

Paul Jackson spoke with quiet, deadly calm, repeating the substance of her replies.

"So, while the patient was still on the operating table, the chief operating room nurse, Mrs. Doyle, drew the surgeon's attention to the discrepancy in the hemostat count. And Dr. Martin told her not to bother him because he'd already completed the sutures. That's what happened, isn't it?"

As he pressed her gently, the courtroom held its breath. All eyes were fixed on the shrinking figure in the witness chair.

Miserably she glanced around the room for help that would not come. It was a long time before she replied:

"Yes."

Thatcher saw Andrew Chisolm struggling out of a fog to protest. But Jackson hurried on to his stark conclusion too quickly for intervention.

"And what did Mrs. Doyle say?"

Too late, Marie Gentilhomme remembered her instructions.

"I don't remember!"

Five minutes later, Paul Jackson was speaking with firing-squad cadence.

"Your honor, I find it necessary—once again—to recall Dr. Wendell Martin."

5 Malignancy

NEWSPAPERS and life being what they are, the evening headlines were inevitable:

NURSE TELLS ALL

The violent exchanges between Wendell Martin and Paul Jackson, the increasingly thunderous animadversions from the bench, the testimony of two doctors from Massachusetts General Hospital (unable to give opinions about what seven hemostats would do since at Mass General, etc. etc.), even Pemberton Freebody, were relegated to small print. Marie Gentilhomme's unwitting disclosures catapulted her into brief notoriety.

NURSE SPILLS BEANS, said the tabloids the next morning with an unfortunate photograph showing a dazed Marie trying to hide behind Mrs. Doyle.

"Disgraceful," said Everett Gabler, oldest, primmest and most easily outraged member of Thatcher's staff.

"What is, Ev?" Thatcher asked idly, leafing through some research reports forwarded by Walter Bowman.

"This emphasis upon personalities," said Gabler austerely.

"Oh, I don't know," Thatcher replied infuriatingly. "Here's a situation where a doctor seems to have more or less killed a patient. And the hospital is engaged in a massive cover-up. Now *that* may be disgusting. But it seems excessive to react to the American press. Under the circumstances, they come out looking fairly good. After all, Ev, they have neither slaughtered anybody, nor condoned such slaughter."

Everett Gabler, like Miss Corsa, had developed selective hearing when it came to John Thatcher's whimsies.

"Constantly focusing upon trivialities," he muttered, turning to page four.

But Gabler was wrong. It was not trivia which the newspapers had fastened upon. To lawyers like Paul Jackson, Marie's testimony was a small brick in the great wall of evidence. But only lawyers, and coldhearted institutions such as the Sloan Guaranty Trust and Hanover University, are obsessed with items like one hundred thousand dollars. The world at large, and Southport in particular, found Marie Gentilhomme's revelations incomparably more dramatic than Wendell Martin's virtually uninterrupted histrionics—and almost as engrossing as the question of why Pemberton Freebody had died. Marie was young: not beautiful (despite the newspapers who ignored her solid contours and undistinguished features to describe her as slim and lovely), but young. This, spiced by the distress she could not hide, was enough for the vast majority of the newspaper reading public.

In Southport, things were more complex. In the town, the first flurry of excitement about *Freebody v. Atlantic Mutual* had simmered down to a general, if ill-defined, feeling that a bunch of high-priced outsiders were trying to pull a fast one. Many Southportites had been born in Southport Memorial Hospital, many had consulted Dr. Wittke, many had had gall bladders removed by Dr. Martin. Familiarity, after all, breeds complaisance more often than it breeds contempt; Southport had buzzed for a while, then decided that it probably wasn't true. If it was true—well, these things happen.

Marie Gentilhomme forced Southport to think uncomfortable thoughts.

This was enough to justify headlines.

Inside the hospital, of course, feelings were bound to be stronger. Marie had committed a worse offense than killing a patient; she had let down the side and betrayed a doctor.

She had begun paying for her sins before she was clear of Manhattan.

"But everyone will know that you are not . . . that you could not . . . it was not your fault."

Dr. Kroner had been worried as he tried to comfort Marie.

She had sat in the corner of the car speeding back to Long Island, huddled as far as possible from Mrs. Doyle. The silence remained unbroken, except for an occasional comment from Dr. Kroner.

Dr. Martin would have had plenty to say. Fortunately he had been detained for further consultation with the lawyers. His red-eyed glare had boded ill for Marie: today Dexter Loomis and Andrew Chisolm were dogging Martin with a view to keeping his comments off the record, but there would be no such protection for Marie at the hospital tomorrow—despite Dr. Kroner's comfort.

They debouched him at the high-rise apartments on the outskirts of Southport, and Marie was immediately given a more realistic view.

"Well!" Alice Doyle exploded in a harsh exhalation of smoke.

Marie flinched.

"I've got to hand it to you," said Mrs. Doyle raspingly. "You sure blew things sky high."

"I'm sorry, Alice. I . . . I got confused."

Furiously, Alice Doyle ground out her cigarette, slashed at the ashes marring her navy-blue sheath.

"Sorry? A lot of good that's going to do—now! Oh, for God's sake, don't cry! Here, here's your purse. Be a good girl and powder your nose. You don't want your aunt and uncle to worry."

Marie smiled weak gratitude and subsided.

Alice Doyle twisted and retwisted her gloves. "I told you! Wittke told you! Why couldn't you just say you didn't remember. . . . Now we're really in trouble. Oh hell!"

Marie listened, but Alice Doyle was talking to herself.

"This is really going to be rough. I don't know what they'll do, now." She woke to her surroundings and spoke with grim honesty.

"I just don't know what's going to happen to us—or to you, Marie!"

Her sentiments were shared in many quarters, among them, the offices of the director of nursing. Mrs. Stosser listened to the telephone first thing next morning with tempered resentment.

"Well, of course, Doctor, I *can* remove Nurse Gentilhomme from O.R. duty . . . yes, Doctor? But we're shorthanded as we are . . . yes, Doctor!"

The phone she was holding went dead. Mrs. Stosser pursed her lips. This was the third curt demand made for Gentilhomme's dismissal. As if nurses grew on trees! With the cunning of the cornered, Mrs. Stosser drew forth a large schedule and studied it.

If she took Gentilhomme out of the operating room and tucked her somewhere out of sight, say up in Ward Four, why, by the time this furor died down . . .

Without hesitation, she picked up the phone and dialed the number of the modest bungalow where Gentilhomme roomed with her aunt, her uncle and innumerable nieces and nephews. She reached Marie after some difficulties with Aunt Yvonne. In brisk, no-nonsense tones she gave the girl her new assignment.

Trust Gentilhomme not to understand!

"But, Mrs. Stosser, my uncle Dominic can't pick me up until eleven-thirty. If I get off duty at ten o'clock—"

"You can wait!" said Mrs. Stosser. "This is no time for you to worry about commuting problems!"

Mrs. Stosser hung up, satisfied with her stratagem. She was as devoted to Southport Memorial Hospital as anyone else, but her primary job was to keep a nursing staff. And Marie Gentilhomme was not leaving—not until Mrs. Stosser was convinced that some other people weren't leaving first.

"And I just don't know what's going to happen!"

Through the arteries and veins of the hospital, from the outpatient clinic (in the basement) to Obstetrics (sixth floor, new wing), similar uncertainty percolated. To a large extent it remained unvoiced: hospitals, like armies, have people working with those in whom it would be dangerous to confide. Doctor may talk to doctor—but not all doctors. The nurse network is beyond rational representation.

The only people on whom this hierarchy does not weigh heavily are the orderlies. At Southport, they were not talking about Dr. Martin—or Marie Gentilhomme—because they were not interested.

But hospital routine is one of the most powerful forces known to man, and it functioned at Southport Memorial. The work went on.

Early that evening, Harley Bauer, bouncing up the stairs and bursting into the main entrance, felt a pang of disappointment at the very normalcy that met his eyes. He and Joan had stayed up far too late discussing Southport Memorial. Indeed, it was almost like old times, he thought with a chuckle. When he had been on the staff, he had taken home his troubles—and what troubles they had been!

Perhaps that was why Joan had been so gleeful in writing dialogue for the tricky little exchange before him. She always felt things more than he did.

Still, here he was, back at good old Southport.

Harley Bauer paused, missing Joan's prompting.

On the surface, things hadn't changed. Two harried women were bedeviling the reception clerk, while three men and one small child sat dully in the waiting room. White-coated figures strode importantly in and out of elevators, past swinging doors. Beyond those doors, up on the floors above, carts were moving patients, trays were being loaded, nurses were sneaking smokes, labor was continuing, life was ending.

"Harley?"

Someone was genuinely glad to see him. Eagerly, Harley turned.

Sid Segal, incongruously gripping a package from which long plush ears protruded, had hurried up behind him.

"Good to see you again! I didn't get a chance to tell you how sorry I was you decided to leave."

Harley's departure, abrupt, involuntary and dramatic, had been the last uproar at Southport Memorial Hospital. At the time, he assumed everybody must be talking about it.

And here was Sid, who knew everything. He hadn't known.

"It just goes to show," Harley Bauer thought he would tell Joan, "how they can hush things up!"

Could they hush up Dr. Martin's operation after what that nurse had said?

". . . and your wife. Give her my regards. So, you're practicing in Garden City? Not a bad location . . ."

Sid was continuing, almost friendlier now than when Harley Bauer was dropping into the drugstore daily. Harley was unfeignedly glad to see him. In a world of great men, Sid was a note of humanity. He owned the drugstore and the whole business block adjoining, but he was not above delivering stuffed rabbits to small patients in the children's wing.

"You've come back to see your friends, Dr. Bauer," Segal suggested with a friendly prod and the flattery he always extended to even the youngest doctor.

Tactfully, Harley lowered his voice and confided: "I still haven't cleaned out my locker. While I'm here I thought I could see Dr. Wittke . . . or Dr. Martin, maybe. If he's here . . . ?"

Segal knew about Harley Bauer's insatiable curiosity. Locker-cleaning had waited until Southport Memorial had secrets to hide. He answered the question in Harley's voice. "Oh, *he's* here. A little thing like a trial—what's that to Dr. Martin?"

With clumsy subtlety, Harley said, "He's carrying on as if everything were okay, huh?"

Segal became confidential. "Me, I'd stay away. If he asked me, I'd tell him to stay away. Let things die down. After all, this is only temporary. . . ."

"I wonder," said Bauer, looking around.

Segal bent forward in interest, moving both of them slightly out of the traffic, to facilitate talk.

He was just in time. Like a majestic ship sailing into harbor, Dr. Edith Bullivant swept past them with her customary gracious greeting to the girl behind the desk. Even Segal rated a friendly wave.

Dr. Edith Bullivant looked straight through the substantial Harley Bauer, who gazed stolidly back.

But she had seen him. And, as she moved on, her expression was not pleasant. Edith Bullivant had been a doctor for more years than she cared to remember, and her natural talent for diagnosis had been sharpened. Unerringly, she knew that Harley Bauer was not simply visiting friends. As clearly, she saw that Wendell Martin had opened the door. Soon there would be other enemies of Southport Memorial gossiping, whispering, speculating.

She was hesitating at the door to her office when a familiar figure rounded the corner.

"Phil!" she called out.

Obediently, Dr. Wittke approached. "Edith," he said with a fair assumption of ease. "I've been looking in on a rather interesting multiple fracture. Young Jim"—his forty-year-old son and heir— "wanted my opinion. . . ."

Without qualms, she dismissed this. "I thought you said you were going to talk to that girl."

Wittke projected sorrow. "I did. Poor child, she was frightened by the lawyer. You know, yourself—"

She knew how genuine this sorrow was. Ruthlessly, she cut off further pieties. "Somebody had better do something," she said baldly. "If Wendell goes on the way he's going, we'll all be hurt. And as for that nurse, somebody better remind her that nurses don't talk about operations—to anybody!"

"An understandable sentiment." The smooth new voice was shaded with mockery.

Dr. Bullivant's eyes blazed but Dr. Neverson, who had come up behind them, ignored her.

"Phil, I have to talk to you," he said wearily. Dark circles under his eyes, a stoop to his shoulders, a crumpled jacket testified to fatigue and long hours.

"Now, wait a minute, Roy," Edith Bullivant began.

"This doesn't concern you, Edith," said Neverson in exhaustion. He set off down the hall, and the older doctor promptly followed. Wittke was no coward, but he was happy to escape Edith Bullivant. She was the only person in the hospital—possibly the world—who unnerved him. Although he did not realize it, she infected him with the chill of *déjà vu:* Edith Bullivant had many uncanny resemblances to Philip Wittke.

He followed Neverson to his own office, then tried to regain the initiative.

"Now, Roy," he said, settling at his desk, "I hope you're not going to complain about the nurse. I did what I could. . . ."

"The nurse?" Neverson asked vaguely. "Oh hell, that's the way the ball bounces. No, Phil, this is getting serious. Did you read what Wen said yesterday? Or for that matter, have you talked to Kroner about how he acted on the stand?"

Composedly, Wittke replied that he felt it prudent to evince no unusual interest in *Freebody v. Atlantic Mutual.*

Neverson slammed a tanned hand on the desk. "It's too late for us to behave like ostriches!"

Then, with an effort, he controlled himself. "Is Martin in? I'm going to talk to him. . . ."

"You'll be wasting your time," said Wittke quietly.

Roy Neverson believed him. Behind the pompous façade was a shrewd, calculating intelligence.

Wittke continued. "He is in, and in excellent spirits."

"Well, I'm still going to try to talk sense to him. . . ."

And he was out of the room.

Wittke watched him go unhopefully. If anybody could talk sense to Wendell Martin, the outlook would certainly be brighter. But Wittke prided himself on being a realist. Accordingly, he was worried. Deeply worried.

Dr. Wendell Martin on the contrary was not worried, Roy Neverson discovered. Perversely, he was exhilarated. The reason emerged.

"I finally got hold of that bitch of a nurse!" he said, eyes gleaming. "She's not so cocky now! I told her I'd have her blacklisted! She'll never get a job in a decent hospital again! She's got to go. I won't have her in my hospital. . . ."

Neverson found himself speaking slowly and distinctly once again:

"We can take care of the nurse later, Wen. I want to talk to you about this publicity. . . ."

To himself, he was saluting Phil Wittke's astuteness; there was no use talking to Wendell Martin.

Martin looked through some papers quickly. "Just checking my schedule next week," he explained. "The trial? Let me tell you . . ."

He did. He told Neverson what he was going to say, how he was going to make Jackson eat his words, how Atlantic Mutual would get on their knees to thank him . . .

When he stood in the corridor ten minutes later, Roy shook his head. Was Wendell Martin completely sane? He doubted it. And, despite an intelligence keener than many of his colleagues supposed, Roy Neverson was lost.

"I don't know what's going to happen," he said. "Might as well go home. . . ."

But home was no longer the house at the point with Julie and the children. It was an impersonal apartment. Perhaps this was what reminded Roy of one last chore.

He made his way to the desk on the fourth floor.

Marie Gentilhomme was the nurse on duty. Too late, Neverson tried to hide the irrational flick of irritation this caused him. Pale, moist-eyed, docile Miss Gentilhomme had not meant to add fuel to the fire.

Neverson took a deep breath while the girl looked up at him. Scared to death, he thought. Small wonder, after Wendell Martin chewed her out.

"Yes, Doctor?" she said.

He made his voice gentle. "Miss Gentilhomme, Dr. Myron is going to take a specimen from old Mrs. Guild this evening if he has time. He'll run the tests and bring the results up here. Now, if he does, I want you to call me. . . ."

"Yes, Doctor."

Even this grated. Roy Neverson was too tired and too worried to think clearly. He had to hang onto himself.

"If Myron brings the report up, I want you to call me. If I'm not in my office, call me at home. . . ."

"Yes, Doctor . . ."

Abruptly, he turned on his heel and left.

Marie Gentilhomme looked after him blankly. Like most of the nurses, she admired Dr. Neverson's dark good looks. Like all the nurses, she knew that he was moody. And today, he was tense and tired.

And free to go home now.

There was no such escape for her, although a sick headache pounded her temples. She was still on duty.

Earlier she had been grateful for this duty. Arriving at the hospital, she had shrunk from hostility at every corner. But almost immediately she was caught up in the unceasing demands made on the only registered nurse in Ward Four. Unimaginative by nature, she had no time to think about yesterday or tomorrow, as she checked on patients, ordered special diets, filled in charts, supervised the nurses' aides and ran errands for importunate visitors. The long day had wound slowly into evening, unnoticed under the impact of the endless chores.

But then Dr. Wendell Martin caught her in the elevator.

Marie shuddered, and touched her aching forehead, forcing a smile for Mrs. Perkins, who was passing the desk on her way to the bathroom.

Then, Dr. Bullivant had come up to check on one of her patients. Even Dr. Wittke . . .

It was after ten o'clock when Marie came off duty. She was only dimly conscious of leaden feet and a sense of nausea. Mechanically, she checked the records on her desk for Nurse Dodd, who looked at her strangely but mercifully said nothing. Then she stopped at the telephone in the office and tried Dr. Neverson's number to report that Dr. Myron had left Mrs. Guild's report on her desk.

Numbly putting the phone down, she walked like an automaton to the elevator. She had an endless hour to wait until her uncle drove the battered car up to the parking lot entrance, but she could sink into the merciful oblivion of the Nurse's Lounge. She passed a telephone on the first floor without thinking about trying Dr. Neverson again, turned the corner and saw Alice Doyle sagging against a closed door. Dimmed lights exaggerated the shadows under her eyes; her rouged cheeks looked raddled.

"Going home?" Doyle asked vaguely. Here too was fatigue so deep that it obliterated personality. "There's been an accident . . . they're still bringing them in . . . farm laborers in a truck. Oh hell! Have you got a cigarette, Marie? I left mine in my car. . . ."

Doyle would go back to Emergency in five minutes. Marie did not hesitate. "I'll go get them," she said.

Alice Doyle leaned back again and closed her eyes.

Marie's weary feet carried her down to the basement exit where a naked bulb cast harsh light over the stairs. She was edging toward the modest sedan that Alice Doyle always parked near the laundry ramp when she tripped.

"Wh . . . what!"

Suddenly frightened of the dark, of the fingers of light, of the massive building looming over her, Marie froze. Then, with an effort of will, she forced herself to look down.

She had tripped over an outstretched arm. Unsteadily, she squatted on her heels and peered into the shadow. It was a body. Part of the forehead sloped inward, crushed and bloody.

For a moment, Marie looked at death, as she had looked at death before. Then, slowly, awareness returned. Without moving, she looked in horror at the features.

This was Dr. Wendell Martin.

Although she did not know she was doing it, she opened her mouth and screamed, screamed, screamed.

6   Removal

THESE mechanical, inhuman screams stabbed into the lonely darkness of the parking lot. Almost before Marie Gentilhomme had relapsed into convulsive sobbing, Dr. Kroner, with Alice Doyle at his heels, was hurrying out of the basement entrance. And even as Dr. Kroner and Mrs. Doyle absorbed the macabre tableau, Dr. Philip Wittke joined them.

He took charge with complete authority. Dr. Kroner had dropped onto one knee beside the body. He looked up and reported what Dr. Wittke had already guessed: nothing more could be done for Wendell Martin.

Wittke turned to deal with Marie, who was half-struggling against the restraining arm of Mrs. Doyle.

"The last twenty-four hours have been too much for her," Mrs. Doyle said hoarsely.

"Take her inside and give her a sedative," Wittke rasped. Unconscious of Kroner's puzzled stare, Wittke did not move but continued to stare into space. Then, white-faced, he gave further directions, sharp and clear.

Thanks to these directions, when the state police arrived the body was still untouched. Lieutenant Joseph Perenna reported this to his superior several hours later.

"Not that I needed a doctor to see the guy was dead," he said. "Half his skull was crushed in."

He squinted, conjuring up a mental vision of the cordoned-off parking lot. Troopers guarded the entrance; the hospital staff had been shooed inside. Two cars had been positioned, their headlights beamed on the dead man. A steady drizzle had begun so that the fine raindrops clouded the converging cones of illumination. There had been little blood: it was soon washed away. The head—Perenna shook his own at recollection of the gruesome mess. The crossed lights had erased all shadow so that the body, spread-eagled on the path, looked two-dimensional, like a paper doll. One jacket pocket had been completely pulled out, presumably during a quick search;

the pale lining showed up starkly against the dark gray of the victim's suit.

Perenna passed photographs of the scene across the desk.

The captain adjusted a pair of glasses and studied them closely. At the end of his examination, he frowned.

"Did our doctor have anything to say?"

"Nothing that isn't self-evident. There was only one blow, but it did a lot of damage. An instantaneous death, almost. As for the weapon, it was smooth, rounded, quite narrow and heavily weighted. Any kind of metal bar would have done the job."

"And what about the people at the hospital? They have anything to say?"

Perenna shrugged fatalistically.

"At first they were too stunned to say anything. Then they started to gabble about why the police didn't stop all these muggings."

"They read too many newspapers," his superior grunted. "Southport isn't New York City. There aren't a lot of muggings here. In fact, I can't remember the last one."

The captain was silent for a moment as he prodded one of the pictures with a thoughtful forefinger. At length he asked a question.

"Anything strike you as strange?"

"Everything," Perenna said promptly. "It's the queerest so-called mugging I've ever seen. Our mugger wants to knock out his victim so he swipes him with a metal bar hard enough to crush his skull like an eggshell. Then he neatly removes a wallet from the inside breast pocket, but is so nervous he reverses an outside pocket where no man carries anything valuable. You could say he was just being thorough, except that he leaves an expensive gold watch in full view. He carries away both the weapon and the wallet, even though every fifteen-year-old punk knows enough to ditch the wallet fast. We may find it once it's daylight, but right now I'm willing to bet we won't. To top it all off, our mugger prefers working in a busy, lighted parking lot!"

"Not so busy, at that hour of night."

"A lot busier than a deserted side street!"

The captain nodded. "Yes," he agreed, "and there's another funny thing too. This Wendell Martin has been getting a lot of publicity. Too much. It makes quite a coincidence, his getting knocked off by accident. Hmm . . . who did you say that doctor was, the one who made sure the body wasn't touched?"

"Dr. Philip Wittke."

The captain consulted an exhaustive internal reference file on the personages of Suffolk County.

"He's one of the brass at the hospital. So, he's used to taking charge. On the other hand, he made damned sure we'd get the picture."

"You can't tell at this stage of the game. But how do you want this to go out to the newsboys? They'll be wanting something soon. Particularly with Martin being a name."

The captain's white teeth flashed in a sudden, humorless smile.

"That's no problem. Just tell them it's the latest in our rash of muggings. No sense in tipping our hand . . . yet."

Accordingly, the death of Wendell Martin was trumpeted to the world as a straightforward mugging. Reaction, for the most part, was correspondingly simple.

The Internal Revenue office immediately abandoned plans for an investigation of possible tax evasion. Overnight Wendell Martin had been transformed from monster to victim; more important, he was dead. Any discrepancies in his tax payments would be adjusted when his estate was closed. There was no longer any thought of prosecution.

Various arms of the medical profession announced public sorrow and breathed private sighs of relief. A troublesome problem had disappeared from their horizon.

Only at Southport Memorial was relief tempered by caution.

Philip Wittke cradled the phone. "That was the local medical association," he reported. "They're coming to the funeral."

"I hope they haven't confused Wendell Martin with the GP of the year." Roy Neverson sounded preoccupied. "The last thing we want now is a big public funeral!"

The blotter he had been toying with disappeared between his strong fingers to emerge a crumpled ball. He stared at it for a moment, then tossed it into the wastebasket before rising to pace back and forth before Wittke's desk.

"The quieter the better for us, Phil," he said.

"I know, Roy." Wittke too sounded absent. "But we certainly can count on the medical association. After all, they're as anxious as we are to avoid notoriety!"

"Are they?" Neverson asked softly.

Wittke had not spent a lifetime cultivating imperturbability to be disturbed by unanswered, and unanswerable, questions. Firmly keeping his gaze on the window, he said:

"We all want the same thing, Roy. A dignified funeral for Wendell —to serve as a symbol of his professional achievements over a lifetime of service, instead of anything that reflects this last few weeks, and all the unsuitable publicity inspired by avaricious insurance claims."

Wittke made *Freebody v. Atlantic Mutual* sound like a teen-age orgy, Neverson thought. It was typical of him. Also typical was the unctuous ease with which he was simultaneously denying the existence of a problem, and pondering a solution.

Experience had taught Dr. Neverson that this curious technique rarely impaired the effectiveness of the solutions that Wittke ultimately produced.

Nevertheless, he could not restrain his impatience at a generation content to be clever without sounding clever. This, in turn, reminded him of something else.

"You're right, Phil," he said after weighing Wittke's words. "That's the line for us to take. But one little thing—what about Edith Bullivant?"

Without seeming to, Dr. Wittke relaxed.

"Edith Bullivant is a sensible woman," he said. "She knows that we have to take the long view. That's something you younger men are sometimes apt to lose sight of. We—all of us here at Southport—we all want to remember Wendell as a valued colleague of many years standing. It's all a matter of perspective. And Edith, I am confident, even though she's not on the staff, agrees fully. So there is nothing for us to worry about any more—" He caught that unfortunate sentence in time. "Nothing at all to worry about. Except possibly—Lucille."

The uncertainty in the last comment erased the amusement dawning on Neverson's face.

"Lucille! My God, Phil, I'd forgotten about her! Do you think there's any likelihood that Wendell explained the situation to her?"

Philip Wittke was not relaxed now.

"I think Wendell would not have wanted to burden her with that kind of detail," he said, thinking aloud. "Which means that one of us should have a talk with her. After the funeral, of course. Unfortunately, Lucille and I have never really been close. Perhaps, Roy, you—"

Neverson was decisive.

"Oh no you don't! Not on your life. Lucille Martin has made it perfectly clear what she thinks of me."

He scowled for a moment, then looked up.

"And, Phil, I don't think any of us should get involved with Lucille."

Wittke, rather testily, asked what that meant.

Neverson became persuasive. "What about Al Martin? He's her brother-in-law, after all. It would be better, and a lot more natural, if *he* had a talk with her. Probably wouldn't have to go into detail, at all. You know Al. He'll be coming up anyway to help out. He probably wouldn't want any of us interfering."

Wittke nodded. "Good idea, Roy. He is the best possible choice. And, as you say, that means that there's no real need for any of us to approach Lucille about business. In fact, we won't have to worry about Lucille at all!"

How mistaken he was, neither man realized until Dr. Wittke's secretary announced that the widow was on the phone. The danger was not apparent at first.

"Philip? Is that you?"

The voice was heavy and slow, almost drugged.

"Yes, my dear. I'm so glad that you called. When I tried to get you earlier, your maid said you were lying down. Quite the wisest thing for you at the moment."

"There's nothing else to do," said the lifeless monotone. "Wen is dead. Everything is over."

"Now, my dear, I know you feel that way now. It's only natural. The shock lasts a long time. But life goes on, and you must go on with it."

Philip Wittke was experienced with the recently widowed. The burst of angry denial usually sparked by this kind of consolation was beneficial. The important thing was to arouse an emotional response, any response.

Lucille Martin, however, was beyond the reach of such tactics. She did not argue or hit out; she merely asked, out of vast exhaustion, why he had called.

"I want you to know that you mustn't worry about the . . . the arrangements. I'll take care of all the details, Lucille. I want you to feel that you can rely on me. Anything at all. Now, would you like me to speak with the undertaker?"

"The undertaker?" Mrs. Martin might have been hearing the word for the first time. "A man from Pfost's is coming here in about an hour. He said Wen had already arranged something."

"Then, I'll come right over, shall I? In about forty-five minutes?"

"It doesn't matter. I can't think about that sort of thing now. Nothing matters any more . . . nothing except punishing the man who killed Wen."

Wittke murmured sympathetically. "You don't have to worry about that, my dear. The police, I'm sure, will do everything possible—"

Lucille Martin interrupted him. Not quickly, not vehemently, but with a muted assurance that was almost terrifying.

"But the police are wrong, Philip. Wen would never have been mugged. He was always very careful. Somebody hated him and killed him. Somebody took Wen from me. And he was all I had."

A hint of sharpness entered Wittke's manner. He raised his eyebrows at Neverson, who was listening intently.

"Now, my dear, you mustn't say that sort of thing," he said. "I realize you're upset, but it can only make for unpleasantness, and you wouldn't want that."

"I don't care," she said simply. "Somebody murdered Wen, and they have to pay for it. I'm sorry if it will be unpleasant."

"Lucille!" Wittke was genuinely aghast. "I hope you haven't been saying— Well, never mind that, I'll come over right away."

The widow was very docile.

"Yes, you come right now, Philip. I'd like to talk to you. But I'm right. You'll see."

Wittke let out his breath as the receiver clicked.

"I just can't believe it. Lucille, of all people!"

"What's the matter?" Neverson asked.

Wittke gave him the gist of their conversation.

Neverson stared.

"That's incredible," he protested. "Of course, it's simply shock."

Wittke nodded mournfully. "You can't tell about sudden widowhood. Lucille always seemed so calm about Wendell. She was a good wife but you'd never expect her to go off the deep end."

Neverson hesitated before he spoke. Then he shook his head.

"I think you've got it wrong, Phil. True, she didn't act like an adoring bride. But she raised her children, and after they left home I think Wendell became her child. And she indulged him in a way she never indulged her daughters. If he stormed and raged, she was tolerant as if he were a spoiled child. But, by and large, she saw to it that what Wendell wanted, Wendell got."

Echoes of that automaton voice lingered in Wittke's ear and produced their own doubt.

"You could be right. That's what she sounds like—a mother who's lost a child. That's very bad."

Neverson brooded as he sat in silence. Eventually he came to an unpalatable conclusion.

"It could be very bad if she persists in this business about someone hating Wendell. Because you know the name that'll come to her mind? . . . Harley Bauer!"

Wittke's immediate reaction to this analysis was to reach for his hat. "Don't worry," he said confidently. "I'll quiet her down. She'll have forgotten this lunacy by tomorrow."

"I hope so," said Neverson, following him to the door. "All we need is to have Bauer in this mess. What if he talks?"

"Whatever his faults, Harley Bauer is a doctor." Wittke was at his stolidest. "We can count on him."

Neverson's equanimity was restored by this *volte-face*. Poor Philip must be feeling hard pressed, indeed, to defend Bauer. When they had first learned that Harley was joining a panel medical program, Wittke had apostrophized his conduct as unethical, unprofessional, un-American and downright communistic.

"Oh, I suppose so," he agreed. "Under normal conditions. But I hate to think of what he might say if the widow accuses him point-blank of murder."

"I'll take care of that."

"Fine. While you're at it, I intend to have a word with our other little troublemaker."

Neverson strode briskly toward the group at the end of the corridor.

Marie Gentilhomme was so busy listening to Dr. Kroner and Alice Doyle that she did not see Dr. Neverson until his voice at her elbow made her jump.

"Nurse! I want a word with you!"

She could tell right away that Dr. Neverson was in one of his difficult moods. He wouldn't yell, like Dr. Kroner sometimes did. Instead he would be terribly polite and cutting, every now and then pausing to give her a chance to reply, when he knew very well she couldn't.

"I left specific instructions that I was to be informed of the results of Dr. Myron's test. Did you think that a twelve-hour delay would do just as well?"

"No . . . no, Dr. Neverson."

"I hope you understand how lucky you've been. The test result was negative."

"Yes . . . yes, I know that, Dr. Neverson."

"Yes, you knew it. The point, however, was that I should know it."

Marie was simply enduring. Horrible as this was, she could stand it better than Dr. Martin's savage bludgeoning. Her chin set stubbornly.

"If that test had been positive, an instant change in medication would have been required." Neverson was goaded to fury by her lack of response. "And may I ask why you saw fit to go off duty last night without leaving word with your replacement that I was to be informed?"

A third voice intervened.

"If you excuse, Doctor, I think you cannot understand." Dr. Kroner was prepared to struggle with the English language for the sake of justice. Laboriously he explained that Marie Gentilhomme had been given an injection and sent home in shock after her discovery of Wendell Martin's body.

"Under express instructions from Dr. Wittke himself."

"I see," said Neverson shortly. He had completely forgotten that it was Marie Gentilhomme who had found the body. "Very well, nurse. But if you intend to continue in this profession, you'd better harden yourself to the sight of physical injuries."

With that he turned on his heel and marched away.

"Whew!" breathed Alice Doyle. "I wonder what's eating him?"

"Thank you, Dr. Kroner," Marie Gentilhomme smiled shyly.

"One Bromo, it is," said Sid Segal. "Hard day, Alice?"

"The less days like this, the better, Sid," replied Alice Doyle.

Cautiously she downed half the glass. Sid Segal, with years of experience, waited for exactly the right moment to resume the conversation.

"I suppose everybody's upset about Dr. Martin. Terrible thing. The police ought to do something about these muggings."

"Yes," Alice agreed absently, draining the glass. "But it doesn't help if people start acting up."

"The doctors?"

"You know what they're like."

Nurse and pharmacist exchanged a glance of perfect communion.

"On top of that, I hear that La Belle Dame Martin is making herself interesting. She claims it wasn't a mugging, it was murder."

Sid Segal clucked censoriously.

"Now that, that's not right. She can stir up a lot of ugly talk."

"Oh, I suppose they'll manage to shut her up. But it all adds to the atmosphere."

Collecting her empty glass, the druggist was philosophic.

"It takes a couple of days. Then it'll all blow over."

"My God, I hope so, Sid." Alice Doyle prepared to lower herself from the stool. "At least there's one good thing. We should stop hearing so much about that damned insurance trial."

"And where does Martin's death leave the insurance claim?" asked John Putnam Thatcher as Charlie Trinkam and Kenneth Nicolls assembled in his office to discuss the latest turn of events in *Freebody v. Atlantic Mutual.*

Trinkam was ready with his reply. "As far as information goes, Paul Jackson says that he has the two admissions he wanted from Martin—that Pem Freebody was not on his deathbed when he entered the hospital, and that the presence of the hemostatic clips would have been dangerous for him, quite apart from the bullet wound."

"Those are the tangibles," Thatcher nodded. "I presume there's an intangible as well."

"A very big one. The jury hated Martin so much that Paul figures every minute he was on the stand was so much money in the bank for us."

Kenneth Nicolls was pondering this cavalier treatment of evidence when Thatcher continued:

"Now, what about the hospital? Will they become more flexible now that they have no surgeon to protect?"

"Jackson doesn't think so," Charlie replied. "They've got their own reputation to protect. That nurse's testimony hit them hard. And, if you ask me, that's what really stuck in the jury's craw about Martin. They could have forgiven a simple mistake. They couldn't forgive the fact that Martin and everybody else in the operating room knew the patient was being wheeled out full of surplus metal."

Kenneth Nicolls was still trying to find his feet in the shifting balance of factors. "Do you honestly think those hemostats killed him?"

Trinkam shrugged his ignorance. "It's a cinch they didn't do poor Pem any good," he said cheerfully.

"We don't seem to be getting anywhere," Thatcher said with dissatisfaction. "The reason I called you in is that I've been getting cryptic phone calls from Dexter Loomis at Atlantic Mutual. I think he's putting out feelers for a settlement."

"Just wait," Charlie chortled, "just wait until he finds out what Paul has up his sleeve now."

Thatcher waited with some misgivings. Alone, either Charlie Trinkam or Paul Jackson added a desirable zest to almost any commercial team. Hitched together, their combined *joie de vivre* might well run away with the carriage.

"Yes?" he inquired cautiously.

"Paul wants to see if he can get leave to amend the pleadings, to ask for double indemnity under the accidental death clause."

There was a moment's silence before Thatcher's wary response.

"It has a certain inspired simplicity. Does Jackson have anything to support this?"

"Oh, yes. His theory is that Pem would still be with us if he had been left to bleed privately in his little woodlot, as he had arranged to do."

"I see," said Thatcher gravely. "It was the ghastly mischance of being taken to a hospital that killed him?"

"That's it, in a nutshell." Charlie's grin broadened.

"Tell me, is he considering this seriously, or is it just part of his harassment program?"

"Well, there's no denying that insurance companies bring out Paul's sense of mischief," Trinkam conceded. "I think he would have been willing to give this one a serious try if he had Martin feeding the flames. Now, he's not so sure. He really needs something to take Martin's place."

Thatcher thought a dose of cold water might be beneficial.

"On a statistical basis alone, he is unlikely to find another Martin at Southport."

"No, of course not. Paul has something else in mind. He's got some people working out at the hospital. They're getting the names of patients that Martin had in the post-operative ward during the critical four days."

"And?"

"It seems that there's a lot of coming and going after an operation —doctors checking and consulting, nurses following through. Jackson thinks if he can get evidence that one more doctor knew about those hemostats and did nothing, we'll have it made."

Very slowly Thatcher nodded.

"I see. That would suggest almost a conspiracy against Pemberton Freebody. And we already have at least two nurses who knew of the situation. There might have been some talk. It would depend, I suppose, a good deal on how people felt about Wendell Martin."

Charlie was buoyantly optimistic.

"Well, you remember what he was like. He can't have had many friends."

7 Gall

DR. PHILIP WITTKE was not a sensitive administrator, but he was conscientious. The next few days were extremely busy for him. He rallied to the support of Lucille Martin, impressed his two sons into funeral preparations, established new safeguards for the hospital parking lot and gave a pep talk to the non-professional staff.

The doctors required a more personal touch. Pocketing his own inclinations, Wittke doubled the cordiality dispensed to outside doctors and took time for a public display of affability to Dr. Edith Bullivant, walking with her the length of a corridor and exchanging stately chaff about the population explosion in Southport's delivery rooms. Any nostalgia that Dr. Kroner might have felt for the medical circles of Europe was presumably banished by a cozy chat in which he was assured that Southport wanted to make him feel at home.

Nor was the nursing staff forgotten. Dr. Wittke found an opportunity to hope that Nurse Gentilhomme was recovered from her shocking experience and to convey a few words of warm appreciation to Nurse Doyle for unspecified services. Marie Gentilhomme, as was to be expected, was suitably grateful. Alice Doyle, on the other hand, jolted him severely by responding with a significant question about the forthcoming retirement of Mrs. Stosser, the director of nursing. (And Nurse Doyle was a woman he had thought he could depend on, too. Nowadays, no one seemed to do anything out of a simple sense of duty.)

These responsibilities discharged, Dr. Wittke was ready to call it a day. At this point, however, a worried group of inside doctors took him quietly aside and pointed out that the critical problem remained untouched.

"It's that damned insurance claim," said the chief of medicine. "If it wasn't for that, the publicity would be over after Wendell's funeral."

"But *Freebody v. Atlantic Mutual* doesn't concern *us,*" said a surprised Wittke. "We have nothing further to tell them."

A resident neurologist corrected him. "We can't help being concerned. The way things stand now, there's still a legal quarrel over the cause of death."

Wittke prepared to join in the general anxiety. He was not sure that his colleagues were right. But he had long since grasped one facet of administration. A staff's morale was a reflection of what the staff thought. Whether they were right or wrong was largely irrelevant. Until Southport was relieved of the incubus of Pemberton Freebody, it was not going to be a happy ship.

"Not that there's much we can do about it."

Roy Neverson, who kept in touch with "the younger men" as Wittke called them, had been instrumental in arranging the meeting, but this was his first contribution; it was not calculated to raise any spirits. "Even if we all troop to the stand for the insurance company, we won't get support from other doctors."

There was a sound of gloomy agreement, suddenly interrupted by an exclamation from Philip Wittke.

"That may be the answer, Roy," he said reflectively.

"I didn't realize I was providing any answers," Neverson said.

"You can't go on with a trial if you don't have a case. Wendell was the insurance company's medical testimony. Now they expect *us* to take his place. But, what if we don't? Then, Atlantic Mutual will have to settle. Right?"

There was a respectful silence. Everyone realized that this was the answer, and that it could have been put forward by nobody else. Philip Wittke would have been quick to reject the suggestion that Southport Memorial wash its hands of Wendell Martin—if he had not thought of it himself.

Thus it was that one fine spring day found John Putnam Thatcher on the Southern State Parkway, rolling out to Suffolk County. Paul Jackson had been amused when he announced the conference.

"Of course it's irregular as hell," he admitted cheerfully. "After all, Wendell Martin was subpoenaed as a witness—and only Martin. Technically the rest of the doctors at Southport Memorial aren't involved, except maybe Kroner. But they don't understand that this isn't a routine malpractice claim. I think they plan to sweep the whole thing under the rug, just like one of their closed hearings before the AMA. And let me tell you, Atlantic Mutual doesn't like this meeting one little bit, but they're going along just to see what Wittke's got up his sleeve."

Thatcher said that he shared their curiosity.

"Me, too," said Paul Jackson. "Although I can make a pretty good guess."

At Southport Memorial Hospital's small, bright doctors' lounge (a faintly shabby collection of chintz-covered sofas and chairs, a small table and a free-standing blackboard), they found Atlantic Mutual represented by Dexter Loomis and Andrew Chisolm. Thatcher, Paul Jackson and Dr. Edmund Knox, from the Institute for Cancer Research at Hanover, represented the plaintiff.

Or, as Dr. Knox persisted in phrasing it, the beneficiaries.

Everyone could guess what Southport Memorial wanted. It wanted to be left alone. How they intended to achieve this goal, John Putnam Thatcher, for one, was eager to learn.

He did not have to sit through tedious preliminaries.

"I've asked Dr. Neverson and Dr. Kroner to be with me during our discussion," said Dr. Wittke, "so that you will see just how little information we can give you—especially now, after Dr. Martin's tragic death," he added, in case anybody missed the point. "Both of them were on duty the night that Mr. Freebody was admitted."

The mere fact that Dr. Neverson and Dr. Kroner were both able to maintain unconcerned silence at this point convinced the two attorneys present that Southport Memorial was not going to produce another Wendell Martin. The gathering nodded sober acknowledgment of Martin's death, and Wittke swept on to a disarmingly ingenuous conclusion.

"We'd like to be of assistance, but unfortunately we're no longer in a position to give you any information."

This was too much for Atlantic Mutual.

"As you must realize, Dr. Wittke," Chisolm said sternly, "this claim has now become an inquiry into the exact cause of the death of Pemberton Freebody. He was brought here directly after shooting himself, was operated on here, lived for four days and then died here. Thus, Southport Memorial Hospital is the only possible source of information as to his death. And, much as we all regret Dr. Martin's death, the patient was not in his exclusive care during the relevant period of time. Other people must have seen him."

Having relieved his feelings, Chisolm leaned back in his chair and fell to wiping his glasses savagely.

Philip Wittke frowned. One of the things sustaining him before this unpleasant interview had been his hazy assumption that he would be engaged in a tournament, championing the medical profession against the rest of the world. The arrival of Dr. Edmund Knox had destroyed that illusion—among others. The eminent Dr. Wittke was the product of a small private clinic and a small suburban hospital. In that environment he was a great success. But Edmund Knox was a name that conjured up the giant medical compounds of New York City, the recent Nobel prizes and the latest application of laser techniques to cancer surgery. Dr. Knox was material for *Time* magazine.

Dr. Wittke had counted on dealing with laymen.

He played his next card.

"Of course, Mr. Chisolm. The patient received constant care and attention from many of our staff. The initial examination in Emergency was made by Dr. Kroner."

The insurance brigade stiffened to attention. If Kroner was willing to say that Freebody was as good as dead *before* the operation, Paul Jackson would be left out in the cold. They turned hopefully.

The hope was very short-lived.

"Yes, this patient, I myself see," Dr. Kroner struggled manfully. "The bleeding I stop and I . . . I warn Dr. Martin to prepare himself for . . . for . . ."

"For an operation," Roy Neverson supplied helpfully. His voice was grave but there was amusement in his eyes.

Chisolm glared. No matter what Dr. Kroner was willing to say, he could never say it with any persuasive effect to a jury.

"May I ask a question?" Dr. Edmund Knox sounded happy. In fact, he sounded like a man who had just received a check for a hundred thousand dollars.

"Certainly, Dr. Knox."

Wittke didn't like the way his words came out. They were too damned deferential. But, he told himself, it is hard to hit the right doctor-to-doctor note with a man who has surrendered to the institutions. Everyone agreed that the individual practitioner was the backbone of the profession.

Dexter Loomis was also willing. "That's what we're all here for."

Thus encouraged, Dr. Knox got down to business. "We are happy to have heard Dr. Kroner's views. But the critical time in the patient's condition seems to have been during the four days after the operation. Who, besides Dr. Martin, was involved in the post-operative care?"

Across the width of the room, Neverson and Wittke exchanged glances. Thatcher, seeing this, was prepared to swear they had already prepared their tactics for the occasion.

"I was." Roy Neverson paused. "I was disappointed when he took a turn for the worse the day after the operation. He had been holding his own nicely until then. After that, he lost ground steadily."

Wittke took up the narrative. "Dr. Martin asked me to have a look also, because of my experience in the field," he said, momentarily forgetting Dr. Knox. "Everything humanly possible was done, but the patient did not respond normally to treatment."

"I see," Chisolm said tightly. He shook his head firmly at Dexter Loomis, who was at the boiling point, then stared balefully at the Southport contingent. Dr. Wittke and Dr. Neverson might just as well have said it outright. If pushed, they would testify that the patient had mysteriously started to fail as a result of Dr. Martin's surgery. "I see very clearly. You realize we'll have to call expert witnesses?"

"Naturally." Philip Wittke's cool voice invited him to try to find some. "On the other hand, with such an unusual and complex situation, many doctors may hesitate to answer hypothetical questions. Of course, I know nothing about such matters, but I would have thought that a settlement would be appropriate—where real doubt exists."

John Thatcher almost laughed aloud at Dexter Loomis's expression. It is not often, he reflected, that a third party intervenes to tell an insurance company it should settle with one of its policyholders. Particularly just after having kicked the insurance company in the teeth.

Chisolm's jaw was clenched so tightly, he was physically incapable of reply. But medicine is not the only discipline with professional loyalties. Paul Jackson, in his first observation of the day, took up cudgels on behalf of the New York Bar.

"The parties will naturally give consideration to the possibility of a settlement, as well as other courses of action. As you say, that need not concern the medical witnesses."

"Very fortunately," was Wittke's rejoinder to this snub.

Strangulated speech had now become possible for Andrew Chisolm.

"There is one other way in which you could add to your helpfulness, Dr. Wittke," he said, heavily ironical. "At the outset, this case seemed so simple that we neglected to subpoena Dr. Martin's case records. I presume those records will be available when we require them. I would like your assurance to that effect."

There was a clear implication he wouldn't be surprised to find Wittke burning the files the minute his back was turned.

Dr. Wittke had long ago learned to let little unpleasantnesses like this slide off his back. Roy Neverson favored a more direct approach. Now he smiled openly.

"We thought you might be interested in those records. They're in Dr. Martin's office. As long as they haven't been subpoenaed, why don't you—all of you—come and take a look?"

Despite Atlantic Mutual's gnashing of teeth, John Thatcher and Edmund Knox were on their feet. They knew perfectly well that Neverson was feeding them ammunition. And an early glance at those records could be useful, if only to prepare a rebuttal. Although from what they had seen of Southport Memorial, neither expected its records to be very illuminating.

The procession straggled down the corridor and came to a halt in the doorway of the office entered by Philip Wittke. They could see two women already in the office. One wore hospital whites, the other black.

The one in white spoke first.

"I'm preparing a list of condolence messages, Dr. Wittke," she said, her eyes flashing a warning.

"Of course, Miss Reese." Wittke nodded his understanding and moved forward. "But, Lucille, should you be out? Miss Reese could have gone to you. You should take better care of yourself."

He looked hesitantly over his shoulder and decided against introducing the widow to the men who had scarified the reputation of her husband.

As for Lucille Martin she paid not the slightest attention to the knot of men hovering on the threshold. Even Philip Wittke's arrival barely seemed to register with her. She had always been a placid woman. Now her grief had transformed that placidity into frozen lethargy. Physically, she had barely changed. Her golden suntan gave her a deceptive air of well-being. Only blank, unfocused eyes betrayed inner turmoil.

"I have that list ready, Mrs. Martin," Miss Reese said brightly. She offered some typewritten pages, which the widow accepted like a robot.

"And now, Miss Reese, please get us Dr. Martin's records on the Freebody case. Then we won't bother Mrs. Martin any more."

"Yes, Dr. Wittke." Miss Reese moved swiftly to a filing cabinet. She realized that Wittke wanted to remove his visitors before Lucille Martin recognized the name of Pemberton Freebody.

But Lucille Martin was miles away, waiting for the interruption to end. Torpidly she scanned the list in her hand.

"You can take care of these, can't you, Miss Reese? It's only . . . oh, look at this hypocrisy!"

Something had caught her attention. Suddenly she awoke from her torpor.

"How could they? Where is it?" She began to riffle through the pile of condolence cards. Then she seized one and tore it, halving and rehalving it viciously. "That's what Dr. Harley Bauer can do with his condolences! And that scheming little wife of his! They think I don't know what they did to poor Wen!"

Alarmed, Wittke strode to her side and grasped her hands. "Now, my dear, you mustn't let these things upset you. You've overtaxed yourself, coming out. You must sit down and get control of yourself."

Drawing her to a chair, he saw the pulled-out drawers of the big desk and tried using them to distract her. "And you've been looking for something in Wendell's desk. You only had to ask me. I'll gladly do anything I can."

As quickly as it had flared, the widow's brief spurt of emotion faded. Her shoulders shuddered briefly, and she drew a hand down her cheek.

"I don't think there's anything you can do. It's very strange," she said almost absently, "but Wen hasn't left much money. Next to nothing."

Wittke started back and let her hands fall.

"Money?" he repeated stupidly.

Behind him, John Thatcher's ears pricked up.

The widow's dreamy indifference persisted.

"Yes. At first I thought maybe he hadn't been doing as well as he told me. Wen did so like to boast to me. But then I realized I was trying to avoid the truth. And that never helps, does it?"

With a harassed glance over his shoulder, Wittke patted her arm soothingly.

"We can discuss this some other time, Lucille."

She almost succeeded in smiling at him.

"Poor Philip! How embarrassed you must be. But, putting it off won't make it any easier for me. I have to face it. And I thought I understood Wen. That's what hurts so. It's incredible. That Wen could behave like that and, even more, that I didn't realize it."

Wittke's tone was perfect. In John Thatcher's opinion, however, his wording could scarcely have been less fortunate.

"You must try to understand. Wendell was devoted to you, Lucille. But there are some burdens a man wants to spare his wife."

She was incredulous. "Spare me?"

"Lucille!"

It was a peremptory cry. From behind the visitors, Dr. Neverson pushed his way to front and center. He had decided, Thatcher saw, to end this grotesque encounter.

Brutally, if necessary.

"Lucille," Neverson said emphatically, "there wasn't any other woman in Wendell's life!"

Sleepily she turned to him. "Oh, Roy, you don't have to lie to me. I know that the wife is always the last to know."

There was slyness in her voice as she went on:

"Was it that way with Julie too, Roy?"

Neverson took a step forward. But Dr. Philip Wittke, engulfed by Victorian shock, erupted:

"Lucille, you mustn't say things like that. Or even, my dear, think things like that!"

Lucille Martin stared at him. "What else is there for me to think?" she asked. "Wen's money is gone! It must have been a woman! It's not easy for me . . . to realize I've been a failure. . . ."

Thatcher, obstructed by Paul Jackson and Dexter Loomis, followed this scene with fascinated horror. Neverson, he could see, was also shaken.

But Neverson rallied. He turned away from the widow with eloquent distaste. Then, seeing the faces in the doorway, he turned to the nurse.

"Get those records!"

Miss Reese scurried to obey.

This was enough to remind Dr. Wittke of his bigger responsibilities. He thrust the folder upon Edmund Knox, who stood nearest him.

"I doubt if we can be of more assistance to you. I hope you'll leave those with my secretary. . . ."

The scene had generated its own paralysis, however. Dr. Wittke's guests remained immobilized for a moment. That moment was enough.

"I must know one thing," Lucille Martin said with terrible finality. "Who was she, Phil? Roy, you've got to tell me. . . ."

After this, as John Thatcher would have been the first to admit, neither Jackson & Jackson nor the Sloan Guaranty Trust stood on ceremony.

They fled.

Atlantic Mutual was scarcely a step behind them.

"All in all, it was quite a day," Thatcher said some hours later, as he took a drink from the barman while they waited to file into the banquet room. In the offing was a speech on credit guarantees for export shipments. But at least he was safely back on Manhattan.

Tom Robichaux disapproved. "You should leave your troubles in the office, John."

"I'm not sure these *are* troubles, Tom. In fact it's almost too good to be true. The people in Southport are practically promising to go on the stand and say their surgeon killed our client, simply to get a speedy decision. I find that very odd, considering their united front a short week ago."

"Well, he's not their surgeon any more."

"No, but they should be thinking of the hospital's reputation. It's all very fishy."

"Covering up something?" Robichaux ruminated silently for a moment. "Kickbacks? But, hell, they all do that. Why make such a fuss?"

Thatcher looked up, surprised. Knowledgeability outside the office was not Tom's strong point. Unless Kickbacks, Inc. was being sold on the Big Board, Robichaux should have been lost by now. Of course there was one other way he picked up information. Thatcher narrowed his eyes as he tried to recall.

"Veronica," said Robichaux helpfully. "You remember Veronica."

No, Thatcher said truthfully, he didn't remember any Veronica.

"Hell, I'm not surprised. I was married to her for two and a half years, and I barely saw her. In and out of hospitals all the time. Sort of a hobby."

There was a respectful silence as old memories stirred into life.

"Wonderful the way that woman could eat, considering she was missing most of her digestive system. And money! Went through it like water!"

Thatcher delicately suggested that expenses in every Robichaux marital ménage ran pretty high.

"That's different. But when you can't tell the drugstore bill from the Tiffany bill," said Robichaux in a burst of nostalgic irritation, "I say that's a hell of a way to take your fun!"

Gravely Thatcher agreed. "One of the other features of this Freebody mess is that today Martin's widow said he's died without leaving any estate. She put on quite a bloodcurdling performance. Tom, have you ever heard of a forty-five-year-old surgeon dying poor?"

"Ha!" snorted Veronica's ex-husband. "Don't you believe it! There'll be a safe deposit box, stuffed with cash, somewhere. The tax boys will find it, even if the widow can't."

That, Thatcher had to agree, was possible. But, it was one more oddity to be added to Southport's growing pile. However, he reminded himself that this purported to be a social occasion and turned to other questions.

"Whatever happened to Veronica? Do you know?"

"Oh yes, after a couple of tries, she finally settled down with a gynecologist. Been with him a long time now."

"Of course, it's more economical, that way."

"That's not it. Ronnie wasn't a penny pincher." Robichaux protested unnecessarily. Financial prudence had never been the hallmark of a Robichaux rib. "No, this gives them a common interest. Something to talk about, don't you know."

Thatcher found it impossible to contemplate.

8 House Calls

IN ALL HONESTY Thatcher had, until now, been unable to bring more than a modicum of attention to bear on the entangled affairs of Pemberton Freebody and Southport Memorial. As a man, he had honored the pyrotechnic brilliance used by Paul Jackson to salvage a lost cause. As a banker, he was duly appreciative of the hundred thousand dollars to be netted by this brilliance. The trouble, however, was that John Thatcher did not share the American fascination with doctors and things medical. He appreciated the legal and medical niceties raised by Dr. Wendell Martin's dubious surgery, but he was incapable of following the expert testimony with the genuine relish of Charlie Trinkam. Willpower kept him listening to voices deponing about hemostats and blood transfusions, but it was willpower shaped by his responsibility to the Sloan Guaranty Trust.

Philip Wittke's smooth announcement of his new policy had changed all that. For the first time Thatcher felt a quickening of real interest. The good doctor would have been aghast at this result of his tactics.

Sudden changes of position, particularly following sudden deaths, were, in Thatcher's experience, worth examination. Wendell Martin's death might be simple enough. But the strange reversal at Southport Memorial impressed him as far from simple. Then there was the widow. Her revelations seemed to bear out Tom Robichaux's prediction; there must be a safe deposit box or its equivalent elsewhere.

Safe deposit boxes, not hemostats, were right up John Thatcher's alley.

It was time, he decided virtuously, that the Sloan gave something more than moral support to the efforts of Paul Jackson.

This decision boded ill for his subordinates as Kenneth Nicolls, arriving at the relatively respectable hour of ten minutes after nine, discovered.

"But, Miss Corsa, I've got to finish that pension fund study for Mr. Trinkam by noon," he protested to the phone.

"Mr. Thatcher," said Miss Corsa, in effect dismissing pension funds, Mr. Trinkam and the Western world, if need be, "will require you for the rest of the day."

This announcement, final and adequate for Miss Corsa and possibly Thatcher, left Ken to beard Charlie Trinkam in his den. Charlie was rarely at his best in the morning, and today proved no exception to the rule.

"Oh, great!" he said as Nicolls reported the summons to higher duty and deposited bulky documents concerning the Kosher Butchers' Pension Fund on Trinkam's desk. "Just great! I'll have Phil Cook do what he can, but Gabler has him busy with another cost breakdown on the Pennsy-Central merger. God knows how many Ev wants! Besides, what does John need you for, anyway?"

Ken replied to this unflattering question by admitting that he had no idea.

"I could call and say I need you," Charlie thought aloud. This was an idle threat and they both knew it. Members of the staff did not call John Putnam Thatcher with such comments. Exasperatedly, Charlie returned to his desktop. "Kosher butchers! Still, now that Southport is folding, I suppose I should be grateful for comic relief. . . ."

Ken paused on his way to the door. "You think the *Freebody v. Atlantic Mutual* case is over, Charlie?"

Charlie was already making rapid marginal notes. "Sure. All fini! The hospital is ratting. Even Atlantic Mutual can see when it's being double-crossed. The fun's over. We've got to get back to work . . . kosher butchers!"

As he strode down the corridor to Thatcher's corner suite, Ken reflected that Charlie Trinkam, a determined worker despite his airy manner, deserved the recreation proffered by *Freebody v. Atlantic Mutual*. For his sake, it was a shame that the show was closing.

Five minutes later, Thatcher had once again startled Ken into commencing, if not completing, a protest; the show, it appeared, was not over.

"As I see it," Thatcher announced, "there are two lines of approach. One is through those two patients Jackson's men have unearthed. The other is an inquiry into Wendell Martin's financial affairs."

Kenneth Nicolls permitted his eyebrows to ask the question for him. Reports of the Southport conference had stressed only Wittke's betrayal of Atlantic Mutual.

"Ah, you haven't heard? Martin's widow was making strange statements. Strangest of all, she says her husband left virtually no capital. And he had been a successful doctor for over twenty years."

In many ways Kenneth was still young and innocent. He was not, however, that innocent.

"She's got it wrong," he said with certainty. "Probably there's a portfolio at the broker's or something."

Thatcher nodded. "If so, I think I can undertake to find it. But it will be interesting if there is no such simple explanation. Very interesting."

"Well, yes," admitted Kenneth, "but I don't see what good it would do us."

"You never can tell," said Thatcher enigmatically. "In any event, I want you to tackle the patients. See if they picked up anything at all about the operation on Pemberton Freebody. With luck, you'll find them both out in Southport today. Charlie has the names."

Impetuous questions hovered on Ken Nicolls's lips, only to die unuttered as Thatcher waved dismissal and plunged into some research reports forwarded by Walter Bowman. Not until the door closed did Thatcher permit himself to grin; issuing impossible orders was one solace to the burdens of high office. Then, with a sigh, he paid the price and returned to Bowman's analysis of Major Foods Co., which was planning to expand into a line of polyunsaturated food additives for the weight-conscious canary.

"He wants what?" Charlie Trinkam asked absently, phone at his ear.

"He wants me to start talking to those patients out in Southport," said Ken bitterly.

"Better you than me," commented Charlie, rummaging through his desk for a paper. "Here . . . oh, Ev? Listen, Ev, I want to talk to you about that Pennsy-Central study you've got Phil Cook wasting time on . . . yes, I said wasting time. . . ."

It was after lunch before Kenneth Nicolls drove into what he was already thinking of as Old Southport. He had just treated himself to an elaborate meal on the grounds that he needed it. His morning interview had been frankly terrifying.

There had been no intimation of the horrors in store when he pulled into the driveway before the solid, substantial brick house. Mrs. Furness herself had answered the bell, a trim white-haired lady in sharkskin slacks. Kenneth had taken the trouble to work out a rather elaborate opening, designed to conceal the bare-faced impertinence of his questions. He needn't have bothered.

Mrs. Furness, charmed by his interest, had immediately taken him into her confidence. There had been no question of illness. Far from it. The lady had had an expensive job of face-lifting as preparation for what she intended to be a rambunctious widowhood.

"Edgar died a year ago," she explained. "When I was able to think at all, I looked around at other widows of my age."

She had not liked what she saw. They had all arranged things so that their lives were even drearier than before widowhood. Some of them had gone so far as to marry again—men who were fifteen years older than the husbands they had already lost. This was not what Mrs. Furness had in mind. Edgar had been staunchly conservative. Like a good wife, she too had extolled the virtues of Home, God and Country. She did not rate this experiment a success.

"I gave it thirty-five years," she announced judiciously. "And that is long enough. Now, I please myself."

She was preparing to remove to an artistic enclave in Colorado. She confessed she was not the least bit aesthetically inclined, but— here, the merry eyes twinkled shrewdly—she rather thought that a widow with plenty of money, a desire to entertain lavishly and no rooted objection to overpriced works of art would probably fit in beautifully.

"Because," she concluded forthrightly, "I am interested in men younger than Edgar, not older. Lots of them! And I prefer them as unconservative as possible."

Naturally Kenneth did not inquire into the specifics of her interest. Nor did he understand why he became so alarmed at this point. In any event, it was not a reaction he cared to probe. He did blame himself, however, for allowing his alarm to show.

Suddenly both the twinkle and the shrewdness intensified.

"But, my dear boy," Mrs. Furness laughed, "I can see that you are a very respectable young man, and I am sure you have a very nice wife and children."

Kenneth had withdrawn shortly thereafter, half relieved and half offended at this kindly dismissal. He had a dismal suspicion that he had been classified as a young Edgar. However, no matter what else he had to reproach himself for, he had covered his business. It was abundantly apparent that Mrs. Furness, during her stay at Southport, had been too preoccupied planning her future to have an interest in anything else. And unless Wendell Martin had had unsuspected Bohemian depths, she probably hadn't even noticed her surgeon.

That had been New Southport. He was now entering Old Southport. Kenneth Nicolls realized, not for the first time, that unless a new community is cast up in the wilderness, it never acquires total homogeneity. Where housing developments accrete around an established community, no matter how valuable the land becomes, there is always an old section. The mansions and the estates go, but this remains. It consists of aged ramshackle frame houses whose occupants are mostly old-timers; its storekeepers know all the ins and outs of Main Street business. It wields political power out of all proportion to its population—its residents control the local civil service, win the local elective offices and run the town weekly. This situation persists until a new generation of locals rises to effect a natural redistricting.

The home of Mr. and Mrs. Eugene Perkins was very much Old Southport—sagging porch, weathered siding and all.

"Good God!" Ken's exclamation was involuntary. A venerable gap-toothed picket fence enclosed a small balding lawn and twelve very small children. For a moment Ken fastened on a triviality; why had Southport Memorial put the fecund Mrs. Perkins in the fourth floor Post-Op when sixth floor Obstetrics was all too clearly her spiritual home?

But a second glance dissipated Ken's mental fog; the youngsters, digging holes, playing in the sandbox, swinging in an old tire roped to a malnourished elm, banging on drums and pails, were all of them between three and six years old. It was technically impossible that they should all be young Perkinses.

They were not. A sober fourteen-year-old, rounding the corner with a weeping little boy tucked under her arm, directed him up the walk to the living room and Mrs. Eugene Perkins.

"Oh, call me Nancy," she said exhaustedly, admitting him after he yodeled through the defective screen door. "No, only three of them are mine. But I'm taking care of the others—you see, I simply can't get out to work, not with the children and everything. . . ."

Sinking onto a sofa, she smiled and waved Ken to the overstuffed chair. Ken did see. Nancy Perkins was so thin she seemed transparent; blue lines of fatigue circled her eyes. Only a wiry disheveled mop of curls and the smile showed vitality.

". . . and since the operation I've been so tired! But I'm getting better every day— Freddy! Put that down!"

This last was to an infant who had crawled into view from the adjoining dining room and was purposefully imperiling the end table.

Slowly Ken began to extract facts. They were simple enough. Nancy Perkins had been doomed to die. Dr. Wendell Martin had performed an extremely delicate heart operation. Now, Nancy Perkins was not going to die. She told Ken frankly that she wouldn't be willing to talk with him if Wendell Martin were still alive.

"I wouldn't lie to you," she said steadily. "I just wouldn't let you in. We owe too much to Dr. Martin. But now I'd be willing to help you if I could. What was the date of the operation on Mr. Freebody?"

Kenneth told her.

"Oh, no!" she ejaculated instantly. "I couldn't possibly help. You don't understand. That was the day I was operated on, too. For the next week I didn't really notice anything. I was under sedation most of the time, anyway."

"Then I'm sorry to have bothered you—"

But Nancy Perkins waved him back into his chair. She was frowning and thoughtfully rubbing a snub nose.

"You know, Gene is the person you should talk to, my husband. He practically lived at the hospital all that week. At first, of course, he was terribly worried, but later on, when we knew it was going to be all right, he made friends with everyone. Whenever I was asleep he'd be wandering around, talking to somebody. He might be able to help you."

It sounded very unlikely to Ken Nicolls. A distraught husband, his wife barely snatched from the jaws of death, was not going to be interested in other people's problems. But if Mr. Perkins could be worked in this afternoon, Kenneth was willing.

"When do you expect him home? At five?" He glanced at the battered mantel clock. It was already three.

"Oh, I'm afraid not. He's got the chance to put in some overtime. And, of course, he's glad to get it. We have so many bills to pay off. And even then he may not come back from Houlihan's."

"Houlihan's?"

"That's where Gene works. They do bookkeeping for small businesses. That's why it's hard to reach him during the day. He goes from place to place."

Kenneth nodded comprehension, but at the same time declined offers to set up a meeting with Gene in the evening.

"No. I have to get back to the city. Then I'll check with the office and see what they say. If I wanted to reach your husband by phone during the day, could you locate him for me?"

Nancy grinned. "With a little time I could." The grin faded into a more thoughtful expression. "Yes, you talk with your office. But the more I think about it, the more I realize that, if there was any talk, Gene must have heard it. Why he might even have picked up something at the garage."

"The garage?"

"Yes. That's Gene's *Sunday* job. He's awfully good with cars. I know he always does the tune-ups on Dr. Neverson's sports cars. And I'm almost sure that Dr. Bullivant takes her car there, too."

Kenneth began to wonder about the size of those bills. Here was Nancy taking care of children when she obviously ought to be resting. And the way she said Sunday left Ken in no doubt as to how Gene spent his Saturdays. He looked at the woman on the sofa with sympathy, before he realized the emotion was misplaced. Nancy Perkins had been handed back her life on a platter, and she was still starry-eyed with wonder. Three small children, she had said. Kenneth thought of his own wife and child. No, Nancy Perkins didn't have a single complaint against her world.

But she was quite level-headed enough to understand the positions in *Freebody v. Atlantic Mutual*. As she was seeing Ken off the porch, she had a final word.

"I suppose you don't want me to ask Marie about this?"

"Marie?"

"Marie Gentilhomme. The nurse in the Freebody operation. We got to know her while I was in the hospital, and she's a friend of ours now. She comes over sometimes on her day off." Nancy suddenly smiled with a hint of mischief. "If you'd come yesterday, you would have run into her."

As Ken drove back to the parkway, he realized that his earlier observations had been fully justified. Old Southport was right in the middle of things.

9 Organs

IF KENNETH NICOLLS had taken the trouble to scan the inbound traffic as he returned to New York, he might very well have spotted the figures of John Thatcher and Charlie Trinkam. They, too, had unexpectedly spent the afternoon in Suffolk County.

The phone call from Paul Jackson had come in the morning, only ten minutes after Ken Nicolls had stalked off in the general direction of Montauk Point.

"Sure . . . no bother, Paul," said Charlie genially and untruthfully. "Anything new? . . . What! . . . No! Not on your life!"

He continued in this vein for some minutes, but Paul Jackson was widely known as one of the most persuasive advocates in Manhattan with good reason. After an hour of tremendous productivity that reduced his secretary and one statistician to tears, Trinkam presented himself in Thatcher's office with suspiciously brushed hair and a somewhat shamefaced statement of intent.

Thatcher listened calmly. "By all means go, Charlie. If you enjoy funerals, I'm sure you'll enjoy this one. Mind you, I don't see what you'll get out of Wendell Martin's last rites—but there's no accounting for tastes."

Charlie grinned at him. "Now, John. Paul seems to feel that it's the right thing to do. Ed Knox will be there—and Dexter Loomis, too. I might be able to get a little business in."

Thatcher did not bother to project skepticism. Instead, recalling some of the exchanges between these various parties and the late Dr. Martin, he said: "Am I to take it that this turnout is designed to show that, notwithstanding our bitter business and legal contests, we all have a high regard for Wendell Martin? Or had, rather?"

Everett Gabler, whose conference with Thatcher on the Pennsy-Central merger Trinkam had interrupted, snorted impatiently. The staidest and most proper of the trust officers, he was chronically suspicious of Charlie Trinkam's motives, and currently inflamed by a difference of professional opinion. Since he could scarcely interpret a funeral as one of the extravagant extracurricular ventures so characteristic of Trinkam, he fell back on a second line of attack.

"From what I gather, Martin was no loss to anybody! He was knife-happy!"

Gabler was a firm advocate of Nature's healing power (with proper diet and exercise), so his views on eminent surgeons carried little weight.

"Well, I'm meeting Paul at noon," said Charlie. "Sure you don't want to come, John? Paul is touting this as a golden opportunity to see the entire Southport staff, let alone the mystifying widow. Sure you want to miss it?"

When it was put that way, John Thatcher didn't want to miss it. Moreover, in the hour at his disposal before Everett Gabler beat down the door of his office, he had managed to call an impressive array of financial correspondents in Suffolk County. Several of them might well be present at the funeral. It was this second thought that made him speak as he did.

"All right. But tell Jackson to meet us here. If we're going to do this, we might as well do it right. Miss Corsa can get a limousine for us!"

Shortly thereafter Thatcher realized that he had pleased Miss Corsa. This rare feat was always accompanied by surprise, but this time he should have anticipated it. Miss Corsa had a high regard for dignity and ritual. On both counts a funeral could scarcely fail to please. As for the limousine, she was constantly trying to intrude it into Thatcher's life. She deplored his habit of hopping onto the IRT. The fact that the IRT was more efficient in Manhattan cut no ice with Miss Corsa. She had long since realized that after a certain level, efficiency was no longer quite as useful as it might once have been. But there was always mileage in dignity.

There was also a good deal of mileage on the parkway. The drive was enlivened by Jackson's description of the state of affairs at Atlantic Mutual.

"Chisolm and Loomis both know they have to settle this. But they're stalling, and you know why? Loomis is looking for some medical testimony to square himself with his company."

"You're joking," Charlie accused. "Why doesn't he just file some of the headlines that Martin was getting? He was their star witness."

"It's a big claim," Thatcher reminded him, "and a big settlement."

"That's it. Loomis figures he can't be too careful. He wants a watertight file. I hear he's talked to DeLuca, asked him if he'd do a report once the settlement's gone through.

"He can have *all* our experts, once he's paid up," Charlie offered generously. "If the settlement's big enough, even Ed Knox would probably do a report for him. He can't ask for anything better than a Nobel prize winner."

On this happy note, the limousine came to a smooth halt.

"I'm afraid you'll have to get out here, sir," said the chauffeur, as he stopped several car lengths from the church steps.

Southport, the medical community of Southport Memorial Hospital (as well as St. Anne's and Southport Community), the county medical association, patients, friends, relatives were doing Dr. Wendell Martin proud. The steps before the entrance were already crowded, and as Thatcher, Jackson and Trinkam approached, their car was directed by a uniformed policeman to the end of a long cortege of gleaming black enamel. There, representatives of August Pfost ("Serving Southport for Fifty Years With Reverence and Understanding") were hustling up and down appending tasteful insignia to fenders.

As Paul Jackson and Charlie amused themselves detailing to Dr. Knox their plans for his future employment, Thatcher drew slightly aside.

He was particularly interested in the changes in mourning costume during his lifetime. It was especially noticeable in the women. But on this warm June day, some of the men were hatless. Thatcher could remember that when he had been a very young man, fresh to Wall Street, a senior had stressed the advisability of having a hat at a funeral. It didn't make any difference whether you wore it. That way, old Deming had said, whenever you are in any doubt about what to do at a funeral, you can always lay your hat respectfully across your breast. Thatcher had followed Deming's advice through the years and found it sterling.

"They tell me you're John Thatcher," a voice said in his ear.

He turned to discover a spry, elderly man examining him with interest. He acknowledged his identity.

"Benjamin Edes. Southport National Bank," said the other, extending a hand. "We were on the phone with each other this morning."

Thatcher was delighted at the encounter and again thanked Edes for his promise of assistance.

"Haven't done anything yet," Edes said gruffly. "But I've put some people onto it. Wouldn't be surprised if we had something for you."

"I'd be very interested in that."

The elderly man chuckled.

"Bet you would! Well, can't talk here. Not that I mind a good funeral." He raised a valedictory hand and melted back into the crowd.

Thatcher then found himself being herded into a knot with Paul Jackson, Trinkam and Dr. Knox.

"Yes, it is quite a turnout," said a mellifluous voice. It was not Dr. Wittke but a younger, slighter edition. "Shall we be getting inside?"

The little group obediently began to move toward the church; Dr. James Wittke bestowed a bloodless smile on them and oozed his way to other mourners.

As they entered the First Presbyterian Church, powerful organ throbs drowned Paul Jackson's strictures on this evidence of over-organization. To the mighty strains of "Nearer My God to Thee," the mourners filed in, introducing an antiphon of coughing and shuffling.

By the end of the anthem, the church was filled. Ushers slipped over to close the great doors and cut off the sunlight streaming into the nave. With the sudden dimming of light, the organist began a discreet musical doodling along Bachian lines. There was a collective hush of awareness, like that which greets the bride, then four men, bending slightly to indicate solicitude, escorted a black-draped figure up a side aisle. Behind them was a small, embarrassed band: a middle-aged man, a troubled-looking matron keeping an eye on two teen-agers. Bringing up the rear, a youthful couple, the woman visibly pregnant.

Barely moving his lips, Paul Jackson swayed toward Charlie: "Three to one we get the 'In the midst of life' dodge."

Thatcher was too preoccupied to hear Trinkam's reply; he had caught sight of Mrs. Doyle, watching the widow's progress. Her expression was unfathomable.

Wendell Martin's assorted nearest and dearest finally were ensconced in the front pew. The organist, unseen but watchful, stepped up the tempo. Dr. Rudolph Simpson, Bible in hand, mounted the lectern, looked down sorrowfully at the flower-bedecked, closed casket, raised his eyes and stared pugnaciously at the waiting congregation.

A muted flourish from the organ, and there was silence. Dr. Simpson continued his measured appraisal. Charlie Trinkam shifted slightly, but Paul Jackson watched the minister with professional interest.

Dr. Simpson bowed his head briefly, opened his Bible and fell into silent communion.

From the front pew, there came an ominous echoing moan.

Without undue haste, Dr. Simpson finished reading.

"My friends," he began in a reedy tenor.

A strangled wail, followed by controlled activity in the front pew. To a man, the congregation averted its eyes from the assembled Martins and stared at Dr. Simpson. Dr. Simpson compressed his lips, presumably in a moment of silent prayer, then began again:

"My friends . . ."

"Wendell!" The voice was harsh and rasping. "Oh, dear Lord! They've taken Wendell away from me! And nobody will do anything! Al, make them do something! Don't let them get away with it. . . ."

A positive frenzy seized possession of the front pew; fascinated, Charlie watched one of the men rise and bend over the black-draped figure. At the aisle, an usher hovered. There was a murmur that reached to five pews back.

"Lucille, my dear . . ."

"Do you have a handkerchief, Madge?"

"Please relax . . ."

Cutting through this an octave higher, Lucille Martin's voice rose in lament.

"My God! Wen is dead! Doesn't anybody understand! They're going to let him get away with murder! Why doesn't somebody do something . . ."

Dr. Simpson looked upward, away from the drama roiling at his feet. The rest of the church simply gawked at the front pew.

With unconscious theatrical timing, Lucille Martin shook off restraint and comfort and struggled to her feet. Turning her back on Dr. Simpson, she staggered forward to clutch at the casket, then turned a taut, skeletal face toward the congregation.

"He's dead! Do you understand me? He's dead! Why are you

sitting there? Why don't you find the man who killed him! Just because he's a doctor . . ."

These words broke the spell gripping those present. There was an almost palpable shrinking among the mourners, a frisson of horror. It was, Thatcher realized, trying vainly to locate familiar faces, professional outrage. Or perhaps it was individual apprehension. Whatever its nature, it produced a belated stir of activity. Dr. Simpson waggled his skimpy eyebrows at adjutants who came hurrying up the aisle. From a pew not far behind the Martins, a portly figure rose and began to edge toward the aisle. Philip Wittke, to do him credit, was hurrying to offer his services—which was more than the other doctors present could rouse themselves to do, as Charlie pointed out some hours later to Thatcher. Her family were plucking nervously at Lucille Martin's draperies.

With anguished vigor, Mrs. Martin straightened.

"They know he killed him! They're going to protect him because he's a doctor! But I won't let him get away with it! Harley Bauer always hated Wendell—Wendell told me! He was jealous and he killed him! And you'll let him go! Why doesn't somebody do something? Oh my God, Wendell, Wendell . . . !"

Her voice had risen to an intolerable pitch. With sudden release, she buried her face in her hands and broke into unnatural, inhuman gasping.

Was there a tremor of response at Harley Bauer's name? John Thatcher—and Paul Jackson later confirmed this—was listening but could hear nothing other than involuntary response to Lucille Martin's hysteria. Throughout the church, women wept openly. Many more clutched their escorts with terrified rigidity.

The removal party, led by Philip Wittke, finally converged on Lucille Martin. Under Wittke's whispered directions, two ushers and her brother-in-law firmly but gently eased Mrs. Martin away from the casket. Half carrying, half leading, they bore her to a side door.

The organist alertly plunged into Handel's "Largo."

A rustle of commiseration and surmise was quickly silenced by Dr. Simpson. As soon as the oak door closed behind the weeping Mrs. Martin, he signaled the organist for silence and, this time accusingly, continued Wendell Martin's last rites.

"My friends . . ."

10   Irregularity

THE REST of the funeral was inevitably anticlimax. In whispers, the New York City group agreed that the defensiveness of Southport Memorial against intrusive strangers must have been increased tenfold by Lucille Martin's outburst. There would be no information forthcoming now. Better to slip away quietly after the burial. Veteran funeral-goers to a man, they took up strategic positions and occupied one of the first cars to pull away from the cemetery.

In spite of this achievement, they had not been half as foresighted as some other interests.

Hasty consultation at graveside among the powers of Southport Memorial had resulted in a division of labor. Philip Wittke was needed to speed to the side of the widow, preferably with a good strong tranquilizer. Supported by his wife—a motherly woman already murmuring "poor dear"—he dutifully prepared to undertake this task. More immediately important, however, was the necessity to soothe Harley Bauer.

Roy Neverson was ready to try, but he wanted assistance. Dr. Wittke was a firm believer in the enormous reserves of tact bestowed at birth on every woman (in spite of the evidence of his daughters-in-law, famed throughout Southport for their ability to put a heavy foot in the middle of whatever was going on). He suggested Dr. Edith Bullivant as an appropriate second.

Neverson stared.

"Have you gone mad, Phil? With what Harley knows about Edith?"

"I forgot." Wittke recollected the status of Dr. Bullivant with a start. Tactful she undoubtedly could be. Unfortunately, she would also be a red flag to Bauer.

In the end it was Dr. Kroner who converged on Harley's left flank as Neverson approached from the right.

Harley stood rigid, looking unlike himself. Doggedly he had remained throughout the funeral and accompanied the casket to the cemetery. But he was paying for this endurance. With the shiny, uncreased skin of youthful corpulence, his face was normally a ruddy mask of good nature. Under emotional or physical exertion, it turned bright red.

Roy Neverson knew he was in for trouble at his first look. Harley was dead white; the flesh on his face might have been marble.

"Now, take it easy, Harley," said Neverson, cautiously touching the younger man's elbow. "I know how you feel."

"Do you?" Harley demanded flatly. "And how many times has that bitch accused *you* of murder before the entire county medical association?"

"I know, I know." Neverson almost stuttered in his anxiety. "It was terrible. But, Harley, don't blame us! I'm your friend."

"You're everybody's friend. My friend, and Martin's friend and Wittke's friend. Being your friend doesn't seem to prevent people from getting socked in the stomach."

Neverson bit down hard on a retort. He had spent the better part of a week last winter trying to persuade this pigheaded zealot that only grief would come of tangling with Wendell Martin.

"I'm anything you want, Harley," he said evenly. "But don't go away like this. It's got to be thrashed out. This is an hysterical woman trying to wreck your life."

Neverson's words were making no impression at all. Harley had immured himself in a soundproof cell. But suddenly Dr. Kroner spoke and, in spite of his imperfect English, he spoke with earnest authority.

"I will not permit that you leave alone. You are a boy, and it is your whole life at stake. What you say about the medical association is true. They have all heard, and now they are watching. If you do not wish to speak to us, then it shall be as you say. But you must be seen to leave with doctors from Southport Memorial."

Roy Neverson had chosen his second well. The little European did not pause for argument. He started to turn toward the gate and made of himself a pivot around which the two others could swing. Dr. Bauer marched out of the cemetery between Dr. Neverson and Dr. Kroner.

They walked in silence until they reached the cars. Then Neverson said:

"I thought the three of us could go up to my place for a drink."

Bauer stiffened for a moment, then suddenly he relaxed. Perhaps it was because he had sensed the genuine concern in Dr. Kroner's voice, the concern of an adult holding himself responsible for a young person. For Harley Bauer did feel like a child whose balloon had burst. The funeral was to have given him an opportunity for a few discreet words with old friends at Southport, friends who knew the inside story. Instead he had been singled out from hundreds of mourners and accused of murder. Harley Bauer was almost incoherent with shock.

When they were seated in Neverson's apartment, he exploded immediately:

"The only thing I could think of was 'Thank God, Joan isn't here!' It was the only thing that made me able to go through with it. And she almost came!"

Neverson's bright eyes darkened with sympathy. "My God, that would have been terrible!"

Harley did not doubt his sincerity. Ever since his own wife had divorced him, Roy Neverson had been solicitous about everyone else's marriage. Now that he could give his wife and children nothing but money, he showed more consideration for the sensitivity of others than he had ever shown to anyone, including his wife, during marriage.

Harley thawed further. "I don't know what that woman wants!" he said in a voice more like his own. "They got me thrown out of the hospital, isn't that enough? After all, I'm not the one who's done anything!"

Nothing but fight city hall, thought Neverson silently. He left the vocal response to Dr. Kroner.

"She is upset now, of course. That we understand. But still it is odd." Dr. Kroner struggled for expression. "I think maybe she tries to reject his death. It is easier for her to think of a continuation of his quarrel with you, Harley."

In the doubting silence that greeted this pronouncement, Neverson busied himself making drinks. They were an odd trio sitting there in the luxury apartment surrounded by rosewood bars and stereo tape recorders. Roy Neverson lived next to the boatyard and pursued a sailing, skiing, sports car version of the bachelor life. At first this had jolted colleagues used to associating him with the large split-level house in Green Acres, two small children and a washing machine whirring in the background. Many of their wives still did not like it.

But he looked the part with his bronzed countenance and lithe movements.

Little Dr. Kroner, by the simple expedient of wearing a dark armband to a colleague's funeral, had managed to place himself not only a continent away, but a generation as well. And as for tubby Harley Bauer—in spite of his youth, Mrs. Furness would have instantly diagnosed his oddity against this background. He was hopelessly domestic.

Dissimilar they might be; they were joined by a common problem. Each man wanted to erase Lucille Martin's accusation from the tablet of history. Dr. Kroner remained realistic:

"There is only one thing that can be done. Everyone sees that she is not responsible for what she is saying, scarcely knows what she is saying. It must be made clear that Southport Memorial knows this is nonsense."

"One other thing," Neverson added grimly. "Phil Wittke can damn well make sure she doesn't get another chance to sound off. He's got to keep her shut up."

Harley Bauer laid down his glass and prepared to leave. He spoke slowly and carefully:

"He'd better, Roy. I just don't know how much more of this I can take."

Kenneth Nicolls heard the grisly details upon his return to the Sloan.

"Good lord!" said Ken, belatedly aware that his lot, Nancy Perkins and Mrs. Furness notwithstanding, had been free of naked human passion.

John Thatcher, who shared Ken's instinctive recoil at the thought of female hysterics, was prepared to utilize any information they conveyed.

"Mrs. Martin had mentioned Bauer before, as a matter of fact. When we were at the hospital. At that time, she seemed to have a grudge against both the man and his wife."

"Do you think there's anything in what she says?" Kenneth asked.

"I doubt it. There hasn't been any suggestion that Martin's death was more than an ordinary mugging, and the widow was slashing out at Bauer in any way she could." Thatcher shook his head in dissatisfaction. "It isn't our business, after all. We're interested in the financial situation, and, apart from her wild attacks on Dr. Bauer, this Martin woman didn't really say anything. Nothing about missing money, for example."

Charlie replied by pointing out that Lucille Martin had been hustled away before she could really get warmed up. Then, since he was the kind of extrovert who hated to dash hopes, he added that he personally had no doubt she could have gone on and on.

Ken found both John Putnam Thatcher and Charlie Trinkam regarding him. With a chill, he realized they were weighing the advantages of dispatching him into the orbit of a widow who had just buried her husband. Before he could protest, Thatcher shook his head.

"No, I don't suppose that we can get any more information from Mrs. Martin at the moment. Then, too," he broke off and swiveled his chair around to gaze out his window, "there seems to be a crowd of people determined to shut her up whenever she does start talking. I wonder . . ."

The wave of relief crashing over Ken Nicolls made his ears buzz momentarily. When he had recovered, he found Thatcher looking at him with something like sympathy.

"I don't suppose your day has produced anything as colorful as Mrs. Martin," he said. "Did those patients have anything of interest to say?"

"Well . . ." Ken answered the question with a brief description of his encounters with Mrs. Furness and Nancy Perkins. Thatcher listened, he noticed uneasily, with great attention.

Charlie Trinkam, on the other hand, rose. "Sounds like a washout to me. Unless the Perkins husband's got something. But I'll put my money on the widow. There's something funny going on, and they won't be able to keep her shut up long."

On this cheery note he departed to resume hostilities with Everett Gabler.

Thatcher roused himself from his abstraction. "And I," he said severely, "will put my money on the missing wealth of Wendell Martin. But that may just be the congenital bias of a banker."

Ken had had an unrewarding day, and this emboldened him beyond his wont.

"I thought Mrs. Martin decided the money had gone on another woman."

"A little calculation as to how much money was involved will disabuse you of that suspicion, Nicolls," Thatcher said crisply. "The fact may not have been brought to your attention, but suburban American men do not keep mistresses on the scale of the Shah of Iran."

Kenneth struggled with a sense of resentment. First Mrs. Furness and now John Thatcher! Any minute now, there would be a reference to his nice little wife and child.

But Thatcher had kindly changed the topic. Why, he wondered, was young Nicolls blushing like a sunset?

"I think Charlie was right when he said this Perkins might have some information. The man seems virtually inaccessible during the day. If you have an evening free this week, see if you can catch up with him. I'd keep it as informal as possible, if I were you . . . what? Oh, yes, Miss Corsa, I'm ready to dictate."

Ken marched off, wondering if the life he was leading was too restrictive.

Miss Corsa, dictation pad at the ready, settled herself. Thatcher did not give his preliminary cough.

"Tell me, Miss Corsa," he asked, "what do you and your family do about medical care?"

Miss Corsa rarely indulged Mr. Thatcher, but, given a decently limited question of fact, she was prepared to try to cooperate. Despite this, Thatcher had drawn a blank: Miss Corsa, her father and those of her brothers old enough to work, had a wild array of complex health insurance schemes paid for by the large institutions employing them. Moreover, one Dr. Mario Sodaro was a close family friend, his mother, like Miss Corsa's, having hailed from Termini in the province of Naples. All of this was preparation and no more—despite a diet of saturated fats and carbohydrates, despite girths (excepting Miss Corsa) to turn cardiologists pale, the Corsas were a remarkably healthy and long-lived breed.

"Disappointing," said Thatcher.

Her instincts toward helpfulness prompted Miss Corsa to search her family's medical history.

"My grandfather has high blood pressure," she preferred doubtfully.

"And how old is your grandfather?"

"Ninety-seven," said Miss Corsa. "Dr. Sodaro gives him some medicine, but he always forgets to take it. It's nothing serious."

"I see," said Thatcher.

Regretfully he dismissed the Corsas as a source of information about the peculiarities of modern medicine and turned his attention to the New York real estate entrepreneur whose dubious investment plans were his immediate concern: "Dear Frisch, I have asked our accountants . . ."

11 Deficiency

NOTHING in this world is really certain, doctors and lawyers are in the habit of saying. John Thatcher often suspected this was a rationale for the disproportionately high input of wasted energy and fruitless discussion that characterized both professions.

Still, he had to admit *Freebody v. Atlantic Mutual,* the death of Dr. Wendell Martin and now Southport Memorial's grand right-and-left might justify unusual activity. Whether it did or not, the offices of Jackson & Jackson, like the law department of Atlantic Mutual, hummed. Proposal met counterproposal, references to settlements in Kansas were capped by recondite cases from the Hawaiian Islands. Thatcher, at the Sloan, and Dexter Loomis, at Atlantic Mutual, both grew accustomed if not reconciled to calls bristling with *unpredictable interventions, contributory causes* and *standings to bring suit.*

The medical pot was boiling, too. Up at Hanover, Dr. Edmund Knox and staff, including two young Englishmen boning up on U.S. medicine before ultimate return to the British Isles (or so they claimed), pored over alumni lists to locate allies and drafted complex suggestions for the disposition of one hundred thousand dollars. At the medical grass roots, Dr. Philip Wittke let lesser fry remove tonsils, deliver twins and test overweight executives. He reserved himself for policy-making, namely, holding conferences and keeping a weather eye on Lucille Martin.

Even the police, so Paul Jackson privately assured a surprised John Thatcher, were still asking questions about Wendell Martin's murder.

It was all tiring to contemplate, Thatcher reflected. Yet, on his rarefied level, he too was active, although convinced he was the only one in the whole lot not simply thrashing around.

Of course, when Thatcher decided to look into the financial background of Southport's personnel, he was in a strong position to do so. Over the years, the Sloan Guaranty Trust, with its customary foresight, had dispensed favors to many financial institutions scattered throughout the greater New York area. Possibly more important from the viewpoint of banks in Suffolk County, the Sloan remained a source of future assistance. Since there can never be too many sheet anchors to windward in the money market, Thatcher's inquiries received prompt attention in many quarters and, more to the point, a frank response. Without exception, his contacts promised to call a few friends and check around. With discretion, of course.

As a result, many a luncheon conversation in Islip, in Babylon, in Huntington, was gently steered into channels centering around the names Martin, Wittke, Neverson, Bullivant. Indeed one conversation—on the outskirts of Southhampton—was pushed in that direction by three lunchers simultaneously.

With this kind of wholesale cooperation, Thatcher confidently anticipated information. It came, however, in rather unexpected form.

"Benjamin Edes," his phone identified itself. "Southport National Bank. We met yesterday at the funeral, you recall."

"Yes indeed, Mr. Edes. It's good of you to call. . . ."

Thatcher was interrupted by cackling.

"Never hurts to cooperate with the Sloan," the phone told him candidly. "I understand you're still in the market for that information. Think I've got something for you if you'd care to join me for lunch. . . ."

Thatcher would. Two hours later, he stood in the foyer of the Southport Yacht Club which, Mr. Edes had assured him snappily, served pretty poor food but still the best available in Southport. It was a deliberately ramshackle structure some three miles from Southport Center, occupying a spread of scrub beach. Neither the parking lot to the west, nor the horrors uncovered by low tide to the east, improved its overall appearance. Within, the Southport Yacht Club compromised between the nautical (buoys and nets draped against dark wood walls, windows giving onto the bay) and the suburban (a mature houri hostessing, a well-stocked bar opening off the dining room). In the evening, and possibly over weekends, the Southport Yacht Club might well shelter tanned and happy sailors in sneakers from Abercrombie's; on working days its prime function was to provide a suitable place where business could be talked. The large dining room was exclusively male save for one female foursome growing hilarious over martinis and plans for a dinner dance.

Edes was the spry, angular septuagenarian who had been so chipper at Wendell Martin's funeral.

"Sorry I couldn't come into town," he said, imperiously directing the hostess to place them at his usual table in a choice alcove. "Always like to get into the city. They say it's crashing to the ground, what with race riots and rising taxes. But hell, I've been sitting here in Southport for seventy years listening to 'em say it. Every time I go, it's still there. Hear you fellows want to move the Exchange now." Mr. Edes lowered himself into a captain's chair, waved Thatcher to a seat and examined him closely. "You won't like it much up in New Hampshire."

Thatcher, who had left New Hampshire almost fifty years ago, decided that Edes was going to require a firm hand. (He had no intention of disclaiming personal responsibility for the New York Stock Exchange's more venturesome plans for emigration.)

"I'm very glad to have a chance to see more of Southport," he said firmly.

With patent glee, Edes topped him.

"Reason I couldn't get in," he said, studying the handwritten menu, "is that I'm going to attend a meeting of the Board of Trustees of Southport Memorial Hospital. Wife's been on it for dog's years—I told her she ought to rest today. Only reasonable for me to stand in for her, don't you think? . . . Here! You there! We'll order drinks now. Thatcher . . . ?"

Thatcher, no fool, took Benjamin Edes's measure and left the pace-setting to him. He was not disappointed.

Over cocktails, Edes said:

"Normally would have had my girl ring you back. Then, when things started coming in, I decided you and I ought to talk."

"Yes?" Thatcher prompted cautiously.

His host eyed him.

"Don't know whether you were guessing or not, but you're on to something!"

Calmly, Thatcher finished his drink. This was just what he had wanted. Insurance claims could come and go. His sense of smell had told him that there was something bigger in the wind. Here was Benjamin Edes with confirmation.

Edes was high-handedly ordering lobster for both of them. "Only thing they know how to cook," he confided. Then, without changing tone, he returned to business. "Don't know what it is yet, but there's a helluva lot of money missing!"

Thatcher's reaction was disappointment.

"Money missing, eh? That's what Mrs. Martin was saying—in her way. . . ."

"It's not just Martin," Edes told him severely. "The others, too. Wittke and Neverson. And probably others . . ."

Thatcher savored this.

"Now, that is very interesting."

Edes wheezed happily.

"Knew you'd say that. Said it, myself. Let's see, do you know about the quarter of a million?"

Thatcher put down a breadstick. "No," he said invitingly. "Tell me about the quarter of a million."

"There's about a quarter of a million dollars missing from Martin's estate," said Edes. "The tax people were standing by when we opened up his safe deposit boxes. And do you know what they found? Nothing but junk! . . . Here, boy! Get us some more melted butter. . . . Now where was I?"

With considerable amusement Thatcher told him that he had arrived at a safe deposit box full of junk.

"Oh yes. Well, things weren't like that two years ago. About that time, Martin went into cash. Sold out of the market, slapped a mortgage on his house—turned everything he could lay his hands on into ready money."

Benjamin Edes brandished a claw for emphasis. "And there's no record—at all—where that money went! The only thing left is what he's accumulated in the last eighteen months."

Thatcher thought about this for a few moments. Then he fired a test shot. "The widow must have been upset."

"She was!" Edes was in full agreement. "Not, of course, the way she was later at the funeral. Just stood by the safe deposit box in a trance, moaning her husband's name." He shook his head and added, "I have to hand it to those tax people. They didn't turn a hair. Of course, they run into this sort of thing all the time!" Again he peered at Thatcher with a wicked gleam. "And what do you think! She came into the bank first thing this morning—with Al Martin, Wendell's brother. Back to life! Sad of course—but normal, if you know what I mean."

"And what do you think caused that?" asked Thatcher, who was enjoying Edes.

"She knows where the money went, not a doubt about it. And sure as God made little fishes, Martin's brother told her. He's a stock-broker, you know. Only natural to help his brother out—in money matters."

Thatcher addressed himself to his lobster for a while. "It's natural," he agreed finally. "But that does suggest some sort of family arrangement, doesn't it? Of course, that's just a guess. These doctors seem to follow a policy of studied confusion about money, don't they?"

"Confusion?" Edes asked scornfully. "I'd call it downright stupidity! You should have seen them the day we asked for their social security numbers. That damn fool Wittke made a special trip to inform me that he was not on a salary!"

Thatcher could visualize the scene. "You said that money was missing from other accounts, too?"

Edes nodded vigorously. He was supremely untroubled by this spilling of clients' beans. Perhaps it was his advanced age. More likely, thought Thatcher, it was because of the clients.

"Martin's mortgage reminded me. I recalled some talk, so I checked around. Wittke got a mortgage at the same time. For that matter, so did all the Wittkes. They went to different banks, but the word got around. . . ."

"All the Wittkes?" asked Thatcher, who thought that one was enough.

"He's got two boys," Edes replied. "They're not associated with the hospital. They took over that private clinic Wittke built up. Do very well, let me tell you. No matter what you've got, it's chronic. That means a visit every week. Special medicines you can only buy at their pharmacy. It's a gold mine! Well, all this made me curious. Couldn't approach the Wittke broker myself, you understand. Don't know the man well enough."

Thatcher nodded gravely. "But you know somebody who does."

Edes beamed. "That's it."

Really, it was a shame to think that Benjamin Edes had been wasted in Southport all these years.

"And guess what? The Wittkes sold out of the market about two years ago. The same story. There's nothing in their portfolio except the little they've put in this last year."

Thatcher murmured he felt sure Edes had followed this up by

examining Dr. Neverson's finances. Edes had, but confided that he had hit a snag.

"He's an exception to this rush for cash?" asked Thatcher in surprise.

Edes raised a restraining hand. "Maybe yes—then again, maybe no! You see, Neverson and his wife got divorced just about then. . . ."

Thatcher did see. Divorce frequently triggered financial upheavals —with assets scurrying into hiding. Edes's leisurely description of Roy Neverson's recent business transactions confirmed this:

". . . didn't mortgage that big house of his, but sold it outright. For that matter, it was already mortgaged up to the hilt. He's the only one who doesn't buy his houses free and clear—course, he's younger, you know. Now he's got a cooperative apartment, so that gives him a tax break. . . ."

After hearing Benjamin Edes out, Thatcher summed up. "We know that Wendell Martin took a quarter of a million dollars and did something mysterious with it—something with no records. We know that at the same time, some other doctors were getting their hands on cash. Of course they're not dead, so we can't be sure they didn't do something perfectly aboveboard with the money. . . ."

"Hah!" said Edes, automatically loading a monstrous churchwarden pipe. "It may be aboveboard, but it isn't normal! Not investment in real estate or anything like that! They moved right out of standard banking channels. Otherwise, I'd have heard about it. . . ."

Thatcher believed him and said so. He added that, in all fairness, Roy Neverson had to be exempted for the moment. His financial change of life might be the result of divorce.

A gigantic puff of smoke momentarily obscured his companion. Reappearing, Edes passed judgment on Roy Neverson.

"He's got more brains than the rest of them combined," he said. "I don't think he's pulling any funny business with his divorce settlement. He's still close to his family. Two little girls, you know. They spend the summer with him and his mother. And he pays their school bills—whopping big ones, at that!"

"So you think that his move into cash means that he must be associated with Wittke—all the Wittkes. And Martin, too?"

"I do," said Benjamin Edes decisively. "I can tell you one doctor who isn't, though. That little German. Kroner. You've met him? He and his wife have an open financial life. Not that there's very much of it," he added. "She's some sort of teacher."

Edes pondered his own words, then, apparently at random, commented that he had not finished his research. Next on the list was Dr. Edith Bullivant. She was, he said, a pretty sharp businesswoman. He would be interested to learn if she was involved in whatever it was. Suddenly serious, he put down the pipe.

"That's what I've been wondering about," he said. "You know, I've been around Southport a long time. Hell, I knew Philip Wittke back in the days when doctors weren't rich. That was before Edith Bullivant married that husband of hers. And Martin was in the bank the day he got out of the service in forty-five and settled down here. And I remember Neverson when he was a resident. . . ."

He looked back at his memories and Thatcher waited.

"You know," Edes said, "I can think of a lot of reasons why Wittke and Neverson might be up to something. But Wen Martin wasn't a gambler! He never took any chances! That means that whatever this is—it's a sure thing!"

"A surer thing than being a doctor!" Thatcher amended.

And that, for the moment, was that. Benjamin Edes sincerely advised against any dessert that the Southport Yacht Club could produce. It was over coffee, therefore, that he ducked his head at Thatcher in his first and only conspiratorial gesture.

"Look there," he said. "Martin's brother."

Casually, Thatcher glanced across the room. There, behind the four convivial ladies who had still not progressed beyond martinis, two men were advancing on a table. The short tubby man bore no resemblance to his celebrated brother; the tall dark man with the good looks was familiar.

"Roy Neverson," Edes told him unnecessarily.

He ordered more coffee as autocratically as he had waved it away earlier. "Of course, perhaps they're just friends. Nice chance to get together, after the funeral."

Was Edes being caustic? Thatcher wondered something else.

"I wish I knew," he said aloud, "I wish I knew what they're talking about."

Had he been able to eavesdrop, he would not have been much enlightened.

"I wonder what they're talking about," Al Martin muttered when

Neverson, detained by one of the ladies for a moment, finally sat down.

He had sighted Edes and his companion upon entry.

Neverson looked at him quizzically. "Stop worrying, Al! What difference does it make now? You're too wound up! You should get more rest!"

They had to give their orders (no drinks because of Al's ulcer and Neverson's acute understanding of how Southport likes its doctors to behave, no matter how it behaves) before Martin could reply.

"Wound up! You bet your sweet life I am! And you would be, too, if you'd been through what I've been through. . . ."

Deliberately misunderstanding, Roy looked up from his chowder. "I'm sorry, Al. I keep forgetting that Wen was your brother. . . ."

This insincerity mollified his companion. It also had the less desirable effect of restoring his feeling of intimacy with Neverson.

"You know," he said, "what I keep forgetting? I haven't seen you for . . . God, it must be two years now. I wanted to tell you how sorry we were to hear that you and Julie had split up. . . ."

He blundered on without noticing Neverson's constraint. The Martin brothers, though physically dissimilar, shared certain family characteristics, among them insensitivity. With Wendell, this had been glazed by arrogance. Albert Martin, a much less prickly personality, was just one of those men who are clumsy in personal relationships. He was, however, a competent stockbroker.

Roy Neverson's distaste was not obvious, although anyone from the hospital would have been alerted by his sudden stiffness. A man of many moods, he protected himself from intrusiveness with practiced reserve.

And that, he thought ruefully as Martin rambled on, was one of the costs of divorce—one of many. Divorce was a fissure, flawing the shell that protected vulnerability.

". . . always think of you and Julie and the kids at that beautiful house on the point," Martin was saying. "What a great location, Roy! And the docks . . . !"

"I sold it," said Roy Neverson shortly.

Martin was a fellow boating enthusiast. "You didn't sell that nice little ketch, did you? Remember when we went out . . . ?"

"I traded up. Got a thirty-two footer now."

This, as Roy Neverson had known it would, set Al off on a disquisition on docking charges in Delaware Bay. Interjecting the correct responses left Neverson free to think his own thoughts. These circled and touched down on many subjects these days—he, who had always prided himself on self-discipline. First and always were Julie and the girls. The apartment had every comfort known to man, from maid service to vicuña rugs, but it would never be a home.

Well, maybe Julie was right. He was too self-centered, too calculating to be part of a real home. That was pretty much what Harley Bauer had said, too. Neverson cut into his steak, reviewing the efforts he and Kroner had made to calm young Bauer. That was something else he should check up on . . .

He discovered Al Martin waiting for a comment.

"Why don't you stay over another day, Al?" he said easily. "I could take some time off and we could go out on the boat."

Regretfully, Martin shook his head. "That'd be great, but I've got a seat on the eleven o'clock plane, and I ought to get back. It'll give me time for dinner and another talk with Lucille tonight. . . ."

Neverson was concerned. "You're sure she's all right?"

"She's all right *now*," Martin corrected him. "She's still miserable because Wen is gone"—here he shook his head incredulously—"but I explained things to her. I didn't go into details, you understand. But she didn't want details. As soon as she understood that there was no other woman and that Wen was thinking of her—well, that made the difference. I still don't see why one of you didn't explain things to her before the funeral."

Neverson grimaced. There was no use pointing out that, if anybody had contemplated the unfortunate scene at the church, somebody would have.

"Did she ask many questions?" he wanted to know.

"She didn't ask any." Al was bemused. "Lucille's a funny girl. Really devoted to Wen. I think she'll spend the rest of her life mourning him."

Cleverer men than Al Martin would have found Lucille Martin incomprehensible.

"It wouldn't do any harm if you or Phil ran around to see her once in a while," he began before breaking off suddenly and narrowing his eyes.

Roy Neverson turned.

Benjamin Edes was leading Thatcher out of the dining room. Their path took them near a table where an elegant, white-haired man sat with two younger companions.

"Well, Giles Bullivant!" said Benjamin Edes, all surprised pleasure. "You usually lunch here a little earlier, don't you?"

Confusion on the handsome, if ineffectual, face yielded to recognition.

"Hello there, Edes," he replied in vaguely British accents.

Edes plunged into introductions ". . . and Giles here is Director of Admissions up at our new community college," he told Thatcher. "We'll be having four hundred students this year, won't we?"

"Actually," said Giles Bullivant rather defensively, "four hundred and fifty!"

"You don't say!" Benjamin Edes marveled. "Well, sorry we can't stay. . . ."

As they continued their exit, Thatcher glanced at his host. He was just filled with information.

"Dr. Bullivant's husband?" he inquired.

"What? Oh, yes. Interesting talker. He used to give a lot of time to the club before he got this job. Committees and things like that. He's always been popular. He—and Edith of course—have been members of the club for years. . . . We don't see much of Edith, but Giles is a regular."

As intended, this gave Thatcher more food for thought.

In the dining room, Giles Bullivant took a quick quaff. And, at the table by the wall, Al Martin munched a full lip.

"I don't like it, Roy! That was Thatcher from the Sloan with that old fool Edes. What did they want with Giles? Hell, do you suppose . . ."

As if he had not heard, Roy Neverson looked across the table and said:

"I'm still sorry you can't stay over for a day or two. And you know, I'm not the only one. Sid Segal dropped in my office today. Told me to tell you he was sorry to miss you after the funeral. You should drop in and talk to him. He's a pretty sensible guy, Al . . ."

These observations did nothing perceptible to allay Al Martin's fears.

12 Retention

THERE ARE many rungs on the ladder of banking as in all other careers. While John Putnam Thatcher was lunching with the president of the Southport National Bank, Kenneth Nicolls was arranging to interview Eugene Perkins, bookkeeper, mechanic and cashier.

His arrival in Southport for that meeting after dinner proved that surroundings mirror rank. The Southport Yacht Club, whatever its other deficiencies, had been quiet; Ken Nicolls found himself deafened. Screams, shouts and explosive clatter echoed under the arched low ceiling and smote his ears. More voices were raised, to be crowned by distant explosions.

Dino's Bowladrome was busy. All twenty-four lanes were in full operation; in the banks of seats behind the lanes, many men and women impatiently waited. Threading neatly among them, trimly uniformed waitresses efficiently hurried trays of beer to bowlers and onlookers. In the background, a cash register rang out and a jukebox throbbed tympanically. There were groans of mock sympathy, yelps of pleasure, cries of encouragement rising from every lane, together with the endless swish of heavy bowling balls cannoning down the alleys to strike pins into brittle disarray.

Ken turned and sought out the cashier's desk, where Eugene Perkins put in three nights a week. When Ken learned this, during his telephonic hunt, he had suggested postponing their meeting until tomorrow night, only to be told that it was easier to talk at Dino's Bowladrome than at Grossman's Meat Packing Company where Perkins worked two nights a week.

In view of the din prevailing, Ken wondered about Grossman's as he introduced himself to Perkins, a jaunty carrot-topped young man sporting a red open-necked shirt. Perkins finished dealings with four men labeled "Babylon Hammer and Drill," then invited Ken to join him behind the counter. Between a bowling team from the Suffolk Construction Works and four ominous teen-agers, their conversation continued.

First, Perkins put his cards on the table. "Nancy says she told you how we feel about Dr. Martin?"

Ken ignored the discomfort his sober gray flannel was causing in this sea of informality and replied that the Sloan's interest had shifted away from Dr. Martin himself, to the rest of the staff at Southport Memorial.

"Stands to reason," said Gene, knitting his brows. "Well, the week that Nancy was operated on, I was there most of the time . . . let's see . . ."

His effort, which cost a tremendous scowl alarming several regular customers, was unproductive. This did not surprise Ken, who had chalked Perkins up as an uncomplicated young man, inclined to think the best of everybody, including the new friends he had made at the hospital when his wife was sick. Nobody who accepted things at face value was going to be able to see behind the kindly mask of hospital staffs, particularly when he wanted to trust their professional optimism.

On the other hand, Ken recalled two comments by Mrs. Perkins. Miss Gentilhomme had become a family friend; and Gene Perkins— who must certainly be one of the most active young men in Southport —worked in a garage where Neverson and Bullivant cars were sometimes serviced. So, Ken squirmed on the stool, and listened to an uncritical assessment of Southport Memorial Hospital. Two years earlier he might have cut Gene Perkins short and escaped; tonight he took a leaf from John Thatcher's book and decided to invest the rest of the evening.

"Not that I know anything about the doctors," Gene Perkins said with untroubled humility. "Gosh, I don't think we actually spoke to Dr. Martin more than twice . . . that's seventeen, Mrs. Ballou. Have a good game!"

Suddenly Perkins snapped his fingers and turned a dismayed face to Ken.

"Hey, I forgot," he said in distress. "I hate to break this up, but I've got to take off early."

Perkins was not going straight home. He was detouring to Southport center, to pick up prescriptions at Segal's Drugstore. Already on his feet, he was explaining that, since his car had broken down that morning, he had to hurry to catch the last bus.

Ken seized his opportunity and offered a lift.

"Gee, that'll be a big help!" said Perkins with enough warmth to make Ken feel faintly remorseful. "I've got to change first. . . ."

Thankfully escaping from the tumult, Ken went outdoors to wait. In the warm summer night with its dark star-spangled sky, the world seemed older and homelier, he reflected, firmly ignoring the solid blaze of headlights on the highway and Dino's multicolored neon sign. Within minutes, Gene joined him, now in a sweat shirt since, he explained, they were saving on shirts.

"This really makes a difference," he said, settling in Ken's station wagon. "I won't have time to fix that fuel pump until the weekend."

On the trip to the business district of Southport, Ken learned that Gene Perkins was not only a repairer of his own car, but a baker of his own bread. Under the best of circumstances, the Perkins budget had been stretched thin. Nancy Perkins's operation, together with hospital checkups and special medicines, had blasted the Perkinses deep into debt.

"So, whenever I can," Perkins said cheerfully, "I use elbow grease, instead of dollars!"

His world too had been handed back on a silver platter.

Segal's was fully lit, but far removed from its daytime bustle. A solitary man in Bermuda shorts stood leafing through *Playboy;* at the back door a leisurely janitor was already wielding a long-handled broom. Otherwise, no one was in sight. Perkins threaded his way to the prescription counter without hesitation. Ken, following, looked around with the vague interest of the non-shopper, a tourist in a new country. Segal's was an orderly jumble of clocks, cosmetics, stationery, thermometers, hard candies, deodorants. Everywhere signs featured young women transformed by hair spray into goddesses.

This array of consumer goods triggered the usual husbandly response. Ken decided to buy something for Jane. He moved past candy and mothballs, mouthwash and hair curlers, combs and suppositories, to the glass case filled with perfumes and colognes that stood near the prescription counter where Sid Segal had materialized. Three small boxes stood between him and Perkins.

"I've got two new ones," said Perkins, digging two squares of paper out of a pocket. "Dr. Wittke says that she should take them for a couple of weeks."

Segal clucked. "Still," he said, "she's getting better—that's what counts." Affixing his glasses higher on his nose, he peered through them and mumbled something as he studied the prescription. Just then, he caught sight of Ken. "I'll be with you in a minute, sir . . ."

Gene Perkins's introduction drew Ken into their exchange. Segal disappeared from view with Perkins's prescriptions, but he continued speech.

"Why am I working tonight? I'm working tonight because I've got nowhere else to go. My wife's in Florida. Somebody talked her into trying the west coast and she says she's dying from boredom. But my God, what expensive boredom!"

"But, Sid," said Gene, winking at Nicolls, "why isn't Harry here? Or Art? I thought they usually took over nights."

Sid reemerged with two more small packets.

"Art and Harry? You mean my sons? My sons and their wives have more important things to do. They are spending tonight at the Community Theater! To see a play about a man who sits in a trash barrel! Culture! This is more important than working. Dr. Wittke, he's filling in at the clinic tonight, too. His sons and their wives—they too have to go see this play about garbage! And not just see. They're sponsoring it! Wonderful!"

During this monologue, he was totting figures on a brown paper bag.

"I said to Dr. Wittke today, when we were young, we didn't have bicycles. But our sons—they have to have Rolls Royces! Sponsoring plays! Gene, it's forty-three dollars. Make it forty. . . ."

He sighed fatalistically.

Perkins counted out bills. "Don't worry, Sid. Your friend Dr. Neverson is paying tonight."

This comment succeeded in puzzling Segal. Perkins explained:

"He had a split carburetor on that Jaguar of his," he said. "And boy, do those foreign cars cost a mint! I had to spend four hours on the darn thing. . . ."

With a shrug that dismissed anyone foolish enough to waste money on exotic sports cars, Segal turned to his other customer and the question of perfume.

"Who knows what women will like?" he asked rhetorically. "Here, take this. It's the most expensive so it must be good. . . ."

As Ken was fishing out a twenty, a small fold of white caught his attention.

"Say, I've got a prescription too!"

"It couldn't happen in a better place," Segal assured him. He reached out and again studied.

"No," he sadly decided after consulting a leather-bound volume, "I don't have it. I can order it for you."

Ken thanked him and replied that he would pick it up on Wall Street the following day. He caught up with Perkins, who was waiting at the door.

Segal watched them leave with his usual air of melancholy. Then, pursing his lips, he turned away. "Eddie," he called out. "Switch off the window lights. I don't want any more customers."

Segal's was darkening by the time Gene and Ken pulled away.

Ken had not been in a small town on a summer night for a long time.

"Want to stop off for a beer?" he suggested.

Gene Perkins brightened with innocent pleasure, then rejected temptation. "I'd better get on home. Want to be sure that Nancy isn't overtired. . . ."

"Well then," said Ken.

So, armed with twelve cans of beer they invaded Nancy Perkins's kitchen ten minutes later. Mrs. Perkins, sitting at the table, was glad to see them. Since Ken was able to say, with truth, that she was looking much better, this brought a wide grin to Gene's face. It was good spirits on all fronts—save one.

Marie Gentilhomme, who sat across from Nancy, looked very nervous.

"Let's all go into the living room," Nancy suggested.

"Hey, Ken's not company!" her husband reproved her. "Hi, Marie! You want a beer, too?"

Predictably, Marie shook her head, although she managed a shy smile of greeting. Ken, who drew up a chair and accepted the can that Perkins proferred, knew better than to throw her into total confusion by a direct remark. He simply nodded acknowledgment of introductions and remained silent.

The kitchen, scuffed linoleum, chipped enamel, wheezing refrigerator and all, was gay with yellow paint and bright red and white gingham curtains. Ken could guess who had done the painting.

"No, we don't want glasses," Gene told Nancy. "So what's new, Marie?"

Release came to poor Miss Gentilhomme in the form of a distant honking.

"That must be Uncle Dominic!" she exclaimed, jumping to her feet. "Night, Gene! Mr. Nicolls . . ."

By the time that Nancy Perkins returned from escorting her to the front door, Gene and Ken had passed onto their second beer. She was half resigned, half angry.

"Uncle Dominic," she explained when Gene demanded enlightenment. "He saw Ken's car, and he wants to know who was here . . . you know. I feel so sorry for Marie! They're so old-fashioned."

Gene began to laugh.

"What?" his wife asked suspiciously.

"Uncle Dominic and Alice Doyle!" he chortled.

Ken looked on politely while the Perkinses shared a family joke until Nancy Perkins remembered her manners.

"It isn't really funny," she said, giggling a little, "but do you know Mrs. Doyle? Alice works with Marie, or she did until they transferred Marie. Well, somehow or other Uncle Dominic found out that Alice was getting a divorce. . . ."

"Now, Nancy, if you're going to tell it, tell it right," her husband insisted. "A big fight, you know, and the husband got custody of the two kids . . ."

The look in Mrs. Perkins's eyes told Ken that she would have a few words for Gene after company was gone. "Well anyway," she said, "Uncle Dominic actually went up to the hospital and insisted that it wasn't right to put a young girl next to someone like that! Marie nearly died!"

Gene Perkins listened while his wife described Marie's difficulties at home, meanwhile placing the little packets from Segal's Drugstore in a line.

"Say, drink up. . . ."

By their fourth beers, Ken and Gene were moving to the point that requires wifely indulgence.

"Sure, I grant you medicine's too expensive," said Perkins with tremendous emphasis. "We know that better than most people, don't we, Nancy? But hell, it's not money thrown away! Not like spending two-fifty for a ten-buck item just because your car's a Jag . . ."

"That's the point I'm making," Ken said. "Here you are, working your head off for these bills. And what are doctors doing . . ."

"Have another," Gene interrupted. "Now, Ken, doctors deserve to make money. I don't grudge a doctor his Jaguar even when he doesn't know one end from the other, even when he parks it in an alley full of broken bottles. Look, they saved Nancy's life, didn't they? That's worth money. . . . Look, do you have kids?"

Ken refreshed himself and prepared to clinch the argument. "Sure, I've got a baby, but that just proves my point. I know life is important—but it's no excuse for price-gouging. Just for the sake of the argument, tell me how much Dr. Bullivant charged for delivering your—"

"What!"

It was an involuntary protest from Nancy. She and Gene Perkins exchanged looks that startled Ken.

"Dr. Bullivant didn't deliver my babies," Nancy Perkins said firmly, lowering the temperature by the chill in her voice.

Although he did not understand why, Ken found himself muttering apologies. Nancy Perkins took pity on him.

"Yes, yes, she is very . . . popular here in Southport. A lot of people swear by her. As a matter of fact, Dr. Bullivant is the only thing I do remember about the night when that Dr. Martin was killed. She was up in the ward just when I was going back to my room. She said I looked well enough to be up in Obstetrics."

Gene Perkins was opening another beer can with concentration. This time the words that would bring a wife's censure were not uttered.

"No, Dr. Wittke delivered my babies. Young Dr. Wittke," Nancy continued. "I used to go to Dr. Philip, but he's too busy. . . ."

"Yes," said Ken, who had lost the thread of his argument if he had ever had one. "Well, I only wanted to point out that bringing life into the world is as important as saving life, and it doesn't seem to cost as much. . . ."

"But it can cost more in other places." Gene Perkins picked up the ball. Only the other day, he reported, a drug salesman had been complaining that in Southport he sold far too little. "He said that all the doctors here want to do is cut, cut, cut!"

"Gene!" his wife reproved him.

But the discussion ended indecisively, and shortly afterward the evening did also. Ken parted from the Perkinses amidst warm and sincere invitations to return, to bring his wife. Yet, as he headed home, he was wondering exactly what there was about Dr. Edith Bullivant that proved too much for the Perkins's quite remarkable benevolence.

13   Digits

WHEN Kenneth Nicolls left the Sloan and prepared for the long haul out to Dino's Bowladrome, he was convinced that he had been singled out for one of life's more bizarre tasks. Unknown to him, that conviction was shortly to be shared by John Putnam Thatcher.

With the approach of six o'clock, Miss Corsa finished the last of her letters, closed her typewriter and checked her superior's calendar for the following day. She picked up the letters and crossed to the inner office, smiling.

When the signing ceremony was completed, she spoke:

"Mr. Thatcher, I've left the morning open until eleven tomorrow. So that you can pick out a puzzle for Geoffrey."

Momentarily baffled, Thatcher abandoned the Pennsy-Central report and stared.

"Your grandson," Miss Corsa explained kindly. "It's his birthday next week."

Thatcher opened his mouth to protest. He had been cherishing that free morning in the hope that it would dispose of Gabler's *bête noire* once and for all. Miss Corsa's next words silenced him.

"I've spoken with Mr. Durrant and he's saving several models for you. He has one in particular he wants to show you."

Leaving a cloud of indulgence in her wake, Miss Corsa withdrew.

Accordingly, the next morning found Thatcher emerging from his hotel and deviating from his regular course. Instead of plunging into the subway, he walked briskly toward the large toy shop on Fifth Avenue that enjoyed his patronage. And that patronage was by no means negligible, now that his role as grandfather was extending so dramatically. (His two sons, both late starters, were nosing out their sister in the fertility stakes.)

The day was perfect, not too cool, not too warm, with enough breeze to sweep away the smog and give the illusion of fresh air. Nevertheless, Thatcher felt resentful. He was caught in one of those social traps from which there is no escape.

Two and a half years ago, in preparation for a Christmas holiday to be spent with his son and daughter-in-law, he had been buying some last minute toys. With every name on his list crossed off, he had happened upon a pile of small, complex Japanese wood puzzles, the kind in which all the pieces interlock in an asymmetric fashion defying reconstruction. He had not seen one for over twenty years. Promptly he cut short his shopping and retired to enjoy an evening devoted to mastering the refinements of the post-war models of oriental cunning. Christmas afternoon had been spent relaying this virtuosity to a fascinated grandson.

The spectacle of a gray-haired man and a very small boy absorbed in the same pastime is irresistible to the intervening generation, which suddenly sees itself as the transmitter of a powerful genetic force. Before the holidays were out, family folklore had firmly established John Putnam Thatcher and Geoffrey Kincaid Thatcher as sharers of a common passion for wood puzzles. All very seemly, very proper.

Five months later a letter from his daughter-in-law reminded Thatcher that Geoffrey would be expecting for his birthday "one of those puzzles you and he adore." The letter was opened by Miss Corsa. Thatcher dutifully plodded over to Fifth Avenue, where he was served by the same young man, a Mr. Durrant. The next Christmas, no letter was necessary. Miss Corsa had become self-starting. She called Mr. Durrant, who arranged to hold back three or four specimens for Thatcher family use.

The speed with which a legend can become deeply entrenched is too often underestimated. Within eighteen months, son, daughter-in-law, Miss Corsa and Mr. Durrant were all convinced that they were doing Thatcher a kindness by providing this outlet for an insatiable avocation. On his last visit to the West Coast he realized the lengths to which this process had gone when he found himself being introduced as: "My father-in-law, whose hobby is wood puzzles." He was naturally hardened to that shock of non-recognition experienced by everyone upon being introduced with an erroneous synopsis of salient characteristics. But this seemed excessive. The experience had one salutary result. The next time a lady was presented to Thatcher as mad about pottery, he reserved judgment. She had probably once filled an awkward conversational pause with an innocent query about some vase, thus dooming herself to be publicly branded a ceramics enthusiast from that day forward.

The disheartening truth was that, after unraveling the second puzzle, Thatcher would have been perfectly content to allow another twenty years to roll by before his next bout. He had a shrewd suspicion that this attitude was shared by young Jeff. (Alas, no parent is interested in carrying the genetic seed for a mild and easily satisfied interest. Only a burning passion is worthy of the conduit.) But Thatcher had reconciled himself to the situation. He was, he admitted, not man enough to face his daughter-in-law and say: "Now listen, Susan, I'm fed up with all this wooden puzzle nonsense."

No, the only salvation lay in Jeff's inevitable transformation from small, polite boy, considerate of others, to boorish, self-centered adolescent. Then he would say it for Thatcher. Unfortunately, Jeff showed no signs of being an early-flowering hood. He was still wearing ties and shaking hands.

It was all very discouraging.

Pushing through the revolving doors of the store, Thatcher checked briefly before an enormous stuffed lion with an engaging expression. It was chastely labeled with a price tag for one hundred and fifty dollars. Well, that was one thing to be said in favor of puzzles. At least they were cheap.

Mr. Durrant spied his approach and waved a cheerful welcome. He produced four puzzles, each a marvel of intricacy. Mendaciously, Thatcher discerned a peculiar excellence in the second, thereby sparing himself exposure to the others. Then he selected the present proper—a miniature but powerful set of bagpipes which should settle Susan's hash—to which the puzzle would serve as garnish. Mr. Durrant undertook the mailing of the parcel, and Thatcher was a free man once again.

More than free, almost light-headed. It was like leaving the dentist with no further appointment for six months. (Little did Thatcher know that his expert insights and exacting standards had been a mistake. Dr. Durrant could be a self-starter, too. With his customer's interest now more than confirmed, the young man decided that henceforth he would call Miss Corsa whenever a particularly desirable specimen arrived from the mysterious East.)

Full of virtue at having discharged the requirement of the Protestant ethic, Thatcher contemplated killing the rest of the morning. If nothing had come up at the Sloan, he might be able to find a game of squash at the club. He strode toward the nearest phone booth. Thus do events make the man. Five minutes ago Miss Corsa had been a goad of conscience. Now she was merely a source of information.

"Oh, Mr. Thatcher. I'm glad you called. Mr. Edes has been trying to get you. That's Benjamin Edes of the Southport National Bank."

"Yes, I know. Did he say what it was?"

"No, he was just anxious that you call him back as soon as possible."

"All right. Do you have his number?"

Miss Corsa relayed the endless string of numbers required for direct dialing, repeating them twice. She was always unnerved at the thought of Mr. Thatcher making his own calls. When she dialed a number, she not only got the number, but the party was available. If Thatcher tried to call an insurance company in Hartford, he was infallibly connected to a bar and grill in St. Louis. It was surprising how long conversation could be sustained before the error became apparent.

But this time he was in luck. The reward of virtue, no doubt. Mr. Edes was not only in, he was champing at the bit.

"Thatcher?" he demanded. "I've got something for you."

Thatcher was genuinely startled. He had already had such a lucky strike with Edes that it did not seem reasonable to expect another lode.

"You haven't found out where that money is?" he demanded incredulously. Visions of co-opting Edes for the Sloan's Board of Directors danced in his head.

The old man chuckled with satisfaction.

"No, I haven't found out where it is, but I've got some news about what it's doing."

Thatcher arranged himself comfortably in the booth, propping one shoulder against the wall, with coins at the ready for a prolonged conversation. Not for the world would he have deprived either Edes or himself of the pleasures of a leisurely examination into these latest developments.

"Don't tell me that after taking the trouble to go into cash, Martin let something flow back into his account?" he asked.

"That's it!" said Edes triumphantly.

"How in the world did you spot it?"

"Well now, that account's been getting a lot of attention. The tax people have been examining every transaction." There was a long pause. "Naturally I thought it my duty to assist them."

"Naturally."

The phone cackled in high glee.

"As you can imagine, Martin's account was pretty active. Hundreds of entries every month. There was a deposit for six thousand eight hundred last December. It was a check on his brother's brokerage outfit, down in Delaware. There was another one in March. Nobody paid much attention to them on the first go-round. They were sort of buried in the mess. But I remembered them when I saw the mail this morning. Guess what? Another check for sixty-eight hundred."

Hastily Thatcher recalled the day's date.

"What did you say those dates were again?"

"December 5, March 5 and then June 5."

Edes paused for effect.

"Quarterly dividends," Thatcher murmured unconsciously.

"Sure. And he does his normal investing with a broker here in Southport. If he'd just changed brokers, he would have had the portfolio transferred."

Meanwhile Thatcher's mind had been pursuing a well-oiled banker's track. Absently he obeyed the operator's demand for small change.

"But that," he said in outrage, "is over ten percent!"

"Damn close to eleven percent," Benjamin Edes replied cosily.

There was a moment's silent appreciation.

"We agreed they must be on to something good," Thatcher reminded him.

"It's so good, it's the next thing to counterfeiting."

"My God," continued Thatcher, still digesting Edes's information, "if this is being run like a normal business, they're not distributing anything near their total profits. They'll have all sorts of reserves as well."

"Not to mention expanding the business. And who wouldn't expand this kind of business?"

"I'm not surprised the widow became suddenly carefree after talking to her brother-in-law," Thatcher observed tartly.

"Not exactly carefree. She's just stopped worrying about money and is concentrating on murder, instead." Edes paused discreetly. "You remember the funeral? And what she was claiming about Harley Bauer?"

"I do," said Thatcher. "Tell me, is she still calling him a murderer?"

"She sure is!" said the Southport banker comfortably. "The hospital people keep trying to shut her up, but it's causing a lot of talk out here."

Thatcher was always inclined to clear up finances first; emotions could be dealt with later. He knew perfectly well that this elderly Sherlock had not completed his disclosures.

"I suppose you've checked to see if the others are getting the same kind of income from Delaware?"

"Wondered when you'd get to that. They're all getting checks from the same place on the same date. But not for the same amounts. All of them except Edith Bullivant, as far as I can see. Philip Wittke is getting the same as Martin got—sixty-eight hundred. The Wittke boys are each getting thirty-four hundred. Neverson is getting forty-seven sixty. Got a pencil?"

But Thatcher was already busy casting up sums.

"The way I figure it," the voice rolled on with quiet elation, "if we count Martin and Wittke as having a thousand shares apiece, then Neverson has seven hundred and the boys have five hundred."

"Yes. That's what I come out with. It would be interesting to know how many people in Southport are getting these checks."

"I thought so myself. If you want to hold on, I'll see if anything has come in."

Thatcher braced the receiver and stared bemusedly at his calculations. There was nothing more to be gained from them. He transferred his stare to the glass door of the booth. Over ten percent! By men who were doing far too well in their professions already to take the risk of peddling marijuana on the side. And who wouldn't set up a Delaware corporation to do it, anyway. He shook his head in vexation. There was no point in blind speculation. It was enough at this point to know that Wendell Martin had been mixed up in something very fishy, indeed. And that, as soon as the inexorable spotlight of publicity had been fixed on him, Wendell Martin had very conveniently died.

Thatcher wondered if things were getting out of hand. His modest objective of forcing Atlantic Mutual to cough up one hundred thousand dollars by proving the general culpability of Southport Memorial Hospital and its staff was becoming small potatoes. It was beginning to look as if Southport Memorial was a front for the numbers racket.

Well, closing it down had not been his intention, but, in view of Pemberton Freebody, it did not appear that doing so would constitute a disservice to humanity.

Thatcher's roving gaze at last found something to hold it. Indignantly he noted that someone was actually buying that stuffed lion. Someone in a short skirt and figured stockings who didn't look a day over nineteen. He had assumed the lion was an eye-catcher. In the absence of Christmas he would have regarded it as unsalable. It just showed how old-fashioned he was becoming. He must make an effort to keep abreast of the financial habits of the go-go generation. (Mercifully, duty did not require him to probe other, and less savory, habits.) Not only was the lion being sold, but two men were hoisting a rather mournful elephant into its place. Probably they went through a whole menagerie in the course of a day.

"Thatcher? Still there?"

Thatcher returned to his post.

"There doesn't seem to be anything else. You understand, I can't have the whole place honeycombed. I just had the tellers queried if they remembered anything with reference to doctors' accounts. Just because they don't remember, doesn't mean there isn't something. But we'd have to know where to look." Edes was disappointed.

Thatcher hastened to reassure him. Of course, he wasn't to divert the entire staff into a search. If a specific name came up, Thatcher would alert him. With renewed assurances of friendship and cooperation, they hung up.

All thoughts of squash were now evaporated. Thatcher was beginning to feel on his mettle. Surely, if a little bank in Southport could produce this much information, the Sloan, with its vast resources, was not helpless. He remembered that Ken Nicolls had spent the previous evening on the Great Southport Tangle. It seemed unlikely that he had unearthed anything, but Thatcher intended to hear his report as soon as possible.

"And that's about it, I'm afraid," Ken concluded his summary with a decent show of regret. He could not understand why Thatcher had been so eager to hear the details of his evening expedition.

"It certainly doesn't tell us anything new," Thatcher agreed. He crossed off his name on some routing slips, tossed the attached reading material into the out basket and buzzed for Miss Corsa. Silly to have convinced himself that the boy was going to hand him a solution on a platter. But he had been gripped by one of his powerful, and apparently erroneous, hunches.

Miss Corsa entered, emptied the basket and eyed her employer with disapproval. She was perfectly willing to allow him time off, once every six months, to fulfill family obligations. Playing detective was something else again. Inefficient suicides, inefficient surgeons and inefficient witnesses had no place in Miss Corsa's view of the Sloan. But she was just. She knew this was none of Ken Nicolls's doing and modified her severity in addressing the young man.

"Miss Todd rang through. If you could let her have the tax table back, she'll type up that estimate."

Obediently Nicolls produced an envelope from his wallet pocket and handed it over. Then:

"Oh, just a minute, Miss Corsa. While you're at it, would you give this prescription to Miss Todd and ask her to send out to have it filled?"

Thatcher watched the transaction in some amusement. Did young Nicolls realize that his Miss Todd was beginning to show the powerful organizing potential of a Miss Corsa? She was telling him what to do, and when. She was beginning to edge in on his personal chores. Soon she would be sending him off to buy model boats for his children. Ah well, Nicolls would have to fight that battle himself.

"It's surprising you have any prescriptions left, after an evening in the bosom of a drugstore," he said. Inefficient drugstores apparently could be added to the roster of Southport's shortcomings.

Nicolls confirmed this unfavorable impression.

"I tried to get it filled at Segal's, but they didn't have the right stuff in stock. And just as well, if the prices they were charging Gene Perkins were their usual ones. Did I tell you what he paid for a week's worth of medicine?" Kenneth became heated in recollection. "Why, I figured out that his entire salary from that bowling job must go in—"

"What did you say?" Thatcher suddenly barked.

Nicolls returned stare for stare. Why had his superior stiffened like a lamp pole? Why was his voice accusing him of every felony in the book?

"I said," he replied very quietly, "that I figured out that Perkins—"

"No, no." Thatcher waved Perkins away. "About your prescription." He was leaning forward, coiled for the spring.

Kenneth, a good deal alarmed, mentally reviewed his earlier comments. They could not possibly have offended anyone, he concluded. His jaw came forward. With careful control, he repeated:

"I tried to fill my prescription in that Southport drugstore. But the druggist told me they didn't stock the necessary . . . the necessary ingredients."

"That's it!" said Thatcher incomprehensibly. "That *has* to be it. You had the answer all along, my boy." Face, as well as voice, was now accusing. Suddenly they softened. Sorrow replaced anger. Not a marked improvement, in the judgment of a bewildered Kenneth Nicolls. "Now I want to get this absolutely clear. Why did you and this man Perkins race over to Southport Center for a drugstore in the first place? Were the others already closed?"

Kenneth resigned himself to never knowing what it was all about.

"No, Gene never mentioned that. He said that he had to go to Segal's to get these prescriptions filled. I supposed his prescriptions called for something not commonly stocked."

"Splendid! And we have already established that you, on the contrary, had to go someplace other than Southport with your prescription. Do you know what it is, by the way?"

Nicolls shook his head.

"No, it's for Jane. But it's nothing out of the way. I've never had any trouble before, and she's been taking it for months."

Thatcher beamed at him.

"Exactly so. And finally, you say Perkins has heard salesmen from the drug houses joking about how little they sell to that drugstore or to the hospital pharmacy?"

Kenneth shifted uneasily.

"Yes, but Gene was a little beered up by then. We were arguing about surgeons versus pill-pushers. I think that was just a trade joke, Mr. Thatcher. That business about the hospital believing in nothing but the knife. You've got to realize that Perkins has been in and out of hospitals and drugstores so much lately, he's practically an insider, the way he talks."

"Not an insider, my boy," said Thatcher with gentle satisfaction.

"The insiders are making money, not paying it out. And now we have only one more step necessary for confirmation. To think it was only an hour ago that Ben Edes said he couldn't do anything more without a specific name."

When Benjamin Edes returned from lunch there was a neat note placed on his desk. It said:

Mr. Thatcher would like to know if checks from the same source have been paid into the account of the owner of Segal's Drugstore.

14 Graft

LATE that afternoon an excited Benjamin Edes rang through with the information that checks from the brokerage firm of Martin & Bookerman (Wilmington, Delaware) to the tune of six thousand eight hundred dollars had been deposited in the account of Sidney S. Segal (jointly with Rose E. Segal) in December, in March and yesterday afternoon. Moreover, Edes, to whom a wink was as good as a nod any day, had also examined another account. Deposits from the same source had been made by one Ronald Lawson.

"But he only seems to be in for three hundred shares." Edes was contemptuous. He had no time for small fry. "I think you can guess who he is."

Thatcher thought so, too.

"You did say that Wittke's sons ran a big private clinic, complete with pharmacy," he mused. "Lawson wouldn't by any chance be their druggist, would he?"

"Exactly!" said Benjamin Edes. "Pretty smart work, your tumbling to all this. It's beginning to take shape, isn't it?"

Thatcher agreed that it was and rang off, after making an appointment to confer with Edes tomorrow about further developments. He was amused to find himself full of factional pride; the honor of the Sloan Guaranty Trust had been maintained. It was doing its bit to unveil the dubious financial machinations taking place at Southport Memorial Hospital.

With Segal implicated, things were indeed shaping up, as the redoubtable Edes had said. But the information-gathering stage was over. The time had come to approach one of the many interested parties, if tomorrow were really to bring further developments. Thatcher was weighing the alternatives when he was interrupted by a second phone call; this time from Tom Robichaux.

"You won't forget about this shindig tonight, will you, John?" he inquired mournfully.

"I will if I'm given half a chance," said Thatcher frankly.

"That's what I thought. Wouldn't mind giving it a miss myself."

"Then why are you reminding us both about it? It would have been so easy to let this dinner slip quietly out of our lives," Thatcher said with the brutal frankness of an old friend.

"You don't think I wanted to call you!" Robichaux's voice darkened at this final injustice. "I'm doing it because Cousin Bella made me promise to. Said if I didn't, she would! You're not going to tell me you'd prefer that, are you?"

There was no hesitation in Thatcher's resounding negative. He remembered Robichaux's Cousin Bella (Mrs. Arabella Robichaux Hollingsworth) vividly from past encounters. She was a woman who had been born to be a suffragette. Modern movements proving inadequate, the bulk of her energy was discharged on quailing relatives and associates. It was the kind of situation that made Thatcher believe in professional training for young women. A worthwhile career—say, as an organizer for the Longshoremen's Union—would have gone a long way toward providing Cousin Bella with an outlet for those talents now dissipated on Banning the Bomb and Saving the Old Met.

"She's not going to be there, is she?" he asked, mentally considering the advantages of a fleeting attack by some obscure virus.

"My God, no! It's stag. If you ask me, that's what's got her worked up. She says Amory will make a fool of himself."

Thatcher reviewed the recent activities of Cousin Bella's only son.

"He already has," he pointed out.

"Now look, John," Robichaux rumbled peevishly. "Don't make things even more difficult. We all have relatives! I'll meet you at the bar."

He forestalled further debate by hanging up with a decision far removed from his customary dithering farewells. No doubt it was the suffragette influence at work. Thatcher grinned and abandoned thoughts of further attention to the Sloan. Instead he cleared his desk and set off uptown for the club providing a private suite for the meeting.

The fine assortment of faces which greeted him as he paused to check his hat was a tribute to Cousin Bella's gadfly potential. Her son, Amory Robichaux Hollingsworth, after an undistinguished career drifting along the eastern seaboard from the offices of one family enterprise to another, had decided to place his talents at the disposal of the constituents in his ostensible congressional district. Happily, his forty-two years of life had been so politically inert that he had a rather unusual freedom in determining the party of his choice—as well as the state.

An expensive poll, with stratified subsamples, in a Manhattan district composed almost exclusively of registered Democrats, had brought him to the acute conclusion that it would be folly to sally forth under the banner of Republicanism. He had therefore styled himself a New Democrat. His candidacy had thus far been entirely uncontaminated by association with any organized political group, whether regular or reform.

"Evening, Thatcher," said a voice at his elbow.

He turned to find Dexter Loomis at his side.

"Hello, Loomis. What are you doing here?"

He was reminded of the Hollingsworth interest in insurance.

"Perhaps I phrased that unfortunately," he said as they strolled toward the bar. "I meant what is our presence supposed to accomplish? Do we do anything other than eat our dinner and listen to Amory tell us his plans?"

"God knows! They're calling it a kickoff dinner." Morosely Loomis inspected the martini handed to him. "I was just talking with Carruthers—the downtown lawyer, you know. He says there's not a soul here who has anything to do with politics or who lives in Amory's district."

"A new approach," Thatcher observed blandly.

Dexter Loomis became suddenly combative.

"I can tell you one thing. Amory isn't getting a check out of me. I don't mind being held up for a contribution when the guy is making some kind of an effort, but I'm not subsidizing hobbies!" He looked at Thatcher fiercely, following an unhappy train of thought. "We've got enough money going down the drain these days."

"I assume that means you're settling the Freebody case with us."

"We don't have any choice. But I—"

They were interrupted by the arrival of Tom Robichaux with the guest of honor.

"You know John Thatcher and Dexter Loomis."

"Hello, Amory," Thatcher began.

"Call me Rob!" the candidate trumpeted with a glazed smile.

Remorselessly the amenities proceeded. Dexter Loomis was so hypnotized by the atmosphere that he was soon assuring Hollingsworth that they were all looking forward to his victory over the machine, and ultimately carried him off to meet someone with the makings of a New Democrat.

"Thought Loomis had more sense," was Robichaux's only comment.

Thatcher was more charitable. "He was just carried away for the moment. But I wish you could have waited another five minutes. Loomis was about to say something. There's no justice."

"Oh, things balance out." Robichaux was cheering up now that his responsibilities were over. "What do you think of Amory's Man of the People stunt?"

"Is that why we're supposed to call him Rob?"

"It's all part of the big picture. He's going to put on a sports shirt and tour his district in a station wagon with the wife and children."

It was not an attractive vision, but Thatcher tried to be fair-minded.

"Quite a lot of unlikely people are doing that nowadays. And getting away with it."

"Not with Amory's wife, they're not!"

"Oh." The vision of an all-American family receded. "Difficult, is she?"

Articulate analysis was not Robichaux's strong point. He fumbled for a shortcut.

"She's the sort of woman who keeps reminding herself that she's got to be very, very kind."

"You can say that again!" echoed a newcomer.

Startled, Thatcher turned . . . to find that life's compensations, as predicted by Robichaux, were duly taking place. Before him stood Curtis Hammerton.

And Curtis Hammerton was a vice-president of Japhet Rose, Incorporated, fourth-largest pharmaceutical firm in the United States.

"Just the man I want!"

Quickly Hammerton replied that he made his political contributions to the Republican Party of Connecticut.

"No, no. This is business."

The announcement did not bring the same satisfaction to his companions as to himself.

Robichaux, fortifying himself with another bourbon, said sadly:

"It's creeping up on you, John. Getting so that you can't ever forget business. You want to roll with the punches."

Hammerton's wariness did not diminish. If anything, it increased. Which was not surprising. Hammerton was Japhet Rose's outside man, its announcer of new wonder drugs, its maker of policy statements.

And, of course, in recent years, its testifier before congressional hearings about drug prices, practices and profits.

Poor Hammerton, a man made to exude confident good feeling, had lost weight over those recent years; he was probably braced to discover that the Sloan Guaranty Trust was about to embark upon its own version of the Kefauver investigation.

Thatcher set his mind at ease. With a smile he watched Curtis Hammerton brighten upon realizing that, for a change, he was being asked to consider the malefactions of others.

Briefly Thatcher outlined the financial discoveries of the Southport National Bank, concealing only one fact—the amount of the sums involved. Then he touched lightly on the peculiar difficulties encountered in filling the Perkins and Nicolls prescriptions.

"Of course," he said in innocent conclusion, "it's not very difficult to guess what they're up to. But I'm at a loss as to how to proceed. These people have gone to considerable lengths to conceal their activities, which suggests that they may be unethical—"

"Unethical!" Hammerton broke in jovially. "In New York State, let me tell you, it's illegal enough to get you sent up the river. That is, if what you are talking about is what I am thinking of. And, given these damned money-grubbing doctors, the odds are ten to one that it is!"

Thatcher's eyebrows rose. Only strong emotion could have made a vice-president of Japhet Rose, Inc., "The Doctor's Partner in Medical Progress," resort to language like this.

Thatcher lowered his voice.

"Tell me," he said.

"The latest dodge for doctors who can't keep themselves happy until they've squeezed every dollar out of the patient," Hammerton began, "is to set up their own private drug companies. These companies range from perfectly reputable, if small, laboratories—sometimes with a chemist or even a pharmacist—more often with one or two semi-trained people. These operations may be quite all right in their way—that is, careful, clean and so on. They are not, you understand, capable of research. . . ."

"Yes, yes," said Thatcher to no avail.

"These bucket shops," said Hammerton, his assumption of impartiality crumbling, "are really in business to exploit the discoveries made by the millions upon millions of dollars that firms like Japhet Rose spend in research. Why, our six hundred trained researchers . . ."

All information-gathering exacts a toll. Thatcher listened to a vivid description of Japhet Rose's magnificent laboratories, its unending battle to conquer disease, its exacting standards. Hammerton spoke with a fluency normally lacking in his discourse.

After five minutes, Thatcher cut in.

"About these small private drug houses?" he suggested tactfully.

"What? Oh, sorry," said Hammerton. "I make that speech so often that it just slips out. Well, as I say these parasites are respectable from one point of view. They produce, brand and market the commoner drugs under perfectly satisfactory conditions. From a health standpoint, that is. The gimmick is usually that the doctor writes a prescription calling for a drug produced by the company that he owns—and there goes the price! Usually two or three times what we would charge . . ."

He paused to refuel and continued. "Then some doctors set up private drug outfits that are nothing more than an office and a business address. What they do is import drugs cheaply, usually from Mexico or Italy. They then relabel them—and sell them at a damned good price by specifying them on all their prescriptions. The pharmacist, you know, cannot substitute a different brand. And, I need not remind you, drugs produced in Mexico or Italy are not subject to the searching standards of the U.S. Pharmacopeia. . . ."

"You need not," said Thatcher astringently. One lecture was enough. "Just go on. I'm interested in this price hike. I don't wish to offend you, Hammerton, but my general impression was that prices . . ."

Again tact prompted him to keep the sentence unfinished, and Hammerton emerged from his glass to give him a man-to-man look. "I know what you're thinking! You're thinking that our prices are too high already! Well, let me tell you, the price of a new drug may be high, but think of the research—oh, all right, John. But the fact remains that within a few years, competition brings it down! Look at the antibiotics! Look at penicillin! But when a doctor sets up a firm, he keeps the price up—steadily! He specifies his own firm's drug—no other! So there is no competition—and he can charge what he wants! And these firms do! I'd say that on the whole they are thirty percent more expensive than the open market! And that's not the worst of it—although five dollars for a dozen aspirin is bad enough! But some of these so-called drug firms are a real disgrace! No tests, no safeguards, not even simple cleanliness!"

Curtis Hammerton, carried away by his own emotion, had raised his voice. The mere fact that he was talking about doctors was sufficient to attract the attention of a bystander.

"What's this about doctors? What have they been up to now?" demanded Dexter Loomis with grim joviality.

Curtis Hammerton turned to the insurance executive in surprise. It took him a moment to recover his non-platform manner.

"Thatcher, here, has come up with something interesting. Another little swindle by these doctors."

He began to explain. As he did so, Dexter Loomis's grimness became intensified and the joviality disappeared entirely.

"In Suffolk County, I suppose," he said when Hammerton concluded.

Both men turned expectantly to Thatcher, only to find him lost in thought. Dexter Loomis was appalled to discover the makings of another enormous scandal at Southport Memorial Hospital. Such a discovery would serve to discredit the medical staff more, and further weaken Atlantic Mutual's bargaining position. Thatcher had realized this from the start. He was beginning to realize something else as well. . . .

He shook himself free from abstraction.

"Oh, yes," he agreed. "It's our friends, again."

He did not have to amplify. All of "our friends" were part of a system to make more money. The stark simplicity of the system struck him as peculiar to a peculiar profession; only men who were guaranteed incomes roughly ten times the national average could be so uncomplicated in their approach to acquiring wealth.

Loomis was trying to salvage what he could from the latest debacle.

"So, they've got a little racket going. But what in fact would anyone do about it?" He looked challengingly at Curtis Hammerton.

Tom Robichaux had been a disapproving spectator of the entire pageant. No one seemed capable of having a simple drink in peace. In many ways it was as bad as if they spent the time having a serious discussion of Amory's candicacy. But now, he thought he saw a shortcut.

"Come off it, Curt!" he advised easily. "Let off a little steam if you want. But we all know Japhet Rose makes its money getting along with doctors. You're not going to stir up any stink."

He leaned back, idly twirling his glass as he watched Hammerton and Thatcher.

The representative of Japhet Rose was reminded of his role as public figurehead.

"Naturally, we wouldn't wish to alienate anyone for the sake of . . . the sake of a minor pecadillo," he murmured. "First, we'd call in our own men and get some sort of idea how big the operation was. If it was small potatoes, we'd have a quiet little talk. . . ." He shrugged.

Thatcher inspected the depths of his Scotch. "And if," he suggested calmly, "if it were a million-dollar operation?"

Curtis Hammerton suddenly choked. "Million dollar! We'd raise holy hell! We'd see it didn't spread! We'd . . ."

Under cover of this wave of emotion, Tom Robichaux spoke:

"Nicely done, John," he commented appreciatively.

Within days, John Thatcher learned precisely what Japhet Rose, Inc.—"The Doctor's Partner in Medical Progress"—meant by holy hell. When the Doctor's Partner moved, it moved. Thanks to information swiftly scooped up by an army of drug salesmen and disaffected pharmacists and, just as swiftly, relayed to the district attorney, Thatcher was surveying a rich and satisfying harvest of headlines.

DRUG RING IN SOUTHPORT

FOURTEEN MEDICOS INDICTED

ILLEGAL DRUGS IMPORTED

15　Infected Areas

AMONG the ten milliion people who read these headlines, a surprising number were propelled into some form of action. In Washington, the chairman of more than one congressional subcommittee realized that now, if ever, was the time to resume hearings into drug prices. Officials charged with auditing payments by Medicare, Medic-Aid and every other form of public health assistance instructed subordinates to inspect druggists' bills with special care. Suave lobbyists (representing powerful German chemical interests) spoke persuasively of the salutary effects to be derived from allowing foreign drugs to compete freely in the American market. Several civic-minded groups demanded legislation to regulate the use of trade names in prescriptions.

On a more parochial level, the state police investigating the death of Dr. Wendell Martin also read the headlines with interest. They came to the same interesting conclusion that had caused John Thatcher's sudden abstraction at the kickoff dinner for New York City's New Democrat.

"Makes you think, doesn't it?" ventured Lieutenant Joseph Perenna, drinking cold coffee from a cardboard cup.

His superior agreed stolidly.

"We said that it was too convenient, Wendell Martin getting himself killed just as he was grabbing the headlines. Now we know who it was convenient for. Exactly fourteen people!"

Perenna studied the news story again. After laying bare the bones of the Hyland Drug Company and discussing the role of Albert Martin as its financial front man, the story went on:

> . . . also indicted were Drs. Philip Wittke, James Wittke, Theodore Wittke and Roy Neverson. Sidney Segal and Ronald Lawson, both pharmacists in Southport, Long Island, were also cited as being implicated in the illegal operation of the Hyland Drug Company.
>
> It is understood that Dr. Wendell Martin, slain last month in the parking lot of Southport Memorial Hospital, was a substantial shareholder . . .

"None of these people are the kind who'd ever expect to see the inside of a jail. And Martin was pushing them down the road damn fast! Before he was through, they would have the tax boys after them. First the Feds, then the state, then the Food and Drug people—and God knows who else! To say nothing of flushing a beautiful little money-maker down the drain!"

Several moments of silence ensued.

"It gives us a motive, all right," the captain concluded at last. "But we still don't have much else. The autopsy didn't give us anything new. One blow, which could mean some thug cracked Martin in an unlucky spot, or else—"

"Or else someone intended to kill Martin and knew how to do it with the least effort!" The lieutenant swiveled to throw his cup into the wastebasket for punctuation.

"And nothing new on the weapon," the other continued imperturbably. "Except that they did manage to pick some rust particles out of the wound. Just a plain metal bar. And you were right about the wallet and the weapon. They were never found."

"Probably at the bottom of the bay by now."

"Oh, I wouldn't be too sure about that. These people haven't had much spare time," he flicked the headline of the newspaper, "and we've had a man down at the boatyard to check. None of the boats have been out."

"So all we've got is a motive," Perenna mused. "And not much chance of getting anything else unless we come out in the open."

The captain came to a decision.

"It's time we did! These people are rattled now, and being asked for alibis isn't going to calm them down. I want to get them off balance and keep them that way. We need to know where these fourteen were when Martin was killed. We need to know how dangerous this insurance thing was for them, how much these people had to lose if Martin went on talking. And while you're at it, find out what else is going on at this hospital. This guy Wendell Martin sounds as if he could have tangled with almost anybody."

The lieutenant was not impressed by the difficulties of penetrating hospital security precautions. He nodded easily and rose.

"I'll get started on it right away," he said crisply.

Philip Wittke did not have to call for an attorney to be present during his police interrogation. His lawyer was already there, trying to explain to the assembled Wittkes that they would require different representation during their forthcoming trial for running an illegal drug company.

"Look, Phil, I'm not a criminal lawyer. You need someone else."

"Well, you do trial work, don't you?" Wittke demanded impatiently. "I know you handle all those car accidents. And I don't intend to have a lawyer whose other clients are in the Mafia!"

"Phil, it's your own interest I'm thinking of. The trial is nothing. They've got all the evidence they need, and it's all documentary. What you need is someone who can do a deal for you with the prosecutor's office."

Wittke stared blankly. Blunt talking had thus far been conspicuously absent in his immediate vicinity. He was still laboring under the delusion that everything would turn out satisfactorily. The jury would realize that he had only been exercising his God-given right to benefit from the American system. It was a moment before he appreciated the full implications of what he had just been told.

"Do you mean to say that *I'm* going to be found guilty?"

The voice started as a roar, but in midstream turned into an uncontrolled squawk of horror.

The lawyer sighed and spread his hands helplessly.

"That's right, Phil."

The younger Wittkes shuffled their feet uncomfortably. The conference had been their idea, designed to bring home the facts of life to Father. But until now, their one contribution had been the heavy announcement that their wives were terribly upset by the whole affair. Significantly they did not ask how Mother felt.

James now began to speak hurriedly.

"In that case, we ought to make the best deal possible." He looked nervously at the lawyer, who nodded encouragingly. "It might even be necessary for us to testify for the prosecution. We have to think about the future."

His father looked at him as if he had never seen him before. Then he suddenly took a deep breath and relaxed.

"You're upset and you've lost your head for a moment," he explained magisterially. "What you're advising is totally inconsonant with our professional dignity. And, if there's one thing I've always maintained, it's that—"

"Dammit, Father! Don't you understand!" the younger man interrupted with a howl of anguish. "I won't be a doctor any more if I'm convicted. It's different for us than it is for you! I'm thirty-eight and Ted is thirty-five. You were going to retire in a year or two. But what about us? We don't have your financial resources."

"Financial resources have nothing to do with it," grated Wittke. "We'll fight this thing tooth and nail!"

"For Chrissake, father—"

It was on this scene of family accord that Lieutenant Joseph Perenna was introduced.

"Just a few questions," he said easily, settling back into a comfort enjoyed by no one else in the room. "I'm lucky to have caught you all together."

"This is completely irregular," the lawyer protested. "The prosecutor must know that I'm not going to allow my clients to answer casual questions. They'll answer questions at their trial!"

The lieutenant's smoothness remained unruffled.

"I think we may have our wires crossed. I'm inquiring into the murder of Dr. Wendell Martin."

"Well, why didn't you say so?" Wittke snarled. "And it's high time the police did something about that!" Some malevolent spirit impelled him to develop this theme. "Apparently you have all the time in the world to probe into pharmaceutical manufacturing and other things no layman could possibly understand! But when criminals attack and murder a prominent surgeon, where are you then? Dr. Martin was a valuable member of the community whose death should be rigorously investigated. It's getting so that a doctor isn't safe on hospital grounds. I don't know how you expect hospitals to be staffed under those circumstances."

Lieutenant Perenna was supremely indifferent to the problems of hospital recruitment. He let the tirade run its course, then said:

"Will you tell me where you were at the time Wendell Martin was murdered, Dr. Wittke?"

The stunned silence that greeted this question was broken by the lawyer.

"You don't have to answer that, Phil," he said hastily.

"Of course, if Dr. Wittke prefers to stand on his rights . . ." the sentence trailed off suggestively.

"I . . ." Wittke took a deep breath. "I don't know how you expect me to remember at this late date."

"It shouldn't be difficult. That was not an ordinary night and, according to our records, you were at the hospital when our squad car answered the call."

"Yes, of course. I was working late at the hospital that evening."

"The call was answered at ten thirty-four. You must have been working very late."

"I frequently work very late. You don't run a hospital on a nine-to-five basis."

"Perhaps you can tell me who you were with?"

But Dr. Wittke could not. He had, he said, been on the move. Earlier in the evening he had spoken with Dr. Neverson and Dr. Bullivant. But at nine-thirty his memory seemed to end. He spoke vaguely of looking into empty offices and walking along vacant corridors. He had been informed of the tragedy over the house phone, after having been paged. It was all very unsatisfactory.

James and Ted were able to report, with manifest relief, that they and their wives had been present at a rehearsal (for patrons only) of the Community Theater in Bayshore. It was, Lieutenant Perenna thought, typical of them.

Exposure of the drug company had caused the Wittkes to take counsel with their lawyer. Roy Neverson was taking counsel with his mother. In many ways her advice was as shrewd and as hardheaded as any that could be offered by a member of the bar.

"How bad is it, Roy?" she asked on arrival, wasting no time on empty sympathy.

"Damn bad. I may go to jail."

"That's going to be hard. On all of us."

Beatrice Neverson knew all about things being hard. She had begun learning when her husband deserted her and their six-year-old son. Within ten years she had become china buyer in the department store where she started as a salesgirl. Now, thirty years later, she had an interest in a specialty shop which spent the summer in Southampton and the winter in Palm Springs.

Her chunky bracelets jangled as she reached for a cigarette.

"What do you want to do about the children? Julie was going to bring them to Southampton at the end of the month."

"That's just it. I don't think they ought to come up. They'll still hear about it, but nobody's going to be very interested in their jailbird father up in Michigan."

Beatrice nodded. "Do you want me to talk to Julie about it?"

It was thanks to Julie's affection and respect for her mother-in-law that Roy Neverson saw as much of his children as he did.

Neverson replied tensely:

"Yes, but there's more to it than just that. I don't see how I can share the house in Southampton with you anymore. Money's going to be damned tight."

"All right, Roy. Let's get it out in the open. What are we going to have to do?"

"That's the trouble. I don't know." There was tortured effort behind the words. "I'm going to lose most of my investment in that drug company, and there's not much left over. If I go to jail, God only knows what happens then. The medical association will throw me out. Hell! I don't know how to do anything else. Bea, I just can't tell what's going to happen."

His voice broke. His mother made no comment on these fears, or on the effort and sacrifice that had been required to send him through medical school. But her jaw tightened as she ground out her cigarette. Beatrice Neverson had never had much sympathy for weakness.

"Then you may as well face it, Roy. First, you're going to have to cut down on your payments to Julie. The sooner that's fixed, the better. There's no point in putting it off."

Neverson stared sightlessly out the window. But his voice was as stubborn as hers.

"I don't want to do that until the last minute. You realize what it'll mean? Julie will have to take the girls out of school. Most of the extras will have to go. I'm not going to do that until I have to."

Deliberately she poured cold water.

"They can go to public school. I did. You and Julie both did. It's not a tragedy."

They were still arguing when Lieutenant Perenna appeared. His pointed questions turned Beatrice Neverson rigid, but her son could barely be distracted from his personal anguish.

"Oh my God! So now somebody thinks we murdered Martin! As if we don't have enough to worry about."

"His death was very convenient," said the lieutenant mildly.

"That may be the way it looks to you," groaned Neverson. "From where I sit, it's just another body blow. I suppose it was inevitable, somebody would get that idea. Living or dead, Martin was always trouble. The only thing that would have done any good was infanticide."

"Just tell me where you were at the time of the murder."

"Let me think a minute. Yes, I remember. It was the day after Marie Gentilhomme's brilliant performance in court. I checked out of the hospital about nine o'clock. I came straight home and stayed here the rest of the evening. I didn't find out about the murder until I heard it on the news at breakfast."

"Any confirmation of that?"

"I don't think so. No, wait, I stopped for a bottle at the liquor store on the corner. But they probably won't remember."

"You'd be surprised what people remember sometimes."

Illegal drug companies were not the only headlines Joseph Perenna had seen in connection with Wendell Martin's death. Sooner or later he was bound to arrive at Harley Bauer's house, where the young couple confronted him together.

"These statements by Mrs. Martin are causing a lot of talk. We thought we'd just check into it."

"It's spite, that's what it is," gasped Joan Bauer. "She and I had a fight, if you must know. Right after Harley started at Southport Memorial. She tried to pull the great lady on me. Ever since she's had her knife into us."

"Now, Joan," said Harley uneasily. "The least said about that, the better. Lucille's just upset. Everybody knows Wendell Martin was killed by a mugger."

"Do they?" The lieutenant paused to let it sink in. "Considering all the dark streets in Southport, we think it's funny a mugger should decide to operate in a lighted parking lot with a lot of coming and going. We're ready to look at any theory."

Harley Bauer went white.

"And so," continued the policeman relentlessly, "I'd like to ask where you were at the time of the murder, Dr. Bauer."

"I suppose I may have been at the hospital," Harley said in a half-suffocated voice. "I went over to Southport that night to pick up some of my things. I got there about eight. It must have been about two hours before I left."

"You talked to people while you were there?"

"Yes. As a matter of fact I talked to Martin himself early in the evening. I saw Neverson and Wittke and Sid Segal, too. Then, later on, after I cleaned out my locker I chatted with Dr. Kroner awhile. He was the last one I talked to."

"And you left before any alarm had been raised?"

"That's right."

"And where had you left your car, Dr. Bauer?"

"In the staff parking lot," said Harley through clenched teeth. "All right, I know what you're thinking. My car must have been close to where the body was found. I was a couple of places over from Alice Doyle's car."

"And you noticed nothing when you left?"

"Not a damned thing!"

Harley leaned back defiantly, daring the lieutenant to make something of it. But the lieutenant shifted his attack.

"Mrs. Martin claims you hated Wendell Martin. We'd like to know what the trouble between you was."

Harley began a response which by now had become mechanical. "The disagreement between Dr. Martin and myself was entirely professional. It had nothing to do with his murder, and I see no reason—"

"NO!"

All the protest which Joan Bauer had repressed since Dr. Wendell Martin's funeral exploded in that one syllable. She clutched her husband's arm desperately.

"Don't you see, Harley?" she demanded frantically. "You can't take that attitude about Southport Memorial any more. They stand back and accuse you of murder, and they know they can rely on you to be all ethical."

"Lucille Martin isn't a doctor," her husband objected weakly.

"That's the filthiness of it! They just hide behind her. Do you think they couldn't stop her if they wanted to? Don't you see what they're doing? It's been the same all along at that hospital. They've victimized you from the minute you set foot in there. And they're doing it again. It doesn't matter what *they* do. They've always got Harley Bauer to take the blame. If you don't tell the lieutenant, I will!"

Perhaps Harley Bauer had learned something from his wife's outburst. Perhaps it had occurred to him that he, too, had a woman to hide behind. In any event, he made no further protest as Joan turned stormily to Perenna.

"If there was any hating in Southport, it was Wendell Martin who was doing it. Because Harley showed him up! Dr. Martin was supposed to be such a great surgeon."

"And he wasn't?" inquired Perenna.

It did not seem like a dramatic revelation in view of recent courtroom exposures.

"I don't know how good he was technically. But Harley showed that half the time his operations weren't necessary! He was taking out gall bladders simply to make money!"

"Look, Joan," said Harley wearily. "If we're going to have this out, let me tell it." He shrugged helplessly. "Joan's dramatizing, but she's got the basic situation right. Last year, when I went to Southport as staff pathologist, was the first time they had a compulsory tissue review on every operation. I guess they didn't realize what they were letting themselves in for. Before any results came in, the committee adopted the standards of the big teaching hospitals. The standards tell you how many times a surgeon can diagnose an "acute" appendix that turns out to be normal before being called on the carpet by the chief of surgery. Well, my reports showed that Dr. Martin was operating on far too many normal conditions. The trouble of course was that Dr. Martin *was* chief of surgery. So I was the one who got called on the carpet. He told me in so many words that I'd better change my reports. I refused. Then I got canned. That's the situation in a nutshell."

The lieutenant did not comment immediately. Harley Bauer had described a situation in which feelings could run high on both sides—indeed, he thought, looking at Joan Bauer's flushed face and recalling Lucille Martin's hysterical denunciations, the resentment could extend to both families.

"I suppose this wasn't just a quarrel between the two of you? Dr. Martin had to have support to fire you."

"The Old Guard stood behind him, all right. But they didn't like it much, particularly in view of his other suggestions." Harley was relaxing now that the skeleton was out of the closet. He was more at peace with himself than he had been since the storm broke.

"What were those suggestions?"

"Martin objected to my temerity in disallowing operations by staff members. But he still wanted a check on the outside doctors with hospital privileges. In fact he had the nerve to tell Wittke to cancel some of those privileges on the basis of my findings. Wittke wouldn't go along with that. He had the sense to see he had to be consistent. He took the position that I was a bum pathologist, and Southport wouldn't pay attention to any of my work. But that didn't stop Martin from tearing a strip out of one visiting doctor he didn't like." Harley chuckled in recollection. "They went at it hammer and tongs."

"And what was the name of that doctor?"

Harley stiffened.

"Oh, now look here, Lieutenant—"

It was a full five minutes before Perenna wrote down a name.

The sign read:

> *Dr. Edith Bullivant*
> *Obstetrics & Gynecology*
> 2–4 P.M. *and by appointment*

The house was a handsome Colonial set in carefully landscaped grounds. It was, thought Perenna, a proper setting for the plump, gray-haired doctor.

"Naturally I'll tell you anything I can about Wendell Martin, Lieutenant," she said, handing back the ID card, "but I don't see how I can be of much help."

"We're checking into his relationships this last year. I've been told that you and he had some fairly violent disagreements."

"That's true," Dr. Bullivant agreed calmly. "And it would be true for almost any year during the last twenty. Dr. Martin and I didn't get along."

"I wasn't thinking of your personal relationship. We've been told that this was a professional disagreement."

"It comes down to the same thing. I don't know how much you've heard about Wendell Martin, but you probably know he liked to throw his weight around. He was chief of surgery. Insofar as I am responsible to anyone, it's to the chief of obstetrics. I told him I wasn't in his jurisdiction, and he didn't like it." The lady paused to smile affably. "But he can't have been very surprised. He's been told the same thing by most of the obstetricians on the South Shore."

"I understand he objected to some of the D&C's you performed. That could mean trouble."

"I'm not in any trouble, Lieutenant," she said good-naturedly. "And I won't be, until the objections start coming from the chief of obstetrics. Dr. Martin was no doubt a highly competent surgeon. He was neither qualified nor competent in obstetrics. I am."

She sounded very sure of herself. But then, if Harley Bauer's story was correct, objections from Wendell Martin would have been taken with a grain of salt by the hospital's inner circle. Particularly if he had a long history of poaching on other people's territory.

"I'm glad to get this cleared up. There's just one more item. For the record, we're checking on the location of everybody at the time of Dr. Martin's murder. Can you tell me where you were that evening?"

"Certainly. I was in the delivery room until nine-thirty. The mother was a diabetic, and it was not an easy delivery. I came straight home after cleaning up. I was with my husband the rest of the evening."

Dr. Bullivant's calm remained unshaken during this recital. Lieutenant Perenna duly noted that she was the only witness to display no reaction to his critical question. But that could simply be strength of character. He had a fairly good idea that Edith Bullivant's reactions were under strong control at all times.

Before leaving, Lieutenant Perenna had a chance to meet Giles Bullivant, who unhesitatingly corroborated his wife's story—which was not surprising. The state police now knew what all of Southport had always known. Giles Bullivant led a carefree, elegant life, which was largely supported by Edith Bullivant's efforts. He had more than one reason to desire her continued success and popularity.

Guided by some unconscious obedience to the medical hierarchic structure, Perenna had deferred Sid Segal until last. In many ways, the interview rounded off the day nicely.

"Sure. I know where I was. I was over at the hospital talking to Phil Wittke. I can't have been gone from him more than five minutes or so when they started paging him over the intercom. I found out the next day they were calling him to tell him about the murder."

"That isn't the way Dr. Wittke tells it. In fact, he didn't mention you at all in accounting for his evening. How do you explain that?"

Segal closed his eyes briefly, in acknowledgment of the world's stupidity.

"Oh, I can explain it all right," he said wearily. "And if you've met Phil Wittke, you'll understand. What we were doing is having a nice, long talk about how something had to be done to shut Martin up before he got the rest of us thrown in jail!"

Expressionlessly, Perenna took notes.

"That's very interesting. And whose idea was it that Martin had to be shut up?"

"Oh, I admit it, I was the one doing the pushing." Segal lifted his shoulders. "Wittke agreed it would be nice if Martin shut up. But he was willing to wait; he said there was nothing for us to do. I wanted to get rough with Martin, explain exactly what dangers he was running."

"You mean you just wanted him to talk to Martin? That doesn't seem very rough."

Segal looked at him from the end of a great weariness.

"You ever had anything to do with doctors, Lieutenant?"

Perenna admitted that this was his first experience.

"Well, you don't say to Wittke that Martin is so stupid you have to explain to him as if he were five years old. Wittke had been passing Martin off as some kind of genius for so long that he believed it himself. And Wittke had kidded himself this drug business wasn't really illegal. Irregular was his favorite word. He likes to wrap things up. I don't mind it myself, but I like to remember what's under the wrapping. The result of all this was that Martin was being allowed to barrel down the roller coaster without anybody telling him the tracks ended at the bottom. Neverson had already had a go at Martin. I was trying to spike Wittke into the same thing."

"But why should Wittke object? His interests were the same as yours, weren't they?"

"Sure they were. I knew it, Roy Neverson knew it, Ron Lawson knew it. But Wittke . . . well, according to him, he didn't see we were all sitting on a barrel of TNT."

Perenna leaped on the reservation.

"What do you mean—'according to him'?" he demanded.

"Wittke's not as simple as he looks. *He's* no five-year-old. Not by a long shot!" Segal said with calm certainty. "And sometimes Dr.

Wittke doesn't publicly admit what Phil Wittke knows damned well. But, take it from me, precious little gets by him."

"None of this explains why Wittke doesn't admit to being with you on the evening of the murder."

"Wittke is still fighting the drug charge. The less he admits to being with me, the better he likes it. I don't know why I knocked myself out trying to make him see sense. I've got a lot less to lose than the rest of them. I'm not a doctor, my boys are clean, and I'm a rich man."

Well-regulated disbelief appeared on Perenna's face.

"So you're not trying to fight the drug charge?"

"Not enough to take the rap for someone else's murder."

Sid Segal spoke with complete finality.

16　*Office Hours*

LIEUTENANT PERENNA'S instructions had been all-embracing, and he was a conscientious officer. His earlier interviews had been a necessary part of police routine. But fundamental to the life of Dr. Wendell Martin—and probably to his death as well—had been Southport Memorial Hospital. It was here that Martin had exercised dominion; here that the major suspects spent the better part of their time, practicing their professions, waging political war, advancing or retreating in the hierarchy; and it was here that the Hyland Drug Company had its spiritual home, regardless of the fact that its legal domicile was on the seventeenth floor of an office building in Wilmington, Delaware.

Therefore, the lieutenant spent the next day at Southport Memorial, wandering its corridors, asking questions and watching . . . watching . . . watching. By evening he had learned a surprising amount. He knew how the doctors checked in and out, when the shifts changed down in the service and administration blocks, where the orderlies retreated for a quiet, illicit smoke, when the cafeteria was bursting with people grabbing a quick snack and when it was virtually deserted, what arrangements the nurses had made for their creature comforts, when the tide of visitors swelled and ebbed.

Nevertheless, his mission was a failure. Because he knew something else as well. In spite of the fact that people were being born and people were dying all over the hospital, in spite of the ceaseless clacking of the paging system and the deliveries of food, linen and medical supplies, still Southport Memorial—as it had existed last week—was dead.

He was reminded of one of his police courses taken several years ago. The subject had been how to determine death. The lecturer had moved from the absence of cardiac pulsation through a whole series of corroborative methods ending with the final, daunting statement: *Corruption is an absolute sign of death.*

And corruption was the prevailing smell of Southport Memorial right now. No doubt a new Southport would rise from the ashes, but it would be unrelated to the old. It was only a final galvanic spasm

which moved everyone to consult Dr. Wittke and refer to Dr. Neverson. The courtesies were as meaningless as those surrounding a
dowager queen immediately after the death of the monarch. The title
might remain, the reality was over. The old political structure had
been annihilated. A new king would soon be reigning, new courtiers
would appear, new loyalties and enmities would be formed.

And everyone knew this. However reticent the medical community
may be in its dealings with the outside world, under the best of
circumstances it is not above a cozy intramural gossip with familiars.
Under the worst—and few doctors reading the headlines occasioned
by the death of Pemberton Freebody and the existence of the Hyland
Drug Company could conceive of anything more appalling—the
tribal grapevine can operate with an efficiency that might be envied
by the larger communication utilities. Anybody at Southport Memorial trying to delude himself that he was surrounded by Casabiancas,
stoically embracing the burning deck, had only to listen to the hourly
bulletins emanating from the administrative suite.

Mrs. Stosser had crowned a lifetime's success in bending to the
wind by getting her resignation in first. She had been scheduled to
retire in six months. Now, Southport would be without a director of
nursing within a matter of days.

Dr. Kroner's colleagues, when they thought about him at all, were
wont to pity him his lack of connection with that rich network of
professional contacts which is the heritage of the lowliest graduate of
an American medical school. Accordingly they were surprised to find
the little German second in line. He was relocating, he explained with
unnecessary courtesy, because of a sudden desire to specialize in
dermatology. Happily, there was an opening in Poughkeepsie.

Scarcely had Karl Kroner cleared the office before the morning
mail brought letters from two new residents, expected to arrive
shortly for the forthcoming year. They deeply regretted that it would
be impossible for them to take up their appointments, but due to
personal commitments, unexpected changes, et cetera. An obstetrician, second only to Edith Bullivant in the number of deliveries for
which he accounted, found it expedient to book his patients into
another hospital for the time being. Not so polite as Dr. Kroner, he
explained bluntly that he was getting out fast before any of the mud
stuck to him.

Southport Memorial had never figured largely in the hopes of young interns planning the next step in their careers. Now it ceased to figure in anything but their nightmares.

Marooned on its island, the remaining staff was necessarily prey to a sense of abandonment. Lieutenant Joseph Perenna's presence had the effect of joining to that unwelcome emotion a sense of bewilderment amidst shifting standards.

"But, Alice," protested Marie Gentilhomme. "I don't see what you're so worried about."

"Look, kid," Mrs. Doyle replied, "I've just seen fifteen years' work washed away. And there's no time to gripe about it. I'm too busy wondering whether there's anything that can be done about the next fifteen."

"Well, how can all this affect you? You've just been doing your job."

Alice Doyle produced a travesty of a smile.

"Yeah," she said bitterly. "I've done a good job, too. And do you think I'm going to get anything for it—anything but a boot in the rear? Hell, no! Like everyone else around here, my name's going to be dirt. I'm beginning to think we'd be better off opening up to the police."

"Why, of course." Marie's color rose at her temerity in giving the older woman advice. "If you can tell them anything, you ought to."

There was a pause.

"Well, you know I'm right, don't you?" she insisted.

"Actually, kid," Alice Doyle said at last, "it's you that's got something to tell them."

Nor was Lieutenant Perenna's visit to the Sloan Guaranty Trust the next morning any more helpful. He ended by imparting more information than he received. But at least this interview left its participants in a cheerful frame of mind.

"Now that the police are finally digging, they're bringing up mud by the bucketful, aren't they?" announced Charlie Trinkam. He slung a leg over the arm of his chair as an indication that he was not following the policeman from the room.

The other men in the room had also settled down. The state police had wanted to know about the insurance claim, and they had received the united cooperation of Trinkam, Nicolls, Thatcher and Dr. Edmund Knox. Paul Jackson's professional scruples had debarred him from attending the conference, but he had been on the phone to Thatcher as frequently as Benjamin Edes, both men gathering information in the wake of the police investigation almost as quickly as it developed.

Absently, Thatcher pushed the cigarette box toward Dr. Knox.

"The implications were certainly very nasty," he agreed. "I'm not sure that I understood all the involvements."

"Well, the main thing seems to be the drug conspiracy," Kenneth Nicolls ventured. "That's what would have come to light if Wendell Martin had kept on grabbing the headlines."

"And they were all in it, up to their necks," said Trinkam, who had been following the newspaper coverage avidly. "The whole Wittke Clinic, for instance."

Thatcher shook his head.

"That's not what I mean. That, if I may say so, is the business end of it. I was referring to the medical end—Martin's disagreements with Dr. Bauer and Dr. Bullivant. I find it difficult to estimate how important they were."

Everyone looked at Dr. Knox. The specialist shook his head angrily.

"Medical end!" he growled. "There wouldn't have been any disagreements if these people had been practicing medicine! Every single time, the trouble started because someone was trying to make more money out of something."

This conclusion came as no surprise to three bankers. But they all recognized that Edmund Knox was overcome by chagrin at the activities of his co-professionals. Secrecy was no longer possible. All the activities of Southport Memorial were now doomed to exposure under the pitiless glare of a murder investigation. But the doctor from Hanover had to find his own way to make palatable a discussion of the foibles of the Southport clique.

Trinkam eased into the subject.

"The fight with Bauer is easy enough to understand. The boy was producing evidence that Wendell Martin was operating in a number of cases where no surgery was necessary. I suppose if he'd been allowed to go on producing that evidence, sooner or later the rest of the staff would have found out."

"It's more complicated than that." Edmund Knox glared at Charlie Trinkam as if he were the embodiment of the collective delinquencies of the AMA. "There can never have been any question of 'finding out.' Some of the staff knew all along. You've forgotten they established a Tissue Review Committee."

"I'm afraid I don't see how that comes into it," Thatcher said patiently.

"Bauer's findings didn't go directly to Martin. They went to the committee. Of course, any surgeon is going to be wrong in his diagnosis every now and then. That's why you have standards. And it's only when a surgeon transgresses those standards that the committee reports him to the chief of surgery."

Kenneth Nicolls unwisely belabored the obvious.

"But that means the entire committee at Southport knew about Dr. Martin."

Dr. Knox was now glaring at all of them.

"Yes," he admitted. "That is why Martin was so furious. If the reports had gone straight to him, it wouldn't have involved his reputation with anyone except Bauer. This way, every man on the inside surgical staff would know about it. If they hadn't had the facts, Martin could have explained away rumors of a disagreement with Bauer. He could always say he was having a run of bad luck."

"But with the facts, the hospital would have to do something about it, sooner or later?" Ken persisted.

"They should have done something about it right at the start. How they could hope to have any kind of Tissue Review Committee that would tolerate that sort of thing, I fail to understand!" Knox's heavy eyebrows drew together in massive censure.

"They do seem to have achieved some sort of toleration as soon as they got rid of Bauer," Thatcher pointed out.

A groan was his only answer. Dr. Edmund Knox's life had been spent in the great research hospitals of the big city. His first intimate view of a small suburban hospital was proving a real eye-opener.

"I suppose I shouldn't be so surprised," he confessed. "The last study on the subject revealed an astonishing number of simple operations that were being performed although totally unnecessary."

"What operations are they?" asked Trinkam.

"Appendix, gall bladder and hysterectomy are the common ones."

"I'll remember that," said Trinkam darkly. "Anybody who wants to take a knife to my appendix or gall bladder is going to have a fight on his hands."

"I had my appendix out three years ago," Nicolls contributed gloomily. "I hate to think it was just to satisfy the surgeon."

Knox came to the defense of his profession.

"Quite a few of these operations are necessary." He searched for something else to say but apparently was unsuccessful.

"Well, then, the Bauer-Martin tangle is at least comprehensible. But what about Dr. Bullivant? Jackson was almost chortling with glee when he told me about it." Thatcher wondered if he should admit that he didn't have the faintest idea what a D&C was. He decided to offer bait. "Something about her D&C's. No tissue for the pathologist, or something."

"Ah!" Dr. Knox expelled his breath softly. "That could be grave, very grave."

Trinkam had no inhibitions about launching into a full-scale gynecological discussion. "What's so grave about it? I thought it was the same racket. Just make-work."

"By no means," said Dr. Knox sternly. "It sounds very much as if you're talking about D&C's after alleged miscarriages."

"So?"

"Criminal abortions," said the specialist shortly.

Charlie Trinkam whistled.

"They don't miss a trick out in Southport, do they?" he inquired genially.

"Obviously not." Thatcher sought to depress Trinkam's exuberance, which was having an unfortunate effect on Dr. Knox. "But the important thing is that it could mean a speedy end to Dr. Bullivant's practice."

"Not quite that. It's a long way from a fuss in the hospital to a question of criminal prosecution."

"In Southport," said Trinkam irrepressibly, "the distance seems endless."

Dr. Knox threw up his hands. He had abandoned his halfhearted attempts to find excuses for Southport.

Thatcher groped for a conclusion. "It really depends on the kind of man Martin was, doesn't it? I gather it would be extremely unethical for a doctor at Southport to report Dr. Bullivant to the authorities. But what about ending her privileges at the hospital? Would that be a blow?"

"A devastating blow. An obstetrician, after all, needs a hospital more than most. But I scarcely see how Martin was in a position to exercise any influence in the matter, considering his own history with the pathologist's reports."

"He seems to have had enough influence to fire the pathologist. I wonder just how safe Dr. Bullivant felt, with Martin on the warpath."

They all considered that. Then Kenneth Nicolls raised another point.

"If Dr. Martin was really interested in the pathologist's reports, he might have been threatening other doctors as well. I think the only reason we know about Dr. Bullivant is because she and Martin went in for a big public fight. You can't tell how many of these scenes were taking place on the quiet."

"Bauer would know," Thatcher pointed out.

"But, Mr. Thatcher, Bauer isn't doing much talking."

"The time has come," said Edmund Knox decisively, "for someone to explain to Dr. Bauer that the interests of the medical profession require a thorough investigation of the situation at Southport. The young man seems to have behaved very properly until now—and under singular provocation. I have every sympathy with the principle of professional discretion. Where irregularities can be rectified without recourse to publicity, it is much more satisfactory to avoid washing dirty linen in public. But the main thing is that they *be* rectified. And when a hospital has already bemired itself in so much notoriety, no responsible objections can be raised to stringent inquiries and complete disclosure. Dr. Bauer will understand this when I explain it to him—particularly now that he is assured of professional support."

Dr. Knox spoke quietly, without any of the belligerence or restiveness that had accompanied his earlier explanations. For all that, it was as if trumpets had sounded the call to charge.

Dr. Knox's blood was up. He had coolly resolved to declare war on Southport Memorial, and he had an imposing array of forces to throw into battle. The light of the crusader was beaming from his eye as he left them on this martial note. His destination, he said, was the American College of Surgeons. Both Thatcher and Trinkam were reasonably confident that mighty winds were going to whirl through various medical societies, that much talk about accreditation would take place, that veterans would be summoned to the theater of conflict, that the New Guard at Southport was going to be charged with an awesome cleansing assignment.

"And has it occurred to you," Thatcher mused as he tilted his chair back contemplatively and studied the ceiling, "that may be just what Wendell Martin's murder was designed to prevent?"

Charlie lit a cigarette and prepared to cast off the conversational restraints which he had inflicted on himself (although Edmund Knox would have found it hard to believe) during the good doctor's presence.

"If that was the reason," he offered, "it wasn't a howling success!"

Ken Nicolls's serious-mindedness was too inherent to be influenced by the mere comings and goings of medical luminaries.

"I don't see how you can tell what the motive was," he objected. "There seem to be so many swindles going on at that hospital—dummy operations, abortions, money floating around, an illegal drug company. Once you know what these people are capable of, you can imagine almost anything going on out there. They might even be running an adoption racket!"

This new game appealed to Trinkam.

"Think of the opportunities in the drug company alone! They were letting Martin's brother handle the financial end by himself. He could easily have been taking a cut off the top of the pile that nobody knew about. Then, suppose brother Wendell catches him with his hand in the till?"

"And remember all the cash transactions that have been going on? There could easily be a blackmailer at work in the middle of them."

The more serious Ken became, the more playful was Charlie Trinkam.

"Now that I don't know about," he said easily. "In Southport, if you step out of line, they seem to crack your skull in. That's not the kind of atmosphere in which blackmailers flourish."

Thatcher thought it time to end his subordinates' flights of fancy.

"I think we can take it for granted that Southport could be the home of almost any malfeasance. On the other hand, we have to ignore the ones we don't know about, as a matter of expediency. I don't think that's a serious oversight, because anything that hasn't been dredged to the surface by the publicity of the last week was buried deep enough to be safe from exposure, regardless of Wendell Martin's antics."

"It's not as if that leaves us with any shortage," Charlie encouraged Ken. "We've got the drug business, first of all. Now that was really endangered. Paul Jackson says the tax people were readying an attack on Martin. Once they started to dig into his income, they would have gotten to Hyland Drug in about three days."

Thatcher brought his gaze down from the ceiling.

"And what would that have meant?"

"Plenty! This Martin was a real fruitcake. The others have been declaring their income from the drug company. But not Martin! He was never satisfied. And the tax boys wouldn't have gone easy on him. It wouldn't have been a simple case of paying up what was owing."

"But the Internal Revenue makes compromises like that all the time," said Ken, mindful of several clients of the Sloan Trust Department.

"Sure they do. But not when it's somebody like Martin. After the Pemberton Freebody business, he would have been in about the same position as Al Capone on a tax rap. The tabloids would have been howling for his blood. The medical societies wouldn't have gone to bat for him. For once, public feeling would have been on the side of the Internal Revenue."

Thoughtfully, Thatcher nodded.

"I'm sure that's correct as far as it goes. But in one sense, the conspirators would have been better off if exposure had occurred that way. They would have been able to use Wendell Martin as a scapegoat. The others might have gotten off with a suspended sentence."

"They didn't expect you to come along, John," Trinkam grinned. "They could figure the drug company was safe, once Martin was dead. In any event, he doesn't sound like the kind who'd cooperate about being a scapegoat. He probably would have done his damndest to paint the others as black as possible. He'd have claimed he was an innocent victim who was tempted by the rest. It's a cinch he didn't have the brains to think up that racket himself."

Thatcher's agreement was now more wholehearted. "That's true. And jail or not, they would have lost their investment. Quite a remarkable number of people will commit murder for a quarter of a million dollars."

Kenneth Nicolls emerged from some private world of his own and shook his head in dissatisfaction. But on such delicate ground, he chose his words with care.

"Even so, we know that there's one woman at that hospital who wouldn't stop at anything. And there is no doubt that Dr. Bullivant would have gone to jail if Dr. Martin had pressed charges against her. I'm surprised the police bother to look any further."

"I don't see what evidence you have that the others have an earlier sticking point," Thatcher observed. "They were running a criminal system to extort money from the sick. At least Dr. Bullivant delivered at a price that her patients understood. And delivered a service they presumably wanted."

Not for one moment was Kenneth going to admit that, because Edith Bullivant was a motherly looking woman, he was even more revolted to learn that she was coldhearted and venal.

"It is a matter of denying life," he temporized.

John Thatcher had a very fair notion of what was troubling his subordinate and, out of kindness, did not ask him to define an unnecessary hysterectomy. Instead he said:

"Dr. Bullivant's real protection would seem to be in that final phrase of yours—*'if Dr. Martin pressed charges.'* Ed Knox was sure that most doctors wouldn't. As a matter of professional ethics."

Charlie pounced.

"If anything is clear in this whole mess, it's that Wendell Martin wasn't 'most doctors.' As for medical ethics, look at the way he treated this Dr. Bauer. If Bauer's story is true."

"You doubt it?" Thatcher raised his eyebrows. "They can check with the entire Tissue Review Committee, you know."

"Oh, I'm sure the facts about the pathology reports are true. But the way he tells it, he should have been breathing fire and revenge, and Martin should have forgotten the whole thing. After all, it was a victory for Martin and an infuriating injustice for Bauer—as well as a damned good motive for murder, incidentally. But what actually happened? Martin was the one left breathing fire—he must have been, the way that wife of his is carrying on. She seems to have gotten the impression that Bauer was persecuting her husband!"

"You've already given one answer to that, Charlie," said Ken, abandoning his broodings on Dr. Bullivant's iniquities. "Wendell Martin wasn't normal. Any blow to his esteem and he went berserk. Remember what he was like on the witness stand?"

Thatcher intervened smoothly. "There is another answer. That the widow concocted the accusation out of whole cloth—in order to distract attention from herself. In a way, everyone else's motive was negative—to prevent a possible threat. But after all, she alone had a positive motive and a very substantial one at that—over a quarter of a million dollars. I can only assume she has a watertight alibi. Or the police really wouldn't be looking any further."

"You hit it right on the nail!" Charlie Trinkam laughed outright. "That's the first thing the police thought of. Paul says they were almost disappointed when they found out she was playing in a duplicate bridge tournament at the exact moment her husband was killed."

"Do they have the time down that closely?"

"Oh, yes. Not that they need it in the case of the widow. She was still at the tournament when they went to tell her about the murder. They checked back later to make sure she hadn't slipped out during the evening, but she faded as a suspect right from the start. It would have taken her almost an hour to make the round trip."

Thatcher was almost disappointed himself. It would have been a tidy, straightforward solution. And Lucille Martin had not struck him as an adoring wife, although he was the first to admit he had seen her under trying circumstances.

"It's a different kettle of fish for the people at the hospital," Charlie was continuing. "They just needed five minutes to slip out to the parking lot. And none of their stories are really supported. The ones who say they'd already left may not have left; the ones who really did leave may have come back; and the ones seen on the fourth floor at ten o'clock could always have ducked downstairs."

"The murder was at ten then?"

"They place it at ten-fifteen, give or take ten minutes. The reason they can be so precise is that they got there so soon after the killing. The call came through at ten thirty-four, and the police doctor was there by ten forty-five. On that basis, the Gentilhomme girl found the body at about ten-thirty. She must have practically tripped over the murderer."

"The Gentilhomme girl?" Thatcher sat up in sudden interest.

"Sure. The one that Paul Jackson turned inside out. You remember."

"Yes, but I had forgotten she was the one who discovered the body." Thatcher drummed his fingers idly for a moment. "When you pause to think, she has always been a central figure, hasn't she? She was the one who exposed Martin on the stand. And she was on the scene of the crime within minutes of its commission."

"And," Charlie picked up the tale neatly, "she had a fight with Martin that same day. He was threatening to have her blacklisted. The director of nursing out there is finally coming through with a lot of scuttlebut, now that she's got nothing to lose."

Thatcher was not concerned with the director of nursing's instinct for self-preservation.

"You know," he reflected, "I feel we have neglected Marie Gentilhomme."

17 Nurse's Aide

THE MEASURED silence was broken from an unexpected quarter.

"That's what I thought," said Kenneth Nicolls, "when I met her in Southport."

The two men stared at him. "You do manage to get around, Ken," said Trinkam in congratulation.

Kenneth, on the brink of a hot denial, suddenly remembered Mrs. Furness and desisted.

Thatcher fanned the air with an irritated hand. "Never mind that. Where did you meet her, and did you try questioning her at all?"

"I met her at the Perkins house. No, I didn't question her. I don't think I spoke to her at all. She's a very shy girl. I'd have to get to know her first."

For Thatcher, whose expeditions to Southport had been restricted to the Olympian locales of the Forest Glen Cemetery and the South-port Yacht Club, it was a question of Nurse Gentilhomme, a hospital employee who had tried, albeit unsuccessfully, to parry Paul Jackson's questions. To Ken, who had been among the proletariat, she was Marie, a girl refusing a beer in Nancy Perkins's kitchen.

"What I cannot understand," said Thatcher exasperatedly, "is why you didn't tell me about this when you got back."

Kenneth went onto his dignity. "I don't believe that I ever got beyond the prescription counter at Segal's Drugstore," he said, recalling full well how Thatcher had stiffened like a well-trained hunting dog at that stage of his narrative and then begun telephoning Benjamin Edes.

The beginnings of a reluctant smile dawned on Thatcher's face. He was remembering the same thing. Diplomacy was called for.

"Ah, yes. I believe I may have cut you off due to the importance of your earlier activities that evening. Let's hear what else happened."

Ken recognized the olive branch. He was only sorry that he had nothing to offer in exchange.

"I'm afraid that nothing else happened."

"Tell us anyway." Thatcher had no intention of carrying diplomacy too far. These were no doubt the exact terms in which the boy would have assessed his momentous attempt to fill a prescription with Sid Segal.

But at the end of the recital he was forced to agreement. Nothing had happened, nothing except two men drinking beer in a kitchen while a wife took an occasional companionable sip.

"I could probably arrange it so that she'll be there the next time I go out to the Perkins's," Ken offered as solace. "She might be willing to talk to me on this round."

"Are you going out to the Perkins's again?"

"Yes, Jane arranged everything with Nancy."

"Jane?" Thatcher was bewildered. "Your wife?"

If Thatcher was bewildered, Kenneth was guilty. If he had taken that face into the dock, a jury would have been ready to convict him of almost any crime in the book. Shamefaced, he shuffled his feet.

"Oh, well, when I told Jane about the Perkinses, she started to call people in Brooklyn Heights. She ended up with a station wagon load of children's clothes and toys and things like electric mixers. I'll be taking them out some time this week."

Across the room Charlie Trinkam was showing signs of undesirable jocularity.

"Admirable!" said Thatcher bracingly, determined to avoid emotional quagmires. "If the Perkinses have been put through the wringer by Southport Memorial, I can well understand how they would be hard up."

"They have bills up to the ears. On top of the original operation, they have continuing visits to the doctor, and the weekly checkup at the hospital and druggist's bills. You just wouldn't believe it!"

"I can now. Did you say something about weekly checkups at the hospital?"

Ken nodded, happy to display his expertise on the subject of the Perkins family. "Yes, she goes in one evening every week and stays overnight. They do some kind of tests on her first thing in the morning, when she's barely awake."

Thatcher dismissed the medical details. "But what night? Good heavens, she may have been there the evening of Wendell Martin's murder. Didn't you even ask her?"

"At that time," said Ken stiffly, "we were interested in Pemberton Freebody's death. That's what I asked her about."

"More fool you!" Charlie interrupted cheerfully. "Here you've got a nice, juicy murder and maybe a red-hot witness, and you let yourself be distracted by an insurance claim. What say, John? Shall we shoot him out to Southport again?"

John Thatcher knew what too many newsmagazines, public relations firms and politicians do not: the snowballing of meaningless detail does not, unfortunately, guarantee the production of truth.

Nonetheless, he nodded.

Nancy Perkins had moved the ironing board to the kitchen window in order to be able to watch the play yard as she finished up the laundry. She was so accustomed to policing juvenile disorder and so intent on spray-starching the collar of Gene's shirt that it was several moments before she identified the approaching clamor as adult in origin. That was not the lusty, uninhibited howling of a balked four-year-old; that was the convulsive sobbing of a woman.

Then the door flew open, propelled by a hearty shove from Gene Perkins's right arm. His left arm was wrapped protectively around Marie Gentilhomme; she was red-eyed and hunched over, clutching herself desperately.

Nancy stepped forward in alarm.

"What in the world . . . ?"

"Now, Nancy, nothing to worry about," said Gene. "Marie, here, is a little upset."

Nancy, very properly, ignored this fatuous statement. Instead she pulled out a chair and thrust her guest into it.

"Oh, Nancy, I'm so sorry . . . just silliness . . . thank God Gene was there . . . be all right in a minute . . ."

Marie hunted wildly for a handkerchief, looked up at the concerned face hovering over her and abandoned efforts at self-control.

"Oh-h-h-h!" she wailed, the four-year-old triumphing over the woman. Then she flung both arms on the table, laid her head on top of them and surrendered herself to an orgy of weeping.

Gene Perkins looked alarmed and tentatively patted a heaving shoulder.

"Just leave her alone, Gene, and let her have a good cry. She'll feel much better when it's all over. I'll put the kettle on so that there'll be tea when she's ready for it." Nancy Perkins suited action to word,

then took her place at the table. "And, now, suppose you tell me
what this is all about."

"I don't know exactly where to begin." In perplexity Gene rubbed
the heel of his palm over his crew cut hard enough to raise sparks. "I
was at the garage when Dr. Neverson pulled up—"

"The garage? Today isn't Sunday."

"Oh, didn't I tell you? We've got the car back! Joe found a fuel
pump for us in a Chevvy they were cannibalizing."

"Wonderful!"

For a moment the triumph threatened to distract them both. Nancy
was already planning a massive raid on the supermarket to bring back
gallons and gallons of the milk she had been hand-carrying. Gene
would at last be able to get to the dump with the pile of trash
gradually engulfing the entire yard. Marie sobbed in unabated
rhythm.

"Anyway, Joe was putting it in for me," Gene sternly returned to
the subject. "And Dr. Neverson drove up to drop off a flat he had in
the trunk. I asked him how the Jag was running since I tuned it up for
him. And we were kidding around with each other. You know, he
asked me how come I had to have a mechanic work on my car, and I
said this must be the first time he ever changed a flat himself instead
of hollering for the boys at the garage and, honest, Nancy, he seemed
perfectly normal to me! I didn't notice anything wrong with him!"

He raised puzzled eyes to look at his wife.

Nancy nodded soberly. She knew, as Gene did not, that they were
neither of them very good right now at noticing anything wrong with
people. Since Dr. Wendell Martin's successful surgery, they had both
moved in a cloud of euphoria that they were inclined to extend,
without any basis in fact, to every friend and chance-met acquaintance. Dr. Roy Neverson could have assumed a ceremonial squat,
brandished a large Japanese sword and proceeded through the preliminary ritual of hari-kari without Gene Perkins noticing a thing.

Unless, of course, Dr. Neverson had carefully explained that he
was feeling suicidal. For the first time, it occurred to Nancy that this
might well be the case. The joys of sports cars and boats must fade
pretty rapidly in the shadow of an approaching jail sentence.

"What happened?" she asked nervously.

"Well, nothing happened as long as we were alone. Like I said, we were just kidding each other. Then a car pulled in for gas. It was Alice Doyle, and she was giving Marie a lift."

"Yes?"

"Alice says hello and we say hello, and then Dr. Neverson notices Marie. So instead of saying hello, he makes some kind of crack to me about this being the little woman who started the great big war. He doesn't realize I know Marie. And you know—"

Here Gene broke off to look uneasily across the table. Marie was still weeping, though with less violence. Nevertheless he lowered his voice as if ashamed at some suggestion of disloyalty in his words.

"You know, I think everything would have been okay if Marie had kind of sassed him back. But she doesn't say anything. None of us do, and Dr. Neverson opens up again—but he doesn't sound the same at all—and he says, kind of driving her to the wall, is she satisfied with what she's done, ruining everybody at the hospital, and it's a pretty good act she's got going, pretending to be stupid when really she's spiteful, and he wouldn't be surprised if she wasn't acting for someone."

"Oh, poor Marie! How awful for her!" Nancy said with ready sympathy.

"Wait! That isn't all, not by a long shot! Before I can even budge, Alice Doyle lets loose. I tell you, you never heard anything like that woman. More like a wild animal!"

Nancy sniffed eloquently.

"Now, I know you don't like her, Nancy," Gene began.

"I never said that. I don't really know her. What I said was that she's a cheap tramp. But Marie has always said that she's a hard worker and a good nurse."

"This wasn't just being cheap. I never thought I'd hear a doctor talked to that way. Or hear a doctor talk that way." Gene had been genuinely shocked. "Because Dr. Neverson came right back at her. They're neither of them really nice, you know."

Nancy tried to understand him. She looked at Marie's bent head for inspiration.

"Bad language?" she suggested dubiously.

"That isn't what upset Marie. Although there was plenty of gutter talk." Gene shook his head.

He knew that frank speech is not unheard of in Antigonish, Nova Scotia, where Marie Gentilhomme had passed her formative years.

And even though rural colloquialisms never sound as nasty as the epithets spawned by city streets, that was not what had upset him, as well as Marie. "It was as if they hated each other, it was pure poison. I've never heard a woman sound so venomous. She said what did he mean, was Marie satisfied? Was he satisfied? Said he'd ruined the careers of people who had to sweat for a small salary. Then she called him a cheap bum who couldn't keep his greedy paws to himself even though he was making a fortune just to loaf around, him and that SOB Wittke."

"Oh, no!" breathed Nancy in horrified fascination.

"I tell you it was a real set-to. He got started on how she'd two-timed her husband so bad she couldn't even get custody of her kids, and then she called his wife a stupid bitch who'd milked him dry and then walked out and—"

"And it was simply awful, Nancy!" Marie Gentilhomme was now upright. With a last watery sniff, she apologized. "I'm sorry for crumpling all over you this way but this, on top of everything else! I don't understand what's happened to people. Nobody used to act this way!"

Nancy immediately embraced her warmly, then rushed to the teakettle. "Don't be embarrassed, Marie. These things happen. Now you tidy up and we'll all have tea."

A household which includes three small children, a host of transient children, a young woman who has passed through a serious illness and a young man rushing back and forth among countless jobs while economizing on shirts is used to the spectacle of people far removed from bandbox perfection—people in undress, as it were. Marie's disheveled hair, tear-streaked face and crumpled dress did her no disservice in the eyes of the Perkinses. And paradoxically, the woebegone smile she gave them as she rose lent her attractiveness she never achieved in the starched order of hospital uniform.

"What did you mean by 'on top of everything else'?" asked Nancy as she distributed cups five minutes later. "You mean that everybody's acting oddly?"

"No. There's that, too. But everybody is acting as if there were something odd about me."

Clearly she craved contradiction. But Nancy could only ask:

"What on earth do you mean?"

"I suppose it's Alice Doyle, mostly. She seems to be hinting all the time that there's something I haven't told the police." She searched for further illustrations. "And Gene heard Dr. Neverson hinting about the trial and saying I was spiteful. Why should I be spiteful? I was happy before the trial! Of course, I was new at the hospital and I hadn't been a nurse very long, so I was nervous a lot. But there was nothing for me to be spiteful about. Now even Mrs. Stosser and the patients don't seem to behave normally to me."

"Part of that's imagination," Nancy said with assurance. "No, let me finish. What I mean is that when one or two people are acting oddly to you, it's only natural to think other people are too, to see things that aren't there."

"Well, take it from me, one person who's really being strange is Alice Doyle." Gene Perkins's shoulders shuddered in recollection. "Whew! What a woman!"

"I've never seen her the way she was today," Marie confessed. "But that isn't what I meant. After all, she was sticking up for me. It's that terrible hinting I can't stand."

Nancy studied the salt and pepper shakers with great interest. Her eyes did not shift away from them when she spoke.

"I suppose," she said hesitantly, "I suppose you *have* told the police everything you know about Wendell Martin's murder."

"Nancy!" Marie lowered her cup indignantly. "You were there! What was there to know?"

Both Gene and Nancy were startled by the counterattack.

"Gee, honey, I'd forgotten that. You were there."

"You both were," Marie pressed home her point. "Don't you remember, Gene? You didn't leave until after I'd given Nancy her ten o'clock medication. That was the first time I was on ward duty."

Gene frowned into the past.

"I remember. You'd had some sort of fuss with Martin earlier. You were crying."

"And Nancy cheered me up." Marie smiled tremulously. "Just like today."

"It's all coming back," Gene continued. "You told me you were going to have to wait for your uncle Dominic."

Nancy suddenly moved to a cabinet drawer, from which she drew a pencil and a pad of paper. She tore off the top sheet, which said *two gallons of milk* and *peanut butter,* and announced:

"It's coming back to me, too. Let's write down every single thing that we remember. We can help each other. That way we can settle once and for all whether Marie knows anything."

Half an hour later, Nancy Perkins grounded her pencil. She had been writing steadily except for one dash to the back yard and one dash to the teakettle. She had pages of notes, for the most part representing a minute-by-minute account of the activities of a Mrs. Margolis, who had occupied the bed next to hers. But she had something else as well.

It was that which caused her husband to look accusingly across the table. "You know, Marie, you're just not curious enough, that's your trouble."

"But how could I know? And what should I do? I can't go to the police with a little thing like that."

"I don't know, Marie," Gene said doubtfully. "I think maybe you ought to."

"Well, Marie doesn't have to go to the police alone. We can go with—or, wait. I know. We can call Ken Nicolls. He'll know what to do. Maybe he can go instead."

Everyone was only too eager to lay his problem at other feet. They all had a touching confidence that a banker like Ken Nicolls would carry more weight with the police than they. Cutting off further discussion, Nancy moved to the telephone.

A young woman who is raising three children on no money, however nice at heart, must learn to develop determination in asserting her rights. It was as well that Nancy Perkins had been through her basic training. Because institutions like the Sloan Guaranty Trust employ large numbers of people for no other purpose than to suppress such phone calls.

Marie and Gene watched the back yard from the kitchen while Nancy wrestled with the phone in the hall. Every now and then a bulletin for them wafted across the small living room.

"I've got the switchboard. They want to know who I'm calling for."

Sounds of argument.

"I've got a Miss Todd. She wants me to call back later. Ken is in conference."

Sounds of argument.

"I've gotten a Miss Corsa. She's the only sensible one in the lot. She's getting him."

Sounds of conversation.

"I don't understand. Now he's having a conference about *this*."

And finally, loud and clear:

"Oh, Ken, I'm so relieved you're coming. . . . Yes, of course you can bring Mr. Thatcher with you."

At the Sloan they were just as enthusiastic.

"Well, speak of the devil!" said Charlie Trinkam in the tones of simple pleasure with which he was accustomed to receive any goodies life cared to hand him—whether beautiful women, ridiculous prospectuses, outré social events, outlandish lawsuits or simple opportunities to bait Everett Gabler. "What do you think they've got hold of?"

Ken shook his head. "I have no idea. Nancy sounded awfully solemn. But Marie Gentilhomme is with them now. We'd better go out there, right away."

"Take my car," Charlie offered. "It's at the garage."

But Thatcher shook his head. "No. We're going to Brooklyn Heights first."

"Brooklyn Heights?" Was Thatcher inviting himself to dinner, Kenneth wondered. And if so, was it meat loaf night?

Thatcher looked at him reproachfully. "Naturally we are taking that station wagon load with us." His voice became brisker. "I do not know what the Perkinses have for us, but I will offer odds on one thing."

"What's that?" Charlie was always interested when odds were being offered.

"Three to one Nancy Perkins was in the hospital the night that Martin was murdered!"

18   Quarantine

FOR DR. EDMUND KNOX, busy calling Southport to judgment, the exact day on which Nancy Perkins was accustomed to have her weekly checkup was not important. For that matter, neither was the murder of Wendell Martin. Gripped by an almost biblical fervor, Knox could have watched the annihilation of Southport Memorial's entire staff with no reaction other than a few appropriate references to Sodom and Gomorrah. He was not, however, averse to using that murder to further his own ends.

Dr. Knox had reached a decision in Thatcher's office that he was determined to implement with all the vigor of outraged morality. His methods might lack orthodoxy, but they were grounded in hard-headed realism and unyielding tenacity. Accordingly, as soon as he realized—or was brought to realize—that the success of his campaign could serve other interests and hence command other support, he became an enthusiastic adherent of certain plans advanced by John Putnam Thatcher and Lieutenant Joseph Perenna.

They could not have chosen a better ally. Edmund Knox was a man whose life had brought him into contact with large institutions. He knew all about universities, insurance companies, foundations, banks and medical associations—their power, their inertia, their dislike of trouble, their vulnerability to public outcry. He knew it was hard to make them move and, once they were moving, hard to make them stop. Long ago, he had learned to do both. Within a surprisingly short time, he demonstrated his skill. Fulminating his way the length of Manhattan, he prodded, cajoled, goaded, persuaded and bullied a good cross section of these institutions into agreement with his program.

His hand with individuals was just as sure. When his bristling eyebrows and ringing denunciations burst into a freshly outfitted examining room in Garden City, an emotional compound of gratitude, awe and sheer fright effectively reduced Harley Bauer to an extension of Dr. Knox's will. Stammering with excitement the young pathologist promised full cooperation. Even when it developed that this cooperation was expected to range over some rather surprising territory—which no stretch of the imagination could place within Dr. Knox's province—Harley Bauer was not inclined to cavil.

Edmund Knox's public platform was simplicity itself. He was going to lower the boom on Southport Memorial Hospital.

Present at the boom-lowering were representatives of the American College of Surgeons, Atlantic Mutual Insurance, the Sloan Guaranty Trust and various medical societies. Representatives of the New York State Police hovered, unseen, in the wings. Edmund Knox had shed his worldly affiliations for the occasion. If he was representing anything, it was some powerful abstraction—Justice or Nemesis.

It was certainly a more satisfactory role than that being enacted by the bewildered group in the center of the room, eleven local dignitaries who composed the Board of Trustees of Southport Memorial, and into whose collective lap the whole mess had been deposited. Ordinarily they, together with the absent twelfth trustee, worried about the selection of architects for new wings, the ever-present threat of unionization of non-skilled workers, and fund-raising, fund-raising, fund-raising. Service on the Board was a symbol of achievement, a sign of esteem from the burghers of Suffolk County and an acknowledged form of civic participation. It had nothing to do with knowing about hospitals. The doctors ran the hospital and, to do them justice, until now they had shouldered the blame for any failures in its performance.

"So, what does it have to do with us?" one Board member asked querulously.

Dr. Knox was ready with a stern answer.

"You," he said, "have been responsible for persuading the community to ante up some fourteen or fifteen million dollars' worth of plant and equipment. This investment is placed at the disposal of doctors for the practice of their profession, but it remains the property of the community. It is the responsibility of you, the chosen overseers, to ensure that this loan is used for the benefit of the community, rather than the personal enrichment of the doctors. Failure to fulfill that responsibility constitutes a breach of trust on your part which, in its negligence, is almost as reprehensible as these acts of overt venality. Your laxity has permitted theft! Your sloth has invited greed!"

Not surprisingly, the Board member collapsed. Thatcher noted, with alarm, that Edmund Knox's speech was beginning to assume the stately King James cadence of his favorite reading. Before coming out to Long Island, the outsiders had decided among themselves that a touch of Knox in this mood would help bring the Board to its knees. But Thatcher hoped Knox was not going to discharge the full load of his displeasure on the heads of these poor unfortunates, who had thought it sufficient to gather together the millions and lay them at the feet of Dr. Wittke and company. Happily, it was now only a matter of harsh words. The real grapeshot was being reserved for the truants; there the Board would have its innings. Everyone had agreed that it would be wiser if Knox and the delinquent doctors did not meet while Knox was still being an Old Testament prophet. Thatcher realized he was weakling enough to be grateful that he would not have to enter the staff room at Southport Memorial Hospital on the heels of a man declaiming: *Woe to them that devise iniquity!*

One lone trustee remained mutinous.

"I don't see what you expect us to do."

In more explicit detail than was kind, Dr. Knox told him. No one was misguided enough to leave the situation in their hands. They were not expected to do or to decide anything. All necessary action would be undertaken by those untainted with the stigma of irresponsibility. The Board's sole task was to communicate decisions already arrived at. That way, there would be no possibility of error. Failure was unthinkable. The Augean stables were about to be transformed into a model barnyard.

The solitary standout had stamina, if not intelligence.

"And anyway, what do those people have to do with this?" A heated nod toward the corner indicated the assembled financial interests.

"They," explained Dr. Knox, mimicking the gesture savagely, "are capable of ruining Southport Memorial Hospital with accumulated financial liabilities."

A brittle cough from Dexter Loomis resounded.

"If I may?" he said with meticulous courtesy. "Atlantic Mutual finds itself in a position where it cannot continue with a defense against the claim of the Freebody estate. This is entirely due to the fact that the medical staff of this hospital can no longer be viewed as responsible professional witnesses. There is no reason why Atlantic should shoulder the financial burdens created by this situation.

Particularly when we don't have to! We are prepared to bring suit against the hospital to recover our losses. Furthermore—"

"No!" quivered one of the trustees. "If you have a malpractice claim, you pursue it against the individual doctor."

"Not," Dr. Knox intoned levelly, *"not* where there has been a concerted policy by the hospital authorities to cover up, condone and permit further professional misconduct. Failing cooperation by the Board, the insurance companies here represented—who include the writers of the hospital's liability insurance—can subpoena Dr. Bauer's records as staff pathologist and bring to light cases of unnecessary surgery as well as actions open to criminal prosecution."

"What's he talking about?" wailed the innocent trustee.

Two of his colleagues, better informed, whispered hasty explanations.

"Oh my God!" It was a cry from the heart. "That's been going on *here?* Why didn't somebody tell me? We've got to make some settlement and destroy those records."

"On the contrary!" thundered Isaiah in a voice of doom. "Those records are a vital part of the compromise which has been agreed upon. They will be made available to an independent review committee. All offenders will have their association with this hospital terminated immediately. Flagrant offenders will be disciplined by the medical association. The same action will be taken with respect to everyone found guilty in connection with the drug conspiracy. New appointments will be made to the staff from outsiders. This decision will be communicated to the present staff. At once!"

"And who's supposed to tell them?"

For the first time, a hint of humor appeared in Dr. Knox.

"Well, that's the function of the Board of Trustees."

The subsequent meeting between the trustees of Southport Memorial Hospital and the medical staff adjourned in an uproar. The trustees were bent on simple escape. The other participants eddied into the corridors, the lounges and the cafeteria. According to temperament, they were prey to despair, bewilderment or cold fury. The news roared through the hospital like a forest fire.

"This is the end," said Roy Neverson flatly. He was looking into a long, bleak future.

"I don't understand," Dr. Philip Wittke repeated for the fifth time. "How can they do this to me?"

Edith Bullivant's plump good nature had congealed. "If I go down," she threatened, "I will take everyone of these goddamned bastards with me."

"This is very interesting, no?" commented Dr. Kroner as he and a young resident watched the havoc around them. "My wife, she will have much to say when I tell her."

"I've already said I'll do it, Dr. Knox." Harley Bauer was very nervous in the abandoned office. "They should all be down in the cafeteria in another half hour."

This was not the only exchange aimed at the immediate future.

"Marie, you've got to be very careful." Alice Doyle bent the full weight of her personality on the girl. "One false move and everything could be ruined."

Harley Bauer's estimate had been quite accurate. It had taken half an hour for the truth to penetrate. There was no longer any room for maneuver. The support of colleagues, whether obtained by blackmail or friendship, was no longer an impenetrable defense. Little caucuses broke up. Now, at Southport Memorial, it was every man for himself. But still, misery loves company. They started to drift downstairs, one by one, hoping to submerge themselves in common plaint.

Roy Neverson even roused himself to explain to Philip Wittke the full extent of their predicament, taking a twisted satisfaction as he saw a lifetime's complacency crumbling under the first onslaught of despair.

"There's no point in thinking you can wriggle out of it, Phil. They're going to pin us up like a couple of specimen butterflies. It doesn't make any difference how many important friends you had yesterday. You're not going to have them tomorrow."

"But why? Why?" demanded his senior. "Martin was chief of surgery. It's not our fault what he did. We don't know anything about obstetrics. None of that was our fault!"

"They're out to get us, and they're going to. Just like this." Neverson drew a forefinger across his throat with macabre humor. "And to think that it all started with Martin making a fool of himself in court."

"But that had nothing to do with this!"

Neverson was blunt. "You're behind the times, Phil. Nobody's separating things any more. All they see is one big cesspool. They didn't like the way Wendell was so sloppy with old Freebody. They didn't like the way the staff around here was operating. They didn't like what was going on in Obstetrics. No more rope is being given to anybody at Southport. Particularly, anybody at the top. They figure, this big a cesspool, we should have noticed."

Wittke shook his head with a stubborn, angry movement. Despair was beginning to make way for anger. The emotions of an innocent victim sustained him. After all, he had made a life's work of holding his nose. How could he be expected to notice a cesspool? On oath, he would have had no hesitation in saying he never noticed the Hyland Drug Company. He had been content to draw his eleven percent and leave the details to others. He intended to make that very clear at his trial. Now, he was searching for some focus for his anger. He narrowed his eyes as Dr. Edith Bullivant approached their table.

"I hope you're satisfied, Edith," he lashed out suddenly. "You've managed to ruin a life's work."

"I don't know what you're talking about," said the lady with open contempt. "I doubt if you do."

A red flush mounted Wittke's neck and face. This was not the tone he was used to on the grounds of Southport Memorial. In fact, it had been a long time since he had heard it anywhere.

"You know perfectly well. I should have listened to Wendell and cut you off the day he asked me to."

"Even now, you don't know where you made your mistakes," she retorted. "You should have listened to Bauer and gotten rid of Martin last winter. Then none of us would be in this mess."

"You've always wanted to get rid of Martin, haven't you, Edith?" asked Neverson quietly. "You knew he wouldn't rest as long as you were running your little racket upstairs."

"If Wendell was really against it, he was the only one," she shot back. "I never noticed that it bothered the rest of you one single bit."

Wittke sucked in his breath sharply. "What do you mean?" he demanded. "If, for one moment, I had thought that Bauer's work had any substance, I would not have tolerated the situation."

Dr. Bullivant laughed unpleasantly. "What you mean is that you didn't dare stir up trouble about Martin's work. Wendell Martin was never in any position to preach morality. And, let me remind you, neither are you. At the moment I'm the only one sitting at this table who isn't under a criminal indictment."

"That is entirely different, it's only—"

Their voices had grown louder until they were drawing attention from other tables. Marie Gentilhomme and Alice Doyle, a bare three feet away, had abandoned any pretense of conversation. But the muted hum from the further reaches of the room had provided some cover. Suddenly there was dead silence in the cafeteria. Philip Wittke abandoned his protest to stare at the door in disbelief. Roy Neverson turned to look over his shoulder at the cause of the sudden silence.

Harley Bauer was framed in the doorway. He stood for a moment, accepting the dislike, surprise, hostility or speculation in all the faces confronting him. Then he walked quietly toward the coffee urn and drew a cup.

Roy Neverson's quiet voice commanded the room.

"Well, our little collaborator has returned to the fold. You sure picked a great way to get back at us, Harley!"

Solid dignity settled over Bauer's short, round figure. Feet firmly planted, he replied as quietly:

"My collaboration consisted of pointing out the file cabinet where I kept my records and handing over the keys. I don't know what choice you think I had, Roy."

"Handing the key over and giving the learned Dr. Knox an earful, I'll bet," Neverson leaned forward to taunt.

Harley carried his cup of coffee over and set it down firmly. "No, Roy. It wasn't Dr. Knox who wanted my records. It was the police."

Dr. Edith Bullivant went white.

"What were you saying about criminal indictments, Edith?" asked Neverson with malicious satisfaction. "It looks as if you'll be joining our happy throng."

But again Harley intervened.

"I don't think it was that," he said to Dr. Bullivant. "It was the lieutenant who's been asking questions about Wendell Martin's murder. He seemed to think the records would help him with the motive for the murder."

The quality of the silence in the room had changed. Before, it had been a listening silence, curious, intent, but somehow companionable. Now it was the silence of fear, withdrawn and isolated, as each

The statement was made with hypnotic force, the kind of force which was usually very effective with Marie. But the young nurse, lost in some private calculations of her own, was blind to these evidences of coming trouble.

"No," she said shaking her head, "it couldn't have been. I remember very clearly. I'd called Dr. Neverson and I'd already given Mrs. Perkins her medication, so it must have been almost ten-fifteen. That's when Mrs. Perkins is always scheduled for."

The frown cleared as she settled matters to her own satisfaction and looked up, only to meet the blazing fury in Edith Bullivant's face. The twinkling blue eyes had turned into granite chips.

"It's your word against mine!" the doctor spat. "You're covering up something! You weren't with Mrs. Perkins at ten-thirty! And you were right on the spot when it came to finding Wendell Martin's body!"

Marie's face crumpled.

"Oh, no!" she gasped before raising her hands to hide the welling tears.

Philip Wittke viewed the spectacle with distaste. But the opportunity was not lost on him.

"What makes you think your word is going to be so good, Edith?" he asked, sloughing off the professional veneer long since abandoned by everyone else "Do you think the police aren't going to be very interested to hear that you tried to fake an early departure from the hospital? No one can prove that Segal and I weren't together until a few minutes before the discovery of the body. But you seem to have been floating around with an hour to spare. And don't think they're not going to hear about it! I, for one, am through with all attempts to protect you any more. The time has come for things to be cleared up!"

As Dr. Wittke strode masterfully from the cafeteria, he was followed by many eyes.

But one pair of eyes remained fixed on the bent head of Marie Gentilhomme.

person wrapped his defenses about him and eyed his neighbor speculatively.

Curiously, Edith Bullivant recovered first.

"Motive," she said softly. "Of course, they've already been working on opportunity. They know who was here late that night."

She looked challengingly at Philip Wittke.

"Being here has nothing to do with it," he said instantly. His words tumbled out. "I was here, myself, but I was with Sid Segal. I was with him until they paged me after finding the body."

He looked around at the circle of aloof, suspicious faces.

"They only have to ask Segal! He'll tell them!"

"You're not very well informed, Philip," said Edith Bullivant coldly. "We all know Sid Segal would say anything to give himself an alibi. But they asked the girl at the desk, too. She said that Segal had been with her for ten minutes when they started paging you. And that Nurse Doyle had stopped to chat also."

Heads swiveled automatically to the nurses' table. The unspoken question hovered in the air.

Alice Doyle spoke hesitantly, choosing her words with care.

"Yes, I was at the desk when they started paging Dr. Wittke. And Sid Segal was there, too. But I don't know how long he'd been there. Probably the girl at the desk doesn't know either. She'd have to guess. Five minutes, ten minutes, how could she tell?"

It was very well done. The statement contradicted no one, made trouble for no one, left everybody an escape hatch. It was the cautious product of Alice Doyle's training.

But Dr. Bullivant had thrown caution to the winds. She was bent on triumph.

"The girl at the desk has to note times constantly. She is very accurate. She was able to tell the police that I left at nine-thirty to the dot."

"I'm sure she was, Doctor," said Alice Doyle diplomatically. She would have been happy to retreat into the anonymous audience.

But Marie Gentilhomme, a frown of concentration wrinkling her brow, kept the limelight on their table.

"But that was before you came back, Doctor," she said with earnest helpfulness. "Before you met me in the fourth floor ward."

"You've got it all wrong," snapped Dr. Bullivant. "As usual. I saw you before I left at nine-thirty."

19   *Antibodies*

NIGHTFALL transforms buildings. The towering skyscraper that vibrates to comings and goings from nine to five becomes a cold, silent sentinel; the school that is exuberant with youth is a chill shell, forbidding and forlorn, in the small hours of night.

Even buildings not abandoned by humanity have a special night presence different from their solid daytime substance. Wartime always brings the discovery that, in factories running round the clock, the odd, inexplicable or antic invariably occurs during the third shift, from eleven o'clock to seven in the morning. Psychologists search for evidence that night-shift workers differ from their daytime brothers. They do not understand that buildings by night (like nocturnal animals) absorb some of the icy madness of the moon. Alone, they shudder. Occupied, they infect.

Southport Memorial Hospital was set back in a small park, its outer limits lost in darkness. Forsythia tendrils waved in a soft, insistent breeze, snaking shadows over the walk; in the parking lot, the spotlights trembled slightly as the wind rose.

"Storm coming up," said Gene Perkins, grasping Nancy's arm.

"We need the rain," she replied, comforted by his warmth.

Yet their anxiety communicated more powerfully than words, and instinctively they moved closer together. Gene slipped an arm around his wife's waist. They continued up the walk.

"Just think," said Gene Perkins. "This is the last time, Nancy!"

"It's wonderful," she agreed.

He tightened his grip on her overnight case. They knew they must behave naturally.

It was only eight o'clock; to the west, lingering pink streamers trailed the setting sun. Yet already it was clear that tonight was going to be dark, with an inky clear sky studded by distant stars.

At the hospital, lights were already lit, still registering yellow against the curiously yellowed sky. Although the Perkinses knew that Southport Memorial was almost as busy by night as by day, they felt the chill of desolation.

"I'll be here to pick you up tomorrow," said Gene Perkins.

Nancy too had paused, staring ahead with wide eyes. Now she turned to look at her husband.

"But you've got to go to work."

They were under the old-fashioned portico. Gene Perkins spoke more loudly than necessary.

"When my wife comes out of the hospital for the last time, I'm going to be there to meet her!"

"Oh, Gene!"

"Honey!"

She buried her face in his shoulder, then they turned to hurry inside.

Within minutes, Nancy Perkins was in a routine as familiar to her as her own household chores. Yet this familiarity was still miles removed from her home and her life; as always, it was remote and uninviting at first. Only after hours or days in a hospital does its reality obliterate the outside world.

They walked past the waiting room in which only two small lamps glowed inadequately against the darkness. At the reception desk, Nancy was greeted like an old friend.

"You're up in 4C again, Nancy."

Even Dr. Philip Wittke turned aside from his conversation with Sid Segal to smile at her.

"The last time, isn't it, Mrs. Perkins?" he rumbled.

"Yes, yes it is."

"Splendid," he said before turning back to bend his head toward the little druggist.

Nancy Perkins stood on tiptoe to peck a swift kiss at Gene's chin, then slipped the night case from his hand. "Good night, dear . . . Oh, I forgot!"

"Forgot what?"

"My teeth things. We were going to stop and pick some up. Well, I'll just have to do without." She smiled ruefully at the receptionist. "You wouldn't think I could still forget things, would you, Grace?"

Gene Perkins was determined that Nancy's discomforts tonight would not include any that he could prevent. Even a little thing like a toothbrush could loom large under some circumstances.

"I'll pick them up for you, honey. But it'll have to wait until I've gone to the laundromat. Will that be too late?"

"No, that's fine. Marie Gentilhomme will come down for them, I know she will."

"Good." Gene turned with his usual friendly grin to the desk. "I'll leave them with you, Grace, right?"

"Sure. You can leave them in the office. Marie won't be able to come down until the ward's settled in."

Gene nodded, squeezed Nancy's elbow and threaded his way to the door. Wittke and Segal were still busy with each other. A white-faced man huddled in a corner looked up incuriously, then back at his shoes. Nancy Perkins shot him a sympathetic look, then glanced at Grace, who shook her head unobtrusively. They were, they both knew, intruding.

By day, this would not be true. By day, the controlled rustle, the muted footfall, the careful voice of nurse, doctor, visitor, even patient, attest to the demands that illness makes upon life, but conversely they are at once encouraging and soothing, a reminder that life itself, like light and sound, is a powerful primal force.

But by night when vitality is lowered, light and sound are the enemy sapping precious strength. So the quiet is made more quiet, and night lowers the lights, creating shadowy hallways outside rooms where pain and anxiety hold sway. And even sleep, the natural refuge, is suspect. In a hospital, sleep too often indicates not strengthening but the end of resistance. The homely, familiar figures performing welcome chores during the day become furtive intruders at night; terrors held at bay emerge to haunt hospital beds. At night, everyone is alone in a hospital, alone and surrounded by enemies curtained from them only by silence and darkness.

The uneasiness brought by night affects the staff as well as the patients. Night is the easier duty for a nurse in the wards; there are no doctors to visit, correct, blame. There are fewer errands to be run and no distracting visitors to disrupt routine. Yet nurses accustomed to day duty do not like night assignments. They rationalize this by explaining that night emergencies are more demanding, that responsibility is heavier. But they too feel what the patients feel; night is a foretaste of death.

On four, Marie Gentilhomme was sitting at the desk facing the long corridor, bent over some reports, the paper rustling under her fingers as she wrote.

She rose as Nancy Perkins emerged from the elevator and approached.

"Hello, Nancy. This is the last time."

Nancy greeted her. "No," she said when Marie moved to help her with her overnight case. "I know my way."

"Fine," said Marie. "Now, don't stay up too late. Just half an hour . . ."

She was referring to the muted sounds of activity at the far end of the corridor, the patients' lounge. This was a tattered porch-like room filled with wicker furniture, piles of torn copies of *Life* and ashtrays. It was shabby and depressing, yet on the floor it was important. Patients well enough to walk were allowed to visit the patients' lounge to vary the tedium of their days: nurses, doctors, visitors were forbidden. Here, in a strange array of wraps and peignoirs, women with hair carelessly held back by ribbons, with faces naked and plucked without cosmetics, created something fleetingly like the cheerful intimacy of a girls' school. Their talk, inevitably, was of illness, of operations, of doctors, of nurses. Yet there was a certain camaraderie built up by being part of a group, a reminder of what it is to be a human being, not a case. People came and people went, in the patients' lounge, but there was always an authority who knew the ins and outs and advised others; there was always a shy and frightened little mouse; there was always an enigma—a woman who was neither married nor the mother of three children. Despite slow, pain-wracked gaits, hands pressed to sides, eyes bright with fear, the patients' lounge was a haven.

But not tonight. When Nancy Perkins changed into her night attire, put her case in the small closet and slipped down the hall, she found several acquaintances and a newcomer. The newcomer, a brittle, middle-aged woman scheduled for an operation day after tomorrow, was nervous to the point of hysteria and trying desperately to hide it. The other women, who would have been happy to offer unlimited sympathy, could not cope with edgy gaiety. And it was no surprise therefore, that within fifteen minutes, people began drifting to their own beds.

By a quarter to nine, Marie Gentilhomme, looking in to urge her charges to retire, found the patients' lounge deserted. The heaping ashtrays, the neglected pots of ivy, the scattered magazines were no concern of hers—a scrubwoman would make a pass at them early in the morning. Nevertheless, before switching off the light, she walked in, piled the magazines into a semblance of order, plumped a sagging pillow and assembled the ashtrays. Wrinkling her nose slightly at the acrid tobacco aroma that soaked the room, she turned off the light, walked back to her desk, checking right and left as she passed. Most night lamps were already out.

The ward was settling down. Outside, the summer night was just setting and in roadside steakhouses, young couples were finishing their drinks and getting ready to order. But here, in the inner time of the hospital, dinner was long past—served and cleared by four-thirty. Tomorrow would begin by three-thirty in the morning.

Nurse Gentilhomme was at her desk when somebody stopped beside her.

Startled, she looked up. "Oh, it's you!"

"Did I frighten you?"

The voice was hard.

"N-no. But I didn't hear you."

Alice Doyle stood just outside the circlet of light, but the reflection from papers on the desk etched bleak shadows along the bony ridges of her cheeks and forehead, undoing the soft camouflage of cosmetics. It was a harsh and strong death's head beneath yellow hair that looked down on Marie.

"You won't forget what I told you?"

She spoke in her normal hospital voice, low, non-carrying, yet not a whisper.

Marie Gentilhomme reached nervously for the glass of water kept on her desk. After sipping thirstily, she said, "No, Alice, I won't."

With a long last look, Alice Doyle moved away. A moment later, the brief click, then the pneumatic whisper told Marie that she had taken the elevator.

Or had she?

Thirstily, Marie finished the water, then looked over her shoulder. The elevator ranks were around the corner. For all she knew, Alice could be standing in the far corner, waiting. Determinedly, Marie rose and went to refill the water carafe. The thought showed how nervous she was. The next thing you knew, she reflected, letting the water in the small sink in the ladies' room run, she would be getting strange feelings that she was not alone.

Which, in a hospital, was well-nigh madness. Here, within sound of her voice were thirty patients. On other floors, even on this floor, nurses were on errands, an occasional doctor was still checking a patient. Down in Emergency, there might be a great crowd of people. Through the silence, there were gentle stirrings—and elevators moved, people climbed the stairs beyond the fire door, doors opened and shut.

At nine-thirty, elevator doors again whispered. Marie looked up.

She had been wrong in thinking that Alice Doyle had not left the floor. Because here she was, coming from upstairs, deep in conversation—with Dr. Roy Neverson. Exactly as if that scene at the garage had never taken place, exactly as if they were doctor and nurse, conferring about a patient. What could draw them together after that shattering explosion of hatred? Inwardly Marie marveled at the brazenness of it. In spite of herself she strained to overhear their words. That would never do, she told herself severely. She had other things to think about. The empty water glass came into her hand automatically. Irritatedly, she slapped it down on the desk.

There was a thread of tension running through the ward tonight, and there was no denying it. Uneasy tremors disturbed the calm of darkness. Of course, the patients were not comfortable. It was the hysterical woman who had done that. She was one of Dr. Bullivant's patients.

But it was more than patients. Southport Memorial Hospital itself was wounded. And the wound throbbed.

"Marie?"

It was Nancy Perkins standing by her desk. She too had noticed the unlikely camaraderie between Nurse Doyle and Dr. Neverson, but she did not comment.

"I'm sorry. I forgot to tell you. Gene is leaving some things in the office for me. Could I get them?"

She had not mastered the hospital tone of voice. First whispering, then speaking so loudly it seemed that her words, echoing down the hallway, must waken the sleeping.

"Oh, no, Nancy. I couldn't let you."

Marie Gentilhomme was affected by Nancy's nervousness. Her own voice was louder than usual.

The wind outside slapped a branch against a loose pane somewhere. Nancy persisted.

"But Gene went specially to get them."

Marie looked up the corridor. "I'll run down as soon as I have a minute. Don't worry."

The wind must have risen. Now the old building was loosing long, low moans. Nancy Perkins's eyes blazed with intensity. But all she said was:

"No. No, of course, I won't."

Ten minutes later, Marie stood at the elevator. She had brought Mrs. Ohlmann a carafe of water, calmed Mrs. Palfrey's fears caused by the gurgling of the pipes and checked the patients' lounge for open windows. The ward was peaceful. There was no one about and nothing more to be done. She could slip away.

The murderer, too, had just started downstairs. It had been hard waiting for the time to pass, waiting for the right moment.

But it was hardest of all for Gene Perkins, who had delivered his package and then, under orders, had proceeded to act as he had acted on every other checkup night. But this was not an ordinary night, and every move he made was a violation of his love and loyalty. Reluctantly he walked to his car under the swaying trees, while his lips moved soundlessly over the same words, again and again, as if he were telling his rosary.

"I got her into this. I shouldn't just be driving away like this. What if something happens to her? . . . I got her into this."

But in the midst of his despair he remained obedient and did what he had said he would do. He started to thread his way along the obscure shortcut which would bring him home ten minutes earlier. As if he wanted to be home earlier tonight! Dutifully he pulled his car away from the hospital, drove two blocks along the main street, and then turned right into the alley which would allow him to cut over and miss two red lights.

"I got her into this," he thought desolately and his eyes stared unseeingly at the beer cans and broken glass in the gutter, at the blank warehouse walls looming overhead, at the solitary parked car. "If anything happens," he concluded, "it will all be my fault."

The elevator responded to Marie's call and now the door opened. For a moment, the bright garish light in the elevator made her blink. She stepped in, punched the ground floor button but, as usual, other commands supervened. The elevator started to rise.

At six, it halted and the doors slid open.

"Dr. Kroner," gasped Marie as the small man joined her.

"Ah, Miss Gentilhomme," he said sadly, stepping beside her in the elevator large enough to accommodate a stretcher. "So I kidnap you, true?"

The doors clanged shut.

"Ach, these elevators! They are all wrong. But they are not the only things wrong here, now, am I right?"

The penetrating look was at variance with the melancholy of his voice. He was asking something. But what?

Marie was incapable of reply. Perhaps Dr. Kroner expected none. He continued his gentle murmuring.

"Something drastic must be done! Like the cancer—the evil must be cut out! Yes, cut out! Or else . . . ."

They bumped gently to a halt.

"So, here we are!"

With an unhappy smile, Kroner stepped out on the ground floor and disappeared.

Everybody was behaving strangely, Marie thought, licking suddenly dry lips. Even Dr. Kroner. She liked Dr. Kroner, she reminded herself. *She liked him.*

With a shiver, she marched up to the reception desk, now manned only by the switchboard operator. In the waiting room, she noticed, the white-faced man was slumped in the corner. He seemed to be asleep. But he was no longer alone.

Edith Bullivant stood, as if halted involuntarily by an expectant father demanding something from her. Her head remained reassuringly inclined toward him. But, even though she did not change her attitude by as much as a centimeter, her eyes moved in a slow, horizontal sweep so that for a moment Marie caught the full impact of that flat, hostile stare.

Until the revelations in the cafeteria, Dr. Edith Bullivant had had all the protection of a plausible alibi corroborated by her husband. Marie shuddered and was glad when the doctor shook off a restraining hand and stumped away.

"No, nobody's left anything here," the girl replied to Marie's query.

Marie's nerves were again playing tricks. The switchboard girl was speaking too loudly, too distinctly.

"But say," the girl continued, "that little fellow with the red hair was here about twenty minutes ago, just before Grace left. I think she told him to put it in the office . . ."

Wearily, Marie Gentilhomme turned past the desk to the administrative offices that adjoined. Here were the offices of Dr. Wittke, the dietician and the Board of Trustees. However, in the language of the switchboard, "the office" meant the treasurer's office, the long green room with six wooden desks, endless rows of battered filing cabinets and three calculating machines. Here was where the admission records were maintained. It was the last office in the block.

The murderer was already in that block.

Dr. Wittke's office was the first, and light showed through the frosted glass panel. These were hard times for Philip Wittke, and he had been cleaning out his desk today. All the nurses knew that he was staying late tonight. He had explained that he still had "one or two things to take care of."

Marie passed on, turning the corner, into a deserted corridor. Her rubber-soled shoes squeaked slightly on the linoleum floor as she went by two empty, darkened offices. Squeak . . . squeak . . . squeak.

Her rubber-soled shoes, or someone else's? Firmly she thrust back the terror rising to choke her, firmly she refused to vary her slow, steady stride. It would be so easy, by a sudden discontinuity, to test whether other footsteps were synchronizing with her own. Then she came to the treasurer's door. It was closed.

She knew what lay behind that door—the three orderly rows of desks, the angled lamps ready to spotlight typewriters and checkwriters. At the far end of the room were two closets, each big enough to conceal the largest of men. Better not to think of that.

She put her hand on the doorknob, then hesitantly turned her hand slightly. Nothing happened. Her moist hand simply slid around the cold brass. Nerving herself, she clutched tightly and twisted hard, all in one convulsive motion. The door opened swiftly—to disclose an empty room.

The room was not dark, although the overhead light was off. One desk lamp was lit, spotlighting the desk farthest from the door and leaving the rest of the room in shadow. The desk top was clear except for two items. Precisely in the middle of the pool of brilliant illumination lay a green toothbrush in a transparent container and a small tube of toothpaste. Two homey, domestic objects floodlighted as if they were part of a stage set, almost festive in their simple colors. They seemed to beckon to her invitingly.

Temptingly . . . luringly.

Marie hesitated on the threshold for only a moment. Then she forced herself to go forward while the silent, oppressive air around her seemed to shriek at deafening volume: "This is a trap! This is a trap!"

She could feel the blood pounding at her temples. Her ears were blanked out by an inchoate thundering. She must move now, another minute and she would not be able to.

She had almost reached the desk when, behind her, the door clicked shut.

She wheeled about.

He was standing with his back to the door, a dim blurred figure, darker than the surrounding shadow. The outline of his hunched shoulders was feral with menace, the long narrow object trailing from one hand hinted of crushed bone and welling blood.

Terrified, Marie shrank back, gaping at him.

"I don't want to do this," he said in cracked tones that sounded horribly sincere. As if all the insincerities had been burned away by the anticipation of violence. This time he would not have the emotional insulation of a blow delivered in hot blood, out of an unthinking rage. Now he *had* to think; it was the only defense left to him, to think quickly enough to remove all danger. There was danger all around him. "You know too much. I have to do it," he concluded in a lost, lonely voice.

The voice was a revelation. "Why he's lonely!" Marie thought wildly. "That's what murder does to you. We're two lonely people trying to destroy each other."

And then he started to advance, his body well under control even if his voice was not, so that he moved with his familiar lithe silence.

Marie gave an inarticulate moan and scurried behind the desk to stand at bay, back to the closets, with no further retreat possible.

He raised his right arm as he came forward, and the light caught the metal as it arced into the range of the lamp. But Marie did not see this. With one last shudder, she pitched forward on her face before he could reach her.

The two closet doors burst open; the rush of trampling feet sounded in the corridor.

As the overhead lights snapped on, Lieutenant Joseph Perenna was the first man to brush by her recumbent form.

"Okay, Doctor! The fun's over!" he said as he wrested the tire iron from Roy Neverson's unresisting hand. "Hey, Sammy!"

The white-faced man from the waiting room entered.

"Him? Well, what do you know? Okay, Joe. Take him away!"

Blue-coated figures removed Neverson, now dazed and trembling.

"That leaves this poor kid," said Sammy, indicating Marie Gentilhomme, still unconscious.

Lietuenant Perenna was in good spirits. "What better place for it?" Opening his mouth wide, he loosed a booming, unhospital-like bellow:

"DOCTOR! GET A DOCTOR!"

20   *Witch Doctor?*

THE ROOM rang with the buzz of voices, the clinking of glasses, the flaring of matches. Theoretically, it was the formal reception to commemorate the opening of the Freebody wing of the Institute for Cancer Research. Actually it was Edmund Knox's song of triumph. He had crushed his enemies—and brought home the bacon. In consequence, the proceedings were more exultant than is the custom with institutionally sponsored events.

"Glad to hear the girl's all right," said Benjamin Edes, surveying the room with lively curiosity. "Out of the hospital, isn't she?"

"Oh, yes," Thatcher assured him. "She wasn't really hurt. It was more a matter of accumulated nervous strain, than that rap on the head when she fell. And a week of cosseting from the Perkinses and Alice Doyle has taken care of that."

Edes nodded. By now the characters in the final act of the Southport drama were familiar to him, as they were to every newspaper reader.

"I never have figured out what she was supposed to know, why Neverson thought he had to kill her. Though from what I can see, he must have been damn near crazy by that time."

"An accurate assessment, I would say." Thatcher remembered Joseph Perenna's description of Roy Neverson in jail, resigned, half-stupefied, refusing to see his mother. "He had just learned that Marie Gentilhomme could blast his alibi into smithereens! The scene in the cafeteria sent him into a tailspin. Of course, it upset quite a few people. That's what it was designed to do."

Edes inspected him shrewdly. "Telling me you were surprised it turned out to be Neverson? That you didn't know until the end?"

"Oh no. Neverson was the obvious suspect all along, on the basis of motive. He was, I agree, half-crazy. But to suspect anyone else, you had to postulate a complete lunatic!"

"I suppose you mean that drug company we dug up."

Benjamin Edes's brief career as a detective had gone to his head like May wine. Thatcher had a strong suspicion that the Southport banker now spent his idle moments plowing through his clients' accounts in the hopes of bringing to light further conspiracies that had left their trail, like the slime of an earthworm, across the prim statements of debits and credits. And if that hospital were any reflection of the community, God only knew what he would come up with! He might soon be running an operation second only to J. Edgar Hoover's.

"Naturally I mean the drug company. After all, whatever threat Wendell Martin might have posed for Edith Bullivant and Harley Bauer was not being perceptibly increased by his performance in the Atlantic Mutual trial. If Martin planned to discredit Dr. Bullivant, the only effect of the trial would be to distract him. She might reasonably assume that he would have plenty of other things to occupy his mind. But every additional hour he was on the witness stand made exposure of Hyland Drug more likely. It would be too much of a coincidence to suppose that someone else, for an entirely different reason, stepped in at just that moment to solve the problem for Wittke and Segal and Neverson."

"But that's just it. Narrowing it down to the drug racket didn't narrow it down to Roy Neverson. The whole bunch of them were in it up to their necks." Edes, warming to the story, gestured for another drink with the same lordly assurance he employed in Southport, and got the same deferential service. Whatever else the years had done for him, they had taught him the value of making an impression.

"Certainly, they were all in it. But it's a mistake to think they would have suffered the same losses if they had been exposed. What would have happened to them? The certain loss of their investment, the probable loss of their license to practice, a possible jail sentence."

"For all of them."

"Not necessarily." Thatcher raised a cautionary finger. "But even assuming that to be the case, what did it mean to each man? Sid Segal was in the strongest position. I expect he joined them simply because they threatened him with the loss of a large part of his prescription business if he didn't. And prescriptions play a very big role in the economy of that store. But, quite apart from his investment in the drug company, he's a rich man. He owns that entire block, he has a thriving business which could continue with his sons. His family wouldn't suffer any hardship, and he himself would not be an object of moral revulsion, because he wasn't a doctor. He was only the man who filled the prescriptions the doctors wrote. Except for this last point, much the same can be said for Philip Wittke. He, too, was independently wealthy by now. And while professional censure would be a blow to his ego, he was on the point of retiring anyway. He could always slip away—even after a jail term of six months or a year—and spend his golden years in Arizona as if nothing had happened." Thatcher belatedly hoped that Edes did not include Arizona in his immediate plans. "In fact, as a general principle, you can say that the older men were not going to be hit very hard, not hard enough to constitute a motive for murder, anyway. It was a very different kettle of fish for the younger men, they were the ones who would suffer. They would lose all their money and their right to practice medicine, with their whole lives still before them. And, bear in mind, these were not ordinary young men. They had all been used to living on incomes which a young man, like Kenneth Nicolls say, would consider fit for a king. You can lose your license to be a real estate agent, or a lawyer, or a pharmacist for that matter, and still have every hope of re-creating the same life in some other occupation. But this is not so with doctors! Roy Neverson, still in his mid-thirties, was making over seventy thousand dollars a year—and without being particularly good at his profession, without being a world authority or even associated with a good hospital. How could he ever duplicate that if he were thrown on the world and told to make his living doing something else?"

"Don't tell me about the young men!" Sounds of displeasure had been emanating from Edes for some time. Now he enlarged on his grievance. "I've heard it all from the Wittke boys. They're selling off their summer place and their boats. Every time they come into the bank, I have to listen to their sob story. Finally told young Jim off! Said he was only getting what he deserved for being mixed up in that swindle. That shut him up." The memory seemed to afford Edes considerable satisfaction. "Hell, why not? He's going to be wanting a loan any day now, and money's tight."

Thatcher was pleased to see that bankers remain bankers under the most outrageous conditions.

"Tight money?" asked an alarmed voice. "My God, what are they up to now?"

Tom Robichaux appeared out of the swirling throng, an unlikely celebrant for the latest attack on cancer. He was reassured on Federal Reserve policy.

"Money's not just tight for doctors in Southport," Edes confirmed with a cackle. "It's non-existent."

"Oh, doctors!" Robichaux waved away the profession and rocked back on his heels to run an expert's eye over the gathering. "Nice little blowout they've got going here. Don't believe I've ever been given decent brandy by a school before."

Somehow Robichaux managed to reduce Hanover University to the level of P.S. 98. But Edes was not prepared to stand on ceremony with him.

"They can afford it," he said dismissively. And, turning back to Thatcher: "So, the Wittke boys were right on the starting line with Neverson."

"Not exactly. They would feel it, I'm sure. But they have something Roy Neverson doesn't have—a rich father. Neverson, on the contrary, was sharing some of his mother's expenses."

Robichaux registered intelligence.

"Neverson? He's your murderer out there. Somehow I expected it to be a surgeon. Nothing they did would surprise me!" He retreated into brooding memories of Veronica.

"That too was a matter of some importance." Thatcher neatly took over the conversation before Tom could carry them all down one of those esoteric, speculative channels in which he specialized. "Because I don't think it's true that all the conspirators would have drawn the same penalties if a prosecution had resulted from Wendell Martin's indiscretions. We were talking about this the other day, and we agreed that a scapegoat would probably have been offered up as sacrificial victim. Naturally, at first sight, it seems that Martin should have been the scapegoat. But Martin undoubtedly would have tried to defend himself. His obvious course would be to claim that he had been led astray by the originator of the scheme. In fact, that he was just a high-spirited boy victimized by a Bad Influence. And, from what Edes here has told me, I don't think there's much doubt that Neverson was the one who masterminded the entire racket."

"None at all!" Edes barked. "He was the only one who had the slightest idea about money. He knew about mortgages and took some interest in the stock market. Hell, the rest of that bunch didn't even understand credit. They took in a lot of cash and put out a lot of cash. Every now and then, they took whatever had accumulated and dumped it with a stock broker. That's about the size of it."

"And the others, bear in mind, were surgeons. Neverson was an internist, what Gene Perkins tells me they call a 'pill-pusher.' He'd be particularly alive to the possibilities of drugs—as well as being the one who was on good terms with Al Martin."

"Put it another way," urged Edes. "He was the only one with the brains to think up that scheme."

"Or possibly with brains enough to comprehend the full menace of Wendell Martin?"

But here Edes jibbed. He shook his head decisively. "No, I wouldn't say that. The one really on the ball was Sid Segal. Still is, as a matter of fact. He's got the druggists association protesting the pressures brought to bear on pharmacists by doctors. I'll bet he comes out of this lily-white. And Phil Wittke isn't stupid, when it comes to protecting his own interests. They both must have known that Martin was a menace. Segal tried to talk to him, and Wittke realized it wouldn't be any use. But that's as far as they were prepared to go. It all comes out of what you were just saying. Neither of them was desperate. And Neverson was!"

Tom Robichaux did not care for these highfalutin emotional flights. It was, in his opinion, a waste of good brandy. He prepared to move on.

"I can see that you're both hipped on this thing. Think I'll find somebody who can chat about something livelier."

It was no accident that his eye rested on an attractive young woman at the bar. She was unaccompanied at the moment. She was also, as Thatcher had been informed by Dr. Edmund Knox, a very promising brain surgeon. Oh well, let Tom make his own discoveries.

"I don't understand what you're doing here anyway," he said to Robichaux.

"Melinda." The gleam in Robichaux's expression was momentarily dimmed. "Seems Hanover has an island somewhere. Melinda's got her eye on it. Well, it keeps her busy."

On this philosophic note, he departed. Things do balance out, as he had once said. Melinda, hot on the trail of her island, would be too preoccupied to notice her husband—also hot on a trail.

"You know, there's another thing you might have considered about Roy Neverson," Edes resumed. "That is, if you'd known him. He really has been a little crazy since his divorce, grimly determined that his wife and children were going to have the best of everything, whether they wanted it or not. He lavished money on them. I think he wanted to prove to himself he was necessary to them, even if his wife did get a divorce. Coming down to a regular job and a regular salary would have been bad enough. Breaking it to his wife would have just about killed him."

Thatcher nodded. He was not going to tell the septuagenarian he had already figured this out.

"That's interesting. And not so uncommon, where the husband resists divorce and the wife doesn't remarry."

"Then there's that mother of his," Edes continued his character analysis. "She's always been a driver. That's the real difference between Wittke and Roy. Wittke thinks everything is coming to him naturally, and he's not inclined to make a push. But Neverson knows you have to go out and take it. When Martin got in his way, his natural instinct would be to do something about it." He twirled the Scotch in his glass reflectively. "And he almost got away with it. Don't really see how he messed things up."

"I don't know that you can say he messed things up. He really didn't plan the murder of Wendell Martin. What seems to have happened is that he made one last attempt to talk sense to Martin on the night of the murder. He was forced to the conclusion that Wittke had been right. Talking to Martin wasn't going to do any good. The Freebody trial was going to go on, with the attention of the entire country riveted on Southport Memorial. So Neverson slammed out of the hospital at nine o'clock, exactly as he later claimed. He stopped for a bottle across the street from his apartment house, where his presence was duly witnessed. There was no premeditation at that point. That's what he's said to Lieutenant Perenna, and I believe him. Otherwise he would never have been so silly. But by the time he'd had a few drinks and reviewed his own position, he'd worked himself into a white-hot fury. If talking wouldn't do any good, then it would have to be action." Thatcher could almost see it. "Scarcely knowing what he was doing, he went back to the hospital and parked his car in an alley. He got out his tire iron and sneaked into the parking lot to look for Wendell Martin's car. It was entirely by chance that the murder took place. The timing hadn't been planned at all. If Martin had already gone home, Neverson would probably have drunk himself into a stupor and wakened the next morning, still frightened about the future but rid of his homicidal rage. In fact, if Wendell

Martin had worked very late and Neverson had been forced to lurk in the lot for a few hours, diving into the shrubbery every time someone appeared, he would probably have thought better of the whole thing. But, as luck would have it, the car was there. Martin himself came out in a few minutes."

"You're right about that. Roy Neverson would never have hung around very long. As soon as he started to calm down, he would have been worried at looking foolish if anybody caught him sneaking around."

Thatcher agreed sadly. "He would have been lucky if looking foolish was all that came of his night's work. After he killed Martin, he had sufficient presence of mind to rifle the pockets and try to make it look like a mugging. Then he went home and faced the fact that he was a murderer."

"Admitted, it's not a cleverly planned crime. But it's the kind they always say has the most chance of success. One biff on a dark night and away you go!" Edes spoke with considerable gusto.

"That's fine as long as a motive isn't apparent. But once the police started concentrating on the drug conspirators, the picture changed. Neverson, of course, simply omitted his return trip to the hospital. His story was that he went home and stayed there."

"What's wrong with that? I'd have said the same thing myself. Nobody saw him, did they?"

"Nobody saw him. But people knew about his activities anyway. He had made the mistake, just before leaving the hospital at nine o'clock, of asking Marie Gentilhomme to call him with the results of a patient's test. It was, he said, very important. So she called him— twice. Once at ten, again at ten-fifteen. There was, of course, no answer. Furthermore, Gene Perkins saw his car. That disaster, Neverson could not have anticipated. Neverson was careful to leave his car in a deserted alley, surrounded by warehouses. But that alley is on Perkins's shortcut home, and Perkins works in the garage that services the car. In fact he services it himself. And it is a noticeable car."

"A big fancy sports car," said Edes disapprovingly.

"Exactly. A Jaguar, I believe. And seen by one of the few men who could identify it without hesitation. Perkins was so impressed he even commented on the doctor's parking in the midst of broken glass."

"You couldn't want anything more damning. One witness busts his alibi, and the other not only places him at the scene of the crime, but in a surreptitious location. No reason in the world for Roy Neverson to park in an alley only two blocks from the hospital."

"Particularly when there was nothing in the alley that he could have possibly been visiting at that time of night. Gene Perkins, of course, did not realize the importance of what he had seen at the time. But he was a man who was interested in the death of Wendell Martin, simply because he has very good reason to be grateful to Martin. And he could therefore identify that night without much difficulty, even a good while later. It was not until afterward that his suspicions were roused."

"That was when the Perkinses and that girl got ahold of you, eh?" It had not been an accident that Mrs. Benjamin Edes was absent from the most critical meeting in the history of the Board of Trustees of Southport Memorial Hospital. But her husband knew Thatcher's conference in Old Southport had been the inspiration for that meeting and all that followed.

"Yes. When Marie and the Perkinses put their heads together, they came up with the phone call and the parked car. Then Perkins remembered something else. Neverson had dropped off a flat tire at the garage that very day, and in the course of so doing became involved in a nasty encounter with Alice Doyle. Naturally everybody's attention was riveted by the quarrel. But when that interest faded, Perkins began to consider the tire. Neverson was a man who had never done anything himself on his car, in Perkins's memory. When he had a flat tire, he called the garage to change it. And rightly so. It was a difficult tire to change. For an inexperienced man like the doctor, Perkins estimated that it would take over half an hour—if he was lucky. Why then, this sudden change in pattern? Perkins couldn't figure it out, but he was suspicious enough by then to tell the lieutenant about it. And the lieutenant hit on the answer almost at once."

"The tire iron? Why didn't he get rid of it? It certainly wasn't still bloody, was it?"

"Neverson was facing up to the problems of living in an apartment house. He didn't dare put it in the garbage, he didn't have the time to take his boat out, he had no means of disposal. Above all, he didn't want to be seen carrying it in circumstances which would make anybody think. Then, he was bothered by the problem of replacement. If he was missing a tire iron the next time he needed a tire changed, the garage would notice. And he certainly didn't want to go out and buy one. So he came to what was probably a sensible conclusion. He decided to leave it in the one place where it would attract no attention. In his car, with the other tools. But almost all the difficulties involved in throwing it away arose when he tried to clean it. He couldn't exactly carry it into the hospital and toss it into a sterilizer. He had to be content with wiping it. Of course, that wasn't sufficient to defeat a chemical analysis. Perenna tells me they are having a field day with it. More important, it might not be enough to escape notice from a mechanic who had used it several times. Neverson was taking no chances. He changed the tire himself."

"All right. Then that brings us to your trap. I don't see how you worked it."

"Properly speaking, I didn't. It was Ed Knox who did. He set up the scene in the cafeteria with young Bauer. It was imperative that Neverson be told about Marie's calls. You understand, he still didn't know about them. When he tried to upbraid her for failing to call him, she didn't try to defend herself. Instead Dr. Kroner stepped in and explained that she had been sent home in shock after finding Martin's body. So Neverson had to be told that Marie Gentilhomme was a danger to him, and under circumstances where everybody else's attention was distracted. Bauer and Marie did a very good job of it."

Edes snorted. "I would have smelled a rat!" he said confidently. "And then you handed him the girl on a plate."

"Naturally." Thatcher was shocked. "You don't think we would invite him to murder her and then leave the time and place to him? Miss Gentilhomme was very carefully guarded until that evening. Then he was given the information that she would be in a lonely, deserted spot at a certain time. I expect he must have been rather impatient by then. They tell me he was trying to get her alone for some time."

"And the Perkinses were in on it?"

"Almost everyone was in on it. The Perkinses, of course. And Alice Doyle was assigned to bring him to the fourth floor where he would overhear Mrs. Perkins asking Marie to go downstairs. That was in case he hadn't picked it up already. They did everything but announce it over the PA system. Even Dr. Kroner was assigned to see that Marie was not in the elevator alone."

"With that much cooperation, it's surprising someone didn't blab."

"People were picked out rather carefully. And being a murderer is a lonely business. I think Neverson realized that at the end." Thatcher had put this interpretation on Marie Gentilhomme's rather disjointed remarks.

"I'm surprised you let this Alice Doyle in on things. She seems to have been acting up herself."

"That was simply a failure in communication. Mrs. Doyle was present when Roy Neverson complained about Marie's failure to call. After the doctor left, Marie explained her attempts to reach him. At the time it was not very important. Dr. Martin's death was being viewed as a mugging. But Mrs. Doyle did realize the oddity of a doctor demanding to be called with a message about a patient and then disappearing without any word as to his location. When the police made it clear that Martin's death was not a casual mugging, that oddity instantly assumed its true importance in her mind. In fact, the importance was so self-evident she ignored the possibility that it had escaped Marie. That woman is a born politician. She instantly assumed that Neverson had squared himself with Marie."

Edes looked knowing. "Blackmail?"

"Not at all. Give Mrs. Doyle her due. She knows what kind of girl Marie is. She never even considered blackmail. Rather, she thought in terms of some explanation by the doctor and agreement by Marie, out of the goodness of her heart, not to embarrass Neverson. That was why she was so furious when the doctor had the gall, in her eyes, to attack his benefactor at the garage. It was righteous fury, mingled with her own disappointments, that led her to attack Neverson so savagely.

"Disappointments?" Edmund Knox joined them, beaming widely and far removed from the Isaiah of Southport Memorial. "Doesn't Mrs. Doyle like her new job?"

"I didn't know she had one," Thatcher confessed.

"Southport's new director of nursing. There was a little opposition to the appointment, but I soon took care of that."

Thatcher could readily believe it.

"Not exactly in the image of Southport Memorial," Benjamin Edes commented fearlessly. His position was that he could eat Edmund Knox for breakfast.

"The sooner they get rid of their old image, the better," Knox announced genially. "She'll make a first-class director, if you ask me. She knows the job, she's a hard worker and she's got plenty of back-bone. Not likely to take any nonsense from anybody!"

It was a quality that appealed to him. Social polish left him indifferent.

"You've been busy," Thatcher remarked. "I hear you offered young Bauer his old job, too."

Knox was virtually running Southport Memorial in addition to his more than adequate regular schedule. He seemed to be thriving on the demands.

"Turned me down flat. He said that he likes general practice now that he's started."

"He'll probably end up being the last GP in the country." Edes was being deliberately provocative.

But Knox was above provocation. He looked around with contentment.

"The medical profession has a good deal to be said for it, in spite of Southport and its little cousins." For a moment he seemed to be readying an attack on the negligence of Southport's trustees. Then he refrained, out of an overriding sense of well-being. "I'm not the only one getting people jobs. You heard about Thatcher's final clause in the Freebody settlement?"

"No," grunted Edes, dissatisfied. "Nobody tells me anything. How did the settlement turn out and who got a job?"

"We got a hundred thousand," said Knox, putting first things first.

"Yes," Thatcher agreed, giving Edes the details he craved. "The settlement was tied in to our little trap. We agreed to drop the double indemnity claim if Loomis would agree to drop his claims against the hospital—provided, of course, that Southport went along with our demands. Loomis was so pleased at finally getting the case off his neck that I was able to talk him into hiring Gene Perkins at a salary that should put a stop to all that moonlighting."

"Nice, very nice. The boy's bank account had even me worried."

"I don't know that I've effected any real improvement in his life. Although he's down to one job, he seems to have some kind of commuting schedule that involves rising at five-thirty."

Knox pointed out the obvious.

"He could move."

Thatcher shook his head. You had to know the Perkinses before you could appreciate their zest for impossible schedules, their talent for overworking themselves, their cheerful concern for the well-being of others. At this very moment, according to Ken Nicolls, Nancy

Perkins was scouring the countryside for young men for Marie. She had her eye on a boy just finishing dental school.

"I don't think it's even occurred to them."

"Well, at least if they stay in Southport, they can continue to protect Marie Gentilhomme. And she seems to need it more than most." Whether this was some obscure comment on Marie's bank account, neither of the two men facing Edes could determine. "Why didn't she tumble to the importance of what she knew earlier?"

"The reason for her obtuseness is very simple," Thatcher reported. "Gene Perkins put his finger on it. She is singularly devoid of curiosity. She never bothered to find out what alibis the doctors were using, even though every orderly was talking about them. She had not the faintest idea that her information was catastrophic, to Edith Bullivant, as well as to Roy Neverson. Not until Nancy Perkins got the whole story out of her."

"Damndest young woman I ever heard of," Edes summarized. "Curiosity is the hallmark of youth."

"Oh, I don't know about that," began Edmund Knox. "One of the troubles we have training researchers—"

He was interrupted ruthlessly.

"Take my grandchildren, for instance." Edes automatically groped in his breast pocket for pictures. "Got seven of them now. But the six-year-old boy is the pick of the lot. Bright as a whippet! Always taking things apart to see what makes them tick. Took my watch apart the other day," he said proudly. "Sometimes he even puts things together again. I tell you it's a real problem keeping him supplied. But you've got to do it. Shame not to encourage that kind of talent. That's the way they develop."

John Putnam Thatcher was visited by a sudden inspiration. He began to speak.

"There's this place on Fifth Avenue . . . very carefully made . . . imported from Japan . . . a challenge to your ingenuity . . ."

He spoke slowly, persuasively, seductively. Ten minutes later, he was saying:

"Mention my name to Mr. Durrant. He'll have just the thing for you!"

The voice was Jacob's voice, but the hands were the hands of Esau.